The BOW STREET RUNNERS

TRILOGY

The BOW STREET RUNNERS

—— TRILOGY ——

3 Acclaimed Novels

CHRISTY AWARD WINNER

MICHELLE GRIEP

ISBN 978-1-63609-556-1
Adobe Digital Edition (.epub) 978-1-63609-557-8

Published in association with the Books & Such Literary Management, 52 Mission Circle, Suite 122, PMB 170, Santa Rosa, CA 95409-5370, www.booksandsuch.com

Published by Barbour Publishing, Inc., 1810 Barbour Drive, Uhrichsville, OH 44683, www.barbourbooks.com

Our mission is to inspire the world with the life-changing message of the Bible.

Printed in Colombia.

BRENTWOOD'S WARD

This book dedicated to:

my sweet daughter,
Mariah Joy,
thank you for your unvarnished opinions

my sweet friend,
Stephanie Gustafson,
thank you for your encouragement in so many arenas

and as always for my sweet, sweet Savior,
Jesus Christ
thank You for saving my soul

CHAPTER 1

London, 1807

"You, sir, are a rogue!" Emily Payne scowled into the black marble gaze fixed on hers, determined to win the deadlock of stares. Horrid beast. Must he always triumph?

Without so much as a blink, the pug angled his head. Sunlight from the front door's transom window streamed over her shoulder, highlighting each of his fuzzy wrinkles. The pup's face squinched into a doggy smile, coaxing a sigh from Emily. Who could remain cross with that scrunched-up muzzle?

"I should've named you Scamp instead of Alf, eh boy?" She smiled then laughed outright when he snuck in a quick kiss on her neck.

Beside her, Mary, her maid, joined in—until Mrs. Hunt, equal parts housekeeper and sergeant major, huffed into the entry hall. Emily glanced at the matron over the pup's head. If the Admiralty were smart, they'd press her into service, and the Royal Navy would learn a new meaning for *shipshape* in no time.

"Sorry, miss. The little beastie got clean away from me." Mrs. Hunt reached for the fugitive, the smell of linseed oil and hard work wafting with the billow of her sleeve. "Hand him over, if you please. It won't happen again."

"Hmm. Don't be so sure." Emily nuzzled his furry head with the top of her chin, well aware he ought not be encouraged, yet completely unable to stop herself.

Mary tsked. "He just can't bear to be parted from you, miss, that's all."

"Which is more than I can say for the males of my own species," she mumbled into the pup's fur. Alf nestled against her shoulder. If only Charles Henley might become so attached, the empty void in her heart would be filled at last. After a last snuggle, she held the pug out to Mrs. Hunt.

But Alf wriggled during the transfer. His back paw caught the lace on her glove, tearing the sheer fabric. Frowning, she inspected the damage. "Oh, bother. Mary, would you—"

"I shall." Her maid turned, but a rap on the front door spun her back around. "Right after I answer the—"

Emily shook her head. "I'll do it. You see to the gloves."

She opened the door to the height of fashion. By faith, the only thing Reginald Sedgewick prized more than his garments was his looking glass. "Uncle Reggie!" She smiled. "A bit early in the day for you, is it not?"

He nodded. Nothing more. Perhaps it was indeed too early for his usual cheerful banter. "Is your father home?" His voice crackled at the edges.

"I've not seen him, though that's not unusual. Come in." She stepped aside, and the scent of bay rum entered with him—or was it? One more sniff and her nose wrinkled. There was nothing bay about it. The man reeked of rum.

He doffed his hat, and she called to her maid, who by now was halfway up the stairs. "Oh Mary, would you be a dear and summon my father before you see to my gloves?"

"Aye, miss." Retracing her steps, Mary scurried past them and disappeared down the same corridor Mrs. Hunt had taken earlier.

Emily turned back to Reggie and swept her hand toward the open sitting-room door. "Please have a—"

The words clogged in her throat as she studied him up close. His cravat knot hung loose. Buttons on his waistcoat did not match the proper holes, and no red carnation adorned his lapel. She shifted her eyes to his. "Is something wrong?"

His jaw clenched, and she suspected his fists might have too. Then strangely enough, the angry wave subsided. "Nothing a good row with your father won't solve, my dear." A ghost of a smile softened the threat, or was that a grimace?

"How very strange. Usually it is I who am at odds with him." She reached for the bellpull on the wall. "Shall I ring for tea?"

"No need. This shan't take long." He paused, turning the hat in his hands around and around. "Hopefully."

A shiver crept across her shoulders. He was not only disheveled but anxious as well? That didn't bode well, not coming from the jolliest fellow she knew.

Behind her, Mary's footsteps clipped onto the marble flooring. "Mr. Payne is unavailable, sir."

Red crept up Reggie's neck and blossomed onto his cheeks. "Unavailable?"

Mary bypassed them both then halted near the balustrade at the base of the stairs. Did she keep such distance from conservation of steps . . .or fear? She studied the floor as she answered, making it impossible to read her face. "Yes, sir. Detained for the rest of the day. I suggest you call back tomorrow, Mr. Sedgewick."

Reggie breathed out an oath then jammed his hat on top of his head so forcefully his valet would need a shoehorn to pry it off come evening. With a curt nod to them both and a ground-out "Good day," he swooped out the front door. A firm thud accentuated his departure.

Emily slid her gaze to Mary, who returned her wide-eyed stare. "That was. . .interesting. I wonder what Father's done to vex Reggie so?" Would it be business related or something to do with the recently widowed Mrs. Nevens? She suspected the latter, for they'd each been vying for the woman's attention.

Mary merely bobbed her head. "I'll see about those gloves, then."

The girl disappeared up the stairs, and a fresh wave of mourning washed over Emily. Instead of tucking tail and running away in the name of duty, her former maid and confidant, Wren, would have listened to her conspiracy theories. Or likely more than that. . .Wren would have added a few of her own ideas to the mix. Emily sighed, frustrated that even a hundred Wren-would-haves wouldn't bring her favorite maid back. Nothing would—except, perhaps, for a miracle.

"Is Reggie gone?" Her father's bass voice rumbled from the corridor. His head peeked out the study door, fuzzy as a downy-haired tot whose nightgown had just been pulled off.

Emily pursed her lips, shedding one glove after the other. "I thought you were unavailable, Father."

"I am." His big belly and stubby legs appeared. "Leastwise as far as Reginald's concerned."

She set the ripped lace onto the calling card salver then looked up at her father's approach, narrowing her eyes. Something was off kilter. He often avoided her, but never his business partner. "Uncle Reggie was quite put out, you know."

"I do know, but it can't be helped."

She opened her mouth to argue with the absurdity of his statement, but before she could speak, Mary descended the last step and held out a set of white gloves. "Here you are, miss."

"Thank you." She reached for the fresh pair, and a keen scowl slashed across her father's face. "What are you frowning at?"

"You are not going out, I hope. In fact, I quite forbid it."

"Don't be silly." She wiggled her fingers into the cool fabric. "Did I not tell you I've an appointment at the milliner's?"

"You own enough bonnets to cover all the heads of Mayfair proper. No, no, I insist you stay home."

"You do?" Her gaze shot to his. For one glorious moment, she imagined playing the part of papa's little girl—finally—even if she was three and twenty. Regardless of the years, her heart leaped in her chest.

Then stilled when he spoke. "I am expecting someone I require you to meet."

Inside her gloves, perspiration dotted the palms of her hands. The last man he'd brought home for her to meet had nearly been her ruination. Never again. She set her jaw. "Father, you can't be serious. This appointment was confirmed ages ago. Besides which, I need one last fitting for my gown, and if I do not attend to it today, it shan't be ready for the Garveys' ball."

"No more about it, Emily. I will be obeyed in this matter. You are not to leave the house this morning." He lifted his chin and peered down his nose. "Am I understood?"

She took the time to straighten each ruffled hem of her sleeves before returning her gaze to his—a stalling tactic she'd learned from the best. Him. "Quite," she answered.

"Good." He wheeled about and disappeared down the hallway.

Disappointment burned at the back of her throat. Would that he might want to spend a day with her instead of foisting her off on one of his business associates. Swallowing the sour taste, she reached for the doorknob. Her entire future depended upon the upcoming ball—a future that did not include one moment more of pining for her father's love.

Mary's eyes widened. "Miss Emily! Your father said—"

"My father said not to leave the house this morning. But, Mary dearest"—she opened the door and winked over her shoulder—"did you know that right now it's afternoon in India?"

Short of breath and lean on time, Nicholas Brentwood sprinted down Bow Street, dodging hawkers and pedestrians. Though patience was one of his assets, it did not make the top ten of the magistrate's virtues. Nearing the station, he splashed through a pool of waste that leaked into the hole of his right boot, but it was not to be helped. He was late.

Darting through the front door of the magistrate's court, he shoved past milling gawkers waiting to be let into the sentencing chamber. With a "Pardon me," he veered right and bounded up the stairway, two treads at a time. Fatigue stung his eyes, anguish his heart. Though he inhaled deeply the smell of oil lamps, ink, and lives hanging in the balance, the stench of disease yet clung to his nostrils.

He bounded down a narrow corridor, shoulders brushing one wall then another in his haste. Through a crack in the magistrate's door, he slid in sideways and breathless.

Sir Richard Ford stood near the window, regarding the streets of London. Weak sunlight filtered through the soot-dusted glass, highlighting the man's shorn head—a head that did not turn when Nicholas entered. Good. Reining in his heaving chest, Nicholas breathed out a thankful prayer that his less-than-decorous arrival had not been noted. Then he straightened the lapel on his dress coat, covering the rip on his vest beneath. "I'm here, sir. Please excuse—"

The man waved his hand in the air, batting away his gnat of an apology.

Galled that he was the offending insect, Nicholas advanced. "If you would allow me to explain—"

"Permission denied." Ford turned from the window. A frown etched lines on either side of his mouth, deep enough to sink any thoughts of rebuttal.

Nicholas widened his stance and squared his shoulders, taut as a sail in the wind. "Yes, sir."

The man's frown deepened. "Sweet peacock, Brentwood, sit down." Ford strode to the overstuffed chair behind a massive cherry-wood desk and lowered his frame. "You make me nervous."

He made the magistrate nervous? The same man who in mere minutes would don a wig as tall as a small child and sentence countless men to their deaths? Nicholas bit back a smirk and sank into the worn leather seat opposite the desk, grateful to set aside running for the moment. "I can only assume, sir, this is about my recent absences. By your leave, I should like to explain."

The old fellow skewered him with a hard stare, one that might divide flesh from bone by sheer will. "I will have no explanations."

Nicholas clenched his jaw. So, this was to be it, then? His career ended now when he needed money most? Not that he didn't deserve it. God knew he warranted much worse than to be dismissed.

But Jenny surely didn't.

Slowly, feeling every year of hard living and lack of sleep, he nodded and rose. "Very well. I understand. It's been my honor to have served—"

"Reseat your back end, Brentwood. You don't understand a thing."

The chair held his weight, his mind a thousand questions. "Sir?"

Ford leaned forward, the desk becoming one with the man. "You think I don't know about your sister? This is an investigative agency I run, with none but the best in my employ. Every officer knows how you care for her, and none fault you for it." He sat back and lifted his chin. "Neither do I."

The tightness in Nicholas's shoulders eased for the first time in months. Though he hated that all knew his business, it was a relief to be able to stop hiding the burden—a trail he'd done everything in his power to conceal. But apparently not enough. He pierced Ford with one of his own pointed looks. "Did you have me followed?"

"Didn't have to. A certain doctor came here, inquiring after you. Seems the fellow doesn't trust you'll be good for his wages." One of the magistrate's brows rose, a perfect arc on such an austere canvas. "Imagine that."

A smile begged for release, but Nicholas refused the vagrant urge. Not yet. The magistrate didn't often keep a courtroom full of brigands waiting. Something else was brewing. "If this doesn't concern my sister, then why the summons? I don't suppose you're holding up court for tea and crumpets with me."

"I've a task in mind for you, Brentwood." Ford propped his elbows on each arm of the chair, angling his head to the right. One of his favorite bargaining positions. The man eyed him as he might a piece of horseflesh to be bought. "A task that must be tended to immediately, and I'm certain you're the perfect officer for the job. In fact, I will consider no one else."

Unease tickled the nape of his neck, and Nicholas rubbed at the offending sensation. Ford was generally spare with his praise. Why now?

"I appreciate your confidence," he said.

"Bah." The magistrate sniffed. "I'm certain you're the man because you're the one with the greatest need for funding. Am I correct?"

Nicholas shifted in his seat. Exactly how much did his superior know? "Go on."

Ford laced his fingers and placed them on the desktop. "A gentleman of some means approached me with the business of procuring a guardian for his daughter. He's willing to pay a tidy sum to see her well cared for."

Scrubbing a hand over his chin, Nicholas chewed on that

information as he might a gummy bit of porridge. Either the man was a reprobate too intent on pleasure to see to his own offspring, or the girl was a hellish handful. A frown pulled at his lips. "Why does he not look after her himself?"

"He sails for the continent on the morrow."

Nicholas snorted. "Seems he ought to have obtained a guardian long before this."

"Yes. . .well. . ." Ford cleared his throat and averted his gaze. "The point is the man is willing to pay a large sum to safeguard his only child, and it's my understanding you could use that money. Yes?"

He tugged at his collar. A marmot in a snare couldn't have felt more trapped. "I think that's already been established."

"Very well." Sliding open a top drawer, Ford produced a folded bit of parchment. "The gentleman, Mr. Alistair Payne, will fill you in on the particulars of the agreement. Officer Moore's got the streets covered and Captain Thatcher the roads, so I shall excuse you from your regular duties until this assignment is complete."

Stabbing the paper with his finger, Ford skimmed it across the desktop toward him. "Here's the address and the agreed upon amount."

Nicholas unfolded the crisp paper. He blinked, then blinked again. Granted, the ink watered into gray at the edges, but even so, a figure stood out sharply against the creamy background. Two hundred fifty pounds—enough to send Jenny to the blessed moon should a cure be available there. He locked stares with Ford. "This is no jest?"

"Really, Brentwood, how often do you see me smile?" His lips didn't so much as twitch. The only movement in the entire room was the pendulum ticking away in the corner clock—that and the rush of blood pulsing in Nicholas's ears.

"Well?" Ford broke the silence. "What do you say?"

The only thing he could. "Yes." He folded the parchment and tucked it into his breast pocket.

"Excellent." Ford pushed back from his desk and stood. "Now if you'll excuse me, I've a few cases to hear."

As the magistrate stalked out the door, Nicholas ignored decorum and sat frozen, too stunned to follow. Amazing, that's what. Did God seriously delight in dropping the jaw of a man such as himself? He rose and glanced at the cracked plaster ceiling, whispering a prayer. "Thank You, Lord. Your bounty never ceases to amaze me."

He crossed the room and stepped into the hallway, hope speeding his steps—and landing him square into the path of a steel-bodied man.

"You're in an awful hurry, Brentwood." A dark gaze bore into his. Though clear of anger, a fearsome enough stare.

"Sorry, Thatcher." Nicholas sidestepped one way, Thatcher the other, an odd sort of dance in the narrow corridor. "On my way to a new assignment. Didn't expect to see you here."

"Surprise to me as well." Samuel Thatcher straightened his riding cloak and planted himself in front of the magistrate's door. "I was summoned for an early meeting with Ford. So early, I neglected to bring up my own inquiries. He still in there?"

Nicholas shook his head. "Not anymore."

"Right." Thatcher blew out a long breath. "Suppose I'll head out, then."

The big man turned the opposite direction, but two steps later, pivoted. "Hold on, Brentwood. New assignment, you say?"

Nicholas nodded. "Guardian position. Ought not be. . .what? Why the grin?"

A smile the size of Parliament slid across Thatcher's face. He backed away, hands up. "Good luck with that one. You'll need it."

Nicholas growled. "What did Ford not tell me?"

Thatcher's grin morphed into a low-throated laugh. He turned and stomped off. "You're just the fellow for the job, Brentwood."

"As are you to haunt the hollows on a horse. That's it, run off like the coward you are." His words didn't stop the man from retreating nor douse the remains of his laughter.

Nicholas wheeled about and strode the other direction. Thatcher was batty, that's what, likely from too much time spent on the byways wrestling with highwaymen. The man probably envied the soft position he'd just landed, holing up in a fine town house, watching over some proper little heiress. For all he knew, she might have a nurse or a governess, and all he'd have to do was recline in the man's study, smoke cheroots, and read the *Times*.

Descending the stairs, he grinned in full at his fortune and entered the foyer. His bootsteps echoed in the wide lobby, empty now that court was in session. He reached for the doorknob then jerked back when it opened of its own accord.

"Ahh, Brentwood." A barrel-chested man entered, not as large as Thatcher but every bit as powerful. All Ford's chosen men were built like bulwarks.

Nicholas nodded a greeting. "Moore. How goes it?"

"Not bad. On my way to testify." Alexander Moore swept past him, shedding his hat and brushing back his wild mane of blond hair. Nearing the courtroom, he called over his shoulder: "And by the smile on your face, I assume you escaped that horrendous assignment ol' Ford was trying to pawn off."

The door slapped shut behind Moore, as soundly as the jaws of Ford's trap snapped down on Nicholas. Replaying the entire interview in his head, the magistrate's throat clearing and his darting gaze stood out as the single tip-off. Apparently the gentleman, Mr. Alistair Payne, had tried to arrange for a guardian long before he set sail, a position both Moore and Thatcher had declined. Nicholas frowned. Ford hadn't chosen him for any special reason other than he was the last resort.

Stepping out into the rank offense of Bow Street, Nicholas flipped up his collar against the chill and cast off any misgivings. After tracking down murderers, gamblers, and whoremongers, how hard could guarding an heiress be?

CHAPTER 2

Before entering 22 Portman Square, Nicholas stood dangerously close to the carriage ruts in the road and glanced up, studying the place. So many windows would be a problem, as would the servants' entrance below street level to the left of the front door. The roof, three stories up, sat below the neighboring town house—an easy leap down for an intruder bent on topside access. No wonder Mr. Payne felt ill at ease leaving a young daughter home alone in such a burglar's playground.

In four strides, he reached the door, lifted the brass knocker, and rapped. Moments later, the door opened to a flint-faced housekeeper who he might've served next to in the Sixth Regiment of the Black Dragoons. Odd that for such a fancy house, neither butler nor footman answered his call.

Nicholas offered his card. "I'm here to see Mr. Payne."

She didn't just take the thing—she held it up to within inches of her eyes and read the sparse bit of letters as if he'd petitioned to view the crown jewels. "So you're Mr. Brentwood, are ye? What business do you have with Mr. Payne?"

With a doorkeeper such as this, mayhap guarding the place wouldn't be as difficult as he first imagined. "I believe, madam, that if you don't already know, then maybe you ought not."

Her eyes shot to his, gunmetal gray and sparking. "A simple 'imports or exports' would have sufficed. Come in."

She stepped aside, allowing him to pass, then cut him off before he could advance any farther. "Wait here, if you please."

Removing his hat, he studied the grand foyer. Flocked paper lined the walls, graced with enough wall lamps and an overhanging chandelier that the light would likely give him a headache come evening. To his right, a carpeted stairway led upward. At its base, three paces past and to the left, a single door. Closed. Opposite, french doors opened to a sitting room before the rest of the home disappeared down a corridor. It smelled of wealth and lemon wax—

And a faint scent of linseed oil as the housekeeper reappeared from the hallway. "This way, Mr. Brentwood."

He followed her swishing skirt as she retreated once more down the corridor. Stopping in front of the next closed door, she knocked, and a "Just let the man in, Mrs. Hunt," bellowed from behind.

Twisting the knob, she nodded at him. "If you please."

Out of habit, Nicholas scanned the room. Two floor-to-ceiling windows and a large hearth, besides the threshold he'd just crossed, presented four possible points of access. Four. In one room. This could prove a very tedious assignment.

"Mr. Brentwood."

The first thing he noticed at Mr. Payne's approach was the fellow's round belly. Apparently Portman House employed a good cook. At least the eating part of this assignment would be agreeable. His gaze traveled upward then stopped, fixated on Payne's amazingly horrible teeth—chompers any beaver would give a hind leg to own. Nicholas squinted. Were the front two really that big or the rest abnormally small? A man of his standing surely could afford to have them pulled and replaced with porcelain replicas. Or at the very least, could he not have the rascals sanded down and even them out a bit?

Before he breached protocol any further, Nicholas forced his gaze higher and held out his hand. "Mr. Payne."

The fellow clasped his fingers in a firm grip followed by a squeeze. Confident and over so. Quite the contradiction to the man's appearance, for the structure of the rest of his face made him look perpetually surprised. Fuzzy hair, thankfully short and sparse, stood on end, as if he'd just taken a great fright. Dark eyes, brown as dried tobacco, sat below wiry white eyebrows, high set and arched—apparently their normal repose. This man surely made children laugh, perhaps even his daughter.

"Have a seat. I understand you're one of Ford's men, eh?" The freakish teeth punctuated his words.

"I am." Nicholas eyed the furniture to keep from staring. Anchored on an overlarge Persian rug, two library chairs faced a glossy desk. Interesting, though, that no inkwells or papers, ledgers or registers favored the topside. It was bare. Completely. What kind of businessman was this Mr. Payne?

The man sank into a seat behind the desk, cushions whooshing a complaint beneath his weight. "Please excuse the somewhat unconventional greeting at the door. I've given my butler a temporary leave. I hope you weren't too put out by Mrs. Hunt. She can be a bit brash at times."

Nicholas met the fellow's even gaze. "Perhaps you ought to offer her the guardian position."

"I said she's brash, sir, not wily."

After his short encounter with the woman, Nicholas was not convinced. That mobcap hid more than aggression. He tipped his head. "I was not aware that cunning was one of the qualities you desired."

"Yet you are, Brentwood. Cunning, that is. Or you would not be employed as one of Bow Street's finest." Mr. Payne sat back and lifted his chin. "Am I not right?"

Nicholas said nothing.

"Very well, man. I can see you'd like to get down to business. My daughter, Miss Emily, is. . ." His eyes followed his brows upward, and he studied the ceiling as if a description of the girl might be found near the rafters. Silence stretched, revealing more than a score of words could accomplish.

A father speechless about his daughter did not bode well.

After excessive throat clearing, Mr. Payne finally spoke: "Let's just say Emily knows her own mind, or at least she thinks she does. Because of this, I charge you with the oversight of her at all times until I return."

"Which will be?" The thought of safekeeping a prideful girl for days on end—one who may have a beaver bite like her father—sounded as diverting as the time he'd lugged ol' Nat Waggins, escape artist extraordinaire, from York down to Tyburn.

"I expect to be gone a month, give or take and naturally weather permitting, at which point I shall award you 250 pounds. It's very straightforward, Mr. Brentwood. Keep my daughter safe, and the money is yours." Payne leaned sideways and slid open a drawer, procuring a carved wooden box with brass hinges. From his waistcoat pocket, he fished out a tiny key. "Though I suppose you should like an advance, eh?"

"May I ask a few questions?" Not that he'd turn down the payment. Jenny's life hung in the balance without it—and perhaps even with it.

Mr. Payne set the key in the box's lock. A click later, he lifted the lid. "Of course."

Nicholas drew in a breath, girding up for a salvo technique he'd mastered long ago. "I gather you are a merchant, hence the travel, and the import/export mentioned by your housekeeper."

"I am."

"Should the need arise, how do I reach you?"

"You don't."

"Then are there other relations I may contact?"

"None."

"Yet you fear for Miss Payne's safety."

"I do."

"Why?"

That stopped the man but only for the briefest of moments. A pause easily missed, one Nicholas had learned to listen for in the voices of swindlers and cons.

Payne scowled, the effect lightened by the ridiculous teeth peeking through his lips. "You can imagine, Brentwood, that a man in my position garners many enemies. Blood-sucking enemies, no less. Emily is my only heir, hence my one vulnerability."

"What exactly is your position, Mr. Payne?"

The man slammed the box's lid shut with one hand and held out a banknote with the other. "Commerce, Brentwood. The world's wheels turn on the hub of commerce, of which I am the center, leastwise in the shipping industry. Now then, here is your advance."

Nicholas leaned forward and pinched the paper between thumb and forefinger, expecting the man's grip to lessen.

It tightened. "One more thing. There's been a slight change of plans. I expect you to set up quarters here. Now. My ship sails by day's end."

A nerve on the side of his neck jumped. He'd have no time to dash over to the Crown and Horn to let Jenny know of his whereabouts. If she should need him, no one would know where to find him. . . unless he paid a courier to deliver a message. He lifted his gaze to meet Payne's. "Then a change in remuneration should be in order as well, I think."

The man frowned, yet the banknote loosened. He pocketed the sum as Payne withdrew another note.

"Very shrewd, Brentwood. I see why Ford's runners have earned such a reputation."

Runner? Heat burned a trail up Nicholas's spine and lodged at the base of his skull. The man might as well have questioned his parentage. He snatched the added check from the man's pudgy fingers then rose and skewered him with a glance. "I shall give you the benefit of the doubt this time, Mr. Payne, for perhaps you are not aware that *runner* is a derogatory term. One I don't take kindly to being associated with. I am, in your own words, one of Bow Street's finest, not an errand boy or Ford's lackey; I am a detective, sir, an investigator. A sleuth. The kind of man who will stop at nothing to hunt down a criminal and bring him to justice at the end of a rope. Now you are educated. See that it doesn't happen again."

"Well. . .I. . ." Payne's Adam's apple bobbed up and down, his brows ending where his white hairline began. "Of course." He busied himself by tucking away the box then stepped to a velvet cord on the wall and tugged it.

Pocketing the rest of the payment, Nicholas allowed his blood to cool. It'd been a hard battle to become a man of integrity, a fight he'd not see belittled by donning a pejorative title.

"Aye, sir?" The housekeeper's head peeked through the door.

"Summon Miss Emily straightaway, Mrs. Hunt." Payne resumed his seat behind the desk.

Nicholas preferred to remain standing and meet the little heiress with the advantage of height.

"I am sorry, but she is gone out with Miss Mary. Will that be all, sir?"

Color started rising slowly, like mercury up a thermometer, slipping over Payne's ears, diffusing across his cheeks, then inching up his nose. Judging by the rapid spread, his head might pop at any moment—and those teeth would be deadly projectiles. Nicholas retreated a step.

"The devil you say! I specifically forbade her!" Payne sputtered an oath. "Never mind, Mrs. Hunt. That will be all."

As soon as the door shut, Payne retrieved his safe box yet again. He removed a fistful of assorted notes and held them out. "Take it, Brentwood."

Nicholas narrowed his eyes. "You've provided a sufficient advance. What is this for?"

A muscle jumped near the hinge of Payne's jaw before he ground out, "Hazard pay, for indeed, Emily is hazardous on more levels than one."

Emily's shadow arrived at the townhome before she did. Mary's lagged behind, shorter and wider. As her maid caught up, hatboxes draped on each arm like Christmas ornaments, Emily stepped aside and lowered her voice. "Now don't forget—"

"I won't." Mary nodded toward the door, bonnet askew. "Would you mind?"

Emily reached for the knob, grateful that Mrs. Hunt ran a well-oiled household. "Good luck," she whispered as Mary passed then took care to shut the door behind her.

One-one-thousand. Two-one-thousand. Mary ought to have made it to the base of the stairs by now. Three-one-thousand, four. Should have ascended at least a few treads. Five-one-thousand, six and seven-one-thousand. . .

Emily pressed her ear to the cool mahogany, shutting out the *clip-clops* and grinding wheels of a passing carriage. Eight-one-thousand, nine. She held her breath. *Wait for it. Wait for—*

Mary's shriek, while a bit over the top, trilled from within. The *thumpity-thumps* of dropped boxes were a nice touch. The girl was starting to grow on her, though she'd never replace the spot in Emily's heart for her former maid, Wren. Nevertheless, a smile lifted the corners of her mouth.

And a deep moan leaching through the door wiped it away.

Muffled footsteps pounded across the foyer tiles. Voices, not words, filtered through the wood, but their emotion came through clear enough. Worry. Pain. Fear? La, it sounded as if the entire household congregated just beyond the threshold. She'd never be able to sneak in undetected now.

Slowly she withdrew her ear from the door then turned and leaned against it. What had gone wrong? Ignoring the fading light and passing coaches, she bit the inside of her lower lip and mulled over her plan. All Mary need do was create a diversion by pretending to have seen a mouse. A squeal, perhaps a feigned swoon, something to get the servants—and her father—to set their mind on something other than her late arrival, and she'd slip in unnoticed.

Now that would be impossible.

A gust of wind swooped beneath her bonnet and snagged loose a piece of hair. She flattened her lips and tucked up the stray. Standing on the stoop all evening wasn't an option, and with twilight's growing chill, tarrying much longer wouldn't be pleasant, either.

Emily folded her arms, calculating her next move as she might in a hand of whist. She could waltz in, pretending as if nothing had happened, that she'd not technically disobeyed her father. . .but that wouldn't stop his censure. Mayhap she might play on everyone's sympathy and develop a cough. No, that would only add further restrictions to her comings and goings. Plus she'd have to remember to cough frequently. That wouldn't do at all. Perhaps she ought—

The door flew open. She plunged backward, mimicking Mary's earlier shriek. Strong hands righted her before she bruised her backside and her dignity.

Regaining her balance, she drew in a breath and turned. "I swear I can explain, Father—"

A man, decades younger than her father, studied her with an intense pair of green eyes—eyes that sifted and weighed the content of her heart and soul in one glance. Desire to run and hide from his curious inspection welled in her stomach—and the reaction annoyed her.

She lifted her chin and returned the stranger's stare. A shadow lined his jaw. He'd not taken the time to shave, yet the look favored his rugged style. Dark hair breached his collar's edge, wild and wavy, not quite long enough to pull into a queue. A good pomade would tame it, but she suspected the man would not give in to such folderol, considering the stark cut of his dress coat and plain-colored vest beneath. He might have stepped off one of her father's merchantmen, but he didn't smell of the sea. . .more like spent gunpowder and boot blacking. She wrinkled her nose. Who was this wild man?

"I should like to hear that explanation, miss, if you please." His arm stretched toward the sitting-room door.

She frowned. Who did this fellow think he was? Hoping to spy Mrs. Hunt or Mary—or at this point, even her father—she rose to her toes, the only way to see past his tall stature and broad shoulders. A single housemaid, Betsy, was all that remained on the stairwell, collecting the last of the hatboxes.

Lowering her heels to the floor, Emily squared her shoulders. "You presume a great deal, sir. I do not answer to you."

"Ahh, exactly what I wish to discuss. Shall we?" He nodded at the open sitting-room doorway.

Emily sucked in a breath. The man was more pompous, and likely as dangerous, as the scoundrel of a captain who'd ruined Wren—and nearly herself—late last summer. She straightened further, posture adding confidence. "I don't know who you think you are Mr.—"

"Brentwood."

"Brentwood." She spit out the name as if it were an olive pit. "This is *my* home. I am no servant to be ordered about within these walls, nor anywhere else for that matter. I owe you no accounting of my personal activities. Furthermore, you may collect your hat and coat, and see yourself out the way you came in."

"Miss Payne"—the man leaned close, his voice intimate and

low—"do you really want to have this conversation in the foyer?"

Her eyes followed the slight tip of his head. Gathered atop the stairway landing, Fanny, a lower housemaid with an armful of linens, had joined Betsy, each trying hard not to appear as if they weren't devouring her every word. Had she truly been talking that loud?

She swallowed, her scratchy throat testifying against her. She'd have to concede, or her business would be all the talk of belowstairs. Still, the smug tilt of Brentwood's jaw was not to be borne. What to do?

Straightening her skirt, she matched his arrogant stance. "Very well, Mr. Brentwood. I shall inquire of you in the sitting room."

Amusement flashed in his eyes. Or was that irritation? Not that she cared, and it piqued her that she'd noticed in the first place. She whirled and strode into the room, the last of day's light blending colors into a monotone. Why had Mrs. Hunt not yet lit the lamps? Where was the woman?

Behind her, boot heels thumped against wood then muted in timbre once Brentwood's feet met the rug. Emily refused to turn. Instead, she peeled off one glove then the other, and laid them on the settee's arm. Tugging loose the bow beneath her chin, she slowly lifted her bonnet and set that aside as well. Behind her, a sigh competed with the ticking of the floor clock, and her mouth curved into a smile. Good. The man, whoever he was, could wait upon her.

"Are you quite finished?"

She cast him a glance over her shoulder. "Momentarily."

"While I've no pressing engagement requiring my attendance," his voice rumbled from behind, "I should not like to spend the entire evening in the sitting room, staring at your back. In short, Miss Payne, your stalling tactics do not amuse."

She spun, the swoosh of her skirts matching the rush of blood through her ears. "How dare you—"

He held up a hand. "I understand your apprehension. It is not so much daring on my part as it is obligation, for currently I am under your father's employ. Had you obeyed the man in the first place, as a dutiful daughter should, this scene would have been avoided."

The sitting-room's shadows suited her mood, dark and growing blacker. "You, sir, are quick to judge. Moreover—"

"Allow me to finish." Challenge thickened his tone, and his words smacked of authority.

When he took a step toward her, she shrank, fear more than compliance dissolving the rebuttal in her throat.

He widened his stance, planting himself but three paces from her. "Your father has recently sailed for business and made you my ward in his absence. You will find me to be fair but firm, and with little patience for antics. Speaking of which, I will have that explanation now for your absence and the subsequent spraining of your abigail's ankle."

Emotions riffled through her faster than she could identify. Her father gone, without so much as a by-your-leave? Not that it surprised her, but did he honestly care that little? Leaving her as the charge of the big man in front of her, a complete stranger? Questions rose like weeds after a spring rain, but only one surfaced. "Mary's hurt?"

He folded his arms. "Is it any wonder? You sent the poor girl up a flight of stairs carrying more boxes than a pack mule."

A slow burn rose from her stomach to her heart. She didn't often own up to remorse—and now she knew why.

She didn't like it.

His green gaze pinned her in place. "Where you went today concerns me less than why. Why would you directly defy your father's wishes?"

"I had an appointment." Her voice sounded small, even in her own ears.

He frowned. "You also had specific instruction from your father to stay home."

"Only for the morning." The petulant quiver in her voice shamed her, and she drew in a breath to mask it.

Twilight's shadows darkened the man's—Brentwood's—face. Or was it her imagination?

"Do you deny you left the house before noon?" His voice boomed.

She threw out her hands, hating the way he exposed her, and worse . . .the sudden desire ripping through her to hide beneath the settee.

"How do you know all this?"

A rogue grin flashed on his face. "Part of my job."

Blowing out a long breath, she considered an entirely new ploy. Truth. "If you must know, Mr. Brentwood, my father sometimes makes unreasonable requests. I'd scheduled the milliner's appointment long ago—at a most exclusive shop I might add—and I wasn't about to miss it for one of his whims."

"His *whim*, as you put it, Miss Payne, was to be able to say good-bye to his only daughter. He'll be gone nigh on a month, perhaps longer. Was that too much to ask?"

She turned from him, glad now that no lamps had been lit, for he'd surely see the tears burning in her eyes. Her father had wanted to say good-bye to her, after all, and she'd missed it. *Oh God, forgive me.*

"And your abigail, Mary. . . Why did you hide yourself outside the front door and send the girl in to meet with injury?"

His question stabbed a hole in her repentance. She whirled back. "I did no such thing!"

The flinty set of his jaw, the steel in his posture left no room for argument. His gaze heaped coals upon her head.

Once more, he was right. She hadn't felt so afflicted since the mumps. "I didn't mean for her to be hurt. Truly. I merely. . . Wait a minute."

Indignation doused the fire in her belly, and she lifted her face to his. "How would you know I waited outside the front door?"

Instead of answering, he stepped toward her. She sucked in a breath as he neared then slowly let it out when he strode past. Her eyes followed his broad back as he crossed the room and halted at the front window. With a tip of his head, he raised both brows at her.

Narrowing her eyes, she followed his lead and peered out the glass—then swallowed. Why had she never noticed this window gave such a clear view to the front stoop?

She drew back, and when he turned to face her, the air suddenly charged.

"I believe you sent the girl in, instructing her to create a diversion as you waited. In the aftermath, you planned to slip in unnoticed. Am I correct?"

She pressed her lips tight, hiding their trembling, and took sudden interest in the baseboards. Better that than face the all-knowing man scowling at her.

But that didn't stop his lecture. "Servant or not, you owe the girl an apology. Furthermore, while you are in my charge, you will refrain from such devilry. Your father may overlook your schemes, but I assure you, I will not. I am a lawman, Miss Payne. I'll as soon shackle your wrists or lock you up, if that's the way you want to play the game."

She jerked her face up to his. Such arrogance was not to be borne. "We'll just see about that, Mr. Brentwood."

"That we shall, Miss Payne." He angled his jaw. "And so the game begins."

CHAPTER 3

Sunlight slanted through the sheer window coverings in the dining room, high enough in the sky to reveal that the morning was well spent. Retrieving his pocket watch, Nicholas flipped open the lid, more to rub his thumb over the sketched miniature inside than to confirm the time. *Oh, Adelina.* His gut tensed. His shoulders. His soul. The old familiar ache, one usually stored in a cellar of his heart, rose like a specter—

Until he snapped the lid shut and shoved the watch back into his pocket, banishing memories as if they were lepers. He glanced one more time at the open door. If Miss Emily Payne hadn't shown for breakfast by now, she likely wasn't coming. Not that it surprised him. After yesterday's threat of locking her up, she'd dived into her chamber and never resurfaced. He drained the rest of his coffee, now cold as death, and reset the cup to saucer, then stood—

Just as the woman glided into the room. "Good morning, Mr. Brentwood."

His breathing hitched for the briefest of moments, increasing his frustration. Such a base reaction, however, was not to be helped. Entire battles had been waged and won for lesser beauties than this woman. For truly, Emily Payne was a beauty. Her blond hair was caught up into a pearl coronet, curls thick enough that once loosened would likely fall to her waist. A heart-shaped face framed eyes brown as drinking chocolate, set above lips that would no doubt taste as sweet. Her white day dress, high-waisted and trimmed in pale blue ribbons, clung to the curves that had stolen his breath in the first place. The woman was deadly—on more levels than he'd care to descend.

Donning a face that had won him many a round of faro, Nicholas pulled out a chair for her. "Good morning, Miss Payne, but barely so. Should you have dallied any longer, a good afternoon would be in order, I think."

She tipped her head, studying him, yet took the offered seat, the sweet scent of lily of the valley traveling in her wake. As he settled her chair nearer the table, she glanced up over her shoulder. "Are you always this growly, Mr. Brentwood?"

"No." He sank into the seat adjacent hers. "Your fair presence tends to magnify my starker qualities."

She removed the linen napkin near her plate and shook it out, the snap of the fabric harsh to the ear. A frown shadowed her lips. "Is that a compliment, sir, or a threat?"

Rubbing the back of his neck, he sighed. "Admittedly, Miss Payne, we've gotten off on the wrong foot. I am not the cad you perceive me, and I doubt my first impressions of you are correct, either. I suggest we call a truce and start over."

A slow smile spread, erasing her frown. Dimples appeared on each side of her mouth, indents he'd not noticed in the spare light of last evening. "Very well. . . Good morning, Mr. Brentwood. I am pleased to make your acquaintance."

"Good morning, Miss Payne." He winked. "The pleasure is mine."

Her dimples deepened. "Apparently your charm is every bit as intense as your—"

Claws scrambling across wooden flooring, accompanied by wheezy grunts, echoed in the hallway then burst into the dining room. A fat pug strained at one end of a studded leash, a red-cheeked maid at the other.

"S–sorry, miss! Excuse me, s–sir!"

The maid stuttered—a small flaw but one Nicholas habitually tucked away in his memory for future reference.

The dog yanked the woman to the table, and she bobbed her head at Emily. "Your Alf here will have none of m–me. I d–didn't know what to—"

"You did the right thing, Betsy." Emily bent and unhooked the pup's leash then scooped him up to her lap. "I'll see to my boy."

As Emily nuzzled her chin to the top of the pug's head, Nicholas would swear in front of a grand jury that the dog smirked at the maid.

"Thank you, miss." Betsy dipped a curtsy before retreating.

The dog craned his smug little muzzle toward him, wearing a mien as haughty as his owner's. Nicholas slid his gaze from the pug to Emily. "May I assume the bundle of fur belongs to you?"

"You may." She held the fat pup aloft. "This is Little Lord Alfred the Terror, commonly known as Alf, or Alfie if you feel so inclined."

Her face softened as she rubbed her cheek against the pug's chubby side. Free of guile and without defense flashing in her eyes, Miss Emily Payne quite stole his breath. No wonder her father had reservations about leaving her unattended.

"Pleased to meet you." He spoke to the dog without pulling his gaze from her face.

His voice rang husky in his own ear, nor did she miss the tone, for her eyes widened as she lowered the pug.

Clearing his throat, he gave himself a mental flogging. The woman was entirely too treacherous. "How is your abigail's ankle this morning?"

She settled the dog in her lap, white teeth nibbling her lower lip—and remained silent.

Which was more indicting than a thousand excuses. He'd witnessed the same discomfited silence time and again from the most hardened of criminals. Nicholas cocked his head, knowing the effect to be hawkish. "So, I gather you were remiss on the apology and have not even checked on her as of yet. I suggest this be your first order of business for the day. Other than that, what are your plans? Any pressing appointments of which I should be aware?"

Her nose edged higher in the air as she bypassed the cold toast rack and reached for a biscuit. "None today, but tomorrow I should like to wear one of my new hats when I call upon Lady Westby. She's asked a select few to her home to view her fan collection."

Lest Alf land on the floor, Nicholas passed the jam dish to within Emily's reach. "Well, then, I shall be happy to escort you."

Her biscuit hovered midair, the crystal jam bowl ignored. "Oh no, I really don't think—"

"Your father is paying me very well to attend you, and I never shirk a duty." He leaned back in his seat and folded his arms, enjoying the way her lower lip shot out. "Not to worry, though. I have a way of blending in with the woodwork."

Without a bite, Emily set down her biscuit and met his gaze dead-on. "Am I to understand, sir, that you intend to be stuck to me like a growth?"

Nicholas smiled. He'd been called many things in his day, but this was new. "An amusing way of putting it, but yes."

"There's nothing amusing about the situation, Mr. Brentwood. You can't be serious."

Lifting his chin, he fixed her with a stare. Sometimes silence and one's own thoughts emphasized his position more than a whack over the head with his tipstaff.

"No." She shook her head. "I won't have it. I won't. There is no possible way you fit into my plans. The season is just beginning, and I can't be seen with you at my side. You'll ruin my chances of—"

Her lips straightened to a thin line.

Nicholas leaned forward. "Chances of what?"

She averted her gaze, taking sudden interest in the silver coffee urn at the opposite end of the table.

Apparently he was on to something. "Come now, Miss Payne, I've been direct with you. I expect the same in return. . .unless there's not as much courage beneath that beautiful face as I give you credit for."

She snapped her gaze back to his. So, the little vixen owned a pride as large as her father's wallet.

"I hardly expect you'd understand." Nudging Alf's head up with her forearm, she stroked the sweet spot between his ears. The dog's tongue lolled out in a canine smile. She caressed the animal as if he were the only lover she'd ever—

"Ahh. . ." Nicholas nodded. Of course. He should have known. "Allow me to hazard a guess. You're what. . .two and twenty? Three, perhaps? At any rate, of prime age and social status to shop around for a suitable mate at the marriage mart, eh? I suspect your grand design for this season is to snare a husband. You feel my presence might hinder your efforts." His grin broadened. "And by the way your fair cheeks have turned quite a pretty shade of red, I assume I am correct. Yes?"

Her blush turned murderous. "You are very direct, Mr. Brentwood."

"And entirely accurate?"

Sunshine backlit the bits of her hair not woven in as tightly, creating a golden halo—but the scowl she directed at him was less than heavenly. "Whether I own up to your absurd imaginings is hardly the point." She snipped her words, sharp as scissor blades. "The fact is you, sir, are hardly attired properly to be my escort."

Clothing? This wasn't about marriage but garments? Holding up his sleeves, Nicholas checked each elbow. No rips or tears, and he'd taken great pains to cover the hole in his vest by creasing his lapel just so. His pants, recently purchased and tailored after ruining a pair hunting down old Slim Gant, were too new to even be raveled at the hem. Moving on to inspect his dress coat, he detected only a few frayed threads. Not bad, and indeed far dandier than he'd expected. How could the woman possibly object to his attire when her own was likely plagued with dog hair?

He shrugged. "I surrender. What is wrong with my clothes?"

"They are severe, Mr. Brentwood. Too severe. While quite the match for your personality, if you plan on shadowing me to every function"—her upper lip curled, the same look from eating too much horseradish—"then I insist you invest in more stylish garments."

Though he hated spending money on himself with Jenny so in need, the flare of Emily's nostrils and sharp set of her jaw left no room for debate. Leastwise a debate that wouldn't draw blood. He shifted in his chair, the hard wood of the arm bumping into an ill-healed scar at the base of his ribs—a tangible reminder to choose his battles wisely. "I suppose I could do with a new dress coat, maybe a vest or two. You'll stay put if I go out?"

Alf's fur ruffled with her sigh. She lifted both arms toward Nicholas, jostling the pup, and held out her hands, wrist to wrist. "Bring out your fetters if you wish, though I doubt that is what my father had in mind when he hired you."

Nicholas smiled in full. "Shackles will not suit your fine skin, Miss Payne. Your word will do."

Her hands lowered, but her brows shot up. "My word? Really?"

That she thought him an ogre was not a surprise. That it pricked like a knifepoint did. He softened his tone. "Think of it as a child's game of blocks. You're building trust with me, and I with you. By keeping your word today, you'll lay a foundation upon which to build. Cast the block aside, and I'm not likely to hand you any more until your father returns. The choice, Miss Payne, is yours."

She narrowed her eyes. "Is that not a risk?"

"Yes, considering what I know of you."

A pretty pout twisted her lips. The flash in her eyes was even more beguiling. "You are harsh, Mr. Brentwood."

He curled his hands around the chair arms and stood. Better to gain distance than to reach out and smooth away her sulky frown. "I prefer to think of myself as honest, Miss Payne. A trait you may one day come to value, and one I expect from you in return. Are you up to the challenge?"

Alf snorted at the same time as his mistress. "I never shrink from a challenge, sir."

"No, I suppose you don't." And neither did he. As he bid her leave, though, the real question hammering in his temples was exactly how big of a challenge Miss Emily Payne would be.

Glancing down at Alf, whose squat little body stood at attention at her feet, Emily tried to mimic his compassionate gaze. Why she felt compelled to go through with checking on her maid irked her more than the act itself. Still, it would be satisfying to swipe the superior look off Mr. Brentwood's face next time he asked after her abigail. And honestly, it was her fault Mary lay abed. Before she changed her mind, she lifted her hand and rapped her knuckles on the door adjoining her chamber. "Mary?"

"Come in, miss."

The muted words didn't sound stilted, which would have made this task all the more difficult. Good. Truth be told, she never would have made such a fuss over apologizing to Mary had her horrid guardian not prompted it. Guardian, bah! The thought of the man curdled the tea in her stomach, especially because—though she'd never concede it aloud—she knew his suggestion was the right thing to do.

Emily pushed open the door, Alf tagging at her heels, then stopped short. Across the small chamber, Mary sat in bed, propped atop her counterpane, needlework in her hands. Swaths of linen covered an ankle the size of a small cabbage, so unnaturally fascinating, Emily could not pull her eyes from the sight. The longer she stared, the more grotesque it became. Comfrey and mugwort lay heavy in the air, the words on Emily's tongue even thicker. "Oh, Mary! I am so sorry—"

"La, miss. Think nothing of it." A smile as warm as a hearth fire lit the girl's face. "It doesn't pain me overmuch, as long as I don't stand. Besides, it's a grand excuse for me to loll about all day, leastwise for the next few weeks. Why, I feel like royalty. Please, have a seat. It's nice to have company."

Only one chair graced the room, a rocker, near the coal grate. Emily sank into it and pulled Alf up to her lap. "You're so good, Mary. I envy your charitable heart."

"Go on with you, miss." The girl's laughter bounced from one painted wall to the other—an easy feat in such close quarters. "So much praise is likely to make me ask Mrs. Hunt for a raise in wages, though I daresay your father would have to approve. . .and I hear he's absent."

"That's not the worst of it." Emily rocked forward, careful to keep Alf from toppling off her lap. "My father's gone and hired a guardian for me. A guardian! Can you imagine?"

"Ahh, yes. Mr. Brentwood." Mary's eyes grew as large as her ankle. Sunlight from the single window danced across the girl's cheeks, washing them in a rosy hue. Wait a minute. . . Emily narrowed her eyes. Was that a blush?

"I got a peek at him last night, miss, right after my tumble. 'Twas him who ordered everyone about—even Mrs. Hunt. Rallied the troops, so to speak. Calm yet firm. And if you don't mind me saying, he is quite pleasing to the eye, a real dapper figure, don't you think? All muscle and—" Mary slapped her fingers to her mouth. Apparently whatever tincture the physician had ordered carried a side effect of loose lips.

Emily smiled. Obviously the man had an effect on everyone. "Honestly, Mary, I hardly know what to think. Oh, I'll grant you that he is dashing and all"—her own cheeks grew hot, the traitors—"but underneath is a harsh taskmaster. Do you know he threatened to lock me up?"

Mary's brows shot up, matched by a wicked grin—

A grin her own lips mirrored. "I suppose I did deserve his lecture after causing your accident. Oh, Mary, how will I bear the man's company with you confined?"

"Give him a chance, miss. He can't be all that bad."

Emily blew out a long breath. "He can and he is."

A sharp rap on the door from the hallway cut her off. "Mary? Is Miss Emily—"

"I'm in here, Mrs. Hunt." Shooing Alf off her lap, Emily stood just as the housekeeper entered the room.

"There you are. I've been on quite the search." By the look of her skewed apron and tilted mobcap, Emily didn't doubt her.

"It's about Mr. Sedgewick, miss." She straightened her skirt with one hand while righting her cap with the other. "He's down in the sitting room and refuses to leave until he speaks with your father."

Emily's forehead crumpled, harmonizing with Alf's. "Didn't you tell him Father is away?"

"Of course, but the man won't relent." The housekeeper threw up her hands—a gesture Emily learned long ago to avoid. Pushed beyond her limits, Mrs. Hunt could make a rat-catcher cower. "He asked to speak with you."

"Very well." She glanced down at her pup then back at Mrs. Hunt. "But you shall have to take Alf."

The housekeeper's lips pressed tight for a moment. Then she bent and opened her arms. "Come on, little beastie. Let's go see what Cook has to offer."

Alf shot forward, his stubby legs scrambling across the wood floor. The words *cook* and *walk* produced the same effect.

With Alf cared for, Emily descended to the sitting room and swept through the door. Reginald Sedgewick stood, back to her, with both hands gripping the mantel. The fabric of his waistcoat strained across his shoulders. He looked as if he'd grabbed hold of God's mercy seat.

"Uncle Reggie?"

He wheeled about, the loose cravat of yesterday now flapping completely untied. Only one button secured his vest, the top. Part of a wrinkled shirttail overflowed the waistline of his equally creased pants. Had he slept in his clothes?

"Good day, Miss Emily." His voice was raw.

Emily stepped closer, but not too much. She paused at the tea table by the window. "Are you all right?"

Raking a hand through his hair, he snorted—bullish and bitter. "Hardly. Forgive my abruptness, my dear, but necessity calls for it. I must know. . . Where is your father?"

The question shot through her as effectively as his bloodshot gaze. Had she obeyed yesterday, she might know. "You're his business partner, not I. Have you no idea?"

"Unfortunately, I suspect that I do." With a curse, he spun and slammed his fist onto the mantel, jarring the urn of flowers atop it.

Emily flinched, her breath catching in her throat. She'd seen her father in a rage many a time—overheard heated words from his study—but never had she encountered anger like this from Uncle Reggie.

Silence stretched, like a thread to be snapped—and once broken, it might fray beyond repair. Should she stay or slip out?

She inched back toward the door. Three steps remaining to freedom, her heel sank onto a loosened floorboard. The creak ripped a hole in the stillness, and she froze.

Reggie wheeled about and stalked the length of the room, nostrils flaring.

Fear tasted brassy. She spit out words, attempting to rid her mouth of the sour tang while appeasing the man she thought she knew. "I am sure my father will return within a month's time. He usually does, you know. Then you can clear up whatever is so upsetting to you."

"A month?" He stopped a pace away, his left eyelid quivering. "By then it will be too late."

He shoved past her, leaving behind a trail of upended emotions and a single burning question. . .

Too late for what?

CHAPTER 4

The grating wheels of a passing dray heaped one more insult atop the din assaulting Nicholas's ears. Lombard Street teemed with barrow men, ragpickers, and not just a few mealy apple sellers. Though people abounded, only one was of interest—one he couldn't see. There was no way to hear the soft footsteps behind him, but all the same he knew they were there, like a rat in a shadow. Edging nearer. Closing in on his coattails. Three, maybe four treads to his one. Timing was everything.

Hold. Hold. And—

Brentwood spun and clamped his hand on a wrist hardly thicker than kindling. Wide eyes stared up at him, the whites of which shone in stark contrast to the girl's soot-smeared face. A swipe of fair skin peeked through dirt beneath her nose, a corresponding smudge on her sleeve where she wiped it. Apparently the girl had a bad habit, though that was likely the least of her problems. Threadbare fabric hung off shoulders so sharp, the sight cut to the marrow, especially since the girl was only eight, possibly nine—though judging by the foul language she spewed, she'd lived a lifetime already.

"Lemme go!" came out amid curses and oaths. She twisted, and her bones ground beneath his grip.

"Surely you know the penalty for thievery, girl."

"I weren't thievin'!" A mackerel on a pike couldn't have wriggled more.

He tightened his grip and squatted, face-to-filthy-face, ignoring the pedestrians flowing past them on either side. "And do you know the penalty for lying?"

"I ain't lyin', you scarpin' cully!"

A frown tugged his lips, and he pierced her with the same stern stare he'd used on Emily. "You can lie to me, girl, but not to God."

"Well. . .maybe. . .maybe I. . ." Her voice blended into the clamor. Beneath his fingers, her muscles relaxed. Her chin, once jutted, now softened to the point of trembling. Angry creases disappeared into the curved shadows of each hollowed cheek. He'd seen that look a thousand times. Despair didn't just weight the soul; it scarred the face.

In the brief space of a blink, Nicholas prayed: *Lord, what am I to do?*

"Don't turn me in, sir." The tear in the girl's eye might be an act. But the appeal in her tone was real enough. "I'm powerful hungry, that's what. I ain't et a morsel since yesterday, and then only a crumb. That's God's truth, sir, it is."

Blowing out a long breath, Nicholas reached with his free hand into a concealed slit inside his waistband. Baring an entire wallet in public was suicide. He pulled out a ha'penny and held it up, both their gazes drawn to the bit of copper. For the street waif, the coin meant life—but would the giving of it hasten Jenny's death?

"What's your name, girl?" he asked.

"Nipper." Her eyes didn't shift from the money.

"Nipper, eh?" He masked a grimace. Beneath that grime lay a girl who ought to be wearing ribbons and twirling about in dresses, not scrounging the streets for marks with fat purses. "Odd name for a girl."

She shot him a glance then zeroed back in on the ha'penny. "Ain't so strange when the one what named me is Maggot."

Nicholas frowned and ran through a mental ledger of criminals in the area. He knew of a Grub and a Fishbait, even a Vermin and a Tick, but no Maggot. "This Maggot, where does he live?"

"Din't say 'twas a he."

"All right. Where does *she* live?"

The girl wriggled, eyes yet fixed on the money. "What for do you want to know?"

He softened his tone yet kept it loud enough to be heard above the street hawkers and coaches. "What do you say, Nipper, if I were to visit ol' Maggot and hire you away from her. Would you like that?"

Her face jerked to his, fire in her eyes. "I might be a cutpurse, but I ain't no bleedin' trollop—"

"No, no. I'm not suggesting anything of the kind." He loosened his grip on her wrist. She yanked back her arm and retreated several steps, but his outstretched coin held her in his orbit. "My sister is in need of care, Nipper, and for the next few weeks, I am not able to attend her. I suspect a small chamber of your own would be a great improvement over some rat hole in a rookery."

Her eyes widened. "How did you know—"

"Do you dispute it?"

She swiped her sleeve across her nose, a nervous reaction that endorsed his earlier guess and sanctioned his new deduction.

Slowly the girl extended her hand, palm up. "All right. Anythin's better than Pig's Quay. I'll take the job. But don't worry 'bout ol' Maggot. She'll let me go, and be glad of it. . .long as I keep her garnished."

Nicholas dropped the coin. She snatched it midair and tucked it away in her shoe.

"You give that to Maggot then scurry back here to the Crown and Horn. There'll be a meal and another penny for you." He stretched to full height and gave a nod down the block.

Her face brightened. Visibly. Like the flame of a match in a darkened cellar. "That I will, sir. You can count on me, or my name's not. . . Hey, what's yer name?"

"Brentwood." He offered his hand.

She inched nearer then snaked out her fingers and shook it, her grip a curious blend of frailty and strength.

And quite the act of faith for a pickpocket. Half a smile lifted his lips. "Besides employment, I should like to give you a new name as well. From now on, I shall call you Hope."

She drew back, mouth agape. "Me? Hope?" Her tongue darted over her lips after she said the name, tasting of it as she might a sugared date. A slow smile brightened her face as effectively as a good scrubbing. "I like it, I do. Hope!"

Then she darted into the traffic and vanished. Speedwise, the little urchin was good at her trade. Hopefully she'd do as well with his sister. He shoved his hands into his pockets and turned, tramping the half street to the Crown and Horn. Had he done the right thing?

Pushing open the tavern door, he shed his hat and threaded his way past men seated in clusters. None looked up. He was as much a part of this pub as the scarred oak tables. The smell of tallow and lard, mutton pasties, and the nutty tang of malt ale curled into his nose and sank to a warm place between belly and heart—home. For the past few years, anyway, and until now.

At this time of day, mostly legal professionals or coach drivers on layover took a draft and a sausage pie, though there might be a random playwright or actor in the bunch. Laborers were too busy toiling the day away, but they'd come later. The cotters, the stave makers, chandlers, and silversmiths, all and more would stop by for a mug on their way home to fishwives and laundry women. Though he didn't envy their lot, he understood the pull of returning to something other than four empty walls and a cold bed each night.

He neared the stairwell entry just as innkeeper Meggy Dawkin barreled through the adjacent kitchen door. In one arm she balanced a platter of cheeses, topped with a loaf of bread. Her other hand gripped a tankard, foam spilling over the rim.

"Good day, Megs. How is she?" Nicholas nodded toward the stairway.

" 'Bout time you showed up, Brentwood. I have a pub to run, and I'm no nursemaid." A red curl fell onto her forehead, and she blew upward to knock it back. "Still, I set out your sister's porridge and a mug o' cider early this morn. When I went to pick it up, not a bite or drop was missing. She gets much worse an' you'll have to move her out."

She leaned toward him and lowered her voice. "Can't let it spread that the Crown and Horn houses diseases."

Her words shaved layers off his faith. God forbid Jenny's sickness should spread. But for the moment, this was the best he could afford. In three or four weeks, though, as soon as Payne returned, he'd have the money to move her out to the country.

Oh God, let her make it.

Nicholas scrubbed a hand over his face, feeling a score older than his twenty-seven years. "Has the doctor been here?"

"Like I said, man, I've a tavern to run. He might've slipped in last night when I was dodging pinches and running pints, but he ain't shown his beak today." She whirled to the catcall of a fellow across the room, and a plop of ale foam landed on the floor. "Keep it civil, Bogger!"

Before she set off to topple the fellow—Meggy ran a strict pub—Nicholas called after her. "Oh Megs, I hired a girl to see to Jenny. Small thing. Quite dirty. Goes by the name of Nipper, or possibly Hope. Give her a room and a basin next to my sister's. She'll need to be fed as well."

Meggy frowned at him over her shoulder. "It'll cost you."

"It usually does."

Her lips curved up. "Cheeky devil."

Ignoring her taunt, he turned and tromped up the stairwell, walls closing in like a coffin. Were a fire to break out—no. Better to not think it.

The stairs were steep, and the beam at the landing low. He ducked and veered right. Thin light seeped through a tiny window at the end of the corridor, feeble as the cough leaching through the door where he stopped. He rapped the wood with one hand and reached for the knob with the other. "It's me, Jen. Nicholas."

The hacking increased as he entered the room. Death lived here, crouching in the corner, biding its time. Judging by the rattle of his sister's lungs and gasps for breath, the beast wouldn't wait much longer.

He strode to her bedside and lowered to the mattress. The wooden frame creaked as he cradled Jenny's shoulders and lifted her up. Bones bit into him, sharper since his last visit. "You're worse."

She settled against the pillow he plumped, chest heaving. "Good day. . .to you too. . .Brother."

"Ahh, Jen. You know I wish you the best of days." He coaxed back the dark sweep of fringe from her brow—hair that should've been pulled up and fastened with pearl combs as any other young lady her age. Her green eyes, dulled almost to gray now, followed the movement. Ahh, such a beauty she'd been before disease came calling. Choking back a sob, he forced a smile for her benefit. "How are you?"

In return, a weak smile quivered across her lips. "Dandy and grand, as always."

He stood, pacing the length of the room—eight steps one way, eight back. That she kept such a sweet spirit attested to God's own grace, but why did it anger him? He spit out a sigh, knowing the answer lay deep in his own wicked heart—a reaction he'd have to face one day. But not this one.

He stopped at the foot of her bed. "When was the doctor here last? What did he say?"

The lines of her mouth softened, and for the briefest of moments, a flash of the sister he knew peered up at him. "You worry too much. At seven and twenty, you ought be fretting over a wife and children, not your sister."

Oh, no. Not that topic again. He folded his arms and widened his stance. "You're stalling, Jenny. The truth."

She pushed herself up farther, the effort expelled in another bout of coughing. "That is the truth, Nicholas. You do worry too much. Leave me in God's hands, for there am I content. He alone has numbered my days, and try as you might, you can't change that. You are not God, you know."

Though the Brentwood family tenacity served him well in catching thieves and solving cases, it wasn't nearly as agreeable when employed upon himself. "Very well. I shall leave the matter. . .for now." He grabbed the single chair next to a small table and dragged it to her side. "I've got good news and bad. Which would you have first?"

Her gaze darted from one of his eyes to the other, as if she might read the answers without him speaking a word. "Let's get the bad out of the way."

"As you wish." He reached for her hand. "I won't be able to check in with you as often, if at all. I've a job over on the West End, Portman Square. I'll be tied up for three, maybe four weeks."

"That is bad news." She freed her fingers from his and brushed away his own unruly hair from his eyes, her fingertips cool against his skin. "For who will smooth away those lines on your face?"

"Bah. No one even notices, save you." He caught her hand in both of his, ignoring the clammy flesh beneath his touch. "Now, for the good. I've hired a girl to see to your needs while I'm away. She ought be here later today. She's a street waif, but I believe one with a true heart. I think you'll like her. And should you require, you can send her to fetch me."

"But the cost—"

He let go of her hand and pressed a finger to her lips. "Let me finish. By the time I complete this assignment, I'll have enough to see you and the girl moved to the country. Think of it, Jenny, fresh air and lots of it. Sunshine to warm your bones. I am sure God will have you on the mend in no time."

Her brows lifted. "That must be some wage, but for what? Please don't tell me this is dangerous."

"Only for my patience." He smirked. "I'm safeguarding a lady whose father is off on business, though *lady* is hardly a fitting term. Miss Emily Payne is more wily than a brothel madam."

"Nicholas!" Jenny gasped, setting off a spate of coughs and ending with a strained clearing of her throat. "I doubt you're being fair."

He shook his head. How to sum up what he already knew of the woman? "She's everything you're not, Jen. Petulant. Defensive. A rebellious streak as deep as her father's pockets, paling only in size to her pride. One thing she does share, though, is your beauty, in an opposite kind of way. Where your hair is dark, hers is golden. She's got brown eyes to your green. Her skin is pure cream, a shade fairer than yours, and her wit is a bit more prickly."

Jenny's gaze bore into him. "Seems you've observed quite a bit about the lady in your short time with her."

"I'd have to be blind as old Billy Moffitt not to notice her ways. In the space of one day, she disobeyed her father, caused the injury of her maid, and now demands I purchase some gaudier clothing." He threw up his hands and stood. "If she thinks I'll preen about as a pet peacock, all foppish and—"

"She can't be all that bad."

"She can and she is." Bending, he straightened the blanket riding low on her lap. Jenny would defend a bare-fanged badger if given the opportunity.

"Nicholas?" The tilt of her head was their mother's. . .one if not heeded, often earned him the switch. "You asked me to give this street waif of yours a chance. Seems to me you ought do the same for Miss Emily Payne."

Heat filled his gut. Her logic chafed, stinging and raw. Of course, she was right.

But that didn't mean he liked it.

CHAPTER 5

The sway of the carriage usually made Emily sleepy. Not today. Not with Nicholas Brentwood sitting across from her, the bothersome man. All her nerves stood at attention—an uncomfortable and recently frequent sensation.

While he looked out the carriage window, she jumped on the opportunity to study him undetected—a rare occasion. For the most part, he observed her and her ways, questioning what she did and why she did so. After nearly a week in his presence, she'd discovered very little about him. He, on the other hand, had an irritating way of always turning a conversation around to his benefit.

Streetlamps cast spare light, silhouetting his broad shoulders and pensive face—a face more handsome than she cared to admit. The slope of his nose was straight, the cut of his lips full. His dark good looks gave him an edge, eclipsing thoughts of how much he might be worth, making one wonder for the briefest of moments if it truly mattered anyway.

Faint creases lined the corners of his eyes. Apparently the man laughed, and often, though she'd not witnessed much of his humor. What made Nicholas Brentwood laugh?

A crescent scar curved downward near the apex of his jaw. Not arge nor unseemly, but noticeable. When she'd first met him, she'd sensed a certain ferocity held in check, a layer beneath his wit. This arched white line confirmed it. She frowned. Merriment and violence were an odd combination. A swirl of leaves cast about in the wind would be easier to sort through than the character of this man.

"You analyze me as you might a bolt of fabric. Why?"

His gaze remained fixed outside the window. Good thing, for he'd surely notice the fire blazing across her cheeks—and the feeling irked her. Perhaps, as in cribbage, the best defense would be offense. "A few rules, Mr. Brentwood."

He snapped his face toward hers, the green of his eyes deep and searching. "Rules?"

A smile lifted her lips, victory tasting sweet. For once she'd gained the upper hand. "Yes. After our disastrous shopping excursion the other day, I think a few guidelines should be set."

He snorted. "I'd hardly call that a disaster. Still, you make a good point." A flicker of a grin lifted his mouth. "I think a few guidelines are in order."

The carriage wheels bumped and ground over a hump in the road, the springs creaking as he spoke. Had she heard him correctly? Surely he wouldn't give in so easily.

He held up his index finger. "Rule number one, then, is—"

"No, no, no! I meant *I* have a few instructions." Boorish man. Did he honestly think she'd ask for more requirements from him? She shifted on the seat, facing him dead-on. "Rule number one is do not hover about me like an overbearing governess. I would rather you put to use those fade-into-the-woodwork skills you boast of."

Light twinkled in his gaze. "Did I not perform to your satisfaction at Lady Westby's? As I recall, I waited in the carriage."

"Yes, but you called for me to leave far too early."

"An hour was not enough time to view some fans?" He snorted. "Does the lady own the market?"

"Certainly not. I just didn't want to be the first to leave." She cleared her throat, hoping to cover the whiny tone that slipped out.

He rolled his eyes.

Drat. . .he'd noticed.

Nicholas folded his arms, cocking his head at a rakish angle. "What about the day before last, when you insisted on visiting Bond Street? I was a dutiful baggage handler, nothing more."

"Nothing more? It was quite the scene at Mabley's Lace and Glove when you apprehended that shoplifter." Which was an understatement. Who'd have thought that the tiny shop could hold so many gawkers? And she was still hard pressed to decide which horrified her more—the way he manhandled a thief until a constable arrived or that Mrs. Mabley had assumed he was her beau.

"What would you have me do?" His voice rumbled lower than the carriage wheels. "Stand by while the place was robbed?"

Her lips pulled into a pucker. He'd cornered her again. The only correct answer was one she didn't want to voice.

No, better to forge ahead. "Rule number two. You are my cousin Nicholas."

His eyes widened. "Say again?"

"I can't properly be seen with a nonfamily member unchaperoned. What would people think? And worse...what would they say? I will not become this season's scandal." She lifted her nose, hopefully mimicking his own commanding posture. "You shall be my cousin Nicholas, visiting from out of town."

He shook his head, sending a dark swath of hair across his brow. "I will not lie for you, Miss Payne, nor anyone, for that matter."

"I'm not asking you to." She sighed. An abigail was so much easier to manipulate than this bully. "Simply don't say anything to the contrary. That's not lying."

"No. It's deception."

His words peppered the air like gunshot, and she flinched. "Must you always be so obstinate?"

"I'm not always. Sometimes I'm cynical and other times downright—"

The carriage pitched to the right, and her head snapped to the side. The pearl comb in her hair slipped, digging sharp ends into the flesh at her temple as her head smashed against the window. Vague shouts from the driver ricocheted inside her skull, as did the bark of Mr. Brentwood's reprimand to the man.

"Emily!"

Her name floated midair, like a puff of dandelion seeds. Something warm wrapped around her shoulders. Something cool pressed against the side of her head. She inhaled sandalwood and strength.

"Just breathe."

Slowly, shapes took on edges. Colors came back. Her cheek rested against a white shirt, which stretched across a solid chest, strong and—

A chest?

Emily pushed away, trying hard to ignore the staccato hammering inside her skull—and the way the sudden loss of Nicholas Brentwood's warmth cut to the quick.

The carriage door flew open and the driver popped in a reddened face. "My apologies, my lady, sir. A blasted crack-brained jarvey cut me off, the half-witted—"

"Mind your tongue and see that it doesn't happen again." Nicholas shifted so that she couldn't see his face, but it must've been a fearsome glower he aimed at the man, for the driver stuttered an "Aye, sir" and resealed the door.

When Nicholas turned back to her, though, nothing but compassion shone in his gaze, warm and strong as when he'd—

"Rule number three, Mr. Brentwood." Her words trembled as much as her body. "Is never, ever hold me like that again."

Nicholas frowned. "You hit your head, Miss Payne, and if you will not have me apply pressure to your wound, then perhaps you ought."

He held out a handkerchief, a red stain in the middle.

Her fingertips flew to her temple, meeting with sticky wetness. "Oh." Her voice was a shiver.

"With your permission?" He lifted a brow.

She nodded then wished she hadn't. Her brain rattled around in her head like dice in a cup.

"Turn a bit, this way." He guided her face aside with a gentle touch. The carriage jerked into motion once again, and even so, he compensated for the abrupt movement, never once applying undue pressure. "It's looking better, though perhaps. . ."

This close, his voice rumbled through her, filling places in her heart that she didn't know were vacant. A tremor ran the length of her spine. This was silly.

"Perhaps we ought return home."

"No, I'll be fine." She inhaled, drawing in determination. She might as well take a gun to her head—though in truth it felt she had—as miss the opening night of *The Venetian Outlaw* at the Theatre Royal. "It's merely a scratch, is it not?"

He leaned closer, his breath feathering against her forehead like the kiss of a summer sun. Smoothing back her hair, he lightly refitted her comb. Why was it so hot in here?

"I've seen worse." He drew back, the tilt of his jaw granite. "And I suppose I'll not hear the end of it if we do turn around. But if you feel nauseous or the slightest bit off center, we shall leave. Immediately and without debate. Is that understood?"

"Yes." Remembering the throbbing from last time, she omitted a nod.

"May I have your word on the matter?"

She nibbled her lip. The man placed far too much value on one's word. "Another building block?"

He answered with half a grin.

"Very well, Mr. Brentwood, you have my word. The second I feel I'm about to swoon, we shall return home." She bit back a smile. She'd never swooned in her life, and she certainly didn't intend to start now.

By the time the carriage eased to a stop, she felt certain she'd arranged her hair to hide her bump. Nicholas descended first then offered his hand. When their fingers touched, even through the fabric of her gloves, a quiver ran up her arm. La...she had hit her head harder than she thought.

She shook off the feeling, but once her slippers touched ground, a new one swirled in. Dizziness. She straightened her skirts, concealing a sway, and blamed it on the bright lanterns and commotion of the Theatre Royal. After all, scores of other women must surely be as lightheaded with the prospect of seeing and being seen.

Nicholas offered his arm.

Her stomach tensed. Had he noticed? "I'm fine."

"While I agree there is none finer here tonight than you, Miss Payne, still I insist." He bent, speaking for her alone. "Or shall I heft you over my shoulders as a ragpicker's sack?"

"Have I told you that you're a—"

"Yes. I have duly noted your opinion of me many times over." He settled her hand into the crook of his elbow. "Shall we?"

They swept into the grand foyer, large enough to house the entire population of Grosvenor Square and Mayfair combined, though by now the crowd thinned, most having taken their box seats.

"Your wrap, Miss Payne?" Nicholas stepped behind her and waited as she unfastened her buttons.

While he went to check her pelisse, she darted her gaze from one dress to another, hoping to spy her friend, Bella Grayson. No red curls caught her eye, but a certain blue velvet jacket with golden trim did. Emily pinched her cheeks and tucked up any loose hairs near her injury. Should Charles Henley glance her direction, she'd look her best or die in the trying. With a quick smoothing of her skirt, she took two steps toward him—then a hand on her shoulder pulled her back.

"One moment, if you please."

The loud words traveled on a cloud of rum—hot and sickly sweet. Charles Henley's head turned, and Emily spun before he could identify her. . .hopefully.

Bloodshot eyes stared into hers. Since when did Uncle Reggie imbibe in public? "Good evening, Uncle. I hope this evening finds you in better sorts than our last conversation."

"Any word from your father?"

Her nose wrinkled from the tang of his breath, and she glanced over her shoulder. Charles no longer looked her way. Worse. He engaged in conversation with Millie Barker—the biggest flirt this side of the Thames. "Oh, no." She spoke as much to herself as to Reggie then shifted her body to keep Charles and Millie in the corner of her eye.

"Nothing at all?" Reggie stepped in front of her.

Emily frowned. Her uncle all but blocked her view. "Not a word." She craned her neck one way and the other. No good.

"It's imperative I know the instant you hear anything. Do you understand?" Thunder boomed in her uncle's tone, rolling across the room. Had Charles heard?

Standing tiptoe, she slipped her gaze over Reggie's shoulder while answering. "Mmm-hmm."

Before she could read the expression on Charles's face, her uncle's fingers bit into her upper arms, pinning her in place. The red crawling up his neck matched the lines in his eyes. "Listen to me!" He emphasized each word with a shake.

Her head pounded, centering like a hound to the kill on the tender spot she'd smacked against the carriage window.

"Unhand the lady. Now."

The deadly calm voice of Nicholas Brentwood breached the ringing in her ears—and the glance of Charles Henley her double vision.

If looks could kill, the man scowling at Nicholas would swing from a Tyburn gibbet for manslaughter. Why had Emily spoken to the rogue in the first place? Nicholas had turned his back for what. . . thirty, maybe forty seconds? The woman's magnetism was positively horrifying.

The man looked past Emily to him, smelling like a pirate and looking no better. Granted, his attire was impeccable, but his face twisted into a ruthless mask. Criminals didn't frequent only alleys and shadows. The fellow sniffed, as if he were the one considering something rotten. "Mind your own business."

Nicholas threw back his shoulders. "The lady *is* my business." With one hand, he lifted the edge of his dress coat, just enough for chandelier light to glimmer off the golden spike of his tipstaff.

Slowly, the man's hands lowered. A sneer rose. Emily scooted aside.

"So, you're a runner, eh? Here at the theatre?" The man's voic was a growl. "Should you not be out fetching a call girl for your magistrate or running some other useless errands for the Crown?"

Both Nicholas's hands curled into fists. The spark of fear in Emily's eyes kept them at his sides, but that did nothing to stop the flash of white-hot anger surging through his gut. "May I suggest, sir, that you nick off to Gentleman Jim's if a knuckle bruiser is what you're about.

Unless intimidating women is the extent of your courage."

The man's eyes narrowed. "Are you calling me a bully, sir?"

"I don't have to." Nicholas widened his stance. "You've said it for me."

The man swung back his fist. "Why of all the—"

"Uncle, no!" Emily flung herself between them, stopping Nicholas's heart. If the man let loose now, her face would bear the brunt.

He reached for her. "Emily, don't!"

She shrugged off his touch while facing her. . .*uncle*? Nicholas shifted his weight. Something didn't add up. Why would a family member be such a brute? And hadn't Mr. Payne owned that there were no nearby relations?

Emily wrung her hands. "When I hear from my father, I vow I shall let you know. Please, don't do this."

The man's arm lowered—though his fingers did not uncoil.

"Thank you, Uncle. Now if you'll excuse us." She turned to Nicholas, eyes pleading, and laid her fingers on his sleeve. "Shall we?"

His heart pumped, muscles yet tense, fingers still itching to feel the satisfying smash against cartilage and bone.

But then he'd be no better than the sod in front of him. He tipped his head toward Emily. "Very well."

He led her toward the grand staircase, and once out of ear range of the blackguard, he shot her a sideways glance. "Are you all right?"

"Yes." She gazed up at him, lips quirked. "Reggie's interrogation was no worse than one of yours, albeit a bit more. . .physical."

A frown pulled at the corners of his mouth. Likely if he lifted her sleeve, even now he'd see angry red imprints from the man's grip. "Is all your family so harsh?"

"Family?" Her nose wrinkled, and she kept her silence up the first set of stairs. "Oh, he's not really my uncle."

Nicholas shook his head. "Another one of your faux relatives, eh? Tell me, Miss Payne, do you consider all your acquaintances as kinship?"

She pulled her hand from his sleeve and huffed past him. "Don't be silly."

The pout on her face before she turned matched her earlier expression in the carriage. His biceps tightened, the memory of holding her etched indelibly into his arms. As he followed her down the corridor, sconce light slid over each lock of her pinned-up hair, stunning enough to shame the sun. Shadows lingered along curves he ought not notice. A long-forgotten feeling roused deep in his belly. He hadn't looked at a woman like this since Adelina.

No. Better not to go there. Not now.

Or maybe ever.

He increased his pace and caught up to Emily. "So, tell me. What did this Uncle Reggie want?"

She paused in front of a box marked 22A, hand resting on the knob. Her teeth toyed with her lower lip for a moment. "For some odd reason, he's rather put out that my father left town. He's asked me several times to let him know the instant he returns."

She pushed open the door. Venetian accents poured out, the actors already in full boom.

But before her head filled with intrigue and romance, he stalled her with a light touch to her shoulder and a low voice in her ear. "What is the real relationship between Reggie and your father?"

"Something to do with business," she whispered back then stretched her neck to peer into the box. "May we go in? The play's already started."

Nicholas held his ground—and her shoulder. "Is the man always that forceful?"

"No." A glower as dark as the box accompanied her answer. "Not any more than you're being right now."

The truth of her words splayed his fingers. He followed in her lily-scented wake, scoping out the box as they entered. Eight seats, four to a row, and not a one occupied. Either Mr. Payne enjoyed his own private box, or attendance was lacking—not likely on opening night, though. Emily sank onto a velvet-cushioned chair center-front, and he took up the seat next to her on the right. She leaned forward, her face softening as she focused on the stage.

He tensed and swept the auditorium's perimeter to detect any danger. Twice. Finally satisfied, he leaned back and fixed his gaze on the actors, eyes unseeing. Something wasn't right about the exchange between Emily and her. . .*uncle*. A man so heated over the mere absence of a business partner on a routine trip didn't add up.

Unless the trip wasn't so routine after all.

CHAPTER 6

Reginald Sedgewick loosened his cravat as the hackney he rode in jittered over cobblestones. Breathing had been a forgotten priority for so long that his fingertips tingled. Rage, now spent, left him unhinged—though the rattling his bones suffered could be blamed on the horrid driver. It figured he'd get the broken-springed coach with the one-armed jarvey. Blasted luck.

The cab lurched to a stop. " 'Ere we are then, guv'ner."

A scowl twisted his mouth. Even through the walls of the hack, the driver's voice grated like an off-tune fiddle. Reggie flung open the door and teetered out, one hand clutching the crooked cab for balance. His stomach roiled, and he swallowed back a sour taste.

Now that his feet touched ground, why did the world still tilt?

He paid the driver then paid even more with each painful step to his front door—head throbbing every time his boot met pavement. He should stick to bourbon and leave the rum to pirates and thieves—like Alistair Payne. Fumbling with his fob, he sorted the keys by feel, the slow burn of anger rising once again. The man was a rotten villain.

And what burned him even more was that's exactly how he felt. Twice now—or was it thrice?—he'd treated Emily as if he himself were the rogue. Dastardly behavior. What had gotten into him?

He unlocked the door, stepped inside, then froze. The smell of Burley tobacco curled out from the sitting room, and suddenly he knew the exact cause for his recent ill manners.

Fear.

Drawing in a deep breath, followed by another, he removed his hat, unbuttoned his greatcoat, and hung both on the brass tree. Then he straightened his cravat and while he was at it, brushed out any possible wrinkles in his trousers. He'd known deep in his gut this meeting would come, but that didn't make it any less odious.

Painting a smile on a face as stiff as canvas, he strode into the sitting room. Hand extended, he greeted the lanky fellow puffing on a pipe near the mantle. "Captain Norton, pleased to see you safe and sound. Rather late in the evening for a visit, is it not?"

Norton bent and tapped his spent tobacco into the hearth then stood. Slowly. Like the uncoiling of a king cobra. In three strides he closed the distance between them, his hand snaking out. The captain's grip was no less crushing than the last time they shook, but the flesh more leathery. Calluses were the only calling card the fellow needed to prove his identity. "Aye, it's late, but callin' earlier don't seem to do me no good. You're either out or. . .*unavailable*."

The man's American accent boxed his ears more severely than the hackney driver's ragged tone. Reggie swept his arm toward a chair. "Please, have a seat. I admit I've been rather occupied as of late. My apologies, Captain."

Norton's eyes followed his arm to the chair then retraced the route back up to his face. "This ain't no social visit, Sedgewick. Pay up what you and Payne owe, and I'll be on my way."

"Yes. . .well. . ." Sweat dampened his palms. Good thing they'd already shook. "Surely you realize that at this time of evening no banks are open. And naturally, I do not keep such an amount on hand." He shrugged. "No, no. Times are too dangerous for that. I suggest you call back, say. . .next week, and I'll have a bank draft written up for you."

"Next week?" A sneer slashed across the captain's face. "My ship's been unloaded nigh on a fortnight, now. Time is money, Mr. Sedgewick. The longer I sit idle, the more it costs. . .if you catch my meaning."

The rum in his belly inched up toward his throat, leaving a burning trail the length of his torso. Brash American. Money grubbers, the lot. The very seed of America's rebellion. Reggie sniffed, hating the captain and all that he stood for. "Of course. I shall include a little extra for your trouble."

"Aye. See that you do." Norton pocketed his pipe and stalked to the door then paused on the threshold. "And see that next time I come to call, the money's a-waitin' for me, for I will have my payment . . .one way or another."

A fine mist collected on the edge of Emily's hood where she stood outside the theatre. The fat droplets hung there, daring her to move. One quiver would loose the floodgates and wash her face. So she stood, still as a Grecian statue, and as thoroughly chilled.

Ahead, Nicholas stepped back from the row of carriages lined up like infantrymen in front of the curb. In the rush of departing patrons, his figure alone commanded her gaze. How could he, without a word, make such demands?

As he strode over to her, greatcoat clinging to the hard lines of his body, she shivered. Water rained down, and she couldn't decide which annoyed her more—that she'd noticed his physique, or the cold rivulets trickling down her cheeks and nose. Retrieving a handkerchief, she dabbed away the moisture on her eyes.

"Are you well?" Nicholas's words hung suspended in the mist, lower in timbre than the chatter of passing theatre patrons.

Fighting a yawn, she made a quick assessment, for a simple yes or no would undoubtedly warrant further questions on the matter. A dull ache loitered at the edge of her hairline—though no more painful than the aftereffects of one of her father's lectures. Cold nipped her toes, and she was slightly thirsty, but other than that, she couldn't complain. Tipping her face up to his, she smiled. "I am fine, though in truth I am looking forward to a good night's sleep and to lounging about on the morrow."

His eyes searched hers, lamplight softening his sharp green gaze. Or—an involuntary tingle ran up her arms—was that concern?

Lips quirking into a wry grin, he cocked his head. "What. . .no shopping or visiting? No running about whatsoever? I fear you hit your head harder than you admit, lady. But I am happy that, for once, you will stay put."

Her smile faded. She'd never said she'd *stay put.*

"Your carriage is tenth in line, Miss Payne," he continued. "Should you like to remain here or walk?"

Tucking her handkerchief back into her reticule, she pulled tight the cords before answering. "It would be faster to walk, I think."

He crooked his arm, and she set her glove atop his sleeve, discounting the muscle beneath—though the memory of his embrace would resurface in an instant if she'd care to reel it in. She sniffed. Such nonsense. The man was a brute, nothing more.

Four carriages ahead, the bob of red curls beneath a royal blue bonnet disappeared into the coach, and a wonderfully wicked idea emerged. Without missing a step, she turned to Nicholas. "I noticed Miss Grayson paid you an inordinate amount of attention during the intermission."

His jaw shifted. No words came out. His stride didn't alter a beat.

"I think Bella finds you quite intriguing, as did several others. With all your observational skills, did you not notice the pretty heads you turned?"

He stared ahead, as if dodging patrons and strolling past the remaining carriages were more valuable than a derby prize. "I have no idea what you mean, Miss Payne."

A slow smile lifted her lips. She was getting to him. "La, Mr. Brentwood. You paid more attention to those in the auditorium than the action onstage. Why. . .I don't think you could sum up the play should I ask you to."

He shot her a sideways glance. "The only way to prevent trouble, Miss Payne, is to identify the danger before it strikes. I am not employed to appreciate performances but to look out for your well-being."

"Danger. . .here?" She swept out her hand at the merry theatergoers ducking into coaches. The worst offense she could see was an ill-matched Cheshire frock coat paired with sateen breeches that were much too tight. "There's not much threat at the theatre, sir."

"I beg to differ—"

"Miss Payne! Emily! Pray, hold up."

The voice behind crawled up her spine and settled at the base of her neck, raising the finest of hairs. Did Nicholas Brentwood always have to be right? Sure enough, seconds later, danger in taffeta swished up to her side.

Pink-cheeked and slightly breathless, Millie Barker fell into step beside them. "My carriage is just behind yours. Such a coincidence, for I'd meant to speak with you earlier."

Emily choked. The woman had time for no one unless they wore breeches and bathed in money. Coughing into her glove, she hid the snappy retort then forced a pleasant tone to her voice. "By all means, you should join us."

"You remember my aunt, of course." Millie nodded her head over her shoulder.

Emily followed her movement. At least ten paces behind, a dark shape hustled to catch up—a terrifying sight were they in a back alley. A black veil topped off a black cape with black bombazine skirts billowing out like a cloud of death. The woman draped herself in mourning, although her husband had been dead at least a decade.

She turned back to Millie, but before she could respond, Millie looked past her to Nicholas.

"And this is?"

Emily narrowed her eyes. Of course. Nicholas was the bit of breeches Millie had noticed. And what would Miss Barker's face look like when she discovered the man's chilly personality and even emptier wallet? The thought tasted as sweet as one of Cook's pastries. "I am pleased to introduce my cousin Nicholas Brentwood."

Emily studied his face, eager for a reaction. He didn't disappoint, though she doubted whether Millie could see the jump of a muscle along his jaw.

This could be fun. A chance to vex Nicholas and send Millie sniffing down a trail that would take her off the scent of Charles Henley. She didn't have to fake her smile anymore. "Mr. Brentwood, please meet Miss Millicent Barker."

"Miss Barker."

His stiff nod was hardly a cause for the rapture deepening the color on Millie's cheeks. "I am pleased to make your acquaintance, Mr. Brentwood."

He made no further response, but that didn't lessen the blush on Millie's face. She smiled as if the man had just spouted some epic poem about her beauty. Then she turned toward Emily. "Apparently my invitation to you for dinner tomorrow evening was lost, for I have yet to receive your response. Do say you'll come. It's Aunt's birthday celebration."

Emily clenched her teeth. Lost? Hah. She'd never once been invited to the Barker estate. "Oh?" Her voice lilted with just the right amount of we-both-know-you're-not-telling-the-truth in her tone. "Well then. . . I suppose I'll have to check my schedule."

Stopping in front of their carriage, Nicholas turned at the open door and frowned at her. "But you said—"

Millie cut him off. "I'm sure you'll want to rearrange your calendar, dearest. Not only will your friend Bella Grayson be in attendance, but Charles Henley as well."

"Now that I think of it," Emily shifted her gaze from Nicholas's scowl to Millie's hopeful eyes, "yes, I do believe I am free."

"Excellent." Millie beamed. "See you tomorrow evening then, Miss Payne, Mr. Brentwood." His name lingered on her lips, her eyeballs on his form. Then with a huff to her aunt to "please try to keep up," she darted down the row to her own carriage.

Nicholas's chin twitched as if he ground his teeth. "So much for lounging the day away on the morrow, hmm?"

She replied by grasping his offered hand and stepping into the coach. Let him wonder all he wanted. Millie would wind him around her little finger, leaving her free to entice Charles Henley.

She straightened her skirts and smoothed her pelisse as she settled onto the leather seat. As much as she yet again hated to admit Nicholas Brentwood was right, he was. Her goal this season was to snare a husband, but not just any man.

The prize stag—Charles Henley.

CHAPTER 7

Wine splashing into goblets, silverware clinking—all sounds receded and time stopped for Nicholas. A fine bead of sweat cooled his brow, and he tugged at his cravat. Four glistening blobs of gray taunted him from their half shells on a gilt-edged plate. Mayhap by loosening his cravat, the oysters would slide down his throat without inducing his gag reflex. This was wrong. Whoever conceived of wrapping one's lips around cold pieces of raw mollusk in the first place? The delight of a warm slab of mutton pie far outweighed this epicurean nightmare. For the tenth time in as many minutes, he thanked God he'd not been born a wealthy man.

Across the table, Emily's eyes laughed at him over the rim of her cup. The little vixen ought to be an officer herself, for her gaze didn't miss much. Three more weeks of this—four if Payne was delayed—and he'd be back to dragging corpses from the Thames or hunting down a murderer bent on a killing jag. And it wouldn't be soon enough. Nothing was more torturous than dressing in garments tighter than a straightjacket while eating fish bait served on fine china.

Picking up her dessertspoon, Emily tapped her wineglass, drawing everyone's attention. "Millie, dear, may I be the first to thank you for your gracious hospitality. How thoughtful it was of you to serve your cook's famous oysters. Don't you agree, Cousin?"

Nine pairs of eyeballs skewered him—Millie's shining, Emily's lit with wicked amusement. He picked up his fork. Very well. Two could play at this game.

"My thanks as well, Miss Barker." He glanced at the pale man beside him. "Though my apologies to you, Mr. Henley. I suspect even the smell of seafood swells your throat."

Emily snapped her face to the fellow, her lips flattening. Indeed, Charles Henley had pushed his chair as far from the table as decorum allowed.

Henley reared back his head and pierced him with a look. "How would you know that, sir?"

Nicholas smiled. "Even now a slight flush creeps up your neck and, though concealed, you scratch the back of your hands as if chafed by wool."

"Very good, Mr. Brentwood! Do tell..." Miss Barker leaned forward, one long curl draped over her bare shoulder. A sultry light smoldered in her gaze. "What can you say about me?"

That she was a lioness? A jackal? A leech on the lookout for blood? Without breaking eye contact, he lifted an oyster to his lips and tipped the shell, blocking a retort that ought not be spoken in mixed company—or any other for that matter.

"Come now, sir." Her mouth curved into a feral smile. "Can you detect any secrets simply by observing me?"

She leaned farther, the slant emphasizing her cleavage and the tilt of her lips admitting she knew it. The oyster landed in his gut like a bomb. Once again, the weight of all eyes around the table pressed in on him.

"Why, Miss Barker," he forced a pleasant tone to his voice, "like a fine wine, a woman's secrets are better left to cool in a dark cellar until ready to be served, lest a sour taste remain in the mouth."

"Well said, man!" Beside him, Henley rallied, though it was hard to tell if it was from Nicholas's answer or the fact that a servant had removed his plate of poison. To his left, one man over, a colonel in dress uniform exclaimed, "Hear, hear!" and the fellow next to Henley lifted his glass in a toast.

Millie's eyes narrowed. "I wonder, Mr. Brentwood, what secrets do you harbor?"

"Perhaps you ought ask Miss Payne, for I daresay her eye is as keen as mine."

"Why. . .yes! What a delightful dinner game." Millie flashed a smile at Emily. "Well? What intrigues does Mr. Brentwood hide beneath that cool exterior?"

"My cousin is"—Emily sought his eyes—"orderly to a fault. Demanding as a magistrate. Entirely concerned with honor and justice. Why, I daresay with those traits, he ought be a Bow Street Runner."

Millie's fingers flew to her mouth. "Scandalous!"

Henley snorted. "Imagine."

And the fellow next to him, an Italian named DiMarco, leaned sideways and elbowed him. "You going to sit there and take that, Brentwood?"

"Ahh, but Miss Payne is correct." He threw out the words like a sharp right cross. Blunt truth had ever been his weapon of choice. "With my keen sense of honor and justice, it would hardly serve were I to rebut her in public."

Emily yanked her gaze from him, defeat obviously as desirable to her as a mouthful of oysters to him.

"Judging by that silver tongue of yours, Brentwood," the colonel's voice rumbled louder than the din of chatter that'd slowly resumed, "I'd say you're a lawyer. Tell me, what is your business?"

Nicholas tossed back a swallow of wine. He couldn't very well say he was Emily's nursemaid, though in truth, that was what he'd been reduced to. Replacing the goblet, he paused as the next course was served—a dish of bombarded veal and ragout. His taste buds slowly awoke, and he smiled at the colonel. "I am staying at Portman Square upon Mr. Payne's request."

The colonel nodded. "Completely understandable, given the situation."

The rest of the meal went untasted. Nicholas smiled and parleyed in all the right places, but the colonel's response lodged in his mind like a stone in his boot.

When the women finally departed and the port decanter passed from man to man, Nicholas sat back, glass in hand, drink untouched.

"Looks like you're the prize stallion again this season, Henley." Puffs of cheroot smoke punctuated the colonel's words.

"Yes, and once again I intend to dodge the golden noose of matrimony." Henley downed his port in one large gulp then swiped his hand across his mouth, leaving behind a rogue smile. His hair, the color of a mug of ale, was cropped short and held in check by pomade, stylish, yet not garish—the kind of man who hid behind a carefully constructed mask. "Why purchase the wine cask when sampling grapes from an entire vineyard is so much sweeter?"

"You might get a bit of competition from Brentwood, there." Mr. Barker aimed the red tip of his cheroot across the table. "You seem to have caught my daughter's eye. So? What about it? Which filly will you choose?"

Staring down the barrel of the loaded question, Nicholas tightened his jaw. No good answer could be given without trapping himself. He lifted the glass to his lower lip as if to drink.

"Mr. Henley is correct, no?" DiMarco filled in the silence for him. "These English women are a garden, *molto belle*. Roses to savor in bouquets." The man's eyes twinkled. "It is not the *italiano* way to limit oneself to a single bloom."

Nicholas set down his glass, biting back a grimace. These were the men Miss Payne hoped to snag?

Barker took a long drag on his cigar, the end glowing as bright as his eyes. "Henley might think otherwise when his harem suddenly changes to your tent, Brentwood. Your arrival, I think, is fortunate."

"Oh?" His muscles tensed, desire urging him to jump on that comment and ride it into the ground. Instead, he ran his index finger around the rim of his glass, following the action with his eyes. Better to wait for the quarry to circle back before striking.

"Bully, Mr. Barker, and I vow that Major Hargreave would agree with you." The colonel's bushy eyebrows waggled at Nicholas. "When the old boy catches wind of this, he'll be taut enough in the sails to hear you've jumped on board, especially if it buoys Payne's boat a little higher in the water. Owes him quite a tidy sum, as I understand."

Nicholas tucked the name—Hargreave—along with the remark, into a chest stored deep in his memory.

"I suspect your uncle—was that on your mother's side or your father's?" Barker ground out his cheroot while the truth burned on Nicholas's lips. How to answer that?

"No matter." Barker flicked his fingers, negating a response. "The point is, I suspect Payne is rather in a dither over this whole slave act passing last week. Though it was very insightful of him to expect the passage and summon you to town. At any rate, it's a deuced good thing he's got your fresh blood for a new venue. So tell us, Brentwood, without the slaving industry, what's Payne's game to be now?"

DiMarco, Henley, the colonel, and Barker stared down the table at him. Expectation charged the air.

Lord, please, do not let me shame You with a lie. The prayer barely formed into a coherent thought when a footman swooped into the dining room, small silver tray in hand, and set it on the table in front of him. "My apologies, sir. The messenger said it was urgent and refuses to leave without your answer."

A folded paper sat atop the tray. Nicholas retrieved it, disregarding all the eyes that followed his movement. Sparse words and an ink blot suggested the note had been written in haste:

237 Hancock Lane
Moore

He pursed his lips, inhaling deeply through his nose, then pulled his eyes from the note. He nodded toward the colonel's cigar. "Excuse me, Colonel, might I?"

The man's brows connected, yet he stretched out his cheroot. "Highly irregular, man."

Nicholas connected the tip of the paper to the glowing end, leaving it there until a wisp of smoke and a red spark grew into a flame. Pulling back his hand, he held the burning note over the tray. When nothing but ash littered the silver, he stood.

"Gentlemen." He strode out the door, a thousand questions piercing the black wool of his dress coat.

Bella's lips pulled into a pout. "I still can't believe you never told me about your cousin. Mr. Brentwood is striking in more than one way. I understand why you kept Millie in the dark, but me? Are we not closer than sisters?"

Emily's mouthful of sherry soured on her tongue. "I suppose I am a horrid person, Bella."

Licking her lips, she averted her gaze. Across the sitting room, Millie sat enthroned on a rosewood wingback, holding court with Catherine, Jane, and Anne. Emily leaned sideways and bumped shoulders with Bella. "But I'm not as bad as Millie."

A wicked smile spread across Bella's face. "You don't know the half of it."

Keeping one eye on the other women, Bella lowered her voice to a whisper. "It seems Mr. Henley took quite a break from his political intrigues to start a scandal of a much more intimate nature. I heard that he and Millie—"

"May I assist you with your wrap, Miss Payne? We are leaving." Nicholas Brentwood swung into the sitting room, his bass tone masking the rest of Bella's words.

Frowning, she glanced up at him. He stood before her, holding out her pelisse like a mandate. Authority surrounded him, magnified by his broad stance and even broader shoulders. The severe cut and dark color of his coat added to his stark manner. Could the man never relent from ruining her fun?

"I am hardly ready to leave now, sir." She turned back to Bella.

"Yet I insist."

Those three simple words pulled her to her feet, though her fingernails dug into the heels of her hands. *Yet I insist* meant an ugly confrontation simmered just below that cool green gaze should she refuse. She'd experienced his strong will often enough in the past week—each time she'd thought to have her own way. The man ought to give up law keeping and apply as tyrant of a small country.

"Is something wrong, Mr. Brentwood?" Millie flew to his side, hands clasped, eyelashes fluttering. The consummate hostess concerned for her guest. Emily choked back a snort. Millie's only concern was that she'd not had time enough to garner the man's attention.

"Not at all, Miss Barker. Simply a matter of business." A small smile softened his explanation. "My apologies for such an abrupt departure."

Millie's lower lip folded, and she turned to Emily. "Men and their business. Entirely too tedious. Why, you and I have had no time to visit at all. I suppose I shall have to call upon you on the morrow, hmm?"

Though phrased as a question, it wasn't. It was a verdict. Or maybe a threat. From the corner of Emily's eye, she caught Bella's raised brow and could feel her own forehead crease. Millie Barker had never once come to call at Portman House.

Emily slid her arms into the sleeves of her pelisse, the heat of Nicholas's hands still warming the shoulders where he'd held the fabric—and then she knew. Millie's call would have nothing to do with herself.

Emily locked eyes with Bella. "You'll stop by as well?"

Bella's gaze strayed to Nicholas. "My pleasure."

"Ladies, I bid you good evening." Nicholas nodded and turned on his heel. "Come along, Miss Payne."

His long, hard lines disappeared through the door. Emily huffed. Was she a dog to trot after him at his command?

Bobbing a thank-you curtsy to Millie and murmuring a "good evening" to the rest, she scurried to catch up with him on the front steps. "You had better have a stunning good reason to pull me from this household at such a breakneck pace, sir."

He glanced at her but didn't answer until he offered his hand at the carriage door. "I'm not entirely sure of the purpose, but not knowing how long I'd be gone, I deemed it best to bring you along."

Emily narrowed her eyes at him on her way up into the coach box. "You don't know where we're going?"

He paused before hefting himself up. "I didn't say that."

Exasperating man. The leather seat creaked as he settled in, his manner as nonchalant as if they were taking a drive in the country. She blew out a breath, long and low. "You don't know *why* we're going?"

"That is correct."

The carriage lurched into motion, as abrupt as his answer, and the jostle triggered a slight headache. Or maybe it was Nicholas who triggered the twinge at her temple. Streetlight reached in through the windows, feathering over the strong planes of his face, sweeping along defined cheekbones and jaw, and resting on the curve of his full lips. A fierce scowl assaulted her own mouth. Oughtn't an ogre look repulsive?

She lifted her chin. "So you're telling me, sir, that you've ruined my chances to charm Mr. Henley, giving Millie free rein to bat her eyelashes at the man for the rest of the evening, and you don't have the slightest idea as to why?"

"Yes, yes, and yes." He cocked his head at her, challenge lighting his eyes. "You ought to thank me, you know. Mr. Henley is a louse."

"Oh, spare me! What would you know of Charles Henley, other than the fact that he has an aversion to seafood, which I think was merely a lucky guess on your part."

"Really?"

She curled her fingers to keep from righting the smug tilt of his face. "You are hardly omniscient, Mr. Brentwood. How would you know the heart of a person?"

"I never claimed to read hearts, just behaviors. Details as well." His eyes held hers, driving home his point. "A person's character is most clearly seen not by what they show, but what they hide."

"Such as?"

The carriage wheels ground over cobbles. A watchman cried the hour. She could even hear Nicholas's body moving inside his greatcoat, the creak of leather as he shifted on the seat, but other than that, silence reigned. Eventually, her gaze strayed out the curtained window, traveling from one passing hackney to the next.

"You will keep what I say in confidence?"

His quiet tone and the implication it carried snapped her gaze back to his. "Do you not trust me, sir?"

The sharp cut of his jaw softened. "I trust in God alone, Miss Payne, and that is enough."

She gaped. "What a lonely way to live!"

"Not at all."

There was a fullness in those words. A kind of naked truth that reached into her own heart and illuminated a hollow shell. If she didn't know better, she'd say that Nicholas Brentwood and God were on speaking terms. No, it was more.

He spoke as if God was his intimate confidant.

The very thought unnerved her, and she ran her tongue over dry lips. "I assure you, Mr. Brentwood, any observations you share shall remain with me. Now. . .what did you see?"

"I assume you mean something besides the hired help palming a pickle fork."

"Seriously?"

His smile reached to his eyes. "No. The Barkers' servants all appeared aboveboard."

She rapped him on the arm as if he were Alf. "Beast."

"It's an offense, you know, to strike an officer of the law." His eyes sparkled as playfully as her pug's. "So. . .this DiMarco fellow, what do you know about him?"

"Not much. He's in town for the season. A family friend of the Barkers. Millie tells me he's on the prowl for a wife."

"He's already had one, you know, or mayhap still does."

She shook her head. This one she knew for certain, and the pleasure of bringing down Brentwood charged through her. "Impossible. Millie says—"

"Millie may parrot what the man has told her, yet the slight indentation on the third finger of his left hand cannot be hidden without gloves, which I noticed he wore until forced to remove them at dinner. And speaking of dinner, did you notice Miss Felton's plate?"

Her attention yanked from DiMarco to Jane. She could do nothing more than repeat his words. "Her plate?"

"Full, or nearly so, at the removal of each course. On the other hand, she drained her cup at least six times before dessert. I've seen sailors keel over with lesser amounts of liquor, yet the lady didn't so much as wobble."

Her jaw dropped. Words stuck in her throat, and it took great effort to coax them out. "Are you saying that Jane Felton. . .tipples?"

Even in the chill evening air, his smile warmed her through. "The woman could drink a Gin Lane sot beneath the table then stand to order another round."

She laughed, the carriage ride suddenly more entertaining than Millie Barker's parlor. "Go on, Mr. Brentwood. Tell me more."

He leaned toward her conspiratorially. "If the colonel should ever regale you with his exploits in the Battle of Trafalgar, don't believe a word of it. I doubt the man's ever set foot in the hull of a skiff, let alone a man-of-war."

"La! Surely you weren't aboard the *Victory*, nor do I believe you to be on speaking terms with Lord Nelson. That being said"—she shifted on the seat, gaining a clearer view of his face—"how would you know?"

"Watch his eyes, Miss Payne. The man's gaze darted about like a caged sparrow, looking anywhere but at me in the telling. And the way he scratched behind his ears, I purposely chose to take a turn about the room lest I caught fleas."

Her eyes widened. "You can tell when people are lying?"

"Frequently."

The carriage pitched to the right, and she flung out her hand for balance, the jolt as unsettling as his words. Not that she lied, but sometimes small falsehoods crossed her lips. Could he detect those as well? Better to change the subject. "Of all those in attendance tonight, surely you couldn't find fault with Mrs. Allen. She is the picture of virtue."

"True. . .but her husband is not."

"Aha! Caught you." She folded her arms, triumph sweet on her tongue. "Her husband was not even present, sir."

"No. I suspect he'd want to keep his swollen knuckles hidden from polite company."

She frowned. How in the world would the man know that?

Before she could ask, Nicholas interrupted her thoughts. "Tell me, is Mrs. Allen proficient with a brush and oils?"

"Quite. But I don't understand how you could know such information."

"Deduction. Besides the cobalt stain inside her wrist, just about even with her sleeve, the lady painted—and quite well I might add—her face."

"You can hardly fault Mrs. Allen or her husband for her cosmetics, sir."

"Of course not. The fault lies in Mr. Allen himself. The coloring around the lady's eye deepened from ivory to beige, with the barest hint of purple, noticeable only when she chanced to pass too near a wall sconce. Had she stepped any closer, I daresay her layers of makeup would've melted to her collar. Mr. Allen bullies his wife quite brutally."

Emily sank back against the carriage seat. "Poor Catherine," she breathed out. "I had no idea."

"My apologies, Miss Payne. Perhaps I ought not have—"

The regret in his voice signaled the ending of the game, a checkmate she wasn't ready to concede.

She sat up straight. "One last thing. You avoided this question at dinner, yet I will ask it again. What have you to say about Millie?"

His eyes darkened, blending into the shadows of the carriage. "I claim Mr. Henley is a louse, yet you don't believe me, so perhaps you ought ask Miss Barker about the content of the man. I suspect she's been jilted in a very. . .personal way."

The wheels jerked to a stop. So did her conceived notions of Charles Henley. Was that what Bella had been about to tell her? Or was this some kind of horrid jest on the part of Mr. Brentwood?

She studied his face every bit as intently as he did hers. If he'd discovered that much information in merely the space of a dinner, what of the entire week spent with her? Had he found out about—no. Her meeting with Wren wasn't even until tomorrow's early hours. Still. . .

"What of me, Mr. Brentwood?" Her voice sounded dry. Crumbly. Like autumn leaves skittering down a graveled road. She swallowed and tried again. "What do you know of my secrets?"

The carriage door swung open. A smile flashed, kind and cunning, illuminating Nicholas Brentwood's face an instant before he vanished into the night, taking his answer with him.

Horrid man.

Gathering her skirts, she ducked her head out the door—then froze.

Why would they leave Millie Barker's dinner party for a visit to Uncle Reggie's?

CHAPTER 8

Death was in the air. Heavy. Ominous. Nicholas could feel it in his bones. He inhaled a fresh waft of Emily's lily-of-the-valley sweetness, but if his surmise was correct, a stench was soon to come. The only way to know for sure was to keep trailing the grim-faced butler who ushered him and Emily down a short corridor of a three-story townhome.

Men's voices spilled out an open drawing-room door, one in particular lilting with a poorly concealed Midland drawl. Three heads turned at his entrance. Only one broke from the huddle.

"About time you hike your skirts over here, Brentwood." Fellow officer Alexander Moore strode across the room.

Emily drew up beside him, demanding answers, but Nicholas ignored her. "What's this? Smugglers not keeping you busy enough?"

"Later." Moore pulled him away from the door and lowered his voice. He gave an almost imperceptible tilt of his head toward Emily. "She a stable one?"

Nicholas rubbed his jaw, unsure of how to answer. Emily Payne was constant in tongue wagging, steady with frustration, and solid with determination to have her own way, though he doubted any of that was what Moore had in mind. "Come again?"

"Is the woman given to. . .swooning?"

He glanced over his shoulder, more from reflex than actual consideration. As he suspected, Emily stood near the door right where he'd left her, her gaze leveled at him like a well-aimed kidney punch—one that bruised even when he turned back to Moore. "She can hold her own, but what has she to do with—"

"Good. We've no time to waste. Bring Miss Payne."

Moore's brawny frame dwarfed Emily as he swept past her. Nicholas knew that gait. Moore was on a mission and wouldn't stop to explain anything until due time.

With a sigh, Nicholas shepherded Emily forward. "After you."

Her steps dragged, enough that he soon drew abreast of her.

"I don't understand." She slanted him a cool glance. "Who are these men? Where is Uncle Reggie?"

"This is Reggie's house?" Nicholas stopped, paces away from a door guarded by an armed constable—the same door Moore had disappeared through, expecting them to do the same. Blast it! No wonder Moore had questioned Emily's constitution. Squaring his shoulders, he turned to her. "I didn't know. Perhaps you ought to wait back in the sitting room. I'll—"

"It's now or never, Miss Payne." Moore's head popped out the door. The constable didn't flinch, but beside Nicholas, Emily did.

Nicholas frowned. "Listen, Moore, as her guardian I don't think this is a wise—"

"I can think for myself, Mr. Brentwood." In a flash, Emily shot past him and past Moore.

This wouldn't end well. He dashed after her.

The ticktock of a grandfather clock competed with her sharp intake of air. Understandable. Likely the worst crime she'd witnessed in her life was her precious pug stealing a biscuit or two from Cook.

"Uncle!" She rushed ahead and sank to her knees next to the divan, all but shoving a mouse of a physician out of the way.

The doctor scowled at her. "Now see here—"

Moore's hand on the doctor's arm ended his complaint. "You said yourself nothing more could be done. Care to revise that prognosis?"

The doctor's nose wrinkled. "No."

Moore jerked his head toward the threshold. "Then there's the door."

The doctor's lip curled as if he'd bitten into a rotten bit of cheese.

Without another word, he snatched a black leather bag off the desk and evil-eyed Moore as he retreated.

Nicholas crossed to Emily's side, all the while cataloging the room in a sweeping glance. The wall safe was open. Curtains marshaled in cold night air. A rat's nest of papers was strewn atop a desk. All in all, the room was as torn up as its master.

Reggie lay ashen faced, still alive but barely. Right of center on the man's chest, a deep stain spread across his open waistcoat. His shirt was ripped apart, blood darkening a poultice left over from the doctor's futile ministrations. Pink foam dribbled out one side of the man's mouth. Indeed, he had minutes left, if that. A pistol ball to the lower lung was a miserable way to go.

Emily took up one of Reggie's hands in both of hers, chafing them as if the fellow were dying of cold instead of a bloody suffocation.

"Thank. . .God. You're not. . .hurt." Reggie's words rasped with fluid, his lips sucking air like a landed fish. His eyes closed with the effort.

"But you. . .oh, Uncle," Emily's voice broke, her own chest heaving. "Why would someone want to hurt you? Or me?"

His eyes reopened, mortality a gray film over each. Hopefully the man knew his Maker, for he'd soon meet Him. "Your. . .father. . ." He wheezed, his fight for air forcing Nicholas to tug at his own cravat.

"I fear for you. . .Emily. . ." Reggie struggled to lift his head. "You must be careful." The words drove him back, flattening him against an overstuffed cushion.

Suddenly, seconds were precious.

Nicholas dropped to his knees next to Emily. He hated to be the one to interrupt what might be her last exchange with the fellow, but prudence was a harsh taskmaster. "Of whom, sir? Be careful of whom?"

Reggie's eyes gripped his. Tight. Pleading. The loneliest moment of a lost one's life was often the last. His lips moved, but no sound came out.

Compassion burned a trail from Nicholas's gut up to his mouth. "Call on Christ alone for mercy, man. Now is the time."

Maybe Reggie did. Or not. Hard to tell, for an instant later, his wheezing stilled. His gasps ceased. His struggle for life ended in dismal defeat.

For one horrific instant, Jenny's face superimposed over the dead man's, and Nicholas's own heart stopped.

Emily's wail rent the air. She splayed her fingers, dropping Reggie's lifeless hand. Sobs followed. Turning, she buried her face in Nicholas's shirt.

He wrapped his arms around her, one hand patting her back, knowing full well that shock often accounted for the most unlikely of embraces. She trembled, frail and vulnerable, a whole new facet to the fiery woman.

Glancing up, he met Moore's gaze. The set of the officer's jaw confirmed that condolences would have to wait. Even so, Moore stepped outside to give them a minute.

Nicholas pulled Emily to her feet. Sniffling, she retreated a step, a little wobbly but bearing up.

He retrieved a handkerchief from his dress coat and held it out. "Forgive me. Had I known, I never would have brought you here."

"No, don't think it. It's better he had someone he knew with him for the final moments." Her gaze strayed to the dead man on the divan. Color drained from her face. "He. . .he. . .what about my father? What did he mean? Why must I be careful?"

Each word grew shriller, her chest fluttering as if she'd taken the bullet. Nicholas stepped in front of her, blocking her view of the corpse. "Miss Payne—"

"I. . .oh my. . .what if—" She swayed, her eyes dark holes in a face white as cotton. If the woman didn't breathe, and soon, he'd have two bodies on his hands.

Grabbing her upper arms, he forced his face into hers. "Emily!"

Startled, she met his gaze. A faint bluish line rimmed her lips.

"There is nothing to fear. I'm here, and no one will take you from me. Do you understand?" He measured his words, doling out each one like a lifeline, willing her to grasp onto the strength in his voice. "Upon my word, I'll keep you safe. I vow it, on pain of death."

Her throat moved with a swallow. A lost little girl couldn't have looked more exposed. Slowly, color crept back into her cheeks. The trembling beneath his fingers stopped.

"Good." Half a smile tipped his mouth. "You're doing better already."

"Thank you." Her voice was a whisper. A shell. Hardly more than a piece of chaff on the wind.

But it was a voice, nonetheless.

He smiled in full.

Officer Moore, maid in tow, cleared his throat as he entered the room, cuing an end to consolation. Nicholas released Emily's arms, pleased that she remained straight and tall. "Now then, you shall return to the drawing room. Mr. Moore and I have a bit of work to do in here."

Her eyes widened. The lovely pink in her face fled once more. "But—"

"None of it. You're a strong one, you are." Lifting his chin, he looked down his nose at her. "Unless my assessment of Emily Payne is incorrect. Do you hide a yellow streak beneath those skirts?"

She set her jaw, a blue spark of anger lighting her eyes. "You, sir, are a—"

"Rogue. I know." He nodded toward the maid while turning Emily to face her. "Go."

"This way, miss." The maid spun, apron strings fluttering behind her. Clearly, sharing a room with her deceased employer didn't top her list of favorite duties.

When he felt sure they were beyond hearing range, Nicholas lifted his eyes to Moore's. "So, what have we got?"

Moore stalked to the open window, a hunter on the trail. His long legs stretched with the grace of a lion. His dark blond hair, longer than decorum allowed, blew back with the breeze, adding a mane-ish effect. "As you see. Point of entry."

"Don't you mean exit?"

"That too. I queried the servants. No one was admitted by the front door. In truth, no one suspected anything other than that Reginald Sedgewick was alone in this study."

Nicholas rubbed at the tension in his neck. "Then what?"

"Some kind of heated debate, I suppose. One which Mr. Sedgewick lost." Moore swept his hand toward the mess on the desk and the overturned chair behind it.

The clock in the corner kept a steady beat as Nicholas studied the room. He fingered through the documents. Correspondence mostly, notes inquiring about shipment arrivals or departures. A few invoices, all headed with Sedgewick & Payne. Stepping around the desk, he righted the chair then peered into an open wall safe. Empty. He frowned. "But why lose a heated debate when he obviously handed over all his valuables? Unless..."

Nicholas squinted and ran his fingertips over the locking mechanism. A Bramah, without so much as a scratch. No surprise, though. As far as he knew, no one had yet collected the two hundred guineas promised by the manufacturer for picking one of their locks. He turned to Moore. "No sign of force."

Moore rubbed the back of his head. "Unless he was shot first then told to—"

"Unlikely. If that were the case, Reggie there would be sporting a blown kneecap, not a hole in the chest. Why comply when death is imminent?"

"True." Folding his arms, Moore nodded. "It could be the vault was empty when he opened it, hence the argument, leading to rage and eventually murder."

"And if the suspect left here unsatisfied, monetarily speaking, then that would explain Sedgewick's warning." A growl rumbled in his throat. "Which is clear enough on Emily's part, but what of her father? Were Reggie's last words a warning *for* her father or *from* him?"

Moore shrugged. "What exactly is Mr. Sedgewick's tie-in with your ward? Why spend his last moments on earth to see that not only Bow Street was summoned but Miss Payne in particular?"

"Exactly." Nicholas ran his hand through his hair. "That's what concerns me most."

And it did. More than he cared to admit.

CHAPTER 9

After hours of tossing and turning, recounting ghastly images of her uncle's lifeless eyes, Emily was glad to focus on something else—even if that something else taxed her in ways that were every bit as nerve-racking. Slipping out of the town house an hour before dawn for a clandestine meeting with her former maid had seemed like good idea at the time she'd arranged it. But now. . .

Clutching her package to her chest, Emily glanced over her shoulder. A dark, empty street stretched behind, made all the more ominous by a fine mist suspended midair. Her footsteps alone echoed off the brick townhomes. At this hour, only an occasional carriage or a dray bent on an early delivery run traveled the lanes of Portman Square. So why the breath-stealing impression that eyes followed her every move?

She resettled the pack over her shoulder and tugged her hood forward. Nerves. That's what. Barely six hours ago Uncle Reggie had died right in front of her. No wonder jitters marked her every step. If Wren weren't counting on her, she'd still be curled up under her counterpane, sleeping off the dreadful experience. Leaving the safety of her bed had taken more courage than she'd realized.

And what would Nicholas Brentwood say were he to find her chamber empty?

She quickened her pace. She'd just have to make sure he didn't. Two blocks down, she turned right. Ahead, near a cabstand that wouldn't house a hack for at least another hour, a lone figure lingered beneath a sputtering lamppost. The shape was slight, short, and entirely Wren-sized. Emily shot forward.

Her former maid met her halfway. "Oh, miss! So good to see you."

Emily slung the bag down to the wet cobbles and folded Wren's hands into her own. Cold flesh chilled through the fabric of her gloves. "It's always good to see you, Wren. How are you holding up?"

"I'm well, miss, as is the babe." Wren pulled back her hands and rested them on the swell of her belly. For a brief moment, half a smile lit her face. "Thanks to you, that is. Without you. . .why, I don't know what I'd do."

"None of it. You're a strong one, you are." The same words Nicholas used for her tasted sturdy and warm in her own mouth and hopefully lent similar courage to Wren. "Please tell me you've found a place to stay."

"I have. I've got four walls and a bed of my own, which is more than I can say for other girls in my. . .condition." Wren's gaze lowered.

Anger lifted Emily's chin. "It's not fair, Wren. None of this is. That scoundrel of a captain ought to be scratching out his existence in the streets instead of you. And my father"—she sucked in a sharp breath, mourning afresh her mounting loss of respect for the man—"why I'm still so furious he let you go without references, I can hardly stand it."

"Don't fret. It's all right. Truly. I've found peace." She reached out one hand and squeezed Emily's. The sharp angles of her cheekbones softened, and through the mist and dark, light sparkled in her eyes. "I know it's strange to hear me say so, but I forgive them both, your father and Captain Daggett."

"Wren!" *Forgive them?* The words boxed her ears, foreign and completely abhorrent. Emily yanked back her hand. "How can you? They ruined your life!"

"No, miss. It's not like that, not at all. I see it different now." The peaceful look in Wren's eyes spread to lighten her whole face, or was that simply streetlight reflecting off the mist on her cheeks? "Only by losing everything could I gain the one thing I would've overlooked."

"What's that?"

"Need."

Emily frowned. "You're telling me that need, want, the lack of shelter, food, and clothing, is a *good* thing?"

"Didn't call it good, miss, but it is a blessing." Wren's smile would shame the sun, and mayhap did, for along with it the hint of dawn barely bleached the sky. "Aye, miss. I know it don't make sense, but I've found that God is more than enough, even in the direst of situations."

Emily couldn't help but shake her head. "You're starting to sound like Mr. Brentwood."

"Mr. who?"

She sighed, for truly. . .how to put into words her conflicting emotions about the man? One minute a bully, exacting and demanding, the next consoling her as a dear friend. Even now, if she closed her eyes and thought of it, she could feel his solid arms circling her, breathe in his peppery shaving tonic, lean into his strength.

A fresh waft of morning fires being stoked banished the memory. Nearby, households awakened. She bent to retrieve the oilskin bag and held it out to Wren. "Here is an old dress of mine I've let out in the front. It ought hold you over until—when did you say?"

Wren hugged the pack to her chest. "Nigh but two more months now, near as I can figure."

Emily lifted her chin, a gesture she'd seen Mrs. Hunt use to rally the servants a hundred times. "Well then, there's some tincture in the bag from the apothecary, good for you and the babe. A spoonful at night and one in the morning. I've included a spoon."

"Ahh, miss. You're always thinking."

The warmth in Wren's voice burned a trail to her heart. How she missed the girl and her sweet ways. "Tucked deepest inside is a coin purse. There's enough to hold you over in food until we meet again next month. Same time and place?"

"If you don't mind. Thank you. One last thing, though I hardly deserve more. My mother, does she. . ." This time there was no mistaking mist for the single tear sliding down the girl's face. "Does she ask after me?"

Emily's lips pressed into a tight line. Must it be her lot to break the girl's heart afresh? "In truth, Wren, I've not told her yet that I've been meeting with you. I've meant to, but the time's never been quite right. Oh, I've hinted around and such, but your mother's as adamant as ever when I bring up your name. I feel sure, though, that once the babe is born, once she sees the sweet little one, she shall change her mind."

"Aye. Mayhap." Wren's voice was hollow. She settled the pack over her shoulder and dipped a small curtsy. "Good day, miss."

Emily nodded, for truly there was nothing more to say. Watching Wren retreat spent the small account of optimism she held for the girl. To what part of town would Wren's feet take her? Who would be there for her should something go wrong? Except for Wren's growing belly, she was so small, so vulnerable.

Shivering, Emily turned her back to the desolate figure. Dampness soaked into the leather of her shoes while she retraced her steps. As she neared the corner, a quiver shimmied along her shoulders—but not from cold. The distinct thud of boots pounded dully in the mist behind her.

She increased her pace and refused the urge to look over her shoulder, denial lending some confidence. *Please God, may it be one of those coal heavers on an early delivery.*

But the boot thuds upped their tempo as well.

Fear settled low in her stomach, making her feel as if she might vomit. The ghastly memory of Uncle Reggie lying waxen and gray added to the nausea. She'd made a huge mistake coming here by herself. The realization burned white hot, like the pretty red coal in the grate she'd touched as a tot. She'd discovered its danger too late . . .just like now.

Still, maybe the fellow behind her was simply in a hurry. After all, she—

The world spun. Her back slammed against a brick wall. Every nerve shrieked a warning, but she couldn't scream.

A glove covered her mouth.

Hot breath blazed across her forehead. "I'll remove my hand, but upon my word, you scream and this will go all the worse for you. Do you understand?"

Emily's head moved beneath Nicholas's fingers. A stingy nod, but an acknowledgement nonetheless. Her hood had fallen back. Lengths of blond hair cascaded over his sleeve. He lowered his hand, bypassing the pretty neck he'd love to wring, and clamped his fingers onto her upper arm instead. "You little fool. What are you doing out here alone?"

"You frightened half my life away!" Her voice shook, as did the slim arms beneath his grasp. "I was meeting a friend. Nothing more."

But he would not be moved. Not yet. "Only criminals meet by shadow of night."

"Wren is a friend! One who needs my help. How dare you infer anything other." Her body writhed with each word. "Now let me go."

"Not until I've had the whole story."

"I told you—"

Was the woman truly that daft? "Blast it! You saw what happened to Reggie." He clenched his jaw instead of shaking her like the empty-headed rag doll she playacted. "How am I to keep you safe with a handful of half-truths?"

Instantly she stilled. The whites of her eyes glistened abnormally white. "Surely what happened last night has nothing to do with me."

"Honestly, Miss Payne. This is not a child's game we're playing. Why do you think your father hired me in the first place?" He jerked his head toward the spot where she'd been standing only minutes before. "I suppose you didn't take the time to notice the cutthroat across the road from the cabstand."

Her gaze slide past his shoulder. "Don't be ridiculous. I don't see any. . .oh my. . ."

"And I'll wager you also didn't see the blackguard trailing you on your way here, either. What sorry state do you think you'd currently find yourself in had the flash of my pistol muzzle not guarded your steps?"

Her eyes widened. "You mean you—"

"I mean you can thank God for waking me when I heard the floorboard squeak outside your chamber door!"

Her face blanched, gray as the dawning daylight. She tipped her head back until it rested against the brick wall. Moments passed, as did an early morning carriage behind him, the ground-level fog muffling the grind of the wheels. Perhaps it was a bit much for her to take in, but finally—mayhap—she understood the gravity of her situation. A small victory. Nonetheless, every successful battle, no matter how slight, led to winning the war.

With a sigh, he released his hold on her and stepped back. "Who is this Wren that so desperately needs your help, enough so that you'd endanger your own life?"

Once again her gaze darted toward the cabstand, as if by looking the woman might magically reappear. "Wren—*Lauren*—Hunt was my abigail before Mary. I've known her for years. Wren and I practically grew up together." Her voice softened. Apparently she was very fond of the girl. Then quick as a spring cloudburst, a shadow crossed her face. "She was forced to leave several months ago."

"Why?"

"She is. . ." Emily's gaze shot to the ground. "Wren is with child. Because of me."

"You?" He snorted. "Hardly possible, and is in fact an impossibility altogether."

She snapped her face back to his. "Do not think to school me in the specifics of nature, Mr. Brentwood. Would you have the story or not?"

He raised both hands. The woman could change emotions faster than a cutpurse in a crowd. "Go on."

She took her time gathering the loose ends of her hair, tucking them behind her head, and reseating her hood before she continued. "It was late last summer. We'd just settled at Abingdon, our country home. Father had a guest in for an early season hunt. The weather was hot, oppressively so. I'd ventured out late one evening, seeking air, and Father's guest, Captain Daggett, chanced upon me—though now I realize it likely wasn't chance."

She paused, her face hardening into a brittle mask. "I managed to fight the man off, but Wren, well. . .when she came looking for me, Daggett took her instead."

Nicholas rubbed his jaw. How much of this was true? He didn't doubt Emily could scare off a baited bear with her tongue, and the figure she'd met at the stand was with child, as stated. But was Payne such a rogue as to throw out a long-standing servant into the street? "Surely your father—"

"Father chose to believe Daggett's pack of lies." Her tone took on a hard edge—one he hadn't heard before. "And I suspect were it me instead of Wren, he'd still have sided with the man." She nodded toward the stand. "That could just as easily be me."

The woman ought to be onstage. Drama was in her blood. He shook his head. "You must be mistaken. There's got to be more to it, reasons your father chose not to share with you."

Her gaze locked on to his, resolute and slightly unnerving.

What he read there chilled him to the marrow. These were no theatrics.

"Business is my father's life, Mr. Brentwood. Without money, I daresay he'd stop breathing. Once set on a deal, he'll allow nothing or no one to alter his plans, whether that means banishing a dear family servant. . .or his only daughter. Fortunately for me, it didn't come to that. But sweet Wren—"

Her voice cracked along the edges, and if the tears shining in her eyes spilled over, he'd rip off his gloves and wipe them away.

Instead, he simply said, "Thank you."

Her brow crumpled. "For what?"

"Your honesty. Truth is a gem to be admired and very pretty when it comes from your lips."

Were the sunrise not obscured by clouds, it would be chastened by the blush rising on her cheeks. This was no pretend pleasure. It was real. Fresh. And entirely alluring. A charge passed between them. He could see it in her eyes, feel it in his gut.

"Yes. . .well. . ." The fine lines of her neck moved as she swallowed. "I'm not usually so candid. Do you have this same effect on criminals?"

"What effect is that, I wonder?" He tucked his chin and purposely lifted one eyebrow, knowing the result it would have.

She leaned forward, a breath away. He heard the small sound of her lips parting, but he daren't lower his gaze to them. Danger didn't issue only from the barrel of a gun.

For the good of them both, he retreated a step and pivoted. "We should return."

Before she could answer, he set a brisk pace, feeding off her protests to slow up and using her indignation to cool the warmer feelings he ought not entertain. Caring *about* a client was one thing. Caring *for* a client was quite another animal altogether.

Still, she had shown an extra amount of compassion for her former maid. Quite in contradiction to her sometimes shrewish demeanor. Perhaps, underneath it all, she hid more heart than he suspected. Unique thought—one he'd mull over later.

By the time they reached the townhome door, they both were breathless. She from the insane pace he'd set. He because of the figure stepping from the sheltered nook leading down to the servants' entrance.

Perhaps Hope hadn't been the best choice to name the little urchin, for her appearance meant anything but.

CHAPTER 10

Please, God. . .grant that I get there in time. Nicholas spent the entire carriage ride from Portman Square to Lombard Street alternating between silent prayer and peppering Hope with questions.

It was the longest ride of his life.

Before the hackney wheels stopped turning, Nicholas bounded out the door. Hope's feet hit the ground behind him. Though still early morning, Lombard Street was in full bloom, which for some odd reason irritated him. The hawkers were too loud. The horse droppings too foul. The world had turned brash and harsh and entirely too precarious. He flipped a coin to the driver without missing a step.

Ducking into the Crown and Horn, he strode the length of the pub, avoiding eye contact with Meggy Dawkin as she delivered a plate of mutton hash to a customer. Nevertheless, he felt her stare. She wouldn't condemn him for all to hear. She didn't have to. The way she thunked the plate onto the table voiced her opinion in no uncertain terms. Mistress Dawkin wanted his sister out of there, and so did he.

But not in a wooden box.

He took the stairs two at a time, crediting Hope for the deft way her footsteps tapped behind his. By the time he reached the second-floor corridor, the doctor was already stepping from Jenny's room. He was a tall man, angular in an almost grotesque way. His black greatcoat shrouded his length like a shadow, an eerie image of the grim reaper.

Nicholas closed the distance in a heartbeat. "Is she—"

Dr. Kirby held up a hand. "She's resting, for now, but she won't stand another attack. I suggest you say your good-byes."

The incendiary words scalded his ears then burned deeper, branding his soul. How exactly did one let go of their last family member? He met Kirby's even stare. "Is there nothing you can do?"

Hope hovered at his back, but Nicholas felt his own optimism dwindling as Kirby shook his head.

"I told you from the start, Brentwood, I'm no miracle worker. Better you bring your requests to God, if you think He's listening." The doctor sidestepped him with a nod of his head and an added "good day."

Nicholas stood stunned. Of course God was listening—but that didn't mean God would answer in an agreeable fashion. Sucking in a shaky breath, he twisted the knob and eased open the door. No sense waking Jen if she'd just gotten settled.

His care was wasted. Her eyelids raised the instant his boot crossed the threshold. Overlarge eyes, framed by gaunt cheekbones, gazed into his. The slow move of her pale fingers drawing up the bedclothes spoke of weariness. The downward slope to her brow, resignation. His chest tightened. He'd seen that look many times on the battlefield and more recently on Reggie.

He knelt on the cold wooden floor and lifted one of her hands in both of his. His posture mimicked Emily's from the night before, but hopefully this prayer would see a different result.

He forced a smile, though likely it looked more like a grimace. "Ahh, my sweet Jen. How are you today, hmm?"

"Dandy and grand. . ." She winced. "As always."

Her voice was a thread. Thin. Fragile. Instinct urged him to buoy his own with enough strength for the both of them. "I suspect, then, that there shall be no end of the balls I must take you to or the dinners you should like to attend. And the suitors. Well, I suppose I'll have to beat them away with my tipstaff."

Her frail smile disintegrated. "Dear Brother. When shall we stop this masquerade?"

He swallowed, but it did nothing to relieve the lump in his throat. "Never."

The word came out harsher than he intended. Carefully, he tucked her hand beneath the blanket then stood and raked his fingers through his hair. "Two weeks, Jen. Only two, and my employer shall return. I'll have the money to see you off to the country. You'll breathe easier there—I know it—and you'll find that this isn't a charade after all."

He knew he was rambling, but it couldn't be helped. "You'll be dandy and grand—" His voice cracked, the following words nothing but a whisper. "As always."

Her gaze pierced his soul. "For one who values truth, Brother, you employ a lie with ease."

"Jen, I—"

"Don't make excuses." Morning light streamed through the single window, a bright contrast to this deathly conversation. The lone sunbeam slid along her skin-wrapped bones like a knife, cutting and severe. Already she looked like a cadaver.

"Allow me this moment to speak my heart, for I may not have many more. I shall miss you, dearly, but please understand, I am going to a better place. A place I want to be." She paused, her chest riffling the blanket with her quickened breaths. "Let me go, Nicholas."

He clenched his hands into rock-hard fists. God help the next criminal that crossed his path, for this depth of emotion could not be contained for long. It wasn't fair. None of it. He should've died a hundred times over for his wicked ways, not her.

"I should like to rest now." Her voice was a fragment of a whisper, barely pulling him from his thoughts. Slowly, her eyelids closed.

"Of course." He bent, kissing her brow as a benediction, unable to keep from wondering if it would be the last time. "Sleep sweet."

Straightening, he lingered, casting a long look at the shell housing his sister.

Then he turned and stalked out.

Hope stood exactly where he'd left her, leaning against the corridor wall. She looked up at his appearance. "Is Miss Jenny dea—"

He scowled at her. "Don't say it."

The girl's decorum was nonexistent. Not surprising. Death played alongside the street children, ever present in their games, ready to steal another one of their companions when they weren't looking. 'Twas a gruesome round of hide-and-seek.

Nicholas shook off the morbid thought. "My sister is resting. Have some broth ready when she wakes. I'll return as soon as I can, but don't hesitate to fetch me once more if she. . .no. That won't do."

Jenny ought not be left alone. He scrubbed his jaw, stubble pricking his fingertips. The late night and early morning hours he'd kept slowed his mind. *Think. Think.*

Digging out another precious coin from his pocket, he handed it to Hope. "If my sister needs me, hire a cab, just like I did this morning, and tell the driver to deliver the message. Can you do that?"

Hope bobbed her head. "Aye, sir."

"Good." He tromped down the hall and flipped up his collar as he descended the stairs. A small barricade to hide behind, but he had no stomach to argue with Meggy about moving his sister now. As his foot left the last tread, he scanned the public room. The last swish of her skirt hem, followed by streaming apron strings, disappeared through the kitchen door. He hustled past the diners finishing their breakfasts and slipped out the front.

Relief lasted only until a brawny man in a dun-colored greatcoat rounded the corner and plowed through the pedestrians, straight toward him.

Nicholas frowned. "I don't suppose you're frequenting the Crown and Horn for the hash, eh, Moore?"

Alexander Moore's hat sat low on his brow, making Nicholas aware he'd neglected to don his own. "You've given me quite the rundown this morning, Brentwood."

Nicholas fell into step beside him. If Moore had taken the time to track him, something was up. "You know me. I like to keep on the move. Where are we going?"

Moore shouldered past a knife grinder blocking their way, barking about the quality of his sharpening services. "There's someone you ought to see down at the dead house."

Nicholas shot him a sideways glance. "Who's that?"

"That's exactly what I'm hoping you can tell me."

Emily stifled a yawn, the third in as many minutes. She straightened her back, but the settee cushions beneath her felt softer with every tick of the clock. If she sat here any longer, she'd curl up next to the little pug snoring at her side.

"Really, Emily, I've far overstayed my visit. In truth, I may have set a record." Across the sitting room, Bella turned from the window. The sheer curtain shimmied into place. Displaced daylight backlit her red hair, creating a radiant halo. "There's no sign of Millie. Do you think she'll really call?"

Standing, Emily wiggled life back into her feet. Alf jerked up his head then must've decided the effort wasn't worth abandoning his comfy bed. His scrunchy face flopped back down onto his paws. Emily sighed—better that than another yawn. "You're right. And you're a dear. I owe you for frittering away your morning with me."

"Pah! You saved me from having to shop with Mother. You know how much I abhor traipsing from one merchant to another."

Ringing the bell for the maid, Emily smiled. What woman in her right mind wouldn't want to browse for new shoes or a bonnet? "Remind me again why we are friends?"

"Opposites attract, or so I'm told." Bella returned the grin then stooped to pat Alf between his ears. "Good thing, for you shouldn't like to be compared favorably to your wrinkly pup now, would you?"

"Not if I'm to attract Mr. Henley this season."

Bella straightened, humor draining from her face. "Have you listened to a word I've said? After all I've told you about him and Millie, why would you even want to interest that man?"

Emily stepped forward and placed a light touch on her friend's arm. "Not that I doubt you, but honestly, I don't feel I have a choice. Father won't put up with me forever. You know it's only for my mother's sake—God rest her soul—he's been gracious thus far. Besides," she continued, squeezing Bella's arm, "if only half what you shared is true, don't you think Millie is the one to blame every bit as much as Mr. Henley? For goodness' sake, Bella, you've seen the woman in action. She's nothing but a lace-covered tart."

Bella's lips twitched. No wonder. She was probably battling over whether she should gasp or giggle. "True, but that hardly means Mr. Henley should have, well. . .you know. Once word of this gets out, which shan't be long if you and I already know, Millie will be ruined, and Henley will merely get a pat on the back."

Emily frowned, the double standard grating her sensibilities as a tooth gone bad. It was as ludicrous as Wren's situation and about as just. No doubt Millie deserved whatever she had coming, but Wren didn't. Why should she have to live in a hovel while the lecherous captain sailed the high seas, free to prey on the next ruffle and bow? Her frown deepened into a scowl. "Whoever came up with such ridiculous societal rules is a bird-witted cod's head."

"Emily!"

A wicked grin erased her glower. "Sorry. I didn't mean to say that aloud."

The maid pattered into the room, holding Bella's pelisse aloft. Turning from Emily, Bella shrugged into her wrap—but not fast enough for Emily to miss the twist of her lips. "Please, Em, rethink your options. Mr. Henley isn't the only available man in London."

"But he is the richest. And at three and twenty, I find my options get more limited with the passing of each season."

"Just. . .be careful." Bella's eyes sought hers. "I'd hate to see anything happen to you."

"Have you ever known me to act without thinking it through first?"

Her friend's pretty lips parted, but Emily beat her to it. "Go on with you. I'll see you tomorrow at church, hmm?"

"Do yourself a favor and pay attention to the sermon for once. Who knows, perhaps God will change your mind about Henley. You're obviously not listening to me." Her tone softened as she headed toward the door. "And give that yummy Mr. Brentwood my regards whenever he returns, in a discreet fashion, of course. Until later, Em."

Bella's departure left a void, one that fatigue quickly filled. Emily arched her back then snapped her fingers, rousing the pug. "Come along, Alf. A cozy counterpane is calling our names."

She crossed the room and hall. Doggy toenails tip-tapped double-time to her pace. Each step up the staircase required effort, hers because she was weary, his from stubby legs. Perhaps she ought not have spent the entire morning waiting around for Millie. At least that's the premise she'd hide behind for now—for if she cared to peek around the sides of that flimsy excuse, she was afraid of what she'd see.

Nicholas Brentwood. Horrid man. Why should she give a fig about where he'd disappeared to with that waif of a girl? Yet it bothered her to no end. Not that it was her business. She ought to be reveling in the freedom she'd enjoyed from breakfast until now.

So why wasn't she?

Another yawn stretched her jaw as she padded down the second-floor corridor to her room. Passing by Mary's door, she slowed, and Alf bumped into her hem. One of Mrs. Hunt's stern reprimands leached through the paneling. What in the world had her abigail done to warrant such a scolding? Though she was still unable to walk, Mary had worked wonders with her needle, stitching fine designs upon nearly every one of Emily's day dresses.

With a shush to Alf, Emily leaned her ear to the door, removing the muffle from the housekeeper's words. "Your last warning. One more slipup like this and you'll be out the door with nary a reference. And don't you think I won't. Why I—"

"M–miss?"

Emily jerked upright and spun, biting back an unladylike oath. Alf didn't hold back though—he yipped. Emily shushed him then turned to the maid. "Betsy! For heaven's sake, don't sneak up on me like that."

The maid's head dipped, scarlet darkening her cheeks. "S–sorry. There's a c–caller for you. Shall I turn her away?"

"Yes." Emily inhaled deeply, calming her racing heart. Was this entire day to be fraught with one startling moment after another?

Mrs. Hunt's tirade continued without pause, and as Betsy turned to leave, Emily once again leaned toward the door—then immediately straightened.

"Betsy, wait." She turned to the departing maid. "Did you say the caller is a woman?"

Near the top of the stairway, the girl paused. "Aye. A Miss Barker."

Drat. Should she socialize, eavesdrop, or cave in to her fatigue and snuggle up with Alf?

"Mind the dog, Betsy. I'll attend to my guest." She swooped past Betsy, tucking up loose bits of hair as she descended the steps. No sense handing Millie a reason to judge her appearance.

Emily swept into the sitting room, sizing up Millie in a glance. She wore a periwinkle gown, which peeked out from a matching pelisse and was topped off with a bonnet so lacy and ruffled and large, that if taken apart, the thing might clothe several little girls. Emily frowned, calculating when she could scoot over to the milliner's and have her latest purchase redone to such a standard, then greeted her guest. "Miss Barker, how kind of you to call."

Retreating back to the door, Emily reached for the bellpull. "My apologies. I am mortified Betsy didn't take your wrap."

"No need. I shan't be staying long, unless. . ." Millie ran a gloved finger along the length of the mantel as she strolled the room. "I am disappointed you feel the need to address me as Miss Barker. Are we not on a first-name basis by now, dearest?" She circled back. "For I feel sure, Emily, we shall be the best of friends."

Emily pressed her lips together, remembering the warning Nicholas had spouted days ago. *"The only way to prevent trouble. . .is to identify the danger before it strikes."*

Oh, yes. A close friendship with Millie would be quite the hazard.

Pasting on a smile, she crossed toward the settee. "Shall we sit, Millie?" The name left a tart taste in her mouth.

Millie stopped near a framed silverpoint study. Either she took a deep interest in such artwork, or she was snubbing the offer on purpose. "That was quite an abrupt departure you made from dinner last night." Millie spoke without facing her. "I hope your cousin's business was profitable, whatever it was."

Unbidden, the awful gray face of Uncle Reggie surfaced. Emily shifted on the cushion. "Not really."

Millie turned then, a feline smile curving her lips. "Too bad. Mr. Henley asked after you."

"He did?" A secret thrill raced through her. Perhaps she was making progress, after all.

"Did Mr. Brentwood happen to make mention of me?"

Only that he suspected she'd been jilted—in an intimate way. Emily bit her lip. She couldn't very well spout that, so she said a simple, "Yes."

A tiny squeal squeaked out of Millie, not unlike Alf when a bone was involved. She abandoned the silverpoint and sank into the chair adjacent the settee. "You must tell me about your cousin, dearest. His likes. His dislikes. He will be accompanying you to the Garveys' ball next week, will he not?"

"Hopefully not."

Millie's eyebrows nearly lifted her elaborate bonnet off her head.

Though it was God's honest truth—Mr. Brentwood would be proud—still. . .she couldn't let it stand without revealing to Millie her reasons why. "I mean to say hopefully he will not decline, though I don't suppose he will."

"I see. Well," Millie leaned forward, "you know how I adore games. Why don't we play one?"

Emily tilted her head. "Such as?"

"For every secret you tell me about your cousin, I shall give you one of Mr. Henley's. Would you like to play?"

Millie seemed relaxed, but in that one drawn-out moment while Emily debated an answer, she could see by the thin set of Millie's lips and the slight tic along her jaw just how eager the woman really was.

And so was Emily.

CHAPTER 11

The east side of the Thames, though geographically not far from Portman Square, was a world away from the pretty ladies and their dandier counterparts on the western edge of town. Even on the brightest spring days, sunshine didn't stretch to warm these streets. Nicholas tugged his coat tighter as he kept pace with Officer Moore. On each side of the narrow lane, buildings stooped like rheumy old men, hunched at the shoulders. Snuff-colored laundry hung overhead, laced from window to window. Nicholas eyed the patched fabric on a pair of frayed trousers and shook his head. Why bother to wash such a drab garment in the first place?

"Something doesn't meet with your approval?"

Moore's question cut into his thoughts—and his conscience. "I think my time spent at Portman Square is making me into a snob."

"You always were a bit priggish, if you ask me."

Nicholas frowned over at him. "I didn't."

"Fair enough." Moore spoke without slowing a step. "Oh, I nearly forgot. It seems Ol' Georgie isn't the only one on the list of 'who Americans love to hate.'"

His frown deepened. Moore liked nothing better than to toss out his nuggets of information, one crumb at a time—an annoying tendency. "What's your point?"

"Apparently your 'Uncle Reggie' isn't a favorite with the Yanks."

They parted momentarily, a mound of horse droppings splitting them as effectively as a rock in a streambed.

"After you left last night," Moore continued, "Sedgewick's valet remembered a caller about a week ago. The man left no card, yet the valet recalled not only the man's drawl but his name—Captain Norton."

Nicholas grunted. "I shouldn't think that would be unusual. Sedgewick & Payne are a shipping company, after all."

"This one, however, left with a threat. Said he'd return in a week."

"Sure fits the time frame. Perhaps we ought make a call on this Captain Norton."

Moore grunted. "We?"

"If you've the time."

They rounded a corner, which channeled them into an even narrower lane surrounded by soot-blackened tenements. How a corpse cart heaped with a body or two could fit through this lane without scraping its sides was a wonder. Moore took the lead, in silence. He remained quiet for so long, Nicholas redirected his wondering away from the carts to if the man would ever answer.

"I suppose I've the time to hunt down this captain," Moore finally said.

Above them, a woman draped over a windowsill whistled for his attention. She pulled aside a tattered shawl, revealing skin the color and texture of porridge.

Nicholas averted his eyes, ignoring her ribald comments. He had to take two quick steps to catch back up with Moore.

"Scurvy smugglers. Blackjack and Charlie aren't cooperating with my investigation. You'd think they'd packed up and moved shop. Though I shouldn't be surprised if they heard it was me, the infamous Officer Moore, who's the one looking for them."

Nicholas rolled his eyes. "Your pride never ceases to amaze me."

Moore shrugged. "I'm an amazing type of fellow."

Moore stopped in front of a gloomy building, known simply as the Plank Street Dead House. The brick walls wept chunks of mortar to the ground. In the resulting pits, black mold grew in cancerous welts. High-set windows near the eaves, open for ventilation, added a noxious stench to the fetid air wafting in from the nearby muckyard. Add a few flames, and truly, the place could be hell on earth.

Moore shoved open the door. "After you."

Nicholas swept past him into an office barely larger than a casket.

Randall, the clerk, smiled at their entrance. He sat behind a tall, narrow-legged desk, ink smudges marring his thin cheeks. Minus the smears, he'd be the same color as the bodies he housed. "G'day, guv'ners. Come to visit my little lovelies, 'ave you?"

"That we have." Nicholas took the offered pen from the clerk. He dipped the nib in the ink and signed his name onto the ledger.

Moore sketched his name after him then lifted his sleeve to his nose. "How you stand the stench is beyond me."

Randall inhaled deeply, his chest straining the single remaining button on his waistcoat. "Ahh. Why that's a sweet perfume, it is. As long as you can smell it, you know yer still a-kickin'."

Nicholas elbowed Moore. "He makes a good point, you know."

Moore planted his coat sleeve against his nostrils ever tighter.

"Righty, then." Randall slammed the ledger shut and pulled out a key ring from the top drawer of his desk. "This way."

He jingled over to the door, and as he fumbled with the lock, Nicholas asked, "I've often wondered, Randall, is that really necessary? Are you keeping your '*lovelies*' in or the body snatchers out? Seems a bit pointless with you at the guard."

"Policies, mostly. You know, big-wigged rules and all. We may be a dead house, but we ain't no fleetin' fly-by-night kind of joint. And don't forget the effects. Sometimes a swell or two comes my way and you never know what's in their pockets. Pays to keep it locked up." With a final jiggle of his key, the bolt finally clicked. " 'Ere you go then."

The door swung open to a dimly lit room, chilled by a row of ice blocks lining two of the walls. Nicholas took care crossing the threshold. The stone floor slanted toward the farthest wall, the side facing the muckyard. At that end, melted ice and runoff funneled into a great drain. He frowned, resisting the urge to wipe his hands over his waistcoat.

"Identify as many as you can. Wouldn't mind cleaning house a bit." Randall's voice was dull in the big space.

Moore lowered his sleeve, but only long enough to get out a rush of words. "I got a tip-off from one of my regulars that you took in a bloater day before yesterday. Come in from one of the Skerry warehouses down by the Wapping Wharves. Said the fellow was picked over pretty good. Stripped, actually. Likely was one of those swells you mentioned, but scavengers got to him before you. This ringing any bells?"

"I may not know my lovelies' names, but I knows 'em intimate well, I do. Come along." Randall darted forward, trotting down a long line of marble slabs. Apparently he didn't house the same qualms about slipping.

Nicholas trailed behind Moore. Rarely did death make him flinch. Bodies were part of his job. Even the stench of putrefaction, while not pleasant, didn't trigger his gag reflex. No. . .something deeper unsettled him. Something pregnant with hideous possibility. As Nicholas passed by sheet-covered corpses, he wondered where each soul had gone. It was here in this gallery of decay that he felt the enormity of eternity—and it stole his breath.

God should so bless everyone with a visit to the dead house.

"'Ere's the one." Randall stopped halfway down the row and peeled back the cloth. Though he professed great affection for his wards, Nicholas noticed the man took care not to let his sleeve come in contact with the sheet.

"This the chap yer lookin' for?"

Moore stepped aside and inclined his head toward Nicholas, never once removing his arm from his nose. "You tell me."

Nicholas closed in.

It was a man, distended to eye-popping proportions, though he'd probably not been a reed of a fellow to begin with. He wore the marbled color of one who'd died a fortnight ago, except for his legs. From midthigh on down, the skin was tar colored. The top half of his head was ragged, chewed to bits, probably by rats, judging from the bite sizes.

Bending, Nicholas studied the cadaver's neck. A ligature mark cut deep, and if he cared to look closer—which he didn't—he'd likely find a sliver or two of hemp. He glanced up at Randall. "Does the impression go all the way around, or is there a gap?"

"Gap at the back, guv'ner. Weren't no strangulation. He were hanged."

Nicholas nodded. "Then the only question that remains is was it self-imposed or not? Though I'm not quite sure why you needed me to confirm what you already knew."

Randall shrugged, and Moore mumbled something. Hard to tell with a sleeve blocking his mouth. Nicholas cut him a lethal glance.

Slowly, Moore pulled his arm from his nose. "Fine. Have it your way. But if I lose my stomach all over your shoes, don't complain."

Nicholas frowned. "Go on."

"About a fortnight ago," Moore began, "one of my informants—goes by the name of Badger—bumped into this fellow down near the wharves. Badger's always on the lookout for me, let's me know when something's out of place. Like this fellow." He nodded toward the body. "Said the man looked nervous, and well he should. Dandy clothes ought not be worn in that nest, as you know. A week later, he found the fellow's body hanging in an abandoned warehouse two piers south. He let me know about it early this morning as I left my flat."

"Why didn't he come to you right away?" Nicholas interrupted. "Why wait to tell you about it?"

"Badger feared he was being watched. That mob I'm hunting suspects his loose lips. Rightly so. Badger waited till it was safe. By then, the body was taken down, gone over by ragpickers and street waifs, and delivered here to Randall."

Nicholas studied the body one more time. A fat dead man who may or may not have committed suicide. A mystery, but one he didn't have time for at the moment. He shifted his gaze back to Moore. "I fail to see what this has to do with me."

"Badger told me he caught the fellow's name. Badger's that good. Got a way about him that loosens—"

Moore continued talking, but Nicholas didn't hear him anymore. His heart beat too loud in his ears. He snatched the soiled sheet from Randall's hands and used a corner of it to shove aside the swelled tongue protruding from the corpse's lips. Teeth stared back at him.

Large.

Overlarge.

Nicholas scowled, holding back the base response that rose to his lips. He'd been right. There wasn't anything even remotely routine about the business trip Payne had taken.

Emily jerked awake then reached to massage the resulting kink in her neck from having dozed off on the settee. Her arm prickled as well, a sudden rush of blood stinging the sleeping flesh.

She frowned, realizing she was in the drawing room. Had she dozed off? La, she'd much rather have stayed in dreamland. Leaning her head back, she closed her eyes. If she concentrated on the soothing tick-tock of the corner clock, maybe she could pick up where she'd left off. Mr. Henley was sweeping her around a ballroom, eyes fixed only on her, whispering sweet—

"Hie yourself off!"

Mrs. Hunt's outburst carried in from the front foyer, shattering her fantasy once and for all. Straightening, she turned an ear toward the open drawing-room door and caught another round of Mrs. Hunt's warning volleys. What in the world?

Emily stood, wobbling momentarily on stiff legs, then crossed the room. An involuntary cringe tightened her shoulders as more of Mrs. Hunt's words sliced through the air. A butcher's cleaver couldn't cut to the bone as deftly as her sharp tongue. The last hapless peddler that'd ventured upon their front stoop had lost his hat when he'd fled from her scolding.

And he'd never returned to reclaim it.

With a quick pat of her hair to tuck up any strays, Emily slipped into the foyer. "Is there a problem, Mrs.—"

The door burst wide open. The housekeeper stumbled backward, tripped on her skirt hem, and crashed to the floor.

A brute of a man shoved his way in. His oilskin cloak smelled of whiskey and salt and danger. Emily held her breath when, for one heart-stopping moment, he shoved his face into hers.

"There's no problem as long as I see Payne." His voice was low and discordant, like an unresined bow skidding across a cello string. "Where is he?"

Emily stiffened, fear clouding her thoughts. She couldn't piece two words together if her life depended on it—which it might.

"Stupid English wench." The man's greatcoat whapped against her as he wheeled about. He stalked over to the sitting room, stuck his head in the door, then stomped down the corridor and repeated the process at each room he passed.

Emily spun to Mrs. Hunt. By now she'd propped herself up against the entry table, face pale as washed parchment.

"Quick," Emily ordered, "go get Mr. Brentwood."

"He's not returned yet." Mrs. Hunt nodded toward the open front door. "Run! Get yourself to safety."

Emily hoisted her skirts, eyeing the door. She took two steps then hesitated. This was her home. Before she could form another thought, boot heels thumped back into the foyer behind her.

She turned, straightening her shoulders, and willed courage into her voice. "As you've seen, my father is not here. Now leave."

The man tramped toward her, a dark light in his gaze. Cold perspiration dotted the tender skin between her shoulder blades. This was entirely too much like what happened to her and Wren last summer . . .but in a different way.

A murderous way.

"Where is he?" The man stepped so close that his breath coated her forehead and slid over her cheeks. If she inhaled, he'd be part of her.

"Gone. On business." Each word was a chore.

A muscle jumped in the man's jaw. His eyes bore down hard, the blue-black color of rage. "His business was with me."

Emily lifted her chin, hoping confidence would follow.

It didn't.

He pressed closer, his cloak rustling the muslin of her day dress. "Maybe I should switch who I do business with, hmm?"

She ought say something, anything, but her mouth had dried to dead leaves. Could he feel her body trembling?

Mrs. Hunt sprang forward, heaving her shoulder against the stranger's arm. "Leave her be!"

Only the fabric of his sleeve moved.

Emily's heart thumped in her chest, pulsing a sickening beat in her temples. "My father will return in a fortnight. I suggest you call back then."

The man's lips pulled into a hard-edged smile. Mouse-colored teeth flashed beneath his moustache. "Perhaps I'll stay and wait for him here."

"Perhaps you won't." Behind him, Mrs. Hunt advanced, a brass candlestick wielded high over her head.

He turned. She swung. Metal cracked against bone.

The man staggered, the growl of a wounded bear ripping from his throat. The candlestick clattered to the tiles.

Without missing a step, Mrs. Hunt shoved him in the chest with both hands. As he toppled backward out the open door, the housekeeper grabbed Emily's arm and yanked her aside then slammed shut the door and drove home the bolt.

They both stood motionless, breathing hard, blinking. The maid Betsy gaped from the stairway landing. Even Mary had hobbled to join her side. Cook tromped down the corridor, rolling pin in hand. "What's the ruckus?"

Though surrounded by familiar faces, Emily felt eerily isolated.

"I'll be back!" The man shouted through the door. "You hear me! I'm coming back!"

His curses leached through the front door, pinning her in place. But only for a moment. Hiking her skirts, she bolted up the stairs, shoving past Betsy and bumping into Mary. She ought to stop and apologize for Mary's grunt of pain, but her steps didn't slow. She ran to her room and slammed the door shut, turning the lock into place.

Across the room, the looking glass reflected her image. Pale. Shaken. And the longer she stared, the more she saw Wren's face overlaying hers. Last summer's wretched scene replayed in her head until she leaned back against the door and closed her eyes to escape.

But that didn't stop her from seeing the stranger's savage smile—a leer that would visit her in nightmares and linger even in daylight.

Suddenly she longed for the safety of Brentwood's strong arms.

CHAPTER 12

"Are you out of your mind?"

Nicholas focused on the remaining daylight pooling on the floor in the magistrate's office. He ought lift his head, show a measure of respect, but the cold wooden planks were preferable to the fire in Ford's eyes. He sucked in a breath and held it, the tightness in his chest matching his taut nerves. Would this day never end? Keeping a foolish woman from harm, comforting his failing sister, finding his employer dead, and now this. Not that he'd never been dressed down by the magistrate before, but with fatigue fraying his tightly woven resolve, the man's censure nipped particularly deep.

"Bah! I'd expect such an appeal from a simkin like Flannery, not from a seasoned officer such as yourself." The scrape of Ford's chair and the accompanying footsteps pulled Nicholas's face up.

The magistrate leaned back against the front of his desk, arms folded.

Nicholas worked his jaw. He knew exactly what was coming—and he deserved every bit of it. It'd been a foolish request to begin with. No. . .worse. A cowardly one.

"The fact that your employer is dead is neither here nor there, and well you know it." Ford's tone scolded harsher than a fishwife's. "You are committed, now more than ever, to remain with this case until it is solved."

It wasn't often he argued with Ford, but this time, with his sister's life on the line, he matched the magistrate's even gaze. "For all I know, it could've been suicide. Case closed."

Ford scowled. "Merely conjecture, and you know it."

"For now, it's all I have." The words were ashes in his mouth. He shifted, the creak of the chair's worn leather complaining with his every movement. Of course the magistrate was right. It was nothing but desperation that prodded him to ask to be relieved of the case in the first place. But unless he received another offer for hire—and soon—Jenny's life would be forfeit.

"Have you given thought to Miss Payne?" Ford's question pierced, sharp and precise.

Nicholas deflated with a long breath. How to tell Ford that other than his sister, Emily Payne invaded more of his thoughts than any woman since Adelina?

Slowly, he reached into his pocket and retrieved his watch. Flipping it open, he ignored the time and instead rested his gaze upon the small image pressed inside the cover. The ink on the portrait's dark curls had bleached to gray. The eyes, the nose, the crescent lips—barely distinguishable. When had the likeness faded so much? Why, when he tried to recall Adelina's voice, could he only hear Emily's?

Re-pocketing the watch, he lifted his eyes to Ford's. "Of course I've given her thought. Either way, murder or suicide, Miss Payne will have scandal attached to her name."

And her hopes to marry well—her future—would be dashed. The image of Emily's friend, the pathetic figure clothed in fog and a thin cloak, rose like a specter. Without money, Emily could become that figure.

Nicholas swallowed the chalky taste in his mouth. "She'll be ruined."

Ford's gaze bore down. Hard. "You sound as if you care."

For a snippet of a pampered girl who ran headlong into trouble? Did he? He shifted in the chair.

Should he?

He snorted. "What I care about is the rest of my payment for this assignment. How am I to collect from a dead man?"

A shadow crossed Ford's face. "Avarice? From you? I expected better."

Nicholas clenched his teeth and looked away. Ford was right. And if he looked deeper—which he wouldn't—he suspected the roots of his anguish went far beyond the lack of money for Jen.

But for now, he'd cling to that buoy. "My sister worsens, sir. If I don't get some funding soon—"

"Payne promised you a total of 250 pounds," Ford interrupted. "How much have you received?"

He snapped his face back to the magistrate. "Half, roughly."

"And the second half was to be yours upon his return, yes?"

Nicholas cocked his head. "That was the arrangement."

"I'd say, Brentwood, that Payne has returned." Ford unfolded his arms and strolled back to his seat. "Though not quite in the state you expected, eh?"

He pondered that for a moment. Was Ford seriously suggesting…? "What are you getting at?"

"I know that, second only to your precious pocket watch, is your lock-picking kit. I daresay it's even now in your breast pocket, am I right? I merely propose you employ your skills and retrieve the balance of that payment for your sister's sake. Then remain on the case until it is solved for Miss Payne's benefit."

The idea lodged in his mind like a stone in a stream. Everything else circled around it in a silent whirlpool. Payne's lockbox was in the bottom drawer of his desk. It would be easy enough to take what was owed him then bundle Jenny off to the seaside—and also free him to pursue unhindered some kind of justice for Emily.

Nodding, he stood.

"And, Brentwood," Ford matched his stance, "I think it best if you keep Miss Payne in the dark about her father's demise, for now, at any rate. I understand your hesitation about labeling Payne's means of death, but it is undeniable his partner was murdered. If the two are related, you ought keep a sharp eye on her. For reasons we may not know, she might be next. Hearing of her father's demise will be hard enough. Heaping fear for her own life atop that would be worse. Needless to say, the sooner you solve this, the better."

Ford's ominous deductions shadowed Nicholas as he stalked out of the room, clung to him when he stepped into the twilight of Bow

Street, and haunted him for the entire cab ride to Portman Square. Emily's future was as precarious as Jenny's—and both depended upon him. His heart missed a beat with the weight of it. As the hackney rolled to a stop, he swiped his tired eyes with the back of his hand and breathed out a prayer: "God, do not let me fail them as I did Adelina."

He smacked open the door with his fist and landed heavy feet onto the cobbles. After paying off the jarvey, he retrieved his key and unlocked the Payne's front door.

Two steps past the threshold, he froze.

Only a small vigil lantern on the sideboard lit the foyer. No chandelier glowed overhead. To his left, nothing but shadows gathered in the sitting room. He squinted down the corridor. The dining room was dark as well. If not for the subdued dong of the study's clock chiming half past seven, he'd swear it was well past midnight.

Nicholas frowned. Emily never turned in this early.

A sharp intake of breath spun him around. There, in the single highback gracing the entryway's corner, Mrs. Hunt jerked awake.

"I beg your pardon, Mr. Brentwood." The housekeeper shot to her feet, face flushing deep enough to be seen even in the spare light. Straightening her skewed mobcap, she bobbed a hasty greeting then wrinkled her nose.

Immediately, he retreated a step. Though he was immune to the dead-house stench that had woven itself into the fibers of his clothing, apparently Mrs. Hunt's nose was not. "My apologies for the odor, Mrs. Hunt. I shall change garments straightaway and send these off for a good cleaning. Now, please explain what the deuce is going on."

Her lips puckered, as if she were deciding whether to continue the conversation while inhaling such a stink. "Miss Payne asked me to keep watch by the door until you returned, and I regret to say I must've dozed off. It's been a rather trying afternoon."

His frown cinched tighter. Trying afternoon, indeed. Had the pug escaped? Or the milk curdled before teatime? He shrugged out of his greatcoat and reached to hang the garment on the coat tree, nearly stumbling on an upturned corner at the edge of the rug hidden in shadow. Straightening it with the toe of his boot, he turned to Mrs.

Hunt. "Did Miss Payne bid you douse the lights as well?"

"That she did."

He spread his hands wide. "What on earth for?"

"She wanted to give the impression she'd gone out for the evening." Despite his smell, the housekeeper took a step closer and lowered her voice. "In case the man returned."

He froze. "What man?"

"Around four o'clock, a blackguard came to call. Refused to give his name, merely insisted he see Mr. Payne. I informed him that Mr. Payne was gone on business, but he would have none of it. Pushed his way right in and searched the whole of this level. He took liberties with Miss Emily"—she nodded toward the candlestick on the side table—"so I cracked him a good one on the skull to get him out."

Nicholas's fingers curled into fists. "What kind of liberties?"

"Pressed her flat up against the doorjamb, the filthy scoundrel. Then he fingered her hair, plain as you please!"

Heat surged through his veins, but he kept his tone cool. "A description, Mrs. Hunt. Distinguishing marks. Manner of speech. Anything you can remember."

The dull lantern light traced a grimace on the housekeeper's face—which suddenly paled. If a simple memory of the man had such an effect on this bulwark, the fellow must be fearsome indeed.

The housekeeper closed her eyes, the white of her apron whiffling with a shiver. "Dark eyes, ruddy complexion. What I could see of it, that is. His head was bald as a babe's, with a birthmark the color of port spilled down the back. He were short, as far as men go, but stocky. Solid. Like he were no stranger to work. An outdoor fellow, if you ask me. I shouldn't wonder if he were one of Mr. Payne's captains, though I've never seen the likes of him before. But of one thing I am sure."

Her eyes popped open. "Miss Emily has every right to be anxious. He'll be back, and no doubt about it."

Filing away Mrs. Hunt's prediction along with the rest of the information, he carefully kept out one word to explore further. "A *captain*, you say? Did the man have an American accent?"

The housekeeper curled her upper lip, more pronounced than when she'd first detected the dead-house odor on him. "I pride myself on keeping as far from those filthy beasts as possible, Mr. Brentwood. Still . . .I suppose he could have been, now that you mention it. He called Miss Emily an *English* wench."

"Thank you, Mrs. Hunt. You've been most helpful." He turned and took the stairs two at a time. It was either that or punch a hole into the plaster for the slur to Emily's character.

Ignoring convention—and the clipped steps of Mrs. Hunt ascending the stairway behind him—he stopped in front of Emily's chamber and rapped. A single wall sconce flickered in the corridor, the resulting shadow a monster against her door. "Miss Payne, are you all right?"

Mrs. Hunt kept watch, but at a distance. Smart woman.

No sound came from Emily's chamber. Not even one of Alf's yips.

He pounded harder. "Miss Payne?"

Nothing. Not an indignant "coming" nor a "by your leave, sir." Just quiet.

This time the wood rattled in the frame against his fist. "Emily!"

More silence—except for his own pounding heart and the gasp of the housekeeper down the hall.

Blood rushed to his head, heat to his gut. Gads! What if the man had breached the wall to her window? Or lowered himself from the roof? Was he too late already?

Nicholas reared back, preparing to kick the spot just below the knob. Sweat soaked his shirt. One. . .two. . .

The door opened several inches, and a sleepy-eyed Emily peered out—eyes that popped wide when she took in his stance. "Mr. Brentwood! This is highly irregular."

Should he gather her in his arms or scold her for nearly getting a boot to the belly?

He opted for stomping toward her. Bracing his hand against the frame, he leaned inches from her face. "Why did you not answer immediately?"

The question came out harsher than he intended, no surprise with the way his nerves jittered on edge.

Her lips flattened. "Really, sir, besides the fact that your stench preceded you, would you have had me open the door in my nightgown?"

Involuntarily, his eyes strayed lower, past the hollow of her throat, to the ribbon tied below her collarbone. The wall sconce brushed a warm glow over skin that was likely even warmer. And softer. Here was a woman that angels would envy.

A tremor ran through him, and suddenly breathing took entirely too much concentration.

"Did Mrs. Hunt not explain to you the situation?" she asked.

Her question snapped his gaze back to her face. What had gotten into him? Slowly, he let his hand fall and edged back, straightening his shoulders. "Mrs. Hunt is not at fault. I merely came to see that you are all right."

A strange glint flickered in her eyes. Was it simply the spare light, or something more?

"I am whole, if not a bit shaken." Her teeth worried her lower lip. Either the woman was coaxing out the rest of what she had to say... or hindering the words.

"I am happy to hear it." A small smile tugged his own lips, especially when she sulked at his faux pas. "What I mean to say is that I am happy to hear you are whole. It does not please me that you are shaken."

"Of course, and..." She inhaled. Deeply. A curious act with the stench he wore.

"And?" He prodded.

"Merely..." Her pert little nose lifted an inch. "Thank you for inquiring."

He nodded. "It is my—"

"Yes, I know. It is your duty." An unreadable shadow snuffed out the gleam in her gaze.

It was an unaccountable loss—one he'd dearly love to replace. He reached toward her, but at the last minute curled his fingers to his palm instead. "Miss Payne, I—"

"No matter." She shook her head. "Suffice it to say I appreciate now that my father hired you. I am indebted to you for your service until he returns."

"Yes...well..." A kidney punch would have been less stunning. His short nails dug grooves into his palms—into flesh that was clammy and moist and sickening. How to explain to this wide-eyed young woman that her father wouldn't be returning home?

Ever.

Emily narrowed her gaze. Was that a tic in the corner of Brentwood's right eye? Hard to tell, but she'd swear the strong lines of his throat tightened. Was she imagining it, or did her words affect him as deeply as they moved her? They were sincere—which was slightly shocking and a whole new sensation. But indeed. . .she *was* indebted to the man for her safekeeping. Something about Brentwood, knowing he was here now, housed beneath the same roof, made her feel protected. Sheltered. A feeling she'd not experienced since before last summer, and especially not earlier today.

Her gaze returned to his—and she froze.

He stood silent. Statuesque. Nicholas Brentwood's sudden stillness spread from the hallway, wound through the gap in the door, and wrapped around her shoulders. Filling her. Quieting her. Quenching the hundreds of questions that burned on her tongue while igniting thousands more in her head.

Tension heightened with each breath, until breathing was out of the question.

Nicholas broke the spell first. He retreated several steps, shadows blurring the black outline of his frock coat. Dark hair spilled over his brow as he nodded. "Now that I see you are safe, Miss Payne, I bid you good night."

His deep voice caressed her an instant before he turned. Darkness bathed his body as he stalked down the corridor until he was submerged, leaving behind nothing but a shiver.

"Good night," she whispered then pressed the door shut and leaned her forehead against the cool oak.

What was that all about? The air between them had been more charged than a lightning storm—and as unsettling.

"Is all well, miss?"

Mary's voice spun her around, heart racing. Across the room, propped against their adjoining door and clutching a makeshift crutch in her free hand, her maid cocked her head. "I heard the knocking and got here soon as I could."

Emily frowned. Two, nearly three weeks, and still the girl couldn't serve properly. A trifling injury never would've slowed Wren to such an extent. Still. . .her gaze lowered to the maid's misshapen ankle. She'd never asked Wren to. . .what was it Mr. Brentwood had called it? Be her personal pack mule?

"No need to fret, Mary." Emily padded across the carpet and sat on the edge of her bed. "All's well."

"Are you certain, miss?"

The way her pulse fluttered? Or with the fine bead of perspiration dotting her brow? Emily sank against the propped-up pillows, losing herself in linen and lavender.

No. She wasn't certain at all.

CHAPTER 13

Morning rain pelted the window that reached from the floor to the ceiling of Mr. Payne's study. The fat drops sounded like grapeshot to Nicholas, who paced the floorboards. Should he go through with this, or not?

The gray light filtering inside the chamber suited his mood. The night before he'd wrestled with more than the bedcovers; he'd spent hours struggling with Ford's suggestion to *"retrieve the balance of that payment for your sister's sake. Then remain on the case until it is solved for Miss Payne's benefit."* It seemed fair. It wasn't like he was stealing. He'd work for it, after all. And in truth, by the time he'd figured out the identity of Reggie's killer, he'd likely be owed a great deal more than what was in Payne's strongbox. The fee he'd been promised was for a simple guardianship, not the solving of a murder.

Slowly, he pressed the door shut then turned and surveyed the room before he crossed it. Two framed pictures of a fox hunt adorned one wall, a stag's head mounted between. To his right, a row of hip-high bookcases supported a bust of Plato and a large cigar box. Neither sported a speck of dust, nor did the clock in the corner or the potted fern by the window. As he neared the big desk, he suspected that if he cared to bend over it, he'd likely see his stubbled jaw and bleary eyes reflected quite clearly.

Pausing, he sniffed. Linseed oil and cherry tobacco. Yes, indeed.

The Portman House staff did a fine job of keeping Payne's sanctuary preserved.

Scooting behind the desk, he slid out the right bottom drawer, just as he'd seen Payne do when they first met. It was empty. He shoved the drawer back in place and moved on to the next. And the next. Odd. No parchment. No blotters. No ledgers, quills, or sealing wax. The desk was completely cleaned out. Either the man had something to hide, or he'd never intended to return—

Or someone had been here before Nicholas.

He sank back in the chair, lacing his fingers behind his head and mentally ticking off everything he knew for certain. The list was short. "Painfully short, my friend," he whispered to the stag head, whose glass eyes stared into his from across the room. "You saw everything that happened in this study. What, I wonder. . . ."

He shot to his feet and closed in on the trophy. Cleanliness was one thing, but the odd-colored paneling below the stag's right shoulder was quite another. No wonder he'd not found the strongbox in the drawer.

Grabbing hold of the twelve-point buck, he lifted, twisted slightly, then slowly retreated a step. He stifled a grunt as he lowered the heavy head to the floor. By the time he straightened, his biceps burned—and so did his curiosity.

Unstained by cigar smoke, hearth fumes, or daylight, the outline of the trophy preserved not only the wood but also the sanctity of a small door. Nicholas patted the buck's head in thanks before pulling a leather kit from his breast pocket.

With ease, he opened the panel, revealing another door. This one was outfitted with an ornate circular lock cover inlaid with brass. A slow smile slid across his lips. Good. Looked like a lever tumbler, one that would require a bit of time and skill, but entirely doable.

Retrieving a short pick and a counterweighted lever arm, he re-pocketed his pouch and inserted the lever into the keyhole. It took several tries, but eventually he found the right balance, applying a gentle yet firm pressure to the lock inside. With his other hand, he inserted the pick.

Now came the thorny part.

Using minute movements, he fished around for the tumbler giving the most resistance, while at the same time, keeping his other hand deadly still. When the pick's tip sent the barest tremor up his finger, he lifted, slowly, and. . .victory. The tumbler's slot caught on the bolt's post.

He inhaled deeply. Halfway there.

The fingers on his other hand tingled from inactivity, but he held them steady. One slip now and he'd have to start over.

Footsteps clipped from the other side of the study door. Nicholas froze. Judging by the timbre and speed, Mrs. Hunt was on a mission—hopefully not one involving the dusting of a stag's head or the polishing of a desk.

Was it right to ask God to keep him from being detected?

As the steps faded, he slowly let out a breath. Gathering his scattered concentration, he jiggled the pick half a hair's width to the left. Two wiggles later, the second lever lifted. With both bars trapped in the slot, he shot the bolt and swung open the door.

His shoulders sagged, and he sighed. The box inside had a lock as well.

Jamming his tools between his teeth, he slid out the chest and padded over to the desk. This time he'd repeat the process sitting down.

He used the steady thrum of the rain against the windows to fall into a deliberate trance. The tumblers in this one were worn—all the easier to skim the pick's tip from lever to lever, yet trickier to get them to stay in the slot. Mrs. Hunt's footfall returned in the corridor, but this time he dismissed the threat. She'd not enter the room. She'd send Betsy.

When finally all the levers were wedged, he slid the bolt, opened the lid partway, then once again froze.

Tapping steps echoed in the corridor and stopped just outside the study door. He slipped off the chair so fast, a muscle pulled in the back of his thigh. A bolt he didn't want to hear clear a metal plate sounded from across the room, followed by the barest grind of hinges.

How would he explain to a maid why he crouched like an overgrown bird behind his employer's desk while clutching the man's strongbox?

"Betsy?"

Mrs. Hunt's voice carried from the back of the house. Yes! *Go, Betsy. Go see what your—*

The hinges ground slightly more. One footstep crossed the threshold. Nicholas's heart stopped. Did the girl have a hearing problem as well as a speech impediment?

"Betsy!"

This time the housekeeper's tone was steel. The door clicked shut. Tapping steps retreated.

And a single drop of sweat trickled down Nicholas's temple. Briefly, he closed his eyes. *Thank You, Lord. I can only assume that Your protection thus far means something.*

Swiping his brow on his sleeve, he regained the chair. He grasped the lid, opened the chest. . .and frowned. Disappointment—and dare he admit relief?—drained the last of his fine motor skills. He reached in and pulled out the single item gracing the velvet-lined box.

At least the decision to take what was owed him had been made.

Lifting a fat chunk of wax to within a hand span of his eyes, he squinted then flipped the piece over and inspected the other side. It was a key mold, and judging by the telltale starburst-shaped end, it was designed for a Bramah lock—

Like the one he'd seen in Reggie's study.

He lowered the template and scrubbed a hand over his jaw. Why would Payne want to empty out his business partner's store of money? Wouldn't that be like robbing oneself? He pondered that, until one of his earlier thoughts reared its head for the second time this gray morning.

Unless Payne had never intended to come back. But why—

Sharp yips bounded down the corridor and stopped at the study door. Nicholas slammed shut the box's lid. No time for further pondering.

Pocketing the mold and his pick set, he dashed across the room and slid the chest into the safe. He eased the door shut—while little paws scratched at the other—then bent and hefted the trophy back to its perch.

Thankfully, the barking subsided as he straightened the stag's head, and by the time he finished, the scratching had stopped as well. Glancing at the ceiling as he headed for the door, he shot up a quick prayer.

Thank You, God.

Then he reached for the knob, swung open the door—and came

face-to-face with a fuzzy muzzle held by a frowning young lady.

"What on earth are you doing in my father's study?"

Alf squirmed in her arms, and Emily bent, relegating the pug to the floor. His paws hit the ground running—in the direction of the kitchen. Fickle pup. Just as well, though. She straightened and studied the man in front of her unhindered. Nicholas Brentwood's face was shadowed by stubble and possibly fatigue, creased somewhat at the brow—and completely unreadable. If she'd surprised him, he sure didn't show it.

"The more pertinent question, Miss Payne"—his green eyes searched her face like waves lapping against a shore, wearing away the sand grain by grain—"is why you suspected I was here in the first place?"

She frowned, hating the uncanny way he had of always making her feel like a half-wit. "You don't corner the market on deductive reasoning, sir."

"Oh?"

She lifted her chin, a more ladylike gesture than lifting her palm and slapping the smirk off his face—though not nearly as satisfying. "First, you were not at table in the dining room. Second, Betsy said your chamber was empty when I asked if you were up and about. And third. . ." She paused. Should she admit that she really hadn't known he was in here? No. Better to let him think she was as keen an investigator as he.

"Alf and I"—she nodded down the corridor where the pup had disappeared—"are an unbeatable pair."

"No doubt." His gaze bore into hers, and he advanced a step, crossing the threshold and pulling the door shut behind him.

Everything about the man was intense, and standing this close, the urge to run pounded with each heartbeat. She drew back, but only two paces—enough distance so she could breathe easier yet not enough to show retreat. He smelled of risk and possibility—faintly spicy and very masculine. With a definite hint of sandalwood soap. Interesting, though he'd not taken the time to shave yet this morn, he'd apparently washed off the sickening smell that had clung to him last evening.

"Now that I've answered your question, Mr. Brentwood. . ." she matched his stare, daring him to be the first to look away, "it's only fair you answer mine. So I repeat, what were you doing in my father's study?"

His gaze darted down the corridor, followed by a sweep of his arm. "Shall I explain on our way to breakfast?"

A small smile curved her mouth, victory tasting as sweet as one of Cook's raisin cakes that she hoped waited for her on the dining-room sideboard. "Very well," she conceded then turned and headed down the hall.

Nicholas fell into step beside her. "Your. . .visitor, shall we call him? Obviously the man who barged in so rudely yesterday afternoon was looking for something, some key bit of information only your father could supply. Other than the study or your father's bedchamber, where else might that information be?"

She felt his eyes upon her as they walked, but no, she'd not get sucked into that green whirlpool again. "My father's affairs are as foreign to me as they are to you, sir."

"Are you really so surprised, then, that I investigated the room?" He stopped, allowing her to pass him by and enter the dining room.

Did he always have to be so logical? Ignoring his question, she crossed to the sideboard and selected the largest piece of raisin cake on the platter. Apparently Cook had been reading her mind—and good thing, too, for she would've requested the treat had it been absent.

She waited for Nicholas to pull out her chair. Then she sat and lobbed another question. "Did you find anything in Father's study?"

He sank into the seat adjacent hers and reached for the coffee urn. At her nod, he filled her cup first then his own. By the time she stirred in a spoonful of sugar and a dollop of cream, he'd drunk his, refilled once more, and retreated behind the crisp sheets of the *Chronicle*.

Emily frowned. Her father often escaped in such a manner. Why was her guardian trying to avoid her?

"Well?" she prodded. "*Did* you find anything?"

His eyes peeked over the top of the paper. "Yes."

The paper shot up, hiding his face and ending his side of the conversation.

But not hers. She leaned forward, reached out her butter knife, and slit the paper right down the center. The noise masked the rain buffeting the windows, but not his growl.

"Miss Payne, do you honestly think such antics—"

"You can't possibly expect that I'll let you get away with that snippet of an answer. Tell me, here and now. What did you discover?"

He sighed and folded what was left of the paper into a mound at the side of his saucer. For a moment, she wondered if he'd still refuse to reply. What recourse would surpass slicing his newspaper in half? Her eyes slid to the crystal pitcher next to the coffee urn, and a half smile begged to be released. Perhaps a cold bit of water over the head—

"What I discovered was a curious woman and her nosier pup."

She sank back in her seat. Had she really fallen for that bait? "Droll, Mr. Brentwood. Very droll. Should Bow Street ever dismiss you, I daresay you've a career on Drury Lane writing dramatic dialogue."

A rogue grin lightened his features and, as much as she hated to admit it, lightened the dreary gray morning, as well.

"I'll take your advice under consideration, Miss Payne. So tell me, why was it you—and Alf, I suppose—were seeking me out?"

She speared a piece of raisin cake with her fork and savored the sweet bite before responding. "I did have other callers yesterday besides that blackguard that barged in. Miss Barker in particular." She eyed the man across from her, but the mention of Millie's name didn't so much as twitch his eye. Hmm, that could be a problem, considering the deal she'd cut with Millie.

After one more bite for fortification, she continued: "Miss Barker reminded me that the Garveys' ball is but a week away. Naturally, I've already got my gown, but I should like to add a few accessories—"

"No."

She blinked. Was he objecting to the ball, the gown—though he'd not seen it—or her desire to purchase a new hair coronet and matching earbobs? "What do you mean, no?"

"Are you about to ask me to follow you about town while you shop for said accessories?"

Pleased that he understood her the first go-around, she loaded her fork with one more bite of breakfast cake. "Yes."

"No," he answered.

Her fork hovered midair. "Mr. Brentwood, you can't expect me to stop my life just because some misguided fellow pushed past Mrs. Hunt and entered our home. I admit it was a frightening event, but—"

"Have you forgotten about Mr. Sedgewick's murder?"

She set down her fork. Eating now was out of the question. Outside, a gust of wind rattled the dining-room windowpanes like bones in a grave. She shivered. Horrid thought, as bad as the image of Reggie's final breath. "Of course I've not forgotten, but I find it hard to believe that his situation has anything to do with me. I am not now, nor ever have been, associated with business intrigues."

"Are you really so self-centered, Miss Payne?" Brentwood's voice lowered in timbre and gained in strength. "Did you ever consider it might have something to do with me?"

Her gaze shot to his. "What are you talking about?"

He sighed, giving her the distinct impression he chose his words as carefully as for a tot. "Let's review. I'm charged with your safety, yes?"

"Yes."

"Your father's partner is murdered, a stranger breaks into your home, and your father turns up—"

He stopped. Suddenly. His eyes grew distant and hard. Either his coffee didn't sit well on an empty stomach—for he had yet to fill a plate—or he'd been about to say something he ought not.

She leaned forward. "Turns up what?"

He reached for the coffee urn yet again. Three cups?

"Turns up unable to be reached, Miss Payne." He took a sip before he continued. "Though he prepared us for that much before he left."

The beginnings of a headache lurked behind her eyes, ready to spring out if this conversation became any more complicated. She reached for her own cup in hopes of drowning the pain. "I fail to understand what that has to do with shopping."

"I need you to stay put for the day while I make a few calls of my own."

Behind her, the rain thrummed against the glass. No one would call on her in such weather. The day would stretch unbearably long. Surely she could think of something to change his mind. And if that beastly fellow happened to return—*aha*!

She straightened in her seat. "I wasn't safe here alone yesterday, Mr. Brentwood. What makes you think today will be any different? Perhaps if I accompanied you—"

"Don't worry. I've already sent for a colleague to watch the place. You see, Miss Payne, I generally try to think two moves ahead of the game." He bit into his bread and chewed, deliberately holding her gaze.

Drat. As much as she hated to admit it, he really did think of everything. She pushed back her chair, appetite completely gone, and cocked her head at the same angle she'd seen her father employ time and again before he sealed a bargain. "I'll make a deal with you, Mr. Brentwood."

"Really?" He finished off his bread and wiped his mouth with the napkin. "Why do I sense that wagering with you just may involve the selling of my soul?"

She tipped her head farther. "Is it for sale?"

"No."

"Then you've nothing to worry about, hmm?"

She waited, holding, as if they played at nothing but a simple card game instead of the possible fate of her future.

At last, Nicholas broke the stalemate. "I suspect I may regret asking this, but what do you propose, Miss Payne?"

She flashed him a smile that had earned her many a dance with an unsuspecting beau. "As a reward for my best behavior today, you shall take me to Bond Street tomorrow."

What went on behind those eyes of his, dark as a forest and with depths she could only guess at? If he'd not agree to this. . .then what?

"Your *best* behavior?" he finally asked.

Her smile widened, and she tilted her chin. Millie wasn't the only one with an arsenal of flirtatious moves.

His eyes narrowed, clouding to rival the storm outside. "That tactic might work with Mr. Henley, but it does not with me."

Her shoulders sagged. Rotten man. She bit her lip to keep it from quivering.

"Nevertheless. . ." he leaned back in his seat and folded his arms, "I suppose I can't expect to keep you under lock and key. You're hardly a criminal, are you?"

She bit harder. The only criminal in the room was him. Big bully.

"If I accomplish all I hope to today, I shall be at your disposal on the morrow."

Her mouth dropped, quivering lip discarded along the way. "My complete disposal?"

A shadow crossed his face. "What have you in mind?"

She sniffed, going for a blend of proud vexation. "What makes you think I have anything other than shopping in mind?"

"Let's just say I have my suspicions."

She mimicked his smirk. He could suspect all he liked—for he had a right to. With him absent for the day, she'd have all the time she'd need to dream up and put a few newly formed schemes of her own into motion.

CHAPTER 14

Nicholas left behind the Payne townhome and crossed the street, sidestepping a mound of horse manure, then flipped up his collar against the rain. The shower was steady enough to drench any exposed skin. Annoying, but not enough to make him turn back for an umbrella. One more encounter with Emily, and she just might try a new tack to get him to escort her shopping. He'd rather take a bullet to the head than traipse around Bond Street today.

Or any day.

Entering the arched opening to the Portman Square garden—at the center of all the homes on Portman Lane—he cut an immediate right. Ten paces off, a tree trunk appeared to divide as a figure, dressed in deep brown, stepped out from behind it.

"Sure and it be a fine day to have me put on surveillance, Brentwood." While Flannery spoke, he swiped his thumb and forefingers along the front brim of his hat, sending a spray of droplets off to the side. His red beard dripped with the excess. "I hope yer doublin' what yer payin'."

Nicholas smirked. "I wouldn't complain if I was you, nor ask for further compensation. Ford doesn't take kindly to mewling harpies."

Flannery threw back his shoulders. "Watch it, or I've a mind to keep to meself the scrap Moore asked me to pass along."

"Let's have it." Nicholas held out his hand.

Flannery reached inside his oilskin coat and produced a folded parchment. "What is it I'm watchin' for, if I may be so bold?"

The question bounced around in Nicholas's head as he opened the paper and read Moore's scrawl:

Captain Norton. Billingsgate dock. Best I can do.
Watch your back, for I can't. Off to Dover.

"Well?"

Nicholas refolded the paper before answering. "Keep a sharp eye for anything out of the ordinary. Though this"—he held up the note—"might lead me to the fellow you're guarding against."

Grant that it may be so, Lord. Pocketing the slip, he savored the first tang of hope he'd tasted in a long time. If Norton was the murderer, there'd be a fat chest of money somewhere on board his ship. He'd haul the captain down to Bow Street, collect his share from that chest, deposit the rest with Miss Payne, then see his sister off to better health. He closed his eyes. *Yes, Lord, grant that it may be so.*

He opened his eyes and fixed his gaze on Flannery's sharp blues. "One more thing. On the off chance Miss Payne exits, follow her. She's not to escape your sight. Understood?"

"Aye." Flannery nodded then cocked his head. "But if she slips out the rear, I can hardly be held—"

"Drago's covering the back. Any other questions?"

A sweep of wind howled in from the west, shaking the overhead branches. Even with his hat pulled low, Flannery took the brunt of the wet onslaught. He rubbed his face and flicked the water from his fingertips. "Ye'll be puttin' in a good word for me, then, with the magistrate?"

"Keep my ward safe, and..." Nicholas shrugged and stalked off.

"And what?" Flannery's voice trailed him. "What, Brentwood?! Ye can't be leaving me without knowin'—"

"Mind what I said about mewling," he called over his shoulder. Better the man should be vigilant, prepared for dangers unknown, than slack about his mission. He winced as that thought hit him head-on. Did God ever use the same tactic with him?

After hoofing it past Seymour Street to Duke and another half mile down Oxford, he finally found a hack available for hire. The rain shield was missing and the springs were gone on the left, giving the cab a perpetual list to the side, but at least it had a roof.

By the time he reached Billingsgate, though, he wondered if a soaking walk mightn't have been a sounder choice, for the driver had bumped through every rise and dip in the road. His teeth rattled even when his feet hit solid ground.

Thames Street, rain or not, bustled with people. Nicholas shoved past fruit sellers and fishmongers and veered into the nearest lane. Soot-smudged warehouse walls towered on each side of the narrow avenue leading to the river. The overpowering stench of mackerel and bloaters smacked him in the nose. Why on earth would an American merchant choose to dock at the largest fish port in London? Granted, a fair amount of other goods passed from deck to dock in this area, as evidenced by the added odor of Spanish onions, but a Yankee merchant . . .here?

He set his jaw, chewing that one over. Something wasn't right.

All manner of vessels lined the river on this side of the bank. Many were small, wherries and skiffs, a single Gravesend shuttle sitting among them. This early in the day, most of the fishing rigs were still out to sea.

But directly to his left, a two-masted merchantman hunkered low in the water, no doubt ready to soon set sail. On deck, a few hands stowed ropes and tightened riggings. A leather-cheeked sailor descended from the gangplank. He was so raw-boned and angular, it hurt to look at him.

Nicholas increased his pace. "You there."

The man lifted his face toward him. "Aye?"

Up close, the wrinkles in the fellow's skin were as deep as a peer's pockets. Nicholas slid his gaze to the man's eyes. "I'm looking for Captain Norton. This his ship?"

"Who's askin'?"

Nicholas shifted, allowing the bulge of his tipstaff to peek from beneath the flap of his coat. "The name's Brentwood, on business from the Bow Street magistrate."

"If this has anything to do with the papers, you best hurry over to Customs." He lifted his chin, indicating the ungainly building that crouched like a beast on the waterway. "Too late."

Nicholas frowned. "Too late for—"

"Is there a problem, Skully?" A raspy voice came from behind, heavy with an American accent and followed by the woodsy scent of Burley tobacco.

Nicolas turned and offered his hand to the captain—or was he a killer? "No problem, Captain Norton. Just a few questions. My name is Nicholas Brentwood, Bow Street officer."

The captain's gaze darted from his, to Skully's, then back again before he reached out and gripped Nicholas's hand. His fingers were strong enough to right a keeling ship on a raging sea, steady enough to train a pistol barrel at a man's chest, and firm enough to shove past a housekeeper—

But his face was nothing like Mrs. Hunt's description. Disappointment added to his weariness.

"So tell me, Brentwood," Norton drew back his hand, "why should I answer to you?"

Nicholas hitched his thumb over his shoulder. "Like I was telling your friend here—"

"First mate." Pride sharpened Skully's tone—the same wounded egotism Nicholas used when someone labeled him a runner.

"Fair enough. As I was telling your first mate, I'm on business from the Crown." Once again, Nicholas parted his greatcoat at the hip, making the tipstaff as clear to Norton as he had to Skully. "Shall we?" He tipped his head toward the boat.

The captain folded his arms. "Here will do."

Nicholas studied Norton's face, set as granite. The man's gaze didn't waver. No hint of a smile played on his lips. Apparently this was more about power than evasion.

"Very well," Nicholas conceded. "I understand you had some business with a Mr. Reginald Sedgewick."

"Sedgewick!" A storm darkened the man's eyes. On the side of his neck, an earthworm of a vein emerged. "Rotten scoundrel!"

And then, spent as quickly as the fury of the spring tempest, a smile dawned on Norton's face. He grabbed Nicholas's shoulders. "You've righted things for me? Have you my money?" He looked past Nicholas to his first mate. "Hear that Skully? We're not taking it on the chin, after all!"

Shrugging off the man's grip, Nicholas scrambled to make sense of the abrupt change. Either the captain was playing him like a well-tuned violin, or this was a dead end. "Where were you two nights ago, Monday, April 6?"

Norton's grin faded. "What's that to do with—"

"I'm the one asking the questions here."

The granite look returned, colder. Harder than before. "Then you should snippin' well be asking Sedgewick, not me. He's the criminal. Filthy thief."

"Sedgewick's dead, Captain, and unless you satisfy me, I'll haul you in as the number one suspect." Behind him, a whiff of air sounded. Nicholas spun. He caught Skully's forearm before the man's fist dented his skull, then he snapped the sailor's arm around his back. If he yanked upward any harder, Skully's shoulder would dislocate.

Which would be quite the nasty sight should the wiry man's bone decide to pop out as well.

"This is exactly why America rebelled," Norton sneered.

"I'm waiting, Captain. So's Skully." He nudged the man's arm. Skully grunted.

And several guns cocked behind him from aboard deck.

Facing death wasn't new, but it never failed to ramp up his heart rate. Nicholas skewered Norton with a stare. "Call them off, or prove yourself to be worse than Sedgewick."

The captain's jaw contracted. Tension twanged the air as real as the four warning bells off London Bridge.

Finally, Norton lifted his eyes to the men aboard his ship. Without a word, hammers eased back.

Nicholas released a breath and tightened his grip on Skully, lest the man think Norton's gesture would slacken his resolve.

The captain scowled. "Monday night I was at the Bull's Head, meeting with a merchant, Thomas Gilroy, of Mandrake and Gilroy.

He paid for Sedgewick's shipment, at half rate of course, and cut me a deal for a new trade. Square it with Mr. Gilroy if you don't believe me."

Norton stepped forward, leaving no room to doubt his claim. "My papers are cleared, and I'm sailing today."

That the captain hated Reginald Sedgewick was plain enough—but his alibi was easily confirmed. Mandrake's office was just down the block. Nicholas could confer with Gilroy before the captain's spyglass caught sight of the estuary.

"I suppose you'll need your first mate, then." Nicholas released his hold and stepped back, giving Skully plenty of swing room should he feel the need for retribution.

The first mate didn't disappoint, but the captain stayed the man's arm with a curse. "We don't need more trouble, Skully!"

Nicholas sidestepped them both. "Good day, gentlemen."

Ignoring the foul barrage of name-calling as he stomped down the dock, he wondered how much money one must lose to instill such a passion. Exactly how much the captain had lost was anybody's guess, but gold was nothing in comparison to how much Emily or Jenny would lose if he didn't find the real culprit.

And soon.

Beeswax rained onto the envelope, each drip puddling into a melted pool. If Emily squinted so that her eyelids were just about closed, everything blurred, making it look like a splotch of molten gold—a far brighter hue than the colorless gray outside her bedroom window. Before the wax hardened, she picked up the brass seal and pressed the Payne family crest into the center. There. Signed and sealed. Now to deliver. She hoped Millie was home—and that Nicholas Brentwood hadn't instructed the man across the street to stop her from paying a call.

A slow smile curved her lips as she peeked out the lace sheer at the miserable-looking fellow. Standing under a tree for the better part of the morning, soaking up drizzle like a giant fungus, surely he couldn't be enjoying himself. Her smile grew. She could remedy that. With a few bats of her lashes and maybe a giggle or two, she'd gain an escort to Millie's.

She stood and crossed to a wardrobe solely committed to hats. Just opening the doors sent a thrill racing through her tummy and wafted the fresh scent of lavender into the room. Her friend Bella collected shoes, Millie men, but bonnets? Ahh. She'd take a new bonnet any day and every day had she enough space to store them.

Placing a finger to her lower lip, she scanned the shelves of hatboxes. Her eyes caressed each one like a lover returned from sea. Most were tall, some short, several fairly wide, but finally she settled on a pale pink box with gray stripes and freed it from its wardrobe prison. She padded over to her bed, anticipating the moment when the lid lifted and a brilliant flash of a puffed red crown would—

"I've a mind to dismiss you now!"

Mrs. Hunt's voice slid through a crack in the door adjoining Emily's room to Mary's. Emily paused, hatbox in hand. What could the maid have possibly done wrong? Her ankle, considerably shrunken but yet painful, certainly kept her out of the way.

But perhaps that was the issue.

Setting the box on the end of her bed, Emily turned and crept to the door between her chamber and Mary's. She missed most of Mary's reply, except for a few sniffles that punctuated her last words. "You can't blame me for being laid up."

"I don't." The housekeeper's tone, though quieter, was still terse. Emily imagined the accompanying scowl etched onto Mrs. Hunt's face.

"But that doesn't get your work done," she continued. "Betsy and I are doing double-time what with your chores and ours. I should think that you could at least get through that pile of mending in a timely fashion."

"I was hired as a lady's maid, Mrs. Hunt, not a seamstress for the entire household. That my sewing skills don't meet your approval is as much out of my control as healing my own ankle."

Emily stifled a gasp then leaned closer. Even without a visual, this was as entertaining as a night at the theater.

"That sort of cheek will send you packing," Mrs. Hunt's voice hardened. "And without a reference, I might add."

The threat jerked Emily ramrod straight. She knew that tone. She knew those words. Mrs. Hunt hadn't spared her own daughter—Mary wouldn't stand a chance if she pushed her situation any further. Though she wouldn't miss Mary to such a degree as losing Wren, she had grown accustomed to the girl. The thought of breaking in yet another lady's maid was tiresome.

Emily shoved open the door and sashayed in. "Mary, dear, would you mind reading to me today? Everyone else is too busy, and I feel a headache coming on. I'm so glad you're available like this. Oh!" She fluttered her hand to her chest and widened her eyes at Mrs. Hunt. "I didn't realize. . . Did I interrupt something?"

The housekeeper's face was pinched so tight, even Emily flinched.

Smoothing her hands on her apron, Mrs. Hunt darted a glance at Mary before she answered. "I suppose I'm finished here, miss. I am late for a meeting with John as is."

"Oh? He is returned?" *Thank the Lord!* Casting off her plan to sweet-talk Mr. Red Beard, Emily swooped over to Mrs. Hunt, letter outstretched. "Would you see that this is delivered to Millie Barker as soon as possible?"

If the woman's face scrunched any more, her eyeballs would be lost. "I'll have John see to it." But before she disappeared out the door, she volleyed a parting shot at Mary. "At least the butler has resumed his post."

Mary sagged in her seat near the hearth, a heap of garments draped over the rim of a basket at her side. "Thank you, miss. You'll never know—"

As the girl sat there, eyes shining with tears about to spill over, Emily couldn't help but be reminded of the day Wren had sat in the very same spot, telling her the ugly truth of a fate that could have easily been hers.

She swallowed the sour memory and forced a smile that belied her words. "I know more than you ever should."

CHAPTER 15

The following morn, Emily opened the door and finally—*finally*—escaped the house. Intent on a shopping spree as triumphant as Trafalgar, she had to discipline herself not to skip to the carriage.

Hours later, fingering a pair of amethyst drop earrings, she wasn't so sure about a victory. After three stores, not one package sat in the carriage. She'd been uninspired at Dalton's Lace and Glove. The clerk at Fairmont's outright ignored her, and it still vexed her as to why Rollins Slipper & Shoe had suddenly instituted a new policy of pound-notes-up-front.

She set the earbobs onto the glass counter and heaved a sigh. Posted near the front door, Nicholas mimicked her. The sound satisfied. The earrings did not. Purple, though her favorite color, wouldn't give her the dazzle she hoped for with her golden ball gown.

"These aren't quite right," she told the clerk behind the counter—who promptly sighed as well.

As the narrow-nosed fellow replaced the jewels, she sidestepped down a ways, her gaze traveling from stringed pearls to emerald pendants. Leaning in for a closer look, she blinked. A glimmer flashed at the corner of her eye. She turned her head to look, and her jaw dropped.

There, beneath the glass, a universe of tiny stars sparkled, lit by a ray of sun reaching through the front window. Her breath caught as she eyed a tiara sprinkled with diamond chips. Whoever wore that crown would be the queen of the ball—and she'd long since felt she was royalty.

Noting her interest, the clerk pulled out the magnificent piece and held it aloft. Brilliant glitters of light dotted her vision, so stunning her lips parted and thirst parched her throat. For a second, she was speechless.

He lifted it higher and looked down his thin nose at her. "Should you like to try it on?"

To her right, a green skirt swished into view. Emily glanced over. Eyes wider than a beggar's ogled the sparkles on the tiara. And next to the gaping girl, an older woman—presumably her mother according to the droop of her jowls—stepped forward. The pair looked like bloodhounds on the hunt.

And her tiara was the prey.

Emily jerked her face back to the clerk. "No need. Package it, if you will, please." She upped her volume. "I shall take it with me."

Boot steps thumped across the floor. Nicholas Brentwood drew up alongside her, blocking the sunshine and snuffing out some of the glitter of her new headpiece. "Do you really think that's wise, Miss Payne? A fine jeweler such as Asprey's will send an armed delivery—"

"Don't be silly." She pasted on a pleasant smile, all the while keeping track of the duo on the trail.

"Excuse me," said the clerk. "I shall return shortly." He took his long nose and the tiara with him, backtracking down the counter. Either he sensed the coming battle, or he simply went to box up her piece.

Emily watched until he disappeared through a side door then turned on Nicholas. "I see no need for delay. You are armed, are you not?"

The creases of an impending—and by the looks of it, quite magnificent—scowl started at the corners of his mouth. "I was hired to protect you, not a frivolous piece of jewelry."

"It's not frivolous!" She stamped her foot. An infantile reaction, but gratifying in every respect save for one.

It made the bloodhound in the green pelisse step closer with a look of hope in her eyes.

Emily lowered her tone. "That tiara is necessary, not that I expect you to understand. What would you know about a woman's accessories?"

He folded his arms, a common lecture stance her father often employed. "If you can't catch the eye of a man without the aid of trinkets, then I suggest the man's not worth catching at all."

"It doesn't hurt to embellish the package."

"I beg to differ. For you see, Miss Payne—" he bent toward her, so close his breath warmed her ear—"your *package* needs no further embellishment."

The quiet words sunk deep, sending ripples out to her fingers and toes. A compliment? From him. . .for her? Now that was as stunning as the tiara—

Or was it his unwavering gaze that suddenly seized her heart?

She turned and faced the glass case before he noticed his effect and was rewarded by the return of the clerk. Immediately, her brow puckered. Why did he carry her sparkles unwrapped? And who was the buttoned and bowed man next to him?

"Miss Payne?" The other man's shiny black eyes fixed on her. His dark frock coat clung tight, leaving a wide opening in front where a white starched shirt stretched over his belly. A snowy cravat looped into circles at his neck. All in all, he looked like an illustration she'd once seen of a penguin.

"Yes, I—excuse me." She snapped her gaze back to the long-nosed clerk. With one hand he straightened the velvet bedding beneath the glass, and with the other, replaced the tiara. What a dolt. "Perhaps I was not clear. I should like that boxed up."

The clerk's lips parted, but the other fellow spoke. "Miss Payne, unless you can produce a banknote for five thousand pounds, I'm afraid you'll have to wait. There is an unpaid balance on your account."

The man's words rattled around in her head like rocks in a tin can. She had to wait? What did that even mean? She returned her gaze to him. "I'm sorry. Who are you?"

"Mr. Davitt." He lifted his chin, and if his chest puffed out any farther, one of those buttons would pop. "Manager of Asprey's."

"Well, Mr. Davitt," she matched the pretentious tilt of his head. "There must be some misunderstanding. Whatever the balance is, rest assured my father will see to it as soon as he returns to town."

"Miss Payne," Nicholas's voice curled into her ear from behind, "we should leave."

She cut him a sharp glance over her shoulder. "You, sir, promised to shop all day."

Then she forced a smile she didn't feel and dazzled it on Mr. Davitt. "Now then, please deliver the tiara—"

"I'm afraid that is out of the question."

His refusal pulled her gloved fingers into fists, but popping a penguin in the chest just didn't seem right. Poking at his pride, however, was altogether fair game. "Apparently you don't understand, sir, so I'll speak slowly and clearly that you may follow along. My father, Mr. Alistair Payne—that's p-a-y-n-e—is a name to be trusted, and when he hears of this insult, you'll be lucky to find yourself the manager of the thimble store in Cheapside."

If the man's nose lifted any higher, a nosebleed would follow. "Allow me to be plain. Until the account is cleared, there will be no further deliveries or purchases from Asprey's. I bid you and the gentleman a good day."

"But—"

Mr. Davitt spun, the tails of his frock coat whapping the counter. The clerk merely sniffed. And a combined gasp—both female—came from the left.

Ignoring them all, Emily traced the outline of the headpiece with one finger on the glass. The tiara sat so near yet was trapped beyond her reach. Her whole head ached, knowing the snug feel of those diamonds nested in her hair would never be a reality, leastwise not in time for the Garveys' ball. And if she didn't land Mr. Henley this season. . .moisture welled in her eyes, blurring the glittery little universe into washed-out gray. What was to become of her? Live as a spinster in her father's house until death? If he allowed her, that is.

To her side, the horrid girl stifled a giggle—a girl who might very well purchase that crown and live happily ever after.

Unlike her.

"Emily."

She spun. Had Brentwood seriously used her Christian name? In public?

"I suspected that might grab your attention." Half a smile tipped his mouth. "Let's go."

He offered his arm. Walking out of here would admit defeat. But honestly. . .what choice did she have?

The solid muscle beneath his sleeve lent her strength, enough to straighten her shoulders and force her eyes dead ahead as they crossed to the door. The burn of the girl's stare scorched her back.

Outside, as Nicholas led her down the block to their carriage, other shoppers bustled by, each trailed by servants carrying packages and parcels. She flexed the fingers of her free hand. Why did emptiness weigh so much? What was going on? She'd never been refused service. She'd never tasted the hot green sting of humiliation quite so bitterly.

Deep in thought, she slowed her steps. Nicholas gave her a sideways glance.

"Don't fret. It's for the better that you didn't purchase that gaudy bit of frippery. Your smile's brighter than any tiara." He nudged her. "Come on, let's see it."

She lifted her face to him. "Are you trying to be kind, sir?"

A grin slid across his face. "Is it working?"

Her lips twitched, but she pursed them. "Not yet."

"Well then, I shall have to try harder." He stopped in front of their carriage and waved off the driver then reached for the door himself. Once opened, he turned to her, his smile fading. "I meant what I said, you know."

Her brow crumpled. "What. . .that the tiara was too frivolous a trinket or too gaudy?"

"No." He locked eyes with her. "I meant that you don't need diamonds to attract a man."

The sincerity of his words shivered through her. She'd heard flattery before. Enough to distinguish counterfeit from real. For all his bluster, Nicholas was genuine in a way she'd never experienced—a way that drew her in and wrapped around her shoulders.

He broke the spell with a nod toward the open carriage door. "Shall we?"

When she clasped his offered hand, a queer shot of heat raced up her arm. She smoothed her palm along her skirt as she seated herself—a vain attempt at wiping away his touch, for to admit his effect would be scandalous. But the action did nothing to remove the sound of his voice directing the driver outside.

Immediately, she popped her head back out the door. "Stop first at the Chapter Coffee House, if you please."

Nicholas looked up at her from the street. One of his brows rose—only one. . .his I-know-something's-up look. "Since when are you interested in political or literary debate, Miss Payne?"

She slunk back inside the safety of the carriage and busied her hands with pressing the wrinkles from her skirts. Just because shopping had been a dismal failure, didn't mean the rest of the day must be a loss.

She had larger battles to win than Trafalgar.

CHAPTER 16

The carriage lurched to a stop in front of the Chapter, but the thousand swirling thoughts in Nicholas's mind kept right on rolling, even as he opened the door and delivered Emily to the threshold of the coffee and chocolate drinking establishment. Was he doing the right thing? A woman of Emily's caliber ought not deign a visit to a coffee shop, so something unique was obviously pulling her in. Not that she'd admit to it. Her pretty lips had remained sealed the entire ride, and she'd taken great interest in staring out the carriage window, humming a little tune.

Among those *how come*s and *wonder why*s, he was preoccupied as well with their shopping experience. Either the merchants' aversion to offering Emily service meant that Payne's debts had finally caught up to him, or word of her father's death had leaked out. And if common shopkeepers knew, it was only a matter of time before Emily discovered it—

A truth, he determined, she should hear from his lips and none other's. He'd never overridden a directive from the magistrate before, but this time, he just might have to.

Not now, though. He clenched his jaw and pushed open the shop door. The scent of cigar smoke floated above the earthy tones of coffee and chocolate. For a brief moment, he allowed the aroma to work its magic and loosen the tight muscles in his shoulders; then he handed over their penny entrance fee.

Emily touched her fingers to her nose. Apparently the smell didn't appeal, which made her request even more curious than the silence he experienced on the ride over. The refusal at Asprey's had shaken her in a way he didn't understand.

Nor could he grasp her sudden urge to risk her reputation for the sake of a cup of hot chocolate or mug of coffee. Each morning he'd taken breakfast with her, Emily barely sipped half a cup of either. Something else was afoot—something she'd not own up to—so he'd have to let it play out. He doubted very much, though, that it had anything to do with an education in politics or bookselling, which was most often the case with these patrons. He studied her as she scanned the room then lowered her hand to reveal a small smile.

Ahh, that explained it. Intrigue had everything to do with this stop.

He chased her skirt as she wove past small tables and paused at one midway across the room. Horrendous position to defend, but all the perimeter seats were filled. Worse, every eye was drawn to the arrival of a female—one of only three in the room, unless servers were counted.

Charles Henley rose from his chair and leaned toward Emily, closer than decorum dictated. He snatched her hand, brought it to his mouth, and pressed his lips against her glove longer than customary.

Stepping up behind her, Nicholas scowled at the man. "Henley."

The man's gaze lifted. Slowly, he released his hold on Emily's fingers. "Brentwood. . .I didn't expect to see you here."

"Funny. You don't seem a bit amazed to see Miss Payne."

Adjacent him, and still seated, Millie Barker beamed. "Oh, Mr. Brentwood, Emily, what a surprise!"

"Isn't it?" Emily flashed him a smile over her shoulder. "What luck!"

A groan surfaced at the back of Nicholas's throat. This explained the flurry of couriers Flannery reported going in and out of Portman Square yesterday. How many missives had it taken to arrange this meeting?

Henley was quick to pull out the empty chair to his right and offer it to Emily. The only seat left to him, then, was between Millie and her aunt, who dozed, chin to chest. The drone of a dozen conversations took the edge off the woman's snores; still, each inhale was thick and snorty. Some chaperone. He slid out a chair of his own, giving credence to the rumors he'd heard of Millie's exploits. Mr. Barker ought to invest in a guardian of his own for the woman.

Gritting his teeth, he ordered chocolate for Emily and something stronger for himself. He'd never frequented this particular shop but hoped their coffee was a kick in the head. He'd need it to survive this little tryst. Narrowing his eyes at Emily, he frowned. He never should've given in to coming here in the first place.

Millie bent toward him, eyelashes aflutter. "What a delight to see you, Mr. Brentwood."

He leaned back, better to view Emily and Henley but with the added bonus of evading Millie. "I didn't realize literature or politics was your game, Miss Barker."

"Hmm?" Her smile grew, the slight movement of her lips setting the feather atop her hat bobbing slightly.

"A coffee shop is the least likely place I'd expect to find a woman for it is most often visited by those interested in partisan discourse or the bantering of philosophical ideas." He cocked his head. "And you don't strike me as one with such interests. . .unless there's something you're not telling me."

She leaned closer. "Oh, Mr. Brentwood, I'd tell you anything."

It took every muscle in his body to keep from rolling his eyes.

"Though I must say it's nothing like that." She giggled then nodded at her snoozing chaperone without varying her gaze from his face. "Aunt here was positively in need of refreshment, for as you can see, she tires easily, poor dear. Our carriage happened to be passing by, and so I thought we should stop. Kind of a novelty experience, you see. Imagine my surprise when Mr. Henley hailed us to his table."

"Happened by, eh?" he asked Millie but kept his focus entirely on Emily and Henley. Millie's flirtatious conduct paled in comparison to Emily's, for she employed hers in a more subtle way. The tilt of her head, the parted lips, a coy smile—he sucked in a breath. Why she felt she'd needed that gewgaw at Asprey's to make herself more appealing was a mystery. If Henley's lips weren't shut, his tongue would loll out of his mouth like the dog he was.

"Truth be told, I've never actually been to a coffee shop, Mr.

Brentwood." Millie's voice was a gnat in his ear.

"But you have, am I correct, Mr. Henley?" His question pulled the man's gaze off Emily and landed it squarely on him. A cheap victory but worth every cent.

"Of course. During the day I frequent the usual haunts, but at night. . ." A slow grin bared Henley's teeth.

"Wherever you go, sir, I am sure you add much to the conversation." Emily's words puffed out the man's chest a full two inches before he turned his face to her.

Henley leaned in so close, his breath ruffled the fine hairs at her temples. "I excel in conversation, among other things."

A sudden urge to deliver a right uppercut tingled through Nicholas's fingers. Though he understood Emily's precarious social standing—more so now than ever—that didn't mean he had to like it.

Or Henley.

Next to him, Millie tucked up a curl of stray hair then trailed her hand down the curve of her neck, around to her collarbone, where her fingers settled on the bodice of her gown—a move that couldn't have been carried out better by a strumpet in an East End brothel.

"Oh!" Her fingertips fluttered at the crest of her bosom. "My brooch . . .it's gone!"

"How horrible. Do you think it was stolen?" Emily's sentiment was true enough. Her timing and tone, questionable. Henley said nothing.

"Yes! Oh, it's so clear to me now." Millie answered after a perfect pause—too perfect. "I believe my brooch was stolen. It must've happened back on Oxford Street when Aunt and I encountered a street beggar. Mr. Brentwood. . ."

Her hand flew to his sleeve. He stared her down.

"Emily's told me of your strong sense of justice. I daresay you could right this in an instant. Would you accompany me? I'm certain Mr. Henley and Emily wouldn't mind our absence. Nor would Aunt."

If he didn't stop this now, Millie's dramatics and Henley's advances would steal any pleasure he might find in the mug of coffee headed his way. He removed Millie's hand from his arm. "No need, Miss Barker."

"No need?" Her brow wrinkled, causing the feather on her hat to startle. "Whatever do you mean?"

At long last, the serving girl delivered a cup first to Emily then to him. He downed a big swallow before answering Millie, singeing his tongue in the process and glad for the pain. "If indeed your brooch was stolen, the thief would have already hocked it down at St. Gile's, though I doubt very much it was pinched in the first place. Unless you happened to embrace said beggar, I should think you'd notice so close an encounter."

Millie's lips tightened into a line, not nearly as pretty as one of Emily's pouting poses—and for some reason, that pleased him.

He nodded toward the door. "I suggest you search your carriage floor, Miss Barker. Most likely it fell during the process of getting in or out."

Millie exchanged a glance with Emily. A storm raged in her blue eyes then just as suddenly, calmed, and she tipped her face back to his. "Why, you're a genius, Mr. Brentwood. I feel sure with your sharp eye helping me, we'll find my brooch in no time. My carriage is just outside."

This time when she leaned toward him, she twisted in such a way that the fabric parted, giving him a most advantageous view of her bosom.

"Shall we?" She rose slightly, leveling her chest even with his eyes.

Sighing, he set down his mug, coffee sloshing over the rim. "Do sit down, Miss Barker, and describe for me your brooch."

For a moment, her lips pursed, and then she sank. Slowly. He fixed his gaze on her face instead of her provocative movements, all the while keeping Henley within his line of sight. If the rogue nudged his chair any closer to Emily's, he'd acquaint the man's skull with the metal end of his tipstaff.

"My brooch is gold, naturally, about a finger span in width. There's a flower at center, a ruby in its middle. Two turquoise-studded flowers sit on each side. It's really very pretty. Scrolled leaves cover the entire piece like this." She traced a loopy pattern in the air with her finger.

She needn't have. Her words confirmed his suspicion without further embellishment. He lifted his cup and swallowed a few good gulps before answering. "Your description has revised my opinion of the matter."

Millie's brow crumpled, and Emily cut in: "Really, Mr. Brentwood.

The chivalrous thing to do would be to help, not simply change your mind."

"Chivalrous, yes, but necessary?" He turned to Emily. "No."

"Here, here!" Henley said, raising his cup. "Chivalry is overrated."

"Not my meaning at all, Henley, though I don't suppose you know the definition of the word in the first place."

Emily gasped.

Henley merely smirked, the action narrowing his eyes. . .or did he do that purposely? "You're not so scrupulous yourself."

Nicholas stiffened. What dirt did this snake in the grass think he'd make public? But ladies first. He turned to Millie. "Lest you think I'm heartless, Miss Barker, I believe your brooch is at home. A piece of that magnitude would leave quite a visible pinhole in the tight weave of your dress. I see no such evidence. It may be that you intended to wear it but simply forgot and left it on your nightstand."

Her cheeks flamed as he nodded toward her chest. Were it anyone but Millie Barker, he'd suspect embarrassment as the cause. In her case, it was probably because her plans had been thwarted.

Shifting his attention, he sliced a deadly gaze at Henley, sharpening each word like a blade's edge on a whetstone. "Now then, Mr. Henley, what would *you* know about morals, mine or otherwise?"

Millie's head reared back, eyes wide, ears likely wider. Emily babbled about weather and carriage traffic, throwing out one trivial bone after another.

But a dog's fangs, once bared, were not easily diverted from a bite. From her angle, Emily couldn't see the tightening of Henley's jaw, but Nicholas didn't miss it.

Henley faced him squarely across the table. "I'm not the buffoon you think I am, Brentwood. I've studied you with as much finesse as you track my every move. I'd wager your sudden appearance while Payne is gone is no accident. I don't believe for a minute you're here to lift the prospects of the man's business."

Henley leaned forward, his voice low and even, meant for him alone. "You're here to lift the skirts of the man's daughter."

Nicholas seized Henley's collar and hauled the man to his feet. The table tipped sideways. Their chairs crashed. And then. . .silence.

All eyes trained on them. Whispers rustled in the corners of the room, like dead leaves skittering across cobbles. Aunt, coffee in her lap, was wide-awake now.

Henley's face turned purple. His fingers clawed at Nicholas's grip. He'd pass out soon if Nicholas didn't loosen his hold—not that he wasn't tempted. Whether Millie had asked for it or not, Charles Henley had already ruined her. Emily would not be his next conquest, if he had any say in the matter.

But not if he ended the man's life here and now.

Henley's body started to sag.

God, help me.

"Let him go!" Millie shrieked and slapped at his arm.

Nicholas shoved the man away. Henley toppled backward, landing with a satisfying thud on his backside. Twisting on the floorboards, he turned aside and coughed until he retched. Nicholas brushed his hands, content with his work.

But satisfaction vanished the instant Emily turned on him.

The clear brown of her eyes changed to the angry, muddied waters of the Thames. Her disgust tore at him, her rage drowned the last breath from his lungs.

"How dare you!" Her voice was as dark as night.

He clutched his hands into fists, helpless against the sudden realization that thunked low in his gut. No, this couldn't be happening. Not here.

Not now.

"Out! Get out!" A knife-wielding shopkeeper burst from a back doorway. "Take your fighting to Gentleman Jim's or I'll call a constable!"

Irony tasted bitter in Nicholas's mouth as he tipped his hat in compliance. He was a lawman.

And he was in love with the woman who gaped at him with hatred.

CHAPTER 17

Bracing both feet against the sides of the carriage door, Emily gripped the handle with a death hold. If Nicholas Brentwood thought she'd allow him a cushy ride home after ruining her life, the insufferable man could just think again. Crouching inside the carriage in a most unladylike fashion, she pulled so hard her fingers were beyond aching—they were numb.

Outside, Nicholas bellowed, "For the last time, open this door, or I'll—"

"You'll what? Choke me like you did Mr. Henley? You can walk. Drive on, Mr. Wilkes!"

The carriage didn't move. Hadn't Wilkes heard her orders? Maybe her guardian had him writhing on the ground as well.

"Do you have any idea how much attention this is attracting?" Nicholas's voice was a growl, low, threatening. . . .

And likely correct. Horrid man. She could only imagine the onlookers gaping in a semicircle outside the carriage. Theatrics attracted more crowds than a hat sale.

But just as in netting a bargain, timing was everything. She tightened her grip. The muscles in her arms quivered with the strain.

"So be it." Nicholas's voice was lethal—as would be his next tug on the door.

Listening with her whole body, Emily heard him shift his weight, plant his feet, and then—

She let go.

The door flew open. Nicholas stumbled backward, plowing into the spectators.

For the first time since her life ended moments ago at the Chapter Coffee House, Emily smiled. Then she turned and scooted to the farthest side of the carriage. Smoothing her skirts, she sank into the seat and gazed out the window, pretending she was alone. Perhaps, if she tried hard enough, she could even pretend Millie wouldn't gossip and Henley would overlook the entire incident.

The carriage tilted to the side as Nicholas climbed in. The wheeze of the seat across from her suggested he'd sat. A latch clicked, and her head jerked as the wheels began to eat ground.

"Emily, I—"

"Do not presume to call me by my Christian name, sir."

His coat rustled as he shifted. "I merely want to—"

"I'd prefer not to discuss it." She clipped out each word, like scissors snipping holes in a paper.

Nicholas's sigh filled the carriage, expanding to envelop all of London by its enormity. The seat creaked, and she couldn't be sure, but it sounded like he turned his head to look out the opposite window, completely dismissing her.

Which annoyed her even more. Giving up the silent treatment, she turned to him. "I don't know how you can sit there so calmly, knowing you nearly killed a man and ruined my life, all within the space of an instant."

"Your life is hardly ruined, *Miss Payne*."

"Then allow me to make things plain to you, Mr. Brentwood." She spit out his name as prickly as he'd stabbed the air with hers.

He didn't even blink.

By faith, he was bold! How dare he look so unperturbed—and handsome, which pushed her anger to a whole new level.

"Millie will spread this from Mayfair to St. Martin's before we get to Portman Square. Mr. Henley won't give me a second look at the Garveys' ball next week, nor will any other man if he's to expect a sound beating from you as the result. Why, I've never been so mortified in all my life. And when my father gets home—"

"I thought you said you didn't want to talk about it!"

She narrowed her eyes. "Your smugness is rivaled only by your callousness. I don't expect you to understand my situation, but you could at least show a little compassion."

He ran his hand through his hair, his gaze holding hers. It took him a full minute to speak. "Truly, I am sorry for the embarrassment I caused you. I let my anger get the best of me—a foe I've not completely mastered. Thankfully, God is patient. I pray you will be, as well."

His apology chipped away the sharp edges of her resolve. His soft, green gaze sanded it smoother. She straightened each finger of her gloves before answering. No sense letting him think he'd won so easily. "Fine. Apology accepted. Still. . ." She matched his earlier sigh. "Mr. Henley may never approach me now, not after this."

A muscle moved on his jaw. "One can hope."

"He is my best prospect!"

"But he's not your only prospect." Nicholas leaned forward, as if by proximity he might drive home his words. "Marriage is a lifelong commitment. Do not run headlong through a door that will lock tight behind you, without first discovering what's on the other side."

The truth was loud in the space between them. His words echoed what Bella had warned her against. A queer jolt ran from shoulder to shoulder. Was that really what she was doing? What did she know of Henley, now that she thought upon it? What if he really was as lecherous as Captain Daggett?

Thunder shook the carriage, and she grabbed the seat's edge for support. Impossible. Sunlight yet streamed through the window. Had they collided with another carriage?

Nicholas banged on the carriage wall. "Wilkes, is there a problem?"

Outside, a man's cry answered—followed by a rough "Hyah" and crack of a whip. The carriage picked up speed, much too fast for a London street. Had highwaymen now taken to attacking city folk?

Emily scooted down her seat, bumping her bottom along the leather bench. As much as she hated to admit it, the closer she drew to Nicholas, the safer she felt.

He didn't give her a second look as he jiggled the door handle.

"What are you doing?" Her thoughts rattled along with the carriage wheels. "Shouldn't we wait for Wilkes to stop the carriage before you open the door?"

"Get back," Nicholas ordered.

"What's going on?"

He threw his shoulder against the door. The thing didn't budge.

Emily frowned. "Stop it!"

The carriage lurched, and the wheels rumbled faster. What was Wilkes thinking to drive so insanely?

And why would Nicholas want to get out now?

He turned to her, danger flashing in his eyes. She'd seen him look at her sternly before, but never like this. Coldness gripped her heart.

"Move!"

In the space of a breath, his back was to her, blocking her view. He shoved his hand inside his greatcoat and withdrew a gun.

Not needing to be told twice, she scrambled into the farthest corner of her seat.

Sparks flashed. A gunshot snapped, sharp and brittle as a broken bone. The acrid stench of gunpowder filled the coach, burning the inside of her nose. Outside the door, a man's deep cry competed with the horses' pounding hooves.

Nicholas jammed his free hand into his coat and pulled out a pouch. He worked so fast, his muscles flexed and rippled beneath the taut fabric of his coat. The tension in him was magnificent—and completely horrifying.

A scream stuck to the roof of Emily's mouth, barely letting words escape. "What's happening?"

"Quiet!"

There was no question of disobeying that voice, even if she wanted to. Something was wrong—very wrong. Fear thudded deep in her chest. More than anything she'd ever wanted—even the tiara—she suddenly longed for a faith the size of Nicholas's. Would God hear a desperate cry from her?

She squeezed her eyes shut. If nothing else, she'd meet death without gazing upon its face. *Please God, don't let me die. Don't let Nicholas die. Help!*

The world shifted. Her eyes flew open. She flailed as the carriage careened around a corner. Wheels skidded. Horses screamed their protest. And then—

She was tossed forward as the carriage stopped. The sudden lack of movement was as jolting as the wild ride. Before she could think, Nicholas shoved open the door. On her other side, glass exploded over her.

A wooden club flashed in front of her face then disappeared. Emily stared at the sparkly shards in her lap, her thoughts as hard to piece together as the awful jagged edges.

"Emily!" Nicholas's voice broke as sharply as the window.

She turned her face to him, but her body jerked the opposite direction. Pain grabbed her arm, sliding a sharp line from wrist to elbow. Someone pulled her from outside the window, forcing her up and out. Her skin screamed over spikes of broken glass. Fire shot from elbow to armpit. She'd never fit, not through that hole.

Not in one piece.

From inside the carriage, a warm grip wrapped around her waist. With a grunt and a heave, Nicholas yanked her back.

"Switch places." His voice was a growl in her ear as he shoved past her, using his body as a barrier between her and the window.

For a second, she breathed easier.

Then fingers bit into her arms from behind and hauled her backward. Downward. Outside.

A scream ripped up her throat and ended as a man's gloved hand smashed against her mouth.

"Don't fight this, pretty lady." Hot breath burned into her ear. "It'll all be over soon."

A rag was shoved into her mouth before everything flipped. A man's hard shoulder cut into her belly, and her face smacked against his back. He carried her as casually as a sack of yesterday's bread. Her head pounded with a rush of blood, her heart with panic. Would Nicholas even notice she was gone? And when he did, would it be too late? Tears slipped past her lashes.

Either God hadn't heard her prayer—or He didn't intend to answer.

As soon as Emily was safely behind him, Nicholas ripped off his greatcoat and shoved it over the windowsill then leaned forward and scanned the situation. Bricks walled his sight, hardly two feet from the carriage. Either they'd stopped perilously close to a building, or they were in an alley.

From above, arms shot down. One pair. Good. He could deal with a single man on the roof. Nicholas snagged one of the arms, dug his fingers into flesh, and yanked downward.

Then let go.

A head, followed by a body, plummeted past the gaping hole that had been the window. Bone cracked against wheel rim. Curses ended with a grunt. Breathing hard, Nicholas turned. Surely Emily would have plenty to say about this.

But she wasn't there.

Before the realization fully sank in, darkness filled the doorway, taking on the shape of a demon. Or was it a cloak-covered thug? Nicholas leaned back and kicked. His boot heel smacked against bone and flesh, sending a man sprawling into a wall hardly three feet from the carriage.

So, this was an alley.

And that was a thug.

Nicholas snatched his gun off the seat and vaulted out the door.

Like a lightning bolt, a knife blade flashed toward him. He jumped back and cocked the gun with his thumb. Dark eyes peered into his, twin pools of depravity—and something more. Was that a memory skimming across the man's face, recognition flaring his nostrils? No time to decipher it now. Nicholas lifted his gun.

The brigand turned and ran.

Edging sideways, past horses pawing in their harnesses, Nicholas tore after him. "Stop!"

The thug glanced over his shoulder. Big mistake. His foot shot out on an oily patch of God-knew-what, and he fell. The knife flew from his hand. Before he slid to a stop, Nicholas towered over him.

And fired.

A bullet at close range was never pretty. Neither was the man's scream ricocheting off the bricks.

Nicholas dropped to one knee and grabbed the man's face, forcing his mouth shut. "Get to a surgeon. You might lose the leg, but you'll have your life as a prize. Thank God for that, for I'd as soon have killed you."

Bolting up, he tucked the gun in his belt and shot forward, following blood splats in the gravel. Maybe one day he'd be thankful for the gruesome trail that would lead him to Emily.

But not now. Not with visions of what he might find. Two paces later, he stopped dead.

His heart twisted like a groan.

Ahead, clearing a corner in the T-shaped alley, a Sampson-sized brute carried Emily over one shoulder. She bounced like a plaything gripped in a dog's teeth as he pinned her with one arm. His other hand held a gun, the muzzle aimed at Nicholas's chest.

Nicholas pulled his own gun and lifted a prayer. The screams of the man behind him foreshadowed that this might not end well—especially since he hadn't the time to reload. Schooling his face, he bluffed. "Drop the girl, or you're a dead man!"

The man stopped, twenty paces off. "Son of a jackanapes! If it isn't the mighty Brentwood. Come to aid the damsel in distress, eh?"

Nicholas squinted, the voice dragging a memory from a pit of nightmares he'd long since banished. "Nash!" He spit out the name like a rancid bite of meat. "I should've finished you off when I had the chance."

Emily struggled on the man's shoulder, her elbow catching him hard in the back of the skull. His head jerked forward, but that did nothing to stop Nash's grin. "Aye, ye should've."

"Not to worry." Nicholas lifted his gun higher, eyeing along the muzzle as if about to shoot. "Now's as good a time as any."

"You wouldn't take the chance of hitting a lady." Nash's face tightened into sharp angles. "Drop the gun."

"Drop the girl!" Nicholas countered.

Nash threw her to the ground, her backside grinding into the broken bits of glass and other splinters of refuse that made up the alley floor. The cruel blackguard! Apparently happy with his deed, a smile slashed across Nash's face. "Your turn."

Nicholas's heart pounded in his head. What to do? Think. . .think! *Lord, a little wisdom here—now—would be appreciated.* Immediately, a scripture came to mind. The speed wasn't unusual. The passage was.

"And the great dragon was thrown down."

"Drop it!" Nash hollered.

The rest of the passage drowned out Nash's voice. . . *"He was thrown down to the earth, and his angels were thrown down with him."*

Nicholas gritted his teeth. *Is that really what You want, Lord?*

"Last warning, Brentwood, if you want to live."

The scripture condensed into three solid words. *Throw. It. Down.*

His gaze shot to Emily, who scrambled backward like a crab on sand. As soon as she cleared just enough space to keep her safe, Nicholas splayed his fingers. The gun crunched against gravel. Was this it, then? His life ended here in an alley? Not that he wasn't ready, but what would become of Emily?

And then he saw it.

Nash pulled the trigger. Sparks flew. Metal clicked. Then—

Nothing. No bullet. No searing pain.

The gun did not go off.

Nash's jaw worked as his thumb reset the cock. Stupid move. The action wouldn't help him—and it gave Nicholas time to snatch up the other thug's dropped knife.

Stooping, he grabbed the handle, flipped the knife up into the air, and snatched the blade. Then he whipped it back and snapped a release. The blade sailed true, gouging into the fleshy part of Nash's gun arm. The weapon dropped against the cobbles and went off with a roar.

The bullet ripped through flesh, muscles, tendons, bone, and shot out the other side of Nash's lower leg.

Nicholas took off at a dead run. Passing by Nash, who now howled on the alley floor, he pumped his feet in time to his racing heart. Once again, Emily was out of sight. Surely God hadn't brought him this far to lose her now.

Did You, Lord?

He flew around the corner, chest tight, lungs burning, his muscles flexed to face who knew how many more men.

Then he slowed.

Emily was alone in the passage, pounding on the only door in the dead-end part of the T. Her hair ravaged over her shoulders and down her back, her hat long since lost. The sleeves of her pelisse and the gown beneath hung in shreds. Blood dripped off one elbow.

In four strides, he swept her up and cradled her in his arms. *Thank You, God. Thank You.*

Her tears dampened his shirt. Her blood warmed his skin. A fierce protective instinct stole his breath as she choked on sobs.

"You're safe now," he comforted.

Her body shuddered against his. "I was so. . .afraid!"

"Shh. It's done." He bent his face to her ear, breathing in her lily-of-the-valley scent. "I've got you, and nothing will take you from me. You hear?"

The tightness in her body slackened, though her weeping continued. Perhaps it was what she needed.

"Go ahead," he whispered. "Cry it out."

He turned, fighting against a rising desire to return to Nash and kick him in his bloody leg for the fear he'd caused her. No doubt Nash was the ringleader of this little escapade. . .but why? Maybe a few kicks more would loosen the scoundrel's tongue—and if not, all the better, for he'd be forced to utilize other, less pleasant techniques.

Clearing the corner of the brick wall, Nicholas stopped. He set Emily's feet onto the ground and stepped in front of her.

The alley was empty.

CHAPTER 18

Ambrose de Villet rubbed a hand over his skull. Stubble pricked his palm. Was a decent shave in this godforsaken rat hole of a country too much to ask? And now this. He slugged back a shot of bourbon, relishing the burn as it sank to his gut, then carefully set his glass next to the crystal decanter on the desk.

Turning, he nodded at Skerritt and Weaver, the two men who flanked the makeshift office door. Neither said a word as he strode past them. Their footsteps simply thumped in rhythm to his as they fell in line, echoing from floor to rafter in the abandoned warehouse. Daylight streamed in through cracks in the walls and holes in the roof. The place was a sieve of rot. Half a smile twisted his lips. Funny how all the rays of light pointed accusing fingers at the battered man propped against an empty crate.

Nash. Stupid dog. He should've known better than to hire such a buffoon.

Ambrose halted five paces from him. Nash grimaced in his shirt-sleeves, one of which was torn and slick with blood. His coat was wrapped like a growth around the bottom half of his leg, the fabric wet and dark. Drip by drip, Nash's life wept onto the warehouse floor.

Ambrose cocked his head as he studied the man. A mere girl couldn't have done that much damage.

Glancing over his shoulder, he locked eyes with Skerritt, who in turn looked at Weaver. Both men stalked forward, until Nash stood in the center of their triangle.

"So, my friend." Ambrose folded his arms. "Where is the girl?"

"Wasn't—" Nash gasped. A spasm clenched his jaw then slowly faded before more words flowed. "Wasn't as easy as you said."

Ambrose sniffed, unimpressed with the English dog's pain. "What happened?"

"Brentwood happened!" Nash's voice was as angry as a bruise.

What was this? A code word? Some local jargon? A vein throbbed on the side of his neck, pulsing his skin against his starched collar. "Brentwood?"

"He's a runner. One of the best." Nash turned aside and spit then pushed away from the crate. "I'm done with this job, and I'm done with you, Mr. Dee. I came to collect what's owed me."

Ambrose slid his gaze to Skerritt and lifted his chin. A slight movement, but economy most often produced wealth.

Skerritt shot forward. Two quick jabs sent Nash to his knees, bone crunching against oak. His howl screeched as off pitch as bootnails sliding down a slate roof.

Ambrose paced forward, stopping inches from the man. "Before we discuss your. . .resignation, tell me of this man. This Brentwood."

Nash's chest heaved. Curses were as thick as his breaths. A fresh trickle of blood leaked from his shoulder. What a pathetic fool.

Ambrose circled him, planting one foot after the other, counting his steps. Counting the last of Nash's heartbeats. At full circle, he stopped. "I'm a businessman, Mr. Nash. Your lack of decorum is somewhat unsettling. If you hope to walk out of here alive—and I hold that phrase loosely, considering your leg—then I suggest you cooperate."

Nash lifted his face. Hatred poured off him, vile as his sweaty stench. "Have it yer way, then. Brentwood is ex-military. Keenest eye I've ever seen, with a wit to match. Trained Portuguese gunners in '01."

The beginning of a smile lifted Ambrose's lips. "We all know how that one turned out. Oranges for Queen Maria. Disgrace for England. Perhaps the man's not as invincible as you say."

Nash shook his head and squinted, a shard of sunlight piercing his eyes. "You don't understand. The Portuguese would've beat back the scarpin' Frogs had Brentwood stayed on to help fight. You can be sure of that. It took Lord Nelson to finally clean up that mess, didn't it?"

Ambrose stooped, eye level with the man. His shadow shut out the daylight on Nash's face. In a measured tone, quiet, firm—deadly—his mother tongue slipped past his lips. *"Le sang français traverse mes veines."*

Nash's eyes widened. His lips moved, though it took quite a while before sound came out. "You. . .you're. . ." His head swiveled, wrenching a glance from Skerritt to Weaver. "He's a Frenchie!"

Ambrose smiled in full, mirroring the grins on the other men. Nash's jaw dropped like an unhinged skeleton's.

"My full name is Ambrose de Villet, though Mr. Dee suits me better in situations such as these." Stepping back, Ambrose once again folded his arms. Let the dog think on that for the last few moments of his life. Looking past Nash, he met the gazes of Skerritt and Weaver. "We've a few things to work out, then. Not only has Payne vanished, but his daughter appears to be unreachable so long as this Brentwood is in her attendance. Yet appearances often deceive, hmm?"

Skerritt shifted his weight. Weaver lifted a brow. Neither said a word.

Ambrose continued. "I will not return to Sombra without the money. One way or another, I will have it. For the moment, Brentwood or no, I think a ransom is still our best option. Men?"

Skerritt and Weaver nodded.

Nash scowled. "You're crazy. Brentwood will kill you."

Laughter tasted sweet, and for one long, intense minute, Ambrose savored the humor of Nash's words. Unfolding his arms, he fisted his hands on his hips. "You think I care about dying?"

"Like I said. . ." Breath by ragged breath, Nash pushed up to stand. The blood drained from his face—what little he had left. "I want out. I'm done."

"Oui, mon ami." The smile slipped from Ambrose's lips. His eyes shot to Skerritt's.

And his next words were as sharp as the knife sticking out from Nash's back. "You are done. . .and so is Brentwood."

CHAPTER 19

"Ahh, miss, you're an absolute vision! You'll turn every head at the Garveys' ball."

Mary straightened in front of her, and Emily glanced down at the yards of silk settling in a golden shimmer around her legs, landing a whisper's length above the carpet in her chamber. Hand-sewn pearls embellished the gilt embroidery at the hem, catching the lamplight like tiny beacons afloat a sea of richness. The skirting rose to just below the bust, where it drew in tight. Appliquéd embellishments wove an intricate pattern around her ribs. More pearls, more gold, crisscrossed at the center of the bodice and cinched together at the top then fanned into a lacy ruffle that feathered across a low neckline. A modest amount of flesh peeked out to entice the eyes of any man.

As Emily crossed the length of her room and sat in front of the vanity, she frowned. Why wasn't she sure anymore of which man she wanted to attract?

Mary's skirt swished behind her, a soothing rustle though slightly offset by the lingering limp in her gait. "I beg your pardon, miss, if I were too forward."

Emily waved her off. "No, Mary. Nothing of the sort."

Closing her eyes, she gave in to her maid's tugs with the hairbrush. How to explain that for the past week, ever since the attack on their carriage, she couldn't shake the feel of Nicholas's strong arms holding her? Or the way he'd taken down every last man to get to her in spite of the threat to his own life? Would Mr. Henley have done the same? A sigh slipped past her lips. Henley couldn't even take on one man in a coffee house.

"Are you well, miss?"

Her eyes popped open, and she blinked at herself in the mirror. Her skin was a shade paler, her cheeks a little sharper. Or mayhap the lamplight simply painted odd shadows and leeched her rosy color. "I am well. Why do you ask?"

"You've been a mite quiet, as of late. Not that I think you're a great talebearer to begin with. Still. . ." Mary's hands twisted lengths of hair as she spoke. "You've hardly been out of the house."

"Mr. Brentwood's been too preoccupied to escort me."

"He has been in and out a lot, hmm?" Two hairpins stuck out at the corner of Mary's lips, adding a lispy quality to her voice. "But you've not taken any callers, either."

"Mr. Brentwood thinks it's wise if I don't receive anyone unless he's in attendance." She tilted her head to the right, allowing Mary to gather up some stray wisps.

"Yes, well, it's certainly not the preball flurry I expected." Mary removed the last of the pins from her mouth and secured the bulk of Emily's hair on top of her head. "No packages, appointments, or fittings. If I may be so bold, is something else amiss?"

Emily grimaced, though if she was honest, it wasn't only caused by Mary's use of the curling iron too near her ear. Something was amiss. If she could verbalize it, she'd likely feel better, but slippery emotions she could barely hang on to—let alone name—dangled just beyond her reach. "I suppose that attack left a mark on me. A shadow, so to speak."

"It were dreadful, miss, that's what." Lowering the curling iron, Mary bent closer. "You don't think that tonight, I mean. . .surely nothing more will happen. . . ."

Mary's voice died out, yet the words floated in the air like unmoored phantoms. Emily shivered.

In the looking glass, Mary's gaze bored into hers. "Are you sure you're up to this ball, miss?"

Was she? What *was* wrong with her?

Lifting her chin, she forced a smile. "I am confident Mr. Brentwood will have everything under control. He usually does."

Mary lifted a brow. "You speak of Mr. Brentwood as freely as you mention Mr. Henley."

"Which is none of your concern." The harsh words slipped out before she could snatch them back.

Mary straightened, lips pinched, and silently resumed curling loose tendrils of hair.

Emily sighed. Truly, she'd not meant to be so severe. Mary's observation simply rankled her in a way that rippled unease clear to her fingertips. Since the moment she'd met the man, her world had flipped topsy-turvy. Nicholas Brentwood vexed her to no end. He invaded her home, her time, her thoughts. No wonder she spoke of him as much as Mr. Henley.

Mary's fingers tugged a little harder than normal, prickling her scalp—and conscience. Just because she was unsettled didn't mean she must snap at her maid.

"Nice work, Mary." She offered the girl a half smile as a peace offering. "Lovely work, truly. You are a magician when it comes to hair."

The tight lines around Mary's mouth softened. She pulled on a spiral of hair, and a single stylish curl draped from the crown of Emily's head, past her bare neck, and onto her shoulder. "There, miss. I shouldn't be surprised if by tomorrow morning you don't have several offers."

Emily reached for her perfume bottle. Mary's expectation was a very real possibility—one she'd hoped for, planned for, anticipated as reality.

So why did her stomach suddenly twist as tightly as the bun on her head?

Dabbing on some lily-of-the-valley-scented oil, she tilted her head and listened. Doggie claws scratched at her chamber door. Poor pug. She'd neglected him as much as her callers. Once again, she met Mary's eyes in the mirror. "Will you let in Alf?"

As Mary disappeared from the glass, Emily leaned closer. Her hair gleamed golden, done up in a simple pearl coronet. Nothing like the tiara, but. . . She turned her face slightly. Yes, some pink glowed on her cheeks, and the chocolate brown of her eyes, if not as stunning a color as Bella's blues, were at least shiny and bright. Perhaps an offer or two would roll in tomorrow morning. What would Nicholas say to that?

What would she?

After a few yips and scurry of paws, Alf jumped up on her lap. She scooped him aloft, rescuing herself from questions she couldn't answer and saving her skirt from his toenails. "Little scamp!"

Tongue lolling, Alf cocked his wrinkly face at her, and she smiled. "But I can never stay cross with you."

"I'm waiting, Miss Payne." Nicholas's voice bellowed up from downstairs and through the open door.

"You're as ready as you'll ever be, miss." Mary held out her hands for the pup.

After transferring Alf, Emily stood and tugged up her gloves as high as the fabric would stretch then lifted her arms. "Nothing's showing?"

Mary pitched her head right then left. "Not that I can see, miss. No one but Mr. Brentwood will know of your scratches."

Emily rolled her eyes. "They're hardly scratches, Mary. More like ugly gouges."

"Yet they are completely hidden."

"Miss Payne!" Nicholas sounded as if he ordered a squad of soldiers to battle.

Emily lowered her arms and gave one last pat to the wrinkles on her skirt Alf's paws had inflicted. "I suppose I'd better hurry along. I'm sure Mr. Brentwood's mood is foul enough from having to wear new evening clothes."

Mary smiled. "That were a fine battle, I hear tell."

Emily returned a grin. "I suppose it wasn't fair to force the issue with Mrs. Hunt in the room to back me up, hmm?"

"It worked, didn't it?"

Emily nodded. Though Mary wasn't a thing like Wren, she'd earned a place in her heart all the same.

"Miss Payne!"

"Oh, bother." Emily scooted to the door then paused and looked over her shoulder. "Don't wait up on my account, Mary. I'll wake you when I return."

"As you wish. Enjoy the evening, miss."

Emily rushed down the hallway and, as she neared the landing, heard the distinct sound of footsteps pacing a route at the bottom of the stairs. From the sitting room, the last chimes of the hour vibrated through the air. La, was it already nine o'clock? Had it really taken her that long to get ready?

She lifted her skirts and hastened down the stairs.

At the last step, she paused, her jaw agape. Who was this man in her foyer? In her life? Suddenly she wasn't so sure she had the courage to take the arm of such an imposing gentleman and head out into the night.

For a gentleman he was. Nicholas Brentwood's severe appearance had been subdued into that of an aristocrat. Not that he was foppish. In fact, he could hardly be accused of frill or fanciness at all. Rather, an aura of elegant power cloaked him as neatly as the plain black tailcoat stretching across his shoulders. Beneath, he wore a dark waistcoat, highlighted with fine silver embroidery—his one concession to extravagance. A white shirt contrasted in stark defiance, made all the more stunning by the silk neck cloth he'd secured around his neck with a single pearl pin. His fitted trousers—black, of course—ran the length of his long legs down to plain but shined leather shoes. Though he'd shunned the traditional light-colored pantaloons and stockings preferred by most men, the way his clothing rode the lines of his body, convention be hanged.

His gaze traveled over her, softer than a summer breeze skimming past leaves, and when his green eyes finally settled on hers, she caught her breath. Stillness spread out from him. Time slowed. Space and air and life—everything stopped for the briefest of moments. Silence breathed with him, as did she, for he commanded it without a word.

Then just as suddenly, all shifted back into a normal cadence.

Her mouth curved into a smile. Whatever had passed between them was intoxicating. Forbidden. Impossible, really. . .yet wholly and completely heady.

As she descended the last step, she mulled over Mary's parting admonition and decided to take her advice. No matter the outcome of what the morrow may bring, she would enjoy this evening.

Very much.

Nicholas snapped shut his watch and tucked it back into his pocket. He needn't have looked. The chiming of the sitting-room clock verified what he already knew. They were late. Not that he cared a fig about some silly ball, but regardless of the occasion, tardiness grated on him like skidding bare-fleshed on gravel.

And he had the scars to prove it.

Finally, silk swished behind him. The pad of slippers on tread turned him around. High time she quit her dilly-dallying and—

He froze. A jolt of heat hit him square in the chest. The only words that came to mind were *fear not*.

For an angel stood in front of him.

Emily paused on the last step, wide-eyed, lips parted. Lamplight brushed a soft glow over her shape. Warmth radiated from her, golden and brilliant—as if all the stars in the universe met and mingled in one focused point, igniting the space between them with risky possibility.

His gaze traveled the length of her, memorizing every line and curve, each delicate fold and shimmer of her gown. Then slowly, like a man gazing at a lover as he's led to a noose, he lifted his eyes to her face, for indeed, she held his heart in her hands. She could snuff the life from him if she knew.

Her cheeks wore the first blush of a spring rose. Her eyes gleamed with amber fire. His fingers longed to reach out and discover if her skin was as soft as it promised.

She descended the last step, her sweet lily scent pulling him toward her. The sweeping arc of her lips mesmerized. . .so full, so red. His heart beat a primal rhythm, wild and deep. Three paces, that's all, just three and he could wrap his arms around her slim waist, lower his mouth to hers, and—

A shudder ran through him, settling low in his belly. If he didn't contain this here, now, the evening would end with regret.

He scowled and wheeled around. "About time you deigned to make an appearance, Miss Payne. I've been waiting the better part of an hour. Does it really take that long to make yourself presentable?"

"Well!" She huffed behind him. "Good evening to you, too, Mr. Brentwood."

He grabbed her pelisse from the coat tree near the door and held it out. "We're late, thanks to you. Don't expect me to be pleasant about it." He suppressed a cringe as his own harsh tone boxed his ears, but better to anger her. Better she keep her distance.

Better he keep his. *Oh God, help me, please.*

She frowned up at him. "A real gentleman would have first remarked on my gown or my hair before laying blame, if indeed he blamed at all."

Turning, she allowed him to guide in one arm after the other into the sleeves of her wrap. Her movement enticed. Her nearness stole his breath more effectively than the ridiculous neck cloth choking his throat. He stepped back and wrenched open the door with more force than necessary, welcoming the slap of cool night air against his face.

"A true lady would value punctuality, and furthermore"—he offered his arm—"whatever gave you the idea that I was a gentleman?"

"My mistake." She lifted her chin and bypassed him without a look.

Good. At such a rate, hopefully she wouldn't notice the absence of Wilkes—her usual driver. The man now gripping the reins sported a shock of red hair beneath a felt hat. His jacket bulged with a brace of loaded pistols. And a seasoned driver would've set the wheel brake instead of allowing the horses to jitter the carriage back and forth.

Nicholas locked eyes with Flannery, sitting in the driver's seat, a second before assisting Emily into the coach, then he swung up behind her.

Emily sat center on the seat, the farthest point from either window. Smart girl. He sat opposite her, his back covering the fine line in the seat cushion where he'd modified a small hidey-hole to store extra firearms.

Her hands gripped the seat's edge as the carriage lurched into motion, and she turned her face from him. He bit back a smile. Her anger was a useful tool. Freed of the burden of conversation, he listened for the rush of feet, hooves, wheels, anything that suggested an imminent attack.

The ride, however, was uneventful—and that set his teeth on edge.

It'd been nearly a week since Nash's ambush. Why nothing more? Nicholas's jaw ached from clenching it, and he rubbed his chin. Even bribing his best informants, he'd gained no new knowledge about Nash nor uncovered anything about her father's death. Though at first he'd been reluctant to follow Ford's advice to keep Emily in the dark about the man's demise, the magistrate's wisdom had finally sunk in. Grief was hard enough borne without the closure of all the whys, whens, and hows. And so he'd pursued every possible lead, wearing down precious boot leather in the process. The only certainty he'd gained was further confirmation that his sister hadn't much longer to live.

And that chilled him more thoroughly than Emily's silence. If he didn't conclude this case soon and obtain the rest of his payment from Payne's estate, he'd never move Jenny to the country in time. Tucking his chin, he breathed out another "God, please."

The carriage stopped. He descended. This time when he offered his hand, Emily's fingers rested atop his. Music spilled out the open foyer door, growing louder as they gained the marble stairs facing a towering estate on the western edge of London. So many torches and outdoor lanterns burned on the front lawn, the sun need never make an appearance on this street.

Two footmen in crushed velvet livery flanked the entrance. One held out a white glove for the engraved invitation Emily produced from her beaded reticule. With his free hand, the dandy servant extracted a monocle tethered to a golden chain and lifted it to his eye. Either the Garveys were particularly discriminating, or they simply wanted to make a show of their highly trained, man-sized monkeys.

Once inside, Nicholas paused. His gaze darted from the crowd on the stairway, to the people clogging the corridors, to the sitting room on the right filled with giggling girls and their matrons, then beyond to the open veranda doors. He let out a long, slow breath. No wonder Nash had bided his time. Guarding Emily in this throng would be impossible. If he was going to strike, this would be the perfect place.

Especially when she loosed her fingers from his arm and shot forward, vanishing into a swirl of taffetas and satins and shiny brass buttons.

Nicholas slipped sideways through the crowd after her. A search of the first floor earned him nothing but a few sneers from uppity fops afraid he was closing in on their territory, and several unabashed ogles from ill-chaperoned women. What kind of looks was Emily attracting without him at her side? He took the stairs two at a time, dodging couples and servants alike.

By the time he spotted her laughing with Bella near a punch table on the far side of a dance floor, he couldn't decide if he should throttle her or blend into the crowd undetected to watch the beguiling way her dimples deepened when she smiled.

Across the room, her gaze shot to his.

He wove past spectators, keeping a wide berth from the dancers at center, until he closed in on Emily and her friend. "Good evening, Miss Grayson." He tipped his head to the pert little redhead then turned on Emily. "Miss Payne, I'll thank you to consider that I am not as familiar with this household as you appear to be."

"Ah yes, my apologies." She dazzled a grin at him. "I forgot that a gentleman would've known his way about."

"Touché." He quirked half a grin in return. "Shall we start over? Completely, that is."

He bent at the waist, first to her then to her friend. "Good evening, Miss Payne. Good evening, Miss Grayson."

Bella's brow crinkled. "But you already—"

Emily cut her off with a sweep of her hand. "Don't mind him. My cousin is in a rather ill humor tonight."

"As will you soon be." Bella set down her punch glass and leaned toward Emily. "Don't look now, but here comes Mr. Shadwell."

A ripple teased the fabric of Emily's skirt from bodice to floor. Either she'd just clenched every muscle or she'd repositioned her feet for a good sprint. Nicholas snuck a glance over his shoulder and suddenly understood why.

Plowing through the last square of a cotillion, a red-nosed man, with a belly that further attested to his love of spirits, headed straight for them. Mr. Shadwell gave a cursory nod at Nicholas and Bella then bowed low before Emily, grabbed her hand, and planted a kiss upon her glove.

Nicholas smirked. She'd had the nerve to suggest *he* didn't behave in a gentleman-like fashion?

"Miss Payne, how delightful!" Shadwell straightened, wobbling slightly—as would anyone so off center with a belly like his. "I've been waiting with bated breath for a glimpse of your beauty tonight."

Baited was right. A distinct waft of anchovy pate filled the air. Nicholas cocked his head, curious to see how Emily would handle this affront.

She edged closer to him, away from Shadwell, though she did greet the man. "Mr. Shadwell."

Shadwell smiled. "I insist that the next dance belong to no one but me, my dear."

Emily grabbed Nicholas's arm. "So sorry. I'm afraid I've already promised the next dance. Am I not right, Mr. Brentwood?"

Her eyes sought his, her brown gaze pleading. He studied her closely. Was she holding her breath?

He opened his mouth, but the yes that came out wasn't his.

Behind him, a voice curled over his shoulder like smoke. "The lady is right."

Nicholas turned.

Henley peeled her hand off his arm and tucked it into the crook of his own. "Miss Payne's next dance is spoken for by me."

CHAPTER 20

Emily licked her lips, her mouth dry as bleached bones, though she'd just drunk a full glass of punch. In the midst of the dozens of dress coats filling the ballroom, only two interested her. Her eyes shot from Mr. Henley, to Nicholas, then back again. Both set their jaws, but Nicholas's held a sharper edge, his challenge loud, though he said nothing. He simply stood, shoulders back, stance wide. She'd never been to a cockfight before, but she now understood the desire to wager, for she'd bet all her money on Nicholas were a scuffle to break out.

Which is exactly why she pressed her fingers into Mr. Henley's sleeve and smiled up into his face. "The music has already started. Shall we?"

"I protest!" Mr. Shadwell whined like a tot who'd been told no. "Clearly, I was here first."

Nicholas glowered at the man. Shadwell blanched and took a full step back. Why had the ninny dared approach her so boldly?

"You are mistaken, sir, for I accompanied Miss Payne to this ball in the first place." Nicholas cocked his head, studying Shadwell as he might a bit of manure on his shoe. "Furthermore, I defend the lady's prerogative to dance with whomever she wishes."

He turned to her then. So direct was his gaze, she might very well be the only other person in the room. He lifted his brow, and once again the strange sensation of time stilling wrapped over her bare shoulders like a whisper.

She swallowed.

Next to her, Mr. Henley opened his mouth, but Nicholas held up a hand. Could he command a storm to stop as well? "Miss Payne, is it your wish to dance with Mr. Henley?"

Moisture prickled across her forehead, her palms, the crease behind her knees. It was a simple enough question, but the implications were legion.

She cleared her throat, looking—hoping—for words. Was he trying to bully her into defying him? Or killing her with kindness?

"Yes." It was the only logical reply. The right answer. One to which she shouldn't give a second thought.

So why did her voice sound empty? Her heart turn cold?

Fighting back a shiver, she coerced her lips into a smile then turned and allowed Mr. Henley to lead her across the room to the end of the dance line. Her guardian's eyes burned into her back with every step. She wasn't sure how to feel about that, other than acknowledge the little flip in her stomach that she couldn't control—and try to ignore how lifeless her hand felt on Henley's arm instead of resting on Nicholas's warm sleeve.

With her free hand, she massaged her temple. This was insufferable. Finally, her chance to sway Mr. Henley into pursuing her, and she brooded like a moon-eyed schoolgirl over Nicholas Brentwood, Bow Street Runner. What was wrong with her?

Mr. Henley patted her hand and shot her a sideways smile. "I've been waiting for this moment."

"You have?" She gazed up at him, searching his eyes. Nothing inside her tingled or zinged or. . .anything, really.

And when had she started to prefer green over blue?

She forced her smile to deepen. "What I mean to say, sir, is that I, too, have been waiting for this moment. I am honored you sought me out."

But her smile faded as they swept past the dancers and out the door, leaving the ballroom behind. Mr. Henley's pat on her hand turned into a strong-fingered grip.

Her brow puckered. "Have the Garveys added on a new ballroom elsewhere?"

"Not that I know of." He led her down the stairway, slipping her a glance from the corner of his eye. "I merely wanted to have a word with you. Alone. Without your guard dog."

"Mr. Brentwood is not my. . ." The rebuttal lay like a heap of ashes on her tongue. Wasn't that exactly what her father paid him for? What kind of dolt was she to have feelings for a man who was little better than a servant, if indeed the odd sensations were anything other than some tea that didn't set well in her stomach?

As they sped along, she stole glances at Mr. Henley. Centuries of money echoed in his steps. Aristocracy fit him as neatly as his imported Italian shoes and fine silk shirt. The spicy scent of costly cedar aftershave tweaked her nose. Here was a true gentleman, one with wealth, connections, poise. A future.

Her slippers patted double-time to his long strides. Faces blurred past. Conversations blended into a dull roar, and her lungs started to burn. "I object, sir! Must we go this fast?"

"Sorry." Yet his pace belied his apology. He strode out the open french doors, across the veranda, and descended the steps into the garden.

"Mr. Henley, really!" She yanked her hand from the crook of his elbow and pressed it to her chest, gasping. "I can barely breathe."

Behind them, torches twinkled. Ahead, nothing but hedgerows stood black against the night sky, soaking up the moonlight between them. Clearly the party ended at the veranda.

Henley stretched out his hand. "Come along, my dear. There's a seat, not much farther."

The queasiness in her stomach increased, not unlike the sensation when she'd escaped the captain's advances late last summer. Surely, though, this was different.

Wasn't it?

Slowly, she smoothed her hands along her skirt, shoving down memories. "I don't think I should—"

"Honestly, Miss Payne. I've seen you alone countless times with Mr. Brentwood." Mr. Henley's teeth glinted in the faint torch glow reaching this far from the festivities. "Surely you won't hesitate to sit with me."

Emily frowned. "You forget, sir, that Mr. Brentwood is my cousin."

"Is he?"

A chill leeched up through her slippers. "What is that supposed to mean?"

His upper lip quirked. His gaze cut to his offered hand then back to her.

Should she? Wasn't this what she'd hoped for all along? So why did her slippers drag as she stepped forward?

Bella's warnings, Nicholas's concerns, her own gut feelings screamed an alarm, but Mr. Henley's grip engulfed her glove, pulling her along. His grin flashed white in the darkness, skeleton-like. He led her deeper into the garden, along a path lined on one side with boxwoods as tall as her head.

Ten more paces and he stopped. Letting go of her hand, he inclined his head to an alcove cut into the hedge. A small wrought-iron bench nestled in the recess. Torchlight didn't stretch this far. Music and voices and laughter lapped at the far edges of the night.

"Please, have a seat." Henley's tone was mild, his gesture non-offensive.

Still, her heartbeat pulsed through her veins and throbbed in her wrists. Clearly he had much to say, for her ears alone, or he never would have brought her here. Something as important as a proposal, perhaps? But if it weren't, was the risk to her reputation worth otherwise?

What to do?

She lowered to the cold metal and lifted her face to where he stood. Shadows hid his expression, making it impossible to guess at his emotions. La, she could barely name her own.

But she could guess. "Are you cross about the coffee-shop incident? I assure you—"

"On the contrary." His words ended with a small laugh. He sank next to her, his outer thigh pressing against hers. "I am delighted it happened."

She scooted away from him until the arm of the bench cut into her side. "Why would you say such a thing? Mr. Brentwood embarrassed you in no small way, sir."

"Ahh." He nodded, and a swath of his hair fell forward on his brow. "But you see, Miss Payne, it made me realize just how much I want you."

In one swift movement, he closed the distance between them, bringing with him the smell of pomade and desire. His breath fanned over her cheeks as he pulled her into his arms. "Emily, there is something I should like to ask you."

She bit her lip. This was it, exactly what she'd wanted. What she'd been waiting for. Working toward. Counted on as the very beginning of her new life.

Or was it?

His lips crushed against hers, forceful, seeking. Bruising. She wrenched from him, wriggling to free one hand.

Then she slapped him for all she was worth.

"Please, Mr. Brentwood?"

Though it was hardly more than a whisper, Miss Bella Grayson's request piggybacked on the vibrato of a cello string, pulling Nicholas's scrutiny from the dance floor. Next to him, the pleading eyes of Emily's redheaded friend sought his as Mr. Shadwell reached for her hand.

"I know 'tis a great honor I bestow upon you, Miss Grayson." Shadwell's head bobbed, as did the flap of skin beneath his chin. "I understand your hesitance to dance with a proficient light-foot such as myself. But don't let it overwhelm you, my dear. I often have that effect."

"It's simply not possible for me to say yes, Mr. Shadwell." Bella Grayson slipped to Nicholas's other side, putting him smack between her and Shadwell's big belly.

Casting a last glance over his shoulder—and seeing no flash of Emily's golden dress nor Henley's blue suit among the dancers—Nicholas flexed his jaw. Perhaps he could save a damsel in distress and gain a better view of Emily at the same time. He turned and offered his arm to Miss Grayson while speaking to Shadwell. "What the lady is so graciously trying to say, sir, is that she's dancing with me."

Bella's fingers clung to the curve of his forearm like a drowning woman clutching a life preserver. Nicholas led her to the end of the dance line, leaving Shadwell blustering a few *I nevers* and a distinct *who'd have thought*.

As Miss Grayson took her place, she smiled. "Thank you, Mr. Brentwood. You saved my life."

"Happy to be of service, but in all honesty, I must admit ulterior motives." He stood opposite her and scanned the row of merrymakers as the lead couple skipped down the center. Not Emily or Henley, but a flash of gold at the other end of the line blazed for a moment like a shooting star.

As he and Bella sidestepped, moving up the line, Bella leaned toward him. "I can't help but notice your preoccupation with Emily. Why did you let Mr. Henley sweep her away from you?"

"You heard her. She wished it." He bowed as the next couple skipped down the middle, hating the frivolous steps. Whoever invented such a ridiculous custom in the first place? Still, Magistrate Ford's requirement of logging hours with a dancing master came in handy for assignments such as this—he'd give the man that.

"Pardon me for my boldness, Mr. Brentwood, but you don't strike me as one who easily gives in to a woman's whims." Bella arched a perfectly curved brow as she circled him then stepped back to face him. "And by now you've surely discovered that Emily is often whimsical."

He suppressed a snort. That put it more than mildly. "You are perceptive, Miss Grayson."

Dipping right then left, he held the position a second longer than decorum allowed, gaining another glimpse of gold from the far end—and a glower from the woman next to him.

"So, why did you?" Bella's question circled around him, and then she paused, once more standing in front of him. "Allow Emily to dance with Mr. Henley, I mean."

"Not only perceptive but determined, hmm?" He retreated two steps, as did she, allowing yet another couple to hop-skip down the inner aisle.

"And your answer is?" Bella smiled sweetly as they sidestepped up another rank.

Nicholas couldn't help but grin back. Bow Street could use as dogged a pursuer as this one. Flannery could even learn a thing or two from her. "I meant to keep Miss Payne occupied and somewhat corralled. Mr. Henley was simply a means to that end."

A flash sparked at the edge of his sight. He craned his neck forward then back, straining to see past the other dancers for a glimpse of Emily's golden skirt—but even without looking, the tightening of his chest confirmed what he already knew.

She was gone.

Nicholas broke the line, calling to Bella as he swept past her. "Excuse me, Miss Grayson."

A sharp tug on his sleeve turned him around.

"Hear me out, Mr. Brentwood." Bella stood tiptoe, garnering raised brows for her bold behavior. She leaned nearer, ensuring his ears alone would hear. "I'm not sure what Emily means to you, but I speak with a certain knowledge that she means nothing to Mr. Henley. Pray do not let her be alone with the man. Ever. He is not to be trusted." He nodded, her words echoing in time to his heartbeat as he wheeled about. Of course, he couldn't be certain it was Henley who'd led Emily away, but for now, he must assume. He descended the stairs two at a time and scanned the reception hall before his shoe hit the last tread. No gold. No Henley.

His search of the sitting room ended with giggling girls and several wagging fingers from their matrons, but no Emily.

A huge buffet had been set up in the ground-floor promenade. Tables of food, ices, punch fountains, and ornate pastry towers stretched the length of an entire wall, but not one gilt-threaded skirt swayed among the rainbow of colors. Suddenly his cravat didn't just smother. It choked. Tugging it loose, he reentered the reception hall and shot down a different corridor. Pianoforte music poured out an open door at the far end, followed by applause. A swarm of heads began to enter the hallway—tricky to dissect at eye level.

But not atop a chair.

Backtracking, Nicholas dashed down the hall and swung into a small sitting area, sporting a table, two side chairs—

And Millie Barker.

"I thought I saw you pass this way." She stepped toward him, laying a hand on his shoulder. "You're just the man I was looking for."

"It will have to wait, Miss Barker." He sidestepped her and grabbed one of the chairs.

"Such theatrics, sir. Planning on taming a lion, are you?"

Behind him, laughter and footsteps grew louder. He strained his ears. Did any voice carry Emily's light tone?

Nothing about Millie's tone, however, could be construed as light. "Put down the chair, Mr. Brentwood."

"I've not the time!" He turned. If he didn't get out there now, he'd miss his chance.

Millie shot around him. "Not so fast, sir. I have some information you might like to hear."

Beyond her, couples began to stroll past the double-wide doorway. Nicholas frowned down at her. "Not now!"

"La, I should think you'd like to hear this now." She batted her eyelashes, though her attempt at innocence merely annoyed him further.

She mumbled something, but he shoved past her. Only when he cleared the threshold of the sitting area did her words strike home. He pivoted back around. "What did you say?"

Sconce light sharpened the bones of Millie's cheeks, the skin nearest her eyes creasing as she smiled. "I said, Mr. Brentwood, that I know what happened to Emily's father." Her smile widened with her nod. "I know *exactly* what happened to Mr. Payne."

CHAPTER 21

How dare you!" Emily drew back her fingers, palm stinging. Her anger pooled on Mr. Henley's cheek in the shape of a small handprint, visible even in the spare moonlight. She shot to her feet, swallowing the lump in her throat, unsure if it tasted like fear or relief.

She'd never doubt Bella or Nicholas again.

Fire sparked in Henley's eyes. Before she could run to the sanctuary of the Garveys' ballroom, his arm snaked out. Strong fingers dug into her forearm, trapping her in place. Shadows hid half his face, the other half lit with a grin. A feral cat could have produced none better.

"I wager Brentwood has dared more than a simple kiss, my dear." His tone was sensuous. The way his eyes skimmed over her, defiling.

"Beast!" She yanked her arm, but his grasp tightened. "Let me go!"

"So quickly? I think not. . .not when it's taken me this long to get you alone. It is my understanding, Miss Payne, that you've wished for this all along."

"Wished for what? Brutality? Humiliation? You are mistaken." She tugged, yet his fingers bit deeper, drilling into the barely healed wounds beneath her glove.

Suppressing a wince, she glowered down at him. "Millie may have given in to your charms, sir, but I am not Millie. And you are no gentleman!"

With one swift yank, he twisted and pulled. Her bottom hit the metal bench so hard her teeth juddered, and for an instant, tiny dots of light danced like fireflies in the night.

"Must you insist upon such drama?" His fingers slid up her arm then clamped onto the back of her neck, holding her in place. "Should we not talk this over like civilized human beings?"

"There's nothing civil about you." She arched away from his nearness—but was blocked by the arm of steel at her back. "And I have nothing to say, other than to repeat, let me go!"

Her voice bounced from boxwood to boxwood, the effect muffled and impotent. The alcove they sat in closed in on her, as stifling as the heat from Henley's body as he pulled her closer—oppressive as the captain who'd done the same last summer.

He reached up and caressed her cheek with the back of his knuckles. "I have it on good account that it is your intent to marry this season."

She jerked her face aside. "Are you daft? So it is for half the women in London."

"I've also heard. . ." He leaned in, nuzzling her neck. His voice was a hot whisper. "That I am your intended prey."

She froze. Only Bella, Millie, and Nicholas were privy to that information—and she was pretty sure which one had told.

"I entertained such a notion. . .once." She sharpened her voice to a razor's edge. "But no longer. And I'll thank you to remove your hands."

Wriggling in Henley's arms, she gained a tiny amount of space as his head drew back. Why had she ever thought him handsome? Worse, why had she ever thought him the only one who could make her happy? As much as she hated to admit it, Bella and Nicholas had been right, and the truth slapped her with as much force as the mark she'd left on Henley's cheek. The perfectly fitted suit in front of her housed nothing but the bones of a rake. His gaze violated to a depth that sank low in her stomach, and she shivered.

Slowly, a grin slashed across his face. "Ah, my dear, it pains me, this sudden coldness you own. Perhaps I ought to warm you up."

A queer glimmer shone in his eyes. Either the moon had finally risen to such a slant as to drop in a spare glow of light into the alcove—or an intent she'd rather deny simmered within him.

She shoved him with both hands. Still, his grip would not lessen.

"I will have none of it. And I will have none of you! If you don't let me go, I shall scream."

"Such a feisty kitten!" His grin widened. "But hear me out. Millie did, and to her benefit, I might add."

Not that she'd completely doubted the rumor of a tryst between Millie and Henley, but what had any of this to do with her? Emily scowled. "I don't understand."

"You see, my sweet, there's a reason I've avoided the matrimonial noose thus far." Henley's free hand lowered to his pantaloons.

Emily's heart stopped. Surely this wasn't happening.

"I find that women long for financial security much more ardently than a simple band on their third finger. A lifetime pension need not be restricted by fidelity. I intend to make you my mistress. You'll be well cared for. Is that clear enough?"

"No!" She sucked in a breath then yelled even louder. "Stop!"

"Don't bother playing the innocent. The secret is out about your *cousin*. What you see in Brentwood baffles me to no end." The moon's light broke over the top of the hedges in full, lighting Henley's skin to a deadly gray. "I don't understand the ruse, my dear, but I should like a turn at the game you play so deftly with Brentwood."

Her heart was loud in her ears, each beat dredging up memories she thought she'd drowned. Panic choked her, blocking out all but a ragged whisper. "What game?"

"This one."

The back of her head smashed onto the cold bench seat. And then he was atop her, his body a sword, all edges and violence.

"No!" She screamed a dark, throaty roar.

Henley merely laughed. "Holler all you like. I rather like it. Besides, your runner's not around to defend your reputation this time. I believe Millie has him occupied."

As her skirt slipped up, her panic sunk deeper. Fabric ripped. So did her last remaining hope.

And she suddenly understood exactly how Wren had felt last summer.

Nicholas held the chair aloft, gripping the back so tight his fingers turned numb. Behind him, chatter from passing couples filtered into the small sitting area, each female giggle a reminder that Emily was out there. Somewhere. He narrowed his eyes at the raven-headed tart in front of him. "If this is a ruse, Miss Barker, I swear I'll—"

"Do you really think I'd trifle with an officer of the law?" She lobbed the question like a grenade then stepped toward him, eyes glimmering. Her red lips pulled into a pout—but not sullen or innocent. It was a sultry pucker, one only a trollop could perfect.

For the moment, he dropped the chair. Wooden legs thudded onto carpet, wobbled, then stilled. Though the timing wasn't his choosing, he discarded the guise of being Emily's cousin with as much relief as stepping out of a pair of leg shackles. "What do you know?"

"Ahh, so I finally have your attention, do I, Mr. Brentwood. . .Bow Street *Runner*?" Her lips flattened into a sneer. "You're less than a commoner. I can't believe I was ever interested in you."

"And I am not interested in your opinion." He sidestepped the chair and stalked toward her. Grabbing her shoulders, he barely restrained the urge to shake her. "I care only for the facts, and so I repeat, what is it you know?"

"Such violence, sir." Her eyes slid from one of his hands to the other, then she lifted her face and smiled in full. "I rather like it."

He dropped his hands, but not without curling them into fists at his side. This woman was more vexing—and dangerous—than Emily.

Millie craned her neck past his shoulder then crooked a finger at him. "Come. Why don't you pull up that chair, and I'll tell you a little story."

Running a hand through his hair, he sighed. He didn't have time for this. Emily still needed to be accounted for, though as long as she was with Mr. Henley, he supposed she was likely protected from abduction by Nash. Somewhat, at any rate. And Millie's eyes did gleam with a knowledge she ought not possess.

"As I've said, I think you'll want to hear this." Millie's voice cut into his mental debate. "Unless Emily's father is of no importance to you."

He grabbed the chair and set it opposite the table where Millie sat like a queen about to behead a subject. Her jasmine perfume, overdone to the point of irritating his nose, disgusted him to the same extent Emily's lily scent pleased him.

"Make this quick, if you please." He sat so forcefully, the table jittered, rattling a crystal vase and sending ripples through the rose petals.

Slowly, Millie ran a manicured nail across her lips. "No small talk, no sweet nothings, no. . .soft words before the act, hmm?"

On the streets, he frequently encountered women such as this. The only thing that made Millie different was the grand trappings with which she operated. A scowl was his only response.

"Hmm, I daresay you're as puritanical as Aunt." She toyed with a loose curl near the nape of her neck. "You've already met my father, but I don't believe you've had the pleasure of meeting my grandfather . . .on my mother's side, that is. His name is Lowick. Mr. George Lowick."

Lowick? The name landed like a handful of rocks thrown into a pond, agitating a hundred memories, until at last one single ripple lapped up to shore.

"The newspaper mogul?" he asked.

"The very same." When she nodded, sconce light brushed over her face in such a way that the angle of her nose, the tilt of her brow, agreed with her claim. She did, indeed, resemble a much younger and feminine version of Lowick.

"Go on," he said.

"Apparently there's quite the story soon to print. Something about a certain body found hanging from the rafters over on the Wapping Wharves. One of Grandfather's newsmen took an interest in it." While she spoke, she wrapped then rewrapped the coil of black hair around her finger. A nervous reaction, but not enough to indicate lying.

Yet.

He cocked his head. "Bodies in that part of town are tuppence a dozen. Why would a newsman take note of some bloated cadaver?"

"Mr. Nibbens, or Nibbs as Grandfather calls him, has been investigating a ring of resurrection men. I suppose a man in your profession would be familiar with that trade. At any rate, these body snatchers operate near the old Skerry warehouses, and so it was strange that a fine, fresh body hadn't been sold when all it would've taken was a swipe of a knife to the rope." She shrugged, as if the import of her words had nothing to do with a man who'd lived and breathed and loved. "The corpse ended up over at the Plank Street Dead House, all parts attached and intact. . .even the teeth. Kind of you to identify the fellow."

He narrowed his eyes, the merry sounds of the Garveys' ball receding.

"It's too bad, really. Your intelligence intrigues me, your skill at subterfuge, as well. And your strength. . ." She leaned forward, reaching across the small table to trace little loop-de-loops on his arm. "Positively delicious. I suppose I could lower my standards for one night."

He shot to his feet. Emily was light and air compared to this death trap in a dress. "You've not told me anything I don't already know, Miss Barker. Now if you'll excuse me, I have—"

"Oh, sit down. I'm not going to bite you." She leaned back in her chair and shook her head, her ringlet dangling like a noose. "La, such a man of business. I haven't finished my story yet. I should think you would want to hear the rest."

Duty weighed heavy on his shoulders, pressing down, smothering. But where exactly did his duty lie? With the deceased Mr. Payne or the out-of-sight Emily? He folded his arms and planted his feet.

"Quite the warrior stance, sir." Millie's eyes raked over him. "Ah well, it's to be expected, I suppose, from a man like you."

"Just finish your tale, Miss Barker."

"Very well," she sniffed. "Besides a cultivated relationship with all the mortuary clerks in the city, Nibbs has ties to the underworld. Acquaintances that a lawman such as yourself couldn't make. Too risky. Smugglers tend to shy away from men with tipstaffs." Her eyes slipped to his waist then returned to his face. "Though I don't see any bulges on you tonight. Pity."

Nicholas frowned. "You know an inordinate amount of seamy information for a lady."

"One of my specialties. . .among others."

Beauty, wealth, and corrupt to the core. He swallowed back scorn and measured out his words. "Miss Barker, either you get to your point, or I'm leaving."

"Very well." She sighed. "Nibbs is tied up with his resurrection story, but Grandfather tells me an investigation will be made into the possibility of Mr. Payne's dalliance with smugglers."

Unfolding his arms, Nicholas rubbed the back of his neck. It was a small bone she'd thrown—one easily verified by Moore. Her tidbit didn't surprise him nearly as much as the source. "Why would your grandfather tell you that?"

"He didn't. Not outright." Her smile grew. "Nibbs isn't the only one with connections. I intend on marrying well, Mr. Brentwood, and knowledge is power. I gather it where and when I can, and I use it as efficiently as you might wield a pistol."

He thinned his lips into a sharp-edged grimace. "Women like you sicken me."

Her smile vanished. She rose and stepped toward him like a black cloud about to burst. Anger flashed in her eyes. "And women like your simpering Emily Payne sicken me. The more fools like her that I crush on my upward path, the better. The nerve of her leading me to believe you were her cousin. Her father is dead, and I can't wait to see her face when I tell her!"

Millie's words spread like a cancer in his bones. He should've told Emily, despite Ford's urgings. He should've borne her grief, lent his shoulders to her tears. He clenched his jaw so tight, it crackled. What had he done? If Emily heard of her father's death from Millie, the blow would not be kind.

It would be deadly.

The victory in Millie's tipped chin and bright eyes was too much to bear. Rage boiled deep in his gut. He flexed his fingers, keeping them from curling tight. He should count before he spoke. . .one to keep it civil, two to keep from wringing Millie's neck, three to—

Forget it. He stepped toward her. "If you breathe one word about this to Emily, I swear to God it will be your last."

Millie lifted her face to his, standing so close her skirt hem brushed against his legs. No fear lit her violet eyes. Only guile. "You don't strike me as the type to seriously harm a woman, Mr. Brentwood. You've not got it in you." She shook her head. "Too gallant."

With a growl, he shoved her back, pinning her against the wall. Sconce glasses chattered like teeth. "Grand thoughts toward someone who's less than a commoner, wouldn't you say?" He kept his voice low and hard. "You're right, though. I wouldn't hurt you, not personally. I'd have you locked up. I hear hell's a kinder home than the bowels of Newgate Prison."

Her throat bobbed, and finally—*finally*—a shadow of terror snuffed out the gleam in her eyes. "Let me go!"

Funny how the pleasure he expected to feel withered into shame.

He dropped his hands and retreated then wheeled about before leaving. "Tell me, Miss Barker, for I am curious. What did you hope to gain by informing me of all this?"

She stood where he'd left her. But slowly, as she stepped from the wall, an interesting transformation took place. Her smile returned. The tilt of her head, the lift of her shoulders, all spoke of renewed confidence. And if he looked closely enough, he thought he detected a bounce in her step.

Her pretty lips opened like a grave and issued a single word. "Time."

Time? What was that supposed to mean? Her answer echoed through his head like the slamming of a door in an empty house. She'd hoped to gain nothing but—

His blood ran cold. He'd been duped.

Nicholas fled the room and tore down the corridor, ignoring the huffs he left in his wake. How many precious minutes had he wasted? A quick sweep of the first level turned up no golden gown. He took the stairs three at a time and burst into the ballroom. Those nearest the door gaped at him upon his entrance; those farther when he skirted the room. He was a beast, circling in a cage of preening birds, none of which wore the bright gilt of Emily's skirts.

"Mr. Brentwood?"

Bella's voice halted him. He paused long enough to ask, "Have you seen Miss Payne or Mr. Henley?"

"No." A fine gathering of lines troubled the skin on her brow. "You don't think—"

Her voice faded as he dashed out the door and down the stairs, darted through the sitting room, and sprinted onto the veranda. Everything in him wanted to cry out Emily's name, hear her answer, but he stopped and stood dead still. The few couples dotting the terrace already slanted curious glances his way.

To his right, along the side of the mansion, was a vast courtyard, unlit and uninhabited. Directly ahead, paths stretched into blackness. Every nerve on edge, he blocked out the party chatter and listened to the sounds of the night, staring into the darkness, and—

Nothing.

No sinister shadows crept about in the dark. No screams of panic rent the air above the music filtering out from the Garveys' mansion. His shoulders sagged, as did his spirits. She wasn't here. Emily was gone. And if she'd been taken out the front, off the property, only God knew where she was. He lifted his face to a sky spread with stars and a moon that saw all.

But God, You see more. Show me where she is. Wisdom, Lord. I ask for Your wisdom.

He hoped that wisdom would come on the fly, for he had no further time to remain idle. Sighing, he pivoted toward the open veranda door and—stopped, inhaling deeply. A faint scent of lily of the valley wafted on the night air.

A flower whose blooms had already withered for the season.

CHAPTER 22

Nicholas spun and sprinted to the edge of the veranda, not caring what the other couples on the terrace thought of his bizarre behavior. Three main paths, like spokes on a wheel, branched off the rounded platform, each leading into a different maze of hedges. All were unlit, rife with sinister possibilities. Which one to choose?

"Emily!"

Her name scraped out his throat in a voice barely recognizable as his own. Behind him, drifting out the open windows, the vibrato of violas and cellos skipped from string to string. To his side, a few murmurs of "poor man" or "what's he about?" added to the noise. All masked any cry that Emily might have issued.

He leaped down the few stairs, chose a trail at random—the closest—and bent to study the walkway. It was pea gravel, lined by bricks set in a sawtooth pattern. Indents troubled the surface at regular intervals,wide set and deep. A man, or a very tall, heavyset woman had last traversed this path, neither of which described Emily.

Unless the man had carried her.

Filing away the possibility, he dashed to the center path and stooped yet again. Footprints pitted the pebbles in a similar pattern. Yet next to those depressions, the gravel blurred into two scattered ruts, a curious combination of dragging and scampering.

And not nearly so deep.

His shoes kicked up a spray of rock as he launched down the center trail.

He left behind torchlight and safety. Ahead, a light-colored flash peeked out from the hedges a little below waist level and then disappeared just as quickly. Was it a signal? A warning? A discreet plea for help?

Slowing, he blended into the backdrop of boxwood. Millie had been right about one thing. He carried no tipstaff tonight. Stepping onto the brick edging to eliminate the crunch of gravel beneath his shoes, he pulled out a dagger tucked inside his waistcoat.

As he crept, the sound of labored breathing traveled on the air. A man's grunts. A woman's whimpers. His fingers wrapped tight around the hilt. Whether he surprised a young couple in the throes of passion or had indeed discovered his missing ward, the act he was about to interrupt would not end well.

When he finally gained a view into the moonlit alcove, he paused. A dark dress coat lay discarded on the ground, a sateen waistcoat pooled upon it. Bare legs, likely what he'd seen kick out, were now trapped beneath a man—a sandy-haired man who straddled a wriggling woman. One of his hands covered her mouth. The other tugged at his unbuttoned trousers. Golden fabric bunched around the woman's hips below him.

Rage quivered along each of Nicholas's nerves. This would not end well at all.

Shoving his knife back inside his vest, he then stowed his anger as well. If either remained in his grasp, he'd kill Henley—not that he couldn't be certain he wouldn't anyway.

God, help me.

He sprung from the shadows and grabbed Henley's shoulders from behind. In one swift move, he whumped Henley to the ground and threw all his weight atop him. Shock widened Henley's eyes an instant before Nicholas smashed his fist into his face. Never had the crunch of bone and snap of cartilage sounded sweeter. Slick warmth coated his knuckles as he pounded him again. Henley's body slackened. The assault didn't. The filthy cully deserved every bit of a sound beating and—

"Nicholas!"

Emily's voice shattered his concentration like a rock through a window, jolting him to awareness. Lungs heaving, he stood and staggered back. Retrieving the man's cast-off waistcoat, he wiped the blood from his swollen fingers then threw the fabric down and turned to Emily.

She stood, arms wrapped tight around her waist, huddled to the side of the alcove. One sleeve hung loose, ripped at the shoulder seams, the other was gone completely. Her pearl coronet was missing as well, and her golden hair hung wild to her elbows. Moonlight glistened on the single teardrop sliding down her cheek.

His breath caught.

So vulnerable, so out-of-sorts, she'd never been more beautiful.

"Are you all right?" He stepped toward her, shoving down a swell of resurging rage that made him want to turn back and kick Henley in the head. "Senseless question, I realize, but I must know, did I get here in time? Did he. . ." He stopped inches from her and studied her face, hoping, wishing. . .praying. "Did he hurt you?"

Her lips pressed tight. Though spent tears streaked her face, the slight shake of her head uncoiled every muscle he'd been clenching. Closing his eyes, he breathed out a thank-you to the One who'd guided and hastened his steps.

"I've been so wrong." Her voice was wobbly and small, yet strong enough to snap open his eyes.

"You and Bella. . .you were both right," she continued. "Henley wasn't the man I thought he was, hoped he was. He's. . .he's not like you." Her eyes shimmered with fresh tears. "There's no one like you."

He sucked in a breath. Women looked at him all the time, but never the way Emily did in that moment. Never this unguarded. Not even Adelina had, the girl he'd loved so long ago. The admiration shining in Emily's gaze was so intense, so pure, the pressure of it slammed his heart against his rib cage. If he gathered her in his arms now, he'd never let go.

So he retreated a step and ran a hand through his hair—anything to keep from reaching out to her. "I'm not the paragon of virtue you think I am, Miss Payne. In truth, you may revise your opinion when I say what I must."

He paused, memorizing the look of esteem softening the lines of her face, for it would likely be the last time he saw it. Yet if he didn't speak now, Millie surely would. "There's something I've kept from you. Something you should know. This is the worst possible time to tell you," he swung out a hand toward Henley's body. "But I must."

Her nose crinkled in the funny little rabbity way he'd come to cherish. "What is it?"

Absently, he rubbed his smarting knuckles. He'd told countless people of the demise of their loved ones, but this was different. This was entirely too. . .personal. How to tell the woman he'd come to treasure that her father's body lay in a holding crypt until the investigation into his death ran its course? That the man she depended upon was gone forever? Whether suicide or murder, the scandal would be such that she'd never again hope to make an advantageous marriage match.

As if she could hear the course of his thoughts, she shivered and ran her hands over her upper arms.

"You're chilled. Allow me." He shrugged out of his dress coat and wrapped it around her shoulders. The silk of her loose hair caressed his fingertips in the process. The warmth in her "thank you" weakened his resolve. She'd never let him this near her once she learned of his deception.

He breathed in so deeply, his chest strained against his shirt. Beating a man senseless was easier than this. Retreating to arm's length, he planted his feet into a fighting stance, though it didn't provide nearly the amount of confidence he'd hoped for. "Your father . . .well, you see, he's. . .gone."

She cocked her head like a robin, alert to a possible danger. "Gone?"

Behind him, a deep groan rumbled in Henley's chest—a moan teetering on the edge of consciousness.

"I'll explain, but come along." He stretched out his hand to her. "Or we'll be attached to more scandal than either of us will care to admit to."

Emily slipped her arms into the long sleeves of Nicholas's dress coat. The fabric yet carried the heat from his body, and she shivered in response. As she pulled the coat tight around her, it felt like an embrace. His embrace.

Safe. Warm and protected. The cloth smelled somewhat metallic and sweaty, just like the man, but she didn't care. She couldn't. The breakneck speed of her emotions—fear, despair, relief, longing—dazed her in a way she'd have to sort through later.

She lifted her hand to his. As his fingers wrapped around hers, her lips parted. Strength flowed up her arm. Despite the degradation of the evening, she had no doubt that from now on, everything would be set to rights.

He led her through the garden maze, the dark hedgerows not nearly as suffocating as when Henley had dragged her out here. Though Nicholas had rescued her in time, the touch of Henley's hands, the bruise of his lips against hers, sullied her in a way that had crawled under her skin and taken up residence.

Oh, how Wren must suffer.

Light from the mansion flickered into view. As they neared the veranda, Nicholas paused and turned to her. "You've been through enough this evening. If you like, we can avoid putting our bedraggled selves on display and cut through the side yard instead of exiting via the house."

A genuine smile tugged her lips. For all his rugged bluntness, inside beat the heart of a true gentleman. "Yes. I'd like that very much."

"Stay close, then. I'm poor concealment, but I'm afraid I'm all you've got. We'll move fast. Ready?"

She nodded.

He wasn't jesting.

Gravel nipped the thin heels of her kidskin slippers as she raced to keep up. Nicholas sprinted from shadow to shadow, never resting in a dark hollow long enough for her to catch her breath. It was an odd dance, replete with ghostly bars of a quadrille hovering on the night air from the gala inside. From shrub to shrub, they skirted the open grounds nearest the mansion, avoiding the attention of the couples on the veranda. Thanks to Henley, this was by far the most unorthodox exit she'd ever made from a ball.

Nicholas didn't stop until they reached a twelve-foot-high wrought-iron fence—a fence with no gate in sight.

Emily threw a hand to her chest, panting. "Now what?"

Nicholas dropped her other hand, a low groan in his throat. Hopefully he was forming some kind of solution. She was too busy breathing.

"Take off the jacket." Nicholas's voice cut into her apprehension.

She lifted her face to his. Had he really just told her to remove his coat? "I beg your pardon?"

"Do you trust me?"

Her heart answered before she could dissect the question. "Completely."

"Then hand it over." He held out his hand.

She peeled off his dress coat and shivered from the chill that immediately gripped her arms. Nicholas threw the coat to the ground, missing her scowl as he bent and laced his fingers together.

"Whatever are you doing?" she asked.

Shadow masked half his face as he looked up at her. "Step into my hands."

"But—"

"Ah, ah, ah," he shook his head. "You said you trusted me completely."

She scowled, her own words tasting like soured milk. Slowly, she lifted her foot. As soon as her heel rested in the palms of his hands, the world rushed down in a blur. Instinctively, she stretched out her hands and grabbed the rail at the top of the fence, using the momentum to pull herself atop it. Her already ruined skirt snagged on a jagged edge and ripped further, but she held on and threw one leg over the fence, teetering astraddle like a ropewalker she'd once seen at a carnival.

Clutching the top rail like a saddle horn, she gaped down at Nicholas then gasped. He looked so small. So far away.

And there was no one to boost him. Unless he possessed superhuman qualities she'd not yet seen, there was no way he'd be able to follow her.

"Catch my coat," Nicholas shouted up at her.

Before she could ask what in the world he was talking about, a swish of fabric hit her dangling leg. Holding tight to the fence with one hand, she swiped down the other and barely snagged the hem of his coat before it fell away.

"Tie the sleeve around your wrist, tight as you can, then dangle the rest of it down to me."

Clearly the stress of the situation had skewed his thinking. Merely the weight of his jacket balled in her hands made her wobble. " But. . . I can't pull you up."

"Just do as I say and remember what you said about trusting me."

The man was a dog with a bone. She'd have to live to her nineties to outlast her hasty plea of trust in the fellow. She fumbled with the fabric, but tying a knot one-handed was hard. Doing it while clinging to the top of a fence, impossible.

"How's it coming?"

"Slowly, especially if I have to keep answering you." Eventually, though, she managed to secure it around her wrist and cast the rest of it downward, dangling the fabric just above his head.

He grabbed the sleeve. "Now jump."

"What?"

"Trust, Miss Payne. Trust."

Anger pushed her over the edge. Literally. She leaped into a free fall, but not for long. Her arm yanked, and for a single stunning moment, she hung suspended. Then plummeted. The sudden jerk on her arm made his plan clear. He'd never intended for her to pull him up with her own frail strength. By soaring downward, her body acted as a counterweight to boost him skyward.

Though none of that mattered when her feet hit the ground. Her knees buckled, and she crashed, jarring through every bone. A *whoompf* landed somewhere beside her.

"Let's go." Nicholas's voice breathed into her ear. His grasp hefted her to her feet. Was she on her feet? Hard to tell. The world tilted one way then another. A strong arm wrapped about her shoulders, straightening out sky from ground.

Nicholas ushered her to the line of carriages snaked along the drive, taking care to keep to the shadows. Not that he had to, really. Coach drivers were either too preoccupied in passing small flasks among themselves or too unaware as they snored on their benches. Normally, if she'd caught Wilkes so engaged, she'd have censured him. This time, just to have him present and able to get them out of there quickly, she might kiss his cheek.

By the time she reached the family coach, however, she lacked the energy to even care. Nicholas swung open the door and hoisted her up. The familiar smell of leather and axle grease eased her nerves a bit as she sank onto the seat. Soon all this would be over. . .ended with as much finality as her dream of marrying Henley. A dream that was better cataloged as a nightmare, now. Why had she never noticed the rotten content of the man's character before tonight?

Leaning her head back, she closed her eyes. The answer pained her as much as the throb in her shoulder. She'd been far too busy looking at Henley's bank account to notice.

Outside, Nicholas's deep rumble conferred with another man's, one bearing a distinct brogue. Either Wilkes had some Irish blood in him that she'd never recognized, or she was way beyond tired.

The carriage tilted. The door shut. The cushion she sat on jiggled, and her eyes popped open. Moonlight seeped in the windows, pooling on the broad shoulders next to hers.

Nicholas sat a breath away, on her side of the carriage, wearing a mantle of silver light.

"You all right?" Concern warmed his voice as he reached for her hand. She'd not even noticed his coat was yet shackled to her wrist.

"I hardly know." She watched his fingers tug at the knot. One of his sleeves flapped open, revealing a forearm just as knotted with muscle. He freed the ruined coat then flung it onto the empty seat across from them.

Yet he did not move away.

"It's been quite the eventful evening." His murmured words blended with the turn of the coach's wheels. He lifted her wrist to eye level, examining it. In the space of a heartbeat, a frown darkened his face. "I'm afraid you'll have a bruise here come the morning."

"Then it shall match the rest of my body, I suppose."

She ought pull her hand back. She ought move away. Indeed, a lady would protest at his nearness. But the little circles his thumb whispered over her inner wrist held her in place.

"For that I am sorry indeed." His eyes slid from her wrist to meet her gaze. Compassion, genuine and intense, caressed her more gently than his touch.

Without a word, she leaned closer, pulled like a flower toward the sun.

He bent nearer.

Then immediately released her hand and looked past her, out the window.

An odd sense of loss shivered through her. Following his line of sight, she turned and peered out the glass into the night. This far from town, no streetlamps lit their route. Fear that had never really packed its bags and departed knocked against her ribs. She turned her face back to his. "Do you think we'll be followed?"

"It's happened before." He returned his gaze to her, though a smirk lightened the intensity. "But don't fret. Flannery's more skilled in evasion than your Wilkes."

"Flannery?"

"The fellow who's driving. I'd have told you," he shrugged, "but I didn't want you to worry."

His words in the garden barreled back with astonishing speed. He'd been about to tell her something when Henley groaned. Something she wasn't entirely sure she wanted to hear, for whatever it was couldn't be good.

But she had to know.

She shifted on the seat, allowing the fullest measure of moonlight to fall upon his face, intent on listening with more than just her ears. "There's more you've kept from me. You said so yourself."

A muscle rippled at the apex of his jawline, as if words he didn't want to speak were shouldering their way to break an escape.

Emily swallowed. Suddenly she didn't want to know why. Not really.

But words tumbled out her lips before she could catch them. "What did you mean when you said my father was gone?"

A shadow darkened his face, though hard to tell if it came from without or within.

"I'm afraid I've sorely underestimated you. You show a rare courage, the caliber of which I don't see in half the officers of Bow Street. So bear up. What I'm about to tell you will no doubt hit you broadside." He paused long enough to reclaim her hands and cradle them both within his. "Your father is dead, Emily."

Dead? The word exploded into a thousand pieces. There was no way to gather in all the implications, for they traveled too fast and too far. She wrapped her fingers tight around Nicholas's and held on.

He squeezed back. "You have suffered much. It's all right to weep."

She gasped. No, it wasn't all right. It was impossible. Unspent sobs clogged her throat and a wealth of tears burned her eyes, but she could no more cry than speak. So she stared into the black wall of the carriage opposite her, refusing to look at the light in Nicholas's eyes or the glimmer of moon outside the window. Either would be her undoing. For now, darkness was her friend.

How long she sat, she could only guess to be an eternity, but at last, Nicholas spoke.

"Emily?" Worry poked holes into his voice. "I vow before God I'll find out what happened to your father. Justice will be served. You have my word on it."

She turned her face to his. Lines creased his brow. Lines put there by her. After all he'd been through on her behalf, she owed him. At least a little. Especially truth, for dearly did he value it.

"He. . ." Was that squeak her voice? She cleared her throat and tried again. "He wasn't my father."

CHAPTER 23

What the deuce are you talking about!" As soon as the heated words spewed out his mouth, Nicholas clenched every muscle in his body. Control. That's what he needed. Breathe in, breathe out, subdue the tremor running along every nerve. Anger led to mistakes. And it was no mistake he'd lived through war on two continents or survived the thugs terrorizing London's streets for this long. Not that he hadn't gained scars, but how big of a jagged red mark would this woman leave on him?

Emily flinched and edged away from him, stopping only when her back hit the carriage wall. "You've no right to be so cross. You've not been straightforward with me, either."

Unlocking his jaw, he forced a calm to his voice he didn't feel. "Do not think to play me like a flash game of wicket. If I am to help you, I must be told everything."

Spare starlight from the clear night streamed in through the window, casting a ghostly glow upon half her face. Her eyes were wide. A loose curl trembled over her brow, begging to be brushed aside. Besides a darkened smudge of dirt on her cheek, her skin was the pale hue of exhaustion.

She'd been through a lot this evening. He'd grant her that. Blowing out a long, slow breath, he softened his tone further. "I will have the truth, and I will have it now. All of it. Am I clear?"

Her hands clenched together in her lap, bunching the fabric of her already ruined skirt. "All?"

He nodded. "If we're to sort through this mess, then yes. Indeed."

Fine, white teeth nibbled her lower lip before she answered. "Very well. Go on. Tell me if you're keeping back any more information from me."

His first thought was to smile. The second, to throw her over his knee and supply the sound thrashing she deserved for such cheek. He went with his third impulse and merely eyed her with a growing admiration. "A gentleman always allows a lady to go first."

"A gentleman also keeps a lady's secrets, and so I ask. . ." Her eyes sought his, looking deeply into one then the other. "I know I said I trust you, leastwise I did in the heat of the moment, but can I? Really?"

He cocked his head and studied her in return. "If I am to continue to protect you, then I'm afraid you must."

Her lips, yet swollen from Henley's abuse, curved downward. "And I am afraid you're right."

Though she'd agreed with him, she fell silent. A faraway glaze shone in her eyes. Only God knew what thoughts she chewed on, though judging by a poorly concealed wince, none were sweet. As he waited for her to continue, he took to counting the seconds then moved on to tallying how many times the rolled-up window shade banged against the top of the glass. Still, he waited. Sometimes truth ripened at a rate slower than the plodding horses Flannery guided.

The grit of wheel upon gravel changed to the smoother grind of cobblestone as they drew closer to the inner city, and at last, Emily's lips parted. His every sense heightened to full alert, a skill honed to a sharp edge by countless interrogations—as both the examiner and the examinee.

"Quite honestly. . ." She started slow, her words picking up speed as she spoke. "I have no idea who my real father is. I was raised as Mr. Payne's daughter, for he dearly loved my mother, so much that no one suspected she'd carried anyone's child but his own. Oh, he loved her all right, but the truth is—" Her lips flattened into a straight line. "He never loved me."

"How can you say that?" He raked a hand through his hair, though the action did nothing to reconcile her twisted logic. "The man hired me, for more than a fair amount, to see to your safety. That hardly sounds like the action of a man who doesn't care."

"He wasn't protecting me. He was protecting his name." She flourished her fingers through the air. "The grand Payne family legacy."

"Come again?" Leaning back, he watched her, closely, grateful for the streetlamps now adding an extra measure of brightness through the coach windows. From the flash of light to shadow and back again, he searched for any hesitation, the slightest bit of nervousness—a twitch or tic. Any movement out of character that would brand her a liar.

She swept away the loose curl with one hand, but before she spoke, it sprang back again. Was everything about the woman wild and defiant? "The world knows me as Emily Payne, daughter of the illustrious and wealthy merchant Alistair Payne. I am his only heir, albeit counterfeit, so how would it look if he didn't show some responsibility toward me? Though I suspected all that would change soon enough should the recently widowed Mrs. Nevens have returned his ardor and conceived him a son. Only Uncle Reggie hindered that plan. He and my father may have been business partners, but they were rivals concerning that woman."

"If what you say is true—" He held up a hand, stopping her rebuttal. "I'm not saying it isn't, but if you are not the man's offspring, then I don't understand why he claimed you in the first place. You once told me all he cared about was business."

A sad smile—or was it a grimace?—pulled at the edges of her mouth. "As I've said, because of my mother. She was the one thing he cherished above money. On her deathbed, she made him promise to look after me as his own. And he did. . .materialistically. Nothing more. So forgive me if I do not cry a thousand tears of grief for a man who was little more than the business manager of my life. And believe me—" Glistening eyes belied her brave words. Her voice lowered to a whisper. "It wasn't for lack of trying to make him care. He was the only father I'd ever known, and I dearly wanted him to love me."

He saw her clearly, then. Like the air cleared of soot by a fresh rain. The confident woman sitting before him, the feisty Emily Payne, was nothing more than a little girl looking for affection. Nicholas sucked in a breath, so stunning was the revelation. Indeed, she'd spoken more than truth. She'd bared a glimpse into her soul.

To him.

He reached for her, every inch of his skin yearning to pull her close. Shelter her. Show her that despite her father, she was worthy of love—and indeed, had garnered all he had to give.

But he pulled back his hand. After what she'd been through with Henley, he'd be a rogue to act in the same manner. So he simply said, "I'm sorry."

And he was. Sorry that the most important man in her life had shunned her. Sorry her future teetered on a precipice. Sorry that the thought of kissing her overruled common sense and decency.

"Don't be." She looked out the window with a sigh. "It's the way of the world."

Her voice wore all the starkness of bones left to bleach in the sun. Abandoned. Dead. His heart broke at the sound.

"No one escapes this life without scars, Miss Payne. Not even God." He kept his tone even and soft. Not that he could heal her hurts, but he knew the One who could. How would she receive it, though?

Slowly, she turned her face to his, one fine brow arched.

It was all the permission he needed to continue. "How you grew up, the coldness of the only father you ever knew, it wasn't right. And it didn't go unseen. You will face your Father one day, your true Father. And I can promise you this: He will welcome you with open arms if you but turn to Him now."

Her eyes narrowed. "You speak as if I am nothing more than an upset child."

"Is that not what you are?"

Though she didn't think it possible, a flood of new tears burned Emily's eyes. Her heart beat loud in her ears. Nicholas's question pinned her in place, every part of her, like a butterfly skewered onto a display board. The turn of this conversation required a toll she wasn't entirely sure she could pay, and by this point, she had no more reserve from which to draw.

He was right of course. Mostly. Upset was too small a word to cover the broad river of emotions flowing through her. But one thing was for sure—

She'd never felt more of a child than now.

Her gaze lowered from his eyes to the strong cut of his jaw, traveled past his broad expanse of shoulders, and rested upon his chest. His black waistcoat, once so becoming and stylish, was unbuttoned and torn. The shirt beneath, splattered with blood. Truly, it ought repulse her, yet there was nowhere on earth she'd rather rest her cheek right now. If she could lay her head there, for only a few minutes, would everything be made right?

And if she did as he said and turned to God, would heavenly arms wrap around her?

The carriage jolted out of a rut, flopping the runaway piece of hair back into her eyes. Gathering the loose curls together with one hand, she pulled it all back from her brow and looked him full in the face. She'd think on all he'd said. . .but not now. "We are not speaking of me, but of my father. So now it's your turn, Mr. Brentwood. Tell me what happened. How did he die?"

He cocked his head. "You still refer to him as father, though I know the truth?"

She did. She would. For always. She owed him that, at least. "The man may not have loved me, but he did provide for me. I will honor that as much in his death as I did while he yet breathed. What. . .why are you smiling?"

The gleam of Nicholas's teeth brightened the dark. "You are an enigma. You know that, don't you?"

She frowned. "And you are evading my question."

"If nothing else, you are determined. I'll give you that." Nicholas scrubbed a hand over his face then sighed. "I am still trying to piece together all the snippets of facts concerning your father's death, which is why Chief Magistrate Ford suggested I not inform you in the first place. Suffice it to say, you may take heart in knowing that your father's end was relatively swift."

"That doesn't tell me much."

"No, it does not." His eyes glimmered with knowledge—much more than he spoke—yet his lips pressed tight. Was he trying to safeguard her. . .or himself?

"I was honest with you, sir. The least you can do is the same." A fishwife couldn't have sounded more bitter. How on earth did he evoke such extremes in her?

He lifted his chin and looked down his nose. A fine, strong nose. It annoyed her that he could sit there and look so confident, so. . . handsome. And it annoyed her further that she noticed.

"I assure you," his voice lowered, "I am being quite forthright."

She threw up her hands. "But you've not told me any details!"

A smile spread across his face, and he leaned toward her. "Did you know that your nostrils flare quite prettily when you're angry?"

"And your eyes flash a brilliant green when you're resolved to keep information to yourself." The carriage slowed. Her heart rate didn't. Frustrating man! "If you think you can charm your way out of this, sir, then you don't know me half as well as you credit your powers of observation."

"I never laid claim to charm, but I assure you, my observations are as keen as ever. Did you also know you've an enchanting dimple when you realize you're not going to get your way?" His grin grew. "Yes, there it is." He lifted his hand and his thumb brushed against the side of her cheek.

A trail of fire burned where he touched. This was ridiculous. She'd slapped men for lesser infractions. But now. . .her hands lay limp and motionless in her lap. Traitors.

"And just before your lips pull into a pout, there's a tiny quiver here." His fingers slid lower, tracing her jaw. Then, gentler than a whisper, slid back up and cupped her cheek.

She leaned into his touch, pressing into his warmth. "You. . ." Swallowing back the tremor in her voice, she tried again. "You notice my chin?"

His features softened, and he slid across the seat, moving closer. So close, his breath feathered over her skin as he spoke. "I notice everything about you and have since the day we met."

The carriage stopped—or mayhap the world did. Her gaze fixed on his mouth. She'd breathe if she could remember how. Deep in her stomach, a quiver shimmied upward, and the sensation frightened.

But mostly delighted.

Without thinking, she closed her eyes, inhaling his scent of spice and passion and possibility. A faint groan rumbled out from him, primal and altogether enticing. He wanted this, then, every bit as much as the desire pulsing through her veins. She lifted her face to the heat of him.

And the carriage door opened. "Here we are, safe as ever. And I'll be thanking ye to mention that to ol' Ford, aye Brentwood?"

CHAPTER 24

Nicholas froze, his ardor cooling to the same temperature as the hard leather carriage seat. A musket ball to the head would've been as welcome as Flannery's voice. Emily's eyes shot open and peered into his, blinking. It couldn't have been for more than a second, but what he read in those brown depths embedded into his heart for an eternity. Loss, pure and raw, gaping like an open wound. But loss of what? Discretion? Restraint?

Or the loss of his kiss?

She shoved past him as he whispered her name, the only word able to slip past the guilt closing his throat. He never should have taken advantage of her jumbled emotions. Not tonight. Not ever. What a wretch. He was no better than Henley.

He tried again. "Emily, wait."

But it was too late. She clasped Flannery's upstretched hand and fled out the carriage door before he could turn her around.

A groan rumbled deep in his chest. Leaping to the cobbles, he scowled at Flannery. "Your timing leaves much to be desired."

"What are ye goin' on about?" Flannery lifted his cap and scratched his head. The spare moonlight, more than half hidden now by a cloud, muddied his usual red locks to an earthy tone. "Did I not do a fine job of seein' ye here in one piece?"

The slam of the town-house door jerked Flannery's gaze away. When he looked back at Nicholas, his brows raced to his hairline. "Don't tell me you and the lass were. . .why, stars and thunder! That was a handy move. To be sure, what a grand way to guard a lady."

Nicholas ducked aside, narrowly escaping a sound clap on the back, then froze. Something more than the unwelcome praise grated on his nerves. . .but what?

He scanned the area. No suspicious figures skulked about. No riders or coaches approached the Payne household. In truth, the street was completely empty, leastwise as far as he could see, which in the dark wasn't too far. Pivoting, he studied the townhome's facade for anything unusual—a gutter pipe askew, perhaps, or a rope dangling from a chimney.

Flannery followed his lead, his head craning back and forth. "Something amiss?"

Nicholas grunted, for truly, nothing else could be said. Narrowing his eyes, he strained for one more look into the black shadows draped over the townhome like a shroud. Not one thing was out of place besides him and Flannery, standing on a curb in the dead of night, gawking up at the house in the dark as if they might purchase the thing.

And then he knew.

He broke into a run and flung open the front door, holding hard to the knob to prevent it from banging against the wall. Surprise was a weapon he'd learned long ago to heft with precision. Flannery's footsteps trailed close behind. Glancing over his shoulder, he touched a finger to his lips then turned and raced up the stairs, two at a time.

When he reached the landing, his heart skipped a beat. Emily stood halfway down the hall, hand poised to push open her chamber door. If he called out to stop her, the noise would alert the intruder he suspected, who in turn would escape. Clue lost. Dead end. But if he didn't and she walked into that room, a knife might be pressed to her throat before he could reach her.

"Emily, no!" He raced down the hall before half a question passed her lips. When he reached her, he grabbed her shoulders and steered her to the opposite wall. The action widened her eyes.

"What is happen—"

"No time. Stay put." He wheeled about and drew his knife in one movement then nodded at Flannery to flank him. Flinging wide the door, he listened. A *thwunk* sounded out, brass hitting plaster, not flesh. No one behind the door, then.

Nicholas edged to the left, jerking his head for Flannery to go right. There were plenty of potential hiding places in a woman's bedchamber. Inside the wardrobe. Beneath the bedskirt. Behind an overstuffed wingback in the corner. But he sheathed his blade and stalked past all to the sheers swinging in front of a half-open window. He bent and leaned over the sill. In the narrow courtyard between the two townhomes, footsteps pounded into the night.

Flannery joined him. "Shall I make chase?"

Though he'd like nothing better than to serve the scoundrel justice, preferably at the end of a rope, Nicholas shook his head. "By the time you catch your balance, he'll be long gone."

Flannery scooped off his cap and slapped it against his thigh, uttering a curse. Two sharp gasps—Emily's and another's—sounded behind them at the door.

"Mind your tongue, man." Stepping back from the window, Nicholas turned. A pale-faced Emily and a scowling Mrs. Hunt peered in from the hallway. "Ladies, a moment, if you please."

Emily's gaze darted from the window to him. "Where are we to be safe, if even my own chamber can be breached?"

He scowled. It wasn't right that such an ugly fear had crawled into a corner of her heart—and even worse that he was helpless to remove it, for truly, she was correct. There was no safe place for her now. "As you can see, no one remains. Await me in the sitting room, and I'll attend you shortly."

The housekeeper murmured something into Emily's ear as she took her arm and ushered her away. Their skirts barely swished from view before Flannery threw up his hands. "What tipped ye off? I didn't see a blasted thing out of the ordinary."

"Nor did I." Nicholas turned and pulled down the window. When he faced Flannery once again, the man's mouth had twisted into quite the question mark.

"Ye make about as much sense as a ravin' bedlamite."

"Think on it. When was the last time we passed a carriage?"

"Maybe two or three crossroads back." Flannery's eyes studied the ceiling corner, far left, but Nicholas doubted the man saw plaster from molding. Flannery was back on the road, driving a carriage in his mind. Seconds later, his gaze shot back to Nicholas. "Aye, 'twas two. I remember a dray aside the road on Wigmore and Duke."

"A dray? In this neighborhood? At this time of night?" He doled out the questions like bread crumbs, leading Flannery to draw his own conclusion instead of cramming it down his throat. If the man didn't learn to think for himself, Ford would never hire him on as an officer.

Flannery cocked his head. "What are ye getting at?"

"Whoever was here had point men out there. Granted, this is a residential area and the hour is admittedly late, but did you not think it odd we were the only two on the street? Those men allowed us to pass, but none others."

"But why? Why not attack at that point?"

"Remember when I signaled you to quiet your steps?" He waited for Flannery's nod before continuing. "Silence is a weapon often more dangerous than outright attack. It's easier to haul off a wriggling bit of a woman if no one's around to call an alarm or even knows she's been taken in the first place, and it would give them the advantage of lead time, cooling their trail."

Flannery's eyes widened as those seeds of information took root. "And so you'd not have me give chase for I'd be outnumbered, eh?"

He nodded. "As I said, your timing leaves much to be desired. By the time you dropped, rolled, righted yourself, and reached the blackguard, he'd have a few strong-arms with him to put an end to your evening and possibly your life."

With a last deep inhale of the leftover lily of the valley permeating the room, Nicholas strode to the door and, without pausing, called over his shoulder. "Come along."

"I've a feeling this is going to be a long night," Flannery grumbled from behind.

Mrs. Hunt and Emily rose as they swung into the sitting room, both overflowing with questions.

Nicholas held up a hand. "Ladies, answers are in short supply for the moment, and I fear what I am about to say next will merely add more confusion. But there's nothing to be done for it, I'm afraid."

Reaching into the half-torn pocket of his waistcoat, he retrieved his pocket watch and flipped it open. "You have five minutes, Miss Payne, to change into the drabbest gown you own and tuck whatever necessaries you need into a small satchel."

She recoiled as if she'd been slapped. "Whatever for?"

"We're leaving. Now."

"You can't be serious!" Mrs. Hunt stormed up to him like a thunderhead. Flannery retreated a step.

Nicholas held his ground. "I've never been more serious."

"Taking my lady into the night? Whoever was in her room is lurking about out there." Light from the single lantern sparked off her flinty eyes. "This is madness! You might as well be leading her into a lion's den."

He sidestepped her, lining up for a clear view of Emily. "And now you've got four and a half minutes."

"You can't possibly expect me to—"

"I can, and I do. . .four minutes fifteen seconds."

He watched her closely. Color crept up her neck and flushed her cheeks. Good. Anger would serve her better than fear, for if she suspected where he was taking her, she'd dig in her heels.

As if she'd read his mind, her shoulders stiffened. "Where is it that we're going? Where are you taking me?"

"Better that you don't know." Turning on his heel and crossing to the door, he breathed out a prayer. Was he doing the right thing? *God, please, let it be so.*

Emily tensed and cast one last glance at her chamber window. If a man's face popped up against the glass, she'd scream. Or faint. Possibly both. What a horrid nightmare this evening had turned into—the night that was supposed to have been a dream come true.

Outside her door, boots thumped down the carpet runner, growing louder with each step. Time was running out.

"Hurry, miss," Mary said behind her.

To her left, Mrs. Hunt rattled about at the vanity, clearly as upset as she. The normally pragmatic housekeeper ransacked through hairpins and cosmetics as if Emily were packing for a Midland holiday instead of escaping to who-knew-where.

Spinning on her heels, Emily turned to the wardrobe and bent. She reached deep into a corner then yanked out an old bonnet from the top of a box she'd meant to set out for the ragpickers. The half-starched head covering was a macabre substitute for the tiara at Asprey's. With one hand, she twisted her hair and piled it atop her crown. With the other, she pulled the worn fabric over her head, capturing most, but not all of her curls.

A sharp tap at her door shattered her already broken nerves, and she flinched. Mary gasped.

"It's time." Nicholas's deep voice seeped through the wood.

Mrs. Hunt laid a hand on her arm. "Don't you think you ought to stay here, miss? Going out with Mr. Brentwood, not knowin' where he's taking ye? It's scandalous, that's what."

Emily licked her lips, her gaze darting from the housekeeper to the window, then back. "No more scandalous than what would've happened had Mr. Brentwood not stopped me from entering my chamber when he did. Extraordinary situations call for extraordinary measures, is that not what you always say?"

Mrs. Hunt's mouth pinched as tight as a spinster's corset. "Fine time to start listening to me now."

Nicholas shoved open the door and stepped aside without a word.

Mrs. Hunt squeezed Emily's arm then gave it a pat and let go. Turning, she faced a somber-jawed Nicholas. "See that you take care of Miss Payne, or I'll rain down brimstone upon your head. And don't you think I won't."

"I don't doubt it for a moment, Mrs. Hunt." He held out his hand for the small satchel in the housekeeper's grip. "Nevertheless, you have my word. I shall return in the morning. Until then, Flannery's keeping a lookout, so rest easy."

Then he cocked his head at her. "Shall we?"

Emily let her gaze linger for a moment on the white counterpane spread atop her bed. Every muscle in her cried out to snuggle beneath the quilt and draw it up over her head, shutting out the evening's insane turn of events.

But instead she inhaled and stepped toward the only man remaining whom she could trust.

"I'll be praying for you, miss." Mrs. Hunt's words followed her down the hall, as did Mary's uneven footsteps.

Nicholas wheeled about. "I'm sorry, Mary, but you'll have to stay. I take Miss Payne alone."

"But—" Emily's and Mary's voices swelled into one big objection.

Which was promptly cut off by the raising of his hand. "It will be difficult enough for me to bring one lady where I intend. Two, impossible. I will be trusted in this matter completely, or not at all. What is it to be?"

Mary opened her mouth, but Emily shook her head with a sigh. "I'm afraid he will not be persuaded, Mary, so save your breath."

"Are you sure, miss?"

Was she? Thus far, she had found her judgment of a man's character sorely lacking. Was she wrong about Nicholas, as well? Her stomach tightened, but even so, she nodded. "Yes. But I would covet your prayers as much as Mrs. Hunt's."

Mary's eyes glistened. Were those tears? For her?

"Of course, miss. Godspeed."

Emily pulled her gaze from her maid back to the man beside her, hoping she'd made the right choice. "Satisfied?"

What went on in that head of his, she could only guess at, but the grim set of his jaw did not bode well. "Come along, Miss Payne."

As Nicholas led her toward the back of the house and down the servants' stairs, she noticed his fine silk trousers were replaced with the serviceable woolens he'd worn when she'd first met him. The ruined dress coat and embroidered waistcoat had been exchanged for a heavy greatcoat—the one that smelled of bootblacking and gunpowder. His dark hair was loose, no longer tamed for a gala ball. A black hat hid most of it. And it truly had been bootsteps she'd heard, for the shiny leather shoes he'd donned for the dance were probably now lying on the floor in his chamber. What a far different picture the two of them presented, slipping out of the rear of the townhome, than that of a few hours earlier when they'd strolled out the front.

Nicholas paused at the gate to the back alleyway and turned to her, his eyes moss green and hooded. "It's quite a hike I'm expecting of you. Are you up to it?"

She swept her hand toward the carriage house, the building so close that if she cared to sidestep a few paces, her palm would slap against the wood. "We have a small gig."

He shook his head. "Afraid not."

She narrowed her eyes. "Then why ask?"

Just then the moon escaped its half cloak of a cloud, lighting a wicked grin on his face. "I could heft you over my shoulder if you like."

She scowled, which was more of a response than he deserved.

"Right, then." He pushed open the gate. "Onward."

He wasn't jesting. Though she'd worn her most serviceable shoes, they were meant for a promenade through town, not a hike down rough cobbled passageways. Before long, pains crept up her shins, and she faltered over the hem of her skirt to keep up with his long-legged strides. When her big toe hit an upcropped bit of stone and she lurched forward, Nicholas reached back and grabbed hold of her forearm.

"The offer still stands." His face was shadowed, his gaze unreadable beneath the brim of his hat.

She sniffed then wished she hadn't. The closer to the city's innards they drew, the worse the stench. "I will not be toted about like a sack of puppies, if that's what you're hinting at."

Was that a smile that flashed in his gaze?

"At least take my hand," he offered.

His fingers wrapped around hers, and though at first she kept up, the longer they walked, the more her steps lagged. He led her down one dark alley to another, the buildings progressively closing in the farther they went. The effect was smothering. Cobbles gave way to gravel then eventually thinned out into nothing but worn dirt, littered with broken gin bottles and piles of refuse. Occasionally the whites of eyeballs flashed in dark recesses as they passed, and more than once Nicholas growled out a "shove off" to a bawdy suggestion or an outright threat.

Emily sped up. Viewing the greatcoat stretched across his shoulders from behind wasn't nearly as comforting as feeling the muscle of his arm brush against hers when she managed to remain by his side. There was safety in the heat of his body, shelter in his strength. And the fact that she trusted him so completely was as frightening as the dreadful neighborhoods they passed through.

When the alley narrowed so much that soon single file would be their only option, he pulled her out into a street. They skirted the sprawled body of drunkard who smelled overly ripe for the grave, and for a moment she feared the man actually was dead, until a snore erupted from his open mouth.

A few steps later, a woman emerged from the side of a building, her bosom spilling out of a bodice two sizes too small. Bolder than a king's man, she swung her hips over to Nicholas's side and slipped her arm around his. "'Ave a go at it, mate? Yer li'l princess there could learn a trick or two from me. For a spare coin, she can watch, if ye like."

A slow burn worked its way up Emily's neck and spread onto her cheeks as the woman's words began to make sense. Why had he brought her here? Had she misplaced her trust?

"Not interested." Nicholas shrugged off the woman and looked down at Emily without slowing his pace. "Sorry. You've seen and heard more this evening than a lady ever should."

Her lips twisted into a wry grin, surprising herself that any shred of humor yet remained. "In truth, I wonder if this evening shall ever end."

His eyes held hers a moment more before he faced forward. "We're almost there."

Tired buildings stood elbow-to-elbow, leaning against one another for support. The windows were so sooted over, it was hard to tell what kind of merchants or craftsmen inhabited the bottom levels.

Without warning, Nicholas led her into an alcove and produced a key from his pocket. After two locks clicked their release, he turned to her. "It's tight quarters, so you'll have to follow me. Make sure to slide the bolt on the door once it shuts. I'm afraid it will be dark until I can light a lantern, so you should locate the bolt before you close the door completely. Can you do that?"

She could feel her brow wrinkle with trying to keep back the many questions flitting about in her head. Still, she nodded.

He swung wide the door. There was no threshold, merely the tread of the first stair leading up into blackness. What kind of place was this? He ascended the staircase, narrow as a coffin, and quickly disappeared from view. No wonder he'd asked her to lock the door. For him to even turn around in such a tight space would require an acrobat's skill.

Locating a steel bar as thick as two fingers and long as a child's foot, she rested her fingertips against the cool metal and pulled shut the door with her other hand then slid the bolt over until it caught home. Though she could yet hear the rhythmic thud of Nicholas's boots somewhere above her, the ensuing darkness reached in deep, stealing what was left of her composure.

"Nicholas?" Her voice was a kitten's mew, but it was not to be helped.

"Wait there if you like."

Another bolt clicked above, likely at the top of the stairs. Hinges complained. Floorboards creaked. Several sharp strikes of a flint carried surprisingly loud in the darkness, and then—

Light, blessed and brilliant. Nicholas stood at the top of the staircase like an avenging angel, banishing the darkness back to the netherworlds.

Relieved, she started upward. The steps rose sharply, each one adding more of a burn to her thighs. A lifetime of handprints darkened each side of the walls, and she was glad her arms didn't brush against the filth. She clutched her skirts tighter, keeping the fabric from contact, and pushed away thoughts of what might cause the underlying smell of sweat and toil and desperation.

Nicholas stepped aside when she reached the top, allowing her to pass in front of him.

But she didn't. She stopped and faced him. Better to hear straight up his intentions than give in to wild imaginings. "What's to become of me?"

His jaw locked.

She held her breath.

"For now..." he said slowly. The muscles in his neck gleamed in the lantern light as he looked down at her. "A warm bed and some much needed sleep."

"And then?" she pressed.

A shadow crossed his face, darkening his eyes to haunted green pools. Then he tipped his mouth into a smirk. "Do not borrow trouble from the morrow when tonight's given you a fair enough wage, hmm?"

She frowned. Not exactly the comforting words she'd hoped for, but in light of the situation, they would have to do. She turned and crossed the threshold into a desolate room. On one wall, a table and a single chair kept company. A small hearth graced another wall, with a coal bucket and a tinderbox to its side. Nicholas entered behind her, shedding light onto a wooden-framed bed pushed against a third wall. At its foot, a large chest with a huge padlock sat like a bulldog. Only one window graced the small chamber, barren of curtain and smudged by lantern smoke. This was no Portman Square townhome.

She turned to Nicholas. "What is this place?"

He shrugged off his greatcoat and draped it over the chair then turned to her with folded arms. "It's my home."

CHAPTER 25

With a last glance at Emily, her lashes feathered against her cheeks as she slept on his bed, Nicholas pulled shut his door and locked it. He padded down the stairwell and took care sliding open the bolt on the outer door so it didn't screech. Such a measure likely wasn't necessary, for she slept sounder than a babe in arms, but he'd not risk waking her now. It'd taken too much convincing to get her to surrender to sleep in the first place. Not that he blamed her. She'd never shared a bedchamber with a man before, and it hadn't been easy to persuade her to do so.

Stepping into the street, he rolled his right shoulder and winced from a kink that refused to loosen. A fitful few hours of rest had done him no good. Perhaps the floorboards in front of the hearth would've been a kinder mattress than the chair.

In the early morning light, Eastcheap wasn't nearly as formidable as when trekking it in the dark. Directly across the street, a one-legged man with more gums than teeth sat on a stool, selling rags from a basket. Two washerwomen darted past, scurrying to collect their loads for the day. A smudge-faced chimney sweep trudged after a larger fellow carrying an assorted load of brushes on his back. None were as fancy or tidy as those strolling about the West End of London, but neither were they the vermin that arose when the sun set.

After a quick check-in on his sister—who grew weaker with each passing breath—and a thorough going-over of instructions with Hope, he hailed a hackney. He begrudged the spent coin, but it was not to be helped if he intended to return before Emily awoke.

Yawning as the coach rolled along, he reviewed once again the details of an idea he'd hatched in the predawn hours. By the time the hackney turned onto Bow Street—clogged with traffic, as usual—he'd patched up the last remaining holes in his plan. If Ford didn't go for this, well. . .he rubbed his tired eyes. Would that his charm influenced the magistrate as soundly as it had Emily.

He paid off the jarvey several blocks from the station and hoofed it the rest of the way, increasing his pace when he glanced at his pocket watch. Men buzzed around the front door, and he darted through the swarm. Inside, he shouldered past an overflow of people spilling into the foyer then veered left and pounded up to the second floor. Halfway down the corridor, Emmanuel Whinnet was just pulling shut the magistrate's door.

Nicholas eyed the thin clerk as he strode toward him. Even as a twig, the man would be a poor piece of kindling. "Ford in there?"

Whinnet blinked at him. "Aye, but be forewarned. The Baggley boys are on the docket this morning, and he's in the hanging mood. Perhaps you ought come back later."

Nicholas frowned. "Not an option."

Whinnet tugged at his collar. "Watch your neck then, Brentwood."

He smiled at the outspoken clerk, though truth be told, were the man not blunt as a bludgeon, he would not have lasted long at Bow Street.

Nicholas raised his knuckles and rapped on the magistrate's door.

"Whinnet!" Ford's voice boomed from behind the oak. "I clearly told you fifteen minutes and not a second less. If you wish to swing next to the Baggleys, then keep it up."

Nicholas leaned toward the wood and lowered his voice. "Whinnet's tucked his tail and run, sir. It's me, Brentwood."

The door flew open. Ford's mouth twisted into a glower darker than sin. Nicholas straightened his shoulders to full attention.

The magistrate had not yet donned his tall wig, and as he spoke, a sheen of perspiration glistened atop his shorn head. Whinnet was right.

Ford was steamed up this morn.

He skewered Nicholas with an evil eye. "I can only assume that things are wrapped up on the Payne case?"

Nicholas cleared his throat. This wouldn't be easy. "May I come in, sir?"

Ford's brows drew together, as if the solid line might block him from entering. "Make it quick."

Nicholas strode into the room and planted his feet next to the chair in front of the magistrate's desk. A queer odor assaulted his nose, and he sniffed, trying to pinpoint the stink. Curiously, the acrid smell was strongest when he faced forward, where Ford took up residence behind his desk.

"I see the question on your face." The magistrate reached down and pulled up his judicial wig. Normally a dulled ivory color, it now bore a blackened ringlet of singed curls on one side. "Whinnet was heavy handed with the iron this morning."

Nicholas suppressed a smirk. The Baggley boys had no idea what kind of wrath they'd be facing today.

Ford dropped the hairpiece like a dead cat. "Now that that's been cleared up, perhaps you can make it quick, as I requested."

Nicholas lifted his chin and widened his stance. "Miss Payne has suffered two abduction attempts. I won't allow a third."

Ford sank into his chair. The whoosh of leather matched his sigh. "Let's have it then. What do you need?"

"Moore."

The magistrate shook his head. "He's not yet returned from Dover. If he doesn't sort out that smuggling mess and soon, our patrons are likely not to be so. . .patronizing."

"Must be pretty bad if the revenue men and Moore are getting the runaround."

"Quite." Ford drummed his fingers on the desk, the *tat-tat-tat* like a cascade of grapeshot. "Why the sudden yearning for Moore? Is Flannery not working out?"

"No, it's not that. I'll use him. It's just. . ." Shifting his weight, he debated how much information to feed Ford. Judging by the creases on each side of the man's mouth, he ought serve it all up—on a platter. And quickly. "I intend to lure out whoever's responsible for the abduction attempts, Sedgewick's murder, and likely Payne's demise as well. For that, I need someone with me I can trust. Someone who's proven."

Ford cocked a brow. "Your plan?"

"I'll escort a Miss Payne decoy into a compromising situation, allow the capture of said decoy, then follow the culleys back to whatever rat hole they're hiding in."

"Where you'll go in with guns ablaze, I suppose, assuming of course that you're still in one piece after. . .*her* abduction."

His mouth quirked. "You know my style."

Ford shook his head, frowning. "Who would be daft or desperate enough to don a dress and play the part of a helpless lady, knowing that if he's found out, his throat will be slit?"

Reaching up, Nicholas rubbed the back of his neck. If only the action would loosen some persuasive words from his tongue. "That's the part I need to talk to you about, sir."

Ford's fingers immediately stilled. "What is this going to cost me, Brentwood?"

"An officer's commission, nothing more." *Hopefully.*

Ford leaned forward in his chair. "Let me guess. Flannery."

Nicholas said nothing. To flatter the magistrate by congratulating his intuitiveness would only stoke the man's ire.

The corner clock's ticking replaced Ford's tapping, each tock chipping nicks into Nicholas's strategy. If Ford wouldn't agree to this, he'd have no choice but to use a real woman. But who?

At last the magistrate planted his hands on his desktop and pushed up to stand. "I can think of nothing better at the moment. Very well, then. I shall offer Flannery a commission on the condition you vouchsafe his service brings no shame to Bow Street."

A muscle tightened at the side of his neck. Was the man worth such a wager? Should he allow Flannery to hold his reputation in his hands? Hard to say, but of one thing he was certain—the woman on the run and holed up in his room was worth every risk.

"If he lives through this assignment," Nicholas measured out each word, "then yes, I think I can heartily recommend him."

"Well, if he's foolish enough to give it a go. . .I daresay you ought have him shave first." Ford scooped up his wig, wafting a fresh wave of burnt-hair stink through the room. He scowled as he jammed it atop his head. "And what of Miss Payne, while you're racing about town chasing down villains?"

"Not to worry." In his mind's eye, he could yet see her sleeping like an angel beneath his bland woolen blanket. "She's safely tucked away where no one will find her."

A kaleidoscope of images flashed against the back of Emily's eyelids—her standing like a princess in a golden gown, the twist of Henley's lips before he'd wrestled her down to the bench. Nicholas's green gaze gently holding hers when he'd hovered so near her in the carriage. White curtains billowing into her chamber like ghosts from the grave. A tremble spidered across her shoulders, and she was unable to decide if the skin on her neck was clammy from fever or fright.

Her eyes fluttered open, focusing on a plaster wall inches from her face. For a few moments, her gaze traced hairline cracks from nick to ding as she tried to pretend the pattern was the tiny yellow-flowered print that papered her room. It might have worked, were fatigue still fogging her brain. But the longer her eyes remained open, the more reality seeped in, hard and angular as the lump in the mattress biting into her hip. Still, there was a slight amount of comfort when she inhaled, the thin pillow smelling of Nicholas's musky scent. Stretching, she rolled over, intending to ask him what the day would bring.

Instead, she gasped.

Fathomless blue-gray eyes stared into hers, half of one hidden by a swath of straight, dark hair. Emily clutched the blanket to her neck in reflex, though it was naught but a slip of a girl staring at her, perched on a chair next to the bed—the chair she'd last seen occupied by Nicholas. The girl couldn't have been more than eight or nine, but judging by the tilt of her head and sober pucker to her mouth, she'd already lived a lifetime.

"Who are you?" Emily asked.

"Hope's me name, m'um. Better than Nipper." The girl leaned closer. "Don't you think?"

Slowly, Emily lowered the blanket and rose up to settle on the edge of the bed frame. She'd slept fully clothed, so no need to worry about indiscretion, though she did methodically smooth out wrinkles from her skirt. As she did so, she simultaneously scanned the small room for Nicholas's muscular form. A study in futility, for she would've noticed him right off.

Not even his greatcoat remained.

"Yer pretty."

The squeaky little voice pulled her attention back to the girl on the chair. "Oh. . .thank you. I vow I must look a fright, though I suppose that doesn't matter now. Could you tell me where Nic—" Emily bit her lip. Why did the man's Christian name rise so easily to her tongue? Was this what came of sharing a bedchamber with him? She cleared her throat and tried again. "Where is Mr. Brentwood?"

"Dunno. Din't tell me." Hope hopped off the chair and walked the few paces over to the table. What a cryptic little mouse.

The fabric of the girl's dress scraped over sharp shoulder blades as she reached forward. She pulled a drab square of cloth off a basket then uncorked a squat, green bottle. Apparently finished with her task, she turned and leaned back against the tabletop, crossing one ankle over the other. The pose added years to her small body. "Mr. B sent me to see to your needs. I brought ye some water to freshen up a bit, and a loaf of bread with some jam."

"Thank you." Emily stood and arched her back, wondering which of the hundreds of questions she should ask first. "May I inquire as to how you know him? Mr. B, that is, as you call him."

A smile spread across Hope's face, and for the first time, Emily noticed the girl scrunched up her nose much like she did. She couldn't help but return the girl's smile. Hope unearthed and partially filled a long-forgotten space deep down in her heart for a little sister.

"Why. . .ye're as kind as Miss Jenny, I can tell. Miss Jenny's been teachin' me to speak real proper like." Hope bounced on the balls of her feet. "How'm I doin'?"

The girl's zigzaggy line of conversation was hard to follow, but the way she rose higher on her toes, Emily sensed it was important for her to try. In the depths of the girl's gray-blue eyes, a yearning for approval glistened like sunlight off glass. Was this how she'd looked at her own father?

"You're doing very well, Hope." Emily crossed over to the girl and bent to eye level. "But as for Mr. Brentwood?"

"Tha's right. Got sidetracked, I did. Now, let's see. . ." Her teeth worked her lower lip, and she looked down. The index finger of one hand tapped over the fingers of her other before she finally lifted her gaze. "I reckon 'tis been 'bout three, mebbe four weeks now since he plucked me from the streets."

"Plucked?" She frowned.

Hope laughed. "Ain't as awful as all that, m'um. I guess I shoulda said saved, for so he did. Weren't no better day than that morn I tried to poach Mr. B's purse."

Saying nothing, Emily straightened. What was there to say? Hope's quirky statements made as much sense as the mess she currently found herself in. Bypassing the girl, she retrieved a crust of bread from the basket and took a bite without bothering to spread any jam atop it, though a small jar peeked out from the basket.

Hope watched her for several chews. "If ye don' mind, miss, I bin waiting a long while for ye to wake. I ought be off to see to Miss Jenny. She's real sick, and I fear to leave her alone for so long. Is there aught I can do for ye afore I go?"

Emily returned the bread to the basket and brushed her hands together. Other than wave a magic wand and rid the world of whoever it was that sought her life, there was truly nothing more the girl could do. "Did Mr. Brentwood say anything at all about when he'd return?"

Hope shook her head, the action swinging the swath of hair to cover half her face instead of just one eye. "No m'um."

"Very well. Thank you for the provisions. I suspect your Miss Jenny is missing you as well, so run along." She retreated once again to the bed and sank to the frame. What was she to do here? Alone. Sitting in a man's room, afraid to stay and more afraid to leave? Sighing, she rested her elbows on her knees and rubbed out the lines in her forehead.

A light touch on her shoulder lifted up her face. The girl moved as quietly as Nicholas.

"Don't look so sad, m'um. If Mr. Brentwood's carin' for ye, ye got nothin' to fret about. He's a good man, he is. I knows it, and now so do you."

Little fingers patted her sleeve, earnest as a grandmother's. Emily couldn't help but smile at the girl.

"Tha's more like it." Hope's mouth curved, revealing a dimple on her right cheek. "Hey! I know. Whyn't you come with me to visit Miss Jenny?"

The girl looked at her with such an imploring tilt to her chin, it would be difficult not to promise her a pony had she asked for one. But this request? Probably not the best idea for her to traipse around town with only a pixie of a girl at her side. Emily reached up and smoothed back the floppy bit of hair covering Hope's face before answering. "I don't think that's wise. Mr. Brentwood might get angry were I to be gone when he returns."

Hope shook her head, her bottom lip pooching out in defiance. "I don't think he'll mind a bit."

"You're a very confident young lady, Hope. What makes you so certain?"

She shrugged, her thin shoulders raising little hills at the tops of her sleeves. "Only makes sense he'd search for ye o'er at Miss Jenny's if he doesn't find ye here."

"Really?" She tried, but there was no unraveling of the girl's logic. "Why is that?"

"Pish! Why, she's his sister, m'um."

Emily could feel her brow wrinkle. Nicholas had a sister? Why on earth had he never spoken of her?

CHAPTER 26

Emily stood behind Hope as the girl jiggled a key in the lock to Miss Jenny Brentwood's room. She'd debated long and hard about coming here, but in the end, curiosity won out. That, and the wish to escape the suffocating jail cell of Nicholas's chamber. In comparison to his place, even the corridor of the inn she now stood in was large—though just as shabby. A carpet runner lined the hallway, threadbare in spots and dulled to an allover shade of dirt. Overhead, the plaster was darkened by burnt lamp oil, collecting in black pools above each wall sconce. Mrs. Hunt would have spasms just thinking about the cleanup required were this building left in her charge.

Nabbing a stray lock of hair, Emily worked it into the loose braid at the back of her head and patted it into place. They'd walked quickly to the inn, much like last evening's jaunt, but it was shorter and not nearly as frightening. If anything, with her knack for melding into crowds, Hope led her more invisibly than Nicholas.

Hope pushed open the door and called out in a singsong voice, "Look, Miss Jenny! I've brought you a new friend."

Emily stopped just inside the threshold. Weak daylight spread like a disease from the single window, coloring the small chamber with a gray pallor. The woman lying on the bed matched the colorless hue. Suppressing the urge to turn and run, Emily held her breath. Death lived here. She could smell it.

Maybe this had been a mistake.

Hope rushed over and knelt beside the bed, taking up the hand of the raven-haired wraith lying there. She'd likely been a beauty, once, with her oval face and pert little nose. Now her skin stretched over bones so sharp, it cut to the heart. Sickness was indeed a cruel thief. Jenny's resemblance to Nicholas was striking—and entirely too startling. What if that were him abed and dying?

Sadness, cavernous and cold, wrapped around her shoulders, and she shivered.

Jenny's lips moved, murmuring something to Hope, but her words were too delicate to travel the length of the room.

"Her name is. . ." Hope glanced over her shoulder. Her mouth twisted from one side to the other as if she swished around salt water for a rinse. "Why, I just been callin' you m'um, ain't I? Mr. B told me yer name, but I weren't payin' him no mind at the time." She turned back to Jenny and lowered her voice. "I guess I shoulda asked her name, eh?"

Emily stepped forward. The awkward moment had dragged on long enough. "I am—"

"Miss Emily Payne."

She froze.

Jenny's voice was parchment, frail and thin, yet bolstered with confidence—the same tenor she often heard in Nicholas's words. Emily suppressed a gasp. How could Jenny Brentwood possibly know who she was?

"Have we met?" she asked.

Green eyes stared up at her, paler than Nicholas's, but lit with similar intelligence. "Only through my brother's vivid descriptions. You're every bit as lovely as he said. How I've longed to meet you face-to-face." Shifting on her bed, she lifted a hand. "Hope, would you—"

A deep cough rattled up from Jenny's chest, cutting off her words and her breath.

Emily reached toward her, but what to do? Prop her up and risk breaking her? Offer a handkerchief to cough into or a glass of water to quench the rattle, neither of which she had? Illness was a stranger she'd never dined with nor had the slightest idea of how to serve. Helpless, she turned to Hope.

The girl merely flitted to the table and dragged over a chair, setting it next to the woman who possibly rasped out her last breaths. "Have a seat, Miss Emily, though I think I shall call you Miss Em. Goes nice with Mr. B. . .Mr. B and Miss Em." Her face brightened. "I like it."

"Shouldn't you. . .shouldn't we. . ." Emily threw out her hands toward Jenny. "She can't breathe!"

"Not to worry. Give 'er a moment, miss. She always does this." Ignoring the struggling Jenny, Hope skipped back to a small bench on the other side of the room and picked up two rag figures no bigger than her hands.

The insanity of it made Emily want to scream. Unsure of what else to do, she sat and clenched her hands in her lap, riding out the wretched eternity until Jenny finally relaxed against her pillow.

Emily leaned forward. "Is there nothing to be done for you? Is there anything I can—"

"Don't fret." Blue rimmed Jenny's lips, where a hint of a smile struggled to rise. "I'm dandy and grand, as always. But there is one thing. . ."

Such a shadow darkened her face, Emily bent closer, unsure if words would pass the lump in her throat. "Be at peace. I am listening. I'm not in the best of situations currently, but I vow I'll do whatever I can to help you."

Jenny nodded, the movement as slight as the breaths lifting her chest. "You are very kind. I feel as if we're sisters already. I ask only that you take a care for my brother, would you? My passing, it's. . .it's going to be hard on him, I fear."

Hard? Emily pressed her lips into a thin line. It would be all that and more, judging by the short moments she'd spent in Jenny's presence. The woman had no doubt been a gem. Her death would rip through Nicholas in ways that would leave an ugly scar. Her own heart dried to dust at the thought of the anguish he'd suffer.

Skimming the white counterpane, Jenny slid her hand slowly toward hers. Her touch was as cool as the last gasp of an autumn breeze. "You've done him much good, you know. You've taken his mind off me. It's God's plan. I am sure of it."

Emily snorted. "Some plan. I've brought him nothing but trouble."

"You've given him purpose."

A frown etched her lips. Purpose for what? Risking his own life?

"Nicholas has always taken care of me." The play of shadow and light filtering in from the window warmed Jenny's face—or perhaps it wasn't light at all, but adoration. "Always, from the time our parents died. I was five. He, no older than Hope."

Emily sat still, afraid that if she moved, Jenny might stop. The rare glimpse into her guardian's life was a great treasure, one she intended to hoard.

"We managed by God's grace, he and I, though sometimes it's hard for him to see that. Don't get me wrong. His faith is solid, it's just that sometimes. . .well. . ." Jenny smiled in full then, and for one spare moment, her true beauty escaped the shroud of sickness. Kings would fight for a woman such as this.

"Sometimes Nicholas forgets that he's not the one in control." Jenny's fingers patted the top of her hand. "You need to remind him."

Emily pulled away. "I hardly think he'd listen to me on such matters. Besides which, I don't expect he's signed on as my guardian for life."

Jenny's green gaze bore into hers, and this time Emily couldn't stop her gasp. She'd swear before a magistrate it was Nicholas looking out.

"You may be wrong about that," Jenny said at last. "He loves you, though after Adelina, he swore never to love again. You've changed him, Emily, in ways you'll never know."

In her mind, she quickly searched every conversation she'd ever held with Nicholas. Not only had he never mentioned a sister, he'd never mentioned any woman. She leaned closer to Jenny, keen on learning about the man she'd trusted. "Adelina?"

"You ask as though he's not spoken of her. Though in truth, I'd be surprised if he had. Years ago, ahh. . .he was so young. As was the Portuguese girl, Adelina. He met her while on assignment training gunners in Guarda. He's quite the shot, you know. He'd intended to marry her, until he was wounded, and. . ." A shudder rippled across Jenny's shoulders. "Adelina was killed by a Spanish invasion. My brother, he. . .well, he never forgave himself."

Emily sank back in the chair. All the times Nicholas overreacted about her safety suddenly made sense. What a horrific burden he carried. "But surely it wasn't his fault!"

"No." A faint smile lifted Jenny's lips. "Of course not, but such is the commitment of my brother once his heart is given. And make no mistake about it. . .he's given his heart to you."

Emily's pulse faltered as Jenny's words sank deep into her soul. How could the woman speak with such certainty when everything else about her was frail?

"And so I repeat, please. . .take a care for him, would you?" A cough broke out, gargling her words. "Take. . .a. . .care."

Jenny's eyes widened, and a slow trickle of blood leaked out her right nostril. Her hands flew to her chest, her fingers squeezing the fabric of her shift as if the movement might force air into her lungs.

Emily shot to her feet. "Hope! Does she always do this as well? Is she going to be all right?"

The girl dropped her dolls, one rolling on the floor as she ran to Jenny's side. She pulled the woman up to a sitting position, but still Jenny's breaths fluttered out like a bird with broken wings. One by one, stark red drips mottled the blanket.

Hope's eyes pooled with a well of tears. "No, miss. She ain't never been like this. I don't know what to do!"

Nicholas's gaze ricocheted around his room. Chair, empty. Table, littered with a half-eaten crust of bread, a bottle, and a basket. Obviously Hope had been here. The bed was rumpled, a blanket thrown back atop it. At its foot, his campaign chest was untouched with padlock in place. His gaze skipped from there to the window, and he narrowed his eyes. The thread seal he'd attached from sill to glass was still in place—no one had slipped in uninvited. He rubbed at the knot embedded in his shoulder.

So. . .where was Emily?

Relocking the door behind him, he trotted down the steps and examined the bolt on the street-level door. No sign of forced entry marred the wood or the metal. Had she been lured out?

Ignoring the panic welling in his gut, he scanned the street. Afternoon light painted different angles and shadows, but nothing looked out of the ordinary. The barking tune of the fellow hawking rags directly across the road from him added kindling to a newly sparked headache.

"Rags a binny, rags a bone, buy yer rags an' take 'em 'ome."

Nicholas pressed two fingers against his temple. More like the rag seller ought go home and stuff one of his rags in his own mouth, so tatty was his voice. The man had been there since morning. Hadn't he sold enough by now?

Wait a minute. . .he'd been there all day? Nicholas crossed the road at a brisk pace, dodging a passing bandy wagon.

"Rags a binny, rags a—" The one-legged fellow cocked his head like a robin spying a fat worm. "Need a rag, sir? I got the finest 'ere."

Nicholas stopped an arm's length from the fellow. Any closer and he'd gag from the rag seller's sour body odor. If the man smelled that bad, how putrid were his rags?

Nicholas shook his head. "What I need is information."

"All I gots is rags." With perfect balance, Ragpicker kept his seat as he kicked his single boot against the tall basket on the ground. "Ye want one or not?"

Must everything cost him? Reaching into a concealed pocket in his greatcoat, he pulled out a ha'penny and held it up. "Did you happen to see a young lady, very pretty, exit that door over there?" He pointed toward his own lodging.

Dirty fingers snatched the coin from his. "Mebbe. Memory's not so good, y'see."

Nicholas sighed and held out another offering.

The coin vanished as fast as the gummy smile splitting the man's face. "Aye. She were a looker, that one."

"Which way did she go, and was anyone with her?"

The man opened his mouth, but all that came out was, "Rags a binny, rags a bone, buy yer rags an'—"

With a flick of his arm, Nicholas grabbed the man's throat and squeezed. "You've been paid a fair amount already." He let go, giving the fellow just enough time to cough and curse. "Now answer my question."

"North," he hacked. "With a girl."

"That wasn't so hard, hmm?" Retrieving a last penny, Nicholas handed it over then wheeled about and strode down Sherborne Lane.

First he'd chew out Hope for bringing Emily to his sister's, then he'd have a word with Emily for—

His steps slowed, and he squinted. Surely he wasn't seeing this.

Down a block, Emily strolled toward him, alone. Undefended. Unaware. Above her, one story up, a fat woman with a large bucket leaned out a window, about to drop her slops. Behind her, a black-bearded sailor—considering his golden-ringed ear and bowed legs—followed close enough to reach out and reel her in. To her side, a dray passed in the street, heaped so high with barrels, the slightest dip in the road would send one toppling her way. She'd be crushed. And in front of her, two men swaggered out of an alley, each carrying half-empty bottles of gin.

Nicholas shot forward, ignoring her gasp when he grabbed her by the shoulders. In five long strides, he guided her into a sheltered alcove of a nearby glassery, out of the pedestrian flow and away from public scrutiny. His heartbeat pounded in his ears. "You'll be the death of me! How am I to keep you safe?"

Overly large brown eyes stared into his. Her drab bonnet only served to magnify the golden shimmer of the hair beneath. How could she be so beautiful that it tore into his soul?

Blinking, she drew in a breath. "I didn't think—"

"Of course you didn't think!"

She flinched.

He closed his eyes and counted to ten—then reversed from ten to one before opening them again. Sighing, he lowered his voice. "Where were you?"

"I was with your sister, waiting until the doctor settled her with some laudanum." Emily frowned up into his face. "She almost died! Why did you never tell me of her?"

"There was no reason."

"There was every reason! Had I known sooner, before I got into this dreadful situation, I could have helped."

"You?" He stepped up to her, forcing her back against the brick wall. A smirk begged for release, yet he fought it. "Think on it. When I first met you, your world consisted of pampering a pug, hat shopping, and snagging that scoundrel Henley. Would you honestly have wanted to help my sister?"

The longer she remained silent, the more her bottom lip quivered. "Maybe not at first." Her voice was small.

But true.

Curious, he leaned in, inches from her face, and studied the depths of her luminous eyes. Gilt flecks floated atop brown, shimmering like candlelight against dark velvet, but no guile, no deception, swam in those pools. Never had he seen her so open, so unguarded.

The effect stole his breath, making it impossible to speak. Clearing his throat, he demanded an answer he feared. "What's come over you? Tell me what changed."

Saying nothing, she lifted her hand and reached toward him like a lost lover who'd finally returned home. When her fingertips grazed his brow, he turned to granite. The contact was white hot. One by one, she smoothed away every crease, every line that tightened his forehead. Her gaze tracked the motion.

His heart followed her touch.

When she pulled her hand away, he was lost.

"Everything changed," she said.

Simple words, but the huskiness of her voice kicked off a complex reaction in his body. Blood pumped. A pang shot into his belly and sank. Low. Heat poured off him in waves. The thin space between them was a chasm too painful to bear. Pulling her close, he wrapped her in his arms, a groan rumbling somewhere in his chest.

She quivered against him—but did not protest.

Her name surfaced on his lips an instant before he pressed them against hers. She tasted of light, cinnamon, promise. . .all that was right and good. Her mouth moved against his with an intensity that surprised him, burning like the summer sun.

Closing his eyes, he breathed her in, and wondered if he'd ever truly breathed before. Her hands slid up his back, her fingers curling into the hair at the nape of his neck. He slipped his hands lower, locking them into place at the small of her back. Bending farther, he trailed kisses down her neck and pulled her closer, drawing her hips against his.

"Emily," he mouthed her name against skin so soft, he wanted to weep. When she arched into him, he knew he must have her.

And the thought turned his blood to ice.

He released her and backed away. Time stopped. How long they stood there, he could only guess. He gaped, frozen in place by the host of feelings drifting around him like ghosts in a graveyard, each one howling from the separation. The memory of her body fused against his seared into his bones. God. . .what had he done?

She stared at him, drawing the fingers of one hand to her mouth. Slowly, she traced her lower lip, touching the swell. Her gaze was intense, the color in her cheeks deepening with each of his heartbeats. Was she reliving the kiss?

Or regretting?

"Emily—" His voice broke. What kind of guardian was he? "I'm sorry. I'm so sorry."

Behind them, the usual sounds of London's streets continued on as if nothing had happened. What a lie. Something had happened, leastwise for him. He could only guess what he'd done to her.

"Don't be." Lowering her hand, she smoothed the wrinkles from her dress then lifted her chin, proud and defiant as ever. "I'm not."

Her words were as easy to grasp as feathers in the wind, but when they settled, a slow smile curved his mouth. Shaking his head, he grunted. "As I've said, you will be the death of me, woman. Come along. Let's get you off the street."

She fell into step beside him, the bustle of Eastcheap filling the silence until she spoke: "I am worried for your sister. She ought be moved to a nicer place. Somewhere warmer, or cozier, someplace"—she shrugged—"healthier."

He arched a brow down at her, amazed at her shift from passion to empathy. "Why do you think I took your father's offer in the first place?"

Her eyes widened, as if she'd discovered for the first time that he wasn't an ogre. "But, my father, I mean. . .what will you do now?"

"In your case, I have a plan. As for my sister, well. . ." He looked forward, and instead of seeing the busy street in front of him, Jenny's drawn face filled his vision. "I had a plan, once, but it's not so clear anymore."

"Nicholas?"

His Christian name on Emily's tongue jerked his face toward hers. "Aye?"

"She asked me to remind you that God's the One in control, not you."

Once again he directed his gaze forward. The words ought be comforting, for indeed they were solid and true.

So why did he feel as if he were just about to jump off a cliff?

CHAPTER 27

Here you go." Nicholas threw a blue dress across the Portman House sitting room. With the seams let out and a panel added onto the back, it looked like a crippled heron as it flew through the early evening light. Draped across Flannery's shoulders, the bird would come to life in a spectacular way—one that would be talked about down at Bow Street for months to come. Truly, he ought not smile.

Flannery snatched the material with one hand and held the gown up. His scowl grew in size and depth the longer he looked at it.

Before the man could complain, Nicholas retrieved two precious oranges from a bowl on the tea trolley and rolled them across the floor. "And don't forget these."

"What're those for?"

Without a word, Nicholas brought his hands up and cupped them to his chest.

Flannery glowered. "Sweet flying peacock!"

Nicholas dodged the fruit missiles, choosing to ignore the *thwunk* of them smacking the wall behind him.

"No! I won't do it!" Flannery balled up the dress and chucked it to the carpet. "This goes beyond what ye asked in the first place."

Nicholas rubbed his jaw with one hand. Negotiating with Emily for a spot to sleep on the floor in front of the hearth had been child's play compared to this. "Think on it, Flannery. You know as well as I the past few days have produced nothing. Occupying her chamber overnight with the window cracked open. Me spending the bulk of my time absent from the house. Even you donning a bonnet and tooling about town in the carriage didn't attract anything but some lewd remarks from a near-sighted drunkard. So unless you've a better idea, we give this a shot. Besides, who's going to recognize you in a dress?"

Flannery folded his arms, his scowl softening at the corners. Progress.

Nicholas lifted his chin. "Need I remind you there's a commission in this? We catch the villain; you become a full-fledged officer."

His lips leveled to a straight line. Advancement.

"Sometimes duty calls for extreme measures. If you're not up for it, perhaps this isn't your line of work."

Flannery narrowed his eyes. "Did you ever have to wear a dress?"

"No." He paused long enough to let Flannery think he held the winning hand, then played his trump card. "But I did have to pose as a harlot in a molly house to snag a suspected parliament member with immoral tastes. I barely got out of there with my breeches intact. All I'm asking you to do is wear a dress and sway your hips as we walk down a few streets."

"Pah!" Flannery swiped up the gown.

Victory.

Nicholas gestured toward the door. "Go change in the study. I'll see you're not disturbed."

Flannery stomped past him, mumbling all the way. Waiting until the grumbling faded then finally quieted behind the slamming of a door, Nicholas sank onto the settee and tipped back his head.

"Thank You, God, for small triumphs," he whispered and closed his eyes. The past several days had been grueling, to say the least: keeping Emily occupied in a room hardly bigger than a cell at Newgate, keeping his own emotions in check while spending so much time with her—hard to do with the memory of her kiss forever etched onto his lips. It was a tight balancing act between that and despair over Jenny's failing condition.

Failure weighted his shoulders as well, and he rolled them against the cushion. Why had the abductors not made another attempt? Did they know about Payne's death? Was it safe to take Emily home?

A gruff throat clearing and heavy footsteps hauled him to his feet, and when Flannery swung through the door, Nicholas's jaw dropped. Somewhere deep, laughter ignited, but if he let it explode, the game would be off—not that the knowing stopped an openmouthed grin from stretching his cheeks.

Flannery's hand shot up. "Don't be sayin' anything. Don't be sayin' anything at all!"

Nicholas closed his mouth, every muscle in his gut quivering with the strain to keep from hooting. Flannery stood in front of him, for all the world looking like a dog-faced spinster. And an angry one at that. The long sleeves, poofy and opaque, hid his muscles—but not the hairy knuckles he bunched into fists.

"Don't even think it. I'm warning ye, Brentwood!"

It took several deep breaths to assure he wouldn't lose his composure when he spoke. "Fine. Let's get to work then."

Flannery stalked toward the door.

Nicholas snagged his skirt and pulled him back. "Not so fast. We start right here."

"I thought the point of this was struttin' about on the streets, not in some nimbly parlor. Hard to catch a fish when yer bait isn't in the water."

"After seeing you stomp across the room like an overgrown strumpet bent on a mark, trust me, we've got work to do here. With a gait like that, the only thing you'd catch is the pox from a burly wharf ape."

Red crept up Flannery's neck. "Are ye sayin'—"

"I'm saying let's work on your deportment."

"My. . .what?"

"Your poise. Your posture." Nicholas threw out his hands. "Call it what you will, man, but you must learn to walk without losing your oranges."

Flannery's gaze shot to his chest. One fruit migrated south. The other had slid nearly under his armpit. He grabbed them both and resettled them front and center.

"Good." Nicholas strolled to the door, allowing plenty of space for Flannery to practice. "Now then, chin up. Shoulders back. And with a slight sway of your hips, glide."

In an instant, Flannery's eyes changed from seaside blue to the dark gray of a tempest. Good thing the man was armed with nothing more than citrus.

"I will not—"

"Flannery," he growled the name, "if this is to be believable—"

"Who's to be believin' I'm Miss Payne when I nearly equal your height, am wider in the shoulders, narrower in the hips, and a flamin' carrot top to boot?"

Lifting a finger, Nicholas pointed to the window, where even now shadows blotted out the last bits of daylight. "Which is why we'll take our stroll in the dark."

"Oh, bloody—"

"Tut, tut." He wagged his finger in Flannery's face. "A lady never utters vulgarities."

"Fie!" Flannery spit out. "This better be worth it. Chin, shoulders, hips, glide. I got it."

"Then let's see it."

Muttering, Flannery kicked into motion. He tilted his head, shimmied his shoulders, and shifted his behind one way then another. The oranges slipped, the blue skirt swished, and the redhead went down. Hard.

Nicholas bent, riding out a wave of laughter that wouldn't be stopped, until his lungs hurt and his eyes watered. Flannery let loose a barrage of foul oaths, which only made it funnier to see an Irishman in a dress cursing like a gambler on a losing spree.

"I never!"

Behind them, Mrs. Hunt's voice sobered Nicholas enough to straighten and turn. She held out a note with his name penned on the front. As soon as he pinched it between thumb and forefinger, she whirled and whisked off down the corridor.

Flannery hollered after her. "I never did either!"

Nicholas wheeled back to the dour-faced man. "Go on and practice some more. I'll leave you to it for a while."

He retreated to the study and sank into the chair where he'd first met Payne. With the back of his hand, he wiped the moisture from his eyes then broke the seal on the parchment. Perfect timing for a diversion.

His gaze settled on the words, and as he read it twice over, he wondered how one could understand that which didn't make sense:

Come at once. Your sister draws her last breaths.

—Dr. Kirby

For at least the tenth time, Emily flung open the door of Nicholas's chamber and looked out. Once again, her shoulders slumped, tiring of the game. Nothing but darkness stalked up the stairs. Where was he? He'd not left her alone for these many hours since the day he'd first brought her here, which was not only unusual, but undesirable as well.

And entirely unfortunate.

She tugged her cape snug against her shoulders, wishing it was Nicholas's embrace instead of thin wool, then stepped out and shut the door behind her. What else could she do? If she waited any longer, she'd miss Wren. As it was, even with speedy steps, she'd have to meet Wren first to tell her to wait, then retrieve some supplies from the house. Or maybe Wren could follow her back and hide in the shadows. If only Mrs. Hunt would simply relent and listen to reason—and to her heart.

She tripped on the last stair and flung out her free hand, slapping it hard against the wall. The resulting sting assaulted her palm every bit as much as the realization smacking her own heart. Who was she to judge Mrs. Hunt, when unforgiveness toward her father hid like a spider in a crevice of her soul? Sooner or later, she'd have to deal with that. Setting down the lantern, she took a deep breath and made up her mind.

Later. Definitely later. Making it safely back to Portman Square took priority.

She slid the bolt, opened the door, and blew out the lamp. Better to blend into the shadows than blaze like a beacon. Drawing on every trick she'd gleaned from Hope, she stepped out into the street and merged with the night. If Nicholas knew she was out here, he'd kill her.

Unless the footsteps behind got to her first.

CHAPTER 28

Nicholas crashed open the door of the Crown and Horn and tore through the taproom. Cutting too close to a table, he slipped in a pool of spilled ale. His foot shot out, and he flailed, but quickly righted himself. The teetering table didn't. Wood and grog flew, along with the patron's insults and Meggy's threats. Ignoring all, he bolted ahead and took the stairs three at a time.

God, please. God, please. Not much of a prayer, but it was all he had left.

He sprinted down the hall, his pounding feet rattling the sconce glasses in their holders. The sound mocked like skeleton's bones, an eerie portent he'd rather not acknowledge. What if he was too late?

Two paces from Jenny's room, he stopped.

So did his heart.

Hope sat on the floor in the hall, her back to the closed door. Fresh tears slid down tracks already worn on her cheeks. Her mouth opened, but no words came out. They didn't have to.

He knew.

She shot to her feet and plowed into him. In reflex, he wrapped his arms around her. She sobbed, but he didn't feel his shirt dampen or the shaking of her shoulders. He didn't feel anything. He wouldn't let himself. Not yet.

"Hush, child." His voice sounded far away. Lost. Just like Jenny was to him.

Guiding the girl over to the wall, he peeled her slim arms from his waist. "Sit. Wait. I'll be. . .a moment."

She sank to the floor and buried her face in her hands. Surely the waif had seen death many times over—but such was the effect of losing Jenny. And if it moved a hardened street child who'd known his sister not quite a month, what would it do to him?

Turning, he sucked in a breath and crossed to the door. Each step took a force of will, his boots weighted as if his feet were ten stone apiece. But it wasn't just his feet. Everything felt heavy. His lungs. His hope. His faith.

Inside, a single lamp burned on the table. Light brushed a last glow of luminescence over Jenny's pallid skin. Crazy laughter tightened his chest. What need did the dead have of light?

The closer he drew, the more his steps dragged, the habit of walking quickly becoming forgotten. He dropped to his knees beside the bed, and for a moment, he closed his eyes, reliving a nightmare he'd hoped never to have to repeat in real life.

He hadn't been there for Adelina, either. An ambush ending in a firefight between the Portuguese and Spanish had laid him up for months and kept him from her as she lay dying. The Spaniards attacking her village spared no one, caring nothing for women and their screams.

He should have been there.

He should have been here.

"Nooo!" His fists smashed into the bed frame, bruising his hands and jostling Jenny's body, reanimating her if only for a second.

The movement sobered him.

Reaching out, he brushed back the matted hair from her brow. How much had she struggled? How great was the pain?

"Ahh, Jen—" Sobs choked out his words. No matter. What was the use?

Silently, he pulled out of his memory each time she'd answered "*dandy and grand, as always.*" Every "*you worry too much.*" And shook his head at the "*you are not God, you know.*"

A groan escaped him. Oh, how well he knew that.

He drew his hand back and held his breath. Still. Silent. Mayhap, if he listened hard enough, he might hear her sweet voice one last time, faint as the distant sound of chimes in the wind. What would she say?

What would her last words have been?

The sniffle of the crying girl in the hall and the muffled whoops of late-night revelers in the taproom quickly ended such musing.

Rising, he grasped the blanket's edge and drew it up—slowly—his gaze reluctant to let his sweet sister go. She looked peaceful. He'd give her that. And why not? She was now with the One she loved most.

With a last long look, he pulled the blanket higher, covering her face.

But not his shame.

He stepped back and shuddered. He'd failed her, every bit as much as he'd failed Adelina. If only he'd gotten her moved to a better place, been able to pay for better care.

Been a better man himself and come home to her instead of traipsing around foreign battlefields in a search of fortune and fame.

"Good-bye, Jen." The words came out rough and jagged, though truth be told, he was surprised they came at all. Her name hung in the air like a phantom then dissipated into the dark.

He pivoted and stalked out to the hall. Hope sat balled up exactly where he'd left her.

He reached for her. Inches away from patting her head, his fingers recoiled. "Go to bed. We'll talk tomorrow."

Without waiting to see if she obeyed, he turned and stomped off. Meggy said something as he crossed the taproom. Hard to say what, since all he could hear was the rushing in his ears. He ought arrange a time with her for the body to be removed—but thinking of his sister as a body was too foreign an idea to entertain. Too fragile. If he weren't careful, all his thoughts would splinter into sharp points. Maybe if he walked awhile, fast enough and far enough, the fog in his head would lighten.

He stormed out of the Crown and Horn and turned left, hoping with the desperation of a starving man that someone—anyone—would throw him a crumb of interference, for he dearly wanted a fight. The need to pummel and be pummeled quivered in his muscles and ached in his soul.

In a mood blacker than the streets, he wandered up one and

down another, through alleys, along the wharves. In defiance of the chill air, sweat made his shirt stick to him like a second skin. No one stopped him. None so much as commented, in spite of the challenge he glowered into the nameless faces he passed.

Long past midnight, he turned toward Eastcheap. Sleep wouldn't come, but morning would. Emily must be told. Life must continue. All the musts he should attend to echoed in his head, far off but real.

Exhausted and empty, he pulled out his key. No resistance dragged against the bolt when he turned it. Recalling when he'd left—a lifetime ago now—he retraced mentally each step of locking the door. Yes. He definitely had secured it. He was too careful not to. He was always careful. *Oh God, why hadn't I been more careful with Jenny?* A sob rose to his tongue, and he bit down hard, savoring the coppery taste.

Then he yanked open the door and frowned at the lantern on the lower stair. A tremor rolled over his shoulders, traveled the length of his spine, and lodged deep and low.

"Emily!"

Heart racing—surprising, really, to know that it still worked—he flew up the stairs and, on a hunch, shoved the other door without trying the lock. It swung wide, hinges complaining at the force. His gut tightened. Hope plummeted. Entering the room would likely only add to the nightmare, yet it was one more must that couldn't be denied.

God, please. God, please.

Not much of a prayer, but it was all he had left.

Ambrose de Villet stood in the dark, feeding off the blackness, soaking in its sanctification. His mother had died birthing him during the witching hour, and he'd spent each successive minute of his life anticipating the night. It was home, breath. . .sustenance. As satisfying as the rigid stance of the pregnant Englishwoman twenty paces from him. She feared him. He could smell it.

And it was good.

Reaching into his pocket, he pulled out a lump the size of a severed fingertip. Harder, though, and much more sweet in a bitter sort of way.

Saliva rained at the back of his throat. He popped the horehound candy into his mouth, savoring the first tang sliding over his tongue. But the best, the most enjoyable, part was the cool trail that crawled up high and sank in roots just behind his nostrils. When he inhaled, the chill magnified a hundredfold. The shiver running through his bones was delicious.

Too bad it didn't last long enough. Not as long as he'd stood here, waiting for the Payne woman to meet her friend. Stupid girl. Stupid English. Four weeks on their *rosbif* soil had sullied him to the point of scrubbing his hands raw. By this time tomorrow evening, though, the darkness of a ship a'sea would wash clean the entire month of blunder and mishap.

Biting down, again and again, he ground the candy until it was nothing but a sticky memory in the hollows of his teeth.

Footsteps cornered the end of the block, beating a fast clip against the cobbles. Light enough for a female, determined enough that this was no wanderer. He flattened against the brick.

"Wren!" The Payne woman's voice was breathy as she closed in on the big-bellied sow. "I'm so glad you're still here. Sorry I'm late. Things have been. . .difficult."

"Not to worry, miss."

Ambrose relished the quiver in her tone. It vibrated on the air, terrible and sweet, reminding him to reach into his pocket and pull out another candy.

"I haven't had the time to gather some things for you, Wren. Wait here, and I'll—"

"No. You must come with me. I. . .I have something to show you."

"What are you talking about? Where? What?"

The muscles in his neck tightened. He'd been forced to walk a rope lashed between two roofs once. One misstep, one untrue placement of the foot, and failure would rise up from the ground. He liked heights about as much as the turn of the women's conversation.

"Not far. Not far at all, miss. Please! It's important."

"I don't understand. What's going on?"

"Will you. . .will you trust me, miss?"

"Wren, what's wrong?"

Ambrose swallowed the candy whole and stopped breathing. This could all fall apart and fast. Not that he'd mind killing the stupid English whore. A slow smile tugged at his lips. Ending two English lives with one snap of the neck would be satisfying indeed.

His eyes widened. What was the senseless cow doing? She leaned in close, far too close to the Payne woman. This was not part of the plan. Was she whispering a warning? Steeling his muscles, he was about to step from the wall, when the large one turned toward him and began walking. He froze.

"Wren. . .wait! I know something's wrong. What is it?" The Payne woman raced after her.

Ahh. His smile grew. The English whore was smarter than he credited. Whatever she'd said into Emily Payne's ear had apparently worked. She stopped two paces from him, close enough that the pain on her face sent a jolt through his belly. This was going to be far more exciting than he'd expected.

Emily Payne's hasty steps suffered a quick death, ending when her eyes locked onto his. She jerked her face toward the woman with the ridiculous bird name. "Why did you—"

"I'm sorry, miss. I didn't have a choice."

Like a worm yanked out of a fish's jaw, the pregnant woman turned and fled down the street, leaving the Payne woman gaping.

CHAPTER 29

By the time Nicholas reached Portman Square, the first hints of dawn soaked through the fabric of his greatcoat. The air was damper, chillier, and smelled like a musty cellar. The sky had yet to lighten, but that would come soon enough. God's handiwork never failed.

Unlike him.

Drawing in a deep breath, he swallowed a rising tide of despair and unlatched the front door. Surely he'd find Emily here. Mayhap she'd merely had enough of the oppressive walls in his small chamber and yearned for the spaciousness of her own. Maybe she simply missed her little pug. Whatever reason, he'd praise God to see her safe and sound in her own home—then he'd deal her a sound reprimand. Of all nights to vanish without taking his leave, she had to choose this one?

He closed the door behind him and padded up the stairs. No sense waking the entire house, especially if Emily was curled up beneath her counterpane. Of course she would be. She had to be.

Oh God, make it so.

After two quick raps with his knuckles, he leaned close to her chamber door. "Emily?"

Silence.

He pounded harder. "Emily!"

Nothing.

The knob twisted easily—hadn't he warned her to always lock

a door? The same intuition that broadsided him as he stood outside Jenny's room hit him anew. He swung the door wide and looked into the dark chamber. The scent of lilies taunted him on the inhale. So did the shadows reclining on the covers of Emily's empty bed.

If she wasn't here, then where?

Scrubbing his face with one hand, he retreated down the corridor, the stubble on his jaw as prickly as the possibilities of where Emily might be. The prospects were endless, most sinister, and a few he'd not entertain for a king's ransom. He clung to the one innocent hunch left him and descended the back staircase to the lowest level.

As housekeeper, Mrs. Hunt's room was the first on the right at the bottom of the stairs. This time he didn't bother to temper his volume.

"Mrs. Hunt!" The door rattled in the frame. "Mrs.—"

"Coming!"

The bang of a wardrobe, some swooshes, and a whole lot of muttering preceded the slit-eyed, night-capped woman.

"Mr. Brentwood!" The candle in her hand lit half her face, the other was shrouded in darkness. Never had she looked so weary. "Why . . .what—"

"Is Miss Payne here?" He nodded toward her chamber. "Has she sought your company for the night?"

The housekeeper's eyes popped wide open. "Why, I thought she were with you, sir."

He wheeled about, raising both fists. Then at the last moment, he flattened his palms to the opposite wall and leaned his forehead against the cool plaster.

His thoughts leaked out into prayer. "God, now what? Where is she?"

He listened hard, straining to hear or feel anything. A nudge. A direction. A lightning bolt with a note skewered onto the end telling of Emily's location.

"What is it?" Behind him, Mrs. Hunt's voice was as small as Hope's. "What's gone wrong?"

His shoulders slumped as he turned to face her. "I'll tell you what's gone. Emily."

A knock, not as loud but just as urgent, crept down the hallway from the servants' entrance. His eyes met Mrs. Hunt's. "Expecting anyone?"

"No, sir."

He shot down the corridor, the housekeeper's nightgown and wrap rustling behind. Judging by the tap of her slippers, she matched his pace step for step. By the time he opened the door to a very small, very pregnant woman, Mrs. Hunt had gained his side. She swayed then grabbed his forearm.

"What are ye doing here?" The housekeeper's voice was a shiver in the dark.

Nicholas looked from the unexpected visitor to Mrs. Hunt. Apparently this was no stranger.

Without warning, a snippet of memory clicked into place, as deftly as he might pick open a lock—following Emily in the darkest hour before dawn, hiding in the shadows as she delivered a small bag . . .to the woman who now stood before him. Lauren "Wren" Hunt. That was it.

No wonder Mrs. Hunt's fingers dug into his arm.

"Please," Wren said, "just listen."

Behind them, the slap of sensible shoes hit the tiles, preceding the baritone voice of Cook. Should she ever choose to trade professions, there was likely a lighthouse in need of a foghorn somewhere. "What's all this? Half the house awake and I've not even had a chance to boil water yet. Why—" A gasp punctuated her tirade as she drew near. "Look who's come back."

Cook's proclamation prodded Mrs. Hunt like a cattle brand. Loosing her hold on his arm, she instead grabbed Wren's and pulled her inside. She swept past the gaping cook, calling out as she scurried along, "We'll take tea in my sitting room. Mr. Brentwood, don't dawdle."

Nicholas glanced up at the sky as he shut the back door. *Quite an interesting answer, Lord.* Then he turned and hustled to catch up.

Eyeing the small room, he took a position near the hearth. Banked for the night, it offered no heat, not that it needed to. The housekeeper generated enough warmth as she bustled about lighting lamps.

Across from him, a table with an inkwell and a stack of papers sat in front of a window. In the corner, Wren perched on one of two wingback chairs. No pictures graced the walls. No knickknacks adorned any whatnot shelves. Mrs. Hunt obviously kept the maintenance of her own rooms down to a minimum.

While Mrs. Hunt flitted about lighting lamps, he studied the girl. "Have you seen Miss Payne? Has she met with you? Have you any information?"

Wren's eyes glistened a moment before she buried her face in her hands.

"La, Mr. Brentwood. Give the girl a moment." Mrs. Hunt scowled at him then plopped into the seat adjacent Wren. The stern lines of her face masked any emotion. The housekeeper would not only make a great sergeant but a piquet player, as well. "As soon as you're able, Lauren, we'll have the truth, and all of it."

Swiping her eyes, the girl straightened in her chair. After a final sniff, she faced her mother. "As much as you'd like to believe otherwise, I have only, ever, given you the truth. And this time, I beg you hear me out for Miss Emily's sake."

For an instant, the housekeeper's reserve cracked. Her brows connected in an angry line then just as quickly returned as if they'd never met. "You two have always been thick as thieves. It's not right. Not between a lady and a servant."

"Miss Emily's shown me more kindness than—"

"I suggest we leave the past behind, ladies." He upped his volume, redirecting the conversation. "What news have you of Miss Payne?"

Wide-eyed, Wren reached into a pocket and pulled out a slip of paper. "I am to deliver a note to Mr. Payne."

Nicholas crossed the room in three steps. "Mr. Payne is unavailable. I act in his stead."

Wren's gaze moved from his outstretched palm to his face. A hundred questions shone in her gaze. "Who are you?"

"Mr. Brentwood is a law keeper. He can be fully trusted, and in fact may be Miss Emily's best hope." Mrs. Hunt nodded toward the girl. "Go on."

The paper passed easily from her fingers but once fully resting in his palm, weighed heavier than a brick. So much depended on what this note might say. Odors of horehound and fish wafted upward as he unfolded the ripped segment of yesterday's *Chronicle* and read words written with a heavy hand in grease pencil:

Old Saproot Warehouse, Pig's Quay Wharf
8:00 p.m. unarmed and alone
500 pounds

Emily's throat burned. If Alf's water dish were available, she'd shove the pup out of the way and lap it up—were it not for the gag in her mouth. Her eyes were plenty moist, though. Not that crying helped, but she simply couldn't stop, and what else was there to do? She sat on a precarious stack of crates, terrified the act of breathing might be enough to topple her over. There'd be no way catch herself. Ropes cut into her wrists, pinioning her like one of Cook's poultry. If she fell, she'd crack her head against the warehouse floor and kill herself.

But as horrifying as it was to sit here and wonder if she might plummet to her death—or what would become of her even if she didn't—far worse was the stabbing pain in her back. From Wren. Why? She closed her eyes. *God, why?* Betrayal chafed her heart more painfully than the rag biting into her mouth. Finally she understood the black unforgiveness running through Mrs. Hunt's veins, for it pumped through her own, heavy and thick.

On the far side of the warehouse, three sharp bangs rapped against wood. Behind her, heels thudded on planks. The bald brute who'd dragged her here passed beneath her, hollering over his shoulder, "Take her down."

Daylight streamed through cracks in the walls. If they hauled her out of here now, she might have a chance to attract attention and get some help. She clutched tightly to that hope. It was the only one she had.

A freestanding ladder on wheels rolled over to her tower, but climbing up was no prince to her rescue. The stink of sour ale and mutton reached her an instant before his rough hands. He lugged her over his shoulder like a sack of kittens to be drowned. She winced at the horrid thought then complied by going limp. Better to save her fighting strength until she stood a better chance.

"Right, then. Let's see her."

The words barely registered before the world flipped and she stood on her own. A man-shaped shadow stepped out from a row of crates. When a shaft of light flooded his face and his gaze met hers, her heart stopped.

She knew those eyes. The coldness of them washed over her like seawater, leaving behind a wake of panic, exactly as it had late last summer.

Captain Daggett.

Her stomach heaved, and she doubled over. Nausea wasn't an option with a bound mouth. She focused on her skirt hem and counted the embroidered scallops one by one—anything to ignore the convulsing of her belly.

Daggett's laughter rang out, grating as knife against bone. "How much ye askin' for her?"

"Five hundred pounds."

"Gads! I could buy the Queen Mother for that."

At the snap of some fingers, she was jerked upright, her back pressed against the bully behind her, his arm across her chest.

The bald thug opposite her smiled at Daggett. "Ahh, but this one is—"

"I know what this one is." The captain drew so near, his hot breath hit her forehead. She flinched.

Reaching up, he twisted a loose curl of her hair and rubbed it between his fingers. "I know exactly what this one is."

"She'll bring a fine price," the bald man continued. "You'll make your money back and more, if sold to the right buyer. And I have it on good authority you are a man with many connections."

Daggett leaned closer and bent, his breathing loud in her ear. "He has no idea, hmm?"

Then he wheeled about and offered his hand to the bald man. "Yes,

I believe she will bring a good price. I'll take her."

His words spun in her head. Or was that the room? Hard to say. Nothing was solid anymore—except for the fear driven deep into her soul.

CHAPTER 30

Nicholas strode down the narrow lane, his gaze scouring the shadows more thoroughly than a street sweep intent on a coin. Not many figures inhabited this condemned stretch of riverfront. Those who did were cutthroats and thugs. Though plans for a new dock were in the works, as far as he and the river wardens were concerned, it wouldn't be built soon enough. This boneyard of warehouse skeletons needed to be buried. Deep.

At intervals, dark clouds blotted out the moonlight, adding a sporadic inky depth to the night, which had its benefits—and detriments. Tightening his grip on his end of the heavy chest toted by him and Flannery, he could only pray the darkness would work to his advantage and not for the men who'd taken Emily. Filthy scoundrels. If they'd harmed her, violated her. . .

His gut twisted into a sodden, knotted rope, strengthening his resolve.

Anger had its pros and cons, as well.

Beside him, holding up the other end of the wooden box, Flannery cleared his throat. "Not that I be needin' a hand-holding." He slanted a glance at Nicholas. "But I wouldn't mind ye running over those instructions again."

Nicholas snorted. "You nervous?"

A string of mumbled curses unraveled past Flannery's lips. "More than a strumpet in church!"

Nicholas smirked at him. "Good."

"Ye're a cold one, Brentwood."

"A certain amount of fear keeps you careful. It's too much or too little that can be deadly."

Flannery's end of the chest sagged. "Could you refrain from using that word?"

"Your part in this isn't too difficult. You'll be fine."

"Easy for you to say. Ye're not the one whose head might be blown clean off."

Nicholas nodded left. Flannery followed his lead. They entered an alley and stopped halfway down. Moonlight glinted off the perspiration dotting Flannery's brow as they eased the chest to the ground. The Irishman was right about one thing. He very well might lose his head.

But Nicholas's position wouldn't be any less dangerous.

Straightening, they retreated several steps. Nicholas bit back a smirk. As if the added distance of a few paces would save their lives should the chest explode now.

He faced Flannery and kept his tone low. Who knew what ears the wooden walls towering above them held. "All you do is open the lid. Remove the cloth from around the gun hammer, then make sure it's pulled back and locked into position."

"On the inside front, aye?"

Nicholas nodded, choosing to ignore the quiver in Flannery's voice. "Once that's done, pour plenty of gunpowder onto the pan and lower the frizzen. This isn't the time to be stingy nor tidy. Cover it good. You've got the extra powder?"

The question was unnecessary, but he threw it out there anyway. Sometimes confidence had to be touched to be felt.

Flannery patted the bulge at his hip, his hand shaky as a drunkard's. "Right here."

"Then all that's left is to take the string attached to the trigger and fasten it onto the lid. Make sure to close the cover nearly shut before you put the loop on the hook. Close it—gently—and wait, looking as if you're guarding a great treasure. Run toward the river as soon as you see the vermin coming for their payment. I'll meet you there with

Miss Payne. Got it?"

"Lock the hammer. Liberal powder. Lower frizzen. Hook the loop. Er. . .loop the hoop. I mean—"

Nicholas grabbed him by the shoulders, shoving his face inches from Flannery's. He knew that look—the glassy eyes, the pinched lips—and it didn't bode well. "Focus, man. You can do this."

Flannery sucked in a breath so big, his Adam's apple rode the current down. His eyes darted everywhere except to look straight at Nicholas. "I'm not so sure I'm cut out for this." The words were a ragged whisper.

Nicholas clenched his jaw. There was no way he could do this alone. "Flannery, I'm counting on you." He measured out each syllable, slow and dangerous, compelling the man to meet his gaze. *"Ni neart go cur le cheile."*

Though he'd butchered the brogue, apparently he'd pulled it off. The icy blue of Flannery's eyes thawed immediately.

"Ye've a bit o' the Irish in ye, eh?" Flannery's chin lifted, slight but noticeable. "But ye're right. There is no strength without unity, and to be sure, I won't let a brother down. Ye can count on me."

Nicholas released him and retreated a step, refraining from telling the man he was about as Irish as King George. "Then let's be about it. There's a damsel waiting to be saved, aye?"

A half smile quirked Flannery's mouth. "For the lady."

"For the lady, indeed." Nicholas wheeled about and retraced his route then turned left when he cleared the alley's mouth. The closer he drew to the warehouse door, the harder his heart thumped.

He knew exactly how Flannery felt.

Pausing before the thin piece of wood blocking him from Emily, he glanced heavenward. "Go before me, God. Nothing more. Nothing less."

Then he kicked open the door. The force vibrated up his leg, lifting half his mouth into a smirk. Even he needed confidence once in a while.

He entered what might've been a front room at one time. Two strides in, the cold metal of a gun muzzle pressed into the back of his head.

Excellent. At least he knew where the weapon was.

"Stop right there. Hands up, Mr. Payne."

So far, so good. They'd bought the grayed hair and painted-on wrinkles. *Thank You, Lord.*

With a smooth movement, he complied, cataloging information at breakneck speed. The click-drag-click of the hammer meant his skull hosted a breech-loaded flintlock. Judging by the angle and pressure, the man holding it was an inch or so shorter than himself, but his build more than made up for his height. His accent labeled him a Bristol boy, born and raised. The man's accomplice, the one patting his hands down each of Nicholas's legs, was a slighter fellow—but that didn't make him any less dangerous. And neither the news of Payne's death nor his bankruptcy had reached these scoundrels, for they thought him to be the man.

Behind him, the flare of a flint sparked a lantern into life, creating monstrous shadows. He was a meager David amid Goliaths.

"Follow the light, and don't try anything."

The muzzle shoved his head forward, emphasizing the gunman's words. The other man passed him, and Nicholas fell into step as directed.

A bead of sweat trickled down between his shoulder blades. It didn't matter how many times death handed him its calling card, the familiar physical reaction always sent a jolt through him.

They wound their way past a half wall of rotted shipping crates. The moldering stench triggered a tingle in his nose, and he fought to hold in a sneeze. Any quick movements would be a death warrant. If this was his night to die, so be it. But God help him, it had better not be Emily's.

He counted each step. Memorized every twist and turn. Most matched up to what Hope had told him. But not all—and his whole plan hinged on what the girl remembered of this particular warehouse.

They stopped near the back of the empty space. To his left, nothing but rotted floorboards and a broken-glassed window facing the alley where Flannery waited outside. If he listened hard enough, he just might hear the Irishman's ragged breaths. To his right, crates had been gathered and stacked into a wobbly tower. A rusty-wheeled excuse of a ladder leaned into it.

In front of him, a lantern's glow lit a profane halo above the bare-skinned skull of a third man, who stood with arms crossed. "You do not follow instructions very well, Mr. Payne. You disappoint Sombra. You disappoint me."

"Life's full of disappointments, Mister. . ." Nicholas drawled out the last word, fishing for the man's name. Unless the man lied, the name would be French, though the fellow had done an admirable job with a Southwark twang.

"Who I am is not important. Where is the money?"

"You think I can lug in five hundred pounds alone?" He rolled his shoulders and shot a pointed glare at his upraised arms. "I have a back condition, Mr. . . .Frenchie, for lack of a better name. And holding my hands up like this merely aggravates that condition, so if you don't mind. . ." He lowered his hands, measuring the calculation in Frenchie's stare. Though the movement brought him one step closer to disarming the fellow behind, he wasn't yet quite sure how he'd do it.

"Your back is the least of your concerns, Mr. Payne." The Frenchman widened his stance. "Where is the money?"

"Where is the girl? You think I'd hand over a small fortune to the likes of you without seeing her? I'd sooner trust ol' Prinny with my daughter." The question earned him more pressure from the muzzle. If the man pushed any harder, he'd die from a puncture wound instead of a bullet.

The Frenchman cocked his head like a vulture studying a carcass. "You will have the girl when I have the money."

"How do I know she's still alive? I want proof."

A smile rippled at the corners of the man's mouth. "You English. So predictable." Without varying his gaze, he ordered the man with the lantern. "See to it, Weaver."

Nicholas filed away the name. Weaver set the light on a nearby crate, disappeared behind another, then reappeared with a newspaper in hand. He extended it to Nicholas then stepped back.

Nicholas's breath caught in his throat. Emily's signature, shaky but familiar, was near the top of the *Times* header, next to the date—today's. He slid his gaze from the paper to the Frenchman. "This shows me she was alive earlier today. Doesn't mean she is now."

"You'll have to take my word for it."

"The word of a criminal?"

Frenchie unfolded his arms and advanced. Though his hands fisted at his sides, the fellow would not use them. With his thumbs tucked in, he'd break his bones in one swing. This was a man used to having his dirty work carried out by others. What kind of sway did he hold?

"You are in no position to bargain, Mr. Payne. Supply the money, or the girl is dead, and you as well." He stopped six paces away, far enough that should a shot go off, Nicholas's blood wouldn't sully his shirt.

Fie. This was not going as he'd hoped. He nodded toward the alley-side wall. "Look out the window. Your chest is there."

With a single snap of the Frenchman's fingers, Weaver strode the length of the empty space, taking care to step over missing planks. He didn't come at the glass straight on, but edged in sideways, like the snake he was. Smart move, though, in case a sharpshooter waited to pull a trigger. He peered into the darkness then swiveled his head back to Frenchie. A single tilt of his chin was his only response.

The Frenchman laughed—the jagged-edged kind that rang of doom instead of humor. "Did you really think leaving the money outside would assure you of your safety?"

"My man's been instructed that if I don't walk out that door with Emily, he's not to—"

"I'm afraid that's impossible. I said she was alive. I did not say she was here." The man's mouth curved upward like a scythe, his words every bit as sharp and cutting.

Nicholas sucked in a breath. "Where is she?"

"Barbados? America? Who can say?" He shrugged. "The captain did not apprise me of his route. I suppose that depends upon if he intends to keep her or sell her."

Every muscle in Nicholas's body hardened. He'd been duped, double-crossed—but not defeated. Not yet. Timing would be everything. He counted the steps needed to clear Frenchie, the inhales and exhales of the man behind him, and the pounding of his own heartbeat.

Then he smiled. "Thank you. Very helpful. Now, if you'll excuse me..."

He waited, watching for the ripple of disbelief across the Frenchman's face. There. The beginning of a sneer. Check. And the parting of the lips to issue a command to kill him.

Nicholas spun to the left, jerking up his arm. He snagged the gun muzzle under his armpit and thrust his other elbow forward with all the force he owned. Cartilage gave way. Bone cracked. So did a bullet. Fire burned the tender skin of his inner arm. Shouts echoed along with footsteps.

He shoved the man from him and wheeled about. Tearing past Frenchie, he sprinted for the back right corner of the warehouse.

Another bullet lifted the hair on the side of his head. Hope's information was the only barrier between him and his last breath—would to God that the girl was correct. Hard to tell when the lantern light didn't reach this far.

He leaped into the dark corner. Either he'd crash into the floorboards, making him nothing but target practice for the thugs on his heels, or he'd sail through a hole concealed by a burlap bag and disappear down a drainpipe.

Midair, the next shot bored into his flesh.

Ten paces one way. Ten the other. Years ago, Emily had seen a lion at the Tower of London's menagerie. Now she understood the animal's bizarre pacing behavior. Locked in Captain Daggett's quarters, she was every bit as caged—yet deprived of the roar that begged for release. Still gagged. Still bound at the wrists. The only things free were her feet and her mind.

So back and forth, one foot after the other, she slowly wore away the thin leather of her shoes, worrying, wondering, waiting. What was to become of her? A month ago she'd had her entire life planned out. The perfect marriage. The perfect husband. A fresh trickle of tears leaked down her cheeks. The only thing perfect now was the mess she was in.

And this time Nicholas wouldn't be getting her out of it.

At the wall, she stopped and rested her forehead against the wood paneling. Nicholas. Just thinking his name brought a small measure of comfort. The short time she'd spent with him hadn't been enough. Would never be enough. Above, the footsteps of sailors preparing for a dawn departure beat a steady cadence. Would she ever see her guardian again?

A sob rose in her throat. The gag cut it off. She'd never felt so alone in her life. Not when her mother died. Not when her father ignored her. Not all the times she'd clung to her little pug, trying to ease the ache in her heart.

Whirling, she flounced to the single chair in the room and sank. Deprived even of speech, she closed her eyes. *God, why? Why? I have nothing left to hope in. Not my father's provision, not a prosperous marriage match. Not even Nicholas. How will I survive? All I have is the dress on my back and You. Is that enough to live through this? Are You enough?*

"I am!" The words rumbled like the crack of an unexpected thunderstorm tearing from one end of the sky to the other.

Her eyes snapped open. A jolt of heat shot through her. Prickles raised gooseflesh on her arms. Had God seriously just answered her?

"And if you think I am not the sole reason you live and breathe," the voice continued.

She slid off the chair to her knees. *Yes, Lord. Yes, God. You are. You are!*

"Then I'll give you some time to think on it in the brig. Is that understood, Mr. Snelling?"

The door crashed open—but it wasn't God who entered. It was Satan.

Captain Daggett.

CHAPTER 31

Nicholas fell through the jaws of hell. Spikey edges ripped through fabric and flesh alike as he plummeted through the hole in the warehouse floor. It was a great escape route—for a small child. Not for shoulders like his. Splinters lanced into the gunshot wound in his upper arm. Darkness swallowed him and then spit him onto the mucky bank of the Thames. Pain stole most of his breath. Low tide's stench took the rest.

How had things gone so wrong?

Panting, he rolled to his knees and pressed his hand against the torn muscle on his arm. Warmth oozed through his fingers. Dizziness swirled in like an eddy.

And another pair of boots *thwunked* into the muck behind him.

He doubled over, giving the impression he'd been hurt badly, though the added moan was real enough.

Footsteps neared. Closer. Louder. He waited for the telltale whoosh of air, signaling the lift of a pistol handle to crack against his skull.

Then he twisted and sprang.

The heel of his hand thrust into the soft flesh of Weaver's throat. The man's windpipe gave. His head snapped back. He dropped like a drunk on a binge. If he lived, he'd never again hit the high notes of a bawdy song.

Sucking in air, Nicholas forced away the blackness creeping in at the edge of his vision, then turned and ran. Staggered, really. Sludge yanked his boots with every step. The incline of the bank wasn't steep, but that didn't make it any less treacherous. Slipping, he caught himself and pressed on until the mire stopped at a wall of rotted timbers—the barrier marking the alley's end.

The place where Flannery should have been crouched and waiting.

Dread knocked the wind from him an instant before an explosion thundered through his bones. A red flash desecrated the black sky. Both happened within the space of a breath.

Neither boded well.

Nicholas threw himself against the wall and hoisted himself upward, not caring who heard his deep grunt each time he grabbed for a handhold with his wounded arm. Clearing the top, he rolled over the edge, the fire in his arm burning well past his injury.

Gritting his teeth, he forced himself to his feet. The reek of burnt flesh added to the nausea building in his gut.

God. . .no.

Swiping the back of his hand across his mouth, he straightened. Onlookers emerged at the opposite end of the alley, creeping out like life-size cockroaches. Two bodies—or what remained of them—lay on the far side of what had been the rigged chest. The body nearest him sprawled facedown. One of his arms stretched out. Reaching. As if he'd tried to swim the current of the blast to safety. Remorse ran red through Nicholas's veins. . .the same color as the hair on the man lying dead still.

He sprinted and slid to a stop on his knees next to Flannery. Grabbing him by the shoulders, he carefully eased the man over. "Here now, come on. Flannery? Come on, man!"

Sharp bits of gravel pitted Flannery's brow. His eyes didn't open. His lips didn't part. A sour taste pooled at the back of Nicholas's throat. He never should have given such a dangerous task to an untried man.

"Flannery!" His ragged voice bounced from wall to wall.

Somewhere deep inside Flannery's rib cage, a low rumble started. Or was that merely because Nicholas wanted to hear it? To believe it? To not have to live with Flannery's death on his conscience? He bent closer.

Flannery spasmed. His hands shot up, grabbing handfuls of Nicholas's coat, and pulled him nose-to-nose. "Did we. . .did you. . ." His grasp slackened, thin as his voice. When his eyes rolled back, he let go completely.

Nicholas stared, horrified—until the rhythmic lift and fall of Flannery's grit-coated chest caught his eye. He was alive. For now. But how much longer?

Rising, Nicholas hated the choice set before him. He reeled to catch his footing. Should he hasten Flannery to a doctor and risk the possibility that Emily might set sail for God-knew-where? Or should he leave the man here and continue his search?

Rock. Hard place.

His decision was every bit as granite—cold and unyielding.

He cried out as he slung Flannery's limp form over his shoulder. Even so, the white-hot agony in his arm was nothing compared to the torture in his heart.

The instant the gag was cut from behind and pulled off, Emily whirled. Frightening as it was, facing danger head-on was better than a stab in the back. And with the captain's knuckles still wrapped around a knife hilt, that was a distinct possibility. Though doubtful, the way his eyes undressed her.

She retreated until her shoulder blades smacked against the farthest wall—not far, in this tiny cabin. Fear wrapped tight around her chest. Nonetheless, a crazy peace steadied her fingers as she ran them across her lips. God was here. She knew that now, not just in her head but in her heart. Slowly, she worked her jaw, surprised that it still moved at all.

Captain Daggett slipped the blade into a sheath at his waist and advanced. His body blocked the single escape route out the door. The only way around him was to hurdle the table laden with maps and measuring tools—or scramble across the bed.

His bed.

"You cur!" The words rubbed raw in her throat, sounding more like an animal's growl than a lady's. What he'd done to Wren, what Wren had done to her, the lick of his gaze fondling places that ought not be touched—all of it boiled up and spewed out. "You filthy cur!"

"Ugly words from such a pretty mouth." His words slurred together, and she felt a tremble to his touch as he ran his knuckle along her cheek. He stank of rum and salt and treachery.

She jerked her face aside. "Don't touch me."

"Ahh, but I've waited nearly a year for this."

His breath drifted over her skin, and she shivered. "Beast!"

"You have no idea."

"I have every idea!" She wrenched her gaze back to his. "You ruined my maid then turn your back on your child. You trade for me as if I'm nothing but a—"

"Child?" He staggered then braced a hand against the wall. "What are ye talking about? What child?"

"Your child!" She studied the tic at the corner of one eye. Was he daft as well as drunk and dangerous? "Wren carries your babe, Captain. She's an outcast because of it."

Her words whipped up a tempest. For one sober moment, emotions rippled across his face like waves on a storm-swept sea, too fast for her to navigate the thoughts running through his mind.

"A. . .a babe?" He staggered again, though he still held the wall.

Emily tensed. Was this some kind of ploy?

He lurched from the wall and shored himself against the table, his eyes searching her face. "Are ye certain?"

A fierce frown pulled at her sore mouth, completely unstoppable. The man was either a consummate actor—to what end she couldn't imagine—or he truly was clueless. "How can you be so surprised?"

"Impossible!" The denial draped years onto his frame. Deep lines creased his brow. He stomped to a cabinet door and retrieved an amber bottle.

As he pulled out the cork and tossed back his head for a drink, Emily edged sideways toward the door, careful with her light movement. Too fast and her chance for freedom might shatter, the opportunity thin as glass.

Five steps from freedom, his voice stopped her. "Where is she?"

Slowly, Emily rubbed the chafed skin at her wrists. Though Daggett hadn't been the one to tie her up, that didn't make him a saint. "Have you not done her enough harm?"

"Please." His voice bled like a bruise. By faith, he sounded as if he'd been the one wronged.

She kept her gaze locked on his while daring another step. "Perhaps you ought to explain yourself, Captain."

He lowered the bottle to his side, a long slow breath escaping his lips. His mouth barely moved when he spoke. "I was married once. 'Twas an abysmal match. I was young. Foolish. She was a real beauty, though. A widow. . ." His face hardened. "And a shrew."

He wrenched up his arm and threw the bottle. Glass exploded.

Emily flinched.

"The woman was a harpy! A hag!" Daggett's shout filled the small room. "She came with four extra mouths to feed. Four! Should that not have been enough? Should *I* not have been enough? Yet she wanted one more, one I couldn't afford. One I couldn't produce." His voice lowered until his last word was nothing but a whisper.

Emily watched transfixed as a shiny film covered his eyes. Did he even know she was still there? Maybe not, between his memories and the amount he'd drunk. She dared another step.

"She said the fault was in me. Me! That I wasn't man enough to sire. . ." He shook his head, and for a moment, his shoulders sagged.

When his face lifted to hers, she gasped. A shadow moved across his face. This was no charade. The captain's soul sailed in a sea of darkness. He knew what lay on the other side of pain so deep, so black that no amount of time could separate him from the hurt.

Her breathing hitched. Compassion was a strange friend, calling at the most inopportune time. But now was definitely not the moment to take tea with empathy. "I am sorry for what happened to you, Captain." She snuck another step closer to the open door, speaking as her skirt swished to cover the movement. "But that doesn't justify what you did to my maid."

His sigh could've filled the ocean. "I suppose it does not. But believe me when I say I had no idea there'd be lasting implications. I merely thought the one time, the one night—"

Emily's jaw dropped. "How can you think so lowly of a woman, to use her like that?"

"How can a woman think so lowly of a man, to scorn him in public, make him a laughingstock? Flaunt his impotence to the world!" He barreled toward her faster than she could flee. His fingers dug into her arms, pinning her in place. Anger sharpened the bones of his face. Grief mingled with the rum on his breath. "I never wanted to go a'sea, Miss Payne, but I didn't have a choice! Life on land was hell itself."

Her heart beat loud in her ears. His heavy breaths, all the louder. Everything hinged on this moment. Her future. Her freedom.

His salvation.

"You were wronged, sir," she began slowly, casting the words like a life preserver. "Wronged and damaged, through no fault of your own. So was Wren. And so am I. A wise man once told me no one escapes this life without scars. Not even God."

She paused, waiting for the slightest hint of a break in his stormy gaze. "Let me go, Captain. I am not the woman who hurt you."

His jaw tightened. Nothing more. His fingers still bit into her arms. Overhead, the thumping of sailors' feet readied to sail. She measured time by the vein pulsing on the captain's temple.

After an eternity, she tried again. "Don't add wrong to wrong. I'll see that you're paid back every penny you spent for me if you simply let me go."

A low laugh rumbled in his chest. Then he shoved her, wheeled about, and retrieved another bottle. While he uncorked it with his teeth, she resumed her slow trek to the door.

Daggett swilled half the contents on his way to the porthole, where he stooped and looked out at the inky darkness before dawn. The way the lamplight fell, he couldn't have seen anything other than his own reflection. Emily shuddered. Truly, was there anything more horrific than peering at one's own self?

The image of the broken Captain Daggett branded onto her heart. Even so, she took the opportunity to fly the remaining steps to the door. Would he notice if she slipped out?

Before she crossed the threshold, she turned back. An insane move, as were the words burning on her tongue, but altogether necessary. "I don't know if Wren will have you, Captain, but there's one thing I am certain of."

He didn't look at her. He didn't need to. She spoke as much to herself as to him. "A child needs a father's love. As long as you draw breath, it's not too late to make things right. Think on that."

He grunted then tipped the bottle one more time. Rum dripped down his chin, dampening his collar. Tilting back to drain it dry, he lost his balance and crashed backward. The captain sprawled out flat, his eyes rolled up.

Emily turned and ran into the narrow corridor then paused. Where exactly should she go? Portman Square? Nicholas's room? Neither was safe.

Undecided, she scurried ahead. First she'd have to clear the deck and the docks.

CHAPTER 32

Uncertainty—the only thing Nicholas despised more than waiting. He circled the doctor's small receiving chamber for the twentieth time in as many minutes, turning his back to the jeering clock on the wall. Why must life—and death—hang on the spindly arm of a timepiece? And honestly, how much death could one handle in the space of a day?

As soon as the door to the infirmary swung open, releasing the stinging odor of ammonia and vinegar, he pivoted. The fast action pumped a fresh flow of blood beneath the binding on his arm. The warmth, and pain, reminded him he ought be thankful his own body was not yet counted among the corpses of the past twenty-four hours.

He pinned his gaze and his hope on Dr. Kirby. "How's Flannery?"

Without his hat, tufts of white hair stood at attention above each of the doctor's ears, giving him a perpetually surprised look—and making it impossible to read the truth in the lines of his face. "Did I not tell you to remain seated, Mr. Brentwood?" His chin lifted, and he eyed the growing stain on Nicholas's sleeve. "Even from this distance I can see you disregarded that order the second I left the room. At least your man is a more compliant patient."

Nicholas sucked in a sharp breath. "So he lives?"

"Thus far." Kirby stepped aside, sweeping one arm toward the open door. "Which is more than I can say for you if you continue to stand there and bleed all over my floor. Let's get you patched up, shall we?"

He didn't need to be told twice. Nicholas strode past him, entered a familiar corridor, then turned right, crossing the threshold into a small surgery. Before Kirby's footsteps caught up to him, he tugged off what remained of his shirt and hopped up on the table at center, ignoring the discolored sawdust coating the floor. Practiced from warming this bench a time or two, he focused instead on a bottle-lined shelf.

Kirby snorted. "Someone's in a hurry."

He would have shrugged—but it would hurt. "Have at it."

Instruments rattled. A cork loosened. The fresh waft of alcohol competed with the mix of pungent odors permanently embedded in the pores of the walls.

Kirby's grip held Nicholas's injured arm aloft as he unwrapped the temporary bandage. Nicholas set his jaw against the fiery pain. The doctor's cold fingers did little to offset it.

"I assume you've made arrangements for your sister," Kirby mumbled as he worked.

Nicholas gasped, as much from the fresh reminder of Jenny's passing as from the insertion of a probe. The metal end dug around for a bullet, no less excruciating than the grief boring into his heart. He winced so hard, his eyes cinched tight, making it tough to form words. "Mistress Dawkins. . .is overseeing. . .the details."

"You have my condolences, Mr. Brentwood. Your sister was a rare one."

So was the new agony Kirby inflicted. The white-hot thrust and pull of the extractor blurred the individual bottles on the shelf into a smeared streak. This time, the bottles disappeared. Completely. A primeval growl roared out his mouth, and Nicholas gripped the table's edge with his free hand to keep from falling over. The doctor shored him up further with a steadying hand at his back.

"There now." Metal pinged against metal. "Care to see the beast that bit?"

"Just. Sew. Me up." Wheezes punctuated each word, but at least the glassware on the shelf reappeared.

"Your rough-and-tumble ways are going to catch up to you one day, Brentwood. Soon you'll be more scar than man." Kirby left his side to retrieve a silver tray from a counter.

Nicholas wobbled, missing the doctor's support—then recanted when Kirby returned. A needle dug into his arm. "Ahh!"

"Sorry. As I said, there's not much pristine skin here to work with, and tugging the suture through—"

"Don't explain. Just—" The needle stabbed again. Nicholas grunted. "Finish." His request traveled on a groan.

"Oh? Pressing engagement, have you?" The needle bit thrice more before Kirby's sigh and the snip of a scissor cut through the air.

After the doctor wrapped a fresh bandage over the site, Nicholas slid off the table. Two shelves materialized where the one had been, with double the amount of bottles. He threw a hand out for balance. Kirby was right. His lifestyle was catching up to him more quickly than he'd care to admit. Allowing the doctor to play valet, he eased his wounded arm into his ruined shirt and greatcoat.

Kirby did not miss his grimace. "I suggest you lay low for the day, Brentwood."

The doctor's counsel followed him into the corridor. He didn't have time to answer, let alone lay low.

Not until he upturned every dock from here to the North Sea.

Stepping out into the black before dawn, he set his feet toward the Wapping Dockyards. By the time he turned the corner of Newman Street, a faint sliver of gray lightened the eastern sky. When his boot heels left behind cobbles for wooden walkways, the promise of morning spread across the horizon.

He scowled, the stench of emptied bilge matching his foul mood. Already the vessel farthest down the line slipped its moorings and floated toward the sea—and this was only one of many wharves lining the busy riverway, representing a smattering of the ships already lost to him. If Emily were aboard one of those. . .no. Better to not even brook the thought.

Squaring his shoulders, he approached the first ship, noting any twitchy reactions from those aboard. He gauged the captain's responses to his questions through a filter of presumed guilt, all the while inhaling deeply. The slightest whiff of lily of the valley and he'd tear the vessel apart one-handed. He'd have to. The fire burning in his wounded arm rendered that limb useless.

But nothing seemed out of the ordinary, except for him. His battered appearance drew open stares. Undaunted, he moved on to the next ship—and the next—until he investigated each floating hulk, eyed every passing man, and stalked the length of the quay from one end to the other. Now fully unclothed in the sky, the sun taunted him. In a defiant move to prove it wrong, he fished around in his pocket and pulled out his pocket watch. Ten o'clock. Ten!

Terns screeched overhead, echoing the roar of frustration building in his throat. It would take him all day to scour the Greenland Docks then the East India's. There was no way he could do this alone.

His shoulders sank, the movement releasing a fresh burst of pain in his arm. He needed reinforcements, sleep, faith. . .a miracle. *God, please, just one.* Or more. He frowned. Once the magistrate heard of Flannery's fate, he'd be lucky were Ford to grant him even the lowliest grate cleaner to help him search for Emily. With the back of his hand, he scrubbed at the stubble on his face.

Better to not brook that thought, either.

Crossing to Newton Street, he hailed a hackney, and though he tried, a black cloud of malicious what-ifs and your-faults escorted him all the way across town. Admitting defeat never came easy—especially when it involved those he loved.

But at this point, he'd do anything, say anything, to get Emily back.

Sunlight warmed his face when his feet hit the cobbles in front of Number Four Bow Street. The shaggy blond-headed man leaning against the wall further lightened his spirits. Nicholas smiled for the first time in an eternity. Had anyone ever thought of Moore as a miracle? "You're a sight for sore eyes."

Officer Alexander Moore surveyed him from head to toe, frowning. "And you're a sight. About time you haul your lazy backside to the station. I do all the work for you, and then you've the nerve to keep me waiting."

Nicholas cocked his head, his gaze following Moore's hand as it disappeared inside his coat. He pulled out a leather wallet, and without a word, handed it over.

Shutting out the bustle of carriages and pedestrians, Nicholas honed all his attention onto the money case. A scrolled "P" was engraved on the front—the same crest adorning Payne's strongbox in his office. Judging by the thickness—or rather lack of it—he didn't bother opening the thing.

His gaze locked onto Moore's. "Where'd you find it?"

"Pried it out of the grip of a smuggler down Dover way. The money's long gone, but at least I know what happened to Mr. Payne. . .and it wasn't suicide." Moore shook his head. "Those that deal with brigands never meet with a good end."

"I expect you enacted justice?"

He flashed a grin. "Case closed."

Maybe for Payne, but not Emily. Nicholas's heart lurched. He tucked away the thought and the wallet. "Not quite. I need you to—"

"Tut, tut." Moore's hand shot up. "You should know by now, Brentwood, that I am always correct. I've got one more thing to deliver to you. Come along."

Before Nicholas could grab one of the many questions swirling in his head, Moore's broad shoulders vanished through the front door. By the time he entered the foyer, Moore was halfway up the stairwell, a question of his own spiraling down.

"Were you missing something? Or should I say. . .someone?"

The words stole his breath. His heart—dear God—was it even still beating? Nicholas took the stairs two at a time, nearly crashing into Moore's back at the landing.

Moore stopped in front of the magistrate's public receiving room and turned to him. "It's fortunate the lady encountered me before Ford. He doesn't know about your loose grip on your sleeping beauty, and with the humor he's in today, it might be better if he didn't."

"I owe you." Though Nicholas tried to conceal it, emotion thickened his voice.

Moore smirked. "That you do." Then he pivoted and called over his shoulder as he strode down the corridor. "And Brentwood, I've enough work of my own to care for. Don't lose her again."

"I don't intend to." He grasped the doorknob as firmly as his resolve. "Ever."

A deep voice hung in the thin space between waking and sleeping, balancing on the edge. One false move and the smooth tones might shatter into a thousand pieces. Too many to sweep. Too small to piece together. Emily shifted her head on the settee's pillow—carefully—unwilling that the slightest jostle might fully awaken her. Of all the fitful dreams she'd suffered throughout the last few hours, this one was by far the sweetest.

The jiggle of the doorknob ended that aspiration. Her eyes sprung open, and she pushed up to sit. Officer Moore had encouraged her to rest, but that didn't mean she ought be caught lounging like a slackard.

When the door swung wide, for the briefest of moments she wondered if a heart could explode. Hers pulsed in her temples, her wrists, her knees.

Her guardian stood framed in the doorway. Stillness surrounded him, or was that her breath that stopped? His hair was coated with a fine layer of gray ash. Soot and sweat and fear smeared across his brow. The heat of his gaze spread a wildfire of emotions through her veins.

He stepped forward, filling the room with his presence, banishing all the darkness and terror of the last month. "Emily."

She launched from the settee and ran into his arms. "Nicholas!"

He pulled her close, wrapping his strong arms around her, and pressed a kiss to the crown of her head. "Thank God."

She nuzzled into his chest, breathing deeply. He smelled a musky combination of blood and safety. Always the paradox, this man. Was it his wild unpredictability that drew her or the home her heart had found in his arms? She grabbed handfuls of his coat and held on, burrowing into him. For now she memorized the contour of the muscles beneath his shirt and the feel of his stubbly cheek rubbing against her hair.

"You'll be the death of me, you know?" His voice rumbled in her ear.

"I was so frightened." Tears garbled her words. She closed her eyes, surrendering to the relief leaking down her cheeks, dampening his shirt, washing them both.

"You're safe, now. Hear me?" He pulled back and tipped her face to his. The rough pad of his thumb traced along her chin. "Safe, now and always, for I'll not leave your side ever again."

Pulling back farther, he slid to one knee. His green eyes blazed with a passion so pure, so candid, she shivered.

"This is hardly the time or place, but the past twenty-four hours have taught me nothing is certain, not even the best-laid plans." His voice cracked, and he reached for her hand. He pressed a kiss into her palm before continuing. "You have stolen my heart, Emily Payne, a crime for which justice must be served. And so I ask. . .will you have me?"

Yes, without a doubt, was on the tip of her tongue, but "You're hurt!" flew past her lips. She dropped to his level, her heart breaking at the stained, torn fabric on his arm. Why had she not noticed that first? "Are you all right?"

"I might be." With a gentle nudge, he tilted her face back to his. "If you would but answer my question."

She lifted her hand to his cheek, smoothing back lines of worry etched from years of care. All her dreams and hopes and plans were here, wrapped in the guise of a tattered, scruffy lawman. "I would have no other."

His lips came down on hers, soft as moonlight, hotter than the sun. He tasted of cloves and mystery and sweet, sweet promise. She leaned into him, heedless now of his injury. A tremor shook through him—no. That quivery feeling was inside her. Deep. Low. She ran her hands up his back, feeling desire ripple along each smooth muscle. Unless he held her in place, she'd fall and never, ever be found again.

He groaned and pulled her closer, his lips forming her name against her mouth, her jaw, her neck. The warmth of his breath brushed a shiver along the curve of her collarbone. A crazy rushing sounded in her ears, heady, swirling, entirely intoxicating.

And a sobering voice boomed from the door. "This is not a brothel, Brentwood."

CHAPTER 33

Nicholas shot to his feet, pulling Emily up with him. The magistrate's face was granite. His mouth soured into a scowl that prickled over Nicholas's scalp and crept down his spine. Of all the inopportune moments for the man to enter, he had to choose this one?

Emily huddled at his back. Her trembling filtered through the fabric of his coat—and he didn't blame her one bit. He widened his stance. "I can explain, sir."

Ford's mouth flattened. Was he biting back words or too busy formulating a censure? The magistrate closed the door and advanced across the carpet, bypassing Nicholas without a glance. From the bank of windows, daylight collected atop his shoulders. He pulled it with him as he went, leaving a distinct chill in his wake.

"Pleased to meet you at long last, Miss Payne. I am Magistrate Ford." He bowed his head then offered his arm. "Allow me to escort you to a seat. Brentwood's explanations are entertaining and somewhat long-winded. And judging by the looks of him," he arched one brow at Nicholas, "this one promises to excel on both accounts."

Emily's wide eyes stared into his own, and he nodded his assurance—a confidence he searched for in every nook of his own soul. None was found. As Ford led Emily to one of the settees in an L-shaped arrangement near the hearth, Nicholas made haste to the other. The sooner this confrontation was over, the better.

Ford's "uh-uh-uh" stopped him. "Remain center stage, Mr.

Brentwood. I promised the lady a show, and you will deliver." Flipping out his coattail, the magistrate sank next to Emily then pierced him with a glower. "Start talking."

Nicholas shored himself against the mantel, grateful for the solid brick against his back. His thoughts of how to begin were nothing but vapor. Perhaps the end would work best, leastwise for Emily's sake. "What you witnessed as you walked in, sir, is no stain against the lady's character. I intend our banns be read beginning this Sunday, and in three weeks' time, I would that you officiate at our marriage ceremony."

If the magistrate had been wearing his judicial wig, his brows would've lifted it a full inch from his scalp. "You've outdone yourself this time, Brentwood. Very entertaining!" He slanted a sideways glance at Emily. "Not that he isn't a noble enough prospect, but are you entirely certain about matrimony to this man, Miss Payne?"

A slow smile brightened her face, and though she spoke to the magistrate, she locked her gaze with his. Joy sparkled there—unabashed and sincere. "I'm afraid I have learned to think things through the hard way, Mr. Ford, and while I appreciate your concern, my conclusion is that my best, my dearest, my *only* choice is indeed Nicholas Brentwood."

His name on her lips was as sweet as her kiss, but as Ford turned his frown toward him, he shoved down the memory and stored it away for later. Careful to erase any emotion from his face, he straightened his shoulders.

Ford quirked a brow. "I don't believe charming the lady into oblivion was part of the original guardianship arrangement. Nothing to be done for that now, I suppose. There are a few loose ends, however, that ought be tied up before you two embark on the marital journey. What of Miss Payne's father?" He held up a hand, staying an answer, and turned toward Emily. "I know I promised you a show, my dear, but if you find the topic too sensitive, Brentwood and I can take this into my office."

She lifted her chin. "Thank you, but no. I wish to stay."

"A woman who knows her own mind, eh?" Ford cocked his head back at Nicholas. "She will suit you, I think. Go on with your tale—and this time start from the beginning instead of the end."

The old man didn't miss a trick. A good trait in one who warmed the judgment bench. Nicholas ran his hand through his hair. Ash and soot rained down. "The evening I began my employ at Portman Square, Mr. Payne departed to the Wapping Wharf, his wallet padded with what remained of his fortune and that of his partner, Mr. Reginald Sedgewick. Because of the passing of the recent ban on slavery, they were at odds as to which direction the business should go. Sedgewick favored tobacco and cotton. Payne, something a little more lucrative."

Ford leaned forward. "Such as?"

"Smuggling. Payne needed a large sum of money and fast. Unbeknownst to Sedgewick, he'd gambled their business into quite the precarious position. So Payne took all of what they had and cut a deal with a Spanish smuggling ring led by a man known only as Sombra."

"The Shadow. I've heard of him." Ford stroked his chin. "He's a villain, with quite the grudge against the East India Company. There are rumblings, according to Officer Moore, that the man's intent is to undercut then monopolize the saltpeter and opium trades."

Nicholas nodded. Like colored bits of glass in a kaleidoscope, all the details he'd collected over the past month rotated into a single stunning picture in his mind. He stepped from the hearth and began pacing the length of it, his steps matching the swiftness of his words. "Fearing Sedgewick's reaction to the theft, not to mention the American captain who wanted to be paid for his delivery of tobacco, Payne hired me to see to Emily's well-being until his return. He never guessed that other brigands might get to him first, steal his money, then hang him. . .yet that's exactly what happened."

He lengthened his stride, envisioning a dark-skinned Spaniard waiting for Payne. Lifting his good arm, Nicholas ran light fingers over a ridged scar on the back of his neck. He knew better than anyone what kind of a mistake Emily's father had inadvertently made. "Payne never made his appointed meeting with Sombra—and one should *never* keep a Spaniard waiting. In retaliation, Sombra sent out his watchdog, Ambrose de Villet, to collect the promised amount then kill Payne for standing him up."

"But de Villet had no idea Payne was already dead." Ford grunted. "Interesting."

At the mention of her father's death, Nicholas stopped in front of Emily, searching for a quivering lip or any other kind of reaction. This turn of conversation might be more than she bargained for, yet she remained expressionless, giving no hint she wished to flee.

Ford must've noticed his blunder, for he reached over and patted her hand. "Sorry, my dear. I'm afraid my blunt ways are somewhat ingrained."

"A Bow Street trait, I assume, for I have often noted Nicholas's directness." Her brown gaze lifted to his. "Have I not?"

"Frequently." The smile they shared burned through him from head to toe, so warm, so intimate, a flush rose on her cheeks, and he was glad for the stubble darkening his.

Ford cleared his throat.

Nicholas resumed his pacing—it was either that or a cold bath. "You are correct, sir, that neither Sombra nor de Villet had any inkling Payne had been murdered. Quite the contrary. Because I rarely left Emily's side, de Villet thought I was the man. But here's the twist."

He paused and faced the settee. Both the magistrate and Emily pinned their gaze on him. "All that explains Payne's connection to Sombra and de Villet, but I suspect that when Payne first contacted Sombra, he used his partner's name, Reginald Sedgewick."

Ford cocked his head. "Why the deuce would he do that?"

"With Payne's gambling debts so widely known, he wouldn't have risked Sombra finding out his net worth wasn't quite what he purported it to be. That would explain why de Villet first went to Sedgewick's home for collection. I believe Sedgewick and de Villet found out together about Payne's dubious dealings."

The magistrate shook his head. "That must have been quite the conversation."

"Yes, and de Villet couldn't let Sedgewick live with that much information, so he killed him." Once more he studied Emily's face for signs of grief or remaining horror from that terrible night. Her lips pressed tight, and he waited for her slight nod before he began again.

"When de Villet paid a visit to the Payne household, only Emily was home. He made his threat quite clear—and if nothing else, he is a man of his word. Or was, rather. At any rate, he abducted Emily, held her for ransom, then sold her off while waiting for me to bring his chest full of money, which would have doubled his profits. He'd pay off Sombra and keep the rest for himself. My payment, however, was a little more than he bargained for."

Ford lifted a hand. "Hence your appearance."

"About that." A ragged sigh rippled up from his lungs. The faded green walls of the room closed in on him, the exact color of the guilt squeezing his chest. He rolled his shoulders, wishing the words he had to say might as easily flow. "Flannery didn't fare so well, sir. I never should have given him such a dangerous task. If only I'd devised a better plan. Something safer. His life hangs in the balance because of me."

"Pish!" Ford's stern tone stopped him cold. "Stop flogging yourself, man. Flannery knew the risks involved. Such is the life of an officer. Better he know that up front than find out after a commissioning. I expect nothing more nor less than you see to him and keep me posted."

Of course Ford was right. Nicholas knew it in his head—but his heart would have none of it. Gritting his teeth, he methodically ground the remaining guilt into a thick paste and swallowed it. "Yes, sir."

"Very well. You rescued the fair maiden, and so I find you, a little worse for the wear, eh?"

"Not quite." Nicholas turned his gaze to Emily. "How did you end up here at the station?"

Two pairs of eyes focused on Emily. A bug beneath a magnifying glass couldn't have been more exposed. Shifting on the settee, she ran both hands along her skirt, hoping to coax out enough information without having to go into great detail. "I don't have Nicholas's flair for story telling." Ignoring his snort, she continued. "Suffice it to say de Villet sold me to a captain with whom I'd had previous dealings. After a lengthy conversation, he let me go."

"Let you go?" The magistrate's brows bounced upward. "You must be quite the conversationalist."

"Persuasiveness is one of Miss Payne's hallmarks." Nicholas crossed from the hearth to stand before her, offering both hands. When his fingers wrapped around hers, warmth shot up her arms.

He pulled her to her feet, the green of his eyes deepening to a storm-tossed sea. "Forgive me for not asking immediately, such was my relief at finding you here. Are you all right? The captain didn't hurt you, did he?"

"I am fine."

The worry puckering his brow hinted he wanted to know everything—and the thought of reliving the awful situation here and now added a whole new depth to her exhaustion. Her lips curved into a smile she didn't feel, and she gave his hands a light squeeze. "The captain was too far into his cups to have hurt me, so truly, I am fine, though I should like to go home now. It's been a long night."

For an unguarded moment, his shoulders sank, and an unexplained sadness pulled at the lines near his mouth. Then it was gone. Just like that. Leaving her to wonder if she'd seen the breach of emotion or not.

Dropping her hands, Nicholas turned to the magistrate. "The lady speaks truth. It has been a very long night indeed. If you are satisfied, sir, may we take our leave?"

Ford rose, tugging loose the neck cloth at his throat. "Your long night was nothing compared to that courtroom full of reprobates downstairs. But yes, I think we can officially say this case is closed, though I assume you'll help the future Mrs. Brentwood settle her father's estate?"

Nicholas nodded. "Yes, sir."

"I suppose you'll be wanting some time off as well?"

Emily held her breath. How Nicholas answered might very well be a clue as to where she lined up in his queue of priorities. Would he choose his job over her?

He leveled his gaze at her yet spoke to Ford. "If you don't mind."

"And if I do?"

Nicholas shrugged, and she breathed in all the love she read in the lines of his face.

"Bah." Ford shook his head and turned to her. "For all his rough edges, Nicholas Brentwood is a good man. If he cares for you half as much as his sister, you will be well tended indeed."

Behind him, Nicholas stiffened at the mention of his sister. An almost imperceptible movement in anyone else, but one she now recognized as a serious sign of something important. Something bad. A monster swam beneath his cool exterior, and her own stomach tightened in response.

". . .wish you all the best, my dear."

She snapped her gaze back to the magistrate. How much of what he'd said had she missed? Playing it safe, she flashed him a smile and defaulted to a polite, "Thank you."

"Good day to you both." The magistrate strode from the room.

As soon as Ford's coattails disappeared out the door, she turned to Nicholas. "What's wrong? It's about Jenny, isn't it? I know it. What's happened?"

A halfhearted smirk lifted his lips. "Perhaps you ought think about becoming a Bow Street officer."

His attempt to lighten the heaviness filling the room fell flat. Dread of what he might be covering up squeezed her chest, making it hard to breathe. She reached for him, resting a light touch on his sleeve. "Nicholas, do not dodge the question."

He shook his head, looking older, worn, beaten. She could only imagine all the death he'd seen in his lifetime, more than any human should be asked to bear, but this. . . Her throat clogged.

Oh God, please, not his sister. Not Jenny.

"There was none sweeter than Jen." His voice broke on his sister's name, crushing her heart with the sound.

Tears pooled in her eyes. A few slipped free and slid down her cheeks, landing on her lips. The salt tasted like bitter loss. "I am so sorry."

"As am I." He pivoted and strode to the window, each step carrying him farther away, the space between them an eternity. How to reach him, to console, to comfort? All her years of mourning the lack of love from her father paled in comparison to the heavy weight bending Nicholas's head. She stood in place, clutching handfuls of her skirt, unable to grasp the full nature of his pain.

"I am an officer, Emily." He stared out the window, his voice husky. "There's no guarantee you won't have to shoulder a grief like the one I now bear should I meet as untimely a death as my sister." When at last he turned toward her, the intensity of his gaze weakened her knees. She grabbed the back of the settee for support.

"I won't hold it against you should you decide to change your mind." His face was a mask, as if the real Nicholas had departed and nothing but a shell remained. "I once advised you to think carefully before running headlong into a marriage, and so I do now. Are you certain I am the man for you?"

Was he? This demanding, rugged, by-no-means-wealthy man who'd barged into her life and taken over her world? She walked over to him, aware that her decision would mark them both to their dying day. Reaching for his hand, she lifted his knuckles, bruised and battered, to her lips. He flinched—or was that a tremor?

"My best." She moved her mouth to the next knuckle, speaking against his skin. "My dearest." She kissed another. "My only choice." She lifted his palm to her cheek, all callouses and strength, and leaned into it. "Is you."

Her name was a whisper, wrapping as tightly around her as his arms. It was a distinct possibility this man's days would be cut short on London's streets. But for now, she nuzzled into his chest. It had taken a long time for love to come her way, and she intended to memorize every beat of Nicholas Brentwood's heart.

CHAPTER 34

Descending from the hackney, Nicholas reached into his pocket and flipped the driver a coin before both his boots hit the cobbles. Then he fished around once more to retrieve his watch. Not that he needed to. The morning sun peeking over Dr. Kirby's rooftop said it all.

He was late.

The minute hand stood at attention, which should have indicted him all the more. Instead, a bittersweet smile curved his mouth. The golden needle on the watch face pointed straight up at Adelina's portrait—leastwise, what had been. Nothing but a ghostly collection of watery lines remained of her sweet face. He rubbed his thumb over her memory one last time, breathed out his final regrets, then released at last what could never be undone.

With his nail, he pried out the worn parchment. Holding it up to a gust of wind banking in from Bowler Street, he whispered, "Good-bye," and let her go. Adelina hovered for a moment, caught between earth and sky. He watched, mesmerized. How well he knew that feeling, the in-between and not yet. She spiraled once, twice, then rode a swift up-current toward heaven.

Nicholas turned from the sight. His own heaven on earth waited for him at Portman Square, packed and ready to go. The sooner he finished this errand, the better.

Ahead, Dr. Kirby emerged from his shop, bag in hand and hat on head. He pulled shut the door then stopped, wide-eyed. "Well, well,

Brentwood. Aren't you the dapper fellow today."

"More like uncomfortable." Nicholas tugged at his cravat. He'd rather go hand-to-hand with a back-lane thief than choke and swelter in a suit. Thanks be to God, he'd only have to go through this once.

Kirby snorted. "I've seen you slit-eyed, bled out, and unconscious, and yet you always spring back. Surely a little culture won't hold you down."

"At least not for long, if I have anything to say about it." He nodded toward the doctor's bag. "I see you're leaving. Mind if I step in and check on Flannery?"

Kirby shook his head. "Too late, I'm afraid."

Nicholas sucked in a breath. The doctor's blunt statement rattled through him as chill as the next gust of wind. *Oh God, not Flannery.* He'd seen the Irishman only two days ago. Noticed the first sprouts of new eyebrows growing back. The angry burnt skin on his neck and cheek had cooled into a waxy red patch, and he'd claimed it didn't hurt so much. How could he be gone, just like that? So quickly?

He worked his jaw, forcing words past the tightness in his throat. "Was he. . .did he. . .suffer much?"

"Pah!" Kirby's mouth pulled downward. "The only one suffering around here was me. Ever since I unwrapped Flannery's face and freed his lips, it was all 'oh for the bonny green isle' and tales of his mother's cooking. I couldn't stomach it anymore, so I let him go home yesterday. I'm about to check on him, though. Care to come along—say. . .you feeling a'right?" The doctor paused, narrowing his eyes. "You look a bit pale, though admittedly I've never seen you without bruises or blood coloring your face."

"I'm fine, or rather I was until you scared the life out of me." He straightened his cuffs then nailed Kirby with a glower. "Your bedside manner, Doctor, is lacking."

"Yes, so you frequently tell me." The next windy draft knocked Kirby's hat to a rakish tilt. With a swipe of his free hand, he straightened it then stepped away from the shop. "I'm off. You coming?"

Nicholas shook his head. "Just give Flannery my regards, would you? I. . .uh. . .have a more pressing engagement that I ought not miss." He scrubbed his neck, hoping the doctor would not detect the rising heat burning a trail clear up to his ears.

"Oh? Yet another of your famous pressing engagements, eh?" Kirby's gaze assessed him. "Yet it appears this one is of another nature from your usual. Well, I shan't be back until this afternoon, though from the looks of it, I doubt this engagement involves any fisticuffs."

Nicholas grinned as he watched the doctor set his long legs into motion. Somehow, Kirby had guessed—or come close to a correct conclusion about—what Nicholas would be doing this day. Did love show on a man's face? Even one trained not to tip off his emotions?

But the good doctor was right. He wouldn't need Kirby for bandaging or stitches. Fatigue, maybe, for he intended to show Emily just how much he loved her—and that would take a very long time.

Nibbling on her fingernail, Emily narrowed her eyes at the image in the mirror, blurring her focus to see more clearly the outline of her shape. Mary had worked hard the past few weeks to refashion this gown into a wedding dress, but the maid was no skilled seamstress. White silk poofed out a little too much at the waist, and. . .wait a minute. Emily turned, cocked her head, and yes. Just as she suspected. The fabric behind billowed out in a most unbecoming way.

She spun to Mary, the quick movement attracting her pug. Alf scampered over with a yip, and she bent and wagged her finger. "Do not even consider it, little prince."

He parked his chubby little body at her feet and tilted his head at a sharp angle. One eyebrow rose then the other, back and forth until she couldn't help but smile. "Scamp!"

Straightening, she pointed to the dressing table, heaped with ribbons and lace. "Mary, could you bring over the blue satin? I think it will be just the thing."

Her maid retrieved the shimmery trimming and pursed her lips. "I like the idea of a splash of color, but where exactly would you like it?"

She pressed the poof against her rib cage, flattening the fabric into place. "Tie it as a sash, and make sure to catch up the extra bit of fabric behind me."

"Ahh, good idea, miss." Mary smoothed the ribbon into place then scooted behind her to tie a bow. "I'd like to thank you again for recommending me to Miss Grayson, though I daresay you'll miss having a maid."

"Did I not tell you?" She quirked a glance over her shoulder. "Mr. Brentwood has secured a wonderful new assistant for me."

"Oh?" The maid's tone pinched as tight as the ribbon she knotted.

"Chin up, Mary. You know I'd keep you if I were able, but an officer's salary doesn't stretch very far." In spite of herself, Emily smiled. Trifling over expenses would indeed be a challenge—one she'd forget about every night when Nicholas held her in his arms. "My new maid is nine years old, a sweet young thing he rescued off the streets. In time, Hope will become proficient, but until then, you're right. . .I shall feel your loss."

"You're very kind, miss."

A rap on the door and a yip from Alf ended the conversation. Mrs. Hunt peeked in, frightening the pug into the corner. "There's a gentleman downstairs to see you, miss."

Emily sprinted, heedless of the impropriety and Mary's complaints. Why care if a bow was looped to perfection when green eyes and broad shoulders waited for her in the sitting room? Shoving past Mrs. Hunt, she flew down the stairs and raced across the foyer, not slowing until she dashed through the door.

Then she froze.

Broad shoulders met her, all right, along with a barrel chest and cinder-grey eyes. Captain Daggett stood stiff as a ramrod, his hat clutched in front of him with white knuckles. "Good day, Miss Payne. I wasn't quite sure if you'd see me."

"Well, I—" she bit the inside of her cheek, holding back the *had I known it was you, I'd have turned you away.* At the very least, she should call for John or Mrs. Hunt, for this rogue was not to be trusted. She opened her mouth, then paused. Where was her fear? Pounding heart? Why did his presence not instill any trepidation?

On second look, his shoulders sagged. The usual hard set to his mouth softened with humility. Even the haughty gleam in his gaze was gone. For the most part, the outside trappings of the man were the same, but something was different on the inside.

Taking a deep breath, she searched for the right words. "Good day, Captain. Excuse me if I seem a bit surprised at your visit."

He cleared his throat, looking for all the world like a man about to face the gallows. "Rightfully so. I merely came for. . .what I mean to say is. . ."

The bill of his hat crumpled into a tight wad beneath his fingers. Morning sun from the window highlighted a fine sheen on his brow. If she didn't know better, she'd swear the man was every bit as broken beyond repair as his hat.

A small ember of empathy sparked in a dark corner of her heart. "Go on."

His chest swelled and ebbed with a sigh. "What you said in my cabin, that it's never too late to make things right, well. . .I took that to heart. By God's grace, I am a changed man. I wish to make things right with Miss Hunt and. . ." His gaze darted from door to ceiling and finally to hers. "I acknowledge I have no right whatsoever, and in truth expect to be turned down on all accounts, yet I feel compelled to ask. May I speak with your maid, Miss Payne? Fully in your presence or anyone else's, of course. I should not like to frighten her, or hurt her any worse than I already have."

Emily pressed her lips tight to keep her jaw from dropping. Was he serious?

"Wren is no longer my maid, Captain. She lost her employment when it was found she was with child." She cast the words slowly, watching for his reaction as they sank in.

Emotions rippled across his face, one chasing another. His hat, or what remained of the mangled bit of banded felt, dropped to the carpet. "Please, I. . ." He fumbled inside his greatcoat and pulled out an envelope, offering it over to her. "I know I shall never be able to compensate for what I've done, yet I wish to make some kind of amends. If nothing else, I would like to support the child and its mother. Would you see that she gets this?"

The envelope weighed heavy in her hand, padded thickly with what felt like a small fortune. "I would be happy to, Captain."

"Thank you for your time, Miss Payne. You have been more than generous with me." He swept up his cap and strode past her. "Good day."

She stood there a moment, hardly believing what had just happened, then crossed to the curio desk to tuck away the envelope. What a strange and wonderful oddity. Wren would want for nothing, leastwise financially.

Out in the foyer, the click of the front door closed, then clicked open again. What more could the captain possibly have to say? When she turned, her heart caught in her throat. The long lines of Nicholas Brentwood's body filled the doorway. His dark hair was combed back, his face clean-shaven and smooth. Sunlight brushed along the strong cut of his jaw. His white silk cravat stood out in stark contrast to his midnight-blue tailcoat. Matching breeches rode the curve of his thighs.

"I came to escort my bride to her wedding." He lifted his chin, pinning her in place with his green gaze. The space between them charged with desire and promise. "Have you seen her?"

She crossed the room in a heartbeat and thumped her finger into his chest with each of her words. "You, sir, are a rogue."

"And you, miss"—his voice softened—"are beautiful."

She tilted her face toward his, and when his lips came down, she raised to her toes. Closing her eyes, she surrendered to the urgency of his kiss and the strength in his embrace. His mouth moved along the arch of her neck to the hollow of her throat. The sweet sensation radiated through her, stealing her breath, her thoughts, her heart. He tasted of distant horizons—altogether consuming and far too heady.

He groaned and loosened his hold, setting her at arm's length. "No more." His husky tone shivered through her. "Not until I can finish the job." His eyes glimmered with the knowledge of what lay beyond, after the ceremony, when vows were committed to action.

The heat in his gaze sent a tremor up her arms and down her back, settling in her legs and turning her knees to jelly. She swallowed, praying to keep her quivers from warbling her voice. "Then we'd best be about it."

A slow grin slid across his face. Capturing her hand, he tucked her fingers into the crook of his arm. Steely muscles moved beneath the fabric. "So, I was correct about your grand designs all along, was I not?"

Her nose scrunched up, and she was glad he reached for the door instead of noticing her likely resemblance to her pug. "Whatever do you mean?"

Pausing, he turned to her. "The first morning we took breakfast together, you all but admitted your goal for the season was to garner yourself a husband."

Fire spread across her face. Had she really been that shallow?

"Don't be embarrassed, my love." He bent and pressed a kiss against her brow. "For indeed, that is exactly what you have done."

AUTHOR'S NOTE

Who Were the Bow Street Runners?

Traditionally, every male householder in London was expected to police the streets in their neighborhood, and every citizen was to report anyone they witnessed committing a crime. This changed in the eighteenth century because of increasing concerns about the threat of dangerous criminals who were attracted by the growing wealth of London's middle class.

Prompted by a postwar crime wave in 1749, Magistrate Henry Fielding (who himself was a playwright and novelist) hired a small group of men to locate and arrest serious offenders. He operated out of Number Four Bow Street, hence the name "Bow Street Runners."

Fielding petitioned the government and received funding, but even so, he soon ran out of money to pay these men a worthy salary. Still, the runners were committed to justice, so they took on odd jobs such as watchmen or detectives for hire or even—as in the case of Nicholas Brentwood—guarding people or treasures.

What attracted my interest as an author was an old newspaper advertisement put out by Fielding. It encouraged the public to send a note to Bow Street as soon as any serious crime occurred so that "*a set of brave fellows could immediately be dispatched in pursuit of the villains.*" I wondered about those "brave fellows" and what kind of villains they might come up against, and thus was born Nicholas Brentwood.

Despite Bow Street's efforts, most Londoners were opposed to the development of an organized police force. The English tradition of local government was deeply ingrained, and they feared the loss of individual liberty. So, as gallant as the runners were in tracking down criminals, the general public did not always view them in a positive light. Even the nickname given them by the public—Bow Street Runners—was considered derogatory and was a title the officers never used to refer to themselves.

Bow Street eventually gave way to the Metropolitan Police, and by 1839, the runners were completely disbanded.

Interested in further reading? Here are a few of my favorite resources:

Beattie, J. M. *The First English Detectives: The Bow Street Runners and the Policing of London, 1750–1840.* Oxford: Oxford University Press, 2012.

Cox, David J. *A Certain Share of Low Cunning: A History of the Bow Street Runners, 1792–1839.* New York, London: Routledge, 2012.

Hale, Don. *Legal History: Bow Street Runners, Scotland Yard & Victorian Crime.* Coast & Country, 2013. Kindle edition.

THE INNKEEPER'S DAUGHTER

Dedication

Jennifer Pérez Díaz, a beautiful friend and aspiring writer, and to all the other hopeful novelists out there yearning to be published. Keep writing—your day will come.

And as always, to the Keeper of my soul. I shall keep believing—for my day will come, as it will for us all.

CHAPTER ONE

Dover, England, 1808

Numbers would be the death of Johanna Langley.

Three hours of sleep after a night of endless—or more like hopeless—bookkeeping. Two days to pay the miller before he cut off their flour supply. And only one week remained until the Blue Hedge Inn would be forced to close its doors forever.

Numbers, indeed. Horrid little things.

A frown etched deep into Johanna's face as she descended the last stair into the taproom. Stifling a yawn, she scanned the inn's public room, counting on collaring their lone boarder, Lucius Nutbrown. His payment would at least stave off the miller. Six empty tables and twelve unoccupied benches stared back. Must all the odds be stacked against her?

To her right, through the kitchen door, an ear-shattering crash assaulted the silence, followed by a mournful "Oh no!"

Johanna dashed toward the sound, heart pounding. *Dear God, not another accident!*

She sailed through the door and skidded to a stop just before her skirt hem swished into a pool of navy beans and water. Across from her, Mam eyed the flagstone floor, one hand pressed against her mouth, the other holding the table edge.

Johanna sidestepped the mess. "You all right, Mam?"

Smoothing her palms along her apron, her mother nodded. "Aye.

That crock were a mite heavier than I credited."

"As long as you're not hurt. You're not, are you?" She studied her mother's face for a giveaway twitch in her poor eye. Unlike her father—God rest his soul—her mother would make a lacking card shark.

"I'm fine. Truly." A weak smile lifted the right side of Mam's mouth.

With no accompanying twitch.

Johanna let out a breath and grabbed a broom from the corner. First, she'd tackle scooping up the beans and earthenware shards, then mop the water.

"Where is Cook?" Johanna asked while she worked. "Why did you not let her carry such a load?"

"Ana's gone, child. I let her go this morning."

The words were as vexing a sound as the bits of stoneware scraping across the floor. Though her mother's declaration was not a surprise, that didn't make it any easier to accept. A sigh welled in her throat. She swept it down with as much force as she wielded on the broom. Sighing, wishing, hoping. . .none of it would bring Ana back.

She reached for the dustpan. "I suppose we'll have to forego the plum pudding this year then too, eh?"

"Pish! Oak Apple Day without plum pudding?" Mam snatched the dustpan from her hands, then bent in front of the crockery pile. "You might as well hang a Closed shingle on the front door right now. What's next. . .leaving off the garland and missing the prayer service as well?"

"Of course not." Setting the broom aside, Johanna grabbed Mam's hands in both of hers and pulled her to her feet. "God's seen us through worse, has He not?"

"Aye, child. That He has." For an instant, the lines on her mother's face softened, then just as quickly, reknit themselves into knots. "Still—"

"No still about it. If we fail to trust in His provision, what kind of faith is that?"

"Aah, my sweet girl. . .you are a rare one, you are."

The look of love shining in Mam's good eye squeezed Jo's heart. She'd smile, if she could remember how, but she didn't have to. Boyish laughter from outside the kitchen window cut into the tender moment.

Thomas!

Johanna flew out the back door and raced around the corner of the inn. Boys scattered like startled chickens, leaving only one to face her in the settling dust.

Folding her arms, she tried to remember that Thomas's wide eyes and spray of freckles made him appear more innocent than he really was.

"What are you doing here?" she asked. "You should've been down to the docks long ago. If Mr. Baggett or the Peacock's Inn boy beat you to it, and we miss out on new guests—"

"Aww, Jo." His toe scuffed a circle in the dirt. "You know I'm faster 'an them. 'Sides, the ferry's not due in for at least another hour."

"Even so, if you're not the first to persuade those arrivals to stay at our inn, I fear we won't. . ." She paused and craned her neck one way then another to see behind the boy's back. Her brother shifted with her movement—a crazy dance, and a guilty one at that. "What are you hiding? Let's see those hands."

His shoulders stiffened. Times like this broke her heart afresh with longing for her father. As much as she needed him, how much more did the young boy in front of her?

She popped her hands onto her hips and stared him down. "Now, young man."

A sigh lifted his chest. Slowly—any slower and she'd wonder if it physically pained him—one arm stretched out, then the other. When his fingers unfolded, crude wooden dice and several coins sat atop his palms.

"Thomas Elliot Langley!"

"Well I won, din't I?" He cocked his head at a rakish angle, his freckles riding the crest of a wicked smirk. "And against Wiley Hawk and his band, no less. Pretty good, eh Sis?"

"You were gambling?" The word filled her mouth like a rancid bit of meat. Sickened, she pressed a hand to her stomach. "Oh, Thomas, how could you? You, of all people, know the evils of such a pastime."

"We were just playing. That's not gambling." A scowl darkened his face, matching the low-lying blanket of grey clouds overhead. "It's fun. Something you wouldn't know anything about."

"What I know is that gamblers are never to be trusted. And worse, you lied about it. Is that the sort of reputation you want spread from one end of Dover to the other? Thomas Langley, the liar? What will Mam say? What do you think this will do to her?"

His toe scrubbed the dirt once again. What had been a scowl morphed into a grimace. "Don't tell Mam, Jo. Please don't."

Was that glistening in his eyes authentic? Hard to say—and even harder to remain cross with his quivering lip and thin shoulders slumping like an old man's.

"Very well." She stretched out her palm. "Hand over that ill-gotten gain, and we'll keep this between ourselves."

With a sly grin, he sprinted off, bits of gravel spraying up from his feet. As he raced, he yelled over his shoulder, "Sorry, Jo! I've a ferry to meet."

Picking up her skirts, she dashed after him, then lessened her pace as she neared the main road. What would people think of her, chasing her scamp of a brother? She'd never catch him anyway. Oh, what a day this was turning out to be.

She slowed, then stopped, her eyes narrowing. Was that a flash of yellow-stockinged legs dangling over the inn's front-door awning? She flattened against the wall and watched.

A loosened shingle smacked onto the ground ahead of her, followed by the thunk of two feet. So that's how Lucius Nutbrown snuck in and out without her knowing.

Girding herself mentally for a conversation that was sure to be ridiculous, Johanna pushed from the wall. "Mr. Nutbrown, a word, if you please."

For an instant, his body stiffened into a ramrod. Then he turned, the creases around his mouth settling into a smug line. For a man so lean, how he managed to gather such extra skin on his face was a wonder. When he reached into an inner pocket of his dress coat, Johanna rolled her eyes. Indeed. This would be ridiculous.

Nutbrown's hand emerged, covered with a raggedy court-jester puppet, which he promptly held out front and center. "Sorry, Miss Langley." The puppet's head bobbed side to side, the man's falsetto voice as crazed as the movement. "Mr. Nutbrown is late to an appointment. He shall attend you later this evening. Good day."

Nutbrown pivoted, the tails of his coat swinging wide. Did he seriously think she'd let him off that easily?

Heedless of who might be watching, she darted ahead and stopped directly in his path. "I'm afraid not, sir. This cannot wait."

His brows pulled together, drawing a dark streak above his eyes, yet he shoved the jester forward. "Very well, miss. But make it quick."

"Please, put away your puppet, sir. It gains you nothing." She extended her hand. "Pay up your room and board for the past fortnight, and I shall have nothing more to say."

The jester's head plummeted, his plaster nose pecking her palm.

She yanked back her hand. "Mr. Nutbrown! Really! I should hate to bring the magistrate in on this, but if I must—"

"No." Nutbrown's hands shot up as if she'd aimed a Brown Bess at his chest, the crazy puppet waving like a banner overhead. In three long-legged strides, he sidestepped her, lowering the puppet out at arm's length. "By week's end, Miss Langley, you shall be paid in full. You have Mr. Nutbrown's word on it."

The puppet disappeared into his coat, and Nutbrown scurried down the street.

Wonderful. The word of a jester made of cloth and papier-mâché, and the clown who wore it upon his hand. Yet he was their sole source of income unless she could pry those coins from Thomas's fingers, which wasn't likely. Bending, she gathered up the dry-rotted chunks of broken shingle and frowned. Her world was falling apart as tangibly as the inn—the place she loved most. The home she and Thomas and Mam must leave if they didn't come up with the rent payment by the end of next month.

Holding tightly to the shingle remnant, she closed her eyes. At the moment, her faith felt as crumbly as the wood—which was always the best time to pray.

"Please God, provide a way. Fill the inn. . .and soon."

London

Knuckles hovering to strike, Officer Alexander Moore slid his gaze once more to the left. It paid to think before pounding away, be it in a street brawl or—as in this case—on a door. A tarnished brass relief of the number seven hung at an angle, as if no one had given the slightest thought before nailing up the house number. Considering the man who supposedly lived here, the haphazard detail stayed his hand a second more. Had he written down the magistrate's address incorrectly?

Only one way to find out.

He pounded thrice, then stepped back, ready for anything. Behind him, hackney wheels ground over cobbles, grating a layer off his already thin nerves. Magistrate Ford never—*ever*—invited guests over for dinner. So why him? Why now?

Hinges screeched an angry welcome as the door opened. Lantern light spilled over the pinched face of a tall man shrouded in a dark dress coat, dark waistcoat, and darker pants. Rounding out the theme was a single-looped cravat, black as a crypt, choking the fellow's neck. A ghoul could not have been garbed more effectively. The man didn't say a thing, but even without words, Alex got the distinct impression he read, condensed, and filed away every possible facet of him in a glance—from shoe size to propensity for warmed sherry.

And Alex didn't like it one bit. That kind of intelligence gathering was supposed to be his specialty.

"My apologies. I must have the wrong address." Alex nodded a valediction, careful to keep a wary eye on the figure from the dead. "Good evening."

"Step this way, Officer Moore." The fellow set off without looking to see that Alex complied, nor even that the door was shut or locked. The magistrate would never abide such ineptitude down at Bow Street. Surely this was a ploy, or perhaps some kind of test of his wit.

Aah. A test? A slow smile lifted half his mouth.

With a grip on the hilt of his dagger, he unsheathed the blade and withdrew it from inside his great coat. Crossing the threshold, he left the door wide should a quick escape become necessary and trailed the disappearing lantern down a hall as lean as the man he followed.

At the end of the corridor, the grim reaper tapped twice on a closed door, then pushed it open without waiting for a response. The brilliance of the room reached out and pulled Alex forward. He entered a grand dining hall, incongruous in size and opulence with the street view of the ramshackle building. Crystal wall sconces and an overhead chandelier glittered light from one mirrored panel to another. A thick Turkish rug sank beneath his steps. The place was fit to house a peer of the realm, not a law keeper who served out gritty justice to the malefactors of London.

Directly across from him stood Bow Street Magistrate, Sir Richard Ford, stationed at the farther end of a polished table. Ford snapped shut a pocket watch and tucked it inside his waistcoat, then skewered him with a piercing gaze. "Prompt as always, eh Moore?"

"I try, sir."

Flipping out his coattails, Ford sat, then shook out a folded linen napkin and covered his lap. "Put that weapon away and have a seat. I invited you to dinner, not a skirmish."

The butler stepped forward, offering his arm to collect Alex's coat.

Alex sheathed his knife, then shrugged out of his woolen cloak and handed it over with a whispered warning. "You might want to shut that front door."

Across the long table, Ford chuckled. "Your concern for Underhill is admirable, but quite unnecessary. Though my butler's appearance leaves much to be desired, his service is impeccable. As for the door, by now it's not only sealed but would take a two-ton battering ram to break it in."

Sinking into the chair, Alex cocked a brow.

"You doubt me?" Ford's question dangled like a noose.

"Never, sir. Just curious, is all. Seemed a simple enough slab of oak."

"Oak, yes. Well, mostly. As for simple?" Ford shook his head. "Pulleys, gears, a generous portion of iron reinforcement. Try putting in a monstrosity like that without attracting attention from one end of the neighborhood to the other."

The magistrate paused to ring a small silver bell sitting next to his plate. Before the last of the short chime cleared the air, a housemaid entered with a tray.

Ford ignored her as she set a steaming bowl in front him. "I suppose you're wondering why I asked you here."

Only a thousand times. The retort lay dormant on his tongue. To admit he'd anguished over this meeting would show weakness—a trait he'd vowed never again to embrace. He followed the sleek movement of the girl as she placed his bouillon on the table, then returned his gaze to the magistrate. "The thought crossed my mind that, perhaps, I was to be the main course."

A thin smile stretched the magistrate's lips. "Not that you don't deserve to be after your unorthodox capture of Ned Dooley."

And there it was. What this entire charade was about. Alex leaned forward, bumping the table and rippling the wine in his glass. "Regardless of how it was accomplished, sir, Dooley's conviction ended that smuggling ring, saving countless lives, not to mention the expense spared to the Crown. How you can possibly say—"

Ford's hand shot up, cutting off further comment. "You already know my thoughts on the matter. I daresay neither of us will sway the other's opinion, so let us officially consider this topic closed to discussion. There is a much larger scheme prompting this meeting."

"Must be spectacular." Alex sank back in his chair. "Inviting me here is a singular event. As far as I know, not a runner has ever uncovered where you live, and though I begged you time and again as a lad, you never relented."

"Indeed. Sometimes extreme measures are necessary." Ford shooed away the serving girl with a flick of his fingers, then sat motionless until she disappeared through a hidden panel in the wall. He took a moment to sample his soup. "I would like you to go incognito for a while."

Taking the magistrate's lead, Alex picked up his spoon and downed several mouthfuls of his broth, tasting nothing. Something was not right about the magistrate's request. Ford could've asked him the same thing in his office without the pretense of dinner. In fact, he could've asked any number of other officers or—suddenly understanding dawned bright and clear.

He shoved back his chair. "With all due respect, I've hardly forgotten the assignment you handed Brentwood last year. Am I the only available officer for you to proposition?"

The more he thought of Nicholas Brentwood's previous mission, the hotter his blood ran. He'd sooner quit than be saddled with the care of a spoiled rich girl, as had his friend—even though it turned out well in the end.

Rising, he frowned at the napkin as it fell to the carpet. Let the impeccable butler pick it up. In fact, let Underhill have the assignment. "My thanks for your hospitality, sir, but if that is the case, my answer is no. A firm and emphatic no."

"Alexander, wait."

Ford's tone—or was it the use of his Christian name?—slid over his shoulders like a straight-coat, pinning him in place. Suddenly he was ten years old again, compelled to do his guardian's bidding.

"You," the magistrate continued, "are my first and only choice for this position. This assignment is nothing like Brentwood's. Anyone can be a guardian, but only someone with specialized training may fill the role I'm looking for. All I ask is that you hear me out. You owe me at least that after keeping your hind end out of trouble the past decade and a half."

The few sips of soup, the glittery sparkle of the room, the pleading in Ford's voice combined into a wave of nausea that sank to the pit of his gut. He was indebted to Ford, more than he could ever pay back. Had not the man taken him in as a ten-year-old orphan, he'd have perished on the streets...or become like the criminals he hauled in. He sagged into the chair like a rheumy old man and locked eyes with his benefactor and superior. "All right. Let's hear it then."

Sconce light glimmered in Ford's eyes. "You will pose as a gambling rogue to ferret out a suspected traitor. A dangerous, highly connected traitor."

"Traitors instead of smugglers, eh?" He chewed on that for a moment. "Might be a nice change of pace."

"Nice? Hardly." Ford downed another mouthful of soup, then pushed the bowl away and stood, his gaze unwavering. "You should know that once I've told you the details of this particular mission, I will deny ever having said anything about it. And if this operation fails, I shall refute any knowledge of this conversation, to the point of watching you swing from a gibbet if necessary."

Denial? This was new. The danger in the magistrate's proposal crept down Alex's backbone. He straightened his shoulders, counteracting the eerie feeling. "Then, as always, I shall make it a point not to fail. Go on."

Ford grunted as he strolled to a narrow trestle table. He pounded twice on the top then twisted a knob on the middle drawer. Below the table, about knee height, a hidden panel in the wall slid open. Bending, the magistrate retrieved a leather pouch. By the time he crossed over to Alex, the wall looked as solid as ever.

The bag thwunked onto the table with a crashing jingle. By the sound, he didn't have to open the drawstring to know it wasn't a bag of measly farthings sitting next to his plate.

"As you can see, you are now a wealthy man, Mr. Morton."

Alex's gaze shot from the bag to the magistrate. "Mor. . .ton?"

"You heard correctly. From now on, you are no longer a Moore, but a Morton, less chance of a slip up if your alias is a close cousin to your true surname. You are a dealer in fine wines, a buyer and seller for your father." Ford reached inside his waistcoat and withdrew a sealed envelope, the new pseudonym engraved in gold on the front. "This coming Saturday, you shall attend the finest Oak Apple Day soiree Dover has to offer."

"Dover? I can't possibly go back there. My face is known."

"True. A detriment, that. Yet you shall travel in a higher echelon of society this time. This invitation"—he handed over the envelope—"is your ticket into the estate of the Viscount Lord Coburn. How you maintain connection afterwards is your affair, which I am sure will be no problem for you. Nor do I want to know how you operate. In truth, until you discover who is involved in this mess, I give you full and free rein."

Alex's brows lifted. Free rein? This *was* some scheme, and an enticing one at that, even though he'd left behind a few enemies in that part of the country—enemies whose anger likely still festered. Returning to Dover now might be a death warrant.

He slugged back a drink of claret, the challenge of it all leaving a bittersweet aftertaste. Setting down the glass, he gazed at the magistrate. "What exactly is this mess, sir?"

Ford's mouth hardened into a grim line. "Someone's been communicating with the French. I'm not at liberty to say how I know. Merely that I know is enough. To what extent military intelligence has been shared, and for what purpose, is up to you to find out. There is a traitor in our midst, and I want him brought to me at any cost. The MP funding this mission has deep pockets. Survive this assignment and you'll be able to retire from the force—in style."

Alex blew out a long, low breath. He'd purposely distanced himself from anything smacking of French intrigue or the military. The London streets were what he knew best.

But how could he refuse Ford's earnest gaze bearing down on him? If it weren't for the magistrate, he'd most likely be moldering in a pauper's grave by now. And retirement at his age? Other than his life, what did he have to lose? He raked a hand through his hair. "Very well, but what if I should need backup?"

"Officer Thatcher will be your only means of communication with me, though he too, will be under strict instruction to deny you should your true identity become discovered. You'll both be under a vow of secrecy, sharing information between yourselves and me alone. No one else. Do you swear it?"

A queer chill shivered across his shoulders. This was quite an affair, for he'd never been asked to pledge such a vow before. He shoved down the foreboding quaver and lifted his chin. "Yes, I swear it."

"Good. Then Thatcher will check in with you regularly."

"What does that mean?"

"Whatever you want it to." Ford walked the length of the table and reclaimed his seat, leaving his cryptic answer floating on the air.

But gnawing upon a bone was a trait Alex had perfected. "Where shall I connect with Thatcher, or rather, he with me?"

Amusement lifted one side of Ford's mouth. "You will station yourself at the Blue Hedge Inn."

A groan ripped from his throat. "You're jesting."

Ford quirked a brow. "I take it you are familiar with the establishment?"

Alex pressed his lips tight before harsh words escaped. No longer hungry, he pushed away his bowl of soup. The Blue Hedge Inn.

He'd rather sleep in a pig wallow than that dilapidated hovel.

CHAPTER TWO

The driver tossed down Alexander's bag from the roof of the coach. With a grunt, Alex caught it before the canvas hit the cobblestones, then turned to face the Rose Inn—the last stop on the London-to-Dover run. Sunlight glinted off two banks of windows draped with oak leaf bunting. Deep red bricks, too new to be coated over with soot, contrasted with the green foliage. The building stood like a proud soldier, pinned with honorary banners for the upcoming Oak Apple festivities. A patron exited the front door, patting his belly with a smile and a sigh, the aroma of freshly baked bread and sweet cider wafting out with him.

Alex's mouth pulled into a scowl. Was it too much to ask for lodging such as this if his life was to be on the line? Apparently, yes, though he'd done his best to talk Ford into changing his mind through the remainder of last Monday's dinner.

Turning, he stalked down New Street, then headed south on Canon. As he travelled from city center toward the outskirts, buildings cowered in the shadow of the old castle on Tower Hill. But even here, sporadic vendors had already set up their wares for the upcoming holiday. Across the road, one hawker claimed his oils and tinctures cured everything from gout to gluttony. To his side, cinnamon-spiced nuts roasted over an open fire. Ahead, a gamer ran a coconut shell scam, promising a cash prize for anyone who could pick out the shell with a pea hidden beneath.

In front of that booth, a scrawny-limbed lad jammed his hands into his pockets, then turned and began shuffling away. Behind the boy, a wicked grin slashed the face of the gamer. Alex clenched his jaw. It didn't take a Bow Street officer to figure out the low-life had stolen the boy's last farthing.

"You, boy!" Alex waited until the lad cast a glance over his shoulder. "I'm looking for a strong arm to carry my bag."

The boy's steps slowed, not completely, but enough that he turned and faced him, walking backward. "Ye willing to pay?"

Alex paused in front of the gamer's booth. "Aye."

The boy stopped. The gamer leaned forward. Alex smirked. With one word, he'd purchased their attention. A few more, and he'd own them. "I've a coin or two I can part with."

Immediately, the gamer threw his shells into the air, juggling them into a merry circle. "Step right up! Try yer luck! Are you smarter than a coconut?"

It was hard not to groan at the poor verse, nor smile at the boy as he ran back and tugged his sleeve. "I'm your lad, sir. Thomas is me name. Where we going?"

The gamer shouted louder, adding the pea into his juggling mix.

Shrugging the bag off his shoulder, Alex handed it to Thomas, then nodded sideways toward the gamer. "First stop is right here."

The boy's face paled. "I don't recommend that, sir."

"While I appreciate your advice, the truth is," he squatted nose-to-nose with the lad, "I *am* smarter than a coconut."

Thomas shook his head, the gravity of his puckered brow adding years to his youth. "That's what I thought, too, sir. But I were sure wrong."

Righteous anger curled Alex's fingers into a tight fist. *Vengeance is the Lord's* he reminded himself, but it still took a conscious effort to keep the grin fixed to his face. "Perhaps, boy, it wasn't the coconut you were competing against."

The lad's nose scrunched, bunching his spray of freckles into a clump.

Resisting the urge to laugh, Alex rose and stepped up to the booth. He reached into his pocket, pulled out a penny, and slapped it down on the plank separating him from the gamer. "I'll give it a go."

"Very good, sir. Very good." One by one the coconuts collected onto the gamer's open palms, the pea being the last to land. Above his bony wrists, the hems of the man's sleeves were threadbare, more so than the rest of his dress coat. If nothing else, the gamer knew his trade. Given the chance, Alex had no doubt the fellow could hide an entire pianoforte up that sleeve, and by the appearance of it, perhaps he had a time or two.

"Let's see if ol' fate smiles on you, eh sir?" With much swirling and swooping, the man made a great show of arranging the shells into a neat row in front of Alex. He lifted the middle coconut, then set the pea beneath it. "All ye gots to do, sir, is watch carefully."

Thomas planted his feet beside him, pleading with wide eyes. "Ye won't win, sir. He's good, he is. It's not too late to take yer coin back."

Before Alex could yield to the boy's warning, the gamer snapped into action, sliding shells one way and another, even tapping and clacking their edges now and then. Thomas leaned closer, his gaze fixed on the man's hands. Alex ignored the showman's flourishing fingers and instead studied his eyes. The content of a man's soul could be summed up in a blink—or lack of one. Snakes never blinked.

Neither did the gamer.

"There you have it." The man swept one hand back and forth over the top of the shells. "Which one hides the pea? Say the word, and if ye're right, you'll walk away with a jingle in yer pocket."

Alex looked down at Thomas and cocked a brow. The boy bit his lip then edged one finger up to point at the farthest coconut.

"Are you certain?" he asked.

"Aye, sir. This time I know I'm right."

"Well then, I choose. . ." Alex slanted his gaze back to the gamer, whose hand hovered over the far shell.

"This one." He shot his arm across the plank and grabbed the gamer's other wrist. The man screeched like a little girl, but to his credit, he didn't open his hand. Alex squeezed harder, grinding the man's bones to within a hair's breadth of snapping. Tears leaked out the gamer's eyes, and finally, his fingers sprung wide.

There sat the pea.

Thomas flipped open each of the shells. All were empty. "Dash it!

You're a flamin' cheater! Gimme back my money!"

"It's the way of the game, that's all." The gamer plied and pried and tried to wriggle free of Alex's death grip. "Let me go!"

"Be a shame to break these delicate bones. Why, you'd be out of commission for all of the Oak Apple Day festivities. Yes, sir"—Alex dug his fingers in deeper and leaned closer—"a shame too, if we spread word about how your little game is played, hmm?"

The gamer's face turned an ugly shade of purple. "All right! All right. I'll give the street-rat back his money."

Alex let go. The gamer recoiled, rubbing his wrist and whimpering on the exhale. Alex folded his arms, waiting until the fellow handed over not only Thomas's farthing, but his own coin as well.

Snubbing the man behind the booth, Thomas flashed Alex a smile, wide with teeth he'd not yet grown into. "Thank ye, sir."

Alex couldn't help but mirror the boy's grin. "My pleasure, lad. Shall we?" He nodded down Canon Street, then waited for Thomas to tuck away his money and heft the canvas bag over his shoulder.

The boy fell into step beside him, two paces to his one. His words flew just as fast as his legs. "That were something. That's what. Why, ye needn't pay me nothin' fer carryin' yer bag, sir. Ye got me my coin back and all. Oh, and you must stay at the inn my family runs. Ye'll be treated like a king. Leastwise by me. Don't know 'bout my sister. I stay out of her way, mostly."

"Oh?" Alex continued at the intersection, though his feet itched to turn southward. The Maiden's Head was halfway down that street—the last of the reputable inns on this side of town. Blowing out a long breath, he glanced down at the boy. "Why is that, I wonder? Is your sister such a shrew?"

"She's all right, I guess. It's just that, well. . ." The boy's toe hit a rock and sent it skipping ahead. "She's such a girl, sir. Makes big to-do's outta nothin'. It's no wonder she's not married."

An undertaker's tone couldn't have been more solemn. Alex bit back a laugh. "Can your father not manage her?"

"Father's dead and gone, sir."

"Sorry to hear that." He studied the boy out of the corner of his eye. Honest emotion rarely met a full-faced stare.

"It's not bad as all that, sir. Never knowed him. He died a'fore I was born." Catching up to the rock, the boy kicked it again, displaying no grief whatsoever.

"About this sister of yours," Alex paused as the boy veered around a corner. How on earth could the lad know he'd wanted to turn here? "She runs the inn herself?"

"Nah." Thomas shook his head and skipped ahead of him—quite the feat for lugging a bag Alex knew weighed at least a stone. Why would the boy speed up when he didn't know how much farther would be required of him?

"She and Mam run the inn. Well, and me too," the boy continued. "Mam can't get along without us, with her bad eye and all. Oh, this way, sir. Shortcut."

Thomas cut into an alley carved into the space between two warehouses. Looking past the lad, Alex squinted. At the far end, the shortcut spilled out onto Blue Lane. "Hold up a minute, Thomas. How is it you know exactly where I'm going?"

The boy pivoted, facing him. "Why I told ye, sir. You must stay with us. Ye'll be treated like a—"

"Yes, I know. A king. Let me venture a guess, hmm?" He closed the distance between them and once again squatted nose-to-nose with the boy. "Are you taking me to the Blue Hedge Inn?"

Thomas's mouth dropped. Awe sparked in the depths of his dark blue eyes. "How'd ye know, sir? I ne'er said the name."

An easy enough guess when that was the only remaining lodging this far from the center of town, but if the lad wanted to credit him with hero status, who was he to deny him? Reaching out a hand, Alex tussled the boy's hair and stood. "Let's be about it, then, aye?"

"Aye, sir. Only. . ." Thomas's mouth scrunched one way then the other, as if the words on his tongue tasted sour.

"Only what?" Alex prodded.

"Just that we do have one other boarder ye should know about."

"Why's that?"

Thomas kicked his toe in the dirt, averting his gaze. "Ye'll be sharing a bed with him."

Sharing a—blast! Alex's toe itched to kick more than the dirt. A dilapidated inn. A shrewish spinster running it. And now he'd be rooming with a stranger. Could anything else possibly go wrong with his stay in Dover?

Setting his boots into motion, he headed down the alley and considered pulling his knife as he turned the corner. The way this mission was beginning, who knew what he'd encounter next?

Johanna frowned at the pathetic green-and-brown pile that was supposed to be a garland. It looked like a heap of ratty leaves raked atop a mound of twine scraps. Bending, she picked up one end of the garland, then stood, pressing her lips tight to keep from mumbling about her brother. If she hadn't had to do that rascal's chores, she could've created a proper swag, every bit as stunning as the one on the Hound's Tooth Inn. Yet there was nothing more to be done for the sorry-leafed trimming draped over her fingers. With the parade scheduled for tomorrow, she could ill afford to wait any longer to adorn the Blue Hedge's facade—leastwise not if she hoped to attract holiday lodgers.

Casting a last glance up one side of Blue Lane and down the other, she gave up expecting Thomas to climb the ladder and hang the bunting. No smudge-faced boy darted about anywhere.

But neither did anyone else. The street was empty, save for a horse hitched to a cart halfway down the lane. If she acted quickly, she wouldn't be caught mounting a ladder like a hired man.

Grabbing the rail in one hand and holding tight to the garland with the other, she worked her way upward, rung to rung, then stopped at eye-level with the shingled overhang. No sense going all the way up to the roof. The awning would do just as well.

She poked the end of the bunting into a gap between the wooden shingles, then tugged it a bit to make sure it was caught snugly. Satisfied a good wind wouldn't coax it loose—though there was no telling if Lucius

Nutbrown's foot might not snag it if he made another escape through the front window—she pulled up slack from the coil on the ground, then searched for another gap, and. . .there. To her right. A bit farther than she'd like, still, she might be able to reach it if she leaned far enough.

Or she might fall and crack her skull.

Narrowing her eyes, she gauged the distance. Moving the ladder each time she wanted to secure the garland would only add extra effort and take more time. The lane was empty now, but that didn't mean it would stay that way. Nothing to be done for it, then.

Wrapping her fingers tight around the ladder, she stretched her arm toward the crevice. So close! But not enough to wedge the garland into the crack.

She sucked in a breath, held it, and leaned a little farther. Her fingertips brushed the breach this time. Barely. Perhaps if she stretched just a hair closer, like so, and shifted her weight the tiniest bit, then—

Wood cracked. The world tipped. Johanna flailed, fingers seeking something—anything—to grab on to. A splinter pierced her skin as wood scraped her palms. She tumbled headlong, a scream to wake the dead ripping out of her throat.

She squeezed her eyes shut, tightening every muscle for impact, and—

Landed on a pair of outstretched arms that scooped her up against a solid chest.

"Careful there, missy."

A deep voice rumbled against her ear, reminding her of an autumn day, all golden and warm. Her eyes flew open. The man holding her matched the voice perfectly. Shoulder-length hair, the color of spent leaves fallen to the ground, framed a face kissed by the sun, browned yet fair. His coat, rough against her cheek, smelled of bergamot and wood smoke, spicy but sweet. If September were flesh and blood, it would look exactly like the man holding her.

She blinked, speechless, breathless—and totally drawn in by his brilliant blue gaze.

"Miss? Are you all right?" he asked.

"I. . ." Her voice squeaked, stuck somewhere between mortified and mesmerized. She swallowed, then tried again. "I am fine. Thank you."

"Well then, let's see if your legs work better than that ladder." He bent and set her down.

Released from the safety of his arms, she wobbled, and he grabbed her elbow. La! She must look like a newborn foal.

Behind her, laughter rang out. "What a catch! You should've seen the look on your face, Jo."

A slow burn started somewhere low, her toes maybe, or her tummy, melting her embarrassment and stoking up a hot rage. She reeled about and planted her fists on her hips. "This was your chore to finish, Brother. Had you been here, I'd not have fallen."

The man stepped between them. "Don't be too hard on him, miss. The boy had his own fall from grace."

"Really?" She took the time to fold her arms and dissected her brother's wide eyes. He directed a don't-say-it sort of gaze at the man. "What have you been up to this time, Brother?"

"Filling the inn, that's what." Thomas's chest puffed out a full inch as he lifted his chin. "I got us another guest, and good thing too, or you'd have smashed your head like a—"

"Alexander Morton, at your service, miss." The man cut Thomas off with a bow, chivalrous to a degree that nearly made her smile. Her brother could learn a thing or two from this fellow.

Stuffing down her irritation, she dipped her head toward Mr. Morton. "Thank you, sir, for indeed, your service was welcome. I am grateful you stopped me from breaking any bones, though I own my pride is a little scuffed." She straightened her shoulders, physically relegating the humiliating incident to the past and resuming her role as hostess. "Welcome to the Blue Hedge Inn. My name is Johanna Langley, one of the proprietors."

"I grant this was an unconventional meeting, Miss Langley, but pleasurable, nonetheless." A rogue wink accompanied his words. "I am happy to make your acquaintance."

His smile scorched through her. Truly, she ought to be offended. So why the sudden heat warming her cheeks? She turned her face to her brother, hoping the fellow hadn't noticed. "See Mr. Morton to the south-side room, would you, Thomas?"

Her brother shook his head. "Can't."

"Why not?"

"Got us some more boarders too."

How had the boy managed to attract more lodgers in one morning than she had in a month? And why was he scrubbing his toe in the dirt? Something smelled more putrid in this than a leftover bit of limburger.

She narrowed her eyes. "How many more? When do they arrive?"

Craning his neck, he looked past her. "Right about now."

She and Mr. Morton turned in unison. He snorted. She sighed.

Coming up Blue Lane was a rickety wagon, painted red and gold, with tassels and banners and more riders than could fit inside. Two dogs played chase around the horses, and even from where she stood, Johanna cringed at the ribald singing and bawdy laughter traveling along with them.

"Oh, Thomas." She shook her head.

Desperate times called for desperate measures. . .but gypsies?

CHAPTER THREE

The closer the gaudy wagon drew to the Blue Hedge, the deeper Johanna's heart sank. From where she stood, she counted at least five adults and three children, and who knew how many more were in back. Unless this ragtag bunch of travellers paid up front, Mam would never be able to feed so many with Cook gone. What had Thomas been thinking? Filling the inn was one thing. Making it the laughingstock of Dover, quite another—and with boarders such as these, they'd scare off any prospect of respectable lodgers.

"No, not them." Her brother stepped past Mr. Morton and stretched out his arm, pointing beyond the monstrosity on wheels. "Behind 'em."

As the wagon closed in, more of the street came into view. Her gaze skimmed past the brilliant colors and landed on black and white. Beyond, six men travelled on foot, garbed in varying shades of dirt and producing the racket she'd accredited the gypsies. The scruffy fellows possessed instruments, haversacks, and—judging by the lyrics of their songs—no morals whatsoever.

Her gaze shot back to the gypsy wagon rolling by. Except for the rattle of tack and harness, and the cry of a babe from within, it was quiet. The driver tipped his head toward her then snapped the reins, moving their cart along without pretense. As it passed, a dark-haired pixy popped her head out the back, merry curtains framing the little girl's face. When her gaze met Johanna's, the girl smiled.

Johanna suppressed a frown and forced a polite nod. Compared to the ragged men behind them, singing of ale and women and something about a dog, the gypsies didn't seem so bad.

The wagon lumbered off, replaced by the six itinerant musicians. One fellow took the lead. Striding away from the group with a jaunty step, he planted himself in front of her brother, overshadowing him but not Mr. Morton. Both men were of equal height, but this fellow was night to Mr. Morton's day. His hair was dark while Mr. Morton's was fair. His deep olive skin contrasted with Mr. Morton's golden tan. And he was lean and wiry, like an alley cat about to spring, compared to Mr. Morton's thick shoulders and broad stance.

Johanna's frown fought to surface again. What business of hers was it to notice the men's differences in the first place?

The man bowed with a flourish. "Greetings my fine, young friend, Master Thomas." He straightened then pumped the boy's hand. "You drive a hard bargain, m'boy. Yet we acquiesce to your business savvy, happy to serve and be served, aye lads?" He glanced over his shoulder and cocked a brow at the fellows behind him. All five lifted their fists into the air, hooting their agreement.

Johanna smoothed her hands along her skirt, fighting the desire to plug up her ears.

Before the whoops died down, the man slid in front of her. How could he do that? She hadn't even noticed his feet move.

His hat, and the dark curls escaping the brim, were coated with a fine layer of dust, the same color as his grey eyes. He smelled of a long day's worth of travel, meat cooked over a spit, and something more musky. Exotic. And altogether dangerous. His gaze glimmered with the knowledge of what lay beyond her world of inns and family and all that was good. The urge to turn heel and run tingled in her legs.

But his eyes held her in place. "And you must be the lovely Johanna. Your brother speaks highly of you."

The man's breach of etiquette was stunning, though expecting a travelling musician to display proper manners was just as outlandish. Still, to use her Christian name, to look her full in the face as if he'd claimed her for his own, made her feel as if she stood before all the world wearing nothing but a shift.

Next to her, Mr. Morton stepped nearer and cleared his throat. So, he'd noticed as well.

"I am Gabriel Quail, milady." The man reached for her hand and bowed over it, resting his lips atop her skin like a benediction. As he rose, he gazed at her through dark lashes, speaking something in French. His index finger rubbed little circles on the inside of her wrist.

She yanked back her hand, ashamed at the warmth where his mouth had touched.

"I don't believe Miss Langley asked for your name, sir." Mr. Morton closed the rest of the distance between them, standing so close, she remembered the feel of his arms when he'd held her. If Mr. Quail took one more liberty, she got the distinct impression Mr. Morton would pop the man in the nose.

Her own hands fisted with rising frustration toward them both. She'd avoided compromise for five and twenty years without anyone's help. She certainly knew how to handle a forward wayfarer without the assistance of a man's muscle.

"Thank you, Mr. Morton, for your concern." She shot him a sideways glance before angling her head at Quail. "You are correct, sir, that I am Thomas's sister. You may address me as Miss Langley. I am pleased to meet you, Mr. Quail, yet I advise you and your companions"—she lifted her chin and speared each man in turn with an evil eye—"that the Blue Hedge Inn is a reputable establishment. We strive to maintain a certain decorum."

Mr. Quail pressed both his hands to his heart and sank to one knee. "Be still, my heart. Be still! She's beautiful, therefore to be woo'd. She is woman, therefore to be won."

Startled, she opened her mouth, but no words came out. What could she possibly say to that?

Next to her, Mr. Morton folded his arms. "Perhaps, sir, you ought save your Shakespeare for a larger audience."

Mr. Quail's gaze lingered on hers a moment longer before he faced Mr. Morton. "And you are?"

"Not that it signifies, but I am Alexander Morton, purchaser of fine wines, and a guest here at the Blue Hedge."

"Wine, you say?" A smile slid across Mr. Quail's face. "We shall get along famously, my friend."

"I doubt it." Mr. Morton's words travelled on an exhale, too quiet for Mr. Quail to hear, but Johanna didn't miss them.

Turning to the group behind him, Mr. Quail swung up both arms as if he offered the inn for sale to a massive crowd. "Lads, we have found ourselves a home for the Oak Apple holiday. Let the revelry begin!"

More hoots and hollers filled the air as the men passed in front of her and entered the taproom. Mr. Quail followed them in, slapping Mr. Morton on the back as he strode by, leaving her and Thomas with mouths agape, and Mr. Morton with an unreadable expression.

"Well, that was. . ." Johanna nibbled her lower lip. "Interesting."

"Indeed." Mr. Morton snatched up his canvas bag where it sat forgotten near Thomas's feet. "I'll stow this and then—" He nodded toward the heap of garland hanging by one end from the awning. "We'll see about getting that bunting up for you, Miss Langley. Right, Thomas?"

Without waiting for an answer, Mr. Morton disappeared through the door, Thomas quick on his heels. Oh, no. The little urchin wouldn't get off that easily. Johanna dashed ahead and snagged the boy's collar. "Hold on, Brother. A word, if you please."

He turned, shrugging off her hand. "Aye?"

"Mr. Quail said you drove a hard bargain. What bargain did you make?"

"Just a trade. That's all."

Sighing, she bent face-to-face with him, trying to decide if he was purposely being obstinate or if his lack of elaboration was simply a bad case of ten-year-old naïveté. "Thomas, this could take us all afternoon if I must pull every bit of information out of you like a plum from a pie. But if that's what it takes, I shall."

He rolled his eyes. "You said yourself that if the Blue Hedge could only have music, a real rig-jigger of a dandy band to play for Oak Apple Eve, why, we'd have customers coming from miles around." He stood a little taller. "That's what I traded for. I got me some business savvy. Mr. Quail said so himself."

Johanna narrowed her eyes. "Please don't tell me those men in there are expecting room and board for nothing but music and merriment."

"All right." He spun toward the door.

With a long swipe of her arm, she snagged his shirttail, thankful for the first time in her life for his sloppy appearance. "All right what?"

He stalled for a moment, casting her a sly glance over his shoulder. "All right, I won't tell you." With a jerk, he pulled from her grasp and bolted through the front door of the inn. Laughter and the drone of men's voices rolled out, quieting only when the door slapped shut.

She'd sigh, but what good would it do? Just last week, she *had* wished aloud for a band to attract customers. Why did her brother have to choose that one instant to listen to her? And if he'd made such a deal with Mr. Quail, what kind of a pact had he made with Mr. Morton?

Her gaze slid upward, past the ramshackle awning with the ratty strand of oak-leaf garland hanging from one end, beyond the top window that wouldn't shut all the way and over the roof, sagging like the shoulders of an old woman. Not a cloud dotted the afternoon sky. Endless blue stretched clear up to heaven—straight to God's ear. Apparently, He'd heard her speak as clearly as Thomas had.

A slow smile moved across her lips, though she had no idea how she and Mam would provide for so many guests. "This wasn't exactly what I had in mind when I asked You to fill the inn, Lord, but thank You for listening."

Descending the last step into the taproom, Alex winced at the noise, hard-pressed to decide which was worse—remaining upstairs in a room the size of a wardrobe that smelled of mushrooms, or taking his dinner amidst an off-key violin, a bodhran that could use a good tightening, and two mandolins dueling to the death. To make it worse, Gabriel Quail belted out a ballad with a voice jagged enough to weather the whitewash on the plaster.

A muscle in his neck tightened. How was it possible he missed the din of London?

To his right, a checkered blue skirt hem peeked out a door, and for a moment, his spirits lifted. Resting his eyes upon sweet Johanna

Langley would take the edge off Quail's singing. His arms warmed with the memory of holding her. And when he remembered the way she'd stood up to Quail, unflinching and unapologetic, a grin lifted his lips. Had he known such a beauty was part and parcel of the Blue Hedge, he wouldn't have given Ford such a hard time.

As the rest of the skirt came into view, his grin faded. It would take two Johanna's to fill that dress. A hefty woman emerged back end first. When she turned and met his gaze, the tray in her hands teetered, and her face paled to the shade of fine parchment. Odd. He often elicited a response from the ladies—even white-haired ones such as this—but it usually involved blushing cheeks or fluttering eyelashes.

He tipped his head toward her. "Good evening, ma'am."

"Evening, sir. I'll see ye have a bowl and a mug straightaway." Above a spray of faded freckles, the woman's brown eyes—the same shade as Johanna's—brushed over him like an artist studying a model to be painted. One eye, however, lagged behind the other. Could she even see out of it?

She turned and crossed the floor to Quail's band of merrymakers. A hitch in her step caused her skirt to ride askew on her left hip—same side as the bad eye. Grey hair made a run for it out the back of her cap, right side, this time. She had trouble reaching with her left arm as well. Johanna's mother obviously had suffered an injury years ago. Perhaps it had something to do with the death of Mr. Langley. Perhaps not. Alex filed the information into a storage bin in his mind to sort through later.

In the meantime, he sank onto a bench in the corner with his back against the wall, giving him a wide-angle view of the room. It might've been a cozy inn at some point, but now the walls leaned in toward the soot-blackened ceiling, giving the impression the entire building wanted to lie down and rest.

His table was one of six and closest to the door. On the other side of the scarred oak, the wall gave way to two paneled windows. Thomas could shimmy through them, but his own shoulders would never fit. The door he'd seen the woman carry the tray through likely led to a back door. As he compiled the list of alternative exits, he traced his fingertip along a set of initials scored into the tabletop. LL. What had possessed

LL to pull out a knife and leave the engraved legacy? Drunkenness? Pride? And where was LL nowadays? Behind bars, dead, or reformed?

His finger stopped. So did his breath. Those initials didn't represent one man, but many. *La ligue la liberté,* a growing group of French rebels. He'd bet his soul on it. Casting a glance about the shadowy room, he assessed for possible Leaguers in attendance, though if any were here, their backsides would most likely be warming this bench. Was that why Ford had ordered him to board at this inn?

Johanna's mother reappeared from the kitchen, striding toward him like a hunter to the prey, her dress swishing off rhythm. "Here ye be, sir."

The bowl she set before him wafted a parsnippy aroma, though considering the minute bits of vegetables floating atop the thin potage, it was surprising he smelled anything other than salty hot water. "Thank you," he said, hoping the words themselves would conjure up genuine gratitude for the lackluster meal.

A mug landed next to his bowl. Were it full, a foamy head of ale would've sloshed over the rim. As it was, he could play kick-a-pin with the wooden tankard and spill nary a drop.

"I understand you're a new arrival here at the Blue Hedge. I am Mrs. Langley, proprietor." She cocked her head to the same rakish angle he'd seen Thomas employ. "And you are?"

"Alexander Morton."

"Mor. . .ton, eh?" Her tongue lingered over his surname, her good eye narrowing. Again with the studying gaze? He'd pay a king's ransom to know what this old woman's fixation was about. Had Ford put her up to this?

She leaned closer, though she needn't have. The music had ceased. Quail and his musicians were too busy slugging back their drinks.

"I'm sorry, but from where did you say you hail?" she asked.

Shrewd. Very shrewd. A smirk begged to lift one side of his mouth. He pressed his lips tight. Was she the plant or was he? Had the magistrate ordered him to stay at this establishment in an effort to toy with him, and in the process, sharpen his vigilance?

He doled out a tidbit from his carefully constructed background. "I didn't say, but I was born and bred a Sheffield boy and am on my way home from Porto Moniz."

"Sheffield?" Her mouth folded into a frown. "Humph."

He smiled. "Is there a problem?"

Her lips parted, but it took a moment before any words came out. "None at all, sir. Forgive an old woman." She tapped a finger against her cap, easing her frown into a half-smile. "The mind is one of the first things to go, you know."

She turned, and he watched her weave her way through the taproom. Her body might be hindered, but her mind was as dodgy as a pickpocket's fingers. Maybe it would be better to avoid the woman altogether.

The front door opened silently, and a dark figure slid in on a draft of night air. Dressed head to toe in black, the man wasn't a mammoth, yet that didn't make him any less dangerous. He was solid, compact, and entirely hidden in shadow. Stealth graced his every movement. Quail and his fellows didn't turn a head amongst them as he eased the door shut behind him, but Alex instinctively reached for the blade at his side.

The cloaked figure stalked toward him. Alex wrapped his fingers around the hilt of his knife and pulled it loose. Lantern light dared an advance beneath the man's hat brim, revealing a stubbled jawline and a gaze that could make a saint flinch.

Alex slipped his blade back into the sheath. "Evening, Thatcher." He waited until the man sat opposite him. "You don't waste any time. I arrived just this afternoon."

"I know." Officer Samuel Thatcher's voice was low timbred and smooth, the kind of tone one heard while wondering why the fellow's lips had not moved.

Alex leaned back in his seat. "You always were a ghost in the shadows."

Thatcher merely stared, his dark eyes hinting at neither pleasure nor irritation.

"And a quiet ghost at that." Alex lifted his hand, hailing Mrs. Langley for a drink for his friend. Who knew how long—or hard—the man had ridden.

Thatcher pulled off his hat and pushed back the damp, dark hair on his brow, which answered that speculation. Why the breakneck pace?

Taking a mouthful of ale, Alex mulled over a few possibilities, coming up short-ended on each. "I am surprised to see you so soon. Which leads me to wonder, how often am I to expect you?"

Shrugging out of his riding cloak, Thatcher took the time to lay the garment beside him on the bench before he answered. "Depends."

"On what?"

"On when Ford has a message for you." Thatcher wrapped both hands around the mug Mrs. Langley held out for him and took a long draw before he set the cup down. "Or you have a message for Ford."

He snorted. "So tell me, how exactly does one conjure a spirit?"

While Quail's discordant music wailed, Thatcher stared at him, the kind of gaze that might raise the fine hairs at the nape of a stranger. The fellow had no idea of social norms, or polite and pleasing manners. This was simply the way he was. Inward. Intense. And altogether unnerving.

Finally Thatcher spoke. "You know the trees behind the rocks at Foxend Corner?"

Alex nodded.

"There's a hole in the base of a dead ash, east of center. Smaller of the two. I'll check it as I'm able." Thatcher drained his mug, yet he did not reach for his great coat. Clearly the man had more on his mind.

Alex folded his arms. "Ford isn't seriously expecting me to have a report for him already, is he?"

"On the contrary." Reaching into an inside pocket of his waistcoat, Thatcher pulled out an envelope and slid it across the tabletop. "He's sent a missive."

"So soon?" Strange. Ford had briefed him long into the night and well into the morning before Alex had packed his bag and set foot on the coach. Reaching for the letter, he studied the wax seal on the back. Not that he didn't trust Thatcher, and in fact would with his life, but some habits refused to die no matter the absurdity.

He scanned the first few words, his mouth slowly dropping. Pausing to blink, he reread the immaculate penmanship, then continued on. Surely not. He shifted, tilting the paper to the best advantage in the dim light. Each word sliced into his soul like an assassin's rapier. "Dash it!" He growled under his breath, anger building with each beat of his heart. "Dash it! Dash it! Dash it!"

Thatcher's dark eyes widened. "Is that your official response?"

"No. This is." He shot to his feet, balled up the paper, and lobbed it across the room into the hearth. Quail and his band turned as one in his direction, but Alex didn't sit until flames engulfed the magistrate's note.

Then he leveled a granite stare at Thatcher. "This time Ford's asked too much."

CHAPTER FOUR

Retrieving his hat from a peg on the wall, Alex clapped it atop his head, then straightened his collar. Good enough, for now. He'd fret over his appearance later this eve, when it really mattered.

Happy to leave behind the tiny bed of torture he'd shared with Lucius Nutbrown, he crossed the small chamber in three strides. Nutbrown. Gads! What a bizarre fellow. Spare of mind and fat as well. Reaching for the door, Alex bit back a wince and pressed a hand against the sore spot below his ribs. Nutbrown's elbows and knees had battered him more thoroughly than the time he'd lost a bare-knuckled brawl to Tom Cribb. Aah, but that fight with Cribb had taught him a trick or two—and so had his evening with Nutbrown.

Tonight he'd bed down on the floor.

He pulled shut the door and headed downstairs, the snores of Quail and his band distinguishable in the empty taproom. Sweet heavens! The ragtag fellows made as much racket asleep as with instruments in hand.

Stifling a yawn, he silently cursed Nutbrown and Quail for the fatigue weighing his steps—but he'd likely have laid awake the entire night anyway. He scowled as he passed by the hearth. Ford's directive taunted him from the ashes. Not that he'd never been asked to put his life on the line before, but this? He'd rather face a hundred musket barrels at point-blank range than even consider marrying a woman he'd never met. Why on earth would the magistrate order him to offer for the viscount's daughter? Thatcher better return with some good answers—or this game was over before it even began.

"Excuse me, Mr. Morton, but have you seen my brother this morning?"

The sweet voice of Johanna Langley turned him around, and all thoughts of Ford and weddings evaporated. She stood six paces from him, fresh as the late spring morning, in a blue dress that had no right to brush over her curves so mercilessly. Wisps of dark hair escaped her hairpins, sweeping across her brow in such an innocent fashion, his fingers itched to smooth it back. How soft would it feel against his skin? Like the down of a gosling or the silk of a—

"Mr. Morton?"

A slow burn worked its way up from his gut. Had she noticed his stare? Giving himself a mental shake, he replayed her original question then shot her one of his own. "The lad's slipped you again, has he?"

"Afraid so." When she frowned, a crescent-shaped dimple in her chin appeared, quite beguiling and—

Oh, no. He'd not be caught twice at the same crime. He purposely focused instead on a point just beyond her ear, giving the impression he looked at her but without the temptation to ogle her like a love-struck schoolboy. What was going on with him to skew his thinking so? Lack of breakfast, perhaps. Or lack of sleep?

That was it.

Relieved to have solved the mystery, he rolled his shoulders and returned his gaze to hers. "I am surprised to find you still here. Are you not attending the parade?"

Johanna retrieved a tipped-over mug lying forgotten on the floor. After setting it in the dish bin near the kitchen door, she turned to him. "The running of an inn does not cease for a holiday."

"Right." He swiveled his head, taking in the taproom from one corner to the other. "Quite the bustle in here, I'd say."

She scowled, or perhaps not. Honestly, how did one tell if an angel grimaced?

The thought made him smirk. "Come now, do you never have any fun, Miss Langley?"

"Not if I can help it."

"Then I shall make it my personal quest to remedy that ailment and see you to the parade myself." He angled his arm in invitation.

Johanna's eyes skimmed over his sleeve, but nothing more. Apparently, she'd have none of his offer.

Well then, if entertainment weren't a draw, he'd use another tactic—something he was never short of supplying. "We might find your brother amongst the merrymakers." He added a wink.

For the first time that morning, a smile dawned on her face, bright enough to shame the sun. "You are very persuasive, Mr. Morton."

"You have no idea." He matched her grin.

"Humph." The sound was an exact replication of her mother's. "Give me a moment to grab a bonnet, then."

"Oh, and don't forget." He pointed to a ragged bit of oak leaf pinned to his lapel. He supposed he ought to feel guilty for ripping the snippet of greenery from the gnarly garland he'd hung yesterday—but he didn't. "You should be thankful it was I who came upon you this morn and not Mr. Quail. When he does finally surface, I've no doubt he'll keep a keen eye out for forgetful misses who've neglected to sport a leaf this Oak Apple Day. . .unless you're intending to solicit pinches?"

Her eyes widened into brown pools, complimented by a deep flush spreading over her cheeks. She spun and stalked off, her skirt swishing fiercely enough to stir the ashes in the hearth.

He suppressed a laugh. Making the prim Johanna Langley blush was good sport, but not his purpose here in Dover. While he waited for her return, he devised his plan for the morning. With the town gathered for the parade, he'd have the best opportunity to study people. Though Ford suspected a traitor amongst Dover's elite, a conspirator rarely acted alone. Most likely there was a disgruntled lackey or two among the common folk who carried out the less desirable tasks associated with intrigue.

"All right, I am ready, sir, though I warn you I shan't stay long." Johanna's voice preceded her as she swept into the room. Her dark hair was tucked beneath a straw bonnet, a brown shawl caressed her shoulders, and yes. . .a sprig of oak leaf was pinned to her collar like a warrior's shield. "My mother will need me to prepare for this evening when the inn shall be"—she mimicked his earlier gaze about the taproom—"*quite the bustle.*"

He smiled. Prim, yet saucy...traits far more alluring than the usual flattering and fawning.

Crossing to the door, he held it wide for her. When she passed, he gained her side, and they proceeded onto an empty street. The low drone of a crowd carried from blocks away, where the parade would begin.

"Tell me, Miss Langley." He glanced at her sideways. "Have you lived in Dover all your life?"

She nodded. "And Mam tells me you're from Sheffield."

He was glad she stared straight ahead, her face half-hidden by her bonnet's brim. The lying part of his job usually flowed smoothly, but this time, with this woman, a queer ripple of conscience came out of nowhere, cutting off his carefully prepared answer. Were she an officer or a scalawag, she'd have caught his hesitation. "Yes, Sheffield it is."

At the corner, they turned right. Latecomers like themselves dotted this street. The distinct tattoo of a drum corps chastened them to up the tempo of their pace.

"How long do you plan to stay here, Mr. Morton?"

"Depends." His answer was as evasive as Thatcher's the night before.

"On?"

He cut her yet another glance, and still she did not meet his eyes. Was she purposely hiding her face? Interesting method. Bow Street could use an interrogator like this woman. "Business."

He expected more inquiry, even formulated a few semi-truths that wouldn't be outright falsehoods, yet she surprised him once again by holding her tongue.

The closer they drew to the festivities, the more they zigzagged around a gauntlet of vendors selling parade whistles and all sorts of sweet treats. A thick hedge of people gathered two blocks ahead along the High Street, where an effigy of King Charles would be borne upon a flower-strewn cart. Alex veered to the left, hoping to avoid the crush of revelers and instead perch upon a stack of crates near the mouth of an alley for a bird's-eye view—though how he'd persuade Johanna to such heights was a mystery.

Good thing he had his tactics.

"Oh, Johanna!" Across the street, a female voice rang above the crowd. "Over here!"

Johanna waved then faced him. "Do you mind, Mr. Morton? I'd like to say hello, if only for a moment."

"After you." He swept out his hand.

The woman they approached was of a slighter build than Johanna. In truth, he feared a stout wind might tip her over—a very real danger this close to the Channel with the breeze gusting in from the southeast. She held a babe, bundled in a thick blanket as if the late spring sunshine were a foe.

"Good day to you, Maggie." Johanna smiled at her friend then fixed her gaze on the child. "And how is little Charlotte?"

"See for yourself." The woman, Maggie, handed the bundle to Johanna.

You'd have thought she'd been given the crown jewels. Her face beamed. *Coo*s and *oh*s and, "Who's a sweet baby?" bubbled from her mouth.

Maggie looked from Johanna to him, then back again. Johanna kept on murmuring endearments to the wee one, oblivious to the awkward situation. If she loved children so much, why was she not married with babes of her own?

Alex stepped forward. "With Miss Langley preoccupied, allow me to introduce myself. I am Mr. Morton."

Maggie dipped her head. "Pleased to meet you, sir. I am Jo's longtime friend, Mrs. Scott. At least we used to be friends, until I had Charlotte. Now I'm not so sure she even knows I exist." She nudged Johanna with her elbow. "Right, Jo?"

"Hmm?" Johanna looked up, then adjusted her voice down a notch from baby talk. "Oh, sorry. May I introduce Mr. Mor—"

"No need, Jo." Maggie slid a grin from her to Alex. "We've already met."

Beneath her bonnet brim, Johanna's brow scrunched, but only for a moment. She turned her face and went right back to gooing and gawing at the babe.

"Mags! Come along, Wife. I've a place for us up front." A shorn-headed man, as excessively stout as Maggie was thin, beckoned from the crowd ahead.

"Sorry, Jo." Maggie held out her arms. "You'll have to play with Lottie another time."

Johanna handed back the babe with a sigh. "I'll hold you to that."

"I have no doubt. I'll stop over in a few days. Good day Johanna, Mr. Morton." The woman nodded toward them both, then scurried after her husband.

By now the drums had passed and trumpeters blasted away. The parade would be over before he could assess the gathering. "If you're up for a little unconventionality, Miss Langley, I've spotted just the place to watch the parade." He pointed toward the passageway across the street.

She frowned, the dimple reappearing in all its glory. "All I see are a pile of boxes."

"Exactly."

Lifting her face to his, she narrowed her eyes. "What have you in mind, sir?"

"There's no time to explain if you want to be able to see the parade—and possibly your brother."

Her brow lifted.

Enough of a consent for him. He grabbed her gloved hand and led her across the road, ignoring another *humph* from her.

Stacking one crate atop another, he assembled a small platform, but with no easy way for a lady to ascend—and he'd used up all the boxes. "Wait here."

He trudged farther down the narrow passageway, scanning the shadows created by the two tall buildings. There ought to be another crate or at least a rock to use as a step. Midway down, a dark figure entered from the other end. With each step, the man grew larger—and each step was unmistakable. One of the man's legs was wooden.

For a second, Alex froze. The village of Deal wasn't that far from Dover, where a peg-legged smuggler had escaped the reach of the law—*his* reach—in the Dooley Affair. A free trader who knew his face.

One who could easily reveal his true identity.

"Aye there, matey," the man called out. "Can ye spare a swig o' the nipper with someone in need?"

The voice was bass, carrying a slight lisp, spoken like someone who'd had half his teeth knocked out. Alex flexed his fists, the scars on his knuckles tightening. No doubt about it. Blackjack Cooper.

Alex wheeled about—

To face Johanna, who'd followed him. "Mr. Morton, are we to see this parade or not?"

Behind her, swinging around the corner of the building and into the alley, came a short fellow with a crop of red hair too wiry to fit completely beneath his hat. "Ay Blackie! Been lookin' for ye."

Alex bit down hard on a curse. Blackjack's accomplice, Charlie Pickens, known as the Axe. Not that he should be surprised. The two were close as scabs on a pox victim.

Sinking a bit, Alex leaned toward the wall, using Johanna as cover. A few more paces and Charlie would gain a full view of his face. But if Alex turned away, he'd expose himself to Blackjack.

His heart pounded hard in his ears. He didn't have any tactics left—save one. Gathering Johanna in his arms, he pressed her against the brick wall.

And kissed her.

Heat spread through Johanna. Feelings she'd never before experienced—let alone would be able to name—made her dizzy and breathless and horrifyingly wanting more. For the second time in as many days, the arms of Alexander Morton held her in a tight embrace. Only this time his mouth burned a fire against hers. Maddening enough, but worse, her body—the traitor—leaned into it, enjoying the swirly-headed sensation of freefalling.

Well, then. There were no other options. She jabbed her knee upward, connecting quite sharply with his most vulnerable area.

He released her at once, doubling over with a groan.

"How dare you!" She spoke as much to herself as to him, hating the way she already missed his warmth.

"Please. . .I can"—he gasped, his voice straining on the sharp inhale—"explain."

She turned on her heel and darted ahead. The explanations of men were never to be trusted, a hard truth she'd learned well from her father.

"Miss Langley, wait!"

It would be satisfying to turn and watch him hobbling behind, but not very effective if she wanted to evade the grasping liar. Had compromising her been his plan all along? If so, she much preferred the libertine Mr. Quail. At least he didn't pretend.

Bypassing two men, one short and one peg-legged, she dove into the crowd, earning herself a few, "I beg your pardon's," and some outright curses. Holding her loosened bonnet atop her head with one hand, she used the other like a plow, turning rows of people and clearing space enough to wriggle through. She dodged a group of schoolboys, skirted an overturned barrel of pickles and an angry vendor, then darted across the street behind a row of redcoats on horseback. The view was not pleasant, neither the odor, but she made it to the other side without slipping in a pile of manure.

The crowd was thinner here, and she soon discovered why. Her dress clung to her moist skin, the sun having full rein to beat down upon the spectators without hindrance. After a glance over her shoulder, she slowed her pace, both from necessity and relief. No broad-shouldered man with hair the color of ripened wheat followed her. For a moment, she considered stopping and watching the last of the parade—until a freckle-faced boy crossed her path.

She snatched Thomas's collar an instant before he could dash off. "How providential, Brother. I've been looking for you. There's an inn full of musicians for you to attend, and they're likely waking just about now. It's chamber pot duty for you, my boy."

"Aww, Jo!" Thomas squirmed in her grip.

"Come along." She tugged him out of the press of the crowd and onto a side street. He rattled off excuse after excuse about why he shouldn't have to work, ranging from an old hoop rolling injury in his knee that he claimed pained him to no end, to pleading he was only a child.

She bit back a smile as she yanked him around the corner of St.

James—then froze. Two paces in front of her stood Mr. Spurge, the man she'd been trying to avoid for the past two weeks.

The lien holder of the Blue Hedge Inn.

"Miss Langley." His dark eyes narrowed as he drawled out her name. He towered above her, his height emphasized by a tall, black hat. "How fortunate to cross paths."

Thomas scooted behind her, the coward. Was this how Lucius Nutbrown felt when she confronted him for rent? "Mr. Spurge." She bobbed her head. "G-good to see you."

"I wonder." He stared down his nose as if he were a king. His white hair and beard were as colorless as his voice. "I've stopped off several times to collect what's owed me. I daresay, judging by the frequent absence of you and your mother, that it's a wonder the Blue Hedge Inn operates at all."

"Yes, well. . .I can explain." Wonderful. She sounded exactly like Mr. Morton. For a moment, she considered shoving Thomas to the front and letting his wily tongue spin a whale of a tale.

Spurge held up a gloved hand. "No explanation required. Simply provide what's owed me by next Friday."

She licked her lips. With any luck, sweet words would flow, giving him reason to put off what she prayed wasn't the inevitable. "Perhaps you ought make that the week after, sir. With all the busyness of the holiday, I'm sure you can understand—"

"What I understand, Miss Langley, is that you and your mother need to face facts. The Blue Hedge Inn is going under. I suggest you bail out as soon as possible."

His prophecy hung in the air, as unpleasant as the stink of the soldiers and their horses. Fighting the urge to run away, she planted her feet a little wider apart and lifted her chin. "We've been in dire straits before, Mr. Spurge. God always provides a way out."

"Funny. I've heard that sentiment many times." The lines of his face hardened into angry tracks. "Until a stint in the workhouse changes that philosophy. One week, Miss Langley. Twenty-five pounds. Nothing less."

"Very well." She lifted her chin higher. "You shall have it."

"Yes, I shall." A sneer slid across his face. "One way or another."

Without waiting for her reply, he tipped his hat, then sidestepped them both.

She watched his camel-colored dress coat disappear into the crowd, her confidence vanishing along with him.

Thomas tugged her sleeve. "Where you gonna get twenty-five pounds by next Friday, Jo?"

She blew out a long, low breath. Miracles still happened.

Didn't they?

CHAPTER FIVE

Alex handed over his invitation to a footman, who was more primped and tailored than some of the guests. If the viscount's servants were this ostentatious, what would the man himself be like? And worse...what of his daughter?

He swallowed back a bitter taste and forced a pleasant curve to his lips. Better to shove aside all thought of Ford's ludicrous directive for now, tuck it away into a back corner of his mind. Given enough time, surely he could come up with some plan that would release him from obeying such an outrageous command—and perhaps he worried for nothing. He could've misunderstood. Thatcher had yet to return with clarification. Or maybe Ford had changed his mind.

Oh God, make it so.

The footman placed the invitation into a basket stationed next to him. "Welcome, Mr. Morton."

Alex strode into Lord Coburn's mansion as if he owned the place, confidence his best ally for the moment. He grabbed a glass from a passing silver tray and drained the contents before crossing the front atrium. The drink was not overly sweet and left a dry aftertaste. No bubbles tickled the back of his throat, but even so, he had no doubt about the origin of the viscount's wine. Sparkling or not, champagne always made him—

He turned aside and gave in to the inevitable sneeze.

Pinching the bridge of his nose to ward off a repeat performance, he entered a wide corridor and headed toward the open doors of a ballroom. With each step, he collected curious glances from strangers. He knew no one, but could name them just the same. The fat merchant hoping to sell his soul to gain a contract with the viscount was Greed. The servant sneaking off for a tryst in an unused closet, Lust. And the pair of matrons whose plan was to allow their charges enough slack to hog-tie a bachelor? Self-serving Languor. Here in a manor home or down at a quayside bawdy house, people were people the world 'round.

The first notes of a quadrille welcomed him into the ballroom, and once past the threshold, he fought the urge to cover his eyes from the brilliance of chandeliers, jewels, and hopeful gazes noting his entrance. To his right, a line of dancers bowed in front of their partners, one dark head and slender figure almost familiar. From this distance, however, he couldn't be certain.

Quickening his pace, he skirted the gathering, hoping to gain a closer look. The woman was petite, shapely, and then completely blocked by an ape-shouldered monster of a fellow. Alex angled for a better view and. . . there. Was it? Could that be Johanna Langley?

But when the woman looked up and bright light bathed her face, blue eyes stared back at him, not brown.

And not angry.

He averted his gaze and moved on. Surely one glass of champagne couldn't have skewed his vision already—but yes. Better to blame the fruit of the vine than a truth he dare not admit.

He could not get the woman out of his thoughts.

Aah, but Johanna Langley was a fiery one when roused. He'd spent the better part of the afternoon trying to chase her down and apologize for the kiss. Every time he drew near, she shot off like a fox from a hound. Not that he blamed her. His behavior had been abominable.

But it had worked. By the time Johanna had stomped out of the alley, Blackjack and Charlie had disappeared down the street.

Unfortunately, the ground he stood on now wasn't much safer. How the deuce had he strayed so close to the punch table? Females of all shapes and sizes eyed him over the rims of their cups. He suddenly understood why a stag froze. The slightest twitch would be conveyed as an invitation, drawing a rush of taffeta and ambition.

Slowly, he shifted his weight, prepared for a quick about-face. Handkerchiefs dropped like a cloudburst. If he picked up one, a frenzy would break loose. There was nothing to be done for it, then. Sometimes the best way out was to simply barrel through. So he did—

And came face-to-face with three matriarchs, cocking their heads in unison, eyeing him like a vulture over a laid-out carcass. He swallowed.

They advanced.

He'd rather take on Blackjack and Charlie's swinging axe than this.

"There you are! Come along, ol' scuffer. We've been waiting on you." A deep voice reached his ear an instant before an arm draped around his shoulder and towed him sideways.

The fellow who led him through the crowd was short, the top of his slicked-back hair even with Alex's nose. He smelled of pomade and cherry tobacco—and *strongly*, to be distinguishable in the midst of ladies who'd bathed in rose water and lavender. He was also no stranger to the viscount's mansion. Instead of crossing the length of the ballroom, he darted behind a three-paned partition near the wall, used to disguise the comings and goings of servants. Behind the panel, the man paused in front of a closed door and turned. "That was close. What were you thinking?"

"I..." Exactly. *Think*. Should he know this fellow? Had he overlooked any passwords or codes given him during the magistrate's briefing?

Swerving away from a passing servant, Alex summed up his options, the best being to play along with this charade—but charades was his least favorite party game. He looked the man square in the eyes. "Do I know you?"

"Likely not." Stubby, yellowed teeth peeked out of a grin that lifted clear to the man's brow. He'd only seen that once before—on a goat. "You're new here, are you not, Mr. Morton? Oh, hang it all. That's much too formal. I shall call you Alex, if you don't mind, or even if you do."

Alex rubbed the back of his neck, stalling for time. Was this man a threat or as big a ninny as Nutbrown? Either way, the fellow knew his name, a distinct disadvantage for him since Alex couldn't credit who he might be.

"Don't think too hard on it, old man. I had the footman alert me should we have the good fortune of the arrival of a new player. You didn't really want to dance, did you?" The man's gaze flickered over him from head to toe. "You don't strike me as a fleet-footed dandy."

"You might be surprised."

"Pah!" He landed a playful punch on Alex's upper arm. "If we're to be gaming partners, I suppose I should introduce myself. I'm Robert Coburn, but call me Robbie. Quite got used to it over there." His head angled toward the west.

"Bristol?"

"Boston. Served some time as a lieutenant. And now that the formalities are over. . ." He turned and shoved open the door. "Shall we?"

"What have you in mind?"

Robbie glanced over his shoulder before entering a dimly lit stairwell. "You can thank me for this later."

Flexing the fingers of his right hand should he need to draw the knife hidden inside his waistcoat, Alex followed Robert—*Robbie*—up the stairwell. The man's surname was the same as the viscount's, but the spring in his step, lack of polished manners, and careless demeanor labeled him anything but. Probably. Not that he hadn't encountered stranger things.

Alex blinked in the dimmer lighting. Were shadows and confined spaces among his fears, he'd likely be sweating. The higher they climbed, the more the music and laughter of the ballroom faded. With this many stairs, he suspected they'd bypassed the first floor and gone directly to the second.

At the top step, for there was no landing, Robbie knocked on a panel with no knob. Two sharp raps, a pause, then five successive taps. The door opened inward. Cigar smoke wafted out. Before Robbie passed through, he glanced back. "You do play faro, don't you, Alex?"

The muscles in his gut tightened. This had been far too easy. Almost like a gambling rogue had been expected to walk through the viscount's door this night. He wrapped his fingers around the hilt of his knife, taking care to keep the blade concealed.

"Alex?"

He forced a half smile. "Sorry. Just trying to recall the rules of the game. Now that I think on it, I believe I have played a time or two."

"Excellent!" Robbie strode through the door.

Alex stopped on the threshold, ready to sprint back down the stairwell if necessary. A few paces away, a manservant near a sideboard appeared innocuous enough. Hard to tell about the three men seated at a round table halfway across the room, especially since a fair amount of ivory betting chips at center indicated a small fortune was currently at stake.

"Look what I found." Robbie beamed a smile and swept a hand toward him. "Fresh meat."

The thinnest of the men, seated nearest the hearth, flicked an ash from his cheroot onto a crystal saucer. He studied Alex as he might a new card, then refocused on his own hand, discarding the new arrival as a non-trump.

The fellow sitting opposite him stuck out his lower lip, considering Alex as if he were a tray of sliced beef or carved guinea fowl. In truth, the man would likely pass up neither. Gaps stretching between the double buttons on his red coat—the pairs of them giving away his rank as major general—attested to his love affair with food.

The third man, seated with his back to them, didn't move. Not at first. Then a slight ripple whispered across the fabric between his shoulder blades, barely perceptible.

Alex shifted his weight, poised to flee.

The man shot to his feet, turned, and fired a black powder pistol.

A scream gushed from Robbie's mouth. Blood streamed from his hand. He dropped to his knees, clutching the injury to his chest. The bullet had passed through Robbie's hand and lodged into the mahogany paneling dangerously close to Alex. It wasn't a killing shot. It was a warning.

Alex clenched his dagger tighter, ready for anything.

The man holding the gun flicked his gaze toward Alex, summing him up with a sweep of his eyes. Alex returned the favor. The fellow was neither large nor gaunt. His dress coat was well tailored in an understated fashion. The cut of his trousers labeled him neither a trendsetter nor outmoded. His hair, greying at the temples and thinning on top, was brushed back into a nondescript style, his face clean-shaven and without blemish. Truly, he was no more interesting or intimidating than a dish of jellied pigeon livers. Yet with a single nod toward the servant, the man commanded immediate action.

The manservant rushed to Robbie's side and helped him to stand. With an arm around his shoulder, he escorted Robbie out of the room, leaving a trail of stains in the carpet and the remnants of Robbie's whimpering.

"Well, I suppose we'll give you a try, being that you're already here." The man tucked away his pistol and locked stares with Alex. "Are you going to stand there or play cards? Oh, and grab yourself a drink first. Drake will likely be busy with Robert for a while."

Sheathing his knife, Alex closed the door behind him, sealing off the ghostly chords from the ball far below. He counted his steps—twelve—over to the sideboard laden with bottles, glasses, and an intricately carved cigar box. Then he estimated the remaining steps—six—to the only other exit from the room, the door Robbie had been ushered through. Sometimes the difference between life and death was a number. Alex added the information to his arsenal, for he might well need it. The only available seat would leave him facing away from the main door. He'd known one too many officers who'd taken a lead ball to the back of the skull from a situation such as this.

Bypassing a crystal decanter of brandy, he grabbed a green bottle of wine and a glass, then seated himself. He poured only enough to leave the bottle mostly full, then positioned it to his right, two hand spans from the table's edge. It made for a poor mirror, but from that angle, he'd at least see should the door open.

"Two-fisted drinker, eh?" The fat major general spoke, his voice distinctive—like the bark of a dog that'd been at it for too long. Though with the thick folds around the man's neck, it was a wonder words came out at all. "My kind of fellow, but let's be about it, hmm? I assume you have the money to front your bets?"

Alex nodded. "If I didn't, I'd have made a dash for it down the stairs by now."

Without another word, the man shoved five chips toward him, and the game was on. These fellows were serious. Conversation was not only an unnecessary interruption, but clearly an unwelcome one as well. A tip of the head. The blink of an eye. Even the lifting of a finger communicated far more loudly than a roomful of sailors embroiled in a round of hazard.

The first card dealt didn't interest Alex so much as the second, and neither of those as much as the cards toward the end of the deck. He had no clue how much a chip was worth, but no matter. The magistrate had endowed him with a sizable sum, and Thatcher could always retrieve more funds for him. He slid his entire stack of chips onto the nine of spades printed on the felt in front of the dealer—the man he assumed to be the viscount. Coburn flipped over the last card.

Alex smiled, then scooped up his winnings.

As the game wore on, he continued his devil-take-all strategy. At first, the others split their bets between cards, but as his stack grew and theirs diminished, their patterns changed. All of them placed the sum of their chips on what they felt would be the winning card. Alex suppressed a smirk. Monkeys, even well-dressed ones, were known to mimic.

And that didn't slow his winning streak. Though the men looked the part of well-versed gamblers, they weren't. Oh, they'd employed a few winning strategies early on in the game, but nothing he hadn't already encountered during his darker, cardsharp days.

When Alex's chips outnumbered everyone's, the dealer threw down the deck of cards and leaned back in his chair. For a tense few moments, nothing but the ticking of the ornately inlaid longcase clock in the corner broke the silence. That and the loud grumble of the big man's belly.

Finally, the dealer leaned forward, skewering Alex with an intense gaze. "Where did Robert find you?"

Alex smiled, offsetting his jaw slightly, the same grin that'd saved his behind more than a time or two. "He rescued me from a rabid pack of debutantes."

The silence stretched once again, but this time only as far as it took for his words to sink in. Laughter, starting with the fat major general, spread around the table.

"I suppose I ought not have reprimanded him so harshly, then. But you must understand, my nephew has been warned on previous occasions to stop bringing uninvited players to my table. He needs to learn I mean what I say. I am Viscount Edward Coburn, the lord of this manor, or what's left of it after your significant fleecing." The viscount lifted a brow at the winnings heaped atop the last bet Alex had placed. After a sigh, he swept out his hand—a large, gold signet ring flashing with the movement—and indicated each man in turn. "And you've also lightened the pockets of Mr. James Conroy and Major General William Overtun."

"Gentlemen, pleased to make your acquaintances, and especially pleased to take your money." He scooped the chips toward his side of the table. It was a hefty sum. Perhaps he ought be more thankful that Ford had given him this assignment. "I am Alexander Morton—"

A sharp rapping at the door cut him off.

Lord Coburn raised halfway, a distinct growl rising from his throat as well. "I said I was not to be disturbed until—"

The door flew open. Every nerve on edge, Alex reached for his knife, then slowly regained his lost breath when he saw the swirl of a skirt reflected on the bottle in front of him.

"I can hold off dinner no longer." The woman's voice, while cultured and resonant, was harsher than a fishwife's. "Either you come down—now—or I shall lead every last guest up here to your little sanctuary, Father."

Father? A cold sweat shivered through Alex. Slowly, he stood and turned.

And looked full into the face of the woman he'd been ordered to marry.

"Will you marry me?"

If her hands weren't full, Johanna would slap the silly, lopsided grin off Mr. Quail's face as soundly as she'd clouted Mr. Morton earlier in the day. She didn't have time for this lunacy, not with a full taproom. Taking care to keep the dishes from toppling, she pulled from Mr. Quail's touch on her arm and turned slightly, wielding her tray of dirty soup bowls like a shield. "How many cups of ale have you downed tonight, sir?"

He clapped a hand over his heart and staggered back, earning himself a tart reply from the redhead behind him. Ignoring her, he kept his gaze pinned on Jo. "You wound me, my fairest, to imply my wits have been compromised."

"Better your wits than me," she shot back.

With a laugh, the redhead craned her neck over Mr. Quail's shoulder. "She's got ye there, she does. Yer better at singin' than courtin'."

"Really?" Mr. Quail shifted his eyes sideways, a tic running along his jaw. "And what would you know about music, except for bawdy house ditties and—"

"Mr. Quail," Johanna breathed out his name as a warning. There was no way he could see the big man approaching to his left, though he might have felt the floor rumble with each of the fellow's giant steps. A brawl now would break more than all the mugs Thomas had dropped this evening.

"There a problem, Lovey?" The man draped his arm around the redhead's shoulder, pulling her toward him.

Johanna forced a smile. "I'd say the only problem is the music has stopped. Should you not be about it, Mr. Quail?"

"That I should." Sneaking in a quick wink, he darted off in the opposite direction of Lovey and her man.

Thomas didn't see him coming. He was too busy weaving in and out of people at top speed with an armful of mugs.

Quail swerved an instant before impact, leaning hard on one foot while swooping his arms to keep him upright.

Thomas teetered like a wobbly top, far to one side, then the other, until there was nothing to be done for it but to throw out his hands like Quail had done.

Six earthenware tankards shattered on the floor. Johanna frowned at them. She ought be glad it wasn't her brother's head hitting the planks—which truly she was. But such an event might knock some sense into the boy. A wicked thought, but one that could not be helped.

Had she not told him thrice in the past hour to slow down?

He scooped up the pieces with a laugh, as if the world were nothing but a riddle and he the jester.

"Oh, Thomas." She groaned and her shoulders slumped, rattling the bowls on her tray. Where would they find the extra funds to replace all he'd broken?

"Don't be hard on him, Jo. He's but a boy."

She turned toward her mother's voice. Creases fanned out at the sides of Mam's eyes. Shadows smudged half-circles underneath. Had she ever seen her mother look quite so tired? A woman her age ought to be dandling a grandchild on her knee, not running foamy heads of ale to and fro like a common bar wench.

But at least they had customers to serve. Last Johanna had checked, the coin jar was nearly half full—not enough to stave off Mr. Spurge, but at least the miller would be paid. Blowing out a sigh and a prayer, she repented of her foul attitude.

"You're right." She smiled at Mam. "Thomas is young. I should be thankful he's working and—"

A scream ripped out the kitchen door. Mam's hands flew to her heart. The music stopped as quickly as it began.

Dropping the tray of bowls, Johanna broke into a dead run toward the howling, heedless of who she shoved aside. "Thomas!"

Her brother tore into the taproom, the hem of his trousers aflame. The faster he ran, the higher the fire climbed.

Jo launched forward, tackling him to the ground. She wrapped her arms about him and rolled. Over and over. Smothering the flames between her and the floor. The stench of burnt fabric and flesh was sickening. The heat of his clothes singed her own skin, but she wouldn't quit. She'd roll back and forth until the flames of hell were quenched if that's what it took.

"Lassie, lassie! It's done. It's over."

The deep voice of a Scotsman cut into her nightmare. Breathing hard, she rolled to a stop and pushed up slightly.

Beneath her, Thomas lay still. Eyes shut. Mouth slack.

"No!" She wailed. "God, please. Not Thomas!"

CHAPTER SIX

Alex studied the woman standing in the doorway. Only one word came to mind. Green. Yet color had nothing to do with it. Her off-white gown was embellished with golden embroidery, all loopy and feminine. If he squinted, the design took on a fleur-de-lis pattern strange icon for an English woman these days. Her hair was dark, her eyes darker. She didn't appear to be ill or jealous, yet all the same she was green. Straight and willowy as a field of grass, lithe as a fern frond, all delicate and wispy. A pleasing sight, one that might turn a man's head—but not his.

She directed a cancerous gaze at her father. "Why will Robbie not be joining us?"

"He is detained." The viscount ground out his cheroot onto an already overloaded salver, creating a small cloud of ash. Then he nodded toward Alex. "I am sure Mr. Morton here will be happy to fill your cousin's seat so that you should not lack for a dinner companion. You will find him a refreshing diversion. Mr. Morton, meet my daughter, Miss Louisa Coburn. Louisa, Mr. Alexander Morton."

Alex kept his gaming face intact, though not without struggle. What an irregular breach of protocol. Why would the viscount seat him, having no knowledge of his heritage or credentials, above known guests who surely bore higher social rank? Clearly the man had no qualms about making enemies or choosing his allies on a whim. Nothing about this evening made sense. What nest of hornets had Ford sent him into?

A scowl marred Louisa's pretty face. "You cannot be serious, Father."

Still, this was an opportunity he shouldn't pass up. Alex advanced, leaving behind the three men at the table. "Your father speaks truth, Miss Coburn." He flourished a bow and finished with a rogue grin. "Not only will I take pleasure in dining next to you, but it is my deepest desire."

Her lips parted, closed, then parted once again.

Lord Coburn snorted. "Flit, girl! Don't stand there gaping like a codfish."

A small dimple—not nearly as charming as Johanna's—indented her chin, deepening when she clamped her lips shut.

Alex crooked his arm. "I should be delighted to escort you."

"Very well." At last she rested her fingertips atop his arm, allowing him to lead her out the door.

He paused. "Left or right?"

Her fingers twitched, the movement frustrating the fabric of his sleeve. "Don't tell me you are too far into your cups to remember which way you came, Mr. Morton."

He glanced sideways. "Not at all, Miss Coburn, though the way I came is a bit narrow for such a wide hem as yours."

"Oh, you are one of those. I expected as much." Her voice held all the warmth of a baited bear. Removing her hand from his arm, she turned left and set off at a surprisingly brisk pace.

He caught up in four long strides. "I am curious about the category you've filed me under. Should I be flattered or affronted that I'm one of *those*?"

"That depends if you consider it a badge of honor to be a member of my father's cronies."

He smiled. Ford would be proud of the progress he'd made in only two days.

Pieces of gilded-framed artwork blurred as they sped down the corridor. When this woman was on a mission, she obviously would not be stopped, a hallmark of determination and danger. He tucked the trait away for later use.

"So tell me, Miss Coburn. Do you fancy him?"

She angled her face, a fine line following the curve of her brow. "Whom?"

"Robbie, of course."

Her step hitched at the top of a grand stairway, and he offered his arm. She ignored it, but the fingers of her other hand gripped the banister tightly. "What a strange question, Mr. Morton. Why ever would you ask it?"

"I noted it was an unwelcome surprise when you discovered Robbie would not be present."

"Which merely indicates I dislike change."

"Aah, but combined with the flare of your nostrils and the heightened color in your cheeks, I wondered if there were something more?"

She descended the stairway without an answer, then stopped at the bottom and faced him. "You are quite observant, sir."

As was she. Her gaze pinged from his left eye to his right and back again, as if he hid truth behind one or the other like the shell game Thomas had tried to master. Her father and his friends bypassed them into the milling guests, heralding the beginning of dinner, but Louisa did not move. Apparently infringing upon etiquette ran in the family, for she ought be leading the other women into the dining room at this moment.

Alex pulled his attention from the daughter to the father, just before Lord Coburn disappeared into the dining room. The man's left foot lingered behind the right, slightly dragging to catch up with each step. Quite the distinctive limp. An old war injury, perhaps? A defect from birth? Or was some disease even now leaching life in increments from the man?

Louisa followed his gaze, her eyes narrowing. "How does Father know you?"

"I am a recent acquaintance."

Her lips puckered like a tot trying to figure out by what means rain fell from the sky. "By what connection?"

"Commerce."

"La, sir! Are you nothing but a merchant?"

He leaned in, close enough to inhale a whiff of civet musk—a scent all the rage in France. "I am a man with many skills, Miss Coburn." He allowed just the right amount of huskiness to his voice, intimating at promises he never intended to make, Ford's directive or otherwise. "The question is what would you like me to be?"

Her pupils widened. The rise and fall of a Cross of Lorraine pendant resting between her collarbones increased. Again, a very curious choice of accoutrement. Surely the traitor Ford sought wasn't this woman.

Or was it? Lord knows he'd collared his fair share of female criminals on London's streets. Perhaps Dover's were no different.

"The hour is late, Mr. Morton, and I have put off dinner long enough." She turned and dashed ahead of him toward the dining room, then slowed her pace to a more regal gait as she entered.

He followed, as did the eyes of every guest awaiting her arrival. Whispers travelled the length of the long table, from powdered women to clean-shaven men, and a fair amount of officers in their regimentals. Louisa sat at her father's right, and Alex sank into the empty seat next to her.

Lord Coburn snapped open his napkin, placing it on his lap while addressing her under his breath. "Must you insist on dramatics, Louisa?"

"I've learned from the best, Father." She mimicked his napkin fanfare.

Alex bit back a smirk. They both belonged on a Theater Royal stage.

Coburn nodded toward the footmen, lining the walls like soldiers. They stepped forward in one movement and opened the tureens of soup. Alex inhaled. Turtle, he'd bet on it.

The viscount sipped an obligatory spoonful before cocking his head at Alex. "I hope you'll give me the chance to win back some of my fortune, Mr. Morton."

"You have but to say when and where, sir."

"Tomorrow evening. Eight, sharp."

Louisa leaned forward. "I was not aware you'd taken to adding common merchants to your circle, Father."

Alex choked back the broth, mind whizzing to line up a plausible rejoinder. Little troublemaker! A common merchant was *not* the professional spin he'd intended to present to the man.

Lord Coburn lowered his brows toward his daughter. "Better a merchant than a slacker, and a dishonorable one at that."

The cut spread a flush over Louisa's cheeks, and she suddenly took a great interest in her soup. Hard to tell if the blush was inspired by shame—or anger.

Alex set down his spoon. "The lady speaks the truth somewhat, sir. I am a connoisseur of wines, travelling the continent to keep my father's vast collection in stock. You may have heard of him, Mr. Jonathan Morton, esquire? Up near Sheffield."

"Don't believe so, no. Unless. . .any military connections?"

"None whatsoever."

"Then it is a definite no." The viscount mouthed another bite of soup, then put down his spoon as well and eyed him. "But what brings you to Dover? Unless I am mistaken, which I hardly ever am, there are no exotic stores of wine to be had in this part of the country."

Alex paused to allow the footman to remove his dish. "I am on my way home from Porto Moniz, escorting a shipment of a fine Madeira vintage."

The viscount lifted one brow toward Louisa. "Hardly a *common* merchant, I'd say."

Her jaw set into a rigid—albeit pretty—line, though she made no further response.

A butler, austere in his black suit and cravat, handed Lord Coburn a folded slip of paper. Turbulence darkened the viscount's gaze as his eyes roved over the words. He balled the note, palmed it, then stood.

"Excuse me." He bypassed the butler and strode from the room.

Another round of whispers ringed the table, making Alex wonder if the guests attended the viscount's soiree for the opulence of the mansion and the richness of the food—or the intrigue that accompanied the event. Surprising, yet fortunate, for now he had Louisa relatively to himself.

He glanced back at her. A half smile softened her lips. Was she glad for her father's departure or the anguish the missive had caused? Whatever, theirs was no simple relationship.

Alex offered her a slice of beef from the platter in front of them and waited for the nod of her head before continuing. "Now that you know what I do, how is it you occupy yourself?"

"Orchids."

Returning the serving fork to the plate, he chewed on her answer before sampling a bite of his roast. Orchids? What the devil could one do with those? Paint them? Sell them on a street corner? Gather them in bunches and decorate the lounges of all the fine women in Dover? "I was not aware that flowers could be so amusing," he admitted.

Either the beef disgusted her, or he did, for she pushed away her plate.

This would never do. Inducing scorn was a far cry from wooing her. He poured all the charm he owned into an earnest tone of voice. "Miss Coburn, I realize I am a poor replacement for Robbie, but truly, I am applying my best effort. It is not my intention to spar with you, for I should no doubt be the one bleeding on the floor."

She frowned. "You are very odd, Mr. Morton."

"And you are very beautiful." The words came out easily enough, but they left a traitorous aftertaste in his mouth. He didn't mean them—leastwise not in the way he would speak them to Johanna.

Johanna? What the deuce? He reached for his glass and drained it. Why in the world think of her now?

"All right, Mr. Morton. I shall be candid as well." She faced him, quirking her brow. "Father wishes me to be on the hunt for a husband, but I fancy working in the garden, hence my orchid preoccupation."

Interesting. Most females relished husband wrangling as a favorable pastime.

"I wonder if gardening is your true love, Miss Coburn, or rather your passion for rebelling against your father?"

"I assure you, sir, I am nothing but obedient."

She turned back to her meal. Providential, for she missed the roll of his eyes. Obedient, no doubt, but not to her father. To herself.

"I think I can help you, Miss Coburn," he drawled.

She didn't look at him, but he'd snagged her attention all the same, for her brow wrinkled. "With what, sir?"

"Hunting."

Dawn was a heartbeat away, but Johanna couldn't sleep. She wandered the empty taproom, righting benches, straightening tables. She wasn't alone, though. Mr. Quail's snores from upstairs kept her company. The single lantern yet burning cast a blend of shadows and light. Fitting, she mused as she knelt to pick up shards of earthenware. Darkness always found a way to encroach into the brightest parts of her life.

"Oh, Thomas," she whispered. "Why you? Why now?"

The slow shush of the front door answered her. In stepped Mr. Morton, cravat askew, hair loosened and sweeping his collar. Not the polished figure she'd seen leave earlier in the evening, and certainly not a man to be trusted. Even so, for one traitorous moment, she remembered how he'd held her, and the thought of running into his arms and weeping away her heartache swept through her.

"You're still awake?" He spoke soft enough that sleeping ears would not stir.

"That's debatable."

His gaze scanned the room as he crossed the floor on silent feet. If she weren't so tired, she'd marvel at his ability. As he drew near and focused on her, he sucked in an audible breath.

Not that she faulted him. She must look a wreck. Dress ruined with char marks. Hair unpinned and fallen down her back. Her cheeks stung, chapped from tears, and her eyes must surely be swollen. If he cared to sniff, he might think he stood in front of the kiln master on Brickyard Lane instead of a woman.

"Looks like you had quite the evening." Though the comment was light-hearted, concern thickened his voice.

"Quite."

He likely expected her to say more, but one word would have to suffice. Hers was a raw wound, too fresh to consider. She went back to picking up broken tankard pieces and stacking them in a pile. It was a mindless task—and for that she was grateful.

The toes of Mr. Morton's shoes entered her field of vision, but she refused to look up. His clothes rustled as he squatted in front of her.

"Care to tell me what happened?"

Her hands didn't slow. She stacked one piece atop another, and when the pile towered too high and wobbly, she started a new mound.

"Miss Langley, I clearly see you are troubled. Though my behavior of yesterday morning suggests otherwise, I am not a beast of opportunity. I am sorry about that kiss, but believe me, it was necessary at the time."

Stack. Stack. Just like his words. She probably ought to care. She had once. What did a stolen kiss matter now? Tragedy had a blunt way of rearranging offenses, or rather, defining them.

She glanced up, surprised to see a bit of color rising on his neck. So, this *was* difficult for him. Perhaps he wasn't as big a scoundrel as she'd pegged him. "Let us forget that incident and move on."

He cocked his head, studying her like a foreign species. "Do you always forgive so freely?"

"It's not my forgiveness that matters. You should have a care for what you'll say to your Maker, for you never know how soon that day will be." Her breath caught as the truth of her own words hit home.

Mr. Morton's clear, blue gaze burned into hers. "Tell me what's happened."

Oh, no. If she answered that, she'd be undone. She snatched the last pottery fragment and set it atop the heap. The pile tipped and crashed into the other. Pieces scattered everywhere, the sound making her flinch. Now she'd have to start over. She reached to begin again.

Mr. Morton's hand wrapped around hers, solid and warm, and entirely too supportive. "You're trembling."

Fresh tears blurred her vision. She blinked, forcing them back, and looked anywhere except at his face—or at the strong fingers entwining with hers.

"Come." He pulled her to her feet.

She allowed him to lead her to a bench near the hearth, in the corner where Mr. Quail and his band had played. Why would this night not end? If she listened hard enough, would she still hear leftover strains of music—or worse, her brother's screams?

A shiver rippled across her shoulders as she sank to the seat.

Shrugging out of his dress coat, Mr. Morton bent and wrapped it around her. Still warm from his body, the fabric carried his scent—bergamot and strength. She shivered again.

Without a word, he grabbed a poker and stirred the banked fire. Ashes knocked back, air breathing life, a flame burst out. Red and deadly.

"Don't!" she cried, then immediately wished she'd said nothing.

He jerked his gaze toward her.

She bit her lip. What must he think?

Without a word, he walked away—and she didn't blame him. If she could, she'd walk away from herself as well. Away from this night. This inn. This life. Closing her eyes, she shut out the evil hearth fire. Where was her faith?

Footsteps returned. The bench jiggled. A cup was placed into her hands. "Here. Drink."

She shook her head then lifted her face to Mr. Morton's. "No, thank you."

"Do it."

It wasn't a harsh command, but a command nevertheless, and one she suspected would take less effort to obey than to argue. When the first sip met her tongue, thirst took over. She drained the mug dry. How could this man know her better than herself?

"There. That wasn't so hard, hmm?" He took the cup from her hands and set it on the bench next to him. "Now then, close your eyes."

Accepting a drink was one thing. What he might have in mind, quite another. "Mr. Morton, I hardly think—"

"Ah, ah." He wagged his finger at her. "Trust me, Miss Langley. Close your eyes." The determined set of his jaw left no room for debate.

Eyelids heavy, she gave in, but not without tensing for a quick exit should he make an untoward move.

The bench jiggled again. A few light steps. Not far. The scrape of one of the instruments left on the table from Quail's band.

And then a single, haunting note on a violin. Followed by another. It was a sweet sound, in an eerie sort of way. The kind of tune that reached in and struck chords in her soul. One she'd hear in dreams to come.

Deep down, a sob began. At first she fought it, scrunching her eyes tighter to keep the tears inside. But the music was merciless, coaxing her to let go.

The next thing she knew, the song was over. Arms wrapped around her. She wept into Mr. Morton's fine waistcoat until it was soaked through.

Finally catching her breath, she pushed away.

He studied her for a moment. The room was no longer dark. The grey light of dawn crawled in through the front window, highlighting myriad questions in his gaze. "Now, would you care to tell me what happened that brought you to such depths?"

"You are very persistent, sir."

He merely cocked a brow.

"I see I have no choice." She sucked in a shaky breath. Could she do this? "It was a busy night. Good business, but as you know, we are short on help. Thomas, bless his heart—" Her voice cracked, and she cleared her throat twice over before beginning again. "He was rushing about. I warned him, but..."

Glancing around the taproom, she collected what was left of her bravery. "I'm sure you've noticed our inn is mostly held together by baling twine. We've needed to replace the spit hook in the kitchen hearth for years now, but a smithy is expensive, and the hearth itself took priority. We replaced that and made do with the rest. The hook is yet functional somewhat, *if* one is careful. Thomas wasn't."

She shuddered.

"Go on," he coaxed.

If not for Mr. Morton's fingers on her jaw, turning her face toward his, she'd not have had the courage to speak another word. "My brother leaned over the hearth to scoop a ladle of stew from the pot. He moved too fast, with too much force. The hook broke. The pot fell into the flames. Coals shot out, one catching in the folded hem of his trousers. He tried to smother it, brave boy, but ended up fanning the flames larger. In a panic, he ran. I stopped him. I thought he was"—she gulped back the lump in her throat—"dead."

All expression drained from Mr. Morton's face. This close, she could feel each of his muscles tensing rock hard.

"Is he?"

"No. I did not mean to imply..." Words failed her. Some fates were worse than death, and unless God acted in mercy, Thomas might very well find that out.

Mr. Morton breathed out, "Thank God," then pushed to his feet. "Where is the boy now?"

"Upstairs. Mam attends him. He will live."

"That's a relief—"

"But"—she cut him off lest she mislead him yet again—"the doctor won't say if he'll ever walk again."

CHAPTER SEVEN

After two nights of listening to Quail's off-tune fiddling, Alex purposely left his gun up in his chamber. If he carried it to the taproom, he'd shoot the man to put him and everyone else out of their misery. Was it too much to ask that a musician actually play music?

He swigged back the rest of his drink and frowned at the kitchen door, willing a blue skirt to appear. He'd had precious few moments to query Johanna on how Thomas or she fared, and he was beginning to think she and Mrs. Langley were avoiding him.

"Looking for someone?"

Alex tensed. The question struck him from the side, flanking him like a well-planned skirmish. He jerked his gaze to the shadow slipping onto the bench beside him. Only Thatcher could steal inside a sparsely populated taproom without being noticed.

Alex scowled at the man. "Must you always sneak up on a body?"

"No, but that would steal the enjoyment of it." Thatcher reached for the mug, then glowered when he found nothing but drops remaining.

"What are you doing here?" Alex leaned against the wall and eyed the man. "You couldn't possibly have met with Ford this quickly."

"I didn't. I met with Flannery on the road."

"Flannery?" Alex winced, both from the screech of what should've been a C-sharp and the mention of fellow officer Killian Flannery. He'd never worked with the man directly, but after the hair-raising tales he'd heard about him from fellow officer Brentwood, neither did he want to.

"Please tell me he's not in on this."

"Only as a pack mule. He brought a message from Ford."

Thunder and turf! This assignment was turning into far more than he'd bargained for. One by one, Alex cracked his knuckles, a vain effort at releasing the tension. "What does Ford want now? Am I to dress as a tart and swing my hips in hopes of luring out the traitor?"

Thatcher's lips quirked—the closest he ever came to smiling. "I'd like to see that."

"No doubt." He held out his hand. "Let's have it."

Thatcher handed over a small paper. Once opened, the scrap was hardly bigger than a playing card. Only five words graced the center.

Clarification: ingratiate, eliminate, then extricate.

Alex blew out a long breath. Refolding the note, he shifted his gaze to his friend. "I'm assuming you've read this."

Thatcher nodded.

"Then let me see if I've got this straight." He angled on the bench, facing the man head-on. "I am to ingratiate myself with the Coburn family by making an offer for Louisa. By doing so, Ford assumes I will be able to identify the traitor—which I'm guessing he expects to be either the viscount himself, Robbie, or Louisa. I arrest said traitor, thus eliminating the threat. At that point, I extricate myself from any betrothal ties before the marriage deed can be carried out. Is that your understanding?"

Thatcher nodded again, his dark eyes giving no hint as to what he thought of the matter.

Which only served to kindle the rising irritation burning in Alex's gut. He purposely lowered his voice, denying a strong urge to shout. "Why the deuce would the viscount or his daughter even consider me as marriage material? I'm a stranger. An unknown."

Thatcher merely shrugged. "You've talked your way in and out of impossible situations before, and it's no secret your. . .*skills* with women are unmatched."

"This is different. Coburn's a peer of the realm. He's not going to let honeyed words alone persuade him."

"Of course not. He'll do a thorough background check."

"For Alexander Morton, a nonentity." He grit his teeth. "Ford better be doing some fantastic slight-of-hand work on my behalf."

"He's sparing no expense on this and is keeping close watch on all that happens." Thatcher leaned forward and lowered his voice. "Though it may seem so, you are not alone."

Alex pressed the heel of his hand to the bridge of his nose, fighting off an ache starting at the back of his eyes. The duplicity of the plan was stunning. So many things could go wrong, the legality of it, the unpredictability of toying with people's lives—the possibility that he wouldn't find the traitor in time to extract himself. It was a dangerous line to walk, but if the scheme worked as Ford hoped, it was likely the fastest way to discover the needed information.

He pinched his nose harder. For the first time in his life, he suddenly regretted his fame for going beyond the rules to bring in a criminal.

"I don't like it," he said at last.

"Because it wasn't your idea?"

He dropped his hand and glowered at the man. "Your job suits you, you know."

Though spare lantern light filled the room, the questioning rise of Thatcher's brow was unmistakable.

"Diplomacy is hardly your strong point," Alex explained. "It's a blessing that riding the countryside gives you little interaction with people."

Thatcher's lips quirked again. Twice in one night? A regular belly-buster of an evening for him.

"Well, I suppose it's not like I've never stretched the limits of how to bring in a suspect." Alex sighed. "But I still need you to meet with Ford."

Thatcher reached for the empty cup and tipped his head back, draining what few drops could be found since neither Mrs. Langley nor Johanna had yet appeared to offer him a drink. He set the mug down and frowned. "I think we both grasp the situation clearly."

"It's not about that. I need more money."

"Gaming skills a bit rusty?"

"No." He laughed. "I suspect I shall have to pay a fine price if I'm to become more enticing than orchids."

"Orchids? Is that a new cipher I need to know?"

Alex clapped his friend on the back and stood, snatching up the empty cup. "Thatcher, I doubt you'll ever need to know about flowers."

Whimpering leached out Thomas's closed door, and Johanna winced. This was her fault. All of it. If only she'd better managed their meager funds, made wiser decisions about what to fix and what not, this whole tragedy wouldn't have happened.

Next to her, Mam frowned, face drawn. "You're doing it again, aren't you?"

"Doing what?"

"Blaming yourself. Stuff and nonsense!" Mam shoved the bucket of soiled dressings into her hands. "Go on down to the taproom and put your mind on other things. I'll sit with Thomas."

"But I—"

"Shush!" Mam shooed her away with a flick of her fingers. "I'll have none of that. Off with you."

Truly, her mother should've been in the military, for there'd be no putting her off. Johanna forced a half smile. "Very well. Come get me if you need me."

Mam nodded and ducked back into Thomas's room. Johanna waited until her mother disappeared, then let her smile fall to the floor. Too bad she couldn't lie there as well. Had she ever been this weary?

Treading down the hall, she descended the stairs and entered the kitchen—where a broad-shouldered man stood slicing cheese. "Oh! Mr. Morton. What a surprise."

"You've caught me red-handed, I'm afraid." He smiled up at her—the warmth of which did strange things to her empty tummy. "Just gathering a plate of cheese and bread for my friend."

"Here, let me do that." She set down the bucket and doused her hands in some water. Mr. Morton's stare burned through the back of her gown. Was he reliving the way he'd held her those few nights ago as vividly as she was?

Shoving down the rising heat of embarrassment, she rehung the drying cloth, then herded Mr. Morton aside by reaching for the loaf of bread on the table. "I apologize for our lack of service the past few days."

"You have been tending Thomas, no doubt. How is he?"

She paused before setting knife to bread, and met his gaze. "Tired of the pain and tired of his room, tired of Mam and tired of me."

Mr. Morton chuckled. A delightful sound. Low and soothing.

"I'd expect no less from a caged boy—and a wounded one at that. I would be happy to sit with him and—"

"No, thank you." She sawed through the thick loaf, using more force than necessary. It was churlish of her to cut him off so, but it couldn't be helped. Tending Thomas was her cross to bear. "Mam and I are managing."

"Johanna."

She jerked her face up, annoyed that he dared to use her Christian name—but more irritated that she wished he'd say it again, for her name on his lips was a curious balm.

He studied her with an unwavering stare. "Let me help."

The knife in her hand weighed heavy. No, her whole soul did. Emotions she ought not be feeling right now swirled overhead and pressed down. He stood on the other side of the table, but the way his blue eyes caressed her, he might as well be holding her in his arms. She frowned. She'd been wise to avoid him the past two days. She bent, sawing off another slab of bread. "You are a guest here, sir. Not the hired help."

"There's only one person I know more stubborn than you."

Finished, she set the knife down. "Yourself?"

He smirked. "You take on too much, you know."

"I must. This inn is our livelihood." She handed over the plate of bread and cheese.

He took it, yet he did not leave. Instead, a great sorrow furrowed his brow. "I am sorry your father is no longer here to help you. This is too much of a burden for you and your mother to shoulder alone."

"While I appreciate the sentiment, the truth is we shouldered the burden long before my father died." She pressed her lips shut. Why had she shared that? How did he manage to pull things from her she didn't even know were buried deep in her heart?

"I am sorry to hear it. Did he suffer long?"

Suffer? The word circled like a vulture, ready to swoop and stab the barely healed scars left behind by her father. "The only thing my father suffered from was too much drink and a lying tongue. I abhor both!"

"So should we all." His tone was soft, low, almost as if he spoke to himself.

"Well," she lifted her chin, "I suppose what does not drive us into the ground only serves to make us stronger, hmm? Now if you'll excuse me, I have a taproom to tend."

She grabbed a cloth and whisked past him, wondering all the while how much stronger God thought she needed to be.

CHAPTER EIGHT

The next day, Alex waited for the light footsteps of Johanna and the bass thwunks of the doctor to pass his door before he cracked it open. Peering out, he paused a moment longer until the fat doctor disappeared down the stairway and his wheezing faded. Ought not a man interested in health take better care of his own?

Easing his door shut, Alex stole down the hallway to Thomas's chamber. He'd tried asking for permission to see the boy, but to no avail.

This time he wouldn't ask.

He rapped once on Thomas's door before entering. It was a small room, walls weeping brown streaks from years of leakage. A single window cast sunlight upon the boy's thin body, lying like a piece of flotsam upon a sea of pain. His eyes were red-rimmed, cheeks pale, and his burnt leg was bolstered up and useless. This was wrong. Unjust in every possible respect. A boy shouldn't be laid out in bed like an old man. He ought to be running, climbing trees, chasing after girls and teasing them.

Aah, Lord, grant Your mercy.

Alex choked down rising emotion with a gruff throat clearing. "Good day, Master Thomas. Did you know you're guarded more heavily than a transfer of gold bullion? Perhaps your mother and sister should give up innkeeping and join a regiment of dragoons." He winked, hoping the effect would lighten the load weighing heavy on the boy's brow.

"They're more like dragons, if you ask me." A smile curved Thomas's lips, then flattened into a wince as he propped his elbows behind him and pushed upward.

Alex grabbed a chair and pulled it to the lad's bedside, straddling it backward. The sudden movement rattled a bottle of amber liquid on the nightstand. Straight brandy or laudanum? He studied the boy's glassy gaze. Could be either.

"How goes it? Have the past three days been non-stop pain?"

"Aye, sir."

Alex flexed his fingers and leaned forward against the chair's back, resisting the urge to reach out and tussle the lad's hair. Regardless of the injury, the boy had already been coddled far too much. "Sir is for fathers and old people. I am neither. You may call me Alex, for are we not friends?"

"Aye, sir—Alex."

"You're a quick study." His gaze strayed to the boy's leg, covered from the knee down with a cloth saturated in some kind of golden syrup. Maybe honey. Maybe not. The skin peeking out above the poultice burned an angry scarlet. He could only imagine what damage lay beneath the wrap. "What did the doctor have to say? Shall you live?"

"Pah! Mam and Jo would kill me if I didn't."

He glanced sideways at the twist of the boy's mouth. True, Johanna and her mother had turned into squawking, overprotective hens, but agreement would only fan the flames of the lad's discontent.

"You know your sister and mother want the best for you. Their concern is very real."

Thomas blew out a harsh sigh, then grimaced when his dramatics jostled his leg.

Alex smiled. Apparently passion ran in the family. "Give it time, Thomas. You'll soon be back on both feet."

"But..." Tears filled the boy's eyes. "What if I never walk properly again?"

Alex scooted his chair closer. "I've a story for you."

The boy's gaze shot to his. Just the effect he'd hoped for.

"When I was a lad, 'round about ten years old—"

The boy's pupils widened, and Alex knew he'd nailed the boy's age, reeling in his full attention. "I had a bit of a mishap myself. Father told me never—*ever*—to handle his pistol when he wasn't around. Easy enough, since he carried it with him wherever he went."

"Everywhere?"

Alex shrugged. "London streets are not as safe as Dover's."

Thomas nodded as if he'd lived a hundred years roaming Cheapside or Spitalfields.

Scrubbing a hand across his chin, Alex hid his smile. "One day, my father was home after an all-nighter, sleeping. I knew better than to wake him. Mother was gone. But I was curious. You know that feeling, that need to know how something works? It fairly crawls under your skin, and you have to act on it, for there's no sitting still."

A small "aah" rode the crest of Thomas's exhale. Good, this was working.

"Well, that's exactly how it was for me on that day. Not that Father hadn't shown me his pistol many a time. I could sketch the bronze muzzle and carved handle from memory. The curve of the steel trigger. The sharp angles of the flintlock. Such a beauty." He paused, gauging the time for the gun's image to spring to life in the boy's mind.

"The thing is, Father had never yet allowed me to shoot it. How would it feel? Was there a mighty kickback? I was certain I was old enough, strong enough to handle it, for is ten years of age not nearly a grown man?"

Thomas's face snapped to his. "I tell that to Mam all the time!"

"Well, it's not." He edged closer, whispering the rest. "And I've the scar to prove it. Would you like to see?"

Thomas's head bobbed in a single, solemn nod.

Alex stood, turned the chair around, and pulled off his left boot. His toe snagged for a moment on a hole in his sock, long past the need for darning, but he finally freed his foot and lifted it for Thomas's inspection. There, at center, just above his toes, rose a bubble of marred skin the size of a farthing and the color of an overripe peach even to this day. A tangible reminder of transgression's cost.

"What happened?" Thomas's voice was reverent.

"As I said, I wanted to try out the pistol, but I also wanted to obey my father. I figured him being in the other room fully met the requirements of having him present. So, I gave it a try."

He tugged his sock back on, followed by his boot, then met Thomas's gaze. "Which do you suppose was louder, the firing of the gun, or my screams when the shot tore through my foot?"

"Caw, sir!" The boy's face paled.

"Laid me up for more than a fortnight, I tell you. Got middling good with a cloth-molded crutch. Shall I make one for you?"

Thomas shifted on his elbows, propping himself up farther. This time, though a very real tremor of pain wrinkled across his brow, his smile belied it. "I'd like that. Oh, I would!"

"Good. We'll have you up and about in no time, giving your mother and sister something to really cluck about, eh?" Hooking his thumbs beneath his armpits, he flapped like an overgrown chicken and squawked.

Laughter shook the boy's shoulders.

Mission accomplished. Alex stood and replaced the chair.

"Thomas? Are you all right?" The door swung open, and Johanna's skirts swept in. She summed up Alex with a mighty scowl, the harbinger of a sound scolding.

"Mr. Morton! Have I not asked you to allow Thomas his rest? I insist you leave at once." She stepped aside from the doorway, as if the action, combined with her command, might usher him out as effectively as a gun to the head.

He planted his feet. "It's been three full days, Miss Langley. The boy needed a diversion."

"The boy needs to rest, sir."

"Aw, but Jo." Thomas's thin voice cracked. "Alex was only—"

"It's Mr. Morton, and furthermore"—Johanna looked past Alex to her brother. "Thomas! What are you doing sitting up? You know your leg must remain elevated. The doctor said—"

"It's still on the cushion," the boy shot back.

"Thomas, this is not to be borne. You will not walk again if you do not listen to the doctor's instruction. Is that what you want?"

Her curt question sagged the boy's shoulders. He deflated onto the mattress, pain seeping out in a groan.

Alex frowned. Her careless words had undone in seconds the small amount of good he'd built in the past twenty minutes. He'd hauled in many a brothel madam who'd not be as callous.

Silently, he studied her. A strand of dark hair escaped one of her pins, drooping over her brow. Shadows darkened half-circles beneath her eyes. And was that. . .yes, the wrinkles in her gown were imbedded deep enough that she must've slept in it. This was not the same woman he'd come to know in the past week. Something more was at work here than simply distress about her brother.

"I would have a word with you, outside, if you please, Miss Langley." In two steps, he clasped her arm and led her out the door, shutting it behind them.

"Mr. Morton, really!" She faced him with a scowl.

"Exactly, Miss Langley. What is this *really* all about?"

Johanna clenched her hands so tight, her nails dug into her palms. Was it Mr. Morton's piercing blue gaze or his inquiry that made her feel so exposed? Either way, she didn't like it. Containing her problems was hard enough without him poking holes into her facade.

She lifted her chin. "You had no right to sneak into my brother's room and excite him in such a fashion."

He drew in a long breath and slowly released it. A curious reaction. She'd expected something a bit more defensive. Even a simple raised brow would've done the trick, but the strong cut of Mr. Morton's face was entirely indecipherable. Even with years of experience reading patrons and guests, this man was an enigma at best.

"I admit it was underhanded to wait to visit your brother until you were occupied elsewhere. For that I apologize. But"—he wagged his finger—"that is the sum of my crime. I took the boy's mind off his pain and fear, and you brought it all back with a few thoughtless words."

She stiffened, his accusation chilling her to the core. Is that what she'd done? Slowly, she lowered her head, preferring to study the hem of her skirt instead of the indictment in Mr. Morton's frown.

"As I suspected." His tone softened. "And so I repeat, what is this really about?"

Clasping her hands in front of her, she debated what, if anything, to tell him. Oh, how she missed sharing her burdens with her friend Maggie, but since the baby had arrived, time was a scarce commodity from her. And she couldn't turn to Mam, for her mother was as overwrought as she. That left no other close confidant save God upon whom to unload her troubles, and the skirt fabric at her knees was already worn thin.

She dared a peek up at Mr. Morton. The hard lines of his face had smoothed into genuine compassion—the same look as when he'd held her in his arms and allowed her to make a sopping mess of his shirt.

She sucked in a breath for courage. "Truly, I appreciate your candor, yet I have already overstepped the bounds of propriety. Haven't you heard enough of my troubles? Should you not be out acquiring some fine wines, or whatever it is that you do, instead of counseling my woes?"

"Aah, still a bit of spunk in you. Good." One corner of his mouth turned upward. "Even so, sometimes it helps to get an outsider's perspective."

Was that what he was? An outsider? Then why did she feel as if she ought put on a pot of tea and pour out her cares to this man? She searched his gaze, her problems rising to her tongue. Clearly his mesmerizing blue stare muddled her thinking. Good heavens. What *was* she thinking?

She turned. "I appreciate your concern, but perhaps you ought leave now, Mr. Morton. I'm sure you've bigger matters to attend, and so I bid you a good day."

"That's the easy way out, Johanna."

Her name from his lips shot straight to her heart and tripped an extra beat. Annoyed at the base response, she whirled. "Why must you insist on calling me by my Christian name?"

"Because it never fails to get your attention." His smile dazzled. "And I find that when I anger you, you're more likely to tell me what's really on your mind."

"You are exasperating." As was this conversation. She sidestepped him.

He blocked her path. "And you're avoiding the question."

Faith! What a bully. She folded her arms and for a moment considered how strong of a battering ram she could make herself if she bent forward and charged. There'd be no other way to put him off—but she wouldn't make a dent in that broad chest.

"Very well." She sighed, resignation both acrid and sweet. "If you must know, I am short on the rent payment and the next hearth installment is due in a few days. Now with Thomas's doctor bills. . .well, unless God acts, you may have to find yourself different lodging soon."

"How soon?" he asked.

"Friday."

"How much?"

"Twenty-five pounds."

"How much do you have?"

"Ten."

His nostrils flared, and she got the distinct impression he sucked in more than air. Her own head spun from the swiftness of his interrogation. If this was how he conducted business, no doubt merchants quaked in their boots to cut a deal with him.

"That's quite a shortfall to gather in three days." His tone was even, placid almost, but his conclusion was deadly accurate.

"Oh, what you must think, Mr. Morton." She retreated to the corridor's wall and leaned against it for support. "Had providence not brought you here, we'd not even have that much. It's not like Mam and I haven't minded our accounts. In truth, there are hardly any to mind. Mr. Quail and his band play nightly, which draws in some patrons, but pays only enough to cover the musicians' room and board." She shrugged. "And I've yet to see a coin from Mr. Nutbrown, despite his puppet's excessive promises. Perhaps the Blue Hedge Inn really is cursed."

"On the contrary. I'd say the inn is blessed, Miss Langley, with your fair presence."

The intensity of his gaze heated her cheeks. "If having no rent money is a blessing, then I'd hate to hear your description of mishap, sir."

"Have we not moved beyond sir and mister? The name is Alex. And as I said, all you need is a different perspective."

She threw out her hands. "From where, the workhouse window?"

"Now there is the quick-witted spunk I admire." He smiled. "I see exactly what must be done to cure your monetary ills. Leastwise, for the time being."

"Do tell."

Advancing toward her, he reached inside his greatcoat and pulled out a small pouch. With a touch as light as a whisper, he grabbed her fingers and deposited the bag in her palm, the leather still warm from his body heat.

Without a word, he wheeled about and stalked down the hall.

She stepped away from the wall. "Where are you going, Mr. Morton?"

He kept walking.

"Alex!"

He turned back. "You see? Christian names work for me as well. Now then, there's a certain patron I shall be happy to evict for you."

Her lips parted. Surely he wasn't hinting at collaring Mr. Nutbrown?

"You can thank me later. Now, go tend your brother. He's got an ear for stories, so if nothing else, make one up." He pivoted and disappeared down the stairway.

She gaped. How long she stood there, she could only guess, but slowly, as one surfaces from a deep slumber, she realized her fingers had gone to sleep from grasping the pouch so tightly. Loosening the drawstring, she poked about at the coins, calculating their worth.

Sweet mercy! She must be dreaming. Twenty golden guineas. . . more than enough to pay Mr. Spurge when he came to call on Friday.

The few bites of porridge she'd managed this morning slowly rose from her stomach, and she swallowed. Nothing good ever came of taking money from a man. Absently, she rubbed the small scar behind her ear. That was a lesson she learned early on. This was more than just rent, and while Spurge may be staved off for yet another month, what compensation would Mr. Morton expect for giving her such a sum?

CHAPTER NINE

Darkness had never been a friend to Lucius Nutbrown. An acquaintance, yes, and a familiar one at that, but not a jolly, hobnobbing comrade. No, not a bit of it. Still, he scrunched his eyes shut, closing out the taproom's meager light—and the lurid image of the meat-cleaver-sized hands reaching for him. Maybe this time his frail childhood belief that if you could not see danger, then danger could not see you would prove true.

Come, darkness, hide me now.

Fingers bit into his shoulders. So much for childish convictions.

"Out! And don't come back, ye barmy beggar!" The words flew out the door along with him. Tuck and roll time. Even with a full afternoon of practice, his elbow caught in a pothole, ripping yet another gash into his greatcoat. Gads! Could not a town the size of Dover pay to even out the ruts in the road?

He bumped to a stop and opened his eyes—then wished he hadn't.

A beast of a horse reared over him, the silhouette ghoulish with the sun behind it. Front hooves hovered above his head, about to spear his skull to the ground like a harpoon through an eel.

Lucius jerked sideways. Gravel shards stung his neck when a hoof dug into the lane, but better bits of rock than bits of brain being splattered about.

The stallion screamed, as did the man atop it. "Mind the horse!"

Lucius staggered to his feet, shooting out his puppet-clad hand.

"Mind Mr. Nutbrown's head!"

The man atop the horse gave him nary a look as he retreated down the road. Lucius flipped his hand around so the jester's painted face looked into his own. "I get no respect, aye Nixie? None a'tall."

"None a'tall," he repeated in Nixie's voice. "Speeding devils ought to look where they're going, Mr. Nutbrown."

"Right as always, my friend." He slipped Nixie into an inside pocket and bent to retrieve his hat, where it lay crushed on the ground. As he punched the shape back into the felt, a quiver ran down his spine. This could've easily been his head.

Two pair of footsteps, one of them kind of thumpy, drew up along either side of him. A low whistle blew from the short man on the left. He smelled like overcooked peas. "That were a sorry pass, squire. Ye might've been flattened."

The other man slung his arm around Lucius's shoulder, maybe for balance, as one of his legs was wooden. "What's this world coming to when a squire such as yerself can't peacefully cross the street?"

Hmm. All day long he'd been shunned. Why the sudden attention? Shrugging away from the taller man's embrace, Lucius put on his hat and pulled out Nixie. The little puppet's head bobbed though he tried to keep it still, the effects of the near-trampling still jittering his nerves. "Mr. Nutbrown is no squire, sirs, but a true and bona fide businessman."

"Why, I said such a thing when we see'd what'd happened, right, Blackie?" The shorter of the two squinted up at the other. "I says, 'There's a businessman, a right true one.' Din't I?"

"That ye did." The big one bent and shoved his face into Nixie's. "Well, well, little man. Ye're shaking like a maiden on her wedding night. Can we buy you and your partner a drink? If you've the time, that is."

Lucius froze. No one *ever* addressed Nixie except for himself, and he wasn't sure how to feel about that. This would take some sorting through. . .and a mug of ale was just the thing for sorting. He splayed his pinkie and thumb, causing Nixie to spread wide his arms. "Yes, sirs. Mr. Nutbrown is finished with his appointments for the day, so he believes he could fit that into his schedule."

The big man straightened, his smile as irregular as a carved squash.

"A right proper businessman, you are, Mr. Nutbrown. We can tell, aye, Charlie?"

"Exactly what I was thinking." The other fellow—Mr. Charlie—lifted the brim of his hat to scratch a patch of shockingly red hair. "It'll be an honor to share a pint with the likes o' you both." He nodded at Nixie and him in turn.

Lucius sucked in a breath. Each of these strangers acknowledged Nixie for what he'd always believed him to be—alive. Which, of course, moved them from the category of strangers to beloved friends.

"Right, let's be about it, then." The big man turned toward the door of the inn from which Lucius had recently flown.

"No!" Lucius swallowed, hating that he'd caused a wrinkle on the brows of his new friends, but mostly hating that he'd slipped and used his real voice. He kicked his tone up a few notches and held Nixie higher. "That establishment would hardly do for men of our caliber. Mr. Nutbrown suggests the Drunken Duck."

Lucius held his breath, waiting for the questioning lines to smooth on his friends' faces. *Please. Please.* The Drunken Duck was the only establishment he'd not been thrown out of yet, ever since Mr. Morton began the awful trend earlier this morning. Dirty scoundrel, usurping him like that.

Mr. Charlie cuffed him on the back with a firm pat. "The Drunken Duck it is, squire."

His lungs released, as did the tension in his jaw. They fell into step three abreast—four, if he counted Nixie—with him in the middle.

The big fellow talked over his head to Mr. Charlie, his words keeping time with the thump of his peg leg. "I told you from the looks of him, he'd be too far above our station."

Mr. Charlie shrugged. "I says we ask anyway. All he can do is say no."

Lucius glanced sideways at the other fellow, his palm feeling sticky and hot beneath Nixie's cover.

"He don't need our money." The man's words hung suspended for a moment.

Until Lucius grabbed them. Money? There was an opportunity here. He could smell it—fresh and green and more pleasant than overcooked peas. He turned Nixie to face them all. "Do you fellows have a proposition for Mr. Nutbrown? He is a man of business, after all."

Mr. Charlie leaned forward, grinning past him toward the other fellow. "We could sure use a businessman, right Blackie?"

The big one—Mr. Blackie, apparently—rubbed a hand over his stubbly skull, his step not missing a thumpy beat as he kept walking. "Well, we do got a regular transaction coming up. One with ledgers and numbers and all kinds o' business type stuff we can hardly understand. We know, though, that it promises to pay real well."

"*Real* well," Charlie echoed.

Nixie stared at him from an arm's length away, bobbing up and down with each step. One of his papier-mâché cheeks bent inward, dented from a piece of gravel. With his free hand, Lucius rubbed his own cheek, then winced. His was scraped as well. That settled it. He brought his little friend closer to his face. "We ought help out our new friends, hmm?"

Mr. Charlie elbowed him. "We'd be mighty obliged."

Mr. Blackie repeated the action on the other side. "What do you say, Mr. Nutbrown?"

A slow smile crawled over his lips. If he looked close enough, Nixie grinned too. In fact, Nixie perked up so much, his little jester head waggled. "Mr. Nutbrown says yes, gentlemen. We'd be happy to lend our business finesse."

Alex strode down the street, wishing for the hundredth time he could ease the ugly questions he'd created in Johanna's eyes. Not that he blamed her. Men didn't usually hand over coins without the tether of expectations. Sidestepping a mound of refuse swept up by a closing shopkeeper, he huffed out a breath. Money was nothing to him. He'd already put out a word for Thatcher to bring him more. It was the woman distracting his thoughts he couldn't afford. He reseated his hat and strode on.

Ahead, a shop matron grunted as she backed through a doorway, each of her hands loaded with a bucket of flowers left unsold for the day.

Flowers? His steps slowed. A seed of an idea sprouted. Might be a bit forward, but sometimes it paid to take a risk.

He upped his pace. Ignoring the CLOSED shingle hanging in the window, he pushed through the florist's door, setting off a jingling bell.

"We're done for the day." The woman's voice travelled from a back entryway.

"Yet you've flowers left. I'll take them."

The woman poked her head out the doorway, wearing a mobcap so tight, it puckered the skin of her brow. "I said we're done. Closed. Finished for the day. Buy your flower on the morrow."

"I don't want *a* flower." He grinned. "I want them all."

"All the. . .you mean. . .*all* what I got left?" Her gaze shot to his hands, her words wadding up as tightly as the roll of bills he pulled from an inside pocket of his greatcoat.

"All. And may I have use of a pen and a slip of paper?"

"You can have use of the flamin' best stationery in the shop!" She dashed from the back room and swiped aside scraps of twine and stem cuttings littering the counter. After a quick wipe down with her sleeve, she pulled out a tray from beneath, containing his requested items plus a few envelopes. "Here ye are, sir. I'll wrap those flowers up straightaway."

As she bustled over to the buckets, Alex uncorked the ink and dipped the pen. Now, what to say to a woman who looked at him with eyes of mistrust?

I can help you. Let me.
~ A. Morton

He blotted the note dry and folded it into an envelope, then turned to the woman. "I should like those delivered to Miss Louisa Coburn."

Her eyebrows rose, the mobcap pinching in a whole new way. "You mean the viscount's daughter?"

"Unless you know another Louisa Coburn. Good day." He stalked out, the jingling bell competing with the woman's *ne'er-would-have-guessed* and *didn't-see-that-coming* mumbles. No doubt Miss Coburn would mutter the same when she received the flowers. He blew out a sigh. As of yet, he'd still not figured out how to accomplish Ford's directive without actually marrying the woman, but he'd come up with something. He would. There was simply no other option.

Glancing at the sky, he calculated daylight. An hour remained, give or take. Was he too late? He lengthened his strides, bypassing those headed home for a warm bowl of stew. Shops thinned out the closer he drew to the beachhead. To his left, white cliffs stood like stark sentinels, watching over the harbor. The castle on top loomed over all, a dark reminder that war had been—and always would be—a present danger from offshore. Ahead, earthen batteries rose along the seafront, providing a small measure of protection should the French decide on a bold affront.

He crested the line of defense and trotted down the other side, his boots grinding into the sand, shells, and rocks of low tide. For now, foreign invaders didn't concern him. The smugglers off to his right were a bigger threat. One he could manage, though.

Lifting a hand, he hailed the three men with a loud voice. "Done for the day, Slingsby?"

The two men with their backs to him turned immediately, hands covering pistol hilts belted at their waist. Dark gazes searched the length of him. He returned the favor. Neither were familiar. Judging by the set of their jaws and shoulders, he'd have two bullets to dodge if Slingsby's memory slipped.

Slowly, the old smuggler stood, leaving the fish he'd been tending over an open fire. His eyes squinted nearly shut, then popped wide. "Well, I'll be a toady-headed cully! That you, Ratter?"

"In the flesh." He drew near and offered his hand. Three shakes, a drawback, then a touch of thumbs, the local code. Leaning closer, he breathed into Slingsby's ear. "But it's Mr. Morton, this time."

"Oh? Morton, is it? A regular gent, are ye now?" Slingsby reared back with a hearty laugh, the cries of overhead gulls squawking along with him. Alex stood and waited. He'd learned long ago the best course of action with the fellow was to let him ride out the wave of whatever emotion swelled inside. The other two men hunkered back down and snatched blackened sticks of skewered fish off the fire.

Slingsby leaned aside and spit out the rest of his laughter along with a stream of tobacco, then lowered his voice. "I'll call ye whate'er ye like, long as yer tipstaff don't bear a warrant with my name on it."

Alex slapped a hand to his chest and staggered back a step. "You really think I'd turn on you?"

"Pah! Save yer playacting." The old fellow dropped to a rock draped with a bit of sailcloth. "Sit yerself down, man."

Alex chose his spot carefully, positioning himself so that his back was to the water and the vista of Dover in front. Napoleon may be an enemy in the rear, but that tyrant was farther away than the thugs before him.

"Thrush, Bane." Slingsby nodded at each of his henchmen in turn. "This here's Morton. I trust him with my life—mostly."

The other men slipped him a slanted glance, then went back to silently chewing their fish. It would take more than an old smuggler's word of endorsement to gain their trust.

Slingsby grabbed a skewer and offered it to him over the small fire.

"Still sore about Ned Dooley?" Alex bit into the fish, chewing slowly to allow Slingsby time to digest his question.

"I admit Ned were a cocklebur of a man." Slingsby shook his head, his dirty neckcloth hanging so loose that it remained motionless with the movement. "Still, Dooley were one of the brethren." He leaned forward, the glint in his eye hardening to flint. "None of us take losin' a brother lightly."

"Dooley was a maggot, and well you know it. Smuggling tea is one thing. Slitting throats quite another. I will not abide violence on these shores." He speared Slingsby with a glower of his own. "Do we have an understanding?"

Thrush and Bane quit chewing. All it would take was one word from Slingsby, and they'd turn on him. He shifted his left foot slightly, just enough to yank out his boot-knife if need be.

"Ye hurt me. Hurt me cruel, ye do." The setting sun cast an eerie glow on Slingsby's face, setting the tips of his grey whiskers on fire. Finally, he sat back, taking the tension along with him. "I've harmed nary a fly."

Alex snorted. "You don't need to." His gaze slid from Thrush to Bane, making his point clear.

"Why, these are naught but honest fishermen. Just finished putting away the nets and boat to prove it. Right boys?"

Bane grunted.

Thrush said nothing.

Slingsby hitched a thumb over his shoulder, indicating a ramshackle wooden vessel pulled inland not far down the beach. "Yessir. Fishing. Wenching. Drinking. Other than that, things been real quiet since you were last here. What's yer game this time, Rat—er, Morton?"

Alex pulled off the last morsel of fish from the stick and popped it into his mouth. Sometimes silence accomplished more than words.

"Holding yer hand close, eh? I respects that, I do." Tossing his fish bones aside, Slingsby dragged his hand across his mouth before he continued. "But I'm guessing this here ain't no social call."

"Just keeping a running account, Slingsby. I like to keep an eye on things." He reached into an inside pocket and pulled out a small leather bag, making sure to jingle a few of the coins inside. Three sets of eyeballs followed the movement. "Any new brothers in the fold?"

The brute to his right stiffened. "Why you askin'?"

"Like I said—" He tossed the bag from one hand to the other. "Just keeping accounts. I hear there's some Leaguers hereabouts. I'd like to have a little conversation with them."

Bane eyed him. "Snitches don't live long enough to enjoy any gain."

"No, no. Nothing like that." A slow smile curved his lips. "I'm a collector. I deal in the trade of black market information. Buying. Selling. Sharing the wealth. Ain't that right, Slingsby?"

"All I know is you ain't ne'er one to play by the rules. Still, my pockets are always padded a little thicker whenever yer in town. Must say, ye always done me right." Slingsby folded his arms. "All right. There's a few new faces that joined the ranks since last you were here. None of 'em Leaguers, though, leastwise not that I know of. I can give you names, but they're as real as Morton or Ratter, Bane or Thrush—"

Thrush jumped to his feet, hauling Slingsby up by the collar. "Watch it, old man! I warned you not to bandy my name about."

Slingsby grinned. "Ye ought be worried more about crossing Morton than me."

By the time Bane turned to face him, Alex had knocked Thrush out cold and gripped his blade, ready to slash Bane if challenged.

Bane hacked out a curse and stalked off.

Slingsby chuckled, shaking out his rumpled coat. "There's always action when yer around." Reseating himself, the old man lifted his face. "I'll only say this once, so listen up. Besides those two ye just met, the new brethren are Beak and Sniper. Oh yeah, and a new fish that showed up just a week ago. Goes by the name o' Que."

"Que?" Alex scrubbed a hand across his face, stalling for time. Short for Quail, perhaps? Blowing out a long breath, he swallowed the idea, leaving behind a salty aftertaste.

Slingsby eyed him. "Bludgeoned you, did I?"

Alex rubbed his stomach, hopefully masking his previous hesitation. "Your cooking did. Thanks, Slingsby." He took a few steps, then turned. "Oh, and watch your back. Blackjack and Charlie are hereabouts."

The old man's face drained of color, as bleached as the bones dotting the sand. "Blast! If they're tangled up with guinea boats again, it'll be the devil to pay for all of us."

"Knowing those two, it's likely that and more."

Alex strode away, then stopped at the crest of the earthen mound ringing the bay. A movement near the cliffs caught his eye. Maybe. Maybe not.

Squinting in the last of the sun's rays, he shaded his eyes with a hand to his forehead. A dark silhouette nearly blended in with the rocks, but not quite. The attempt at stealth was valiant enough, just not successful. The shape wasn't necessarily familiar—but the slight limp was. By the time the figure ducked between two rocks, Alex had no doubt about the man's identity. But what interest did Lord Coburn have in smuggler's hideouts?

Hopefully Slingsby had an extra torch on that derelict he called a fishing boat, for Alex intended to find out.

CHAPTER TEN

Darkness rushed in. Nothing more. Johanna craned her neck to look down one length of Blue Lane, then the other. Not a patron in sight. Stooping, she propped open the front door with a brick. Maybe the enticement of the band making merry inside would call to those outside. The music was certainly loud enough. Still, it was a shame Mr. Morton didn't lead the musicians instead of Mr. Quail, for though the man played with enthusiasm, his notes were just enough short of key to set her teeth on edge.

She braved one more glance down the road, conjuring customers with full pockets scrambling toward the Blue Hedge. A week's worth, no, more like a fortnight's worth of ale-drinkers might give her enough money to pay back Mr. Morton, but the only movement was the streak of a cat darting into an alley.

Rubbing her arms against the chill of the early evening air, she turned and strode through the taproom, trying to ignore the fact that there was only one patron nursing a mug in a corner seat. Perhaps a good chat with her mother would set things a'right.

"Mam?" she called as she entered the kitchen, but the room was as barren as Blue Lane. The remnants of a sliced loaf of bread, a few cabbage leaves, and an uncovered jar of applesauce littered the table. Of course. She should've known her mother would've made Thomas a dinner tray and was likely even now serving it.

She reached for the jar lid, but just as her fingers grazed the metal, she was yanked back by the arm and twirled around.

"A dance, milady?" Mr. Quail spun her so fast, she could hardly breathe let alone answer.

He laughed and pulled her against him, waltzing down the length of the small room and back again.

"Mr. Quail!" She wrenched from his grasp and dashed to the other side of the table, putting a stop to the crazy jig and any other inappropriate ideas he might be entertaining. "Really!"

"Of course, really. And actually, and even truly." Laughter rumbled from deep inside his chest. "Oh, Miss Langley, do not look so aghast. Do you never dance? Sing? Laugh out loud?"

"Not if I can help it." She frowned down at the way her skirt hem had hitched itself atop her half-boot and shook it loose, covering her lower leg. Had he seen?

"Life's too short not to enjoy it, especially for a beauty such as yourself."

Insolent man! She stiffened. "Should you not be out in the taproom?"

He shook his head, never once pulling his gaze from her face. "They won't miss me."

She inched closer to the tabletop—and the bread knife. "Was there something you wanted?"

"Just a few words with a pretty lady." In two long strides, he snatched Mam's stool from the corner and perched atop it. Hooking his feet on the lower rung, he settled comfortably. Clearly the man had more than a few words in mind.

Jo folded her arms, scowling. "You can stop the flattery, sir. It doesn't work."

"Can't blame a man for trying, can you?" A rogue grin curved his mouth, which probably worked for other tavern wenches, but not for her.

"What do you want, Mr. Quail?"

"Aah, direct. I like that in a woman." He curled a swath of dark hair behind his ear, then asked, "What do you know about Mr. Morton?"

Her brow tightened. He could've brought up a hundred other topics, but this? "I am not in the habit of conversing about other patrons. If there's something you want to know, why not ask him yourself?"

"I would, were he here." Quail shrugged. "The man is in and out at all hours. It's hard to corner him."

True. She'd not seen Mr. Morton since he'd given her the pouch of money, and that'd been early this morning. She glanced at the mantel clock. It was after seven now. What did he do all day?

"Tell me, Miss Langley," Mr. Quail's grin faded. The tone of his voice flattened into a gravity he'd never before employed. "Mr. Morton's not asked you to pass off any notes or attend any. . .er. . .meetings while he's been here?"

She frowned. Other than the stolen kiss, Mr. Morton had been nothing but kind. "What an odd question. What are you insinuating?"

He leaned forward. "Merely looking out for your interests."

Her interests—she narrowed her eyes—or his? "No, Mr. Morton has asked me nothing untoward. For the most part, he's been a gentleman, even paid up his rent in advance with guineas."

"He paid you in yellow boys?" Quail's eyes widened. "That is interesting. He does seem a bit well to do, hmm? Clothing impeccable. Grooming exquisite."

She pictured Alexander, standing in the hall where she'd last seen him. His brown dress coat rode the crest of his wide shoulders, cut to perfection. An ivory cravat had been knotted and tucked into a collar set just below his strong jawline. Tan trousers of fine wool followed the long lines of his legs and—Johanna tugged at her own collar, suddenly a bit short of breath. Why was it so hot in here?

"Is it not strange that a man of such means chooses to reside here?"

Mr. Quail's question was a slap in the face. Heat of a different kind curled her hands into fists, and she popped them onto her hips. "And why not? The Blue Hedge is a respectable establishment. Furthermore—"

"Tut, tut, little miss. No disrespect intended." The man stood and planted his hands on the table, leaning toward her. "All I'm saying is that it's a curiosity when a man who rubs shoulders with the viscount lodges at an inn on the farthest reach of town instead of residing in a more fashionable neighborhood."

"The viscount?" Her fists uncurled, and she smoothed her moist palms against her apron. Mr. Quail was right. As much as she'd love to house a grander clientele, why would a man of social standing stay here? With drafty windows, lumpy mattresses, and meals nothing to boast about?

"I hear Mr. Morton's a new gaming partner at Lord Coburn's table, and apparently is quite a favorite despite the rumors of his nightly wins."

Her breath stuck in her throat. Mr. Morton was a gambler? The thought set her teeth on edge—but so did the way Mr. Quail eyed her. She met the man's stare head-on. "How would you know such information?"

"Oh. . .hearsay."

"From whom?"

"Connections." Quail straightened and sniffed. "It pays to know with whom I share a roof. And so I ask, confidentially, of course, what else do you know of the man?"

"Well, I. . ."

What did she know? She gazed at the pots hanging from the rack, more sure about them than the lodger who'd managed to crawl into her thoughts day and night. All she knew for certain was that Alexander conducted buying and selling affairs for his father, had recently arrived from Porto Moniz, and was on his way back home, somewhere up near Sheffield. And that he played the violin with so much emotion it made her weep.

She frowned. That was all she knew. Precious little. Much too little for him to have given her a bag of money and a heart full of feelings she'd rather not sort through. If Alexander Morton belonged in society, why had he befriended her rascal of a brother? Or her, for that matter? What could he hope to gain?

Mr. Quail searched her face as she nibbled her lower lip. Drat the man for raising such questions! And what did she know of the rascal in front of her, a flirtatious, itinerant musician—and a bad one at that. "You, sir, take an inordinate interest in Mr. Morton. Why is that, I wonder?"

"Just looking out for you, my little beauty." He angled his head to a rakish angle. "I'd hate to see him pluck such a delicate flower and crush it beneath his heels."

"I am not sure of your meaning, sir, nor do I want to." She snatched the broom by the back door and swooshed it out as if she might scare off a mouse. "What I am sure of is that you ought be out there with your men, playing music as you promised."

Mr. Quail's hands shot up in the air. "I'm going. But, Miss Langley." He lowered his arms, all merriment fleeing from his voice. "Do be careful. Treacherous times are afoot, I fear."

He stalked out, leaving her alone with a room full of doubts.

Who was the real imposter—Mr. Quail or Mr. Morton?

Alex's foot slipped, sending a spray of gravel plummeting into the crashing waves below. Sucking in a breath, he righted himself and breathed out a "Thank God." From the beach, this route hadn't appeared nearly as treacherous. Spare moonlight slid out from the clouds now and again, but not steady enough to grant dependable light.

Balancing one hand against the rock wall, he set off again. The trail was a little more than the width of his foot, forcing him to put one boot in front of the other. Thankfully, the dirt was compacted, flattened by how many men before him? A fair number, apparently.

He inched his way forward, keeping his fingertips against the cliff, and when his hand suddenly gave way into nothing but air, he stopped. The blackened maw of a cave opened to his right.

Cocking his head, he strained to listen above the breakers. No drone of men's voices came from inside. Gravel didn't crunch. Nor did light of any kind exit the cleft. Good signs, unless someone had heard him coming and an ambush awaited.

A smirk lifted one side of his mouth. No risk, no gain.

Edging inside, he entered darkness so alive, it squeezed his chest. He pulled out Slingsby's torch from where he'd tucked it into his waistcoat, the tang of pitch mixing with the earthy air. Mentally, he added a new shirt to his supply list. Ford was going to love this expense tally.

He bent and planted the torch in the gravel, freeing his hands to feel about in his pocket for his flint. With each strike, sparks dazzled a miniature fireworks show, then finally grabbed hold of the pitch and spread into a flame. He blinked and looked away.

Blackness rushed at him, barely stopping at the edge of his circle of illumination. He'd have to examine the area in increments. Starting at the entrance, he hung to the right, scanning the sand and the rock wall with each step.

Twenty paces in, a crate lay on its side. Stooping, he swiped away a layer of grey dust covering some kind of printing. A large *V*, with a small *o* on the descending slope, and a *c* on the ascending. He grunted. East India Company, though their dockyards were miles away in London. A handspan from the crate, two glass balls, smaller than marbles, lay in the sand—spirit beads, used to distill alcohol to the proper concentration. Was this a rum runner's hideout? The disturbed dust tickled his nose, igniting a sneeze—instantly reminding him of the sneeze at the viscount's home. The man's taste ran toward French liqueurs, so maybe not rum after all.

Straightening, he stared down at the display. A slow smile curved his mouth. That was it. This *was* a display. No reputable smuggler would leave behind his spirit beads, and judging by the layer of dust on that crate, it hadn't been used in quite some time.

Hefting the torch, he continued his search. Twenty paces farther in, a black gap punctuated the wall. He ducked, holding the light aloft. The space was as wide as his shoulders, and about as tall, with a tunnel that stretched farther than the flame dared reach. Might be a cramped walk, but the passageway appeared to be stable enough.

He entered, counting every step, memorizing each jut and twist of the trail. By twenty-five paces, he began to wonder if it would ever end. At fifty, he felt sure it soon must. One-hundred erased that certainty.

And at one-twenty-five, his torch started to sputter.

Sweat trickled down Alex's back despite the damp chill. Shadows and earth pressed in, wrapping around him like a casket. What would it be like to be buried alive? Nothing but bones for a smuggler to trip over. His bones. The flesh eaten off by rodents and insects. Breath stuck in his throat, and he swallowed. Was that his heart pounding in his ears—or the foreboding rumble of a cave-in?

Gah! He gave himself a mental shake. He'd heard of men losing their minds in the dark, and he had no desire to find out if that were true.

Turning around took a bit of shimmying and unwedging, at one point almost catching his hair afire from the dimming flame. He snorted, not so desperate for that extreme, but eager enough that he quit counting steps and hastened back the way he'd come.

Naught but an eerie blue light glowed from his torch by the time he unfolded himself from the passageway and reentered the larger cavern. No time to revel in the wide, open space, though. He'd have to finish fast. He scanned what little he could in the poor illumination. Colors were nonexistent. Only greys and lots of blacks.

With his next step, he pitched forward. Curious, when thus far the ground had been flat. He squatted. The dirt and sand compacted into a trail. One direction led to the opening in the cliff. The other revealed a host of boot prints ending at the base of the cave wall.

Why the devil would so many men walk into a wall?

The blue light fizzled dimmer. Even squinting didn't help. Propping up the torch, he yanked off his dress coat, waistcoat, and finally tugged his shirt over his head. Fingers flying, he ripped the fabric into several strips and tied them at the top of the dying flame. Fresh light blazed.

Ford was *really* going to love this expense tally.

The light wouldn't last long, though. Alex shot to his feet and studied the wall. God hadn't created this. That many stacked boulders and rocks smacked of human hands sealing something in—or maybe out.

There, just about shoulder level, a hole. Three feet wide. A handspan tall. Not big enough for a man to crawl through. Why such an odd size?

He shoved in his torch, but that only served to blind him when he looked through the opening. He needed a light on the inside, which is probably where that tunnel he'd followed earlier led. Even if he stripped naked and torched all his clothing, he'd never make it back there and get out before the light was spent.

Working at breakneck speed, he bent and snatched his dropped waistcoat, fastening it into a knot. He took care to leave a piece of the fine silk dangling and touched that corner to the flame. Once it caught, he threw the ruined waistcoat into the hole. It took a moment before growing into a ball of fire.

Alex stared, trying to make sense of the crazy lines and shadows.

Hundreds of what appeared to be small wooden ladders filled half of a cave larger than the one he stood in. On the other half were triangle-shaped frames. All uniform, stacked in rows. Why would the viscount feel the need to hide wood? What were the ladders and frames for? Somehow they were connected. *Think. Think.*

The flame flared out.

His torch fizzled to near nothing.

Yet a single, horrid idea burned inside his mind, birthed by the memory of an artillery show he'd recently attended at Woolwich. He stood still, no longer dreading the dark. If he were right, there was a much more ominous threat to not only his life, but also to all those in Dover. He'd have to find Thatcher on the morrow and confirm, for the fellow was better versed in artillery than he.

But as a betting man, he'd stake all he was worth on the wager that those frames were for shooting off some kind of rockets.

CHAPTER ELEVEN

Morning sun slanted through the taproom's window, highlighting a gouge on Alexander's left boot. He frowned. The hike back from the cave last night had proved to be treacherous in more ways than one. Sleep had been a miser during the long hours of the night, doling out scant moments of shuteye. Wooden frames absorbed his thoughts as he tried time and again to figure out what they might be used for other than the destruction of life and limb.

A yawn stretched his jaw, and he rubbed his hand over the stubble on his chin. Snatching a peek at his reflection in the glass as he strode across the empty room, he reconsidered doubling back for a shave. No good, for it looked to be seven already, or maybe half-past.

Behind him, a stair creaked, but not the usual grinding of feet tromping down. The wood groaned on the third step from the top, caused by a loose nail on the right. He'd made that mistake only once, having memorized the quietest route. Whoever descended now was trying to remain undetected—and failing miserably.

He smirked. Five to one it was Quail.

Alex darted into the corner near the hearth. Not the best of hiding places, but one that ought work. Two breaths later, a Quail-sized shape darted through the taproom and out the front door. A bit early in the day for a man who usually snored until noon.

Alex followed, taking care to ease the door shut behind him. Ahead, ragged coattails disappeared into an alley. Should he follow and see what the fellow was about? A glance at the sky supplied an answer. Pah! It was more likely eight, and who knew how long it would take to find Thatcher—if indeed the man were about. If not, Alex had a hard ride ahead of him.

Giving up on Quail, he skirted the perimeter of the Blue Hedge and headed toward the back stable yard. Hopefully the inn maintained a mount or two, or at least should, for it had been a coaching inn at one time. He bypassed a pile of cracked shingles, each step mocking his resolve. Who was he kidding? This place didn't even have a suitable roof. The best he could hope for was a swaybacked mare with the mange.

He pivoted, intent on visiting Farnham's Mount and Tack on the west end of town—until a feminine voice turned him back around.

"Just open up!"

He rounded the corner of the inn, then paused.

Across the yard, Johanna pushed against a half-hung slab of wood until her cheeks flamed a most becoming shade of red. A basket lay forgotten nearby as she put her heart and soul into trying to shove open the stable door.

Alex grinned. He'd wager a guinea in favor of the barn.

Crossing the yard, he stopped a few paces behind her. "It appears to me the door is winning."

She straightened, the fabric of her shawl pulled taut against stiffening shoulders. Was she angry her efforts had failed. . .or that he'd noticed?

Turning, she faced him with a small smile—a practiced one, the kind she likely used on any patron. Which, of course, he was.

Then why the surge of disappointment rising to his throat?

"Good day, Mr. Morton. Can I be of assistance?"

He smirked. "I believe that question ought be mine." Sweeping one hand toward the pathetic door, he asked, "May I?"

"Be my guest. The wretched thing is intent on keeping me out."

"We can't have that now, can we?" He drew nearer, glanced upward, and grasped the edge of the wood. Instead of shoving, he lifted, then coaxed the top wheel into the rail it had slipped from. Two breaths later, he shoved the door open wide. The smell of straw and manure wafted out. A whinny from deep inside raised his hopes. Maybe he'd underestimated the inn's capabilities.

He turned to her, expecting a real smile this time.

She frowned. "You made that look entirely too simple."

"It was. You merely forgot to assess the situation first. The easiest way to manage a difficulty is to think before acting."

Her brows lowered, and though she gazed at him, he suspected she didn't see. Her eyes were too glassy. Her fingers clenched together too tightly. Some kind of sour memory trembled across her lower lip. What tormented her?

Leaving the door behind, he closed the distance between them, alarmed that the proper Miss Langley did not retreat. "Are you all right?"

She blinked up at him, her eyes widening when her senses apparently caught up with the present. "Oh!"

The red on her cheeks spread to her whole face, and she bent to retrieve her basket. "You are out early this morning, sir."

The woman was far more deft at wrangling a conversation than a barn door. "Indeed. Seems a great many people are."

"What do you mean? Please don't tell me my brother is trying to move about."

"No, no. Nothing of the sort. I was speaking of Mr. Quail."

She glanced across the yard to the inn. "Is his whole band awake? Perhaps I ought stay and help Mam."

"No, only him, and he slipped out the front. The rest are yet snoring."

Her "hmm" competed with the song of a morning sparrow, every bit as sweet and pleasing to the ear.

"Then if you'll excuse me, Mr. Morton"—she sidestepped him—"I should be on my way."

He followed her into the barn. Rays of light crawled in through holes in the roof, highlighting her curves as she passed from beam to beam. That he noticed was no surprise, and in fact, could not be helped. What did astonish him was the sudden desire to make those curves his own. Permanently. What would it be like to come home to this woman every evening? To wake to that face every morn?

His steps lagged as an even wilder thought hit him broadside. Once he finished this assignment, he'd have more than enough money to return here and ask for her hand—yet that would require taking her into confidence now for her to even consider him then. And that he couldn't do, not after taking a vow of silence to Ford.

He raked his fingers through his hair. What was he even thinking? Pah! He was becoming as batty as Brentwood. Aah. . .that was it. Naturally his thoughts ran toward matrimony, after having witnessed the happiness of his fellow officer's marriage and with his own dilemma to avoid such with Miss Coburn.

He caught up to Johanna, where she set her basket onto the seat of a pony cart.

"I am in need of a horse, Miss Langley. Is there one I might borrow?"

A shadow crossed her face. "I am afraid our pony would not take you very far, and that is all we have on hand. You might try Farnham's Mount and Tack over on the west side."

"Brilliant idea." He bit back a smirk. "I shall, right after I help you hitch your pony to the cart."

"Really, Mr. Morton, there is no need."

Reaching for her hand, he lifted it, turning her smudged fingertips so that she might see. "Your gloves say otherwise, and I think we both know there's no stable boy to help you."

She pulled back, eyes sparking. "How would you know that?"

A smile stretched his lips. The woman was entirely too easy to fluster. Brave, though, for keeping up a respectable front when everything around her was rotting and raw. He aimed a finger at the harness lying on the floor of the cart. "Your tack is in a heap and dirty, instead of pegged on a wall. It smells like the stalls could use a good mucking. And this floor hasn't been swept in what. . .two weeks? Or three? From the looks of it, I'm guessing you had to let your stable boy go, and Thomas has been filling in. Though now that he's laid up, this part of the inn is suffering. Am I correct?"

Moments dragged, as did the slope of Johanna's shoulders. Still, her chin refused to lower.

Brave indeed.

"Very well," she said at last. "Posey is over there."

He followed the tilt of her head. Two stalls down, nearly blending in with the shadows, a rough-coated New Forest stood at the stall door—swaybacked, just as he suspected.

Alex blinked to keep from rolling his eyes and strode over to open the stall. The creature twitched an ear, nothing more. At least she was still breathing, he'd give her that, but by faith, he'd seen better horses in queue for the glue factory. Alex coughed to prevent a "Sweet mercy!" from flying out his mouth. No doubt Johanna would be mortified by his thoughts.

"C'mon, girl." He tugged on the head-collar, leading Posey over to the cart where Johanna stood in breath-stealing contrast to her surroundings. For a moment, he paused, impressing her image deep into his mind. It would be a welcome sight to revisit on a cold, dark night. Except for the raven hair pulled up beneath her bonnet, everything about the woman was light and air.

She clasped her hands in front of her, a strange tension lurking behind her beautiful facade. He got the distinct impression that laughter was a friend who rarely came to call on her. What would it take to cause a genuine smile? How would it feel to be the recipient? A foreign urge ran through his veins to be the man—the *only* man—to make her laugh.

"You look at me as though I may disappear at any moment, sir."

He cleared his throat, hoping the action would rid such strange notions. Releasing Posey's head-collar, he reached for the harness. Better to set his mind on something else. "Tell me, what do you know of Mr. Quail?"

"Funny. He asked the same of you last night."

"Did he, now?" He straightened, chewing on that like a tart bite of apple. Why would Quail take notice of him? "And what did you tell him?"

"Nothing much." Her tone rang true, then lowered. "Which is the sum total of what I know of you."

"Would you like to know me better?" The question spilled out from habit. He'd learned long ago that offense with women was sometimes the best defense, but this time the crafty technique sank in his gut, sickening him.

"Yes—no. Of course not." She retreated a step, the pretty glow of her cheeks flaming once again.

Pulling his eyes from her, he threaded the bridle over Posey's head. The pony resisted the bit, but he stuck a thumb in the corner of her mouth to encourage her to open her teeth. "A word of warning, Miss Langley? Be careful around Mr. Quail. He may not be what he seems."

"Are you?" Her voice was soft but the question pricked.

"Sometimes I wonder." His words travelled on an exhale, too low for her to hear, too bitter to remain in his mouth. He settled the back piece over Posey's withers, buckled the bellyband, then slung the breast strap across her chest and buckled that as well.

"What are you doing here, Mr. Morton?"

He made quick work of the breech strap. "Is it not apparent? I'm hitching your pony to the cart." He crossed the reins over the pony's withers, checked all the buckles, then turned to fetch the cart.

"No, I mean why lodge at the Blue Hedge when you might stay at the viscount's estate?"

"Well, well." A slow grin spread across his mouth, and he paused. "It seems you know more about me than you admit."

Her brows lifted, practically disappearing beneath her bonnet. "You don't deny your relationship with Lord Coburn? You make no excuse for warming a seat at his gaming table nightly?"

He shrugged. "Why should I?"

"But"—her head shook slowly, as if she tried to sort out the workings of the universe—"lying and gambling go hand-in-hand."

"Maybe for some, but not for me. I am not a man given to dishonesty. There is no reason for me to cover up either my association with the viscount or how I spend time with him."

"I—I don't understand. Why stay here"—she threw out her hands—"when clearly you can afford better?"

Hah! If only she knew he was on his way to beg more money from Thatcher. Leaving the cart behind, he closed the distance between them, stopping only when the tips of his boots touched her skirt hem. She bowed her head, as was proper for such a bold advance.

But he lifted her chin with the crook of his finger and stared deep into her endless brown eyes. "Why I remain here should be apparent."

She turned so fast, a swirl of dust rose from the barn floor. "I intend to repay you in cash, Mr. Morton. Nothing more."

So, that was the snake that bit. What had happened in her past to cause her such an assumption? His hands coiled into fists at the possibilities, yet he harnessed his rage and lightened his tone. "Johanna."

She whirled, anger etching lines along her jaw, the exact response he expected. But as her mouth opened, a retort about to launch from her tongue, he held up his hands.

"I expect no recompense. Neither in coin nor anything else. Your friendship, your brother's, your mother's. . ." He shook his head, emotion squeezing the air from his lungs. The long dead, little orphan boy within resurrected with a surprising gasp of air, and he staggered back a step, speaking aloud the realization. "Though I am a stranger, I've felt part of your family this past week. That is payment enough. Truly."

Her lips twisted, and it took all his strength not to reach out and smooth them with his finger.

"You don't believe me?" he asked.

"I suppose time will tell. Nevertheless, I shall repay my debt to you."

"Though an admirable trait, determination may be your downfall. Some things are better left in God's hands."

The lines of her face softened, and she murmured, "Thank you for the reminder." Then her shoulders squared, and she blinked up at him. "Are you almost finished? I shouldn't like to hold you up any longer. Where did you say you were off to?"

"I didn't." The answer slid out from an assemblage of evasive responses he'd collected over the years. This time, however, it left a bitter aftertaste. He'd lay bare his life to one of his fellow officers, but never to a woman. Why the sudden guilt for not doing so now?

He bent to work. Lifting one shaft of the cart, he leaned his weight into it, edging it backward, then pulled forward again, threading the shafts through the harness loops at Posey's sides. The poor nag hadn't moved a bit while he'd been distracted with Johanna. Likely it wouldn't go anywhere at her behest, either, but dashed if he'd let her hitch the cart alone.

All secured, he turned to offer her a hand in. "Here you are." Once she settled on the seat, he gave her the reins. To his amazement, as she adjusted her hold and clicked her tongue, the pony's head came up and ears pricked.

"Hopefully you've not far to travel?" he asked.

She quirked a brow. "Surely you don't expect me to own up to my destination when you guard yours like a soldier." The pony stepped out, and the cart slid past him. "Good day, Mr. Morton."

"*Touché,* Miss Langley."

As she drove off, he stood there. Unmoving. Silent. Counting the beats of his heart to keep from contemplating the desires she created. The more time he spent with Johanna Langley, the more he became a stranger to himself. Who was this man who suddenly envisioned raven-haired children and a wife to warm his bed each night? Family and hearth and home? Blast Ford for bringing up marriage in the first place. He'd managed without a family up to this point in life. He certainly didn't need one now.

He stalked out of the barn with a growl. Better to find Thatcher, finish his mission, and hightail it out of Dover for good—and without a wife.

By the time Johanna reached her friend Maggie's house, a line of foam dripped from poor Posey's mouth. Guilt crawled in, taking root deep in Jo's stomach as she patted the old dear between the ears. "Sorry, girl," she whispered.

Drat that Mr. Morton. She'd pushed Posey harder than she ought, a vain attempt to leave behind his kindness, his curiosity, his rugged good looks. Why was she enthralled instead of appalled that he'd left the inn with a gruff shadow of stubble darkening his jaw? She should have pulled back immediately when he'd reached for her hand. And what did he mean it ought be apparent why he remained at the inn? Surely it wasn't because of her. But if it were. . .a slow burn spread outward from her heart.

She turned and marched toward Maggie's home, putting an end to such ninny-headed thoughts. Shifting her basket into one hand, she rapped on the front door. Behind the wood, little Charlotte's cry leached out, growing louder with each passing second. Sweet thing, probably frazzling her mother to no end. Good. The tension in Jo's shoulders loosened. This might work.

It had to work.

The door swung open, framing her friend's flushed cheeks and bleary eyes. Her apron hung like an ill-pegged shirt on a clothesline, and stains darkened the fabric of her sleeves. Jo smiled. Margaret Scott was a portrait of desperate motherhood.

Indeed, this *would* work.

"Good morning, Maggie. I've brought you some of Mam's famous baps." She set down the basket of freshly baked rolls and opened her arms. "Let me take little Lottie for you."

"Aah, Jo, you're a Godsend today." Maggie passed off her babe and swooped up the gift, then pushed the door open wider. "Come in, back to the kitchen."

A few coos and baby jiggles later, she followed her friend, nuzzling her cheek against the top of Charlotte's fuzzy head as she went. How good it felt to snuggle a little one in her arms. Charlotte must've agreed, for her crying faded into whimpers and ended in a hiccup.

Jo paused inside the kitchen door. "Oh Maggie, what on earth?"

Pots bubbled over on the hearth, except for one—which had a smear of grey smoke darkening the air above it. Yellow pools of stickiness dotted the floor in splotches. Jars and bowls covered the table, some tipped on their sides, a few broken. An acrid smell of rotted flowers and mouldy lemons hung on the air, competing with the sour odor of soiled cloths heaped in the corner.

Maggie threw out her hands, blowing a piece of hair from her face in the process. "Don't say it. I know this place is a disgrace. I've been trying to finish the last of the elderflower jam for Sam to bring to market, and if I don't get it done today, ach! He'll be very cross. He's already delayed his London trip by a fortnight. Any later and, well. . .I suppose you didn't come to hear me rattle, eh?"

"Actually, your words are exactly what I'd hoped to hear."

Maggie pursed her lips for a moment, tapping them with one finger. "All right, then. Out with it. That twinkle in your eye says you're hatching some kind of scheme, and by the looks of it, you might as well sit yourself down. Seems like it might take some explaining, hmm?"

Jo kissed the top of Charlotte's head, hiding a smile. Her friend knew her entirely too well. Snuggling the babe a little tighter, she sat on the chair nearest the door—the only one not heaped with a basket of elderflowers or lemon rinds. "I'm not scheming anything. I merely had a wonderful idea, a brilliant possibility, really, and here it is. . .let me tend little Lottie every afternoon, or as many as you see fit. That simple. You'd be able to keep up your jam business—strawberries are just around the corner, are they not? Sam would have no more late deliveries, and your customers would be happy. Why, you might even be able to net a larger profit and—"

"Hold on." Maggie stepped over to a bubbling pot and gave it a stir, then turned and folded her arms. "Not that I don't think you charitable, but what's in this for you?"

"Well, with you making more money," she shrugged, hoping Maggie would come to a conclusion without her having to parcel out words she didn't want to say.

Her friend merely narrowed her eyes. Stubborn woman.

"I thought you might pay me a bit to care for Charlotte," Johanna finished.

"I knew it." Snapping into action, Maggie cleared off another chair and scraped it across the floor. She sat toe-to-toe, cornering the truth. "For how much you dote on little Lottie, you'd practically pay me to watch her, so what's happened? What's going on?"

A sigh drained the rest of Johanna's confidence. How to explain?

"See this kitchen, Mags?" She gazed past her friend's shoulder. "The spilled syrup, the burnt pots. . .this kitchen is what my life looks like right now."

"Oh dearest, it can't be all that bad."

She frowned at her friend. How much should she tell her? La, what a thought. Mags would pull every thread of the matter from her no matter how knotted it was.

"There's no secret Mam and I have been struggling. The inn is rundown. No one wants to stay there, making income scarce. But to attract new customers, we need money for repairs. Money we don't have. I thought that by taking in Charlotte"—she planted one more kiss atop the babe's head—"or any other little ones who might need tending, I could earn the extra capital to make the Blue Hedge into a destination instead of an eyesore."

"Aww, Jo. I'd love to help you. I would, but we're barely getting by as is." A sizzle at the hearth pulled Maggie to her feet. She dashed over and stirred the largest cauldron.

But defeat was not a friend Jo would skip down the street with just yet. Resettling Charlotte on her shoulder, she stood and neared the fire. "What about other mothers who might like such an opportunity?"

"I applaud your determination." Maggie straightened with a sad smile. "But I can think of no one."

Her shoulders sagged. She'd been certain this plan would work. Now what could she do? Charlotte squirmed in her arms, and she didn't blame her. She felt like squirming too, wriggling right out of debt and burdens and hopelessness. A shaky breath escaped her lips before she could stop it.

Maggie pulled the babe from her arms and laid Lottie in a quilt-lined basket, far from popping embers and direct heat. Then she turned and faced Jo. "Are things that bad?"

She bit her lip. "Mr. Spurge will be coming around for the money I borrowed from him to pay the ironmonger for the new hearth. I've got enough to make that payment, but—"

"That's wonderful, Jo! Perhaps things aren't as dire as you're making them out to be. You do tend to look on the dark side of things, you know."

True. She did have the money—but therein grew the seed of her deepest unrest. Despite Mr. Morton's assurances otherwise, surely he expected some kind of reimbursement for such a generous gift. She took to pacing, taking care not to gum up her shoes in the gooey spots. "I am grateful I'll be able to put off Mr. Spurge for another month. The thing is, though, that the money I'm using isn't mine. Not really. Our lodger, Mr. Morton, gave it to me."

Maggie clucked her tongue, tsking as professionally as her own mother. "There's nothing wrong with a lodger paying his rent. I should think you'd be delighted."

"He paid far more than he owes, Maggie. Who knows what compensation he'll require?" With a huff, she halted and absently reached up to rub the scar behind her ear. "I won't be beholden to a man ever again."

"Of course not." Her friend pulled her hand down and squeezed it in her own. "I understand."

"Please, Mags, can't you think of anything? My head hurts with trying to come up with something to gain funding."

A frown weighted her friend's brow, and she sighed. "There is. . . something. But I know you won't want to hear it."

"I am desperate to return Mr. Morton's money. I will entertain any respectable suggestion. Any!" She hated the pleading whine to her voice, but it couldn't be helped.

Maggie's frown deepened. "I am loathe to mention this, but if things are really that bad for you, there's a rumor going around that old Diggery is laid up with the ague. That means Tanny Needler is short-handed with the oakum delivery."

She snatched back her hand. She'd rather owe money to Mr. Morton than do Tanny Needler's dirty work. "Oh Maggie, how could you. . . how could I?"

"Desperate times call for desperate actions." Maggie's eyes searched hers, compassion drawing creases at the edges. "I know it didn't go well with you when you worked for Mr. Needler, but it got you by after your father died. He never failed to pay, and as I recall, was generous at that."

"I can't. I won't." The words oozed out, her voice sounding as ruined as Maggie's kitchen. Maggie didn't know the half of how Tanny had treated her.

Her friend sighed. "If you're intent on returning Mr. Morton's money and paying your rent next month, you just might have to."

She trudged over to the kitchen door, the weight of Maggie's words dragging her feet. It wasn't what she'd wanted to hear—but it did make sense. She paused at the threshold. "Thanks Maggie. I know you're only trying to help. I shall give it some thought. Enjoy the baps, and good luck with the rest of your jam."

Maggie's eyebrows waggled. "If I had to choose between Mr. Morton or old Tanny, I know which one I'd choose."

She turned away from Maggie's knowing look. Of course her friend would choose Mr. Morton. There was no contest between a dashing young man and an angry, pompous wretch—unless Tanny had changed.

Her stomach tightened. God help her if he hadn't.

CHAPTER TWELVE

In and out at the strangest hours. Dressed and keeping company as a proper gent, yet skilled as a common laborer. No, Mam, there are too many inconsistencies that don't add up." Johanna emphasized each word with a solid punch into the bread dough she worked, relishing every impact. "I don't trust Mr. Morton."

"Your brother does." Across the kitchen, Mam covered a steaming bowl of porridge and set it on a tray. "Implicitly."

Jo opened her mouth. Mam's wagging finger closed it up.

"You can't deny Mr. Morton's been good for the lad, brightening each day with a kind word or a tall tale. Why, yesterday he even brought him a sack of lemon drops. Thomas can't say enough about him, that's a fact."

Johanna smacked the dough with a satisfying whack, trying to decide which annoyed her more—Thomas's incessant hero worship of the man, or the decision she'd made to visit old Tanny Needler on the morrow. "But that's just it, Mam. When Mr. Morton is here, which is precious little, he's entirely too good. Too generous. Why? Why treat us so kindly?"

Mam chuckled as she added a mug of cider to the tray. "Despite my poor eyesight, that's easy enough to see. I've been watching him. There's admiration in the man's eyes when they rest on you—which is more frequent than you realize."

Her tongue—the traitor—ran over her bottom lip, remembering the feel of his mouth on hers when he'd kissed her on Oak Apple Day. An "unfortunate necessity" he'd called it, so why the continued attention? She scrubbed her mouth with the back of her hand, leaving behind a powdering of gritty flour. "That only makes the man's actions all the more suspect. Admiration cannot be bought."

Picking up the tray, Mam eyed her over the top of it. "It may be working, though."

"What are you talking about?"

"Mr. Morton fixed the stable door, broke up a brawl between Mr. Quail's men before they destroyed the taproom, even paid in full for an entire month's residence that he's yet to use. In all the time he's been here, he's shown he's a good man. And deep down, you know that. What's more, I think you admire him."

"Nonsense!" She snatched a dishcloth from a peg on the wall, fighting the urge to snap it in the air. "Why you defend him is beyond me."

"He reminds me of someone. Headstrong. Independent. Kind to a fault, though unwilling to own up to it, and much too good-looking for his own good."

The skin at the nape of her neck bristled. How dare Mam? Choking the life from the cloth, she turned back. "Please don't compare me with—"

"I was going to say your father, Johanna. It's been nice to have a man around here looking out for us. Do not begrudge your brother this time, however short, with a gentleman of good standing. Lord knows Thomas needs it." Mam disappeared out the door with her brother's breakfast tray, leaving behind the scent of oats and apples and disappointment.

Shame sank in Jo's stomach, curdling the milk she'd taken with her tea earlier. The dough in her hands felt heavy and thick. With a little too much strength, she plopped the lump into a large bowl and laid the cloth on top like a death shroud, a fitting end to a grievous conversation.

Hefting the bowl, she crossed to the hearth. Why could she simply not be happy about Mr. Morton? He had been nothing but kind and—except for the kiss—of exemplary conduct. Her mother, Thomas, even Maggie seemed to adore the man. Pish! Who did he think he was? Helping. Providing. Caring. Ever since her father died, those things had been her job. Hers!

The bread bowl slipped from her hands and plummeted to the floor.

Oh, Lord. That was it. She stared, horrified as the bowl landed dough side down—no doubt a punishment for feeling jealous. Shame tasted bitter in her mouth. Should she not be grateful for the kindness of a stranger? Closing her eyes, she begged for forgiveness in the quiet of the kitchen—until a shuffle of feet at the taproom door turned her around.

The day was sunny. The shadow on the threshold was not. She'd seen him before. A man of the night, usually conferring in whispers with Mr. Morton at a corner table in the taproom. His hat was pulled low, the whites of his eyes a stark flash of contrast. Black hair, too long to belong to a person of import, brushed the edge of his raised coat collar. Why did he wear such a heavy mantle on a June morning?

She stepped in front of the fallen bowl, hiding the mess she'd made. "I'm sorry. It's early and we are not yet ready to serve."

"No meal required. I merely ask you deliver this into Mr. Morton's hands." He held out a sealed envelope, gripped loosely in his black-gloved fingers. "He said I could trust you."

Jo advanced a step, then stopped, eyeing the thick packet. The situation smacked too much of intrigue. Did she not have enough drama in her life?

With quick steps, she whisked past the man and his envelope, calling for him to follow. "Have a seat, sir. I shall retrieve Mr. Morton straightaway and you can deliver the missive yourself."

"He's not here."

Stopping at the base of the stairs, she pivoted. "Sorry?"

"I said he's not here."

Tucking a loose strand of hair behind her ear, she re-ran the whole of the morning. She and Mam had been in the kitchen the entire time. They would've heard the departure of any of their guests, so rickety were the stairs.

"How would you know that?" she asked.

The man said nothing, his gaze speaking a language she wasn't sure she wanted to understand.

A shiver crept across her shoulders. Mam's shoes started a rap-tap down the stairway, the familiar groan of the wood complaining beneath her feet.

"Mam," Jo called over her shoulder, "will you knock on Mr. Morton's door and let him know he has a visitor?"

"Aye, child." Her mother's rap-tapping faded back upstairs.

"You're wasting her time, and yours and mine as well." The man's voice was matter-of-fact, but the angle of his chin scolded—or was it the play of light streaming in from the side window, slashing an overlarge glower on his face?

For a moment, she considered running out the front door, away from his stifling presence. This was a man used to being obeyed.

She straightened to her full height. "Who did you say you were?"

"I didn't."

She stifled a gasp. This fellow sounded an awful lot like Mr. Morton. How were the two related?

Seconds stretched into what seemed hours. The man's gaze never wavered from hers, neither did his resolve, for he said nothing more.

Fine. If she must be the one to take the high road, so be it. She forced her mouth into a smile she stored in her dealing-with-bother-some-customers reserve. "I have some water on to boil. May I get you a cup of tea?"

Mam's voice answered from above. "Mr. Morton's chamber is empty, Jo."

Once again, the man's arm extended, the envelope daring her to move forward and retrieve it. "Now, will you deliver this? I've not the time nor inclination to wait, but if need be, I will."

She didn't doubt him. Those dark eyes would haunt the taproom until Mr. Morton returned, and with his irregular schedule, that might be a long time off.

"Very well." She clipped across the floor, the fabric of her skirt adding a swishing accompaniment, then snatched the missive from his hand. "I'll see that Mr. Morton receives this."

For the space of a breath, one side of his mouth quirked up, almost as if he were pleased. "I thought as much. You'll do."

His words trailed a cold quiver down her spine. "I'll do for what?"

He stared a second longer, then pulled down the brim of his hat and disappeared out the front door, so quickly she wondered if he'd been but a dream to begin with.

But the heavy packet in her hand was real enough. There was no address on the front. No name. No writing at all. She turned over the envelope and studied the wax seal on the other side. Deep burgundy in color, but no identifying insignia. Whoever sent this either didn't own a signet ring or chose not to use it.

A sharp rap on the door stopped her speculations. She shoved the envelope into her apron pocket, then opened the door to a brass-buttoned chest with the Viscount Coburn's monogram embroidered in gold on the lapel. Her eyes followed the line of buttons up to a tall, starched collar and farther to a chiseled chin set as hard as granite. The man neither smiled nor frowned, just observed her as he might some droppings on the bottom of his shoe. Beyond him, four fine horses pawed the ground, attached to a gleaming black carriage, a matching emblem in gold on the door.

A curious urge to curtsy nearly buckled her knees. Nonsense. This was her home. She forced a smile. "May I help you?"

"I should like to see Mr. Morton." The man's tone was as dismissive as his gaze.

"I'm sorry. Apparently he's not here at the moment."

His upper lip curled, not much, hardly at all, but enough to knock her off the social ladder. Her smile faded.

"I suppose I shall have to leave this with you, then." He held up an envelope, the size and shape of an invitation. Swirly embellishments adorned the borders, glinting silver and gold in the morning light. Fine black penmanship in strong lines clearly identified the recipient to be Mr. Alexander Morton of the Blue Hedge Inn. This one was an artist's masterpiece compared to the missive in her pocket.

She reached for it, but his grip didn't lessen.

"First, I must have your solemn word you'll give this to none other than Mr. Morton. We can't have just anyone gracing the viscount's doorstep." He sniffed. "Especially from this part of town."

"Well then, perhaps you ought not trust the word of a girl such as me who is from this part of town." She yanked back her hand and opened the door wider. "Come in and wait for the man yourself."

His mouth slanted into a sneer, yet he extended the envelope farther. "For Mr. Morton. None other."

"As you wish." This time the envelope released and came away light and crisp in her fingers.

The footman pivoted without another word. She immediately shut the door, not wishing to suffer any more indignities should he choose to take off at such a pace as to spray gravel at her.

Crossing to the counter, she paused in front of the shelves and pulled the other envelope from her pocket. The missive in her left hand was elegant. The other plain. One came from wealth and importance. The other from a whisper of a man who smelled of horseflesh and leather. Both as mysterious as the enigma to whom they were addressed.

Why did Mr. Morton keep company with a viscount and a. . .whatever the dark-shrouded fellow was? Why lodge at a ramshackle inn—she cringed at the thought—when he could be lounging in luxury? Why did he evade her questions?

And worse. . .why should she care?

She bent and retrieved the strongbox, then tucked away both envelopes. A satisfying slam of the lid accompanied the opening of the front door, ending further contemplation on the matter. She stood, prepared to face yet one more courier entering with a missive for Mr. Morton.

But across the counter from her, Mr. Spurge's black eyes pierced her soul. "My wagon stands ready outside, Miss Langley, the paperwork already drawn up for St. Mary's."

"That won't be necessary." How her voice managed to strain through the anger closing her throat was a wonder. She cleared it, then tried again. "My family and I will be staying right here."

"Theatrics, is it?" He chuckled, discordant and altogether unnerving. "Shall I bring in the magistrate and shackles as well?"

"Only if you prefer the weight of irons on your wrists to the greed in your heart." She sucked in a breath. Had those horrid words come from her?

A tic began at the corner of Mr. Spurge's left eye and spread to a vein in his temple. Throbbing, it grew into the size of an angleworm. He leaned over the counter. "Such insolence will gainsay you the darkest of cells at the workhouse." The vein turned purple. "Or worse."

Faith! The mere thought of a damp cell in a workhouse drove a chill into her heart. She forced a calm to her voice that she didn't feel. "I hate to disappoint you, sir, but. . ."

She bent and remained crouched, unwilling to reveal the strongbox to Mr. Spurge. With a quick turn of the lock, she rifled past Alexander's envelopes and snatched the bag of coins he'd given her. She plopped it onto the counter, jingling the coins on purpose.

The sneer slashing across Spurge's face goaded her like a hot iron. Her chin rose. "On second thought, I don't hate to disappoint you at all. There is the hearth payment. Take it and be gone."

He snaked out his hand and untied the pouch. His brows rose, along with a coin. Slowly, he lifted a guinea to his mouth and bit the metal, doubting, testing, frowning. Chucking the coin back into the purse, he turned and gazed about the taproom. "Not a huge increase in patronage, I see." His dark eyes returned to her, pinning her in place. "I wonder if you have taken up a side profession, Miss Langley?"

"I resent your implication, sir." She measured her words, counting the value of each one, praying to God nothing more would slip out her mouth and indebt her to more time on her knees begging for forgiveness.

"You might want to think on it, for I expect fifty pounds next time." The pouch vanished into his pocket. "And no less."

"What? No!" *Fifty?* She staggered back a step. "But the final payment on the hearth plus rent should be only forty pounds."

"Interest, my dear." A slow smile lifted his lips, uncovering the few teeth holding onto his gums for dear life. "You don't think I allow you the liberty of installed payments for nothing, do you? Fifty it is."

She set her jaw, locking it against the rage building inside. "Then you shall have it."

"You're right. I shall. In four weeks' time, Miss Langley." He tipped his hat. "Until then, good day."

With a groan, she bent and slammed the strongbox lid shut.

"Johanna? Was that Mr. Spurge's voice I heard?" Mam's voice called to her from the stairway.

Jo stood, hoping confidence would rise along with the action. "Yes, Mam."

"Is all well?"

She gritted her teeth then forced a smile. "Yes, Mam."

The words tasted metallic. But it wasn't a lie. Not really. For tomorrow she'd visit Tanny Needler and offer herself to do his dirty work. He always paid well.

But could she afford the loss to her dignity?

The smell of rain hung in the afternoon air. Thick and earthy, pressing down on Alex as he stepped from the carriage. He flipped the jarvey a coin and glanced at the sky. When those clouds broke loose and shook out their fury, the whole of Dover would be washed clean—until the resulting mud splattered up against everything.

As he strode to the viscount's front door, he pulled out the invitation that had arrived earlier in the day, when he'd been out. Not that he'd need to hand it over for admittance, still, being that the time of his requested presence was a full two hours earlier than usual, it wouldn't hurt to have it available. Coburn's footman was a puffed-up fellow. Without proof, the man just might make him wait on the stoop until the customary start of gaming.

He lifted the lion-headed knocker. As it fell against the brass plate, he pulled out his pocket watch. The second hand moved on a downward slope. One. Two. Three. A week of playing cards with the viscount and his cronies had taught him the household ran with military timing—until the cards were pulled out. Then all bets were off, or rather on. Very on tonight, as a matter of fact, since Johanna had handed him an envelope of money from Thatcher.

Four. Five. Six. He snapped shut the watch's lid and tucked it away. The door swung open, as expected. But his eyes widened as a dark-haired beauty greeted him.

"Good evening, Mr. Morton." Louisa's resonant voice poured out like a fine wine.

"Miss Coburn." He doffed his hat and bowed, catching a whiff of civet musk—the same French perfume he'd smelled on her before.

As he rose, he captured her gaze with a rogue grin. "A pleasure to see you again."

He'd bet five to one the flash in her eyes was anything but pleasure—nor was the taste of the lie in his mouth.

"Please, come in." She stepped aside.

His footsteps echoed off the marble tile. Crystal lamps already lit the grand foyer, though evening had yet to leave a calling card, such was the greyness of the day. The footman—his usual escort—was nowhere in sight. Alex waited for Louisa to close the door, then asked, "Short staffed?"

"Not at all." She lifted one shoulder, the movement glinting light off the diamonds on her necklace—the pendant she'd worn to the Oak Apple Eve dinner. Did she never take it off?

She swept past him, casting a backward glance. "I simply sent John on an errand."

In three strides, he caught up to her side. "To what end, when you obviously knew I'd be arriving?"

A smile curved her lips, yet she continued to face forward as she led him down the corridor. "To have you all to myself, of course."

He turned her words over in his mind, examining them from every possible angle. She'd had more than enough opportunities to cross his path the past week. Often arriving early, he'd lingered in the sitting room, waiting for the viscount and hoping she might appear. She hadn't. Two days ago, he'd dined here, yet she'd declined the meal. Too fatigued. He'd even taken to riding the surrounding grounds should she venture out for a walk, making sure to pass the windows of the west wing that housed the family's bedchambers. She would have seen him. She could have ventured out. But no. So why the sudden urge to see him now?

He shot her a sideways glance. "I'd say your plan worked, Miss Coburn. I am at your service."

Finally, she faced at him. "Are you always this pliable, Mr. Morton?"

Pliable? He suppressed a snort. If Magistrate Ford heard that one, he'd choke on his own laughter. "I shall have to quote you on that sometime."

Her expression remained placid. Once while on an information reconnaissance in Paris, he'd viewed the famed *Mona Lisa*. Were Louisa's hair let down and straightened, she might have been the model.

She made an abrupt turn into a hallway he'd never seen. Sconces had yet to be lit in this stretch, so shadows escorted them. There were no doors except for one at the very end, making this the perfect corridor should someone wish to entrap him. As they walked, he listened for a floorboard creak from behind, ready for anything. "Where are we going, Miss Coburn?"

"My sanctuary." At the end of the hall, she pulled open the door.

He followed her out into paradise. Palm trees lined a pea gravel pathway. The hydrangea and ivy were easy enough to identify, but Louisa paused to sniff a flower he couldn't name or even guess as to which part of the world it hailed from. The path skirted the garden, close to a high stone wall encircling the area. Bird chatter was as loud as a gathering of washerwomen. The only thing amiss was the pewter sky, clouds bullying down with grey fists. A curious time for a stroll through a garden.

Louisa veered off the gravel onto a worn trail leading into the middle of the plot. The path ended at a fountain, surrounded by four wrought-iron benches painted white. Louisa sat on the nearest. He joined her, leaving enough space for propriety, though he probably needn't have bothered. If the woman had no qualms about asking a man she barely knew to join her in such solitude, she likely wouldn't mind him sitting next to her.

She turned to him. "Do you like riddles, Mr. Morton?"

He bit back a laugh. Did the little vixen not know she was the biggest riddle of all? No, not quite. Even larger was the question as to why Ford would order him to marry the woman—and how he'd get himself out of the situation.

He forced an even tone to his words. "I do. Perhaps you can help me solve one."

A perfectly arched brow rising just slightly was her only answer.

But it was answer enough. He continued, "Why would an English woman wear French perfume, a Cross of Lorraine, and if I am not mistaken, dress in a gown made of silk from Lyon?"

That same brow sank, as did the other. A woman cornered was a dangerous animal. "And why would a man be informed of such things?"

"Touché, mademoiselle." He covered his heart with his hand, feigning a direct hit. "Then for the moment, we shall leave my questions tabled. Perhaps it was a riddle of your own you wanted to discuss?"

"Yes, which is why I've brought you here. I've spent many hours thinking on something the past several days, yet can find no answer. What is it exactly, Mr. Morton, that you think you can help me with? And more importantly, why?"

Help? The woman dealt out her conversation like a dropped deck of cards. He scrambled to pick up mental clues for a moment, then remembered the note he'd sent along with the flowers. Draping an arm over the bench's back, he leaned against it. "Apparently you do not recall the conversation we had at the Oak Apple dinner. I offered to help you with your man hunt."

"La, sir." She flicked her fingers in the air as if batting away an offending pest. "If you're speaking of my father's wish to marry me off, you're wasting your time. I have no interest in you."

Half a grin lifted his mouth. What a welcome change from having to fight women off. "That is no surprise, Miss Coburn, for I suspect it's Robbie who's stolen your heart."

A rumble of thunder competed with the cascading water from the fountain. Her face gave no hint as to what went on behind those dark eyes. Were she a man, she'd be fabulous competition at her father's gaming table.

She stood, smoothed out her skirts, and walked over to the fountain.

His grin grew. "Do you deny my premise?"

She traced the rim of the fountain with her fingers. She wouldn't answer the question, of course. Nor did she need to. Her movement revealed more than any false words she might string together.

At last, she turned and faced him, stalking forward on padded feet. A lioness to the kill. "I am an opportunist, Mr. Morton, and I sense an opportunity with you."

Her words were as tempestuous as the coming storm. He kicked out his legs, crossing one over the other. "Now that is a riddle. Do tell."

She stopped directly in front of him. "You're new here. A novelty.

One which my father enjoys. I simply ask that you continue the diversion for several weeks more, for I can hardly bear to be in the same room with him after what he did to Robert." The lioness's fangs came out in a small smile. "You will, of course, be well compensated."

"Why several weeks?"

"That's when I plan to leave with Robert. He will pay you well for your distraction."

He smirked. "I was correct, then."

"That's immaterial. Will you do it?"

"I shall, but on one condition."

She angled her chin. A tot couldn't have looked more curious. "What?"

"The diversion is to be of my own making."

She laughed. "Oh, Mr. Morton. I don't care how you manage to keep father's attention, only that you do."

He studied her for a moment. A beauty, but mostly bought, nothing like the natural allure of Johanna Langley. This woman hid her secrets well, all perfumed and tied up with a bow. What was it about her that Ford wanted him to unwrap?

He stood and offered his hand. "Shall we seal the bargain?"

Her fingers were cold against his, clammy and moist. Did his touch unnerve her—or the fact that she'd have no control over his means of distraction?

"You are an enigma, Miss Coburn." He drew back and swept out his arm. "Tell me about this place, your sanctuary."

She eyed him for a moment before answering. "I am in your debt now, I suppose. Come along, and I'll take you the long way back to the house." She turned and bypassed the fountain, choosing the path on the opposite side from the way they'd come.

Thunder rumbled closer, quieting the birds, stilling the insects. Could she not have simply told him about the garden instead of dragging him through it?

When he caught up to her side, she continued, "Perhaps you already know my father's record with the East India Company?"

He nodded.

"That was all before I was born, of course. Such tales, though. So vivid. After Mother died, Father's stories of Punjabis, elephants, and exotic flowers unmatched anywhere in the world, well. . .it was the only thing that quieted me. The only place I could go to escape the pain of losing my mother."

He glanced at her. It was hard to reconcile the steel maiden next to him with a weeping little girl. "You don't seem the sentimental type."

"I am not." The path opened onto a walkway wide enough for a small cart to travel, and she turned left. "Nevertheless, I am human, and as I've said, an opportunist. Father's stories of India filled an empty spot inside me, so much so, that it became difficult to distinguish myself apart from the land. I tried to recreate it in this garden, but the truth is I belong there, Mr. Morton. Nowhere else. Father cannot—will not—understand."

"Aah. . ." He stepped over a small pothole in the trail, all the while looking for holes in her story. Either she was playing him, or telling the truth. But which? "Allow me to hazard a guess. Your father wishes you settled here, firmly planted in English soil. And against those wishes, Robbie's agreed to make your dream come true, hence your little excursion next month. But I wonder, Miss Coburn, what fires you most, becoming a bride to Robbie or to an exotic land?"

She stopped dead in her tracks. As still as the dark air around them. Tension lashed out in her tone, sharp as the crack of thunder overhead. "You are overly perceptive, sir."

For a moment, a very small one, compassion squeezed his heart for the little princess used to getting her own way. Exposure was never a pleasant embrace, as evidenced by the strained lines on her neck.

"Everyone is wild for adventure, Miss Coburn, but forcing one is a dangerous affair. Better you should leave that in the hands of God, hmm?"

Her face cut to his. "I didn't know you were a religious person, Mr. Morton."

"Everyone has faith, Miss Coburn. The question is, Faith in what?"

Storm shadows darkened what daylight remained, hiding her beauty. "I learned long ago that faith in myself is the surest—the *only*—dependable force upon which I may rely."

He smiled. "Then the Indies are the best place for you, and I wish you Godspeed."

"What? No theological debate?" Her voice rose as high as her brows. "No damning of my eternal soul?"

"Not from me." He shrugged. "Your desire will accomplish that, I think. Either that or God intends to grab hold of you as surely as He snatched the fleeing Jonah."

As soon as the prophet's name left his mouth, the heavens let loose. Rain drowned any further conversation. Louisa took off at a sprint down the path. Alex smirked and strolled on. Running wouldn't lessen the drenching of already soaked garments.

"Oh!" A cry competed with the next roll of thunder, just beyond a bend in the path.

He shot ahead. "Miss Coburn?"

Louisa slumped on the gravel, clutching her leg, her skirt pelted with mud. She rocked slightly, moaning with the movement. An embroidered slipper lay upside down behind her, half sunk in a small pool. Pah! Women and their silly shoes.

He dropped to one knee beside her and threaded an arm around her shoulder, the other beneath her knees. Streaks of cosmetics rained down her face as she looked up at him.

"I'm fine. Merely a slip up."

He lifted.

"Mr. Morton!"

"We'll assess inside." He raised his voice, competing with the rage of wind and water. "Hold on."

"Put me down!"

Clutching her against his chest, he dashed forward, dodging falling palm fronds. The flowers around him took a beating, stripping petals, breaking stems. By the time he reached the door of the manor, paradise was battered to death, as was the rest of daylight.

His shoes scritched on the polished floor. He ignored the woman's protests, too busy navigating the inside hallway, for the tiles were more treacherous than the wet gravel outside. Retracing their earlier route, he turned and crossed the grand foyer. The household staff would be up late tonight cleaning his filthy trek onto the carpet in the receiving room.

He bent to set the woman on the sofa near the hearth, but before he loosened his hold of her, a deep voice grumbled from behind.

"Is taking my money at the card table not enough, sir, that you must also take my daughter?"

CHAPTER THIRTEEN

Thunder rattled the windowpanes in the taproom, creating an offbeat rhythm to the music of the band. Jo suppressed a wince at the racket. It was bad enough when Mr. Quail eked out songs on his violin, but at least he had a sense of tempo. Tonight his men were on their own, and judging by the peg-legged sprinting of a folk tune that should ramble, they were quite enjoying his absence.

She handed the customer in front of her a mug, offering him a smile as watered down as the cider.

"Keep 'em coming." His face screwed up like a dishcloth wrung too tightly. "A few more and maybe it won't sound so bad."

"I'll see if they can play something a little less—" *Noxious? Loud? Headache inducing?* She swept back a wisp of hair and finally suggested, "lively."

Glancing at several other patrons nursing mugs, she was satisfied when none met her gaze. It was a shame more benches weren't filled, though with the storm, she could hardly expect less. Winding past empty tables, she paused near the band. Their song crashed to a halt at her arrival, the last jarring notes leaving a ringing in her ears that might never go away.

"Did ye like that one, lassie?" Mr. Quail's wooden flute player, Lachlan, leaned over and nudged her with his shoulder, his behaviour as inappropriate as his music.

She retreated a step, dodging his touch and the question. "I'm wondering when Mr. Quail might be down? I've kept your suppers warmed until he arrives."

"Ach, lass. Did I not tell ye?" Retrieving a cloth hanging off the side of his belt, he rubbed down his instrument while he spoke. "Quail's ailin'. Says his throat pains him, so he begged off for the night. Not to worry, though. We won't let you down."

He stuffed the rag away and lifted the flute to his lips. After two notes, the others joined in, and another hair-raising ballad began.

Johanna bolted toward the kitchen, grateful her long skirt hid the flurry of her feet. Mam turned from the hearth, her good eye widening at such an entrance.

Bypassing the larger mugs on the shelves, Johanna settled on a wooden tumbler and faced her mother. "Have we some licorice root left?"

"Aye, there's a bit." Mam squinted and searched her head to toe. "Feeling poorly, Jo?"

"Oh, it's not for me. Thought I'd take some tea up to Mr. Quail. I can't believe I'm saying this, but the sooner he graces the taproom, the better." She ducked into the larder and reached for the small crockery next to the tea caddy. When she removed the cover, she frowned. Mam might need to change her definition of a "bit." Only a few spare nubbins of licorice root remained.

She emptied the contents, replaced the jar, and returned to the kitchen, where Mam stood with a kettle in hand. The hot water barely changed color once in the cup, but at least a faint whiff of spiciness crawled out.

"Mind checking on Thomas while you're up there?" Mam asked as she set the kettle back on the fire.

"Of course." She scurried over to the stairs, trying to shove down the wish for Mr. Morton to arrive and evict Mr. Quail's band as effectively as he had Mr. Nutbrown. No good. With each upward step, the wish grew with intensity, but at least the music lost some of its sting when she entered the hall and turned toward Thomas's chamber.

She pushed open his door with her free hand. "How goes it, Thom—what on earth are you doing?"

On his belly, Thomas sprawled sideways across his bed, injured leg dangling off the edge. The position allowed him to reach the floor, where he'd lined up small soldier figurines in a mock battle. A fake explosion issued from his mouth, and he whaled a clay marble at half the little soldiers before he lifted his face from the skirmish. "Alex told me England expects every man to do his duty. I'm just doing mine."

"And I suppose Mr. Morton felt it his duty to spoil you with a sizable militia. Honestly, Thomas. You should not accept such an offering. We will never be able to pay him back."

"Don't have to. This were a gift."

"Think on it. Why would a man who's known us little more than a week be so generous?"

He stared at her as if she were daft. "Because he likes us."

She frowned. "More likely he expects something in return."

Thomas rolled to his side, propping himself up on one elbow. "Like what?"

"I don't know." She gnawed on her lower lip, trying to work up a more suitable answer. "But I intend to find out."

"Aww, Jo, you make him sound like a no-good, rotten-faced scoundrel. I won these soldiers off him fair and square. He don't expect nothin' for 'em."

Rotten-faced? With that chiseled jaw and eyes the color of an August sky? The way tiny creases highlighted the side of his mouth whenever he smiled. How his gaze made her feel like she was the only one who mattered. Warmth rushed into her cheeks just thinking of his handsome face.

Shaking off the crazy notion, she crossed to the table—when all of Thomas's words hit her. He'd *won* those soldiers off of Alex? She set down Quail's mug and put her hands on her hips. "How exactly does one win a gift?"

"Alex were teaching me a game, and I bested him. Those soldiers were a prize and a gift. He even said so."

"What kind of a game?"

His cheeks puffed out with a huge exhale. "Cards. But don't be angry with him, Jo. He were just helping me pass the time. You wouldn't begrudge me that, would you?"

"Oh, Thomas, don't you understand by now?" She frowned at the way such honeyed words slipped past his lips. The lad was far too much like Father. "If you would but tell me the truth of things up front, I'd not get so cross. Gambling is wrong because it's a poor way to steward our money—but what is worse is that it always leads to lying. Don't you see? You first told me those soldiers were a gift to hide the fact you won them at a game of cards. I cannot tolerate lying, young man. . .*especially* not from those I love."

His head sank face-first onto the mattress. "Sorry, Jo," he mumbled.

With a sigh, she bent and scooped up the soldiers. When would he ever learn? "Very well, now off to sleep with you. Finish your battle in the morning."

Thomas lifted his face. "Don't you *ever* have any fun?"

His question rankled on more levels than one. She'd known frivolity once, years before, so long ago she barely remembered. But over the years, life had leached out her enjoyments one by one, until she'd learned it was better not to enjoy anything—for that delight would surely be taken away.

She shook her head.

Sticking out his tongue, her brother blew an unsavory noise.

Ignoring him—for truly, any response she might give would only encourage the little scoundrel—Johanna collected Mr. Quail's tea and closed the door on the lad. She scurried down the corridor, hoping to arrive before the drink turned completely cold.

She lifted her hand to knock, but before her knuckles met wood, glass crashed on the other side. "Mr. Quail!" Throwing propriety to the floor, she shoved open the door. "Are you all right?"

Nothing but rumpled blankets slept on the bed and the extra pallets on the floor. A gust of wind and rain charged in through a broken pane on the bottom quarter of the window. Why would glass shatter if no one were in here to break it?

Unless someone had been in here until a moment ago.

She dashed over to the window and peered out. Sure enough, below, a dark shape rolled to a standing position. Hard to tell for certain in the stormy darkness, but it might be Mr. Quail. If he'd exited the window and it slammed shut, that would account for the glass and water now on the floor.

But it wouldn't account for a sick man sneaking off into a storm when he ought be downstairs, playing with his band.

"Care to explain?"

Behind Alex, Lord Coburn's words growled a shade darker than the accompanying peal of thunder, both rattling the sitting-room windows. For a moment, Alex tensed, caught between Louisa's mocking gaze in front of him and the angry father at his back.

Slowly, he released her against the couch cushions and stood. Amusement sparkled bright in her brown eyes, chafing as painfully as the newly formed blisters from his wet leather shoes. Spoiled little rich girl. He clenched his jaw. If entertainment was what she wanted, then far be it from him to disappoint.

"An explanation you shall have, sir." He turned and faced the viscount. Sucking in a breath, he steeled himself to bid more than was judicious. Hopefully Robbie and Louisa would make good on their elopement plans. "I ask permission for your daughter's hand in marriage."

Louisa gasped so deeply, she started coughing.

Lord Coburn grunted, but no words followed.

Alex counted every time the yew branch outside smacked against the window glass—better that than count what a high price he was paying to accomplish Ford's intelligence gathering.

"You are full of surprises, Mr. Morton." The viscount bypassed them both, striding over to the mantel. He made quick work of opening and shutting a carved wooden box, then bent, working to light a cheroot from the glowing coals below.

Skirts rustled behind Alex. Breath scented with cloves tickled his ear. "What do you think you are doing?"

He pivoted partway, keeping both the lioness and the king of the jungle within his range of view. "A miraculous recovery, hmm?" he whispered back.

"I told you I wasn't hurt!" Her words picked up speed. "Had you listened, we wouldn't be in this situation. Furthermore, when I asked you to divert my father, I never meant for you to—"

"Save your lover's whispers for another time, Louisa. Leave the room. And for God's sake, change out of those wet garments. I'll not have you taking ill." Lord Coburn straightened, daring her with a widening stance.

She remained silent, but there was no need for verbal rebuttal. Her stilted movements as she left the room said it all. Rebellion lived inside Louisa Coburn—though there was no hiding the way she favored her left foot, whether she owned up to the pain or not.

The viscount tipped the glowing end of his cheroot toward Alex. "I'd offer you one, but I know you'll only turn it down—and that is one of the few things I do know about you." He sank into the chair closest the hearth. "Come. Warm yourself by the fire and tell me why on earth I should give my only daughter to you."

Wet wool, though finely woven and tailored to perfection, stuck to his legs as he took the viscount's suggestion. He stationed himself in front of the coals, warming his backside and facing Lord Coburn. "There is one simple yet compelling reason why you should grant your blessing to me—because you despise Robbie."

"Do be serious." Coburn huffed. "My nephew is not worth that much passion."

"Neither is a bite of rancid meat, yet one forcefully spits such out."

Coburn took a long drag of his tobacco, the end of which glowed like a demon's eye. A curl of smoke piggybacked on his exhale. The tightness in Alex's shoulders relaxed. He'd seen this behavior at the card table, time and again, right before the man made a move.

"Your wit is a fine match for Louisa's, but do not be mistaken. Louisa will not inherit this estate, for it is entailed. In light of that, it is to her benefit to marry well. Tell me, Mr. Morton, what does a wine merchant have to offer a viscount's daughter?"

Without so much as a flinch, Alex stared down the barrel of the loaded question. He would not lie, though he was not averse to stretching the truth into an unrecognizable shape. Calculating the odds of each answer he might deal out, he finally settled on one. "For the past week you have witnessed my skill at the card table. Do you think I will ever lack for money?"

Coburn's face twisted into a sneer. He ground out his cheroot into the ashtray on the side table with more force than necessary, saying nothing.

Alex held his breath. Had he answered incorrectly?

The viscount leaned back in his chair, a faraway glaze in his eyes. "Fortune is a diseased mistress." He spoke so softly that, had not his lips moved, Alex would've doubted he'd spoken at all.

"You speak as one who's had an affair or two."

"Three, to be exact. The pox of such unions still runs through my veins."

Narrowing his eyes, Alex surveyed the man. Skin clear. Nothing sallow in his gaze. Though greying at the temples, the fellow appeared to be in his prime. Still, Alex was no physician. "My Lord, are you unwell?"

"Would to God it were merely that." The viscount pushed from his chair and paced around it, gripping the back with whitened knuckles. "It's the nightmares, my friend. There's no holding back the incubus of past sins."

Coburn's tone bled with a distinct rawness, and Alex bit back a wince. This was an unguarded side of the man he'd not seen before. Did he tip his cards from lack of discretion or on purpose? Regardless, truth was the only salve for such a wounded statement. "If I may be bold, sir, nothing you have done is beyond God's forgiveness."

"Bah! Spoken like a true innocent." The viscount's hands dropped to his side, his shoulders falling with the movement. "Judas paid the price for betrayal, as do I, every day I draw breath, so spare me your platitudes on forgiveness. There is no erasing the terror in a victim's eyes as you watch the lifeblood drain from his throat." He stalked over to a sideboard, where he snatched up a green bottle.

Alex stared, slack-jawed. What kind of devilry had Lord Coburn committed in his past? Worse, what was he capable of in the future?

The viscount slugged back a shot of brandy and turned, still gripping the bottle in one hand, an empty glass in the other. "Care to rescind your offer to unite with such a family?"

Everything within him screamed yes. . .yet he forced out, "No."

"Good." The viscount lifted the bottle. "Join me?"

Alex shook his head.

Coburn poured another drink, then retreated to his seat and deflated. “It is no secret I wish Louisa married by the time she comes of age in a few months, but Robbie is not the man for her, no matter how much she thinks he is.”

“You know of her feelings?”

“I am unsure how much emotion plays into the equation. Louisa will not rest until she steps foot in India—and God help her if she does. Robbie is foolish enough to accommodate that whim. So I’ve been looking for a safer alternative to secure her future. Are you safe, Mr. Morton?”

“That depends upon your definition.”

“Wily, as always. Yet. . .oh, do sit down. Surely you’ve warmed through by now.”

Indeed, his backside fairly stung with heat, but standing was a more powerful position. He angled himself so that warmth crawled up the front of his trousers. “I’ve already ruined your carpet. I shouldn’t like to damage the furniture. Furthermore, if I dry out my front, I shall be ready for a long eve of gaming rather than wasting time traveling home to change garments.”

“You always have a card to play, and usually one better than my own.” The man skewered him with a glower. “Very well. On the matter of my daughter, I don’t doubt your ability to provide, and your travels might fill Louisa’s need to wander. Still, I must have your word that India is never—*ever*—to be a destination.”

The viscount was as determined as Louisa about the continent, though diametrically at odds. Why? Thatcher and Ford might have to do a little digging into the viscount’s military past for him. He nodded, satisfied on his course of action and on the freedom to concede without deceit. “Agreed, though it’s no difficulty on my part. India is not known for vineyards.”

Coburn ran a finger around the rim of his glass, slow and methodical, his gaze never varying from Alex’s. “And what of your fine Madeiran vintage to escort back to Sheffield? I should think by now your father would be wondering what the delay is.”

"The winnings I've earned at your table provided for a far better escort than I." Or would, if he actually had a precious cargo to transport. "I stayed here because of your daughter."

Setting his glass on a side table, the viscount stood and advanced, slapping Alex on the back. "Then I'd say we have an arrangement, of sorts."

Alex's brow tightened. "What sort?"

"Mere formality. A simple background check. Can't have just anyone finding out my secrets now, can I?" Rounding back to the side table, Coburn snatched up his glass and returned to the brandy decanter. "Nor can I have just anyone joining the family. In that respect, I hope you understand I must be very thorough. Are you willing?"

"Of course." As soon as the words slipped from his tongue, he clenched his jaw. Hopefully Ford had constructed a rock-solid history for Mr. Alexander Morton.

For if the magistrate hadn't, the viscount would put a ball through more than just his hand.

CHAPTER FOURTEEN

Fresh. Earthy. Johanna loved mornings like this, the kind that wrapped around her shoulders like a lover's embrace. She inhaled deeply as she crossed the courtyard from inn to stable. Last night's storm had scrubbed the world clean, leaving behind the trill of birds and a peppery scent. This was the type of day in which she could pretend all was right and good in her life—except for the haunting cry of the mourning dove reminding her of her mission. If she listened hard enough, she might almost believe it cooed *poor girl, poor girl, poor girl.*

She upped her pace, grinding the gravel beneath her shoes a little harder than necessary. Surely calling on Tanny Needler was what God wanted her to do. Every other means of raising money had come up dry. She glanced at the sky, blue and innocent.

"That is what you want me to do, is it not?" she whispered.

Poor girl. Poor girl. Poor girl.

A frown folded her lips. If only she could hear God as clearly as the call of the doves.

Reaching out, she grasped the barn door and shoved. The wood didn't budge. Oh, bother! Again? What was it Mr. Morton had—aah, yes. She gripped her fingers tighter and lifted, just as she'd seen him do a few days ago.

Yet the obstinate thing would not be moved. Perhaps if she bent, then heaved with all her might? She crouched and searched for just the right place to plant her fingers, for there was only a thin space between door and wall. When she found it, she wrapped her hands tight and—

A puppet head jutted into her face.

She shot up, barely containing a scream, and slapped a hand to her chest. "Mr. Nutbrown! You scared the breath from me."

The lines of Mr. Nutbrown's face twisted into a question, as if he were the one affronted. "Why, Mr. Nutbrown is exceedingly sorry, miss." His falsetto voice drowned out the sweet morning sounds. "He merely wishes to give you something."

The silly puppet disappeared into the man's dress coat. And my, what a dress coat. Johanna stared. Sunlight glinted off golden embroidery looped along the edges of the lapel, collar, and cuffs. The material was rich green velvet, deep in color and offset by ivory woolen pantaloons. He still wore his ridiculous yellow stockings, but these were of the finest silk. Not a snag or smudge to be found. What on earth had the fellow been up to the past week to affect such a change?

He withdrew his hand and coins emerged, curled into the puppet's body. Mr. Nutbrown shoved the jester and the coins toward her. "For you, Miss Langley."

She turned over her palm. The money landed with a jingle. Fingering through it, she calculated. Six. Seven. Eight. All that he owed for rent. But why now? Why come back to repay her?

Her brows rose. "Well, I'd say your debt is completely paid off. Thank you."

"But there's more where that came from." The puppet bobbed. "Mr. Nutbrown would like you to share in the riches he's found."

She studied his face, wishing she owned the observation skills of Mr. Morton. Whatever Mr. Nutbrown had in mind, it couldn't be good. The man was a consummate slacker. There was no honest way he could've come up with such an amount of money, let alone legitimately offer her a share. She shook her head. "Oh, I really don't think—"

"Ah-ah-ah! One should always listen to the knocking of opportunity." Mr. Nutbrown's arm shot out, and he rapped the jester's head against the barn door.

Johanna frowned, teetering on the fine edge of how to dismiss the fellow without engaging him.

The puppet popped back into her face. "We would like to invite you to a business meeting this afternoon."

Business? Right. Likely some shady affair. And if not, something absurd. She glanced at the sky. Already the sun crept on an upward arc. "I am sorry, sir, but I have my own business to attend. If you'll excuse me."

The puppet thwacked on the door again. Louder. Longer. Was the man not nervous about cracking the head of his precious little jester?

She sighed, fighting the urge to roll her eyes. Clearly, there'd be no putting him off. "Very well, Mr. Nutbrown. Go on."

His puppet jerked away from the door, facing her. "Won't take but an hour of your time later this afternoon, and it pays five guineas."

Five guineas! Combined with what he'd just given her, that would go a long way toward her upcoming rent payment. At that rate, she might even be able to pay back Mr. Morton. Still, this was Mr. Nutbrown. And a puppet. She looked past the jester, into the man's eyes. "That seems an inordinate amount for attending a business meeting for a mere hour. What else is required?"

The puppet's head shot to Mr. Nutbrown's face. "You were right! She is interested." Mr. Nutbrown smiled, broadly, his elastic lips hinting of something more than satisfaction. Pride? Possibly. But with somewhat of a darker shade. Something sinister.

Before she could think more on it, the jester's body waved in front of her. "Here's the long and short of it. You won't actually be attending the meeting. Too boorish for a lady such as yourself. No, no. All you need do is stand outside. Above the meeting, actually. Next to a small hole."

La! And that would pay five guineas? She should've known. Why had she wasted her time? She tucked the money he'd given her into a pocket. "As usual, sir, this conversation is taking a ridiculous turn. I bid you good day."

Mr. Nutbrown planted himself between her and the barn door.

"Oh, very well," she breathed out. "Finish your proposition so that I may be on my way."

"As Mr. Nutbrown has said, miss, all you need do is wait outside for the duration of the meeting. If anyone comes near, you simply drop a pebble down the hole and walk away."

She smirked. Of course. A known smuggling trick. That's where this instant money had come from. Slowly, her lips flattened. It would be easy, though, and paid the same amount she'd likely earn working for Tanny Needler—but without the pain.

Poor girl. Poor girl. Poor girl. The mourning dove's wail crawled into the tiny crack of indecision. Should she? It's not like she'd be committing a crime.

But the smugglers would.

Folding her arms, she set her jaw. "What you choose to do is your own business. I prefer to come by my money honestly, or not at all. Good day to you, sir."

The ludicrous puppet shot toward the barn wall, on his way to what appeared to be a magnificent knocking session.

Johanna flung out her arm, trapping the little jester's head against the wood. Mr. Nutbrown's eyes widened, followed by a sharp intake of breath.

She leaned toward him, emphasizing each word. "I said good day."

Removing her hand, she retreated a step. The puppet dashed for cover inside Mr. Nutbrown's fine coat. The puppeteer straightened his sleeves, his lapel, and finally gave each shoulder a brisk brushing off. A peacock couldn't have looked more ruffled of feather. At last, he pivoted and stalked off.

Johanna watched the silly man until he disappeared through the gate in the side of the wall, her shoulders sinking with each of his steps. That would have been easy money, much easier than what she was about to undertake. But it wouldn't have been honest.

Would it?

She took a step toward the gate. It wasn't like she'd be doing any actual smuggling herself. Besides, she didn't really know if smugglers were involved. Maybe she should have at least checked further into it.

Sweet mercy. What was she thinking?

She turned her back on the temptation and bent to heave the broken barn door. Using every muscle, she lifted. She groaned. She sweated and strained and even jiggled. The door did not budge. Not a smidgeon.

Poor girl. Poor girl. Poor girl.

Frustration nearly choked her. "Be quiet!"

"I've not said anything yet."

A deep voice wrapped around her from behind, and she shot to her feet.

Though she stood at full height, Mr. Morton smiled down into her face, so imposing was his figure—and so near that on the inhale, she smelled his freshly washed scent of sandalwood and strength. His gaze held her, pulling her close without any outward movement. How could the man command such a thing without a word?

"Oh, Mr. Morton, I didn't mean. . .I mean, I didn't. . .I wasn't—" She forced her mouth shut, well aware she sounded more preposterous than Mr. Nutbrown. When Alexander Morton stood this near, combining words was impossible—yet wholly necessary. She'd hoped to corner him this morn for a bit of a chewing out over his teaching Thomas cards the day before.

She lifted her chin. "Actually I was hoping to run into you this morning."

"Are you?" Sunshine sparkled brilliant in the twinkle of his eyes.

Eyes she shouldn't be so admiring of. She frowned. "Yes, I was hoping for a few words with you. I would appreciate it in the future if you would refrain from showing Thomas any more card games. Gambling is not a virtue."

"I beg to differ."

Her jaw dropped, so stunning the conviction of his claim. "But there is nothing honest about it. You may wish to lose your money in such a fashion, but pray do not teach Thomas to do the same."

"While I yield to your point that gaming can and oft' times is dangerous for those lured by money, at the same time, it is valuable in teaching control and self-discipline—something I think we can both agree Thomas would benefit from. As in all of life, Miss Langley, no risk, no gain, right? The key is to never wager something you cannot afford to lose." The blue in his eyes danced a merry jig. "Now then, would you like more help with the barn door?"

Her mouth dried to sawdust, and suddenly she could drink two full mugs of cider. Not only had the man whittled her mountain-sized concerns over gambling to naught but an anthill, he did it all with a grin and a glimmer. The knack he possessed for calming her worries was positively breathtaking.

And so was the man. She clenched her hands to keep from fanning herself as she stared at him. No one should look this fine so early in the day. How could she help but notice the slope of his nose, the shape of his lips? His clean-shaven jaw was a contradiction of smoothness and hard lines. His shoulders were wide enough to block out the sun. He gazed at her as if she were the only one in the world that mattered. Her. Johanna Langley. She no longer heard the keening of the mourning dove, only the thrumming of her pulse in her ears.

"—the door?"

A jolt shot through her, and she licked her lips. How long had he been speaking? "I'm sorry. What did you say?"

"I said"—he cocked his head, his eyes looking into hers—"did you want to continue your hand-to-hand combat, or shall I assist you with the door?"

"Oh, I. . ." She swallowed. What was wrong with her this morning? This man was a patron. She, an innkeeper. This was business, nothing more. "Yes, truly, I wouldn't mind your help. I tried to lift it exactly as you did last time, but apparently I'm doing something wrong."

"Indeed." He laughed. "Remember what I said?"

Faith! She could barely remember to breathe. Retreating a few steps from his invisible pull, she scoured every memory she owned. Aah, yes. She smiled up into his face, satisfied that her faulty senses had returned to normal. "Assess the situation first. The easiest way to manage a difficulty is to think before acting."

His grin widened. "I am pleased you remembered, but did you understand?"

"Of course, I—"

He stalked away before she finished speaking.

"Where are you going?" she asked.

He held up a hand as he bypassed the stuck door and strode beyond, to the smaller side door at the other end of the barn. Shoving it open with his shoulder, he vanished for a moment. A few scrapes and a knocking noise later, he shoved open the bay door from the inside, grasping a hay rake in one hand.

Johanna frowned. How had he known to do that?

His laughter once again rang out, warm as the early summer morn. "Don't look so vexed. You merely forgot to assess. The wheels hadn't fallen from the track this time. This rake had toppled over on the inside, keeping the door from opening. Tell me, Miss Langley, what will you do when I am no longer here to save you in such situations?"

A sudden sadness tightened her throat. Of course the man would leave when he concluded his business in Dover, but a dark knowledge that the Blue Hedge Inn would no longer be as merry settled deep in her chest. She forced a pleasant tone to her voice, but even in the trying, it came out as soulful as the mourning dove's cry. "I suppose I shall continue the battle of the barn door on my own, yet I thank you for helping me today."

He shrugged. "My pleasure."

"But why? Why take such pleasure in helping my family and me so often?" The questions flew out before she could snatch them back, and she slapped her fingers against her lips. For shame. No wonder he spent his time at the viscount's, surrounded by ladies who likely weren't as bold.

Alex eased the rake against the outside of the barn wall, well away from the door. Sunlight pooled on his shoulders as he strode to stand in front of her, making him appear a being of light. "As I've said, you're good people. Is that so hard to believe?"

She lowered her hand from her mouth. Mam and Thomas—mostly—were good, but herself? No, she'd never believe that. Lifting her face, she met his stare. "Surely there's more to it. There are plenty of good people in the world. Why us in particular?"

"Your brother reminds me of myself when I was a lad. Your mother, well, my own would be about her age now, had she lived. And as for you. . ." He leaned toward her, his hand reaching toward her cheek. The air between them charged like the sizzle before a lightning strike.

If she moved, just a little, she'd feel the strength of this man against her skin. His warmth. His touch. Is that what she wanted? Her breath hitched with a sudden realization. She did. More than anything. To lean into his embrace and forget debt and want and loneliness.

A whinny carried from inside the barn, pulling her back to the stark reality of an aging mare, a rickety pony cart, and the upcoming trek to Tanny Needler's—a fate the perfectly tailored Mr. Morton would have no experience with. Of course he wasn't interested in her. Not like that. He was a gentleman—and she was as outlandish as Mr. Nutbrown.

She retreated a step. "Let me guess, I remind you of your sister."

He shook his head. "I don't have a sister, though I would have liked one as attentive as you. Thomas is fortunate. What you have here, with your mother and brother, your strong ties. . .would that I'd have known such as a lad."

"Surely you and your father share such a bond, else he would not trust you to manage his winery."

"My father?" A shadow darkened his face, though the sun went unchallenged in a cloud-free sky. "Of course."

Aah. Maybe she didn't corner the market on loneliness, for there was a hollow edge to his voice. Clearly the man missed his family. "How long has it been since you've been home?"

"I scarcely know what home is anymore." His voice faded for a moment, then picked up, as intense as the blue in his eyes. "But trust me when I say I am in no hurry to go back."

Her lips parted as she struggled for air. Surely he didn't mean because of her.

But everything in her wished that he did.

The early summer sun burned Alex's back, scorching the fabric of his dress coat. Was it the sun that heated him—or the fire in Johanna's gaze? Grace and mercy! He could get lost in those eyes. Dive in. Swim deep. Never surface for air. Johanna stood so close, so vulnerable, his bones ached to sweep her up in his arms, abandon duty and honor, all that was right and good.

But then he'd be no better than the brigands he brought to justice. And honestly, was he? To have offered for one woman, and fraudulently at that, yet stand here longing for another?

He withdrew a step, yet couldn't resist the temptation to make her cheeks deepen in colour. "Are you warm, Miss Langley? You look a bit flushed."

Her fingertips flew to her face. Too late. Scarlet spread well past what her gloves could cover.

Laughter welled up from his belly. "You are altogether too much fun to tease."

The colour crept down her neck, but in the space of a blink, before mortification gave way to anger, he'd seen it. A flash of desire. For him. What was he to do with that? He didn't have time for a woman, a relationship, a family. Blast! Why did he even entertain such thoughts whenever she was near?

And what would flash in Johanna's eyes when she heard he was betrothed to Louisa Coburn? The urge to tell Johanna the truth here and now welled to his lips, but he pressed them tight. She abhorred liars—and he was the biggest one of all.

He nodded toward the gaping barn door, shaking free of such an unprofitable line of thinking. He could no more marry Johanna Langley than he would Louisa Coburn. "I assume you're in need of a certain pony cart?"

"Please, don't trouble yourself any further." She marched past him.

He followed. "I believe we've had this conversation before. Do we really need to repeat it?"

She stopped at the cart and pivoted, gradations of light accentuating every curve. "You are a most determined man."

And you are most beautiful. He bit back the sentiment before it launched from his tongue. "You make it sound as if that's a crime."

"I can see there'll be no putting you off." She swept a hand toward the little mare. "Be my guest."

He went through the same motions as a few days before, though familiar now with the lay of the stable, his movements were more rote than anything.

Johanna watched, quietly at first, then she finally broke the silence. "Our friend Mr. Nutbrown was here, just a bit ago."

"Was he, now?" Alex looked up from checking Posey's buckles. "For what reason?"

"He paid all his back rent."

Alex straightened. "I wonder who suddenly sprouted morals, him or his puppet?"

A sweet smile lifted Johanna's lips. "Neither. I suspect it was naught but an enticement to ensnare me in his latest wealth-gathering scheme."

Next to him, the horse snorted. Alex stifled one of his own. "Did it work?"

"Really, Mr. Morton, do I look like I'd join a band of smugglers?"

Standing there, caught in a web of sun rays reaching in from all angles, she looked more an angel than a woman. He bent, finishing up the buckles on Posey. Better that than gaping at her like a lovesick sailor. "What makes you think that's his game now?"

"Only smugglers and highwaymen fear gathering together without aid of a lookout."

Satisfied with the tightness of the harness, he faced her. "And when was this gathering to be?"

"This afternoon."

"Do you know where?" Not that he had the time nor inclination to attend, still, intelligence was power—and one never knew when power must be wielded.

An endearing little wrinkle creased her brow. "I did not entertain the idea, and so did not ask questions, unlike you."

"Lives are won and lost in details, Miss Langley. You'd do well to remember that."

Her mouth opened, but the stomp of feet entering the barn cut her off. He wheeled about. Five men—*large* men—blocked the entry.

One stepped forward. "You Morton? Alexander Morton?"

"I am." As he answered, he recalculated the paces it took to reach the side door. Ten. Could he make it before they flanked him?

"What is this about?" Fear wobbled in Johanna's voice.

And stopped him cold. If he made a run for it, would the men give chase—or leave one behind to torment her?

Two of the brutes stalked forward, one pulling out a pair of wrist shackles from inside his great coat. Alex's muscles tensed. Flight having been abandoned, he was left with but two choices. Fight or submit.

Johanna stepped next to him, the fabric of her skirt shivering around her. "Mr. Morton?"

His name from her lips sounded jagged. He glanced down at her and—bah! A fight with these men, with her standing so close, would put her in danger.

There was nothing to be done for it, then. He advanced, guiding her behind him with one arm, hopefully to safety. "The lady asked you a question, gentlemen. What is this all about?"

The man on his left swung behind him, wrenching his arms behind his back. Shackles bit into the bones of his wrists. Johanna's cry stabbed his heart.

"Stop it!" She skirted them all then whirled to face them, the silhouette of an avenging angel the way the sun blazed in from outside.

A shove to the small of his back pushed him forward. "Move along!"

"Step aside, miss." One of the men by the door reached toward her.

A roar ripped from his throat. "Leave her! You asked for me, and so you've found me."

Johanna arched away from the man's grasp. "Mr. Morton is a guest here. You have no right! Where are you taking him?"

The man swiped for her again. "As I said, miss, step aside, or we'll take you in as an accomplice."

She dashed just beyond his fingers, a cloud of dirt and questions in her wake. "For what?"

"Treason."

Alex's heart quit beating. It was bad enough that Ford wouldn't be able to get him out of this.

But worse was the disillusion bleeding from Johanna's gaze as he was led off.

CHAPTER FIFTEEN

Sun burned Johanna's cheeks as she set the pony cart's brake and alighted in front of Tanny Needler's shack. Even so, she shivered from a cold gust driving in from the Channel behind it. Must the weather be as contradictory as she felt, as what she was about to do? As the hundred swirling thoughts about Alexander Morton that wouldn't leave her alone? Clearly the man was capable of many things. Compassion. Strength. Looking entirely too handsome in a tailored suit. But treason?

She could not reconcile the indictment with the man, no matter how hard she tried—and she'd tried the entire journey out to Tanny Needler's Hemp and Oakum.

She reset her skewed bonnet, tired of the mystery and exhausted from the swing of emotions Alexander created in her. For a moment, her gaze followed the circling route of a seagull, screeching overhead. Her own collection of screeches welled in her throat. She hated what was to come, hated even more that there was no escaping it. Were she to look in a mirror, surely she'd see the same wild blaze she'd seen in Alexander's eyes as he'd been led off in shackles.

The gull dove, disappearing behind the carcass of wood and nail that made up Tanny's shack. So be it. She shoved down all her misgivings and advanced on a path of gravel and broken shells. Coils of rope, barrels, pallets—some whole, others in pieces—littered the yard. The closer she drew, the stronger the stink of tar and washed-up seaweed. She tried not to breathe, not to think, to simply do what must be done.

With a whispered prayer for forgiveness, she rested her palm on a door she vowed she'd never again touch, then shoved it open. She crossed the threshold before she could change her mind.

"Awk! Hands on deck! Hands on deck!" A birdcage swayed in the front window, the hook-nosed parrot inside hopping from one branch to another as he squawked.

Ahead, a grey shape turned from behind a counter. How could a man she'd not seen in half a decade look exactly the same? Though truly, she should not expect any different. Other than the covering of skin upon bone, Tanny Needler's appearance would not change were his corpse uncovered ten years after his death.

She shuddered. What a horrid thought.

Deep-set eyes stared her down, nearly lost in the shadows of the sockets were it not for a wet glisten at the corner of each.

"Well, well." Tanny's voice crawled up his Adam's apple, over his teeth and past his lips, all the gruffer for the effort. "Look what the tide washed in. Haven't seen the likes of you for what. . .five? Six years now? Din't think I'd live to see this day." He nodded, a colorless cap atop his skull sliding back and forth with the movement. "Missed ol' Tanny, have ye? They always do. They always come back."

She stopped midcenter of the small room, clutching her hands in front of her. "I am not sure of whom you speak, sir."

"Oh? It's sir, now, is it? I likes that. I likes that real well. Learned you some manners, eh?" He slipped out from behind the counter and circled her, his joints cracking with each step. "Filled out a bit too, I'd say."

"Awk! Filled out!" the wretched parrot repeated. "Filled out!"

Johanna stiffened, enduring the observation. Barely.

Tanny stopped in front of her, close enough that the odor of the fish he'd eaten for breakfast fouled the air she breathed.

"You know the routine, girl." The widening of his stance was a mandate.

She bit the inside of her cheek so hard, the salty taste of blood filled her mouth. That pain was nothing, however, compared to the full weight of understanding beating her down.

Tanny hadn't changed at all.

Slowly, she lowered to her knees in front of him. He held out his hand. Beneath translucent skin, veins crisscrossed like worms unearthed by a spring rain, the gangling mess looking as if that was all that held his bones together. Not that she didn't know this was coming, but still… she'd rather kiss a thousand worms than rest her lips on that cold flesh.

"I'm waiting." A sneer coloured his voice.

She bent and touched her mouth to the back of his hand.

"Oh, that's good. That's very good." Tanny's laughter filled the room, violating her in ways that ached in her teeth.

Recoiling, she fisted her hands at her side to keep from wiping her lips. She'd done that once. The scar behind her ear burned white hot with the memory.

Tanny laughed all the way back to the counter, taking his creaking skeleton with him. "What is it you want, girl?"

"Your Grace." She clipped out the words in even measure. Better to focus on steadying her voice than on the anger throbbing in her temples. She lifted her face, but not her body. To stand before he allowed would merely earn her another scar. "I have come here to do business. I heard Diggery is laid up and perchance you might need a replacement."

"That's right." He paged through an overlarge ledger while she waited. And waited. Outside, waves crashed. Inside, the parrot's claws scratched. Johanna held her position, regardless of the way the hard floorboards ground into her knees. This was a power game, nothing more.

But this time she'd win.

Eventually, Tanny slammed shut the book and looked up. "I might be able to take you on, depending."

"Dependent upon what?"

Leaning sideways, he reached for a switch of briars hanging from a hook.

"Your Grace," she amended quickly. "Dependent upon what, Your Grace?"

"Awk! Your Grace! King of the land! King of the land!"

Tanny tapped the switch on the countertop in time to the parrot's squawks. "Things didn't go so well last time you were under my employ."

She clenched her hands in front of her. "No, Your Grace. They did not."

"You can't expect to frequent a gaol yard, girl, and not take on a pinch or two."

The unfairness of it all stole her breath, leaving behind a sore throat. "About that. . .I was wondering, Your Grace, if you might have a different task for me this time. I've become proficient in figures. I thought maybe I might help you with your ledgers? That would free you to make the delivery."

The switch slapped the countertop, loud and sharp. "No one looks at my ledgers, especially not a snippet of a surly wench like you."

She shrank as he rounded the counter, switch in hand. *Oh, God. Oh, please.* Why had she come here? Stupid, stupid idea. She averted her gaze to the warped floorboards. Hopefully a bowed head might appease him until she could escape.

His scuffed boots stopped in her circle of vision, the switch dangling next to them. She held her breath. Surely he would've struck by now if he were going to. Maybe he had softened, leastwise a little. Slowly, her muscles started to unclench.

"Awk! Surly! Awk! Wench!"

The parrot's voice struck at the same time the switch stung the tender skin between bonnet and collar. Once. Twice. She held back a whimper. To do so would only encourage a frenzy of strikes.

Thrice.

She gritted her teeth. She'd been wrong. Terribly wrong. Tanny had changed—and in the worst possible way.

"Aah. I've missed this, I have. Flogging's been a might scarce since you left." The switch lowered to the side of his boots once again, where she was forced to look upon the wicked barbs up close.

But better that than to gaze up into the black pits of his eyes.

Tanny spit again, the splotch landing next to her skirt and splashing up a dark spray. "It's delivery or nothing, girl, for three weeks. Be here at sunup. Bring a load of tarred oakum to the gaol, reload with the cleaned, then bring it back here, same as always. Pays a penny pound. Take it or leave it."

"Awk! Take it! Awk! Leave it!" The parrot's voice pecked at her back.

She stared at the switch. Three weeks. Only three. Her shoulders drooped, along with her spirit. Three would feel an eternity. She'd hoped for a larger wage, but what choice did she have? If they lost the inn—if *she* lost the inn—what of Mam and Thomas? The workhouse was worse than delivering oakum.

She drew in a deep breath. "I'll take it, Your Grace."

"Knew you would. Like I said, they always do." His empty hand shot out.

This time she barely felt his skin beneath her lips, for it was nothing compared to the chill settling in her soul.

The wagon lurched to a stop, the movement snapping Alex's head and releasing a fresh, warm trickle down his temple. He bit back a wince—and a smirk. Fitting that they'd pulled up in front of the black bones of a scaffold. Ford's words replayed with stark clarity. . .

"If this operation fails, I shall refute any knowledge of this conversation, to the point of watching you swing from a gibbet."

His throat tightened. Perhaps instead of the mantle of the law, the magistrate ought don the robes of a prophet.

"Move!"

A boot to his back jerked him forward. Flanked by two men, Alex edged himself toward the open gate at the back of the wagon, where two more men stood, all wearing scowls and angry, red bruises—except for the fellow on the right. A deep gash bloodied his lip, and the lump on his nose promised to grow into magnificent proportion.

Alex glowered at the men, but inside his heart, he smiled. Truly, he ought not take such satisfaction in the ripped fabric and flesh he'd caused. Wicked? Likely. But not as wicked as the sharp pain cutting from foot to knee when his feet hit the ground. Aah, but that had been some escape attempt. Five to one normally wasn't a problem, but with his arms shackled behind him, it had been an unfair disadvantage. Still, he'd given it a champion try.

Too bad he'd failed.

Standing this close to the Market Place Gaol, he recanted of ever having thought the Blue Hedge Inn a run-down hovel. Sunshine soaked the building's bricks, but the life had been drained from them long ago. If not for the blanket of soot wrapped tightly around the place, the walls would lie down and die, buried beneath the weight of guilt and age. Windows were barred in uneven rows, and the roof curved earthward, like an eyelid shutting for eternity. This was no gaol. It was a pox. A leper's spot. A gangrenous limb of justice that should have been cut off long ago.

"I said move!"

A shove between his shoulder blades thrust him forward. Each step up to the scarred front door shot a new agony through his ribs. One was broken for sure. Hopefully, only one. But that wasn't the only thing cracked. For the entire ride, he'd tried to piece together the fragmented logic of hauling a supposed traitor away from Dover castle—where one accused of sedition would face a military tribunal—and instead depositing him here, at a municipal gaol. Clearly, someone wanted him out of the way for a while. But who?

And why?

The prison swallowed them all in a gulp—him, the four men, light, air, all that was good and true. The stench of death and despair punched him in the gut. In truth, though, losing his breakfast on the shoes of the brutes beside him would be gratifying. Aah, yes. He was wicked, indeed.

Lord, forgive me.

They entered a vestibule the size of a large crypt, which opened into a small, circular room. Farthest from them stood a tall desk, marred with nicks and blackened in splotches by the blood of frantic prisoners. It sat like a sentinel in front of a stairwell leading up into darkness. At either side were two doors. One would be the home of hapless debtors or vagrants, snared into working their way to freedom. The other—oh, that it may be so—the one he'd go through. The door to a holding room for prisoners able to pay their way out of humiliation.

"This the man?" The turnkey's voice boomed from behind the desk. He was perched on a stool, unless the man was of freakish stature. Surely the fellow had been born with a nose, but only two slits remained. His left eye slid halfway down his cheek, and no wonder his voice boomed. He could not close his mouth, for one lip was gone. Completely. Either the fellow had taken a devastating fall from a horse and landed on his face, or he'd been shot in the head with a blunderbuss at close range.

The brute to Alex's right answered the man. "Aye. He's the one."

The turnkey's gaze studied one guard after another, his good eye widening as it travelled from bruise to cut. Finally, it rested on Alex. "Bit of a troubler, are ye?"

Alex's lips parted, but a strike from behind drove him to his knees, knocking the air from his lungs. Sucking in a sharp breath, he fought against pain and doubled vision.

"Not anymore." The brute chuckled at his own joke.

"Right, then take him up."

A yank to his collar nearly choked him. Half-stumbling, half-dragged, he was propelled forward, bypassing the door of hope. Before he fully rounded the backside of the desk, he twisted and launched forward, planting his body against the blemished mahogany. His blood added to the stains left behind by countless men before him. "Wait! Who brings charges against me, and what of the registry? Or the garnish? I can pay, and pay well."

"Oh? Regular jailbait, are ye?" The turnkey leaned sideways, tipping his stool onto two legs. From this angle, his body appeared whole—and wholly knotted with muscles. "But there ain't nothin' regular 'bout this, guv'ner. Take him up, boys."

"No! I demand a—"

A cuff to his head knocked him away from the desk, and he staggered like a sailor on leave.

The turnkey laughed, long and throaty. "Save yer demands for yer new playmates. Like as not they'll be interested. Real interested, and that's a promise."

The men closed in on him, herding him around the desk and up into the blackness of the stairwell. Nothing was right about this. No writ served. No documentation of his stay. Only a verbal charge, but from whom? He could rot here, die here, and the only one who would know would be his nameless accuser, the thugs that led him upward, a turnkey who'd never once spoken his name. . .and Johanna.

He gritted his teeth. Merciful heavens. What she must think of him.

There were eighteen treads up. Add that to the twenty from front door to desk, and give or take nine from desk to stairwell. Fifty. Just fifty paces to freedom. He'd hold on to that number like a beacon, lighting some kind of scheme to break free.

The stairs opened into an antechamber hardly bigger than a wardrobe. Again, two doors punctuated the walls on either side. Thick ones. Pocked with nail-heads and reinforced with iron bands. Women's weeping and hysterical cries leached out from the door on the left. The man with a ring of keys opened the one on the right. The stink of sweat and urine poured out, barely doused by an afterthought of vinegar.

"In you go." Another jab to the back hurled him forward.

He wedged himself against the doorjamb. "For God's sake, take off the shackles."

"God don't live here."

He landed flat on his face, pain riding roughshod along every nerve. The lock clicked behind him. Darkness extended a calling card, one he pushed away. He staggered to his feet and retreated toward a wall, refusing to be circled like a carcass on the side of the road. Near the ceiling, sickly light crept down from barred windows, so thin and ruined, they reminded him of the turnkey's nose. In the shadows, ten pairs of eyes raked him over, measuring, judging, cataloging his weaknesses, assessing his strengths. Some of the prisoners were gaunt, marking them as longtime residents. Others were wiry, built of sinew and possibly madness, for their breathing sounded beastlike. And one of them truly was a beast. All thick and hairy. Only half the men posed any real threat—but a very real one at that. These were convicted felons.

What was one more murder to their credit?

CHAPTER SIXTEEN

Stop! You're killing me!"

Lucius Nutbrown cried out as he flailed for a moment, taking his puppet on a wild ride, then righted himself from a near-slip on the gravel. He jerked his puppet to within inches of his face and eyed the little whiner.

"I've had enough of your grumbling, sir," he shouted at Nixie. As much as he hated to stifle his friend, he really *had* had enough. He opened his great coat and stuffed him inside. "You'll ride it out there, my friend."

He'd also had enough of this horrendous trek up a barely discernable path in the darkness before dawn. Even so, he continued to pick his way, step by step, along the crushed rock trail, glad it was fashioned from the white stone of the cliffs and not the darker flint of the shoreline. Curious choice of venue. Strange time for a business meeting as well. Mr. Charlie and Mr. Blackjack certainly conducted an interesting operation. Their last meeting, two days ago, had taken place on a Saturday afternoon up near Deal, and he still wore the blisters on the back of his heel to prove it. Maybe it was a good thing Miss Langley had declined that one.

Twenty paces to his right, far below, surf crashed against rock, covering up the sound of his footsteps. The path was narrow, but at least it wasn't on the edge of the drop-off. Small miracles did happen sometimes—leastwise that's what his mother had always said. But not big ones. Never big ones. He knew that for a fact.

Ahead, briars congregated like a horde of fat, black monsters against the backdrop of a rising wall of a hill. Good thing Nixie was safe inside his coat. Things were about to get rough.

He slowed as he neared the hedge, then bent, looking beneath the thorny verge. Oh, for a lantern. Though there might be some truth to Mr. Charlie's insistence that he not bring one along. Just like the man predicted, his eyes had grown accustomed to the dark. But these briars weren't merely dark—they were the gaping jaws of hell itself. He padded along, half-bent, looking, searching, squinting until finally. . .was it?

He smiled. A crawlspace punctuated the bottom of the hedge. For a moment, his hand hesitated over his breast. If he pulled Nixie out, his friend would surely crow some praises for this victory. But he'd need that hand—and his knees—to clear the thorny tunnel in one piece. Hopefully this wouldn't snag his stockings too horribly. Taking great care, he shuffled ahead on all fours.

The bristly hedge-tunnel was short and opened up to the mouth of a cave, wherein a lantern glowed sun bright. Voices increased in volume. "Coburn's not going to be happy. This fool can't even pull off the few tasks we've given him. I say we kill him."

Egad! Someone was in for trouble. Lucius rose to his feet and duck-walked through the cave's opening and into a carved-out cavern. Stretching to full height, he dusted himself off—then immediately bent once more, examining his legs. Oh figgity! Flesh peeked out from a tear on his hose, dousing some of the yellow glory from his stockings. His lower lip quivered, then he sucked it in between his teeth. Nothing to be done for the mishap now.

"'Bout time you showed, Nutbrown. We were about to give up on you." A gravelly voice interrupted his inspection.

Lucius met the gazes of Mr. Blackjack and Mr. Charlie, who both sat near the light. They scowled almost in unison, their brows drawn into a V. If he didn't know better, he might almost think they were cross with him—but of course it was only the play of shadows from the inconsistent lantern light.

Mr. Charlie shook his head, red hair the colour of spilled wine in the dim illumination. "So far your performance hasn't met with our expectations. And here we thought you was a businessman."

This would never do. He had a reputation to uphold. He yanked Nixie from his coat and popped him onto his hand, shoving the puppet out to take care of this potential disaster. "Mr. Nutbrown assures you, gentlemen, that you'll find none more businesslike than himself. None at all."

Mr. Blackjack scratched the scruff on his chin, the sound rasping overloud in the contained space. "Let's see...you failed to get us a lookout for our last meeting. This time you're late. We've already spotted you enough money to dandy up an entire gentleman's club, but other than promises, you've given nothing in return." He swung his shaggy head toward Mr. Charlie. "What kind of business you suppose that is, Charlie?"

"Bad, I'd say. Maybe the worst kind of bad. Disappoints me, it does." He reached for the straps on his back, biceps bulging like a butcher's, and slowly pulled out an axe. He tapped the flat of the blade against his palm, the thwapping noise a crazed heartbeat bouncing from wall to wall.

Or was that mad pounding his own heart? Lucius swallowed a sour taste in his mouth and bobbed Nixie's head from Mr. Blackjack to Mr. Charlie. "Mr. Nutbrown is your man, sirs! Don't doubt it for a minute. He'll do anything for his friends. And we are friends, are we not? Friends and businessmen, one and the same."

"A'right. We don't have time for this. We're on a tight schedule, and the gears are clicking into motion." Mr. Blackjack shifted, his wooden leg scraping the ground as he moved, the sound eerily like bone on bone. With a thick hand, he patted the dirt next to him. "Sit yourself down and listen up."

In a trice, Lucius dashed over to the spot and sat, cross-legged, making sure to keep Nixie's head at a pert angle.

Mr. Charlie didn't say a word, but he stopped thwacking the axe against his palm.

"There's a shipment coming in, about three weeks from now," said Mr. Blackjack. "All our groundwork must be in place. Preparation is key. As is secrecy. Wouldn't want word to get out to smugglers now, would we?"

"Smugglers?" Beneath the cloth and plaster of the little puppet, beads of sweat popped out on Lucius's skin. "Horrid creatures."

"Right." Mr. Charlie lifted his gaze from his axe blade to stare at Lucius, bypassing a glance at Nixie. "Which is why we hire only respectable businessmen, such as yerself. But yer not going to be enough. We need a woman to work along with you, just for a small task. Someone who's familiar to the town, of good standing and that sort. We need you to find one of those for us. Think you can do that?"

Mr. Charlie slapped the axe blade against his palm so sharply, Lucius and Nixie jumped.

"Why, of course Mr. Nutbrown can." His voice came out squeaky without even trying—maybe a little too squeaky, judging by the knowing look passed from Mr. Blackjack to Mr. Charlie. Lucius cleared his throat and tried again. "But you gentlemen had no trouble acquiring me. Why don't you find a woman yourself? Ought not Mr. Nutbrown's talents be put to more use like ciphering or scribing?"

"Do we look as proper as you?" Mr. Blackjack shrugged one shoulder, the ripple of muscle as fluid as the swipe of a dragon's tail. "Why do you think we gave you new garments in the first place?"

His eyes dropped to the awful snag in his stocking, and it took all his reserve to keep Nixie atop his hand instead of tucking away his friend and attempting to mend the tear. "Of course. Mr. Nutbrown sees." He whipped his puppet's face to his as if to confer, then held Nixie back out into the fray of conversation. "It will take a gentleman—such as Mr. Nutbrown—to solicit the service of a reputable lady."

"Right. That's your next assignment." Mr. Blackjack leaned toward him, his tone lowering to a near-growl. "And if you fail again, you're out."

Nixie trembled, his little cape shivering against Lucius's shirtsleeve. "Umm, a little clarification, if you don't mind. Out? As in. . .?"

Mr. Blackjack and Mr. Charlie laughed loud and long. Nixie looked from one to the other, trying to understand the joke. Poor puppet. Too bad Nix was of limited intelligence. Lucius reached and straightened the jester's tiny collar with his free hand, trying to impart some sort of dignity to his companion.

Mr. Blackjack slapped Lucius on the back, the movement knocking Nixie's head askew. "We'll see you *and* the lady tomorrow. Five sharp at the Pickle and Pine."

Lucius's eyes widened. Gah! The only woman he could think of—who would even consent to a conversation with him—was Johanna Langley, and she'd never leave her precious inn near dinnertime. "If discretion is of the utmost, sirs—" he yanked Nixie's head upright— "the Pickle and Pine won't do. Too many patrons. Too many ears. Mr. Nutbrown suggests you consider the Blue Hedge Inn."

Mr. Charlie snorted. "That rat hovel on the edge of town?"

Lucius bobbed Nixie's little chin up and down.

"Fair enough. Five tomorrow. Blue Hedge. But don't disappoint us." Mr. Blackjack aimed a pointed stare at the sharp axe blade lying in Mr. Charlie's lap.

Mr. Charlie ran his thumb along the blade, opening a line of flesh, bloodying both skin and steel.

Lucius flinched. So did Nixie.

Mr. Blackjack leaned back and looked down his nose at both of them. "There's no holding Charlie back when he's disappointed."

Lucius's throat tightened, and for a moment, he wished Nixie could speak on his own. "N-not to worry, friends. Mr. Nutbrown will be there. On time. Early, even."

He shot to his feet and darted to the door, forgetting to duck and smacking his forehead in the process. Naturally he'd be there, but how to get Miss Langley to agree to sit and listen?

Johanna clamped her jaw to keep her teeth from rattling. The wagon she drove juddered from every rock, dip, or uneven groove on Dolphin Lane, the ride as merciless as Tanny's switch. Resettling her backside on the unforgiving seat, she flicked the reins, urging the horse forward. The animal was hardly more animated than Posey. Not that she blamed the poor bay. Scars crisscrossed his rump from Tanny's wrath. Though she hated inflicting more pain on the horse, it was a must. She was late.

Passing by the Magpie Inn, she glanced at the pots of roses, periwinkles, and pert little candytufts. Now there was a good idea. She could paint an old barrel in the barn and transplant some wildflowers for the front of the Blue Hedge. It wouldn't cost anything and it couldn't help but perk up the facade.

Farther down the lane, she bumped past the White Horse and admired the green- and yellow-striped awning over the door. A sigh deflated her. New awnings were out of the question for now.

The sun grew brighter on the horizon with every turn of the wheels. She'd already passed a few drays loaded with crates for an early delivery. Pedestrians ventured out. Johanna snapped the reins a little harder and ducked her head when Mrs. Dogflacks emerged out a door, shaking dirt from a rug. If the woman saw her driving Tanny's wagon, she'd spread Johanna's shame from one end of town to the other.

At last the Market Place Gaol loomed ahead, hunched on a foundation of crumbling stone. Five years ago, Johanna had held her breath when driving beneath the archway leading around to the exercise yard. This time she stopped the wagon and eyed the disaster before daring a pass.

The first set of gates stood open, one bent and hanging by a single hinge. The other was completely missing. Light gaped through the ragged openings of the overhead archway, where stones finally gave up their ghost and fell to their death. Maybe if she hugged the right side, she'd make it through without a rock to her skull. Why they'd not torn down this ruin long ago baffled her—and the entire town. Money, likely. It always came back to pounds and guineas.

With a "walk on" to the horse and a prayer heavenward, she rolled onward, not breathing until she cleared the arch and entered the narrow road between two walls. Spiked iron rods jutted from the top of the barrier closest to the gaol. Sharpened flint grinned like jagged fangs atop the other. Lot of good that would do them should an inmate clear the first wall and walk free out the broken gate.

The air was close here. Pressing in. Pressing down. It stank of waste and hopelessness, followed by a pungent waft of vinegar. Her stomach lurched. The stench was even more unpleasant than she remembered—and she was on the outside of the walls. Poor Mr. Morton was locked up inside. Often he'd invaded her thoughts the past two days. How was he holding up? Would she see him today? Did she want to?

She rolled to a stop at the back of the building, then set the brake and climbed down. The bay complained with a snort as she rang a bell next to the rear entrance of the yard. A metal slidey-door shot open on a thin slot. Eyes the color of a great, grey rat stared out.

"Oakum delivery and pickup." Her mouth formed the words from memory, the phrase rising from a graveyard where she'd thought them buried long ago.

Behind the slot, the eyes widened. "Yer not Diggery. Not Tanny, neither."

Retrieving the invoice from a pocket of her work apron, she held it up. "Diggery has been given leave for the next three weeks."

"Has he now? Well, well. I don't mind that."

The slot closed, and before the wide doors opened, she pulled herself back up to the wagon seat and released the brake.

The guard's gaze followed as she guided the wagon through the gate and along the edge of the wall. He relocked the doors and rang for an inmate to unload her noisome cargo. The gravel yard was empty, but not for much longer. Soon the gaol would spit out criminals of all sorts, doomed to spend endless hours picking tar from the used hemp she brought.

Setting the brake once again, she parked the wagon next to a gleaming pile of cleaned oakum—yesterday's work—then frowned at the small size of it. Half a wagonload, at best. And next to that, a gnarly pile yet remained to be cleaned. They'd not even finished it? This wouldn't go over well with Tanny.

Across the yard, the gaol door opened, which prodded her to climb down. Sometimes the rear wagon gate stuck, and it wouldn't do for her to still be fiddling with the latch when the guards brought the prisoner on work duty to unload her delivery. She'd made that mistake once, and discovered Tanny was a sweet-spirited altar boy in comparison to a convict.

She hastened to release both pins—thankfully only one needed coaxing—and lowered the gate. Now to return to her perch of safety in the front. She scooted around the side of the wagon, neared the iron step up to her seat, and—

A grasp on her shoulder spun her back. Rat-grey eyes coated her with an oily gaze. "How 'bout I show you the guardhouse while you wait?"

"No, thank you." She ducked from his hold and turned, reaching for the seat to hoist herself up.

Fingers dug into her arm, yanking her around so quickly, the world blurred for a moment.

"Isn't safe for a skirt hereabouts." His words carried more than a warning, the bass rumble of it weighted with an insidious promise.

She jutted her jaw, well aware the move was less than ladylike, and not caring a bit about it. "Safer than a guardhouse, I'd say."

"Oh, a bit salty, are ye?" A feral smile lifted his thin lips, all sharpness and edges. He leaned closer, reaching with his free hand to fondle the hair fallen loose at her temple. "I like a bit o' salt."

"Leave off!"

It was her thought exactly, but not her voice. It came from behind—and stiffened her shoulders. Unsure if she should be mortified or relieved, she froze. Of all the prisoners to be assigned to unloading duty, it had to be Mr. Morton?

The guard in front of her lowered his free hand—still not releasing her with the other—and looked over her shoulder. "You again? Might've known. Why'd you bring that one, Billy?"

"Bagsley's orders. This 'un needs a good breaking."

He laughed, returning his soulless gaze to her. "As I said, won't be safe for you here. Not with this one nearby. Come with me—"

"No!" She wrenched from his grasp and ducked around him, not wishing to be caught in the coming storm.

As she suspected, a wave of toast-colored hair bobbed amidst a flurry of fists. Three guards. One Alex. Unfair. She raced to the back of the wagon and retrieved the pitchfork used for unloading. Profanity polluted the air, accompanied by grunts, and—oh, sweet heavens! Not the click of a gun. Should she hide or try to be of help to Alex?

A shot exploded.

Then silence—except for heavy breathing.

Time stopped. A host of emotions attacked her from every conceivable angle, pinning her in place.

"Johanna?" Her name was a ragged whisper.

Dropping the pitchfork, she dashed around to the front. Three bodies lay on the ground. All clad in blue wool. Alex bent, head down, hands on thighs, shoulders heaving.

"Mr. Morton?" She stopped in front of him, suddenly unsure of what to do. "Are you all right?"

Slowly, he straightened, and as he ran his fingers through his hair, brushing it back, her heart quit beating. The right side of his mouth was swollen, red and angry. His left eye was purpled and but a slit. One cheek sported a fresh welt, and blood trickled from his nose. His fine clothes were ripped and ruined, a taunting reminder of his fall from grace. All this could not possibly be from a tussle with three guards. What sort of anguish had he suffered the past two days?

Tears burned the backs of her eyes, and her throat tightened. "Oh, Alex. . .what have they done to you?"

CHAPTER SEVENTEEN

Alex's lungs heaved, and he flexed his hands, releasing the leftover energy from the fight—but all the while memorizing the sight of Johanna, the way the morning sun painted her in golden light, the brightness of her blue skirts against the backdrop of ugly grey. Pink brushed along the curves of her cheeks. She was an ethereal contrast to the netherworld of this gaol yard. He'd frown, if his lip weren't so swollen. "What on earth are you doing here, Miss Langley?"

Behind him, across the gravel expanse, shouts issued from the prison's door, a discordant harmony to the moan of the guard laid out on the ground beside him. "And be quick about it, we haven't much time."

"Oh, Alex!" His Christian name came out shivery—

And sent a pang straight into his heart.

"I am sorry for your suffering." Johanna's eyes brimmed with tears, authentic and altogether too alluring.

He drew in a ragged breath. How could she show such compassion when she had no idea the validity of his supposed crime? "Why are you here?"

"I have taken on a side job, oakum delivery." Johanna leaned sideways, glancing past him, then drew near, bringing the fresh scent of lavender with her. "Are you *really* a traitor?"

Fat lip or not, this time he did arch his lips, upwards, into a smile. The woman could make a statue grin simply by the command of her presence. "I am a man of many talents, but not sedition. Never sedition."

Her eyes searched his, and the uncertainty there pained him more than his cracked rib. Much as he'd like to grab her hand and run free, defend his innocence and honor, reality pounded the gravel at his back, kicked up by approaching guards.

He closed in on her, bending to whisper into her ear. "Listen. Write a note. One word. Sackett. Put it in the base of the dead ash, east of center, in a stand of trees behind the rocks at Foxend Corner." Pulling away, he flashed her a last smile. "Oh, and find yourself a different occupation. This is not the place for you. Now, stand back."

He pivoted and strode forward three paces, then dropped to his knees, hands up and behind his head. If he had a white flag, he'd wave that too. Anything to spare Johanna from viewing another brawl.

Four guards surrounded him, all training pistol barrels at his skull. Alex tensed, not from the guns, but from the beast in a grey woolen uniform directly in front, one he'd grown to know intimately well the past few days—leastwise the man's knuckles. *Lord, did he have to be on duty today? Truly?*

"Getting handy with the delivery girl, are ye? We'll have none of that." The fellow to his left flipped his gun around, preparing for a sound pistol whip.

Alex hesitated, one, two, then leaned away at the last instant before the strike, avoiding the whack to the head but not the incoming boot to his belly. Air rushed out in a groan as he doubled over. Agony radiated from gut to ribs. How much beating could a body take before breaking beyond repair?

Johanna's "No!" rode the crest of the brute's "Move him out of here."

Hands gripped him under each arm, hefting him up, dragging him forward, pulling him from Johanna's protests and toward the snickers and slurs of fellow prisoners coming out to the yard. By the time he gained his breath, the gaol swallowed him into a narrow throat of a corridor.

The guards prodded him onward, two beside, one behind, and deposited him where he'd begun two days ago—in front of the slip-faced turnkey behind the scarred desk.

"What's this?" The man scowled down at them all, and Alex tried hard not to give in to the horrid fascination of staring at the ruined flesh that should have been a nose.

Beside him, the biggest man growled out a profanity. "He took out Briggs and Grimley, sir."

"That so?" The turnkey's gazed fixed on him. The man blinked, an odd effect from the offset eyes, like the half-flicker of a dying candle. "Didn't fancy picking oakum today, hmm? And here I thought the honest work would make a new man of ye. Aah, well. We gots other methods."

Though it ripped a fresh wave of torment through his bones, Alex straightened and threw back his shoulders. "You have no right to hold me here. By who's order am I detained?"

"Rights?" A croak of a laugh issued from the turnkey's mouth. "You sound like a flamin' American."

"You have no idea who I am." His swollen lips once again lifted into a smile. "Pity. You ought choose your enemies more wisely."

Purple crept up the warden's neck, crawled over his chin, and bloomed upon his cheeks like a bruise. "What's that? A threat from a scarpin' piece of jailbait?"

"A promise."

The turnkey reared back on his stool. "That's it! Take him down, boys. We've wasted enough time on this one. He can rot."

Fingers bit into the soft flesh beneath his arms, yanking him back into the corridor. The biggest fellow led them on a return path to the yard. At least he wasn't going toward the gibbet. A small mercy, that.

As they neared the door, he considered an elbow jab to the fellow on the right, just for spite, but that would be the best he could manage. Trapped between two guards and spent beyond exhaustion, any resistance he might give would cost more strength than he owned.

The big man opened the door, holding it wide, then swiveled his head to the guards. "Let him go."

The fellow gripping his arm on the left dug his fingers in deeper. "But warden said—"

"I'll do as warden asks—and more." A wicked grin exposed the brute's mustard-coloured teeth. "Just go open the hole for me. That's all."

Alex stumbled, though he was hard pressed to decide if it was from the sudden freedom of being released or the revelation of his new home.

The hole? That couldn't be good.

"Go on." The beast at the door glowered at him. "Move it."

Fine. With a defiant lift of his head, Alex strode out—and a boot to his back sent him sprawling down the stairs. He landed chin first in the gravel, the sting against flesh hardly a comparison to the humiliation of knowing Johanna likely saw from across the yard—if she were looking. For a moment, he lay, stunned. *Oh God, please don't let her see this.*

A yank on his collar lifted him from behind. Airborne, he was driven around to the side of the staircase, where a cellar door gaped into blackness.

"Kneel."

Hardly a command, for the man's fists drove him to his knees.

"Hands behind your head."

A sigh emptied his lungs. Fight or flight? What choice did he have? It was eight stairs up to the gaol door, but then the impossible odds of making it through the corridor, past the turnkey, and out the front. Or, had he enough stamina in store, he could take out the brute behind him and dash across the yard, disable the guards by the gate, and flee in Johanna's wagon. He grimaced. The way his muscles quivered, he'd be lucky to crawl the distance, let alone dash. Blast it!

Slowly, he lifted his arms.

"Yer nothin' but jailbait. Rat bait. Hell bait. Any way you look at it, bait's what you are, and you ought not forget it." Behind him, the man leaned closer, his breath fouling the skin on the back of Alex's hands. "If you move, if you flinch, if you so much as make a noise, that hole in front of you will be your grave. Understand?"

Alex sucked in air and held it, steeling his body for whatever torment the brute had in mind.

Without warning, the sharp point of a knife cut into the flesh at the nape of his neck. Alex bit his tongue, trapping a cry. The blade dug a long line, from hairline to shirt, not deep, not to kill. Just to mark. He bit harder when the point struck again, slicing two curves attached to the line. Warm wetness drained out, soaking into his shirt, sticking the fabric to his back. Sweat dotted his forehead, but still he did not move.

"There's a *B* for you to remember what you are, Bait. Think on that.

Think real well. I'll give you all the time you need—and then some."

While the man chuckled, Alex dove, unwilling to suffer one more kick in the back. He somersaulted down moist rocks, each bump jolting pain deep enough to uproot the marrow in his bones. He landed on muck and rolled over, fighting to breathe.

"That's right, scurry off, vermin." Above him, the man's silhouette was a demon against the sky, but only for a moment. The door slammed.

Blackness attacked, and he blinked as he rose to sit. But no. This was not a blinding dark. It was worse. A crack of light reached down from a weathered scar in the hole's door, taunting him.

Oh, God. Please. Not this.

Rage shook along every muscle, masking the pain of cut and bruise and brokenness, and he pounded his fists onto the mucky earth. Over and over. Not this! Who'd put him here? And why?

Finally spent, he leaned back, ignoring the fire on his neck from the torn flesh. *Don't look. Don't do it.* He repeated the words, shoring up against a coming attack that would leave him more ruined than a knife point.

Just. Don't. Look.

Too late.

His gaze shot upward, and as he stared at the crack in the door over his head, suddenly he was ten years old again. Alone. Isolated. Utterly, completely helpless. As powerless as the day his parents were gunned down.

When he'd watched from the darkness of a closet through a crack in the door.

Johanna pulled back on the reins, halting the old nag. She needn't have. The horse had stopped more often than not on the entire plodding route up to Foxend Corner. Perhaps it was a small mercy the oakum load hadn't been overlarge today, or the animal would've keeled over long ago.

To her left, a margin of swaying grass dropped off to the crash of wave and wind below. She set the brake and climbed down, rounding the wagon in the opposite direction, then hesitated before a pile of leftover boulders. Should she climb over the rocks, or skirt them and fight with waist-high brush and scrub? She sighed and lifted her gaze skyward. *Is this a fool's errand, Lord?*

The trek up here supplied ample time to sort through her thoughts, so why were they still such a tangle? On the one hand, her heart broke afresh each time she replayed the blows Alex had suffered in her sight. On the other, why would he have been arrested in the first place were he not suspect?

She searched the sky for answers. Hoping for. . .what? Direction clearly written on the parchment of a cloud? Maybe she really was a fool after all.

Setting her sights on the stand of trees beyond the rocks, she hoisted her skirts and began picking her way from stone to stone. Were Thomas up and about, this adventure would've suited him. The sun, high now in the sky, was a ruthless taskmaster, as was the gusty wind vying for her bonnet. Perspiration dampened her shift. Her toe caught on her underskirt, ripping the hem and teetering her off balance. Was Mr. Morton worth this much effort?

She paused, her vision suddenly watery. Her last glimpse of the man, bloodied, beaten, and plummeting into some kind of cellar was answer enough. Traitor or not, no one deserved such violence—and he'd taken the brunt of it on her behalf simply by fighting off that ill-mannered guard.

For a moment, she lifted her face to the sky, and prayed for the man who was a strange mix of honor and secrets. A man who took big risks but paid his debts, never seeming to wager what he could not afford to lose. She sucked in a breath as a stunning realization hit her for the first time.

Maybe—just maybe—there was such a thing as an honorable gambler.

The thought was so preposterous and alluring, that she hopped down from the last boulder, landing in weeds up to her knees. This close to the trees, beneath a leafy canopy, the wind took on a chillier note. She'd have to think on such disconcerting ideas later.

Now then, which tree? She scanned the branches and found the leafless limbs, east of center. Swishing through the vegetation, she neared the dead ash and bent.

Just as Mr. Morton had described, she spied a hollowed opening at the base of the trunk. She retrieved the small note from her pocket and poked it into the hole. Hopefully an animal or the wind wouldn't steal it. Ought she put a rock or something in front of it? Well, that would be easy enough to find. Rising, she turned.

Then screamed.

A pace away, dark eyes stared down into hers, what she could see of them, anyway. The man wore his hat brim low, his black hair framing a face better suited to night and shadows. He was a ghost, this one. A spectre. A spirit.

And entirely familiar.

"La, sir!" She slapped a hand to her heaving chest. Had Mr. Morton known his friend would be here? Why had he not warned her? "You scared the breath from me, Mr. . .who *are* you?"

His mouth, set in a flat line, didn't move. Nothing about him did. The man was as hard and unyielding as the boulder pile. Even the blessed wind hardly riffled the tails of his riding cloak.

"Who I am is of no consequence." His gaze flicked past her shoulder and landed at the base of the ash. "More important is what's on that piece of paper."

The next slap of breeze snagged a piece of her hair loose, a usable excuse to stall as she tucked it beneath her bonnet. Should she give him the note? Was this who Alex hoped would receive it? Clearly he had some sort of relationship with this man. Besides, if she didn't give the paper to him, he'd simply take it when she left or maybe even shove past her to grab it.

Bending, she fished the missive out and handed it over.

He unfolded the message, his hat sitting so low it was impossible to read a response in his eyes. But she didn't have to. His jaw clenched, and the muscles on his neck stood out like iron rods. The note disappeared in his fist as he shoved it into his pocket. "Blast!"

She flinched. Not that she hadn't heard coarser language in the taproom. No, it was the roar behind it, the man's guttural, livid tone.

She'd heard once that a tiger's growl could kill a wildebeest just from the fright of the sound. She hadn't believed such a fairy tale—until now.

"What does it mean?" Her voice squeaked in comparison.

Taking the hat from his head, he ran a hand through the tangle of black hair beneath and looked up at the sky. A sigh, long and low, slipped past his lips like a prayer. Finally, he reseated the hat and stared at her. "Better not to know."

She fought her own tigerish growl. Frustrating man. She stared right back. "You are a friend of Mr. Morton, are you not?"

His head dipped, a clipped sort of nod yet fully believable.

"He is in trouble, sir. I think you know that, though I cannot fathom how the single word *Sackett* penned on a slip of paper conveys such a message." She stepped toward him, stopping an arm's length away, willing him to see the desperation that surely must be written in the lines on her face. "Mr. Morton needs your help. He is in gaol, for what I suspect is a wrongful accusation. You must go speak for him."

A shadow crossed his face. What went on behind those dark eyes? Was he devising a plan? Composing a note for her to return to Alex? Deciding which official to speak to first?

Without a word, he turned and walked away.

Johanna's jaw dropped. What? Why would a man turn his back on a friend?

Clutching handfuls of her skirts, she ran after him. "Stop! You owe me an explanation. Both you and Mr. Morton." She grabbed his sleeve, trying to turn him back around. "The least you can do is tell me what I'm involved in."

"I said it's better not to know." He shrugged from her grasp and continued his long-legged pace to where a horse waited near the edge of the trees.

In the few moments it took him to untie his mount, she caught up to him. "Listen, Mr. Whatever-your-name-is, I could barely stand to look upon Alex—I mean, Mr. Morton, without weeping. He is a beaten man, sir. What I know is that he suffers. What I do not know is if he really is a traitor, as accused." She lifted her chin, daring him with a direct gaze. "Nor if you are."

"You would not be here if you truly believed him a traitor."

His words were a blow to her heart. How could he know what she barely acknowledged? Slowly, she nodded. "True, I believe Mr. Morton is a good man. You, I'm not so sure about."

It started small, a tiny twitch, hardly more than a whisper really. Then slowly, methodically, his mouth curved into a full-blossomed smile, his face years younger. Boyish, almost. The look captured her by surprise, for she never imagined this dour enigma could transform into such a dashing figure.

"As I've said before, Miss Langley, you will do, and quite well." Humor softened the edges of his words.

"I can do naught. Will you help him, sir? Will you ride into town and speak to the magistrate?"

Quick as a late spring tempest, his grin disappeared. His eyes sparked gunmetal grey, cold and unrelenting. "I cannot."

"What is wrong with you? You're his friend. You coward!" Her fingers flew to her mouth. What had gotten into her? She'd done what she'd been asked. Delivered the note. End of deed. Why provoke for a cause she owed no further allegiance to?

The wind lifted his collar. Beside him, his horse stamped a snort, and still he did not move. Had she pushed him too far? She retreated a step.

But his quiet words pulled her back. "That word, Sackett. It's a code. Long ago, Giles Sackett was a man imprisoned at Newgate. An innocent, chained for a trumped-up accusation of debt by a vengeful duke. Word got out to his family, his friends, and though they played by the rules, seeking justice in court, they were denied. Treachery begets treachery, and so they devised a plot to rescue him through bribery and violence, stealing him away by dead of night."

He stopped, abruptly, his story like a wagon gone off one of Dover's cliffs.

"What happened?" she asked. "Surely there's more."

Turning his back to her, he swung one long leg up and over the saddle, then looked down at her. "They were all killed, Miss Langley. Every last one. The word Sackett means back away, leave off, which is what I intend to do."

He reached for the reins—as did she. "No! If Mr. Morton is innocent, you can't leave him undefended and alone."

"He is not. He has you." He yanked the leather from her hands and heeled his horse onward, into the tall grass, toward the road leading to London.

Johanna growled at the sky, as deeply primal as the man's earlier roar. What else was there to do?

CHAPTER EIGHTEEN

Johanna opened the door to chaos, then stood there, jaw agape. Nary a space remained on any of the benches in the taproom. Around every table in the Blue Hedge Inn, women chattered, men wiped foam from their upper lips, and off in the corner, four children squatted on the floor, playing a game of pick-up-sticks. All looked to be fed, happy and in no hurry to leave. What in the world?

Across the room, Mr. Quail bounded down the stairway and entered the throng, a smile on his lips and bounce to his step. Clearly the man was not as ill as his friends had claimed him to be the previous evening, nor did he appear any worse for the wear from having fled into a rainstorm.

Johanna loosened her bonnet and tugged it off, then worked her way toward him. "I see you've made a quick recovery, sir."

"Hmm?" He turned at her voice, and a grin spread as his gaze landed on her. "Aah, yes. I am blessed with a strong physique." His chest puffed out, and had he the space for it, no doubt he'd make a show of flexing his muscles. "Nothing keeps me down for long," he drawled.

She clenched her bonnet brim to keep from smacking the leer off his face. "You don't fool me, Mr. Quail."

"The beautiful Johanna can hardly be called a fool. But tell me." He reached out and fingered a loose curl of her hair. "What is it you think you know of me, kitten?"

She batted his hand away. "I know you are responsible for breaking a window last night, and I expect full reimbursement."

"All right."

She froze. That had been entirely too easy. What was his game now? "All right what?"

"You shall have it." He shrugged.

"Good." She sounded like a sulky child.

Yet the smoldering flash in his eyes labeled her anything but.

If Alex had looked at her that way, her heart would beat with warmth. Coming from this man, fury fired in her stomach. "And use the front door next time! The folk around here turn a blind eye to smuggling. There's no need to sneak out."

She fled before he could reply and wound her way past milling customers, frustration upping her pace. Darting into the kitchen, she slung her bonnet on a hook.

Mam looked up from behind the worktable. A streak of mustard was smeared on one cheek, and her cap hung at half-mast.

Anger seeped away at the sight. Johanna reached for her apron. "What's going on? Why this many patrons on a Monday afternoon?"

"About time you return, Daughter. You're becoming a regular scamp like your brother." Mam shoved her cap aright with the back of her hand. "Seems there's a ship not yet in, supposed to pick up that lot early this morn." The tilt of her head toward the taproom undid her previous nudge to her cap, and the white fabric fell askew once again. "I hear tell all the taprooms of Dover are filled. Give that pot a stir, would you?"

Johanna crossed to the hearth and grabbed the long-handled spoon off a hook. "Well, that's a blessing for our strongbox, but I'm sorry I wasn't here to help you."

"About that, I thought you agreed to a morning run only, and here it is afternoon. Did everything go well for you?"

She scowled. Well? Sure, if you counted a whipping from Tanny for being late, an unfruitful conversation with an obstinate man who refused to help Mr. Morton, and the awful violence she'd witnessed against Alexander. Unbidden images of his face came to mind, beaten and battered, bloody and pained. How to explain what she'd seen, and especially how she felt, when she wasn't even sure herself? She scraped the stuck bits from the bottom of the pot and set the spoon aside. If only it were as easy to loosen the conflicting emotions caught on her heart.

Straightening, she faced Mam. "The run for Tanny took longer than I expected. I'd forgotten how much work pickup and delivery can be."

Her mother's good eye narrowed. "There's more to it, I think."

"There's no hiding anything from you, is there?" Jo shook her head and bypassed her mother, grabbing an empty pitcher off a shelf. "Remember when I tried to keep that stray kitten a secret out in the barn?"

Her mother laughed. "For a girl not partial to drinking milk, your sudden thirst was a giveaway. And though you're putting a valiant effort into swaying this conversation, I'll not have you dodging the subject. Tell me, child."

Johanna paused, feeling the weight of the pitcher in her hands and the gravity of what she'd seen. Ought she tell Mam? Her mother had fed the crew of customers single-handedly. No sense adding burden to fatigue. "We'll talk later, I promise. Go put your feet up, and I'll tend the patrons."

"They've been fed and mugs recently filled. They'll hold for a few minutes. You've seen Mr. Morton, and I would hear of it."

The pitcher slipped from her hands, but she snatched it up before it hit ground. "How do you know—?"

"Pish! It doesn't take a barrister's mind to figure that out. You ran a load of oakum to the gaol where Mr. Morton is currently housed. And from your hesitation to speak of it, I'd bet my grandmother's teapot you saw him."

A fierce frown pulled her lips. "Mam!"

Her mother chuckled. "Sometimes you're as dour as old Mrs. Stickleby. Life's not always as tragic as you make it out to be. So, how is Mr. Morton faring?"

Exhaling long and low, she set down the pitcher and leaned back against the tabletop. There was no escaping a mother on an information-gathering mission. "I hardly recognized him. They've beaten him. One eye is so swollen, I doubt he can see from it. There are welts and bruises, and worst of all, a guard pulled a knife on him, cutting the back of his neck. His neck, Mam!" Hot tears burned in her eyes.

With effort, she blinked them away. "How can men be that cruel?"

Her mother's mouth pinched. "You, of all people, know how harsh the world can be, Jo. How is he taking it?"

She swallowed as a memory welled of how he'd shoved her back to safety and stepped forward himself, taking on the guards' brutality singlehandedly. "Bravely." The word came out as a whisper. "He fought only when he thought I was in trouble."

"Were you?" Mam dashed over to her and grabbed both her hands. "I'll not have you going back there if you are in danger, whether we need the money or not."

Her mother peered into her face, driving home her point. New worry lines creased the sides of her mouth, and when had her skin become so transparent? This inn, this life, was too hard on her. On them both.

Lifting one of Mam's hands, Johanna pressed a kiss onto the back of it. "Don't fret. It's nothing I can't handle. Do not fear for me, but rather for Alex—Mr. Morton." Mam's brows rose, as did her own irritation. Why did his Christian name fall so easily from her lips? "Keep Mr. Morton in your prayers, for he needs them more than I. They put him in a cellar. I saw him tumble in. Lord knows if they'll let him up for air or even feed him. I don't know how long he'll be able to last in such conditions. I wish there were something we could do to ease his suffering. Who is to help him, if not us? Even his friend has run off to London."

"The man with the hat?" Mam pulled her hands away and retreated a step. Her gaze travelled every inch of Johanna's face. "When did you see him?"

"That's why I was late. Mr. Morton asked me to deliver a message, up near Foxend Corner. By the time I made it back to Tanny's, he was none too pleased." She tugged on her sleeves, making sure the hems hadn't slipped upward. Though probably less swollen, the welts on her arms from Tanny's switch would be quite the shade of ugly purple. "I'll see to the patrons now. You ought put your feet up for a few minutes."

She turned and reached for the pitcher. A grip on her forearm spun her back around, and she barely stifled a cry.

Mam's eyes burned into hers. "This message, what did it say?"

"Just a name, apparently. I'm not sure I believe the tale behind it.

Regardless, Mr. Morton's friend is of a cowardly nature, for he refused to go help—"

"The word, Johanna." Mam's grip tightened. "What was the word?"

"Sackett."

Mam's fingers fell away. So did the pain, thankfully.

Her mother staggered sideways and lowered onto a barrel. "You're right. I ought put my feet up."

"Oh dear! I knew it. This has been too much for you." Alarmed at the grey shade of Mam's face, Jo dashed to the corner and grabbed an empty crate, then returned and set it in front of her mother. Stooping, she helped set Mam's feet on the wood, one leg at a time. "We'll hire back Ana to cook. We will. As soon as we pay off the final debt on the hearth, that's what we'll do next. And with today's extra earnings, we just might have enough."

Mam shook her head. "Don't be so sure of it."

"If we fail to trust in God's provision, what kind of faith is that?"

Her mother's gaze locked onto hers. "Just make sure it's Him you're trusting, not yourself."

The words washed over her like a bucket of cold water, and she turned away with a shiver. Mam *always* knew too much.

Water. Alex would trade his life for just a sip, for he was surely about to die without a drink, anyway. Throat raw, strength spent, he sat motionless in the darkness, hugging his knees for warmth and finding none. Judging by the angle of light breaching the tiny crack in the overhead door, and from the grumble of prisoners in the yard, picking their fingers to nubs with the oakum, he figured it must be morning, day two of confinement. Or was it three? All he knew for sure was dampness, pain, hunger, and worst of all thirst, for he'd had nothing to eat or drink since he'd landed in this godforsaken pit. A small blessing, he supposed, for truly where would the waste have gone except that he should wallow in it?

He dropped his forehead to his knees. By now the magistrate would've learned of his fate, for none exceeded Thatcher's horsemanship, assuming Johanna delivered his message, of course. Mouth dry, he tried to swallow, but he couldn't even accomplish that. Failure tasted burnt and bitter, as agonizing as the torn flesh on his hands from searching every inch of this pit, clawing, pounding, scratching for a way out. Nothing remained but to wait and see how quickly death paid a visit—and wonder whom he had to thank for his ticket to heaven.

A groan rumbled deep in his chest, but stayed there, too weak to rise out his mouth. What a way to die. He'd always dreamed his demise would be in a blaze of glory, guns afire, upholding justice as Bow Street's finest officer, celebrated and revered. . .not wasting away in a hole in the ground, helpless and hopeless.

Is this it then, God? Will Yours be the next face I see?

Who would even know he was gone? Who would mourn? Ford, maybe. He'd watched out for him since his parents' deaths. Thatcher? Not likely. The man was all rock and iron. Brentwood? Too busy with his new wife and son. And that was it. The sum of his friends. He'd spent a lifetime holding everyone at arm's length, and apparently, he was a champion of it.

But what of Johanna?

He winced at the thought of her. She knew he was here. He leaned his head back against the dirt wall, unable to even sob. *Oh, God.* He had caused the confusion he'd seen in her eyes. She probably yet believed him a traitor and was likely regretting his acquaintance in 484the first place. Ironic, really. The whole situation. Sent to find a traitor and now wearing the placard himself. Locked in solitary, just when he was ready to open his heart.

His fingers raked into the muck where he sat. It would have been better if years ago he had raced out of that closet, shouted in the face of the murderers, and taken the knife as a ten-year-old.

"Why? Why! Why spare me for such an end as this?" The words spewed past his lips, taking the rest of his voice with them. All that remained were ragged breaths, broken dreams, and the vague urge to whisper what might be his last prayer. "Yet even in this, Lord, I suppose I must trust You, for there is nothing else."

The dirt walls muffled his prayer, but the words circled back and slapped him sober. *There is nothing else. There is nothing else.*

Stunned, he blinked. Why hadn't he realized such a truth before? There was nothing else to be done but trust alone. Maybe—just maybe—he'd taken on too much, more than a lad should way back when, more than a man could even now.

"Oh God," he gasped. "There never was anything else, was there? Only You, not me. *I've* been standing in the way."

More than a decade of pride and presumption bled out with the realization. He'd been so busy keeping everything under control, managing all the aspects of his life, he'd missed out on the peace that now slowly wrapped around his soul. Light. Air. Freedom. Everything changed. Oh, the damp darkness of the pit lingered, and maybe even death was near, but had he known such contentment was possible, he'd have given up long ago.

Without warning, boot steps thumped overhead. A key clicked into a lock and snapped it open. Interesting timing. An angel, perhaps? He'd smile, if it wouldn't hurt.

The rattle of a chain scraped against the wooden door. Hinges rasped, and finally, white light, glorious and stabbing, filled the enclosure. He jerked his forearm to his eyes.

"Move it out!" The harsh command came from a devil.

Like an old man, he braced his free hand against the wall and pushed himself upward. His legs shook—and down he went.

"I said move it! Haven't got all day. Unless you want to stay in there, all cozy like."

Alex drew on every remaining morsel of strength left to him. This chance might not come again. "God, please," he groaned as he fought his way up.

Hands reached down and grabbed on to his, wrenching him upward. He landed outside, face-first on the gravel of the courtyard, not caring that it ground into his cheek. Air, fresh and precious, filled his nostrils, and he lay there, reveling in the act of breathing.

Until a boot to his ribs made him curl up with a grunt.

"On yer feet. You've a visitor."

A yank on the back of his collar lifted him. He half-choked and half-gagged as two guards lugged him up the stairs and into the guts of the gaol. His mind raced faster than his feet. A visitor could only be Johanna—or the person who'd put him here. His heart hoped for one, his fists, the other.

The guards led him to a door in the main hall—one he'd not noticed before, hidden in the dark paneling. There, the turnkey stood, tapping his foot. "We'll be waiting out here. Don't try anything, or it'll be the worse for you. Understood?"

Sweet, blessed mercy. He could barely walk and the man was worried about him busting out?

"Please." The word clawed out his throat. "Water?"

A sneer twisted the man's face into a macabre sight, as if his features were made of wax and he stood too near a flame. He said nothing, just nodded at the guards and opened the door.

Jabbed between his shoulder blades, Alex stumbled past the threshold and barely caught himself from tumbling headfirst onto the floor. Behind him, the door slammed shut. In front, two wonders. No, three.

One, Johanna's mother sat at a table, the only furniture in the room besides an empty chair. Two, a plate of meat and a crust of bread sat on a plate. And three—

He lurched forward and snatched a green bottle, not caring if it contained water or cider or arsenic, for it was liquid and he was a desert. With each gulp, life seeped back into him.

"Go easy or you'll regret it." Mrs. Langley's admonition, while good advice, was impossible to follow.

He drained the bottle and collapsed into the chair with a moan. His stomach heaved, and he doubled over. For a horrible eternity, he feared he just might lose what he'd gained.

"Tut, tut." Mrs. Langley clucked her tongue. "You look a sight."

When the wave of nausea passed, he straightened and wiped his mouth with the back of his hand. He worked his jaw for a moment, until he was sure words would come out. "Not to be disrespectful, madam, but what are you doing here?"

"I couldn't very well leave you to suffer in solitary." She pushed the plate of food toward him.

This time he paced himself, starting with a small bite of bread. "So, Johanna told you."

"Aye."

"But how did you do it? Get me out, I mean. You're hardly a magistrate." He chewed on a few possibilities, none of which made sense, unless. . .no. The thought was too horrible. Surely his instincts couldn't be that far off. He stared at her, slack-jawed. "Of all the unholy justice—did you accuse me of treason?"

She laughed, crinkling her nose the same way Johanna did. "I'm many things, but not the bearer of false witness. And I'm afraid you're not free. I merely bribed you out of solitary for a visit, a plate of food, and some water. That was the best I could manage with what we had."

His mouthful of meat turned foul, and he shoved the plate away. "Please don't say you used the rent money on me."

"All right. I won't." Leaning across the table, she nudged the food closer to him. "Now, don't waste my coins."

For one with so many years tucked beneath her bonnet, she still had a lot of kick in her. With a grin, he picked up the bread. "Thomas takes after you."

"And you take after your father."

The bread turned to wood shavings in his mouth. Either she thought she knew Ford's creation of a father up in Sheffield, or. . .once again, the thought was too horrible. Too wonderfully horrible. He sat back in his chair, food forgotten, and tilted his head, prepared to listen with his whole body. "What would you know of my father?"

Her eyes twinkled with knowledge and what? Pity? Grief? No. Neither. A tremor moved deep in his bones, rippling outward, like standing next to a reverberating gong.

She gazed at him with compassion. "What I know is that you're no wine merchant, are you, Mr. Moore?"

He sucked in a breath. If she knew the truth, then how many others. . . wait a minute. . .*had* she been the one to put him in here? If so, the woman belonged on a Royal Theater's stage, so good was her act. But why? Every muscle in his body clenched. Was Mrs. Langley the true traitor? Did she know who murdered his parents? Were the two somehow related?

"Breathe, son. Just breathe. You look as if you may give way at any moment." She glanced at the door then back at him. "And I doubt we have much time left."

He set his jaw, then winced at the pain of it. "Perhaps you ought explain yourself."

"It took me a while to figure things out. The old cogs don't turn as quickly anymore." She tapped a finger to her temple, then aimed it at him. "But it's plain as the nose on your face and the striking blue of your eyes. The hair, that threw me, for Charles Moore's mane was dark, as could be his mood at times. I assume 'twas your mother who gave you the fair streak, in hair and character, hmm?"

He'd been speechless once. Shortly after Ford had taken him in, the magistrate had discovered him playing on a fine piece of evidence—a Stradivarius—down in the courtroom's cellar. Of course he'd been reprimanded, but eventually Ford had awarded him the violin and the continuation of his lessons.

He gaped. This didn't even begin to compare.

"Oh, I suspected," Mrs. Langley continued, "but I couldn't be sure until Johanna told me the contents of the note you asked her to deliver."

He shook his head, but the movement did no good. "How on God's green earth would you know the meaning of *Sackett*?"

She lifted her chin. "I believe the real question is why would Ford place an officer at my inn? What is the old fool up to?"

The room began to spin. Or maybe the entire world did. Pain or not, he scrubbed his face with his hand. "I assure you, madam, I am as baffled about that as you. How do you know Ford?"

She pushed back from the table and stood. "I'll not question you further, nor will I answer any of yours. No one can know we had this conversation. Ever. Now eat and drink as much as you can hold, for I won't be able to do this again."

He shot to his feet. "But—"

"Keep your trust in God, son. It is the best any of us can do. And remember, your present situation is not your final destination." She strode to the door and rapped. "Ready."

The little lady disappeared, leaving him with a full belly, renewed hope, and more questions than ever.

CHAPTER NINETEEN

Dumping the contents of the strongbox onto the counter, Johanna shook it for good measure. No more coins joined the small piles already counted and recounted. Horrid, horrid numbers! They wouldn't just be the death of her, but of them all. One by one, she picked up each pence and shilling, recalculating carefully as she put them back into the box.

Her heart sank. The exact same total—and far smaller than what it should've been.

She slammed the lid shut, relocked it, and set it beneath the counter. *Think the best,* she scolded herself. *Wait expectantly. Hope continually.* Had she not read that this very morning?

Marching toward the kitchen, she prayed with each step. Maybe Mam had simply tucked the money away elsewhere for safekeeping. Of course. That was it. It *had* to be it.

"Mam?"

Her mother whisked about from a basin full of dishes, hands flying to her chest and water droplets spraying everywhere. "My stars, girl! What's going on? Is it Thomas? He's not trying to get out of bed again, is he?"

The bloom on Mam's cheeks kindled guilt in Johanna's stomach, and she pressed her fingers against her middle. "No, nothing so dire. I am sorry to have frightened you. I was just putting away my first payment from Mr. Needler and I noticed a fair amount of money missing from the strongbox. Where did you put it?"

"Me?"

"Surely it must have been you."

Mam turned back to the dishes. "Must it?"

Her fingers pressed deeper, as if she might hold in the dread that bubbled to come out with her last cup of tea. If Mam hadn't moved it, then. . .

"Oh, no. No, no. We've been robbed, Mam! And with only three weeks before Mr. Spurge comes looking for his payment. Now even with my extra work, we won't be able to pay him." She leaned against the doorjamb, shoring herself up. "We are ruined."

Leaving the sink behind, Mam wiped her hands on her apron and crossed over to her. "Such dramatics." She reached up and tweaked Johanna's nose. "A wise woman once asked me if we fail to trust in God's provision, what kind of faith is that, hmm?"

She sighed, her own words boxing her ears—no doubt what Mam intended. "Feeble, I suppose."

"And there's nothing feeble about the Johanna Elizabeth Langley I know. Come on, chin up." Mam cocked her head, looking out with love from her good eye—her bad eye weak and squinty—

And a tangible reminder to Jo that she must remain strong, for Mam's sake, as well as her own. She forced a smile. "You're right, of course. We shall wait and see what God does."

"There's my girl." Her mother returned her grin. "Now off with you. I hear patrons in the taproom, and I've not yet brought Thomas his lunch tray."

Grabbing an apron off a peg, Johanna slipped it over her head and worked the ties behind her back while she swept out of the kitchen. At a table near the door was a big man with eyes so cavernous, she wondered if such depth darkened his view. He sat at an angle, one of his legs jutting into the aisle. Across from him, a crazed mop of red hair topped a shorter man. Both their shirts strained against muscles. These were obviously working men. Dockhands, perhaps, judging by the deep color of their skin and huge biceps. Her step hitched. Something wasn't right about this. At this time of day, they ought be heaving crates, not swilling ale. Good thing she'd thought to hide the strongbox.

She neared them with a professional smile—one that froze on her lips when a pair of yellow stockings slid in the front door. No, there wasn't anything at all right about this.

"Not late. Not late! Mr. Nutbrown is on time, sirs." Lucius and his clown puppet raced to a chair between the two men and sat so forcefully, it suspended precariously on two legs for a moment before thudding back down on all fours. Without missing a beat, Mr. Nutbrown shoved his jester toward her. "Afternoon, Miss Langley. My, but you're looking fine today."

Her mouth flattened. "Mr. Nutbrown. Gentlemen. What can I do for you?"

"Ale for the three of us, miss." The big man jerked out a hand the size of a small frying pan and slapped a coin on the table.

The flash of the golden guinea drew her a step forward. Why would a dockhand flaunt such an amount here? And where had he gotten it in the first place? "I am sorry, sir, but I won't be able to make change for that. Have you anything smaller?"

"Not to worry." He eyed her with a grin shy of several teeth. "No change required."

La! They'd be passed out on the floor before that much ale was consumed. Still, a drunkard's coin was no less valuable than a rich man's. Maybe this was how God was providing? She considered the possibility all the way to the counter, where she filled three mugs.

"Here you are, sirs." She set down their drinks and stepped back, not liking the way the red-headed one kept his gaze pinned on her every movement. "Let me know if you require anything else."

She turned, but a puppet pecking on her arm pulled her back around. She narrowed her eyes and glared. "Mr. Nutbrown! I'll thank you to stop—"

"Mr. Nutbrown has another business opportunity for you, miss."

The beginnings of a headache pounded in her left temple, and from the beat, it promised to be quite a superb one. What a day. First taking Tanny's abuse, then discovering missing money, now this. "I told you before that I will not serve as a lookout for underhanded or illegal activities. I have not changed my mind."

"You'll have to excuse Mr. Nutbrown." The big man leaned toward her, bidding her closer with a crook of his finger and lowering his voice so that only she might hear. "He's a few cards short of a deck, you know."

Across from him, the red-headed man shoved one of the mugs toward Nutbrown. "Put Nixie away now. There's a good fellow. Here, have your drink."

With Mr. Nutbrown occupied, the other men faced her. The big one spoke first. "I'm Mr. Cooper and this is Mr. Pickens." He indicated the redhead with a nod. "As Mr. Nutbrown was about to say, we have an opportunity for a young lady of upstanding character and connections. He vouches for your integrity on both accounts."

Danger throbbed inside her skull. Or was that just the headache? She should turn right around and escape into the kitchen, send Mam out here, anything but consider whatever these men were offering. But the flash of the golden coin on the table held her in place. It wouldn't hurt to listen, and ought she not judge according to looks?

She crossed her arms and nodded at the big man. "What is your offer, Mr. Cooper?"

"Mr. Nutbrown has been doing some paperwork for us. Reading and ciphering aren't our strong points, eh Charlie?" Mr. Cooper lifted a brow at Mr. Pickens.

The redhead slowly brought up his fist, flexing his arm. "No, sir."

She frowned. If the man thought muscles impressed her, he could think again, though she doubted very much he thought deeply about anything at all. The bump of a nose broken too many times showed he used his brawn more than his brain.

Mr. Cooper continued, "Still, we've a business to run, and we're stretched thin at the moment. Mr. Nutbrown suggested you might be able to help. He's doing a little task for us tomorrow down at the harbourmaster's, but, well. . ." He leaned toward her once again. "I'm not completely confident he can do it on his own."

"What has that to do with me?" she asked.

"There's a particular shipment we're expecting, a profitable one. Coming in from Woolwich. We just need to know the name of the ship and the time of arrival."

Reaching up, she massaged her temple with two fingers. This wasn't making sense, no matter how hard she tried to unravel it. "Seems that wouldn't take any reading or writing. Why don't you go and ask yourselves?"

"That's just it, miss. Mr. Pickens and I are expected elsewhere. Were it only reading and writing, why Mr. Nutbrown would do just fine. Champion, he is."

Mr. Nutbrown perked up at the mention of his name. He set down his mug and rummaged in his waistcoat. Surely a ridiculous puppet conversation would follow.

But the big man pivoted on the bench, turning his back to Mr. Nutbrown. "This task requires conversation, miss. As you can understand, the harbourmaster won't likely give out information to a puppet."

While true, the explanation hardly clarified. She folded her arms. "Then why send him at all?"

"Why, to save you a trip, miss." Mr. Cooper smiled, and she wished he hadn't. It was like watching a coach crash, so disturbing was his grin. "You give the information to Mr. Nutbrown, and he'll deliver it to us. Shouldn't take but an hour of your time."

She shook her head. Right now, a cool cloth in a darkened room sounded much better than this offer. "I don't know, Mr. Cooper. I have my own business to run."

"Did I mention it pays five guineas?"

"Five!" She choked, then narrowed her eyes. "Why so much? Are you certain this is not illegal?"

The big man laughed. "Nothing illegal about asking for information, is there? And as I said, this shipment will be very profitable for us. Five's a pittance. What say you?"

She lowered her arms, smoothing her hands along her apron. There was nothing wrong with what he asked, yet it didn't seem right. Still, maybe this was God's provision. And if it did turn into something underhanded, in even the slightest fashion, she'd walk away—or run, if need be.

"Very well," she agreed, but the words tasted sour in her mouth. "Tomorrow afternoon, then."

Once again Alex trod down the gaol's corridor, a guard on either side in the usual fashion. This time, though, no one dragged or shoved him. In truth, the men hardly even looked at him, as if they didn't care whether he tried to escape. That could only mean one thing, possibly two. Either the charges had been dropped, or the gallows in front was rigged out and ringed by a crowd, waiting to watch his demise. A smirk twitched half his mouth. Either way, he would be free.

As they swung around a corner and cleared the entrance hall, he still wasn't sure what to expect. The master turnkey was not at his station behind the tall desk. In the shadows near the main doors stood a short man in a dark greatcoat, back toward him, hat set low. He turned at the sound of their footsteps, and his lips curled up, revealing short, yellowed teeth.

The guards dropped back as Robbie Coburn advanced. Whatever the arrangement had been, or might be, Alex kept his feet moving toward freedom. There'd been no paperwork, no final admonitions, not even a word that his time was up. Quite the irregular release. Then again, his arrival had been anything but conventional. He apparently had Robbie to thank for that—and he would with a sound thrashing.

"Thanks, fellows." Robbie gave the guards a smart salute, then drew up alongside Alex, slapping him on the back. "My, but you're looking a little rugged. Had quite the stay, did you?"

Alex winced, the clap of Robbie's hand managing to whap against one of his more recent bruises. "Quite." His hands curled into fists at his side. Once they were outside, he'd give Robbie a little taste of his stay for putting him here. He glanced at the man sideways. "Am I to thank you for my holiday?"

Robbie laughed, the sound incongruous inside these walls of guilt and desperation. He shoved open the front door with one arm. "No, not me. I'll explain on the way."

Slowly, Alex's fists unfurled, and he strode out into freedom, then paused on the top step and breathed in until it hurt. Early evening air, moist with saltiness, fragrant with honeysuckle, filled his lungs. He allowed the sweetness to wash over him. Dried blood, sweat, and grime remained, but even so, he felt cleaner. He probably ought wonder where Robbie was taking him, but truly, as long as it was away from here, he found it hard to care.

"Not having second thoughts about leaving, are you?"

When he opened his eyes, Robbie was already down to the curb, one foot up on the carriage step. Seated atop, a driver in gold-and-navy livery held the reins to a smart set of bays. Alex descended, straightening what remained of his dress coat. Hopefully the viscount would be in a charitable mood, for if he didn't miss his guess, that's exactly where they were headed.

With a grunt, he hoisted himself upward and sat opposite Robbie. The thick scent of cherry tobacco and leather chased away the fresh evening air. As he sank into the cushions, he wondered for the hundredth time in the past few days if he weren't getting a mite old for this lifestyle.

Robbie retrieved a pocket watch, then snapped shut the lid with a curse. "Bah! Shouldn't have stopped off for that pint, I suppose." He rapped on the ceiling and the coach lurched into action. "The old man won't be happy"— he tucked away the watch with a grin—"but then, he's never happy with me now, is he?"

"Lord Coburn?"

"The very same. You can thank him in person for your recent *holiday*."

The viscount had put him in gaol? Anger shook through him as the coach rattled over gravel. He speared Robbie with a frown. "That explains the anonymity, but why the accusation?"

"Oh, nothing personal, I assure you. My uncle's methods are rarely orthodox." He held up his hand, a thick white bandage yet wrapped around the middle where the bullet had taken one of his fingers that first fateful night they'd met. Robbie let it fall back to his lap without a wince. Apparently the wound was healing well. "My uncle merely needed the time to check on your background. Can't marry his daughter off to just anybody, you know."

His gut clenched. That's what this whole thing had been about? He'd anguished and suffered and nearly given in to failure and doubt, all for the whim of a rich man who needed assurance? Rage prickled along every nerve, too spiky and abrasive for the coach cushions to soften.

"He couldn't have done that without locking me up?"

Robbie's shoulders shook with a good chuckle. "Anger will gain you nothing, friend, leastwise not with the old man. Trust me. I've learned that one the hard way." His tone took on a biting edge, belying the remnant of a smile yet on his lips. "Hence the need for my secrecy with Louisa. He'd never give her to me willingly. Oh, and thank you for your rather timely diversion on the matter. You will be well paid."

Gloaming crept in the open window shades, hiding Robbie's face in shadow. Alex leaned forward, hoping to catch some kind of facial tip off. "Cousins marry every day. Why not you?"

He turned his face, a pretense of staring out at the night, for there was nothing to see outside. Even so, there was no hiding the stiffness of his shoulders. "Let's just say that Uncle and I disagree over politics."

Robbie? Political? He stifled a snort.

"But enough of that morose topic, hmm?" Quick as a summer storm, Robbie pulled out a flask. The silver flashed in the darkness as he held it out.

Alex shook his head. "I think some food would be in order, first."

"Aah, sorry. Didn't think." He swigged back a drink and tucked it away, breathing out the tang of bourbon. "In a fortnight, give or take, Louisa and I will sail away on our adventure, but what of you? What will you do with the tidy sum I intend to pay you? Live large? Chase a few skirts or—no. I know. You'll take it to the table, won't you? Will it be Brook's or White's? Or maybe someplace a little more risqué? St. James's, if I don't miss my guess."

Outside the windows, torchlight flashed bright then dark, bright then dark, indicating they'd pulled onto the viscount's estate. He met Robbie's gaze, slipping into his gambling mask. "I've never been one to turn down a game."

"Thought as much." When the carriage pulled to a stop, Robbie didn't wait for the door to open. He worked the latch himself and jumped down.

Relieved that the elopement plans were still moving ahead, Alex exited and joined him on the drive.

Robbie nudged him with an elbow. "Why don't you see the old man alone. I'm a little gun shy. And with my uncle engaged, there's a certain lady I'd like to entertain."

Without waiting for an answer, Robbie dashed up the front stairs and through the door. By the time Alex gained the entry, the footman stood scowling. His upper lip curled higher when the stench of the gaol, woven into the fiber of Alex's clothing and grease of his hair, met the man's nose. To his credit, the footman said nothing.

But the fat man striding down the hall did. "Egad!" Major General Overtun clapped his hat atop his head then lifted a gloved finger to block his nose. "You smell like a gang of *Coolies* come in from a day beneath the Indian sun."

"Trust me," he smiled, "I feel as beat. Are you not staying for tonight's game?"

"No, not tonight. Duty calls, I'm afraid." The general gave him a wide berth as he edged past. "Good evening, Mr. Morton."

"Good evening, General." He saluted his goodbye.

As soon as the footman shut the door behind the man, he turned and led the way to the viscount's drawing room. Though Alex kept downwind of him, he doubted the servant breathed the whole way. For a moment, Alex toyed with the idea of pausing on the threshold as he passed the man, seeing just how long he could hold his breath.

Setting down a pen, Lord Coburn looked up from where he sat behind a burled oak desk, polished to a glassy finish. "Well, a new suit is in order, I think." He wrinkled his nose. "And a bath."

Alex eyed one of the leather library chairs in front of the bureau. Better to sit and cool down than dash across the room and give Coburn a taste of the violence he'd endured the past week. "Mind if I sit?"

"By all means." Coburn leaned back, steepling his fingers. "Your father speaks well of you."

Taking his time to settle in the chair, Alex wondered what actor Ford had paid to play that part. Whoever, the fellow ought to receive a bonus for pulling it off. He frowned, mixing just the right amount of ire and resignation to the bend of his brow. "I would expect nothing less. I hope you are satisfied."

"And I hope you understand it was necessary. A man in my position cannot be too careful."

"What is that position?"

Pushing back his chair, the viscount stood and stalked to the mantel like a panther on the prowl. He opened the lid of his precious cheroot box and proceeded with the ceremony of lighting and puffing before he strolled back and reseated himself. "It was curious, you showing up here, at such a time. I have many enemies and thought perhaps you might be one."

The viscount took a drag on his tobacco, his gaze skewering him. For a few loud ticks of the corner clock, the man said nothing, then slowly, a stream of smoke curled out of his nostrils like a great dragon. "Of course, I know differently, now. I think, instead, that you were a godsend."

Were he a horse, he'd have reared. There were many things the viscount might've labeled him. A godsend never crossed his mind. "Pardon me," Alex said, "but I didn't take you for a religious man."

"Nor did I peg you for a man of violence." The red tip of the viscount's cheroot glowed, as murderous as his statement.

Alex ran a hand through his hair, giving ample alibi for the flinch he couldn't deny. What had Ford's man told the viscount?

"Yet I am glad of it." Coburn ground out the rest of his tobacco and laid the stub to rest on a silver platter. "Your sharpshooting skills might come in handy. Your father is quite proud of your talent with a gun. Though I suppose that's to be expected in your line of work."

Sweet, merciful heavens. What story had the viscount been fed? Sure, he could manage a muzzle, but put to the test, he was no crack shot. He cleared his throat, unsure how to respond, hoping—desperately—that words would magically appear.

Coburn held up a hand. "No need for false pride. I didn't believe for a moment that you were a simple wine merchant. Your military service is exemplary for one so young. A sorry shame that friendly fire took you out of commission. Had I known of your injury, I'd have paid for better accommodations in the gaol."

Alex grit his teeth to trap a grimace. Not only was he a sharpshooter but an injured one? Well, thanks to this man, at least he had plenty of aches and pains to make that believable—but if Ford were here, he'd get an earful of censure.

"Good thing your daughter is worth it," he ground out.

The gleam in the viscount's eyes hinted at approval. "All water under the bridge, eh? Good. We move forward from here. I'm expecting a shipment in a fortnight that I could use some help with."

Alex shifted in his seat. Though he'd love to throttle the viscount for having him arrested, at least the gaol time had garnered him some capital with the man. "I know very little of shipping, other than the transport of fine wines. What kind of help is it you want?"

"In times like these, I find it best to compartmentalize information. It's safer that way. You'll be given information as needed." Once again, leaving his desk behind, Coburn crossed to the mantel and tugged on the bell pull. "In the meantime, you've a week to clean yourself up. Are you sure you prefer to remain at The Blue Hedge? I can accommodate you here."

Alex ran a finger along his bottom lip, thinking. The man was very cagey, very shrewd. Was Robbie in on this? The timeframe he planned to run off with Louisa matched up. If so, how much did he know? What kind of family secrets mouldered beneath the wealth of the viscount's roof?

"Alexander?"

He startled at Coburn's use of his Christian name, and slowly pushed himself up, using his battered appearance to his advantage. "Er. . .yes, sir. Forgive me. Afraid the past week has taken a toll on me physically and mentally. The Blue Hedge is fine for now, but tell me. . .what exactly is it I'm cleaning myself up for?"

"The betrothal dinner, of course. Get yourself a new suit of clothing down at Featherstones on the High Street, and spare no expense. I'll give word you're coming and that it's to be put on my account. Can't present you looking like a beaten thug dragged from a rookery, can I?"

Alex pressed his lips together. Why not? That's exactly how he felt, though he suspected he'd feel worse when his engagement went public and word spread that he was to wed a woman he didn't intend to actually marry.

CHAPTER TWENTY

Johanna wrung out a cloth so frayed and thin, even a ragpicker would turn it down. Cool evening air stole in from the taproom door, propped open to encourage customers. She frowned at the darkness outside. Closing time already and she'd served only two dray drivers nothing but a mug apiece. Pursing her lips, she set about scrubbing off tables that were hardly dirty. Surely she'd made the right decision to visit the harbourmaster on the morrow.

Behind her, the last strain of a violin chord screeched into oblivion, taking some of the tension in her shoulders along with it. At least one tribulation was drawing to a close. That would be Mr. Quail's last song under this roof if she had anything to say about—and she did. Plenty.

Weaving around tables, she crossed the room to where he packed up his violin. "Excuse me, Mr. Quail, but I must speak with you."

He snapped shut the lid and grinned down at her. "Delighted."

The man was relentless. If he practiced his music with as much dogged pursuit as he did his flirtations, he'd be a virtuoso. "You might not be once you've heard me out."

"Oh? Intriguing." He leaned close, his grin widening. "And I love a good intrigue."

With a sigh, she retreated a step. "Nothing of the sort. I merely wish to inform you that your services here are no longer required. You and your band may pack up and leave in the morning."

He staggered back, slapping a hand to his heart as if shot through the chest with an arrow. "You wound me!"

It took all her willpower to keep from rolling her eyes. "Really, Mr. Quail. Such dramatics. This is a business matter, nothing more. Your expenses far outweigh your benefits, Oak Apple Day is long gone, and so you must leave."

"Ah-ah-ah." He wagged a finger at her. "My band has brought in customers. You can't deny that."

"Not enough to cover food and drink. And let's not forget that broken window for which you still haven't paid me, hmm?"

Like a dropped cannonball, he plummeted to his knees and hung his head. His hands folded in prayer as if she were a goddess to be offered devotion. "Have I not begged sufficient forgiveness for that unfortunate incident, my queen?"

She tried, valiantly, but this time there was no stopping the roll of her eyes. "Yes, of course you're forgiven, but that does not fix the glass. Now get up, please. You have some packing to do."

He rose, snatching one of her hands on the uptake and kissing two of her knuckles before she could yank them away.

"Two weeks, my sweet Miss Langley. Just a fortnight more, and my band and I will gladly move on."

"I am sorry." She shook her head. "There are simply not enough funds to keep housing and feeding you for free."

His face darkened like a quick-rising storm at sea, then evaporated with the snap of his fingers. "I know! Yes! Why, I should have thought of this before." He laughed and snatched up his violin case, waving it over his head like a lunatic. "*I'll have grounds more relative than this—the play's the thing!*"

Though she ran the words through her head several times, he might as well have been speaking Portuguese. Perhaps he truly had become mad. Had she caused him to snap by asking him to leave? She leveled a firm glare at him. "What are you talking about?"

"A play, Miss Langley. Who doesn't love theatrics?" He swung about, taking his violin case for a merry ride.

She opened her mouth, a hearty reprimand on her tongue, when he silenced her with a finger to her lips.

"Tut, tut. Other than you, I mean."

Pulling from his touch, she swept out her arm. "Look at the size of this taproom, sir. We haven't the space to put on a play. By the time you clear an area for a performance, you'll have no room for patrons. A play would not be profitable."

"I see." He rubbed the back of his neck, his gaze darting about. "Something of a smaller scale, then."

"Something of *no* scale." She sighed. "It is time for you to move on. Are you not travelling musicians? I should think you would be happy to get on the road."

She might as well have been speaking to a deaf man. He pivoted, continuing his search for who-knew-what around the room. One brow rose, then the other, and eventually his whole head bobbed. "I've got it."

"Mr. Quail, are you even listening to me? I said it is time to move on—"

"Here." He strode past her and stopped at the counter, littered with her wash bucket and leftover serving dishes. Shoving a tray aside so that the mugs atop it rattled, he bent and eyed the area. "Looks to be maybe two feet wide, seven or eight in length. Some wood, nails, a simple modification is all, and. . .yes. This will be perfect."

She scowled, gaining his side. "Perfect for what?"

"A *Punch and Judy Show*, of course. A few boards, some drapery, and *voilà*. A puppet stage that will take up no more additional space in this room."

La! The man *was* daft. Curling her hands into fists, she planted them on her hips. "And how am I to operate without use of the counter? No. Absolutely not. I have a special abhorrence of puppets."

"We can be ready in a week. I'll make up some handbills and begin spreading them around on the morrow." He flashed her a smile and dashed toward the stairs. "Good night, Miss Langley. Big day tomorrow."

"Mr. Quail, I insist you come back here right now. This discussion isn't over."

But his footsteps didn't slow.

"Mr. Quail!" She growled. Infuriating, pig-headed—

"Angry at Quail again, eh? Apparently things haven't changed much."

She spun at the deep voice behind her. Her jaw dropped, unladylike yet completely unstoppable. Alex stood framed in the front doorway, like a macabre painting of a war scene. The longer she gaped, the more her heart broke into piece after piece, until it was a wonder the thing could beat at all. As a young girl, she'd come across a crushed robin, wings broken by a wagon wheel, flying a thing of its past. She'd run home to Mam, horrified, weeping.

But this time, there was nowhere for her to turn.

She sucked in a breath, frantic for air. The gentleman she knew was gone. His dress coat was ripped and dirty. He wore no cravat. His pristine white shirt was torn and bloodied beneath what remained of his waistcoat, both gaping at the chest. An ugly gash cut across his cheek, disappearing into a growth of beard, matted with more blood. Even his gaze was a bruise. No one deserved that much brutality, especially not a man who'd been nothing but selfless and compassionate toward others. Toward her.

"Oh Alex," she sighed, her voice as derelict as his face.

It took him a moment to understand the emotion in the sag of Johanna's shoulders and that the crackle in her words belonged to him, like a gift from a secret admirer, given without a tag. And he wasn't sure what to do about that. Wrap his arms around her—or run out the door? He settled for shoring his shoulder against the door frame.

Tears shimmered in her eyes, caught by lantern light. She cared. About him. Not that in the past other women hadn't, but this? This was entirely different. His heart pounded hard against his ribs. He harbored such affection for this woman that it cut into his soul she would hurt for his sake.

What kind of man loved one woman yet let everyone believe he'd marry another?

He ran a hand through his hair and winced when his fingers grazed a gouge behind his ear. Good. He welcomed the pain, for only a scoundrel would carry out such a vile act.

"You're back," she whispered.

The quiver on her lips and in her voice, the charged tension between them, was too much to bear. Either he ought kiss away every worry she'd suffered on his behalf—or completely change the subject. The latter was honorable, of course, but the first? Aah. . .desire rippled through him from head to toe.

He settled for clearing his throat. "Still have a room available?"

A smile broke, then. One to shame the brightest star in the heavens. "Of course."

She snapped into action, apron strings flying as she pivoted. "But first come to the kitchen, and I'll fill a basin of warm water. Those wounds need a good cleaning."

He followed, his step hitching halfway across the taproom. The crooked floorboards. The beat-up tables and rugged chairs. The way the roof sloped at the corner near the hearth, debating whether to cave in or not. Alex's gut twisted, but wonder of wonders, not from scorn. This place felt like home. Comfortable. Familiar. Worn by decades of life and love, not tatty by sinister neglect.

He upped his pace. Clearly several nights in a gaol had affected him deeply.

Johanna pulled a stool away from the worktable, and he sank onto it. One of his eyes was squinty from a leftover right hook, so he angled his head and watched her gather a bowl and some cloths with his good eye. "What's Quail done this time that's got you agitated?"

She slammed the bowl onto the table, rattling a wooden mug, then retrieved a teapot from the hearth. "He and his band have overstayed their welcome."

"Sounds like your earlier problem with Nutbrown. Shall I evict them for you as well?"

"No." She dipped a rag into the basin and wrung it out. "I suppose I can put up with them for two more weeks if I must, but you can be certain—"

"Two weeks?" he thought aloud. Itinerant musicians didn't usually operate on such a strict schedule. "Did he say why?"

"He did not. I suppose it's anybody's guess with that lot. I'll just be glad to see them go. Now then, let's get you taken care of." She stood so near, he inhaled her sweet scent of rosewater and heat, alluring as a dusky summer day. Her fingers guided his chin sideways, and she dabbed at the slash on his cheek.

"You have suffered much," she murmured. "Too much, I think."

Despite the sting of it, he leaned into her ministrations. He could get used to this attention. "The suffering is over now. I am free."

She pulled the cloth away, her brown gaze smiling into his. "You are not a traitor after all?"

"Did you not believe me?"

She dipped the rag again. The water in the basin turned pink. "One doesn't usually get thrown into gaol for no reason."

Hah! He could think of at least twelve men currently gracing the cells of Millbank and Newgate prisons whose only crime was being in the wrong place at the worst possible time. "You'd be surprised," he said, and left it at that.

An easy silence fell, as soothing and healing as Johanna's deft touch. She worked with a gentleness that tightened his throat. Each time her cloth plunged into the water, the basin deepened into a murkier red.

Eventually, she stepped back and examined her work. Satisfied, she quirked a brow. "There. Your face is nearly as good as new."

Right. He still couldn't see out of his left eye. "You are a poor liar."

She flashed a smile. "I shall take that as a compliment, sir."

But just as quickly, her smile evaporated. She clenched the rag until her knuckles whitened. "I—I saw what they did to you. That day I was there, when they. . .when you. . . Well, I should tend that wound on the back of your neck, but I suspect you shall have to remove your shirt. Shall I call Mam?"

"No need. While I have no doubt of your virtue, I suspect you've seen more than the average young lady who's not tended an inn—especially with no father to take care of the, er, dirtier business of maintaining a taproom. Am I correct?"

Pink blossomed on her cheeks, but to her credit, she did not shrink from his assessment. "As usual, a sharp observation on your part."

While she busied herself emptying the basin and replacing it with fresh water, he slipped his arms out of what remained of his waistcoat, then shrugged out of his shirt, biting back a cry as the fabric stuck to the dried blood on his back. To save her the embarrassment of having to look him in the eye while he sat bare-chested, he turned on the stool, facing the kitchen door instead of her.

But he almost turned back when she lifted his ragged hair aside and sucked in a sharp gasp.

"That can't be good," he said.

"It's not." She blew out a long breath, warming the skin on his back. "But I suppose in time, and with some of Mam's famous salve, it will clear up. The wound is quite infected. I'll have to trim your hair so it's not in the way."

"Doctor, innkeeper, cook, and now a barber as well? You are a woman of many talents."

While locks of his hair fell to the floor, he pondered what she'd mentioned about Quail. Why would the man want to stay a fortnight more? Did this tie in somehow with Robbie and Louisa's planned elopement in two weeks? And what of the viscount's shipment arriving in that very same time period? Some thread knotted them all together.

"What does it mean?"

Johanna's question mirrored his thoughts—but she could have no way of knowing. Could she? "What does what mean?"

"This mark on your neck." She laid the scissors on the table next to his elbow, then leaned closer, her warmth heating his exposed flesh. "It almost looks like the letter *B*. Why would someone cut you like that?"

He gritted his teeth, shoving away the painful memory when knife met flesh. "Despite God's edicts, man is not always kind."

"True." The weight of the world hung in her single, exhaled word. She knew exactly what he was talking about—and the knowledge kindled a rage deep in his belly. It was one thing for him to experience the depravity of man, but she ought not. Ever.

Her skirts rustled. A jar lid opened. The acrid scent of liniment—a strange mix of turpentine and vinegar—filled the room.

"I am sorry," she said, "but this may sting a bit."

Fire followed her warning, burning to the bone, and spread from his neck down his spine. "Grace and mercy! You trying to kill me?"

"No need. You've been doing a good enough job of that yourself. Now, mind your tone. You'll wake Mam."

He steeled himself and straightened. "Please don't tell me you put this on Thomas's leg."

"Of course not. We used something much stronger. Bear up. I'll work quickly."

Darkness crept in on the corners of his vision, but he kept his breathing steady and forced himself upright. Eventually, a cool cloth pressed against the base of his neck.

"There. All finished. You'll survive, I suppose."

"I usually do." He turned then, catching both her hands in his before she could bustle away. "But this time I have you to thank. You are a rare gem, Johanna. I wonder if you know that."

A cloud darkened her face, like a shadow on the sun, then just as quickly vanished. "Off with you, sir. It is late, and you need rest, but first a good scrubbing is in order, I think. I shall fill a hip bath in your chamber. Wait here. I shan't take long."

She disappeared out of the kitchen, taking along with her the whole of his heart.

He slumped on his chair, weary beyond words. This assignment was wearing on him in more ways than one. Would that Ford had decreed he not only reside at the Blue Hedge Inn, but marry the innkeeper's daughter as well.

CHAPTER TWENTY-ONE

Johanna yawned. Again. Fatigue competed with the refreshing breeze wafting in from the Channel as she paced the boardwalk in front of the harbourmaster's office. The briny droplets in the air ought keep her awake, but she'd spent the night tossing one way then the other, the memory of tending Alex both repellant and attractive. She'd been called many things by past patrons, but never a gem. Not that the compliment meant anything, for flattery was a commodity she was often paid. No, his words were nothing extraordinary. It was the huskiness of his voice, the clench of his jaw, the earnest way he'd stared into her soul when he'd spoken. He meant what he said, but more than that—he wanted her to believe it as well. Why would a man care what she thought of herself?

She spun on her heel and retraced her steps, searching the boardwalk for yellow stockings. If she waited for Mr. Nutbrown any longer, Mam would wonder at her absence. She never should've agreed to work with him in the first place and more than likely would have better luck inquiring at the harbourmaster's without him and his preposterous puppet.

Mind made up, she stopped her pacing and pushed open the office door. The room was small, made even more claustrophobic by stacks of papers piled atop the counter. Good thing the front windows gave a grand view of the harbor, for otherwise the place might as well be a crypt.

"Afternoon, miss. Can I help you?"

Though the man's question and gaze required an answer, her tongue stuck to the roof of her mouth. This was no man. He was an ostrich. La! What a neck. The fellow looked as if someone had grasped the top of his head and pulled until giving up on the endeavor. The length from cravat to chin had to be a good eight inches. Was such a neck a requirement of the job—or an unfortunate result of gawking over stacks of paper?

"Miss?"

"Sorry, yes, of course you can help. Forgive me." She spoke as much to God as to him. "I am here to inquire about a ship's arrival."

"All right. Which one?" He folded his hands atop the papers in front of him, and though she ought not be surprised, the length of his fingers was equally amazing. Another job hazard from paging through documents?

"Er. . ." She bit her lip. Had Mr. Cooper or Mr. Pickens told her the name of the ship? She revisited the conversation in her mind, but honestly, she'd not paid much attention until the payment part. Forcing her gaze to remain on the harbourmaster's spectacles instead of his neck or fingers, she offered him a brilliant smile. "Once again, sir, I apologize. I am not quite sure of the name."

"Very well. We can likely pin it down if you can tell me where the ship is coming from."

Victory! She knew this one. "Woolwich."

"Aah." His brows lifted then his head dipped. Like a lighthouse beam, he surveyed the stacks of documents upon his desk and reached for a binder to his left. "Dock number?"

Her smile faded. So much for victory. Drat that Mr. Nutbrown for his tardiness! Did he know these missing pieces of information? "I am afraid I'm not quite sure of that."

The harbourmaster stopped rifling through the packet, his gaze spearing her like a hook through a codfish. "Well, what type of ship is it? Merchant? Brig? Cutter? Sloop?"

"It is. . ." She licked her lips. How to answer? "Of the floating variety."

His mouth pulled into a frown nearly as long as his neck. "What about the kind of shipment, then? Chartered? Licensed? Packet? Military or civilian?"

Glancing over her shoulder, she longed to see yellow stockings crossing the threshold.

"Allow me to hazard a guess, miss. You're not quite sure of that, either."

She turned back to the man. "You are very perceptive, sir."

He shook his head, and for a moment she worried that the movement might topple the thing from its long perch. He paged through the documents in the binder, then set the folder back down. "Sorry. Don't see anything in the next few days arriving from Woolwich."

"Well, it might not be that soon. Would you mind looking further into the future? Over the next several weeks or so?" She fluttered her eyelashes.

Which worked, somewhat. He flipped through more pages, but the accompanying scowl on his face could not be missed. "No. There is nothing. Are you sure Woolwich is the port of departure? You know that's a military arsenal, not often used for common shipments. Maybe you're mistaken. Was it Weymouth? Worthing? Westham?"

Hmm. Was she sure? Tapping her lip with her finger, she recalled the entire conversation. She could've sworn Mr. Cooper had said Woolwich, but then again. . . "I suppose I might have heard incorrectly. Would you mind checking on those?"

He stood and turned, rifling through pages on another counter against the wall. Hopefully that's all it would take.

The door flung open. A puppet entered, followed by Mr. Nutbrown, his long legs encased in crookedly sewn hose.

Her eyes widened as he opened his mouth. If he spoke now—or rather the jester did—her chances at finding out the information would be lost. She shoved the puppet down and glowered at the man. "No!"

"Sorry?" The harbourmaster turned back.

"Oh, my friend here just arrived, reminding me we are running late." She forced a small giggle. "If you wouldn't mind?" She wiggled her fingers toward the back counter.

She waited until he busied himself with the documents, then scolded on a low breath, "Put that puppet away."

Mr. Nutbrown pursed his lips, then shot out his arm, the absurd puppet front and center over the desk.

"Don't!" She warned, pulling on his sleeve.

He shot her a glance from the corner of his eye, then opened his mouth.

She batted his arm, a little too forcefully. The jester bobbed.

So did Mr. Nutbrown. His arms flailed, smacking into the stacks. Papers flew, some behind the desk, some in front. A snowstorm of documents.

The harbourmaster's head swiveled at the noise—a disconcerting sight on such a neck. "What's going on?"

"So sorry! My friend lost his balance. We shall pick these up straight away." She yanked Mr. Nutbrown down to the floor with her.

"Put that puppet away," she whispered. "You're ruining everything!"

For a horrible eternity, he shoved the puppet into her face. If the harbourmaster gawked his long neck over the counter, he'd see the spectacle and kick them both out the door. But thankfully, after a huff and a flare of nostrils, Mr. Nutbrown started picking up papers—the puppet still attached to his hand.

She gathered the documents scattered on her side of the tiny room, then paused as she scooped up the last one. There, written at the top in neat, black letters was the word Wool with a long line after it. Could be Woolwich, or maybe not. Looked like the name of a ship beneath it, and a date. She held it closer—

And Mr. Nutbrown snatched the page away with his free hand.

This was more than anyone should have to bear. "What are you doing? Why—"

"My sentiments exactly." The harbourmaster's head craned over the counter, directing them both an evil eye—which suddenly narrowed. "Get out! Or I shall call the constable immediately."

Johanna shot to her feet, setting the stack of papers atop the counter. "My apologies, sir. My friend here is a little, well, he's—"

The puppet popped up beside her. "Mr. Nutbrown is exceedingly sorry for the commotion. Won't happen again."

"Out!" A squall raged in the thunder of the harbourmaster's voice. "Both of you!"

"But Mr. Nutbrown sincerely—"

Johanna grabbed the silly man's sleeve and tugged him out the door, leading him down the boardwalk while his jester squabbled. When they cleared the warehouse at the side of the office, she stopped. "Really, Mr. Nutbrown! When will you learn that not everyone welcomes your absurd puppet?"

"Not to worry, Miss Langley. Our mission is accomplished, and here you are." He pulled a small pouch out of his pocket.

She shook her head. "How can you say that? All we saw was a slip of paper with part of a departure name, not where the ship is set to dock, or even what kind of ship it is. I don't feel I can take the full amount, for surely Mr. Cooper and Mr. Pickens will not be satisfied."

He shoved the pouch into her hand and bobbed the jester in front of him. "Mr. Nutbrown assures you they will be very satisfied, for he's got the eyes of a snake. All the information is safe and sound." He tapped the puppet against the side of his head. "You may take the payment in good conscience."

A sigh deflated the rest of her fight. She had found the paper, he had read it—and she desperately needed the weighty little pouch in her hand. "Very well," she conceded.

"Many thanks, Miss Langley. Must be off, now. Mr. Nutbrown is late." The puppet disappeared around the corner of the warehouse, along with the man.

Johanna peered into the small pouch, poking through the coins with a gloved finger. All as promised. This was a good start to rebuilding the empty safe box, but not enough to satisfy Mr. Spurge.

And she had only a little over two weeks left to come up with the rest.

Whistling a tune to keep Nixie happy, Lucius sped down the High Street, dodging afternoon shoppers. It wouldn't do to be late. Not again. His business partners surely were not the cheeriest of fellows and at their last meeting had been downright abrasive. It was much more pleasant to work with Miss Langley—even if she didn't acknowledge Nixie.

A cramp bit into his calf, and for several steps he hop-skipped on one foot while trying to rub away the pain. It didn't help. Fig-niggity! This would slow him down.

Pausing, he leaned against a brick wall and kneaded out the spasm. Thick stitches of thread marred his hose. New stockings would be his first order of personal business once he received the next payment. He glanced at the sun while working out the knot. Perfect. He ought have enough time to collect his fee and make it to the hosiery store before it closed. Just the thought of luscious, new stockings drove away the remnants of his cramp, and he darted back onto the walkway.

Two blocks down, he turned into Barwick Alley, then took another turn into a gap between two buildings. If he stretched out both hands, he could touch the walls on either side. How cozy. As if each structure were the best of friends with the other, wanting to be so near. He patted the papier-mâché lump in his waistcoat. Just like him and Nixie.

Ahead, two dark shapes took form. Mr. Charlie sat atop a barrel. Mr. Blackie propped himself against the wall on his good leg. They were bosom companions as well, yet they'd taken him and Nixie into their circle. Perhaps he ought not think ill of them.

Mr. Charlie jumped down off his barrel. "You got the information?"

Retrieving Nixie, he held out his partner and cleared his throat. "Mr. Nutbrown sometimes may not run according to schedule, gentlemen, but he always accomplishes his purposes."

Without moving away from the wall, Mr. Blackie held out his hand. "Let's have it, then."

He tapped Nixie to his temple. Twice. "It's all up here."

A shameful word exploded out of Mr. Charlie. Strange. Was he having a cramp as well? Maybe, judging by the way he lunged forward on one leg.

Mr. Blackie left the wall and shot out his arm, holding back his friend. "Not yet." Then he angled his face, ignoring Nixie and drilling a black stare into Lucius's eyes. "You don't have the document, but you know what it said?"

He bobbed his puppet's head. "Of that you can be sure."

"Well what did it say?"

"Confidential."

A worse profanity fouled the air, this time from Mr. Blackie. "Of course it was confidential. Besides that!"

Nixie looked back at him, giving him time to recall everything he read before he turned the jester's little head forward again. "It said there's an East Indiaman due sometime late July third. No actual arrival time listed."

"Cargo?"

"Confidential."

Mr. Charlie strained against Mr. Blackie's arm. My! Despite his wooden leg, Mr. Blackjack was a strong fellow. His muscles bulged beneath his shirtsleeve.

Even his voice was strong as he bellowed out, "I said besides that!"

"No, you don't understand." He shook Nixie's little head back and forth, emphasizing the word. "That's what was written on the line after the word *cargo*."

"Humph." Mr. Blackie lifted a brow at Mr. Charlie. Some kind of conversation went back and forth between them, but a silent one. Finally Mr. Blackie looked back at him—once again ignoring Nixie.

"And the point of departure is Woolwich, you're sure of it?"

"Well. . ." Nixie's voice stalled out.

Mr. Blackie dropped his arm. Mr. Charlie sprung forward and grabbed Lucius by the throat, lifting him to his toes.

Precious little air made it to his lungs. Even less made it to Nixie's, but the brave little fellow managed to choke out, "Mr. Nutbrown. Is as sure. As he can. Be."

"Axe!" Mr. Blackie shouted. "Drop him."

Mr. Charlie let go.

Lucius rocked back on his heels, rubbing his neck with his free hand and coughing. Nixie spluttered too. When they finally caught their breath, he held out Nixie to explain. "Because of the nature of the document, the departure was shortened to Wool with a dash after it."

Mr. Charlie shot a glance at his partner. "Could just be from Wool. We can't afford to make a mistake."

"Could be. But not having the cargo listed, and. . .hmm." A raspy noise bounced from wall to wall as Mr. Blackie scratched his jaw, then he leveled a deadly stare—at Nixie. Lucius shivered.

Mr. Blackie glowered at Nixie. "You're sure there was a dash after Wool?"

Nixie bobbed his head so hard, for a horrid moment Lucius feared it might pop off. "Yes! Yes! No doubt at all."

A low breath grumbled out of Mr. Blackie, but then he pulled his awful gaze from Nixie and faced his friend. "That's got to be it."

Mr. Charlie narrowed his eyes. "For our sakes, I hope so."

"You and me, both." He faced Lucius. "You'll have to write down that information so's we can deliver it."

"But why can't you just say it like Mr. Nutbrown—"

This time Mr. Charlie leapt for Nixie. Lucius snatched him back, horrified. Indeed. He much preferred working with Miss Langley. Despite her sometimes scolding tone, at least she didn't resort to such violence.

"Not yet, Axe." There was no denying the command in Mr. Blackie's voice. Mr. Charlie retreated—but only a step away.

"What do you think we're payin' ye for?" Mr. Blackie pulled out a money pouch, the jingle of the coins inside sounding like new stockings. "Now then, I said write it down."

Confusion bowed Nixie's head. How was he to write here? No proper desk. No ink or parchment. He held Nixie in front of him, lifting his brave little face. "Mr. Nutbrown hasn't pen nor paper."

Mr. Blackie snapped his fingers. Mr. Charlie pulled out a folded scrap tucked inside his belt and held it out.

Lucius retrieved the piece of rag paper. It was small, but with several folds. If he opened it, he could easily fit the information on one side. Nixie flung out his arms. "There's still the issue of a pen, gentlemen."

A growl rumbled in Mr. Blackie's throat—and a knife whipped out from a sheath at his side. Before Lucius could blink, Nixie was plucked from his hand and thrown to the dirt. Pain, worse than the cramp, stabbed his fingertip. Blood swelled. Deep red.

"You better write quickly." Mr. Charlie laughed.

Nixie whimpered from the ground—or was that him? He leapt toward the wall and opened the paper full, glad for the size of it. Flattening the paper against the bricks, he bit his lip as he scrawled words with his fingertip. His letters were thick as he wrote. *July 3. Late. East India* . . . the pain began to ebb. So did the blood. Sweat beads popped on his forehead as he looked up at Mr. Blackie's dark scowl. Oh dear, sweet mother! The man might sever his entire hand if he didn't finish the message. He shoved his finger into his mouth and sucked on it, drawing a fresh flow. Finishing the last letter, he pulled his hand back from the gruesome sight.

This time Mr. Blackie laughed. "Good. Now read the other side."

He hesitated, worried for Nixie. Worried for himself. Worried about what might be written on the flip side.

"Do it!"

Mr. Charlie's harsh bark forced the page over. Lucius's eyes skimmed from word to word.

"Out loud, you idiot."

A lump lodged in his throat. How was he to speak without Nixie? He shot a wild look to where his friend lay facedown in the alley.

Mr. Charlie rolled his eyes, but scooped up Nixie and handed him back.

Aah. Glorious unity. Nixie trembled, and so did he. With his free hand, he gave the paper back as Nixie relayed the message. "The note says, '*Arrange for transport of frames to Ramsgate on a vessel large enough to suit. Hire a minimal crew.*'"

Tucking the paper back into his belt, Mr. Charlie faced Mr. Blackjack. "If the Indiaman's coming here, why we taking the frames to Ramsgate?"

Mr. Blackie shrugged. "Dunno. Not ours to question." Then he shoved a finger into Nixie's chest. "You, lay low and stay put. We'll find you when we next need you. And here." He dropped a bag onto the vacated barrel. "I suppose you've earned this."

Shoving past him and Nixie, they disappeared down the neck of the alley. It took all his power to simply breathe. Nixie too. That had been completely disagreeable in every possible way. Slowly, Nixie turned his little head toward him. "Why do you suppose picture frames require such a covert enterprise?"

"I don't know, friend. But I have a feeling these gentlemen aren't so gentle."

CHAPTER TWENTY-TWO

Alex swiped his hair over his eye, covering the ugly purple and green remnants. Not that Thomas would mind, and in fact might think the bruise a trophy to be admired. But there was a fine balance between concealment and blocking his vision, so it took him several tries. Finally satisfied, he snatched the crutch resting against the wall and yanked open his door.

Out in the hallway, Quail stopped and pivoted at the sound. "Well, well. . ." He dissected him with a smirk. "Look who's returned—and not looking too good at that."

Alex pulled the door shut behind him and faced the man. "You know, for an itinerant musician, I wonder that you're still here."

"And I wonder that a. . .how did you put it? Aah, yes. Why would a *purchaser of fine wines* remain in Dover? Not a hotbed of vineyards."

"Nor is it a sufficient market for entertainers."

"Never at a loss for words, eh Morton?" Quail narrowed his eyes, the squinty effect likely meant to be intimidating. "Neither am I."

Alex stifled a smile. The man posed him no danger whatsoever—physically, at any rate. But if he were somehow tangled up with the traitor, or in fact was the traitor himself, well. . .better to let the man think he held the superior cards. He remained silent.

Quail took a step forward and lowered his voice. "Nor are you at a loss for money, apparently. Miss Langley tells me you pay your rent in guineas. However do you manage that?"

Alex froze. What the deuce? Why would Johanna tell him that? And what other information had she served Quail along with a mug and crust? He took his own step closer, matching the man's accusing tone. "Tell me, how do you manage to survive from that cat screeching racket you call music? But I think we both know you are not a musician."

Quail's nostrils flared. "Nor are you a gentleman."

A clean swipe on Quail's part, but Alex parried with a smile. "You admit it, then."

One by one, Quail's fingers pulled into fists. "As neither of us are who we claim to be, then I'd say this is a draw, Morton. But I suggest you stay out of my way. Who knows? I might even return the favor."

The man stomped down the hall and disappeared into his chamber. Alex hesitated, unsure if he ought file the conversation away under *Curious*, *Inconsequential*—or *Threatening*. He opted for *Risky* as he strode to Thomas's door.

"Thomas?" He rapped the crutch against the wood. "Feel up to company—"

"Yes!" The answer came before he finished his question.

Tucking his gift behind him, he entered and drew near the boy's bed.

"Caw, sir! What happened to you?" Thomas lifted up on his elbows. "You look worse than the time I took a tumble from Nanny Shuttleworth's apple tree and she chased after me with a switch."

As if making a solemn vow, he held his free hand over his heart. "May you never see the inside of Dover's gaol, young sir."

Wide brown eyes blinked up at him, an interesting mixture of horror and respect shining in them. Alex couldn't stop a smile—nor did he want to. His heart hitched a beat, taking him completely by surprise. How could a scrap of a lad evoke such a strong emotion? He shoved down the feeling and pulled the crutch from behind his back. "Think you could put this to good use?"

Thomas beamed. "Aye, sir!"

"Shall we give it a go?"

"Aye, but. . ." The boy's smile faded, and he looked away.

"But what?"

"Will it. . ." Thomas's lips pressed into a thin line, and he slowly lifted his face. Whatever he had to say would cost him dearly. "Do you think it will hurt awful fierce?"

No wonder the boy's voice quavered. Pride always exacted a price.

"Not if you keep the weight on the crutch instead of your sore leg." Alex crouched, face-to-face. "But if you like, I'll help bear you up for the first try."

At Thomas's nod of approval, he helped the boy to a sitting position, propped the crutch beneath his armpit, and prayed he'd calculated the height correctly. "On three, all right?"

At one, Thomas bit his lip. On two, he paled. But when Alex said, "Three," the lad sucked in a breath and pushed up with all his might. Brave fellow.

After several halting steps from bed to door then back again, he helped Thomas lower onto his mattress. Sweat dotted the boy's brow, and his thin arms shook, but a sweet smile lighted his face.

"There now. That wasn't so hard, was it?" He tussled Thomas's hair, then straightened. "We'll practice a bit each day, and within a week, I wager you'll be getting about all on your own."

Thomas blinked up at him. "I didn't know, I mean. . .well, having a mam and a sister is all right, I guess, but having you here—I. . .I missed you, that's what. And I didn't know I missed having a father either, not till I met you."

Alex stared. The boy's hero worship was a knife to his heart. What a sorry hand life had dealt the lad. Thomas ought have a father to admire—a real father—not a deceiver such as himself. He swallowed the bitter aftertaste of that truth and forced out words he meant more than the boy could possibly know. "I missed you too, Thomas."

Behind him, the door swung open. "What's this?"

He turned at the question.

Johanna glared at the crutch in his hand. "What is that?"

He leaned the boy's gift against the wall—making sure to keep it within arm's reach should Thomas be brave enough to practice without him. "I had some time yesterday. Can't simply lie around, can I? And neither can your brother."

Thomas bounced on his bed. "Alex thinks that if I practice a little bit each day, I'll be able to get about by myself within a week—just in time to see the Punch and Judy show Mr. Quail promised."

"That's a bad idea." She scowled.

"Aw, Jo!" Thomas matched her glower. "You never have any fun, and you never let anyone else have any fun, either."

Alex stepped between them and faced Johanna. Sometimes the best way to squelch a brawler was to block the view of the opponent. "You can't keep the boy in here forever. He's on the mend, and surely you'll want his help again soon."

A sigh bowed her shoulders. "I suppose." She rose to her toes and peeked over his shoulder at Thomas. "But at least wait until the doctor comes in two more days. If he says it's all right, then all right."

Alex gifted her with a grin. "Well done."

She arched a brow, clearly partaking of none of his charm. "But in the meantime, knowing the both of you, I'll hold on to that." Leaning sideways, she reached past him and grabbed the crutch, the effort lifting her sleeve away from her wrist and inching the fabric slightly up her forearm—where three bruises ugly enough to match his own marred her skin.

His smile disappeared. God help the man who'd put them there.

He stepped to the door. "A word with you, Miss Langley. Out in the hall, if you please."

She clutched the crutch to her chest. "You're wasting your time. I'll not change my position until we get the doctor's go-ahead."

He shifted a pointed gaze to her arm. "It's not about the crutch."

Johanna stiffened. Drat! Though she'd tried to keep her sleeve close to her wrist, Alex's face had hardened when it slid upward. Did the man miss nothing? She'd known him for barely a month, yet she knew what that offset angle to his jaw meant. And the rigid line of his shoulders. He'd have his way or die in the trying. He'd evicted Mr. Nutbrown for a simple lack of payment—and quite forcefully, at that. What would he do to Tanny if he found out the man roughed her up now and then?

Not that Tanny didn't deserve a good dose of his own medicine, but still. . . Alex yet wore the bruised remains of gaol on his face. Another visit and he might not have a face left at all.

She darted past him and scurried down the hall, calling over her shoulder, "Sorry, no time now."

"I won't be put off so easily." His footsteps kept time with hers, down the stairs, through the taproom, across the kitchen—even out the door and into the back courtyard. Really, the man ought to go into business with Mr. Spurge, so fixated was he.

She dashed toward the stable.

His shoes pounded the gravel, close behind. "Not that I mind the view from back here, but how long will you keep up this merry chase?"

She ignored him, upping her pace. To face him now would only encourage his roguish charm.

"Johanna, for the love of all that's righteous, just stop. I'll not give up. And if you think you can hitch up Posey to outrun me—"

Gritting her teeth, she whirled and planted her fists on her hips, cutting him off. "There is nothing to discuss. Go about your business, and I shall go about mine."

Afternoon sun lit golden strands in his brown hair, highlighted even more as he closed in on her. "Fine, but first roll up your sleeve. I wish to see your arm."

Pah! He was as bullish as Mr. Needler. But as she breathed in his warmth and sandalwood shaving cologne, her knees weakened in a completely different way than when she faced Tanny.

Still, he had no right to be so demanding. She didn't budge.

He reached for her arm.

She retreated a step. The outright boldness! "You may wish all you like, sir, for I will not roll up my sleeve. I am no servant to be ordered about, nor am I a loose skirt."

Instantly, his hand dropped to his side, a grimace pulling at his lips. "My apologies, for you are correct on both accounts. My directness suits for my work, I suppose, but I never should have used such a manner with you. Forgive me?"

He hung his head while peeking up at her through his lashes. A sheep caught in a briar couldn't have looked more contrite. She stifled a growl. Who could stay cross when facing this?

"Yes." She sighed. "I forgive you. Now, if you'll excuse me." She spun, returning to her previous mission—retrieving a big bucket for Mam.

A tug on her shoulder turned her back around. "Even so, I will see your arm, with or without your cooperation."

Once, on the High Street, she'd seen a mule dig in its hooves, refusing to pull a cart one more inch despite the railing of the driver. Curses, blows, even the offering of a carrot would not convince the animal to budge.

Such was the ripple of resolve lining Alexander's brow—right at the point where his discolored bruise faded into tanned skin. Was tenacity the reason he bore such wounds?

She scowled—but slowly pushed up her sleeve, then held out her forearm like a peevish four-year-old.

Stepping near, he cradled her arm in his big hand and bent over it, his breath warmer than the June sunshine against her skin. Her heart beat loud in her ears. Curse the man for making her feel so precious, like a teacup to be mourned for the chip on its rim. She had no right to feel this cherished. His gentle grip cupped her elbow, treating her as if she were delicate and prized and dearly loved.

He studied the marks with a penetrating gaze, then carefully pulled the fabric back down to her wrist. When he let go completely, she nearly wobbled from the loss.

"How did that happen?" His voice was low and dangerous.

She bit the inside of her cheek. What to say? If she named Tanny, surely Alex would seek retribution. But to lie. . .well. . .was that not as ugly in God's eyes as Tanny's brutality? She'd be no better than her father.

Even so, a perfectly plausible falsehood sprang to her lips, and she bit her cheek harder. Suddenly she knew exactly how Thomas felt when she cornered him. . .how her father had when confronted by her mother.

Alex lifted a finger to her lips and tapped lightly. "And do not deign to tell me those marks were somehow caused by accident, for they were not. You are a woman who prizes honesty, as do I."

She swallowed, suddenly overcome. This man was nothing like her father, despite his gaming ways, for he valued truth as much as she. Maybe it was time for her to trust God and take a risk of her own in allowing herself to love Alexander Morton.

"Very well." She lifted her chin. "I was late in my oakum delivery to Mr. Needler."

"Blast!" Anger banked in his eyes, turning the blue to a smoldering ash—and threatening to flare into a red rage. "You are finished there. Do not go back."

She'd laugh if bitterness weren't closing her throat, and it was a fight indeed to force out any words. "That's easy for you to say."

He shook his head. "There are other means of gaining income, if that's what you're about."

"You don't understand. There *is* nothing else." She cast her hands wide, wishing she could as easily cast all her troubles to the wind. "Believe me, I've tried. Needler's oakum and Quail's silly Punch and Judy show are my last hope to pay the rent in two weeks."

There. She'd said it. Aloud. And voicing it made the workhouse all the more real and dreadful and—the world turned blurry. Hot tears burned at the back of her eyes. No. She would not cry, not in front of a bruised man with enough troubles of his own.

She pivoted and fairly ran toward the stable.

"Johanna!" He darted around her, quick as a jackdaw, and stood immovable in her path. "You're right. There is nothing else, but not in the way you mean it. As valiant as your efforts are, all this striving of yours is but a puff of wind. I had a lot of time to think and pray while in solitary, and I learned something that may be of help, for I see some of the same tendencies of mine in you. Would you like to hear it?"

She sucked in a shaky breath, shoving back the good cry that threatened. Not trusting her voice, she gave a stiff nod.

"It's a simple truth. One I've overlooked all my life, and here it is." Running a hand through his hair, he tipped his face up to the sky. "There is nothing more—nor less—than trusting in God. Therein surrender, and you will find rest."

"Rest?" She spit out the word, despite his earnestness. "What kind of rest is there in the workhouse? I can't let that happen."

His face lowered to hers, his stare unrelenting. "It's not up to you, Johanna. It's up to God. Do you believe that?"

"Of course I do."

"Your actions say otherwise, the way you're running yourself ragged, the worry I see in your eyes, the sharpness with your brother."

She shrank back, her gaze driven to the ground. Truly? Was that what she'd been doing for all the world to witness? For Alex and Mam and—she sucked in a breath. For God to see? Shame twisted her stomach.

Oh God, forgive me. He's right. He's so, so right.

Slowly, she lifted her face. As much as this man rankled and shook her world, she ought give him credit for speaking truth. "Thank you."

A grin spread, making little crinkles at the corners of his eyes. "I'm not the one you should be thanking."

He skirted her and strode toward the inn, leaving her alone in the center of the courtyard. Alone with myriad upon myriad of thoughts.

She lifted her face to the same sky he'd faced just moments ago. "Things might not get any easier, Lord, but even so, Mr. Morton is right. It is You I should be thanking *and* trusting. The thanking part I can do, but the trust? Ah, Lord. . . You know me, better than I know myself. I cannot make any promises to trust You like I should, but I shall try—with Your help, that is."

The sun beat down, pure and strong, as hot and real as the new hope springing up inside her—but would hope alone be strong enough to sustain her and Mam and Thomas should the workhouse be their end?

CHAPTER TWENTY-THREE

Dover was a'scream this early in the morning. Literally. From knife-sharpening hawkers to arguing dray drivers, noise boxed Alex's ears more thoroughly than his shouting match with Tanny Needler. The scoundrel. It had taken all of his self-reserve—and an extra measure gained from an on-the-run prayer—to keep from bloodying the man's nose. He flexed his fingers as he dodged a sausage-seller's cart, temptation to turn back still surging. Needler deserved an uppercut and worse for his conduct toward Johanna.

But a croaky voice echoing in an alley slowed his steps. He cocked his head, listening hard, and there, a layer beneath the hum of commerce and life on the High Street, a familiar twang crawled out from the alley. Alex dared a peek around the corner, though he needn't have. Blackjack's toothless dialect was one in a million.

Two shapes, one tall and listing sideways on a single, strong leg, the other short and squat, with a shock of red hair escaping a hat brim, faced a wide-eyed Nutbrown. If Blackie or Axe turned his way, the knuckle-buster he itched for would be satisfied—but also ruin his mission. And on these crowded streets, he'd not only provide entertainment but newspaper headlines as well.

Alex eased back, remaining within hearing range yet out of their sight.

"But gentlemen, Mr. Nutbrown has said he's excessively sorry to be late once again. Business, my fine fellows. Business is a harsh taskmaster and prodigiously time consuming."

Blackie's expletives punctuated the high-pitched voice of Nutbrown, but the man kept right on talking—or rather, his puppet did. Did he seriously have no notion of the danger he faced?

"For the love of women and song, shut up!" Axe's command was followed by the smack of fist against flesh and then a howl.

Alex gritted his teeth. What to do? Save Nutbrown? Walk on? Or—

Blackie's next words made the decision for him, leastwise for the moment.

"Quit yer whining, Nutbrown. We'll give you another chance, for we've one last thing for you to do. Come along."

Boots ground into gravel, growing louder with each step. Alex shoved away from the building and zigzagged across the street, missing—barely—a skull-cracker of a collision with a wagonload of bottles. Losing himself in a swarm of pedestrians, he upped his pace toward Featherstone's. He might yet have to add saving Nutbrown to his list of tasks to accomplish if Blackjack had a *last* thing for the man to do. The simpleton could have no idea what the villain meant. But for now, Alex had an appointment with the tailor and—judging by the slant of shadows—he was late.

Three blocks later, he shoved open a glass-paned door, setting off a jingling bell. The woolsey smell of merino and cheviot gave a cheerful greeting. Behind the counter, the sour pull of the clerk's jowls did not. Nor did the squint of his eyes, amplified into drawn slashes behind his thick spectacles. This was Dover's finest? How could the man possibly see to cut a bolt of fabric let alone thread a needle? A mystery—but not one tantalizing enough to solve.

Alex offered a smile and a greeting. "Good day. I am sorry I am late."

Understanding dawned on the clerk's face, for his eyelids suddenly lifted like the rising of twin suns. "Aah. Of course. You will find Dr. Swallow's office two doors down."

"Oh? Are you feeling ill?" Alex stepped forward. "Shall I escort you?"

The man's eyes narrowed again. "I meant for you."

"Never felt better, thank you."

"Then you've obviously taken a wrong turn." The clerk's voice pinched as he studied the leftover bruises on Alex's face. "Decker's Boxing Club is over on Priory."

"If boxing were what I was about, then I don't think I'd be standing in a tailor shop now, would I?"

Slowly, the man's glower evened. "I see. What you'll need to do then is head south on the High Street and turn left at Snargate. Bagsby's Thread and Needle is the third building past the fishmonger. Good day."

The clerk turned his back and ran a finger along a tower of fabric bolts stacked on a shelf behind him. Whispered numbers filled the room like so many scissor snips.

Alex folded his arms. Was this to be more of a fight than his skirmish with Needler? "While I appreciate your fine embroidery of directions, sir, nevertheless, I am exactly where I want to be."

The clerk cut a glance over his shoulder. "You do realize this is the most exclusive tailor in all of Dover? We don't serve just anyone. For the last time, I bid you good day, sir."

"You serve the viscount, Lord Coburn?"

The man wheeled about so quickly, the flaps of his neck swished against his collar. Truly, if he were such a crack tailor, could he not do something about tightening up those loose folds of skin?

"Of course the viscount is a client—and you are clearly not!" A fine shade of red spread over the man's cheeks. "Now rid yourself from this establishment before I call the constable."

Alex pulled out a small, white paper from inside his pocket and placed it on the counter, shoving it toward the man with one finger. "I believe he sent word I was coming."

With barely a glance at the calling card, the clerk retrieved a wooden box and flipped open the lid. He paged through a row of index cards, snorting a few *humph*s as he worked. Finally, he pulled out a cream-coloured card and held it at arm's length, his pupils roaming behind the glass of his spectacles like two balls rolling across a carpet. The longer he read, the more his jaw dropped, until at last the index card fell too.

"Oh, my. Oh, sir! My apologies." Dashing around the front counter, the clerk dipped his head, giving the impression of a naughty schoolboy caught cheating on a test. "I never meant, I mean, I can surely see that you are a gentleman of quality."

A second ago he was barely above a vagrant and now he was a gentleman? Alex smirked. "No hard feelings. Let's just get on with it, shall we?"

"Yes! Oh, absolutely." The man straightened and swept out his arm, pointing to a velvet-curtained doorway. "If you'll step into the farthest fitting room on the left, just down that corridor, I'll give you a moment to shed your coat and shirt for some measurements."

Shopkeepers. All the same. Once they detected a jingle in your pocket, suddenly you were their bosom friend.

Alex swiped the curtain aside and strode the length of the corridor. He passed several doors, all of which stood open. Only one was shut—on the left, far end. Had he heard incorrectly? He glanced back at the curtain, entertaining the thought of asking the fellow, but after their already strained conversation, decided against it.

He opened the door. A shirtless man stood on a pedestal, back toward him. Nothing surprising, really. This was a tailor's shop. But just above the fellow's shoulder blade, right side, a dark, puckered scar burnt into the skin an indelible letter *D*. Alex stifled a gasp. You didn't see that every day.

In front of him, kneeling with a mouthful of pins and a tape measure running from pedestal to ankle, a tailor jerked his face toward the door. In a competition, Alex would bet a sovereign that this fellow's glower would easily beat out the front clerk's.

"Sorry." Alex grabbed the knob, intending to make a hasty exit. "I must have the wrong room."

"That you, ol' chap?" The man on the pedestal turned, Robbie's ever-present grin a stark contrast to the tailor at his feet. "Thought I recognized the voice. Had I known you were coming, we could've shared a carriage. Here for your engagement suit, hmm?" A knowing gleam lit Robbie's eyes. "Thought I'd get myself one as well."

This time he did gasp. It would not be contained. "Er. . .yes. That I am."

Behind him, hurried footsteps shushed against the carpet's nap. "Mr. Morton, I've made a ghastly mistake! I directed you to the wrong door. Over here, if you please."

Alex tipped his head toward Robbie. "Duty calls, I'm afraid."

He pulled shut the door and crossed over to the clerk, not hearing another one of the man's blustering apologies—nor anything else he said the entire length of the fitting. Who could pay attention to a pandering shopkeeper when—if he were correct—that branded *D* on Robbie's back labeled him a deserter. But from which branch of service?

And why?

Clicking her tongue, Johanna urged her pony with a jiggle of the reins. But Posey continued to plod one hoof in front of the other. A steady clop. *Clip. Clop. Clip.* Until Johanna wanted to scream. It would not go well for her if she were late to Tanny's. She frowned. Then again, it never went well, were she on time or not.

Still, she'd left Mam with a table full of dirty dishes from the breakfast she'd thrown together. Then there was the bread to bake, the stew to make, and the management of a crazed set of musicians trying to build a puppet stage.

"Oh, Posey, please. Move on!"

Clip. Clop. The horse twitched her ears. Nothing more. Johanna resettled on the pony cart's seat, wishing to do something about her ears as well. The noise of the High Street carried on the breeze even to this side road, two blocks over. Behind her, the hooves of more motivated horses pounded on the dirt. She guided Posey closer to the side, allowing room for the other vehicle to pass.

It didn't. A shiny barouche with the top folded back pulled alongside her. The four horses leading the carriage stood nearly twice as tall as hers, spooking Posey. The voice greeting her set her own teeth on edge.

"Good day, Miss Langley." Mr. Spurge leaned back against his red leather cushions as if he owned the world—which he practically did. "You're out early. What, no guests to serve at the inn?"

"Good morning to you, Mr. Spurge." She forced a prim smile then snapped her face forward.

"I suppose it's good practice for you."

His words dangled like bait on a hook, willing her to bite. She fixed her gaze on Posey's rump. Better that than look at Spurge's smug face. "I have no idea what you're talking about, sir, and I've not time for riddles."

"I hear inmates at St. Mary's are up before dawn, so you see, my dear, you'll have to be a bit more industrious than this."

She squeezed the reins until her knuckles cracked beneath her gloves. The gall! Oh, to give him the evil eye, with a hefty serving of what for. But that's exactly what he wanted, like a boy poking a stick at a hedgehog to see him roll up.

Holding steady, she kept her voice even. "The workhouse will not be my end, Mr. Spurge. You shall have your money, and not a moment before it is due."

"Indeed. I shall. One way or another. Drive on!" His matched greys stepped lively, the barouche finally gaining speed. As a parting gift, Spurge leaned over the side of the carriage and tipped his hat. "Enjoy your last days at the Blue Hedge, Miss Langley."

"That's weeks, sir, not days."

"Days, weeks, a trifling matter, for that inn will soon be mine."

She waited until his carriage disappeared around the next corner before she allowed her brow to sink into a scowl. Wicked man. How could he sleep at night?

Posey continued plodding, but Johanna's thoughts chased circles the rest of the way to Tanny's. In a little over two weeks, she'd have to face Spurge again. The money she earned delivering oakum would put a dent in that payment, but she'd still be short. That better be some Punch and Judy show Mr. Quail put on. But what if it wasn't?

"There is nothing more—nor less—than trusting in God. Therein surrender, and you will find rest."

Alexander's words prickled across her cheeks, as twangy as the gust of wind carrying off the Channel. Even so, her stomach cramped as she set the brake on the pony cart in front of Tanny's. Of course she must trust God, but it wasn't as if she could simply say, "Ready, set, go!" and instantly do it.

Could she?

She hopped down from the cart just as the door to Tanny's shack opened. Tanny emerged, a curse on his tongue and a clip to his step.

And a switch clutched in his fist. "Get on with you. You're done here."

Her stomach cinched tighter, and she dropped to her knees on the dirt, his favorite stance. "I am sorry I'm late, Your Grace. It won't happen again, I promise."

He pulled up in front of her. "I know it won't, because I said yer done."

She forced her gaze onto the scuffed tips of his shoes. "You also said you'd employ me for three weeks, yet I've barely served half that."

"Oh? I'm to have a serving of your salty tongue now, am I?" The switch slapped against his leg.

She flinched. To say anything more might land the thing on the tender skin at the base of her neck.

"Your lover didn't pay me enough for that."

She jerked her face upward. "My what?"

A small pouch thwunked onto the dirt between them. Tanny's lips twisted into a sneer. "Count it. It's all there."

"I—I don't understand." Why would he pay her for unfinished work?

"I don't care a Christmas pudding what you understand. Do as you're told." The switch shook in his hand—a snake to be loosened at the slightest provocation.

She retrieved the bag and opened the drawstring. Five guineas jingled against one another as she dumped them into her palm. Dots of perspiration broke out on her brow. Was this a trap? She lifted her gaze to Tanny. "But why?"

"Tell the big oaf I met his price and kept my word, so there's no need for him to come back here with his threats and impudence."

Suspicion rose like a mist on a moor. Better to know for certain, though. "I don't know who you're talking about."

"Oh? You're a prim lady now, are ye? All high and mighty. A lacy little princess, all buttoned up tight with nary a loose moral." His long legs lifted in a jig, his feet kicking sand against her cheeks. Then as suddenly, he stopped and crouched, shoving his long nose into her face. "I know what you are. You're nothing but a tart. Now, go on. And don't come back."

"But—"

"Go!"

A spray of spittle violated her lips, and she recoiled.

Tanny shot to his feet, raising the switch. "Off with ye before I change my mind."

Clutching the pouch, she dashed to the cart. Even without Tanny naming him, she knew exactly who was responsible for this windfall. The big oaf had to be Alexander, for there weren't many shoulders as broad as his. Of course she'd anticipated him to act, maybe confront her more forcefully about such work or go directly to Mam to voice his concern, but this? Must the man always exceed her expectations?

With a "Walk on," she urged Posey to move, but her thoughts wouldn't be prodded off topic as easily. They never were when it came to Alexander Morton. The man consumed her mind by day and dreams by night.

What was she to do about that?

CHAPTER TWENTY-FOUR

Afternoon sun warmed the taproom, and for the space of a few breaths, Johanna paused on the kitchen's threshold and drank it in. Weather such as this was a rare customer. Salty air wafted inside from the propped-open front door, ushering in the sweet scent of wildflowers where she'd planted them in barrels. Why could not all of life smell as fresh?

Balancing a tray of washed mugs, she crossed over to the counter, then frowned. A monstrosity of wood and nails leaned like a drunken dockhand atop it. If Mr. Quail was so fired up to produce a puppet show, why was he not down here constructing a proper stage? She'd seen nary a hair of him or his band since last night. Nor had she seen Alex.

Alex? Must her every thought be waylaid by the man? For the hundredth time, she mulled over why he'd rescued her from Tanny—and came up short once again. Nor had she been able to ask him outright, for she'd scarce seen him to inquire.

She rounded the counter with clipped steps, the tumbledown stage mocking her every movement. Mr. Quail had already plastered the town with handbills advertising the Punch and Judy show. If that scoundrel thought to leave her with a derelict excuse of a stage and no one to operate the puppets—or the puppets themselves, for that matter—then she'd. . .she'd. . .

She'd what?

Helplessness chafed worse than the poorly darned stockings she'd put on this morning. With a growl, she stowed the mugs, then snatched up a hammer and a stick of wood. She could hardly do a shoddier job than Mr. Quail.

Skirting the counter, she faced the front of the eyesore, deeming how and where best to begin. The rickety frame could use some shoring up, especially at the base. That settled, she set to work.

Each pound of the hammer rattled the entire structure, and she feared the whole thing might fall apart. Thankfully, it held. She grabbed another piece of wood and started on the other side. It felt good to strike hard and see progress, to pound away tension.

Whack! That was for Tanny.

Smack! One for Mr. Quail.

She swung back for a mighty strike against Mr. Spurge, put all her weight into the blow, and—

"Ow!"

Sharp pain crushed flesh and bone. She dropped the hammer and popped her thumb into her mouth.

"Still taking on the world by yourself, are you?"

She whipped about at the sound of Alex's deep voice. Pudding and pie! She'd not seen the man in two days and he had to appear at this moment?

With a quirk to his lips, he held out his hand. "Let's see it."

Emotions pecked her like a flock of martins. Frustration, irritation, but mostly embarrassment that she'd once again appeared the inept female. She yanked out her thumb and hid it behind her back. "No need. I am fine."

His outstretched hand didn't waver. Neither did his gaze. She knew that look, for she steeled her jaw to the same angle whenever confronting Thomas.

Slowly, she offered her throbbing thumb.

His touch was an exquisite agony as he lifted her hand to eye level. His own injuries still marred his face. Purple tainted the corner of one eye, but the edges of the bruise faded into greenish-yellow. The cut near his temple sported new, pink skin where it started to grow together. Doubtful, though, that the carving at the nape of his neck was healed.

He turned her hand one way then another, his breath warm against her skin. His manly scent was familiar now, in a way that connected her to him like a cherished memory.

"I don't think anything is broken," he murmured.

Oh, but he was wrong. Her pride lay in hundreds of jagged pieces. Good thing he studied her hand and not the flush spreading to her cheeks. "I find it curious, sir, that whenever I am in some sort of predicament, you appear. I fear you'll put my guardian angel out of work."

"If the position should ever open"—his blue gaze shot to hers—"I wish to be the first, and only, candidate."

Bypassing the offending thumb, he pressed a kiss to her wrist.

Heat shot up her arm, radiating out from where his mouth touched naked skin. She pulled back her hand, heart jolting. Traitorous body!

Would he now expect such liberties in return for freeing her from Tanny Needler? And why did she hope that he would? Breathing hard, she speared him with a glower, unsure if she were angrier with him or herself.

"Please, stop the pretense, Mr. Morton. I know what you've done, and I ask you to answer honestly." She searched the depths of his blue eyes, desperate for truth. "Why would you do such a thing?"

Panic washed over Alex like a dip in a January pond, frigid and unsettling. What did Johanna know? Had she heard of his fitting for a betrothal suit earlier in the week? Was it common knowledge he was expected at his own engagement dinner tomorrow evening? Or was she asking how it could be that a man would so fiercely love one woman yet agree to marry another?

He schooled his face into a frozen mask—matching the state of his heart. Why *would* he do such a thing? Loyalty to Ford was one thing, but this was his life. If Robbie didn't steal away Louisa soon, he'd have to come up with some other plan to escape the noose of matrimony.

"Mr. Morton?"

Burying his feelings deeper than a sexton on a bender, he forced an even tone to his voice. "What have I done to upset you?"

"Did you think I wouldn't guess?"

He dissected every word or action of the past few days that might've tipped her off. But no, he'd taken care to cover his tracks. Kept his mission at the viscount's manor strictly confidential. Yet maybe it hadn't been him at all, but some other source she'd heard from. Her friend Maggie perhaps?

"Why did you pay off Tanny Needler?"

Her question was scissors, snipping away the tension from each muscle in his shoulders. Was that all that bothered her?

A smile curved his mouth, and he shrugged. "I told you that oakum delivery is not a job for a woman such as yourself. You ought to be attending dinners and dances, not gaols."

Bypassing her, he retrieved the hammer from the floorboards and hefted it.

She huffed behind him. "A gentleman's son may have no shortage of invitations to the viscount's manor, but in case you haven't observed, I am an innkeeper's daughter."

"Oh, do not be mistaken." He turned from the sorry excuse of a puppet stage and stared straight into her heart. "I observe everything about you."

Red flamed on her cheeks. It was entirely too easy to make this woman blush—and for that, he thanked God.

"My point is, sir, that dinners and dances are beyond my reach."

"Were there any justice in the world, that would not be so." He clenched his teeth with the truth of that statement. The justice of this world was a cruel jest. Poisonous women like Louisa Coburn lived in luxury while Johanna scraped to keep a roof over her head. There was nothing fair about it.

"You, my sweet Johanna." Her name rolled off his tongue before he thought. Her eyes widened, but this time she did not denounce his use of her name.

Emboldened, he advanced, stopping a breath away from her. "You deserve ribbons and laces and walks through a garden, not ramshackle puppet stages and the leftover stench of ale."

A sad smile wavered on her lips—lips he very much wanted to kiss.

And he could, if he bent just a little.

"It is kind of you to say." A curious little quiver, almost too faint to discern, shivered across her chin. "But I am not the angel you make me out to be."

He'd taken kidney punches before. This one stunned him most. Despite his best efforts to retain a poker face, his brows shot upward. "What kinds of mortal sin could you have possibly committed?"

She stood like a soldier before battle, bearing up to fight God knew what army of demons. Tears filled her eyes, shining, glossy, a rainstorm held in check by the thinnest of threads, for they both knew if she spoke, the dam would burst.

Every muscle in him strained at the leash, begging to draw her into his arms and hold her forever. But this time, it would have to be of her own volition to seek his comfort, or better, to seek God's. So he held back, barely, and prayed that his words would suffice. "Are you under the impression that what you have or have not done is what gives you worth? Because that is nothing but a vile lie. God stamps His value on everyone—on you—by virtue of His grace."

The truth of his words hung in the air, ripe for the picking. Would she?

Her trembling spread, the skirts of her gown rippling slightly, but she remained silent.

So he plowed ahead. "Tell me, Johanna, is worth the real crux of why you feel you must be the saviour of this inn? Is working yourself to death some kind of atonement?"

"You don't understand," she wailed. "It's my fault. All of it!"

Her tears broke loose, washing down her cheeks until they dripped from her jaw. Though he wished to wipe them away, he clenched the hammer tighter, unwilling to stop the flow, for clearly this was a needed release.

"What do you think is your fault?" He probed carefully, quietly, not expecting her to answer but hoping she would.

Her gaze lifted to his, but he doubted she saw him. He'd seen that look before, in a criminal facing the gibbet, the ugly moment when past sins paraded and blocked out the last few breaths of life.

"I failed," she whispered. Her throat bobbed with effort as she pushed out further confessions. "I failed to tend the fire beneath the soap, and now my mother is blinded in one eye. I have failed to keep up the inn as my father asked. It's my fault I didn't get the hearth hook fixed and now Thomas is scarred." Her voice ratcheted to a keening cry. "I failed! Don't you see? I am a failure!"

She turned from him.

He reached out, staying her with a touch to her shoulder before she could scurry off. "You're wrong, you know. Just because you fail doesn't mean you are a failure. It simply means you're human."

Her backbone stiffened, as did the muscles beneath his touch. She was nothing but bone and glass. The slightest movement might shatter her to a million pieces. So he stood there, suspended, tethered to her by his fingers and the truth.

"You are too kind," she said at last.

Then grabbing up her skirts, she ran as if chased by the hounds of hell and disappeared up the stairs.

A glower carved heavy into his brow. She couldn't have been more wrong about him. There was nothing kind about loving her so deeply while agreeing to marry another. Would to God that Robbie would steal Louisa away before he was forced to sign a contract. Better yet, would that he might figure out who the wretched traitor was and be done with the whole affair.

He seized a board of lumber from the stack, and his first hammer swing collapsed the whole rickety structure. Good. Building a new puppet stage was a far better venture than cataloguing his iniquities.

He pried out former nails, banged them back into straight lines, then overhauled the whole design with a sturdier construction. At one point, a man stumbled in from the street, looking for someone named Grouper, but other than that, Alex worked alone and unhindered. The stage took on a shape he hoped would please Johanna. The desire to see her smile at his accomplishment drove him on. Just one more board and—

"It's a little crooked."

A deep voice came out of nowhere. The hammer plummeted. His thumb was smashed between wood and iron.

And he knew exactly how Johanna had felt.

"Blast!" Throwing the hammer onto the counter, he veered around and faced a dark spectre. Thatcher. He should've known. "Can you not give some kind of warning when you enter a room, man?"

Eyes black as coals glowed beneath Thatcher's hat brim. "That would defeat the purpose."

Alex threw his hands wide. "What purpose? To startle years off my life?"

"That's merely a side benefit."

"Bah!" His thumb throbbed as he stomped over to a table and sank onto the bench.

Thatcher followed, leaving a cloud of dust particles thick on the air behind him. When he sat across from Alex, a fine sprinkling sifted onto the tabletop as well. The man looked as if he'd ridden through the depths of the earth and came out the other side a piece of dirt himself.

Alex propped his hand on the table, any lower and his thumb pulsed too painfully. "Well, what have you? Surely you didn't come all this way to remark on my carpentry skills."

Thatcher loosened the kerchief at his neck and removed it, then proceeded to rub out a muscle in his shoulder. So, it had been a long ride. "You asked me to check into the viscount's background."

Alex grunted. "That bad, eh?"

"I've heard worse."

"Then why such haste?" Alex leaned across the table, shoring himself up to receive dreadful news.

A narrow flash of white grew as Thatcher smiled in full. "Even a ghost needs a drink now and then."

A drink? Alex threw his head back and laughed. The man toyed with him as surely as a cat with a rat—and he'd fallen for it.

Still chuckling, he launched from the bench and retrieved two mugs from behind the counter, then filled them from a keg already tapped. He slapped one down in front of Thatcher and eased onto his own bench. "All right. I'm listening."

Thatcher slugged back several swallows and wiped the leftover foam from his mouth.

"Coburn was part of a military force back in the eighties in India. Bengali to be exact."

Alex rifled through all he knew of East Indies intrigue—and came up shorthanded. Not that he'd let Thatcher know of his scant foreign intelligence. He met the man's gaze. "Sent to quell uprisings or some such?"

Thatcher nodded. "Coburn was good. Some say too good. Prestige has a way of going to one's head. Mix that with greed, and the combination is lethal." He paused to down another swig of his drink. "Coburn wasn't content with his conquests or his military pay grade. When a local rajah approached him, promising gold and lots of it, he sold himself to the devil. A regret I suspect he holds to this day."

Alex blew out a long breath. Coburn had hinted at past sins, and awful ones at that. "What happened?"

Thatcher swirled the liquid in his cup as he spoke. "The Rajah assigned Coburn to lead a contingent of Indian nationals and wipe out a neighboring village. Coburn had no love for the native peoples, so he took the job. But he didn't do his homework. That village contained more than Indians. There were British in residence—a fact he didn't discover until he'd already burned and killed half the population."

Alex's heart hitched a beat. If the viscount had no qualms about killing fellow citizens across the Indian Ocean, what about here? Was he the turncoat?

"Are you saying the Viscount Lord Coburn is a traitor?" Alex listened with every nerve standing at attention.

Thatcher shook his head, his dark hair brushing against his collar. "You'll find no truer loyalist. Once Coburn discovered English blood being spilled, he turned on his own contingent. He barely made it out of the village alive, or out of India when the Rajah heard of his duplicity. Your viscount had to flee the country."

He whistled, long and low. "That must've been a powerful man he crossed."

"The Rajah Bulbudder is the lineal descendant of an ancient family in Hindustani. So yes, Coburn couldn't have aligned himself with anyone of more importance."

"I suppose you don't fear the devil if you're holding his hand." Lifting his mug, he washed back Thatcher's information along with a big drink. "No wonder the viscount forbids his daughter a return visit. I hear the Indians carry a grudge as long as an elephant's memory."

"Aye, well don't get too comfortable holding the viscount's hand, either." Thatcher drained his cup and set it back onto the table. "Coburn has murdered countless innocents. He is not to be trusted."

Alex grunted. The pain in his thumb faded, replaced by a new, more urgent ache in his bones. If Coburn weren't the traitor as he'd suspected, that left either Robbie. . .or Louisa.

He was getting closer.

CHAPTER TWENTY-FIVE

Despite the scuff of clouds draping over Dover like a filthy canvas, the afternoon was most definitely yellow. Lucius Nutbrown couldn't pull his gaze off his beautiful new stockings as he strode toward the Blue Hedge Inn. And as he thought on the golden opportunity he and Nixie had dreamed up, his legs pumped faster, creating a vivid shock of colour along the dusty street.

Rounding the corner, he caught sight of a blue skirt. Fancy that! Just the other colour he'd hoped to spy. He upped his pace. "Miss Langley!"

She turned. A great brown sack in her arms sagged her shoulders. Perhaps he ought offer to carry it, but how to manage that while yanking Nixie out of his pocket? No, quite impossible. He held out his tiny friend as he approached the woman.

"My, but you're looking lovely today, Miss Langley. Mr. Nutbrown is wondering if he might have a moment of your time?" Nixie asked.

Pride swelled in Lucius's throat. How polite. How endearing. Good ol' Nix always knew just what to say and how to say it.

Miss Langley shifted her sack, ignoring Nixie and frowning at him. Sorrow panged an arrow through Lucius's heart. Why could she not see his friend? Acknowledge his presence? As much as he disliked the brutish Mr. Blackie and Mr. Charlie, at least they respected Nix.

"Very well." She sighed. "But only a moment. Come in while I drop this off."

He followed her into the taproom, but as she continued into the kitchen, he stopped—as did all his bodily functions. Breathing. Heart. Hearing, sound, feeling. No, not feeling. Tingles ran the length of him, as did a delicious warmth, bathing him from stocking tips to the sweaty part where his hat band pressed against his skull. Had he died? Was this heaven?

There, right in front of him, was the most majestic puppet stage he could ever imagine. Whitewashed wood framed red curtains with three-inch fringe dangling at the hem. Golden whorls and curlicues embellished the sides of the frame, and in a superb hand, the words *Punch and Judy* reigned above all, like a message from God written for mere mortals.

He barely acknowledged the thump-step, thump-step drawing closer to his side, until a tug at his dress coat forced him to look down.

Leaning on a crutch propped beneath his armpit, Thomas Langley grinned up at him. "She's a beauty, aye?"

Nixie whimpered. So did he. Beauty was too minuscule a description.

"Punch and Judy show tomorrow night." Thomas eyed him. "You coming?"

"Oh!" Nixie squeaked. He'd squeak too, but some of his ecstasy might leak out—and that was something he definitely wanted to savor.

He forced Nixie to look away from the glorious stage and face Master Thomas. "Yes, my fine fellow. Mr. Nutbrown wouldn't miss it for anything."

"Cost you a penny jes' to get in the door. You and Nixie." The boy thrust his chin out at Nix.

The acknowledgement vibrated through Lucius, adding pleasure upon pleasure. Indeed, there had never been a more yellow day.

Thomas lifted two fingers. "That'll mean two pennies."

"No!" Nixie shouted, stunning even Lucius. "No, no, no! A puppet show is worth at least a thruppence per head. Mr. Nutbrown shall pay the full value."

The boy's eyes widened, and well they should. It was an insult asking for a mere penny.

"Thomas, Mam needs you in the kitchen." Miss Langley swept into the taproom.

Instantly the boy's face folded into painful lines. His back hunched like a coal miner's who'd spent decades burrowing in tunnels. He gripped his crutch as if he might topple over at any minute.

"There's still a fair amount of peas to be shelled," Miss Langley continued.

"My leg pains me something awful, Jo. I need a rest, I do."

Lucius exchanged a glance with Nixie. Had his friend noticed the boy's sudden deflated tone as well? But the lad had seemed so perky only a moment ago.

"All right. But see to it you return as soon as you're able." Turning her back on the boy, she faced Lucius. "What was it you wanted, Mr. Nutbrown?"

Nixie wavered between him and Miss Langley, silent. Lucius couldn't help but follow the boy's stealthy movements, especially when the lad lifted a finger to his lips. He skirted the wall, staying out of Miss Langley's line of sight as he edged toward the front door. What a curious place to go take a rest when a perfectly good bed was to be had upstairs.

"Mr. Nutbrown, you are wasting my time."

"Hmm?" He snapped his attention back to the lady in front of him, then raised Nixie a little higher, for his poor friend had slid to an unacceptable height. "Oh yes, there is a new business opportunity Mr. Nutbrown would like to share with you."

She shook her head. "I am not interested, sir."

"Please, Miss Langley, just listen. This venture has the potential to be highly profitable." Inside Nixie's hollow head, he crossed his fingers. This had to work. It must.

"Allow me to be plain." Miss Langley stepped closer and lowered her voice. "Those men you're working with are surely smugglers. I will not entangle myself any further, no matter how profitable."

Smugglers? Ghastly wretches! Lucius tugged at his collar with his free hand, the memory of Mr. Charlie gripping his throat still lingering.

Nixie shivered. "Mr. Charlie and Mr. Blackie are a bit rough around the edges, and that is exactly why Mr. Nutbrown intends on breaking company with them."

"A wise move, sir. Now, if you'll excuse me."

Lucius shoved his hand into his pocket and pulled out a pouch of coins, making sure to jiggle it a little so the money clanked together. "Mr. Nutbrown has developed a new business enterprise, and it has nothing whatsoever to do with nefarious lawbreakers."

Miss Langley glanced at the pouch. She didn't say anything, but neither did she shove him out the door—yet. Emboldened, he bounced Nixie, drawing her attention back to his friend.

"Once Mr. Nutbrown wraps up his business with Mr. Charlie and Mr. Blackie, he plans on. . ."

Just to be on the safe side, he swiveled Nixie's head to scan the room, then pushed him closer to Miss Langley. "You will keep this confidential?"

She rolled her eyes. "I doubt anyone will ask me, but yes, I will."

Perfect! He'd clap Nixie's little hands if he didn't still have his fingers crossed. "There's unclaimed cargo down at Blisty's Warehouse, namely a load of hemp rope what would bring a good price from fishermen hereabouts. We buy the rope at a bargain, then sell it at a profit. You shall be the cheerful face of commerce, Miss Langley, selling a needed product to a worthy people. Mr. Nutbrown shall keep the books and work on finding other merchandise to sell."

A crease furrowed into the lady's brow. "Have you seen this cargo?"

"Not actually, but Mr. Nutbrown has it on good word—"

She brushed Nixie aside and jabbed her finger onto his chest. "You, my gullible friend, must learn to discern. Were that rope anything worth having, Tanny Needler would've snatched it up long ago. It's likely rat-chewed by now, and what isn't has rotted. That cargo will not be a good investment. No one will want to buy it."

Nixie pushed away the offending finger, such a true and loyal companion. "Aah, but that is exactly why Mr. Nutbrown deems this an excellent deal. The fishermen need never know the state of the product until money has first been exchanged."

"That is not honest, sir!"

Not honest? The accusation floated around but never landed, like an annoying black fly, just buzzing, buzzing, buzzing. Why would she say such a thing?

"But of course it is." Nixie shook his head, as puzzled as him. "Money is paid for goods, goods are exchanged for that money, and that *is* the heart of business."

"Mr. Nutbrown, I fear you have no heart at all, nor any sense. As much as I could use the funds, I will not take part in this offer. I am done scheming up ways to provide for my needs and instead shall leave it up to God. I suggest you do the same." She jerked her thumb over her shoulder, toward the front door. "Good day, sir."

"But—"

She shoved Nixie down, and quite forcefully, too. "I said good day, sir."

Nixie's face turned to his, defeat bowing his little chin.

With a last look at the magnificent puppet stage, Lucius tucked his money back into his pocket and sidestepped the silly woman. Clearly she was the one with no sense.

Outside, the day no longer seemed as yellow. It was dull beige, the glitter gone. The colour drained. A flat, soured buttermilk of an afternoon.

"Well, Nixie." He studied his friend's scuffed-up nose. "We gave it a good try, eh?"

Nixie's black eyes stared into his. "That we did. But without Miss Langley, how will we sell to the fisherfolk? Not many take kindly to me."

He patted his precious friend on the head, careful not to snag any of the threads on Nixie's torn jester cap. "They don't know you as I do." His voice hardened to steel, and before that hardness could work its way to his fingers, he pulled back lest he dent Nixie's skull. "But Miss Langley or not, we will prevail. We shall finish our business with the likes of Mr. Blackie and Mr. Charlie, then strike out on our own."

"Excellent." Nixie drew close, nose to nose, and whispered. "I don't like them anymore."

Lucius shuddered. "Nor do I, Nix. Nor do I."

Why was patience a virtue? Why couldn't sweet-blazing-mercy-hurry-it-up be a virtue? Alex stood at the top of the inn's stairwell, waiting, waiting, waiting. Then waiting some more. And still Johanna's blue skirt flashed at the bottom of the stairs, flitting back and forth as she served customers.

Retrieving his pocket watch, he flipped open the lid. Blast! He should've been at the viscount's half an hour ago. Even so—his lips twitched into a smirk—it would be quite the betrothal dinner without the prospective bridegroom.

He rubbed his thumb over the watch's glass face, debating which evil would be the lesser. Dressed in his new suit, clearly dandied up for a special occasion, ought he risk an inevitable run-in with Johanna down in the taproom? Or should he hazard a slip out the window with the possibility of tearing the new garments? He blew out a disgusted sigh. If Thatcher or Brentwood had a peek into his thoughts right now, the teasing would be merciless.

Behind him, footsteps clipped down the corridor. Not the thump-step of Thomas, yet the sound closed in on him from the direction of the lad's room. He turned.

Mrs. Langley stopped in front of him, cap askew, her good eye leveled straight and true on him. "Well, well. . .look at you. You're a hair overdressed for the Blue Hedge. On your way out?"

"I am." He flipped his watch lid closed but held on to the thing. Why did this old woman always make his inner little boy run off on guilty feet? Was it the directness of her questions? The motherly tone? Or did the young lad inside him instinctively know she'd crush him to her bosom in pity if he'd let her. And if he admitted he craved that pity, he'd no longer be a man but a crying ten-year-old once again.

Facing Johanna was better than facing her mother. He shoved the watch back into his pocket and took the first stair. "If you'll excuse me, I am running late."

"Good. Then you won't mind if I hold you up a minute more."

The statement stopped him cold. Since his release from gaol, the woman had avoided him. *Now* she wanted to talk?

"It won't take long. Just a few questions."

Her hook set deep in his craw. The betrothal dinner be hanged! Questions were exactly what he'd love to ask her. He pivoted and reclaimed the top stair, then followed her down the corridor to an alcove at the end of the hall.

The best defense was always offense, so he spoke first. "I thought questions were off the table, madam. You made that quite clear when you visited me in gaol."

"In your line of *work*," she drawled out the word, once again revealing she knew more of him than he did about her. "You of all people should know how quickly things change."

Hmm. . .what had changed? He rubbed his jaw, ransacking memories of the past few weeks, but nothing came to mind.

"I've heard rumours that, thus far, Johanna has not." The short lady lifted her face and impaled him with a glare. "Tell me, sir, what exactly are your intentions toward my daughter?"

A stone sunk to the bottom of his gut. What did this woman know?

Her good eye narrowed. "Do you deny your feelings for Johanna?"

"Yes. No! I—" Words stumbled like drunken sods past his lips, and he shut his mouth. Suddenly he was a boy again, being interrogated by his own mother for using his father's gun.

Father?

The sickening rock in his gut lightened. He could use this opportunity. "Very well, Mrs. Langley. A question for a question. Fair enough?"

The waning light of day leaked in the corridor's sole window, and while weak, it softened the woman's terrible gaze. "All right, but you'll answer mine first."

He sucked in a breath. Was he ready for this? Were any of them? Once spoken, his sentiment would be run up a flagpole for all to see, for words could never be refolded and shelved once expressed.

Widening his stance, he met the challenge head on. "I do not deny that I love your daughter."

There. He'd said it aloud, and despite the awkwardness of professing such deep emotion about a woman to her mother, it felt right, freeing, and he said it again. "I love Johanna with all my heart."

He studied the woman's face, expecting horror, surprise, something. But. . .nothing. The lady could sit at the viscount's table and hold her own.

"And your intentions, sir?" she pressed.

A slow smile stretched his lips. "That is not our deal, madam. The next question is mine." He lowered his voice. Why, he couldn't say. No one was around. Not up here. But even so, it seemed more respectful, almost sacred, when speaking of the hallowed dead. "What do you know of my father, Mrs. Langley?"

Though her expression didn't change, her fingers gnarled into her apron. "In part, he was my husband's associate."

Alex shook his head, trying to make some sense of the information. "But my father was a Bow Street Runner, not in the business of keeping inns."

"Oh, son, I didn't always live in Dover." The hard lines on her face ebbed away. The gleam in her eyes—even her bad one—spoke of years spent, knowledge hard earned. Love won and lost.

She sniffled, just once, then continued. "My husband, William, and I moved here from London, after a murder took place. William and his partner brought the killer in for justice. During the trial, the villain swore a blood-vengeance against those who'd put him there. The man escaped before his execution, and his threat fair shook my husband to the core every time he looked into his baby daughter's eyes. And so he left the force."

Alex gaped. "Are you saying—?"

"Tut-tut, sir." Mrs. Langley wagged her finger. "I have the next volley."

"But—"

"Mind the rules, Alex, or I shall stop the game."

His name on her lips was a smack to the backside. Once a mother, always a mother, no matter the age. He dipped his head. "After you."

"By your own witness, you love Johanna. That being said, what are your intentions? You should know I will not see the girl hurt. She's suffered enough in her young life."

The thought of Johanna's head bent in grief after her brother's injury, the tears, the cries, cut low and deep. He strained to speak past the lump in his throat. "I would never willingly hurt her. She is far too precious to me for that."

"Will you offer for her then?"

Mrs. Langley's question hit him like a boom gone wild, knocking the air from his lungs. Of course he would, in a heartbeat, were he not even now on his way to his own betrothal dinner.

The woman's good eye narrowed, as if she could read into the darkest recesses of his soul.

"No," he said, "I will not answer that question. With our first round complete, we shall have to continue this game another time, Mrs. Langley. As I've said, I am late."

She was silent for a moment, creases etching the sides of her mouth, making it hard to cipher if she were disappointed, angry, or simply amused.

"Then Godspeed to you, wherever it is you're going. I look forward to another round at your convenience."

He schooled his step to keep from running down the hall. Though the match had clearly been a draw, why did he feel like the loser?

CHAPTER TWENTY-SIX

The taproom was a boil of people, bubbling chatter, men bobbing about, air thick and hot and altogether uncomfortable. But even with so many patrons, not many extra coins for the inn's coffers surfaced. Standing near the side window, where the last flames of sunset cast an orange glow against the glass, Johanna arched her back, then bent to wipe another table. She ought be tapping into another keg by now, but hardly any customers were interested in ale. Most gawked at the finished puppet stage. She should've charged an entrance fee just to look at the thing.

Across the room, a flash of burgundy moved at the corner of her eye, and Johanna turned her face toward the rich colour. Immediately, she straightened and gaped, openly, for her jaw would not shut. The rag slipped from her fingers. Without a word or a glance, Alexander commanded her attention.

He strode the length of the taproom in a tailcoat the hue of fine wine, but it wasn't his suit that attracted. It was him. The man. The way each of his steps pounded with determination on his way toward the door. He didn't have to weave through villagers or skirt past anyone. People simply moved from his path.

Wishing away all the sweaty men who blocked her view, Johanna leaned sideways, unwilling to lose sight of him.

Alexander Morton was a king, so regal his bearing, so powerful his stride. His buff trousers were well tailored, the muscles beneath defining the suit instead of the suit defining the man. His hair was brushed back, and as he passed by a sconce, lantern light gleamed streaks as gold as a crown atop his head. His jaw was clean-shaven, creating a strong line above an ivory cravat. And before he disappeared out the door, he clapped a beaver hat atop his head, adding to his height so that he had to stoop when he crossed the threshold.

Johanna dashed to the window, all but pressing her face to the glass, and strained for a last look at him. Sunset sat upon his shoulders, the breadth of them wide enough to hold up the sky. He hefted himself up into a shiny, black carriage, and when the door shut behind him, she gasped at the sudden loss.

She turned from the sight before the coach rolled off. It was too bittersweet a picture. Of course he must attend to his father's business, and the Blue Hedge was not the place to conduct such commerce. It made perfect sense. But all the same, she wished she might put on a pretty gown and join him.

La! Silly girl.

She snatched up her rag and wound through the tables. Maybe if she fried up a fresh pot of pork cracklings, she could tempt some appetites and put her mind on something other than Alex. Aah, but he had been a glorious sight. The stuff of dreams, and one she hoped would revisit her tonight when her head hit the pillow. Wherever he was going, he would surely be the most striking gentleman of all and—

"Oh!" On reflex, she reached out and grabbed Mam's arm to keep her from toppling to the kitchen floor, for she'd run right into her. "Sorry, Mam! I didn't see you."

"Apparently not." Mam's puckered brow smoothed. "No harm done, though. Better you bumped into me than one of those big men out there." She hitched her thumb over her shoulder.

"Yes, well, it's those men I'm hoping to coax some coins from. Thought I'd fry up some cracklin's."

"Good thought. I'll put on the pot of fat."

Jo strode to the crockery of salted rinds and retrieved a bowl full, then set about cutting the pork into smaller bits. While she worked, Mam hummed a folk tune. The melody soon faded, though, as memories of Alexander in his fine suit reinvaded Jo's thoughts. He was so kind. So thoughtful. She'd never met a man like him before, not one of his standing who'd even deign to give her a second look. For the first time in her life, she wished to be something other than a mere innkeeper's daughter.

The blade slipped. Red bloomed in a thin line on her finger, wider by the moment. Dropping the knife, she huffed her disgust and reached for a cloth.

"Johanna!" Mam scooted over to her. "Here, let me do that. What's got you this addle-brained tonight?"

"I. . ." She stepped aside, allowing Mam to chop the rinds. She couldn't very well tell her mother she wasn't thinking straight because of a well-dressed man.

She sighed—again—afraid to admit out loud that truly it was more than smart clothing that befuddled her. It was Alex. He permeated everything and had since the day she'd fallen into his arms. Whew. She fanned her face. The heat of the taproom must've followed her into the kitchen.

"I can see, girl, there's something—or rather someone—on your mind."

Meeting her mother's gaze, she swallowed. What would Mam think if she told her?

"Oh, Johanna." Mam set down the knife and pulled her into her arms. "You've got it bad, don't you?"

"You were right, Mam. You were right all along." She returned her mother's embrace. The top of Mam's head came just to cheek level, and Jo laid her face against her mother's mobcap. "Mr. Morton is a good man. He's a perfectly wonderful man."

"Humph." Her mother pulled back and returned to chopping the rinds, giving the next piece a great whack. She mumbled while she worked, something that sounded like, "I hope so."

Jo cocked her head. Surely she hadn't heard that right. "What was that?"

Mam paused with the blade in the air. "I said I hope so many patrons won't tire you out. Looks to be a full house tonight."

"It is. Though the puppet show isn't until tomorrow night, word has spread." Unwrapping the cloth, she peered at her injury, still leaking red, then rewrapped it. "Mr. Nutbrown sang the praises of the stage from one end of Dover to the next, and now everyone wants a peek at it. Didn't Mr. Morton do a brilliant job on the construction? He is so handsome—I mean handy. He is so handy." She bit her tongue, hard, to keep the thing from further blunders. Hopefully Mam had missed that one.

"Johanna, please." Mam scooped rinds back into the bowl, then searched Jo's face with her good eye. "Be careful."

Despite the warmth in the room, she shivered at the flatness in Mam's voice. Alarm throbbed through her, settling in the cut on her finger. "About what?"

"Just. . .have a care for your heart, my dear. I wouldn't want to see it broken."

"Why are you telling me this?" Her words came out tied on a frayed thread of a whisper.

"Because I'm your mother." Mam reached up and tweaked her cheek, her good humour clearly returning. "And you will do the same for your daughter when the time comes."

She shook her head. "I am already five and twenty. Marriage isn't likely."

"Don't be too sure about that."

"You are very cryptic tonight." She peered at her mother. Who knew what secrets she kept tucked beneath that mobcap? "Is there something I should know about?"

Mam clicked her tongue. A smile broad as a beam lit her face, before she turned her back and toddled over to the hearth.

But Johanna wasn't fooled. Mam knew more than she let on—and it more than likely involved Alexander.

"Are you finished, sir?"

The question rattled around inside Alex's skull like pebbles in a tin can. He was finished all right—with the cloying odor of too much perfume, the congratulations of Dover's finest society gathered around the table for dinner, and especially done with this whole loathsome marriage charade. Tonight he would gather new information about the traitor, or die in the trying—which was one way out of this whole mess.

He leaned back in his chair and speared the servant with a direct stare. "Yes, I am. Thank you."

His untouched plate of lobster cakes swimming in béchamel sauce vanished from in front of him, and he reached for his glass—which was as empty as his soul. The conversation with Johanna's mother had drained him more than he cared to acknowledge. Despite the beautiful Louisa Coburn seated next to him, every time he looked at her, all he could see was Johanna's face and hear her mother's question.

"Will you offer for her?"

He held up his glass. "Refill, please."

Across the table, Robbie mimicked his action, then pushed back his chair and stood. "Attention!" He tapped his goblet with the edge of a spoon. "A toast!" Robbie directed his glass toward Louisa. "To the fairest of the fair, the honorable Miss Louisa Coburn. May you bloom radiant in marriage, like one of the many flowers in your garden."

A round of, "Hear, hear!" circled the table like a chant.

"And to you, my fine fellow and soon-to-be cousin-in-law." Robbie angled his cup toward Alex, the flush of his face indicating he'd had more than enough wine already. "May you find satisfaction with the prize that is sure to be yours."

Most guests smiled and tipped back their glasses, but a few brows scrunched at the cryptic tribute, wheels spinning fast to figure it out. Only he and Louisa could possibly know the meaning—and she gave the loudest, "Hear, hear!" of all.

Not to be outdone, the viscount stood. The movement—or perhaps his glower—drove Robbie back to his chair.

Lord Coburn cleared his throat, then bowed to his daughter and Alex in turn. "To the happy couple, despite the turbulence of the times, I wish you a life of peace."

This time there were a few *amen*s.

Flipping out his tails, the viscount sat. Heads swiveled toward Alex, closing his throat. He'd have to say something. But what? This was not the right time, the right place, and definitely not the right woman that he wanted to speak highly of.

Slowly, he stood on legs that felt a-sea and forced a smile. "To the beautiful Louisa, a bride any man ought to cherish and dote upon. And"—he turned toward the viscount—"to Lord Coburn, a force to be reckoned with—especially at the card table."

Laughter filled the room. Even the viscount chuckled.

Alex tossed back his drink and sat while everyone went back to chattering. This was supposed to be a happy night, as evidenced by the merriness of those around him. But happiness for him was out of reach, even if he strained to grasp it. He stifled a groan, though he needn't have bothered. No one would've heard him anyway. What a sham. What a sorry, wicked, farce he played out, sitting next to the woman he was to marry while only hours ago professing love for another.

Louisa's fingers appeared on his sleeve, and she gave his arm a little squeeze. "Don't look so glum. This will soon be over."

He grunted. "Sooner than you think."

"Oh?" Her gaze sought his.

Setting down his glass, he absently ran his finger around the rim. "Apparently you're not aware your father has decided to skip the banns and has attained a bishop's license ready for me to sign—tonight."

The whites of Louisa's eyes expanded, much like a horse pushed to extreme excitement. "But you cannot!"

He shrugged. What else was there to do? If he could get Robbie alone, he could plead with the man to elope with Louisa tonight—but the fellow had been as slippery as a cutpurse in a crowd. Alex sank back in his chair. Even if he did persuade Robbie, that would defeat the purpose of Ford's assignment. He couldn't very well let the two he suspected most escape at large. No matter which outcome, none were good.

Louisa pulled back her hand. "Well I certainly will not sign such a thing."

She was a spitfire, he'd give her that. "I'm afraid, sweet Louisa, that you already have."

She frowned, and for a moment her eyes glittered cold and shrewd. "What do you mean?"

"Your father signed it for you."

She tapped her lip with a perfectly manicured nail. "We'll see about that."

"Now, now." A large grey-haired lady—the major general's wife—bustled over, stationing herself between them. She smelled of far too much rose water mixed with the leftover scent of pork. "The time for lovers' whispers is not yet. Come along, Louisa. Take leave of your man."

Louisa smiled at the woman, though she spoke under her breath for him to hear. "There's nothing I'd like better."

Alex watched all the painted ladies with their swishing skirts disappear out the door, leaving the men behind with their port. Some stood and arched their backs. A few immediately broke out large cigars from glass cylinders they'd been pocketing. The viscount and Major General Overtun secreted themselves off to a far corner, backs toward the rest of the company and clearly engrossed in some sort of espionage. Alex smirked at the thought, but then leaned forward. Perhaps he'd not been so far off the mark, judging by the way they bowed their heads together. The two hardly spoke even when given the opportunity at the gaming table and were total opposites in personality and stature. So why the bosom friendship?

Robbie's voice pulled him from his thoughts. At the far end of the table, the man had gathered the rest of the gentlemen, and was currently embellishing a ribald tale of his conquest of Lucy Starr, a known slattern over on Parson Lane.

Despite being in a room full of people, emptiness washed over Alex like a North Sea breaker, drowning the life from him. Air. He needed air and lots of it. Taking great care to edge back his chair without garnering any looks, he stood and skirted the table, sticking close to the wall. He moved on silent feet, and had nearly gained the door when a deep voice stopped him on the threshold.

"No matter how crafty you are, you'll not be able to steal Louisa away from the women."

Blast! He turned to face Lord Coburn.

The viscount clapped him on the back. "But I would steal you away. Won't take long."

The man bypassed him into the hall and led him up to the first floor. Alex followed, knowing the way to the man's study by rote. Each step carried him farther from the party below—and from any chance he might've had with Johanna.

Lord Coburn ushered him into his private quarters, then closed the door and strode over to his desk. "Might as well get this part of the deed done, eh?" He held out a pen like a sword.

A cold sweat broke out on Alex's brow. This was it. The moment he'd either lose or gain all, but this time it wasn't a trifling pot of gaming money on the line. It was his life. He'd never before gambled what he could not afford to lose. Was the gain really worth the risk this time?

"Having second thoughts?"

He met the viscount's gaze. "Yes, actually."

"Excellent." A slow smile curved Lord Coburn's mouth like a scythe. "I'd worry if you didn't."

Sucking in a breath, Alex forced his legs to carry him across the room. The marriage license lay on the desk like a mantrap, ready to snap him in half if he got too close. But what were his options? Renege and lose all the confidence he'd built with the viscount? Sign away the rest of his life? Or pray for a lightning bolt to take him out now? He'd been in hard places before, but never one as deadly as this. Blast Ford for being such a high-handed employer!

He grabbed the pen, his grasp nearly cracking it in two. Signing this document was far more than any occupation ought to require—and therein lie the crux of why he stayed when every muscle in him screamed to run off. He owed Ford more than merely being a dutiful employee. He owed him his life for taking him in after his parents' brutal murder.

Swallowing a bitter taste, he bent and signed his name, then threw the pen down. The only thing to save him now was that hopefully this document wouldn't stand in a court of law with the pseudonym of Morton.

The viscount shoved a glass tumbler into his hand. "Here."

He slugged it back—then immediately coughed. A trail of fire burned from mouth to gut.

Lord Coburn smirked. "I thought you'd appreciate an aged cognac."

Alex thumped his chest with his fist, balancing out the pain. "Indeed."

The viscount sank into one of the chairs near the hearth. "I took the liberty of setting the date for the wedding one week from today. That gives Louisa enough time—and me, for I have some preparations of my own which need tending before that."

"Oh?" Setting his glass on the desk, he took the other chair and was glad for the support. His head was starting to spin, a distinct disadvantage when it appeared the man was finally going to say something of importance.

"I'm expecting a shipment to arrive on July third." Flames from the hearth painted a hellish glow on the viscount's face. "I should like you to join me in seeing that it arrives safely."

"A shipment of what?" It took all his strength not to lean forward. Appearing too eager might shut the man down entirely.

Lord Coburn swirled the brandy around in his glass for a long time—long enough that Alex was glad he hadn't held his breath or he'd be blue in the face.

"Better that you don't know," the viscount said at last. "Just in case."

"In case of what?"

"As I've said. . .I have many enemies about. If you were to be targeted because of me, ignorance could be your best asset."

He grit his teeth. It was far better to see what demon you faced than come up against one blindfolded. "My lord—"

The viscount held up his hand. "Edward."

"Edward, I assure you I am capable of dealing with enemies. If you want my help, then you're going to have to be straightforward."

The swirling stopped. The glass clinked onto the table. The viscount leaned forward, his dark eyes studying every inch of Alex's face. "You're not bluffing."

Alex angled his head. "No, I am not."

"Very well. Your blood be on your own hands then, if it comes to that."

"I would have it no other way."

"Well, then. . ." The viscount deflated back into his seat, the leather shifting beneath his weight. "On the morning of the third, meet me here just after daybreak. We'll ride to Ramsgate to meet a ship arriving from Woolwich. Your job is to keep a sharp eye out and have your gun handy along the way. Not that I'm anticipating trouble, but one never knows with Boney's minions about. Nasty little infiltrators." He clicked his tongue as if expelling a seed from his teeth. "We board the ship to ensure it arrives safely in Dover before sunrise, which gives you plenty of time to freshen up before a ten o'clock wedding ceremony later that morning. Is that straightforward enough?"

Alex mulled over the information. It was the most the viscount had fed him at one time, but a queer aftertaste remained. "Why me?" he asked. "Surely a redcoat accompaniment would provide better protection. Why not have your friend the major general supply you with a few good soldiers?"

"And draw attention?" Lord Coburn shook his head. "No, you and I alone. We'll simply be two dockhands on the road to Ramsgate, looking for employment opportunity. So dress appropriately. No finery."

Risky—yet not surprising. The viscount was particularly dodgy at the gaming table. Why not in life?

"All right," Alex conceded. "I understand. This shipment must be very profitable to assume such great personal risk."

"Oh, I assure you, it's more than personal. It's of national value. So what do you say?" Lord Coburn's gaze burned into his. "Can I count on you?"

Of national import? This was intriguing—and perhaps may be the very reason Ford had sent him here to begin with. Though the viscount still hadn't divulged the cargo, once aboard, Alex could surely slip away and sneak a peek. Bag the traitor. Dodge the marriage.

He quirked a brow at the man. "Absolutely. I'm your man."

CHAPTER TWENTY-SEVEN

Blowing an errant curl from her damp brow, Johanna filled two more pitchers and elbowed her way back into the crowded taproom. Even after a full night's sleep and a busy day preparing for this evening's Punch and Judy performance, she still hadn't been ready for this onslaught. Half of Dover crammed into the public room. The puppet show had yet to begin, and already her feet ached abominably, her apron strings hung half tied, and her hair drifted down her back. From now on she'd take better care of what she wished for.

She topped off half-empty mugs, collected more coins, then retraced her steps to the kegs. As much as she hated to admit it, she had to give Mr. Quail credit. His idea attracted more customers than the Blue Hedge had seen since her father died. But would the profit be enough to pay off Mr. Spurge?

Please, God, make it so.

She prayed silently as she shoved her way through the crowd. Nearest the stage, Mr. Nutbrown sat at attention on a bench, front and center, his little puppet quivering at the end of his arm. Now and then, when the stage curtain rippled from a jostling by Mr. Quail or one of his men behind it, Mr. Nutbrown let out a small cry. A dog with a mutton chop couldn't have been more delighted. Hopefully he'd be able to restrain himself and not join the puppeteers. But who knew? Perhaps that would be as entertaining.

From this angle, she stood on tiptoe and scanned from head to head, looking for two in particular. One golden brown, and the other with a shock of hair above a freckled face. She frowned. No sight of Alex or Thomas. If they didn't hurry, they'd miss the show.

Skirting the room as best she could, she worked her way back and was just even with the front door when it flung wide. A spray of freckles hobbled in on a crutch, accompanied by a golden-topped mountain of a man.

Johanna quirked her brow at them. "I was beginning to worry about you two."

"Aw, Jo." Thomas screwed up his mouth as if he sucked dry a lemon. "Quit bein' such a girl."

"Aah, but she can be no less. She is too beautiful to be otherwise." Alex tussled the boy's hair, then faced her with a slow grin. "My apologies. On our way back from posting the last of the handbills, I stopped off for this."

He held out his hand. A small, wrapped package sat atop his palm.

She looked from the brown wrapper into his brilliant blue eyes. "What is it?"

Alex cocked a brow. "Only one way to find out, hmm?"

Cradling her empty pitcher with one arm, she reached for the gift. A single string held the paper together. She tugged it loose and poked the paper aside with her finger. The scent of roses wafted out, a welcome diversion from the sweaty patrons.

"Rose petal soap," she murmured, then shot her gaze back to Alex. "What's this for?"

"A good soak will be just the thing after this." He swept out his hand, indicating the clamoring customers. "Don't you think?"

She blinked, completely tongue-tied. Had ever a man treated her so kindly? With so much consideration and thoughtfulness? He'd taken his time, his money, to stop at a store with the sole purpose of purchasing her a comfort item, that at the end of the night she might strip off her soiled clothing and—

Fire blazed across her cheeks. Had he thought of her undressed in a tub of water?

He leaned close, the warmth of his breath whispering across her ear lobe. "Exactly the effect I was hoping for."

The rogue! She retreated a step and lifted her chin. "I am sure I don't know what you mean."

"The show's about to start." Thomas tugged at her apron. "Did you save us seats?"

She frowned down at him. "Look about you, Thomas. Do you really think I had the time?"

"Not to worry. You shall have a great view." Alex bent and hoisted Thomas up to his shoulders, then winked at her. "I didn't really want to see it anyway."

Wedging his way past her and the other guests, he gave Thomas the ride of his life.

Johanna couldn't help but smile at the man, the boy, and the soap in her hand.

"Miss!"

A call from a back table turned her around. "Coming."

But her steps slowed as she passed two ladies seated next to one another, deep in conversation, for one of them pointed at Alex.

"That's him. That's the one!"

The woman beside her shook her head, the netting holding up her hair jiggling from the movement. "Can't be. Yer daft."

The first lady leaned forward, squinted, then sat back. "I'm certain of it. He's the man. My sister were in attendance last night and told me all about it. Quite the affair."

Johanna edged closer.

The hair-netted lady reared back her head. "Law! What she doin' rubbing shoulders with the likes o' such?"

"She's one o' the hired help at the manor whene'er a big affair is afoot."

Though empty, the pitcher in Johanna's arms weighed her down heavy with guilt. She ought be serving patrons and collecting coins, not listening to two gossipmongers rattling on.

Laughter rang out from the first lady's mouth. "You know when it comes to men, she's got a keen eye. Take a look for yerself. She told me that the man had eyes the brilliance of a June sky, hair the colour of honey taken fresh off the comb, and he were tall and broad enough to make a brigand think twice before aiming a muzzle his way."

The other lady's eyes widened. "Sure looks like him."

Jo agreed.

"O' course it is." The first lady elbowed her friend. "She got a good gander at him, 'specially when he stood in front of God and man and gave his speech."

"Miss! O'er here!"

Duty called, but so did the lure of these two women speaking about her Alex. She froze. *Her* Alex? Where had that come from?

"They'll make a handsome couple," the hair-net lady said. "But one wonders why he boards here."

Couple? Her stomach clenched. Surely she hadn't heard right. On the pretense of passing the ladies, she circled to the back of them, then leaned close.

"That'll change. The viscount's daughter wouldn't set a slippered toe in this place." The first lady chuckled. "She'll be leading him around on a leash in no time."

Sickened, Johanna darted back to the kegs. Such chinwagging natter! It had to be. Nothing but pure, wicked rumours that couldn't be true. With a huff, she shoved the soap into her pocket.

Though it would explain why Alex had looked so fine when he'd left the inn last night.

Funny how dismantling things always took less time than the building—in puppet stages or in life. Alex smirked at the thought as he pried out nail after nail, demolishing the stage. The leftover stench of so many bodies lingered on the air, but at least it was silent now.

While he worked, Johanna bustled between kitchen and taproom, clearing away the last of the mugs and straightening chairs. It was a companionable rhythm they labored in, and for some reason, it caused an exquisite ache deep in his soul.

The front door swung wide, and in stumbled Quail, breaking the magic of the moment, especially when he lurched over to Alex.

"Ha ha!" He spread his arms wide. "Now here's a man of hidden talents. A wine merchant, a carpenter"—the tang of rum travelled on the man's breath as he leaned closer—"and a soon-to-be bridegroom."

Straightening, Alex shot a glance around the taproom. Thankfully Johanna was in the kitchen for the moment.

He faced Quail. "That was a fine show you put on. Didn't think you had it in you." Shoving a finger into Quail's chest, he pushed him back. "I wonder what other talents you're hiding."

"Nothing for you to worry your pretty head over. And speaking of pretty heads. . ." Quail's dark eyes brightened as they followed Johanna's reappearance into the taproom. "Have you told her yet?"

Clenching the hammer, he fought to keep from swinging the thing at Quail's head just to shut him up. He narrowed his eyes at the fellow. "Didn't you say you'd be leaving once this puppet show was done?"

"A week more, then I'm gone." He shrugged. "And what of you?"

He glowered at the man. "That's none of your affair."

"Affair? How apropos." Quail shifted a knowing glance from him to Johanna, then staggered back a step and slapped one hand to his chest. The other he held up in the air, a Shakespearean pose—one that crawled under Alex's skin. "Many a true word hath been spoken in jest."

Tossing down the hammer, Alex grabbed the fool by the collar. "I am not jesting. Stay out of my business."

He released him, and an interesting transformation took place. A thunderhead darkened Quail's face, all signs of mirth—and drunkenness—vanished and was replaced with a deadly stare. Quail's voice lowered, his words sharp as a lance. "I haven't the time for the thrashing you deserve, but you'll meet your comeuppance one day. And I shall be glad to hear of it."

He stalked past Alex and disappeared up the stairs, boots pounding the planks.

Setting down her cloth, Johanna strolled over to Alex. Even after an evening of racing about, waiting on customers, she looked lovelier than ever with her skin aglow and hair loosened to fringe her face. Her fresh innocence stabbed him like a knife in the back—for that's exactly what his announcement would do to her when he told her of his engagement.

And he'd have to now, before Quail bandied the news about.

"Mr. Quail looks none too pleased." She quirked a brow at him. "What was that about?"

"You know Quail. Nothing but drama. It's in his blood." He tried to turn away from her, to avoid telling her what he must, but heaven help him, he couldn't. He knew that. He just didn't know how. Helplessness spread over him like a rash.

She smiled, brilliant enough to shame an August sun. "But he did do an excellent job. We are well on our way to paying Mr. Spurge."

He couldn't help but smile back. "I am happy for it."

She stepped closer, so near, the heat of her lit a fire in his belly.

"There is...something..." For a moment she looked away, as if she might find the courage to speak from the corner of the room. Maybe if he looked there too, he'd find a store of bravery to tell her about Louisa.

"What I mean to say is..." Straightening her shoulders, she met his gaze head-on. "There's something I must ask you, Alex—"

She clapped a hand to her mouth.

He chuckled. Such a prim little miss. Reaching, he pulled away her hand, and against his better judgment, did not let go. "Don't be so mortified. I rather like hearing my name pass over your lips."

Scarlet blazed a flush on her cheeks, and her hand trembled in his grip. "What you must think of me."

He bent close. "Would you like to know?"

"Yes." Her voice was nothing more than a fairy's breath, altogether too alluring.

War waged in his chest, heart pumping blood and guilt and desire. Wisdom screamed to step away, put space between them, tell her of his duplicity then walk off. He should, and he would, but now? Impossible, not with the way hope and yearning intensified the brown in her eyes.

He lifted her hand to his mouth. "I think you are kind." He kissed her pinky. "You are strong." His lips moved to her ring finger. "None compare to your beauty—"

"Not so," she interrupted. "Especially not now."

He pressed his mouth to her middle finger. "That is exactly what I find most attractive about you." Her index finger melted against his lips. "You do not flaunt your loveliness." He finished by pressing a kiss into the middle of her palm, then lowered her hand, hating himself for what he must say next. "Johanna, there's something I must tell you."

"Oh, Alex." His name was a quiver between them. A promise. A vow.

He had to end this. Now. "You need to know I—"

"I love you." She launched forward and pulled his mouth to hers.

Her body moved against him with the heat of a thousand fires, and he staggered from the force—of the kiss, of his desire, of the knowledge he'd already signed a document pledging himself to another. This was wrong in so many ways, on so many levels, too many to count.

And far too impossible to withstand, especially when she fit herself against him.

"Johanna," he whispered against the lobe of her ear, the bend of her neck, the bare skin at the curve of her collarbone. A groan, primal and hungry, rumbled in his chest. This was the woman he wanted, the one he must have, with a need that would not be mastered. A shudder tore through him from head to toe.

"Johanna—" His voice broke, and he gently set her from him. Everything in him screamed to profess his love to her, as she had for him, but he couldn't. It wasn't fair. It wasn't right.

The passion in her gaze rose bile to his throat. The gleam of her smile, with lips yet swollen from his kiss, punched him in the gut.

She reached, and with a touch so tender it cut him to shreds, she placed her palm on his cheek. "I never thought to be this happy—is this a dream? Are you a dream?"

No. He was a vile, filthy scoundrel of the worst degree.

His fingers shook as he gently pulled her hand from his face. The question in the bend of her brow shattered his heart. He'd never be the same.

And neither would she, not after he crushed her with the words he must speak. Sucking in a breath, he retreated a step. In wagering that he could extract himself from an engagement to Louisa, he knew now—and without doubt—that he'd lose the beauty in front of him. Would to God that he'd never thought otherwise in the first place or things might've been different.

"Alex?"

He memorized her sweet tone, the way her lips moved when his name whispered over them, for it would be the last time she ever spoke his name in love.

"Johanna," his ragged voice violated the sanctity of what had been. "I am engaged to another. We are to marry by week's end."

CHAPTER TWENTY-EIGHT

Dazed, worn, cheeks chapped by tears and throat sore from crying, Johanna sat in the stable yard on an upturned barrel, staring at the sky. The sun had risen not long ago—maybe. Hard to tell with an underbelly of grey clouds dragging low. Had she a pin, she'd poke a hole in them to release a torrent. But would that do any good? She'd sat here crying all night and didn't feel the better for it.

Clenching her shawl tight at the neck, she hung her head, glad the sun didn't gloat on her sorrow. Better if it didn't show its face, for she never wanted to see it—or Alex—again. *Oh, Alex.* What a fool she'd been. Her heart constricted, and she folded deeper and lower, hunched like an elder ready to fall into a grave.

The kitchen door creaked, but it took too much effort to lift her head. So she sat, listening to footsteps grow louder but helpless to acknowledge whoever it was that drew near.

"Johanna?"

Mam's voice wavered—or had her hearing begun to shut down as well?

"Oh, my girl."

Arms wrapped around her, tucking her close.

"My precious, only girl." Mam crooked her finger beneath Jo's chin, forcing her to meet her gaze. "What has you in such a state?"

She worked her jaw, but nothing came out.

"Jo?" Her mother peered closer, her good eye searching for truth.

"Alex—" Johanna shuddered. Just saying his name cut sharp. "Alex is to be married." The awful words stabbed so deeply, she winced.

But it was the sagging of Mam's brows, the quivering downturn of her lips that undid her.

She wilted into Mam's arms and buried her face in her mother's shoulder. Grief, sorrow, pain so awful it was not to be borne surged out until her tears waned—and then another, stronger flow convulsed her again.

"I was wrong, Mam," she cried. "I was so wrong about him. I thought he loved me. I truly did. He's nothing but a liar, just like Father."

"In some ways he is—but in many more he is not. Don't be so hasty, my love."

Her tears stopped. The sniffles didn't. Between shaky breaths, she listened hard, waiting for Mam to explain herself, but her mother simply continued to rub a big circle on her back.

Finally, she withdrew and looked at Mam. "What do you mean?"

"Well..." Her mouth quirked, not a smile, for that would be irreverent, but a definite movement nonetheless. "He's not married yet, is he?"

Johanna broke away and set her feet in the rut she'd worn in the dirt from pacing the long night away. "You don't understand."

"Then tell me."

She plodded her way to the broken hay rake then back to the barrel. Again and again. Taking up the cadence she'd developed from hours of practice. Perhaps if she focused on her steps, the words would come easier. "I've never loved a man in this way. I never even knew what love was. Last night I. . .I gave my whole heart to Alex, just handed it right over, and he shattered it into a thousand pieces." She stopped and faced Mam. "What kind of man does that?"

"One who is as confused as you."

Her jaw dropped. Surely Mam wasn't suggesting Alex had been less than brutal. A hundred retorts burned on her tongue.

"Tut-tut. Let me speak." Mam wagged a finger at her. "I suspect it was as excruciating for Alex to tell you of his betrothal as it was for you to hear."

Unbelievable! Her mother stood there defending the man who'd caused her such pain? She threw out her arms. "How can you say that to me? I am your daughter! Should you not care about my broken heart? It hurts, Mam!" She clasped her hands and wrung them, scraping flesh upon flesh, bone upon bone. "It hurts so much."

"I know, my sweet. Well do I know." Mam closed in on her, wrapping one arm around her waist and leading her back to the barrel. With gentle pressure, she guided her to sit.

"It is hard to believe now, Johanna, but love gets easier once the heart is broken. It's a casting away of the shell. Of course it hurts. It's meant to. But broken things are always the beginning of better things. A plant could not grow without first the ground being broken. The most plentiful yields come from a field ravaged by a plow."

The anger she'd been simmering all night boiled into a rage. "I don't care! I don't care about fields or plants or anything. I can't. If that's what love is about, I'll have none of it—ever again."

Mam gathered Jo's hands into her work-worn fingers. Veins spidered blue across the backs of them, tracks enlarged by years of hard living and labor. "Take care, my dear, for your words smack of bitterness."

"I am bitter." Her voice sounded as petulant as a toddler—and she didn't care one whit. "I am angry and ragged and torn. How can God stand by and watch this happen to me?"

"Johanna." With a single word, Mam rebuked more soundly than a month's worth of sermons. "God is not sitting about, watching impassive. Our tears are His. You never—ever—cry alone." She reached and tucked a loose coil of hair behind Jo's ear. "You must bring your broken heart to God—or your broken heart will make you leave Him. What will you do?"

A sigh—as sharp as the pinprick she'd wished for earlier to poke the sky with—deflated her shoulders. "I don't know, Mam. I just don't know."

"It's all right, my girl. Sometimes answers don't come easy. But I intend to uncover a few." Mam turned on her heel, her lopsided gait pounding toward the kitchen door.

Jo stood. "Where are you going?"

Mam glanced over her shoulder, her good eye gleaming. "To strike up a little conversation."

Morning light crept in the window on tentative feet. Alex couldn't blame its weak entrance. If given the choice, he wouldn't want to keep company with himself either. He flung the pillow he'd cursed all night across the room and sat up, fully clothed. Why he'd even bothered to try to sleep annoyed him further. Every time he closed his eyes, all he saw was the shattered, horrified pain in Johanna's eyes. Hurt put there by him. In all his years as a Bow Street officer, he'd locked up many a lesser villain than the scoundrel he'd become. This time he'd gambled everything—and lost.

A rap on his door drew him to his feet. He'd not heard heavy footsteps, so it was a woman, most likely. He'd bet five to one it was Johanna, wanting an explanation, or maybe wanting to vent her wrath. His heart plummeted to the floor, and were it visible, he'd stomp on the thing. When he'd told her last night he was to be wed, the blood drained from her face until he feared she might swoon, then without a word, she'd turned and walked away. No screaming. No tears. No anything. Rage of that caliber had to blow sooner or later. It appeared the time was now—and he deserved every bit of it. Steeling himself, he yanked open the door.

Piercing brown eyes sparked up at him beneath a mobcap.

"Mrs. Langley." His head dipped, driven downward by respect and shame and guilt. He'd prepared for battle with the daughter, not the mother. His stomach roiled like the one—and only—time he'd taken too much libations and was sorry for it the morning after.

"I can only assume this is about Johanna," he mumbled. Apparently even his voice wanted nothing to do with him today either.

"No, it is about you." She bustled past him, forcing him to either step back or be flattened, then she shoved the door shut. "Can you think of a more secure place to talk?"

"No." He dragged over the single chair gracing the room and offered it to her, then sat opposite the woman on the corner of his bed. Her all-knowing gaze, the kind only a mother could produce, sagged his shoulders. He looked at the floorboards. "I'll be leaving today, but before I go, you must know I never meant to hurt your daughter. I hate what I've done to her."

"And I hate what Ford is doing to you."

He jerked up his head, the direction of her words nearly whiplashing him.

One side of her mouth curved. "I thought as much. If you intend to marry Louisa Coburn for the sake of a directive, then you're stepping beyond the bounds of being a good officer into a foolish one."

Stunned, he worked his jaw, but was hardly able to formulate questions in his mind let alone speak any. He shook his head, completely at a loss. "No more games, Mrs. Langley. Please."

She folded her hands in her lap, calmly, as if she weren't addressing the reprobate who'd broken her daughter's heart. "I was young once, beautiful, like Johanna. And just like her, I fell in love with a Bow Street officer."

"At least you and your husband had a happily ever after."

"I wasn't speaking of my husband."

His eyes shot wide. This lady, who ran an upstanding if not ramshackle inn, had dallied with another man?

She chuckled. "Oh, it's not that I didn't love William, for I did, but in a different way than I loved Richard."

Surely she didn't mean. . .but of course. It made sense, if not in a twisted fashion. He leaned forward, the straw tick crunching beneath him. "Richard Ford?"

She nodded. "Richard was never satisfied with mere officer status. He wanted more, to become a magistrate, which was an impossibility for he held no land. He would need an act of parliament. When a high-paying assignment involving an MP came up, he took it, no questions asked, hoping to garner favor from the man." Her lower lip quivered, and she shut her eyes. "The reckless fool."

They sat in silence, save for the muted snores from down the hall. Mrs. Langley's mouth pinched, little ruffles of skin tightening together in fine pleats. Whatever she remembered couldn't be pleasant.

"And the assignment was?" he prompted.

Her eyes fluttered open, and she smoothed her hands along her apron. "Richard was to deliver the MP's daughter safely to her mother, a colonial who'd returned home months earlier. Shortly after setting sail, Richard took ill. Unattended by necessity, the girl was ravished and left unable to identify the attacker. By the time they landed, she knew she was not only ruined, but with child. Richard blamed himself, of course, for such is his strong call to duty. So, risking his own happiness, he married the girl. When I received his letter, I was devastated."

Alex dug deep into the farthest fields of his memories, a fruitless harvest, for he'd never once heard of the magistrate's wife. "I had no idea Ford was married. I am sorry for your loss."

"Not as sorry as I was, though William Langley was a comfort. And, well, I wouldn't have my sweet Johanna or Thomas were it not for him." For a moment, the lines of her face softened, and it was easy to picture her as she might've looked in younger years, when a fellow named William and one named Richard both loved her.

But the creases reappeared, carving row upon row at the sides of her mouth and corners of her eyes. "Richard Ford threw away what he wanted for what he thought was right—but that didn't make it so." Her voice grew hard as well. "If you lose what you love to gain that which you don't, merely out of a sense of duty, such an action can never be right. Think on that."

The words smacked hard, and he stifled a wince—barely.

She stood and rested her hand atop his head. "Ultimately it is God you're accountable to, Alexander, not to me or Ford, to Johanna, or even to yourself. God alone." Her edict hung on the air as her feet pattered over to the door.

She let herself out and good thing, for he couldn't move. He sat dazed, the same slack-muscled, washed-out feeling as after a good row. She was right, of course. Every word of what she'd said rang so loud and true that his head buzzed.

But when he was this close to discovering a traitor, was it any more honorable to back out of the situation and put the lives of Englishmen at risk by the French?

CHAPTER TWENTY-NINE

Step-glide. Step-glide. Lucius practiced stretching one foot forward then bringing up his lagging leg in a smooth motion as he made his way down Wiggett Lane. This late in the day, not many pedestrians remained out and about. A good thing too. Cross looks or laughter didn't help his concentration. He hadn't quite yet mastered the flowing movement he'd been practicing the past five days. Aah, but Punch had made it look so easy as he'd slid back and forth across that puppet stage. If only he could move with such grace.

The last ray of sun blazed on a flash of red, and he jerked his head to the side. Behind a large glass window was a pyramid of all sorts of folded fabric, stacked to attract the eye. His gaze skimmed past the yellows, despite their magnificence, and went to a bit of red wool at the top. The colour was so pure, a shiver skittered from shoulder to shoulder.

He stopped and faced the window. "Look, Nixie. What a jumper that would make for you."

Nixie's little nose pressed against the glass. "It's the same shade as what Punch wore at the puppet show, Mr. Nutbrown."

"I know." He sighed. "I can't stop thinking on it. Seems like yesterday."

Nixie's dented face turned toward him. "You should buy that fabric. Then you can always remember it."

"Brilliant! I shall." Discarding his step-glide practice, he darted toward the door. Even though the shop was likely closed, sometimes all it took was a little persistent rapping and knob-jiggling to get one to open up.

Nixie bobbed between him and the door. "But are we not late to our business meeting?"

"Indeed." Inches from the knob, he pulled back his free hand. Not that he minded the income, but he was worn weary from always having to meet with Mr. Blackie and Mr. Charlie. It cut into his free time far too much.

He patted Nixie's little head. "What would I do without you to care for me, my friend?"

Nixie leaned into his touch. "I will always take care of you."

"Pray do not be offended, Nix. I know you shall."

He tucked his friend into his pocket and set sail once again down Wiggett Lane, then turned sharply onto Bledsoe. This part of town smelled like milk gone bad. He practiced holding his breath instead of glide-walking.

Halfway down the block, he swung into the Broken Brass pub. The stench in here punched him in the nose worse than on the street. Unwashed bodies filled the room, but that wasn't the worst of it. It was the corners. Those dark shadows hid all manner of waste, for more often than not, the drinkers didn't bother with going all the way outside to do their business. He'd stop breathing altogether if Nixie weren't in such need of him.

He wedged his way through muscles and beards and bones, only once tripping over a fellow who'd not even made it to a corner to double over and retch. Near the back door, at the farthest table from the bar, he stopped.

Mr. Charlie lunged up from his seat and grabbed him by the throat. "Yer late!"

His windpipe folded beneath the man's grip. This method of greeting was becoming increasingly annoying. He tried to yank Nixie out to let the man know, but his fingers were starting to feel tingly.

Mr. Blackie leaned across the table with a growl. "Not yet, Axe."

Splaying his fingers, Mr. Charlie dropped back to his seat.

Lucius coughed, sucking in air the wrong way. He pulled out a chair and sank into it. Slowly, Nixie emerged, a little crooked on his hand, but in better shape than he felt at the moment. "Mr. Nutbrown"—Nixie hacked a bit himself—"is excessively sorry for his tardiness, gentlemen. It's the way of business sometimes."

A sneer slashed across Mr. Blackie's face like a wound. Perhaps he'd had a bad day? His big, sausage finger speared a folded slip of paper and slid it across the table toward Nixie. "Read this. Out loud."

Lucius shook out the paper so both he and Nixie could see it. "Load tomorrow," Nixie read. "Deliver to Ramsgate."

Mr. Blackie and Mr. Charlie exchanged a glance, then Mr. Blackie's sausages reached for the paper.

Nixie darted out, front and center. "But there's more."

"Then read the blasted thing! Ye soft-brained coddle-headed—"

Mr. Charlie continued spouting unkind epithets, and likely would for a very long time, so Nixie slid over to Mr. Blackie's face—almost as smoothly as Punch might've. "This paper says you're to make a list of names of the men who serve so they may receive their reimbursement."

"Re–im–burse–ment?" The word jerked and juddered past Mr. Blackie's thick lips. Picking up his mug, he slugged back a big swallow of ale, then swiped his mouth with the back of his hand. His dark eyes sought Mr. Charlie's. "I don't like the sound o' that."

"Me neither." Lifting his cap, Mr. Charlie scratched a patch of hair on the crown of his head. "Don't seem right killing those what help."

A foul curse ripped out Mr. Blackie's mouth, blending in with a host of other off-colour language from the other patrons. "He better not expect us to do the re–im–burs–ing. Let the little dandy dirty his own fine suit with blood."

Blood? Nixie's head angled from one man to the other. "Excuse me, gentlemen, but are you under the impression that reimbursement involves the spilling of blood?"

Their faces swiveled toward him, bypassing Nixie altogether. "Don't it?"

He squirmed on his chair. This much scrutinizing reminded him far too much of his younger years under Mr. Shrewsby's evil eye, the master of Beetroot Home—a shelter for castoffs and misfits.

Nixie rescued him, rising up like a knight on a white horse. "No, sirs. Reimbursement simply means pecuniary compensation."

Dead fish eyes held more glimmer than that in Mr. Charlie and Mr. Blackie's stares.

"It means they'll be paid," Nixie explained.

Mr. Blackie leaned back and drained his mug dry, slamming it on the table when he finished. "O' course I knew that, ye daft muggle. I was jes' seeing if you knew. You passed the test."

Lucius flipped Nixie around and smiled at his friend. My, but they were a smashing team! Such a pair. The best of the best. A finer duo the world had never—

Mr. Blackie's voice interrupted him. "You remember all those men we talked to?"

With his free hand, Lucius tapped the side of his head, but Nixie spoke. "Mr. Nutbrown never forgets a face."

"Good. Bring us the list tomorrow afternoon, three o'clock, and we'll give you yer last assignment."

"And don't be late." Mr. Charlie poked Nixie in the chest. "We'll be giving you your re–im–burse–ment."

Lucius stood, snapping a sharp salute to his forehead with his free hand. Nixie tried, too, but his little puppet hand never did quite reach his brow. "Tomorrow, then, gentlemen."

He turned to go, but Mr. Blackie's voice pulled him around. "Oh, and Nutbrown, this time we'll be meeting out back." He hitched his sausage finger toward the door leading out into a slop lane.

Lucius tucked Nixie back into his pocket. It was a rather unconventional choice of meeting venue, but at least with an appointment that early in the day, he'd have time to buy the red wool for his little friend. The thought was so appealing, he nearly laughed along with Mr. Blackie and Mr. Charlie.

But inside his pocket Nixie shivered as Lucius pulled out his hand. What did his business partners find so amusing?

Plink. Plink. And *plink.* Johanna dropped the last coin along with the last of her hopes into the strongbox. Pressing her fingertips to her temples, she rubbed little circles as if the action might magically move the numbers in her head from the negative to the positive. It didn't. And by the sounds of only two customers out in the taproom, neither would enough magical money appear tonight, either.

She slammed the lid shut with more force than necessary, rattling the wooden bowl on the kitchen table. What a horrid week, as nauseating as the leftover stench of the cabbage soup she'd burned at lunch. She'd lost the man she loved, and it appeared she'd also lose the Blue Hedge. Her head sank in defeat and—as Mam might point out were she not abed with a cough—she was now in the perfect position to pray.

Please, God. Provide a way.

A small sound, not a still voice, but more like a slow and quiet creak answered. She lifted her face, listening with her whole body—then she shot up from her chair and darted to the back door. She yanked it open to a smudge-faced, crutch-leaning, wide-eyed boy.

"Evenin' Jo." Thomas grinned. "I were just coming in to help you with the—"

"Stop it." With a yank on his sleeve, she ushered her brother inside and shut the door. "Do not lie to me. If you wanted to be of help, you'd have been here long ago. Where have you been? And no spinning any tales."

He shifted on his crutch, hiking up his injured leg a little higher—no doubt trying to garner her sympathy. "Out with my friends. That's all. Eew! What's that smell?"

"Humph." She grunted with as much force as Mam, ignoring his diversion tactic. Studying the boy from head to toe, her gaze snagged on a bulge in his pocket. "What were you doing with your friends?"

"Oh, you know. Just jawin' a bit, out behind the Broken Brass. Gotta run now, though. Ought keep my leg up, aye?" He tried to squeeze through the open space between her and the table.

She sidestepped and blocked his route. "I would see what's in your pocket before you go, Brother."

"Aww, Jo! You can't—"

She held out her palm.

Scowling, he shoved his hand into his pocket and pulled out a fistful of coins—which he purposely kept just out of her reach.

"Thomas Elliot Langley! I told you not to gamble anymore."

His chin jutted out, so reminiscent of her father that it tightened her throat.

"You told me not to gamble *here* anymore."

"You knew very well what I meant. There is to be no gaming with your friends here or anywhere else. You are finished." She reached for the money.

He swung his hand behind his back, leaning precariously on his crutch. "I can't just up and quit. My friends are expecting me tomorrow. Wouldn't be right not keeping my word, would it? You're the one always harping on being trustworthy"

"Oh, really? Since when do you care about honesty?" She leaned forward, bending nearly nose to nose. "You will go tomorrow and tell those boys you are done—or I will tell Mam what you've been about."

His head hung, and he mumbled something.

She lifted his face. "Thomas, I mean it. This wagering is a sickness. Once it took hold of Father, it led him—and us—into ruin. He couldn't think straight, couldn't eat, couldn't sleep. It was all cards and betting, nothing else. He lost sight of those he loved until he wasted away. Do you want that to happen to you?"

Thomas's Adam's apple bobbed with a swallow. "I–I'll quit. I promise."

"Good." She straightened, but held out her palm once again. "And I'll take that ill-gotten gain to make sure of it."

His wide eyes narrowed, and she got the distinct impression that had he not a crutch to hold on to as well as a handful of coins, he'd have slapped her hand away.

"You're a shrew!" he shouted. "A rotten, mean, horrible—"

"Enough!" A deep voice with a hard edge made Thomas flinch and her stomach drop.

What was *he* doing here?

She turned, wanting and not wanting to see Alex's blue eyes. Why did he have to come here again?

Thomas used the distraction to hobble past her—but broad shoulders blocked his exit from kitchen to taproom.

Alex stood, arms folded, an impassible, unmovable mountain. "That's no way to speak to a lady, young Thomas. You will apologize. Now."

Slowly, Thomas hobbled back to her. Without making eye contact, he mumbled, "Sorry."

Johanna kept her gaze on her brother. Better that than look at the one she'd been trying to forget.

"You can do better than that," Alex coaxed.

Thomas's freckled cheeks blew out with a puff of wind. "I'm sorry I called you names, Jo."

How could she remain cross with that? Her lips quirked into a half-smile. "You are forgiven."

"There, that's better. Now run along." Alex left his perch on the threshold and strode into the kitchen, giving Thomas enough space to dart as fast as he could with a crutch out the door.

Johanna backed away, putting the table between her and the man she'd sworn to never speak to again. Refusing to meet his gaze, she looked only at his chest, but that was a mistake. All she could think of were the times she'd taken shelter there—and her heart broke afresh. What in all of kingdom come was he doing here again? Walking back into her life and rubbing raw her already ragged emotions?

He stopped on the opposite side of the table. "That was quite a storm from your brother. What is the problem?"

The problem? Did he mean the way her heart twisted and wrenched merely from the sound of his voice? She glowered up at him, breaking her vow of silence. "Nothing you need concern yourself over, Mr. Morton."

Her sharp tone cut the air, and he flinched. Good. She'd like to see him do more than that, to wilt, to droop, to drop to his knees, ruined by a hurt as great as the one that ate her soul. A hundred blistering retorts prickled on the end of her tongue, the urge to see him felled beneath her righteous rage growing stronger with each heartbeat.

But wasn't that just what Thomas had tried to do to her?

She lowered her gaze to the table. "Why are you here? Something wrong at the Rose Inn?"

"No. I came to bring you this."

A pouch landed on the wooden table with a jingle. His big hand shoved it to a stop next to the strongbox.

She retreated as if he'd set down a snake. "Your lodging was already paid. You owe nothing."

"Is your final hearth payment and rent not due soon?"

His words landed like pebbles thrown into a pond, the ripples sending her reeling. All she had to do was reach out and take it. Solve her troubles while maybe putting a dent in his pocket—or at the very least keep him from buying his new bride some baubles or trinkets.

Tempting as it was, she pushed the pouch back to his side of the table. The thought of him with another woman was so abhorrent, not even taking his money would lessen her disgust. "As I've said, sir, it is none of your concern. Now go away."

"Johanna, please." He sighed, the huff of his breath jagged at the edges. "Don't be stubborn and lose all for the sake of your pride. May a friend not do a good turn for another?"

"Is that what you are?" A dark, throaty roar clogged her throat. The audacity of the man! Did he think he could buy his way back into her good graces? She shook her head, again and again. "A friend doesn't inflict a mortal wound, then leave the injured to bleed out alone."

Beneath the tan of his skin, a flush deepened on his face. "If I'd stayed here, would that have not been more cruel?"

She threw out her hands. "Then why come here at all? Go back to the Rose. Go back to your wedding plans. Go back to your happy life and Louisa—"

She spun away. Too many tears threatened to spill. Too much pain twisted her face, far too much to hide—and she wouldn't give him the satisfaction.

Behind her, boot steps pounded on the flagstones, rounding the table.

No! She'd not have it. Darting sideways, she snatched a frying pan from a hook on the wall and hefted it. "If you even think to touch me, I will mark that face of yours worse than any gaol keeper."

He froze. Emotions, too many to count, flashed in his blue gaze. Finally, his shoulders slumped, and he aged a decade in a second. "I am sorry, Johanna. I never meant to hurt you. I. . .I thought I was doing what was right." His jaw clenched, and he looked away. "Yet I hate what I have done."

"That makes two of us." She blew out a long breath and lowered the iron pan. "Go away, Alex. Just go. And don't come back."

CHAPTER THIRTY

Stew bubbled in the pot, and Johanna stirred it absently, watching snippets of potatoes and fine bits of parsnips surface and sink, surface and sink. The sight soothed in a mesmerizing way—the chopped pieces of once-living things now caught in a death spiral at the end of her spoon. Floating and dropping. Just like the last month of her life.

She leaned close and sniffed. At least this stew smelled better than yesterday's failed cabbage soup.

The back door crashed open, but she didn't turn. She simply didn't care. The grim reaper himself could barrel into the kitchen and she'd still stand here, stirring and stirring.

"Jo! You got to see!" Thomas's crutch thudded in time with his words.

"Whatever it is, show it to Mam. I'm busy." The spoon trailed round the edge of the pot, round and round.

He tugged her skirt. "Come on, you got to look."

Blowing a bit of hair out of her eyes, she stared at the stew. Likely he held a toad, or a squirming vole, or some other boyish torture device. "Go away, Thomas."

"Jo, please."

Her spine stiffened. Besides the fact that Thomas never used the word *please*, the panic in his tone alarmed her. Pulling the spoon from the pot, she tapped off the drips and turned.

He held out a dirty scrap of red fabric, all balled up in his hand.

"I found this lying next to the rot pile out back o' the Broken Brass."

Frowning, she set down her spoon, then took the soiled lump from him. She poked at it with her finger, and the fabric unfolded, bleeding over the edges of her palm. It appeared to be stained scarlet wool sewn haphazardly in the shape of a little jumper, with one arm torn off. What in the world? She scrunched her nose at Thomas. "What is this?"

He dug into his pocket and pulled out another lump—and when it landed in her hand, a shiver raised gooseflesh on her arms.

Mr. Nutbrown's puppet, leastwise what was left of it, stared up at her, one eye missing. So was half of its head. The other half was flattened. Only a frayed scar of the jester hat remained where glue held the ripped strip in place. What used to be a painted smile now gaped open in a broken hole. Knife marks slashed a jagged line at the neck.

A shiver passed through her. "Where did you say you found this?"

"Behind the Broken Brass. You gotta go get Alex, Jo. You're faster than me. I'm sure Mr. Nutbrown's in trouble."

Crossing to the table, she set down the crushed head and tattered fabric, unwilling to look at either anymore. "I'm sure he's fine," she mumbled. Drawing strength from her words, she turned to Thomas. "Mr. Nutbrown probably just dropped his puppet, that's all."

But the statement branded her a liar even before it finished passing her lips.

Thomas scowled. "That ain't so, and you know it. You gotta get Alex! He's the only one who can help."

Pinching her lips tight, she strode to the door and snatched her hat off a peg. She'd be hanged if she asked Alex for anything. She could take a quick stroll and look for Mr. Nutbrown herself and still be back in time to serve dinner.

She fumbled with the ribbon beneath her chin. Why were her fingers shaking? "I'll go. I'm sure I'll find some ridiculous yellow stockings roaming the town, looking for a lost puppet."

"No!" Thomas hobbled between her and the door. "It's too dangerous. Alex has a gun, and he's from London. If Mr. Nutbrown's in a bad way, he'll know exactly what to do."

The information stunned. Alex was from Sheffield. . .wasn't he?

"How do you know that?" She studied her brother. What other knowledge lurked beneath those freckles?

He shoved her in the arm. "Yer wastin' time, Jo."

The smashed puppet head on the table implored her with its single remaining eye. Nixie's tiny voice cried silently in her mind, *"Mr. Nutbrown would never leave me."*

Whirling, she slipped out the door and entered the stable yard, then shot toward the broken gate. The afternoon sun bowed to the horizon. She'd have to be quick to make it back in time for any patrons looking for a bowl of stew. But where would someone like Nutbrown be?

She mapped out a route in her head as she turned onto the High Street. If Thomas had found the puppet at the Broken Brass, then that would be the most logical place to start. She upped her pace toward Wiggett Lane, when a shiny, black barouche turned the corner. Her blood drained down to her feet. She'd see Mr. Spurge's sneering face next week when he came to collect his due—a due still short a pound. The thought of an encounter with him sickened her more than the ruined puppet head.

Crossing the street, she darted down a narrow path that led to the harbor. If she skirted the waterfront, she could double back and work her way home through town while looking for Mr. Nutbrown. But trekking on the shingle slowed her steps. It would be faster to hike closer to the water where her shoes could grip firm sand. And she'd have the added benefit of the berm to hide her from Mr. Spurge's eyes on the chance his carriage swung down to Harbor Lane. She hiked her skirts, crested the berm, and pattered down the other side.

Across the beach, a line of men hefted something—boards? Flat boxes? She squinted. Hard to tell. Whatever their cargo, they loaded it onto rowboats that skittered over the water toward a ship anchored just off the coast. A strange time to load. They wouldn't get very far before dark, unless they planned to set sail at daybreak. But why then was the ship not moored in the harbor? She bit her lip, puzzling for a moment, but no matter. It was none of her business.

She hurried to the sand as fast as the rocks beneath her feet would let her. Once there, she lowered her skirts and sped along, making up for lost time. She'd turn away from the men before drawing too close, then head back to the city proper.

But just before she could veer off, her steps slowed. Then stopped. A shape emerged from behind a rock, with a peg-legged gait and a gun pointed at her. For a single, awful eternity, she longed for Alex to be at her side.

Glancing at the berm, she calculated the distance. She could easily outpace the man's hitch-stepped run and make it safely to town—but she couldn't outrun a lead ball. What to do?

"This ain't no place for a lady." The big man, Mr. Blackie, if she remembered correctly, stopped in front of her, and thankfully lowered the muzzle of his gun. "Say. . .you be that girl from the Blue Hedge. The one what helped us, aye?" A glower folded his unshaven whiskers into dark lines at the sides of his mouth. "You were paid, and paid right fine far as I remember. If yer lookin' for more, missy—"

"I am not. I am looking for Mr. Nutbrown." She cut the fellow off before he worked himself into a swirl. Men such as this rarely liked to be parted from their coins, a lesson well learned from Tanny Needler.

But instead of relaxing of his shoulders, Mr. Blackie yanked the gun back up, aiming squarely at her chest.

"Now, now. . .what ye be wantin' him for?"

Drat that Mr. Nutbrown! The man had been nothing but trouble since he set foot in the Blue Hedge—and this time it appeared to be the worst trouble of all. Forcing back a lump of panic, she swallowed and retreated a step. "I suppose it can wait. I see that you must be busy with that ship you were expecting, so I'll just be on my way. Please tell Mr. Nutbrown I have something of his when you next see him."

She turned to go.

The click of the gun and Mr. Blackie's growl stopped her cold. "If it's Mr. Nutbrown yer wantin', I can take you to him."

"No, no. I'm sorry to have bothered you." She forced a light lilt to her tone—yet the words came out strained. "Another time, perhaps."

"Now's the time." Cold metal poked her in the back. "This way. And keep yer yap shut or it won't go well for you."

Prodded along by the muzzle of the gun, he nudged her, step by step, over to the men. She desperately tried to make eye contact with those filing past her, headed toward town. None of them glanced at her, all too busy laughing and talking of women and drink. Several other men swung their legs over the gunwales of their rowboats and set off toward the ship. They'd be no help. Only a few yet picked their way down the cliff face, wooden frames hefted over their shoulders.

A short, red-haired man—Mr. Pickens—was the first to set foot from rocks to beach. He passed off his load to another man, then faced his partner. "What you got there, Blackie?"

"Hold up, girl," the voice at her back growled. "This one's sniffin' around for Nutbrown."

A grin rippled across the shorter man's face. "Then let's take her to him."

Her stomach heaved. Clearly wherever Mr. Nutbrown was couldn't be good.

A wad of spit hit the sand behind her. "Pleasant as it would be, the deed would take too much time. I say we tie her up and leave her."

"That eats time as well, and this is the last o' it." Mr. Pickens hitched his thumb over his shoulder at the remaining four men edging down the rock trail. "I say we kill her and be done with it. Dead men—or women—don't talk."

Her heart slammed against her ribs, and she searched desperately for escape.

Behind her, Mr. Blackie laughed, the coarseness shredding away the last of her courage. Would she die on this strip of beach, surrounded by thieves and murderers? What of Mam? Of Thomas? Why hadn't she gone for Alex?

Another gun behind her clicked.

"That be a waste of a pretty face—and an even prettier amount o' gold." The voice was altogether too familiar.

Her gaze snapped to the man whose boots pounded toward them from the rock face. Mr. Quail's eyes peered out from beneath a mop of dark, curly hair. Her mouth hung open. Behind him, the rest of his band dropped to the beach from the rocks like so many beetles falling off a rotted log, each one hefting lumber on their shoulders.

"What ye jawin' about, Que?" Mr. Pickens flicked sweat from his brow—the movement so sudden she flinched.

Mr. Quail flashed her a smile as he answered. "I say we sell her along with this shipment. Those fancy French gents pay a fine price for the novelty of an English maid."

Alex shifted in the saddle. Thatcher would've thrived on this part of his mission, tearing across the countryside like a crazed stallion on a running jag, but not him. He was better at nabbing thieves on foot. At least after the last swap of horses, Coburn had finally relented and slowed their pace, for they'd made good time. They'd be at Ramsgate by nightfall. He shifted back the other way. After a full day of riding, his backside would appreciate it.

The breakneck pace had given them little opportunity for any conversation—which was good and bad. It gave little time for Coburn to speak of tomorrow's wedding, but allowed for way too much rein on his own thoughts. And they always turned to Johanna. To her welling tears. The betrayal sagging her shoulders. The sharp edge of her voice when she'd told him to go away.

Enough! There was nothing to be done for it now. He glanced over at Lord Coburn, riding beside him. Better to poke a bear than wrestle with monstrous memories. "We're nearly to Ramsgate. No one's around. Now's as good a time as any to tell me what this little venture is really about. I'll find out soon enough anyway."

From beneath the brim of a dockhand's flat cap, Coburn's grey eyes studied him. "We aren't there yet."

"If I were going to harm you or your enterprise—whatever it may be—I'd surely have done so by now."

Coburn faced forward again, the late afternoon sun bathing his profile in brilliant light. "It's not you I'm worried about."

"Then who?"

"I don't know." He sighed. "But I have a feeling someone, somewhere, is gunning for us—for me."

Interesting. Was it leftover guilt from his Indian affairs that left the man suspicious, or did he truly have a deadly premonition? Alex tugged down the brim of his own longshoreman cap. "I am not that man."

"No, I don't believe you are."

They rode in silence for a ways, nothing but the River Stour lapping just past the grassy ridge on the other side of the road.

"You will find out sooner rather than later, I suppose." Coburn scratched at his chin. "Several months back I received confidential intelligence from Major General Overtun."

"Our gaming partner."

Coburn grunted. "My relationship with him goes well beyond wagering. We served together, long ago, in India. But that's neither here nor there. The crux of the information is that Napoleon's planning an attack across the Channel on July fourth."

This time Alex shifted in his seat to keep from falling off. "Tomorrow?"

Coburn smiled at him. "A bit poetic, don't you think?"

More than that. Tensing, he thought aloud. "Using the remnants of their revolution to rub our noses in our loss of the Colonial uprising. But did we not fortify a few years ago and make the Channel secure?"

Coburn sucked air in through his teeth. "Of course."

Blowing out a long breath, Alex scoured every bit of information from the sparse news he knew of the situation. "Last I heard the fellow was busy with Prussia, not eyeing us."

"One can never be sure which rock a snake hides beneath, and it never hurts to be prepared. General Overtun charged me with setting up a little surprise welcome for old Boney, should he decide to visit." He tugged the reins, guiding his horse's mouth away from a tasty patch of sweet grass at the side of the road before he continued. "We are accompanying a shipment of Congreve rockets to be set up along the shore. Before the *Devil's Favourite* can attack, we simply blow him out of the water."

"Cutting it a little close, are you not? Should this not have been done yesterday?"

Coburn chuckled. "Didn't want to tip off the Frogs by showing movement too early. It will be a quick setup. Robbie is getting the frames in position now. And there are plenty of men to operate the equipment from the castle."

"But why did Overtun use you? You are no longer military."

"For that very reason. There are spies about. In a hive of men, there's increased likelihood of an informant, whereas by Overtun appointing me, there's less chance of intelligence being leaked."

"Hence your, er, *compartmentalization*, as you called it." Ducking a swarm of gnats, he urged his horse onward. "But why Ramsgate? Why not simply meet the ship in the dark of night at Dover?"

"These are notorious smuggling waters. I will relieve the captain of his duty on this last stretch of the journey, removing any temptation to sell out."

"Quite the elaborate plan."

"It took some arranging but—"

"Sh-sh." He lifted a finger to his lips and reined his horse to a stop.

"What is it?" Coburn whispered.

Narrowing his eyes, Alex studied the surroundings. On one side, the tall grass, some trees, then the river. To the other, nothing but a rolling sward. The rasp of insects started up, but other than that—hold on. There it was again. He listened with his whole body.

Laughter, coarse laughter.

He angled his head for Coburn to follow and led him off road, up to the rise of a small hillock. From that perch, a good view of the road spread out. Not far ahead, two men led two horses. . .or were the horses leading them? Hard to say for the way they staggered. At least they'd had the sense to dismount before they fell off. But were they truly in their cups?

He turned to Coburn. "That drink you offered earlier. I should like it now."

Coburn's mount blew out a snort, apparently as offset as his rider. Coburn said nothing, but slowly reached in his pocket and pulled out a silver flask.

Alex snatched it from him and poured most of it down the inside of his collar, dousing it on like a lady might bathe in rosewater. Then he pointed at the trees opposite them by the riverside. "Take cover down there."

Coburn scowled. "If you're this concerned, simply shoot those villains now and be done with it. It's your duty as a loyalist and why I brought you along."

He gritted his teeth. Sure, a crack sharpshooter could do such a thing. But not him. Persuasion was his best weapon. "You brought me along for protection, not murder. It's likely nothing but a few drunkards got ahold of some nappy ale, but it never hurts to check. Wait down there, and I'll be back."

Coburn locked gazes with him, the steel in his grey eyes sparking, but then he clicked his tongue and rode off.

Alex gripped the flask in one hand and the reins in the other, riding haphazardly as if he were the one who'd swigged one too many bottles. Humming an old bawdy song, he neared the two men, taking stock of their assets. Two horses, strong muscled, far too expensive for the likes of itinerant drinkers, a Brown Bess strapped onto each. Military guns for this ilk? The men dropped their leads and fanned out onto the road, watching his approach. Neither swayed nor laughed—instant sobriety.

He tipped back his head and drained the remaining drops in the flask, taking care they saw the action but not a flash of silver. He made a show of shaking it, then tucked it away and slid from his horse. "Afternoon mates." He drew close, reeling on his feet. "Got a few drops to spare fer a fellow traveller? Appears I'm out."

The shorter man with a broad nose sniffed the air. "Nab off, ye drunken cully."

"Just need me a sip, boys." He stumbled around, reaching out a hand as if to keep him from tipping over, and slapped one of their horse's in the flank. The mount moved ahead, as did the other. He grinned at the men. "I'm powerful thirsty. Just shared my last bit with a gent a ways back."

"A gent you say?" The other man's voice was strangely high pitched, as if he'd been punched in the throat one too many times. "Well, well, we be looking for a particular gentleman. About yea high," the man lifted his hand to Coburn's height, "and walks with a crooked gait. A fancy gent, nice clothes and all. Is that the man you seen?"

Quite an accurate description of the viscount—almost as if they expected Coburn to be travelling this very road. Alex grinned. Judging by the looks of them, that's exactly what they were up to.

"Not a bit of it." He forced a belch then pounded his fist against his chest. "The fellow what I saw were bow-legged and chin high to a grasshopper, so short was he."

"Well then," the fellow lifted the barrel of his gun. "Like my friend said, be on yer way."

He faked a hiccup, then swiped his mouth and held up his hands. "Ay now, no harm. I'm off."

He lurched around, giving the fellow enough time to lower his guard, then swung back around with a kick to the man's arm. Bone cracked. The gun dropped. The bullet went wild. Horses took off, and before the other fellow could draw his pistol, Alex aimed two guns at him. "Disarm. Now!"

The man's eyes turned to slits, but at least he complied. The other man wailed, holding on to his useless arm.

"Turn around, friends. We're going for a little walk—uh-uh! Hands in the air, gentlemen." He waited until three arms reached, for the broken one would never be so flexible. "That's it. Now head to the river."

They set off, the tall grass breaking beneath their boots. Clearing the downward slope, they stopped at a jutting drop where, over time, water had cut a deep gullet into the curve.

"Jump," Alex ordered.

"Ye daft? I can't swim!" the shorter man shouted.

"Then you'll learn. Off you go." He shot one of the guns just over their heads.

Both men jumped.

He retraced his route to the road and collected the dropped weapons, all the while scanning should there be any more assailants about. His mount had taken off, so he'd have to hoof back to where he'd left the viscount.

Keeping to the cover of the tall grass, he dashed ahead, hoping Coburn would be gracious enough to share his mount. But as he approached the stand of trees where he'd ordered the viscount to wait, that hope fizzled and a new fear kindled. There was no horse and no man. Had the villains he'd dispatched been nothing but a ruse to lure him away from Coburn?

He retreated to the road and crouched, examining the ground for clues. Hoof divots headed into the grass, then about five paces over, headed out, along with quite a kicked up bit of gravel. Some kind of skirmish happened here—and just might again, for something thundered up the road.

Straight for him.

CHAPTER THIRTY-ONE

With each pull of the oars, the shore slipped farther away. Once again Johanna considered heaving herself overboard, but with the rope cutting into her wrists behind her back, she'd sink. Still, a watery death might be preferable. Who knew what the seven men on this boat—or the rest of the scoundrels on the ship they rowed toward—might have in mind. So she stared at the water sloshing at her feet, refusing to look forward or back.

Mr. Quail and his men did the rowing, and with each jerk of the boat through the surf, she cursed him for the villain he truly was. Alex had been right to distrust the man—and she never should've trusted Alex. A scream welled in her throat, already hoarse from pleading and bargaining. Why had she let either of those rogues stay at the inn on that ill-fated May day?

The rowing stopped. The boat bobbed. Johanna lifted her face, then was sorry for it, for a spray of salt water hit her in the eyes. She blinked, trying to work it away, the sting sprouting fresh tears.

"The woman were yer idea, Que." Mr. Cooper's voice rumbled from the bow like kicked gravel. He tossed something to Mr. Quail, or Que, or whoever he was. "Hoist her up and haul her below."

Rising, Mr. Quail held on to the thrown object, but did not pocket it. "I do the work, I expect a cut o' the profits."

"Oh? A businessman, are ye?" The red-headed Mr. Pickens glanced back at Mr. Cooper. "We know what to do with those, aye?"

Their laughter chilled Johanna more thoroughly than her damp gown and wet feet.

Without a word, Mr. Quail stuffed the item into his pocket. Then he grabbed her around the waist, lifted her up, and slung her over his shoulder like a sack of unwanted kittens to be thrown into the sea.

She squirmed, but his grip tightened as he straddled the center thwart. Her face mashed into his broad back, his topcoat as wet as her gown.

"Be still," he warned. "Or we'll both take a dive."

She hung there, balanced between a grave of the deep and a ship full of miscreants, jostling on the shoulder of a man who smelled of sweat and danger. The rowboat bobbed smaller and smaller beneath her as Mr. Quail began climbing a rope ladder, rung by rung. She'd known fear, for Tanny had taught her well, but never anything like this. The shakes trembling through her were unstoppable. No one would help her—no one could. She was alone in this. Horribly, dreadfully deserted.

By the time Mr. Quail lugged her over the gunwale and stood her on her feet, even the afternoon sun abandoned her as it ducked behind a cloud. Men moved about like spiders, creeping in the sudden shade, setting sails and coiling ropes. The silence in which they all worked shivered down her back.

Mr. Quail grabbed her arm. "This way."

She wrenched from his grasp.

He yanked her back.

"I knew you were involved with smugglers." Her words came as fast as the trip of her feet. "I should've turned you in."

He dragged her toward a door. "Good thing for you that you didn't."

"No wonder your music was so awful." It was a churlish thing to say and wouldn't do her a bit of good, but it felt like a small victory.

Without a word, he dragged her down a set of narrow stairs to a corridor below. When her feet hit the bottom, he released her and swung about to face her.

Suddenly she wished for the brightness of the deck, for the lantern light down here emphasized the sharp angles on his face. Her throat closed. When had he grown to be so large? She'd always compared him to Alex, but here, standing solitary before him, he stood at least a head taller than her.

He advanced, and she pressed her back against the wall.

"Listen," he whispered.

She bit her lip to keep it from quivering. Why did he not shout? Or rage? She knew what to do with a man's anger, but this? All the unknowns twisted her belly as sickening as the sudden cant of the ship.

"I've not time to—"

"What's this?" A man stinking of ale and strong cheese stumbled off the last stair. "What ye got there, a little lacey?" He peered over Mr. Quail's shoulder, his black eyes fixed on her. "Oh, a dainty nibble, I'd say. You a mind to share?"

Quail wheeled about. His big back blocked her, and she was glad to not have to face the venom in his voice. "This one's mine. Shove off."

The man scuttled down the corridor like a rat.

Quail turned back to her. "Come on."

He didn't grab her this time, he just pivoted and strode down the narrow passage in the opposite direction of the other man. She stood for a moment, debating on making a run up the stairs and a dive overboard. But the thudding of her heart indicted her for a fool. She'd never make it across the deck—and the tromp of boots coming back down the corridor signaled the return of the other fellow.

She hurried after Mr. Quail.

He stopped in front of a door and swung it open, indicating for her to enter with the tip of his head.

She edged past him, expecting what, she had no idea—but not this. Something dark and furry whisked across the floor just ahead of her. She spun. Were her hands not tied behind her back, she'd drop to her knees and throw her arms around his legs. "Mr. Quail, don't do this. Please, let me go."

Thin light from the corridor lantern lit only half his face, moving over the strong lines of his jaw and straight edge of his nose. "This will soon be over. For your own sake, Miss Langley, stay quiet. I will return."

The door slammed. A key jiggled in a lock. Mr. Quail's footsteps faded.

Johanna stood still, too frightened to move or even think, for it would feed the panic begging release. Blackness so thick it breathed closed over her. So she counted. Numbers. One after the other. Anything to distract her from what she'd first seen when she'd entered the room. But time and again, the scratch of claws scurrying across wood forced her to start back at zero. When her skirt hem riffled from the nose of an inquisitive rat, she abandoned her counting as she'd been abandoned—

And screamed.

Alex dove into the undergrowth at the side of the road, dropping the rest of the guns he'd picked up and loading his own. Better to face an enemy with an old friend in his grip. By the sound of it, two horses neared, so he kept the other guns within reach and flattened belly down in the grass. Timing was his truest asset.

He sweated at the approach and held his breath when the horse drew even. As soon as the second horse passed, he shot to his feet and aimed his muzzle at the back of—

"Lord Coburn?" He gaped.

Heart pounding, Alex released the hammer and lowered his pistol. The viscount had no idea how close he'd come to death at the hand of the man he'd brought along to protect him.

Coburn swung his horse around, Alex's mount following, tethered to his saddle. "Lose something?"

Alex heaved a sigh while retrieving the rest of his weapons and his horse. "I thought I told you to stay put."

"I did—until your mount barreled past me. I figured you'd be needing it." He nodded to where Alex shoved the guns into a pack lashed to his saddle. "Looks like you gained a few new trinkets."

"Found 'em lying on the road. Imagine that."

"And their owners?"

With a smirk, he hove into the saddle, eager to be on the move instead of sitting ducks. "It's a good afternoon for a swim, don't you think? And a ride. Shall we?"

Side by side, they rode the rest of the way to Ramsgate unmolested.

He'd kept a vigilant eye the whole way, but didn't detect any more threats. It would be harder now, though. As they neared the harbour, night fell hard. A half-moon peeked out from clouds, shyly, sporadically, like a scullery maid sneaking glimpses of a stable hand out in the yard.

The viscount took the lead, and when he dismounted, Alex did as well. As Coburn swerved into a narrow lane, Alex took the opportunity to cock open one of his pistols, covering their rear. Years in London's rookeries had taught him well.

They walked the horses down a narrow passage between two buildings. The stink of waste—both of man and beast—hung thick and heavy. Good thing it was too dark to see what his boots strode through. Eventually they came to an opening, surrounded by broken crates and a few overturned barrels missing staves, all sitting on a stone walkway. Water lapped at the other side of it. Across the bay, moored at the nearest dock, was an East Indiaman—but by the looks of it, it wouldn't be there for long. A towboat was even now being attached, readying to haul her out to sea.

Coburn shook his head. "Something's not right."

Alex clutched his gun grip tighter. "How do you know?"

"Captain Fielding was to meet me here." The viscount yanked out his pocket watch, scowled, then shoved it back. "We were to swap clothes, the men onboard that ship"—he aimed a finger across the bay—"being none the wiser."

Alex snorted. "Surely you don't sound the same as the captain."

"No need. Fielding gave the crew express orders the rest of the voyage was to be completely silent and dark. Once he returned—or rather I did—they were to set sail."

"Are we too early? Too late?"

"No." The viscount's voice tightened. "Right on time. I've made sure of it."

"Well," Alex blew out a breath. "The ship's obviously still there, but not for long."

"Then we board her before she sails." The viscount pulled out his gun.

Alex planted his feet on the slick stones. "I don't like it."

"There's nothing for it, man. We must. *I* must! It's of national importance."

"What—?"

"There's no time to explain." The viscount's gaze burned deep into Alex's eyes. "Are you the man I've credited you as, or not?"

Alex hesitated, as uneasy about accompanying Coburn into an unknown situation as he was about trying to haul the viscount against his will back to safety. Either way was a risk. . .but which stakes were the best bet?

"Give me a moment." He slipped back to remove the extra guns from the horse's pack and tucked them into his belt—a mite uncomfortable, but far better than taking a bullet for being unprepared.

He and the viscount secured the horses, then worked their way along the stone walkway and across the edge of the shingle to the jetty, where the ship was docked. Each step of the way ratcheted his heartbeat up a notch.

Before the viscount could set foot off the beach, Alex tugged him back by the sleeve. "Pocket your gun but keep it handy. Hide your face in the shadows as much as you can, but walk with a purpose. Sometimes swagger can save your life."

Just then the moon peered out, casting a milky light on Coburn's scowl. "No wonder you took so much of my money at the table."

Alex bypassed the man and strode down the dock, gaze darting from the sailor untying mooring ropes, to another up near the gunwale, coiling them up. The gangplank remained against the dock for now, but once that sailor finished his task, it would be drawn up. Alex increased his pace.

The viscount's footsteps followed. The sailor looked them over as their feet hit the gangplank. Without slowing, Alex tipped his flat cap at him, and for a heartbeat, he held his breath. But thanks to Coburn's forethought, their longshoreman clothing made them blend in. They navigated the plank without a remark.

The deck was a ghost ship, with inky specters working in silence, save for the scraping of ropes and clanking of tackle as the men prepared to raise sails once the ship was towed out to sea. Danger lurked here, but where exactly? Alex exchanged a glance with the viscount. His face was unreadable in the dark. Well then, why not meet it head-on? Alex stalked toward the quarterdeck, where the captain was sure to be—until a woman's voice stopped him.

"Father?"

Alex turned. The viscount stood where he'd left him, facing a short man with curves like a lady—and the voice of Louisa. No wonder she'd blended in with the sailors, for she was dressed as one. Robbie was nowhere to be seen, and unless he was busy below deck, that left only one plausible conclusion. . .

Louisa was the traitor all along.

Alex crept to the mainmast, flattening against it not only to watch the spectacle, but also to gauge the precise moment to nab her. He shouldn't be surprised, really, that a shipment of rockets was to be offered over to England's arch enemy by the hand of a woman—for had not Eden fallen in the same manner? Suddenly Ford's directive to ally himself with Louisa via a betrothal made complete sense.

"Louisa!" Coburn's voice shook. "What are you doing here?"

Louisa pulled up in front of her father. "The real question is what are *you* doing here, Father? But no matter, not now at any rate. There's a scheme in motion that for once is not of your conniving—one you cannot control. In fact, it's too late for you to change anything. Far too late."

And it was. For all of them. The sailors had already heaved in the gangplank. The ship freed from the jetty, and the deck rocked beneath Alex's feet.

"For God's sake, Louisa," Coburn's voice roared. "What do you think you're about?"

Louisa fisted her hands on her hips, the stance of a gamecock set to kill. "You shouldn't have come. You will have to be put overboard."

"What on earth are you babbling about?"

"How does that feel, Father, to not know what shall happen next? To not comprehend the actions and commands of those around you." She stepped closer to the man, her words gaining in speed. "To have no say whatsoever in what your future might be."

If she meant to cow the man, she'd gone about it the wrong way, for he straightened to a ramrod. "I don't know how you found out I'd be here tonight, but I do know this—your little tantrum has gone beyond bounds, even for you. What was it you hoped to accomplish?"

"Ask all you like, but you will have no answers."

"Looks like I have mine, though." Pulling his gun, Alex strode from the shadow of the mast, aiming the muzzle at the viscount's daughter. "Louisa Coburn, I arrest you in the name of the Crown."

Coburn pivoted. "What's this?"

"I knew it!" Louisa growled, quite the brave act at the other end of a pistol. "I knew you weren't who you appeared to be, Mr. Morton. But there's no crime in elopement. On what charges could you possibly arrest me?"

A sickening feeling twisted his gut. Had he been wrong in his assessment?

But no. . .a woman like Louisa would say anything to gain the upper hand. He cocked open the hammer of his gun. No sense letting the little vixen try to slip her way past him. "You are charged with conspiracy. It took some untangling, but it looks like I've finally found the real traitor."

Another hammer clicked open, just behind his head.

"Are you sure about that, Alex, ol' boy?"

CHAPTER THIRTY-TWO

Alex froze, body stiff with a gun at his back, but his mind took off running. Robbie stood behind him—though he should've been in Dover loading frames. Judging by the wide eyes of the viscount in front of Alex, Coburn was just as surprised to see his nephew here. Only Louisa appeared at ease, gracefully balancing on the deck as the towboat began to row them out of the harbour. Robbie must've paid the captain well to dare such treachery.

"Drop the gun, Morton." Robbie's voice cut the air, a sharp contrast to the relative silence of the sailors scrambling up ratlines and securing ropes.

Releasing the hammer, Alex let the pistol fall to the deck, the clank of it as loud as a shot. No worry, though. Two more guns dug into the tender skin of his waist beneath his coat.

"Good chap. Now, turn slowly, hands in the air."

Alex pivoted. Robbie's smirk was that of a man holding a set of aces.

"Line up with the old man there." Robbie tipped his head, moonlight slicing his face in half. "But keep your distance. You two have held hands long enough."

"For pity's sake, Robert." Disgust coloured the viscount's tone to an ugly darkness. "Lower your weapon. As usual, you've fouled up everything."

"Shut up." Robbie pulled the trigger.

The bullet tore through the viscount's arm. He crashed to his knees, clutching the wound. He didn't howl, but his breathing chopped out in draws and huffs.

"Father!" Louisa dropped beside him. "Robbie, stop it! Are you mad? This ship is full of gunpowder. One wrong shot and we all go up in flames. Just put them overboard and be done with it."

He pulled out another gun. "It's not that easy, love."

Louisa couldn't see Robbie's face as she ripped the hem of her shirt to create a makeshift bandage. But Alex didn't miss the pleasure shining in the whites of the man's eyes.

"The way is never easy for a traitor," Alex murmured.

Robbie shook his head. "I'm no traitor, just an opportunist. As are you, Morton. What's the matter? Did I not supply a sufficient sum in that envelope I sent you? Or were you somehow angling to get more from the old man?"

"Dash it!" The viscount scowled up at Alex, the pain of his wound—or maybe the way Louisa held his arm out to bind it—evident in the stilted movement.

"Really, Uncle, Morton's not worth that much passion. He was merely a pawn in this game of mine, necessary for only a short while."

"You have no idea what you're doing." The viscount's words travelled thick and slow in a strained voice. "Because of you, England now faces an attack."

Robbie chuckled. "Calm down, old man. There's no real threat—not yet, anyway. That was merely a seed I planted in the head of Overtun during a rather exclusive round of cards."

"To what purpose?" The viscount strangled a cry as Louisa tucked in the ends of the bandage.

Alex watched Robbie with hawk-like intensity, looking for an opening. Any opening. But the man kept his gaze pinging between his uncle and Alex.

"Money." Robbie shrugged. "It's always about money, is it not?"

"You. . .you sold out. . .to whom?" It was hard to tell which robbed the viscount's breath more—Robbie's treachery or Louisa's somewhat rough handling to help him to his feet. He wobbled for a moment, then growled, "And why?"

"You should know, Uncle. You've chided me for it often enough. I have no loyalty to a country that saw fit to humiliate, brand, and rob me of everything."

"You deserved that cashiering." The viscount's indictment was as salty as the air.

"I don't deny I deserted, but it was quite by accident. An opportunity arose—it simply took more time than I thought it would to cut the deal." His eyes narrowed. "As you would've known if you'd ever taken the time to listen to me."

Alex studied Robbie's face by threadbare moonlight. Something wasn't right about his story. "There's more to it than that, isn't there?"

"See?" Robbie flashed him a grin, the whites of his teeth skeletal in the dark. "That's what I've liked about you from the start, ol' boy. Ever so keen. You're right, of course. There was also the trifling matter of disorderly conduct unbefitting an officer. Aah, but fleecing that colonel still makes me smile."

"I don't think you'll be smiling when you hang for this," Alex said. The eerie snap of a rising sail magnified his threat.

"They'll have to catch me first, and judging by the looks of things, that'll take quite some doing."

Alex's gaze drifted. He should've noticed before what a minimal crew ran this vessel. Were the viscount not wounded, they maybe would've had a chance at taking charge.

He flicked his stare back to Robbie. "And what of the viscount and me?"

"That is a problem." The moon disappeared, pulling all light from Robbie's face. "I suppose I shall leave you in the hands of my associates once we land."

Alex shook his head. "You know what Leaguers will do to us."

"A pity, that. Good faro players are so scarce."

The viscount swore. Beside him, Louisa didn't so much as gasp. Though why should she? Dressed in men's garments and no stranger to her father's outbursts, it should come as no surprise the lady didn't display ladylike sensibilities. She merely stood, propping up her father with a hold on his good arm.

"*La ligue la liberté!*" The viscount swore again. "You're selling out to the French?"

"The French will pay a premium for a shipment of rockets and frames," Robbie explained. "Enough to fund my travels around the world."

"You mean to India." Louisa let go of her father's arm and stepped toward Robbie.

"Eventually," he said.

"*Eventually?*" The word flamed out of her mouth like a cannonball. She stopped, halfway between her father and her lover. "That was not part of our deal."

Alex rocked back on his heels. Good. This he could use. If he could get Robbie to focus more on Louisa and less on him, he'd have the space of a breath to pull out one of the pistols beneath his coat.

"Tell her, Robbie. Tell her all. You have no intention of going to India and never did. Once a leaguer, a leaguer for life. You are no longer a free man, but a puppet, with failing revolutionaries holding the strings. Miss Coburn"—he shot her a half-smile—"how did you think Robbie, a court-martialed soldier living off his uncle's charity, managed to give you French perfume, that Cross of Lorraine pendant that is even now surely hot against your collarbone, or supply champagne to a viscount's entire household?"

She looked from him to Robbie, face pale in the night. "What does he mean?"

"Don't panic, love." Robbie spoke as to a child. Bad mistake. She'd pick up on it, and it would fuel her rage.

Alex stifled a grin.

"Just a few more obligations, Louisa, and then—"

"Your obligation is to me!"

"Of course, but—"

And there it was. Robbie turned his face toward Louisa.

Alex pulled a gun, cocking the hammer wide open. "Drop *your* weapon, Mr. Coburn."

Robbie jerked his gaze back to Alex.

And behind them all, the hammers of four more guns clicked, followed by a raspy voice. "Drop yours as well, Mr. Morton."

Seven hundred twenty-nine. Seven hundred thirty. Seven hun—

Something warm probed Johanna's toes, just at the tips. But it would move from there. She'd learned the pattern, thanks to the wisdom she'd gained from Alex and a stubborn barn door.

"Assess the situation first. The easiest way to manage a difficulty is to think before acting."

Squeezing the fabric of the gown she bunched in her hands at her back—for she'd also learned the unpleasantness of having a rat trapped between her legs and skirt hem—she waited. Let the nose sniff, the tentative paw poke. Wait for curiosity to throw abandon to the wind, heft a furry body up onto the top of her foot, and—

She kicked with all her strength, then immediately started counting again. Better to focus on numbers than the thwack of the rat's body hitting a crate. Judging by how many times she'd done this, at least an hour, probably more, had passed. Curse that Mr. Quail!

Falling back into a rhythm, she escaped the dark hopelessness threatening to strangle her. There was comfort in counting. Soothing, predictable. . .she stiffened. An off-beat thud of boots scattered her numbers like blown dandelion seeds.

A key scraped in the lock, and the door swung inward. Light flooded inside, not brilliant, just a yellow glow slanting in from a lantern on the corridor wall. Even so, she blinked.

"Told you I'd be back. I. . ." Mr. Quail stopped just inside the threshold, eyes fixed on the floor. "What the devil?"

She followed his gaze. Three furry bodies lay unmoving, long tails a tangle. She frowned. Only three? Surely she'd kicked more rats than that—which meant they'd only return to torment her again.

She scowled up at Mr. Quail. "How dare you leave me in here."

Without a word, he set down the mug he carried and pulled a knife from a sheath strapped to his belt.

Johanna retreated until her back smacked up against a tower of crates. Hands yet lashed together, she'd be no match for the man—and likely wouldn't be even if she were free and held her own blade. "What do you intend? You won't get away with this. Please, Mr. Quail!"

Her breath came so fast, little sparkles dotted her vision.

He grabbed hold of her and spun her around. Two tugs and a yank later, the bindings on her wrists dropped to the floor. She whirled, ready to pummel him if he touched her.

"I am sorry for this, truly." Stepping back, Mr. Quail tucked away his knife and ran a hand through his hair, then breathed out a curse. "I will see you safely to shore."

She rubbed the ache in her arms, which helped some, though it did nothing to remove the pain of what was to come. "I suppose damaged goods will not draw as fair a price once we land in France."

"What?" His dark hair hung low over his eyes, yet no need to see, for the confusion in his voice spoke volumes.

But what did he not understand?

His chin lifted, and he shook his head. "No, Miss Langley. I will not see you sold. That was only an excuse to keep them from killing you."

Her hands fell to her sides, the urge to return to her counting strong. Numbers made sense. Mr. Quail's words did not.

"Why spare me?" she asked—then wished she hadn't. The answer might be worse than rodents crawling over her feet.

He said nothing, just crossed back to the door and retrieved a cup. "Here, drink this."

Her throat tightened. Thirst waged war with her brain, telling her not to accept what might be poisoned. She tested the liquid with her tongue. Tepid. Smelling of nothing other than the damp wood of the mug.

She drained the cup dry. Better to die here than face a life of degradation at the hands of unknown men.

"Better?" Mr. Quail took the cup from her.

She peered at him, his dark curls framing an even darker face lost in the shadows. "Who are you? Really?"

"I suppose, circumstances considered, I owe you an explanation." He pivoted and, with some effort, turned two crates on their sides. He sat on one, and swept his hand over to the other. From this angle, light bathed him like an archangel. "My name is Clarkwell, Miss Langley. Henry Clarkwell. I am a revenue officer, as are the rest of the members of my band."

Slowly, she sank onto the crate. His information, while outlandish, rang true, somewhat. "I knew you weren't musicians," she murmured.

"And it was very gracious of you to allow us lodging despite our shortcomings. You will be compensated, but you must understand that while we were in Dover, we had to remain in character—as we must continue to do until we land."

"What is this all about, Mr. Quai—I mean, Mr. Clarkwell?" The name felt foreign on her tongue—but no more strange than conversing in a storage closet with rats at her feet.

Mr. Quail–Clarkwell leaned forward, dangling the empty cup between his knees. "I came to Dover to uncover and break up a guinea gang. Are you aware of such activity?"

"I know smuggling of all sorts is common."

"Well this sort is the very worst, other than wrecking, that is. It's no secret that gold is in short supply—and in great demand across the Channel. Opportunists ship our guineas over to the French, who pay a premium, trading in lace, silks, and other luxuries. I thought I'd embedded myself in with just such a gang." His words slowed, and for a moment he said nothing. "Turns out, it's far more treacherous."

Something in his voice shivered—or maybe it was she who quivered. She folded her hands in her lap, gripping her own fingers for support. "What is it?"

Reaching for her, he patted her knotted fingers. "Don't worry yourself, Miss Langley. I sent for reinforcements yesterday. As I've said, this will all soon be over." He stood and offered his hand. "Come, let's find you a better place to hide and leave the rats to their foraging."

She stared at his outstretched fingers. Calloused. Nails bitten off. Strong and unflinching and determined. Should she trust this man? Was this a trick? She lowered her face, and her gaze landed on one of the rat carcasses splayed on the floor. Some choice.

She put her hand in his and allowed him to lead her out the door.

"Que!" His name was belted out from down the passage. "Where ye be?"

Boots thudded closer.

"Blast!" Mr. Quail huffed out a curse and shoved her back into the storage room.

"No, not again." She tried to hold on to his hand, but his fingers wrenched from hers.

"Sorry." He slammed the door, leaving her in the dark.

Leaving her with the rats.

CHAPTER THIRTY-THREE

How many rats were on this ship? Closing the hammer, Alex dropped his gun to the deck, as bid by the growling voice at his back. Robbie did the same. Along with the viscount and Louisa, they all turned to face Major General William Overtun. Three soldiers stood at his side, aiming guns their way. So did the general. How many more layers of subterfuge could there possibly be?

"Overtun?" The viscount stepped toward him, relief bleeding from his voice as fluid as that from the wound on his arm. "Thank God for putting a stop to this..." His words dripped to a stop, and his feet froze. "But why are you here? What's gone wrong?"

Overtun shrugged, and Alex flinched. One wrong move with that loaded pistol in his hand could mean someone's corpse on the deck.

"Other than a few anomalies—namely the entourage you seem to be travelling with," the general swept out his free hand, "nothing is amiss. The plan is running along as expected."

Clutching his wounded arm, the viscount swayed. "But you were never to be connected in any way with this mission."

"I believe your nephew stated it more plainly than I ever could. What was it you said, Robbie? Aah, yes, you, and all of you now, I suppose, are 'merely pawns in this game of mine, necessary for only a short while.'" A full grin slashed across the general's face. "Tell me, Robbie, are you certain it was you who planted the seed of an impending invasion during that card game you and I played—or was it *I* who did the planting?" He shook his head, his upper lip curling. "You should've done as your uncle said and stayed with the frames in Dover, boy. But you were never one to follow an order, were you? Nor were you, Edward."

The major speared the viscount with a deadly stare, one that even in the dark gleamed with the threat of murder. "You should've finished the job the rajah sent you on, hmm?"

The viscount staggered back to Louisa's side. "Good heavens, Overtun! Surely you don't mean—"

"Of course I mean it! I've meant to do this since that day years ago when your treachery took the life of my sister and her family in Siswapur. I watched them die. I barely escaped!"

Alex sucked in a breath. The viscount had been right about his past sins, but had the man expected the incubus would manifest here? Tonight?

Overtun widened his stance. "I was merely waiting for the best opportunity to take your life *and* your honor forever. But apparently, I'll be taking your family as well. Goodbye, Edward."

A flash of spark, the sharp crack of a small explosion, and a bullet whizzed through the air. The viscount flew backward, his head split apart before he hit the deck.

Louisa screamed and dropped to his side.

Alex tensed, ready to drop when the soldiers decided to let loose their fire.

The general turned his face to his men, his thick lips opening to give the order—

"Stop!" Robbie shouted, his hands reaching for the sky. "We had nothing to do with the old man's treachery."

Overtun cut a glance to Robbie. "True, but you've seen me now. I can't very well lay the blame on your uncle for this stolen shipment of rockets with you three to say otherwise." He turned back to the soldiers. "On my mark—"

"I can get you more money than you can imagine!" Robbie's voice tightened to a shrewish tone, competing with the wailing of Louisa.

The general's big chest expanded, then he blew out a breath and held up his hand to his soldiers. "I'm listening."

"The frames for these rockets are no longer in Dover. I hired a crew to smuggle them off. That ship is to rendezvous here within the hour. My league contact is paying top dollar, likely more than yours, and expects both rockets *and* frames."

"I should've marked you as a leaguer." Overtun chuckled. "How much?"

"Two thousand guineas."

Alex's brows rose as high as Robbie's hands. That was quite a sum. No wonder the traitor had paid him such a whopping amount to keep the viscount distracted.

"Hmm." The general scratched his jaw. "All right. We'll see if your story is true and wait out the hour. But we won't be needing the others."

"Don't be so hasty, Overtun." Alex lifted his hands as well. "I can beat his deal." Sweat beaded on his brow. *Think! Think!* What could he possibly offer?

The moon broke out again, highlighting the general's thick lips. "You know, Morton, you've been a wild card since the day I met you. What's your bid?"

"Double that."

"How?"

He swallowed. How to make this plausible without being an outright lie? "It's true that France will pay a generous amount, but the Prussians will pay even more. I have connections—unless I'm dead."

"Well, well. . .quite the high-stakes game we've got going, eh? Just like old times."

Overtun turned to the soldier nearest him.

Alex froze, his heartbeat hinging on the general's next words. Around them, sailors crawled up and down the ratlines as if on deck men's lives were of no account. Louisa's sobbing added to the madness. Surely perdition could be no more horrific than this.

"Take them below, Jonesy. One wrong move, shoot them." Overtun pried a pocket watch from his waistcoat and snapped it open. "You've got an hour, Robbie. If those frames show up, we'll sell them to your accomplices. More poetic if the viscount is blamed with a sale to the

French." He snapped the lid shut and stuffed it back. "But if not, I'll go with Mr. Morton's offer."

One of the soldiers stalked out from the rest, the muzzle of his gun urging them to move. The gawky man appeared to be sixteen or perhaps seventeen. A youth, at any rate—with hopefully not much fighting experience. That could be an asset, one Alex tucked away as securely as the last gun that yet remained beneath his coat.

Alex reached for Louisa's arm to haul her up.

"Not the woman," Overtun growled. "Louisa stays here."

She lifted her face to Alex, her wide eyes staring into his, helpless and pleading. "Help me."

"I'll come for you," he whispered.

"Move it!"

The cold jab of a pistol barrel stabbed him in the back. He stumbled forward, catching up to Robbie near the stairs. As they marched down, tripping in the only light from a lantern at the base of the hold, a gunshot rang out.

Alex's gut jerked. The villain! All of them! Coburn. Robbie. Overtun. As scheming as Louisa was, she'd not deserved such an end. He hesitated on the last stair, trying desperately to assess the situation.

But a kick to his backside sent him sprawling ahead.

"Have a seat, boys," Jonesy ordered.

Alex used the momentum of the kick to yank out his pistol and whip around.

The soldier's eyes widened. So did Robbie's.

"Think, Jonesy." Alex spoke low and calm. "Do you really want a gunfight down here, with a hold full of rockets and gunpowder? Put your weapon down."

Jonesy's jaw dropped. His gun didn't. Did the fellow know his threat was empty—that it would take more than a gunshot to fire off this load?

"If you shoot me, you'll have no time to reload before Robbie here takes you out." Alex tipped his head toward Robbie, who lowered into a crouch, ready to spring. "Let it go, Jonesy, nice and easy."

The young man's Adam's apple bobbed, a grotesque movement in the lantern light. But he did as bid, and squatted to lay down his gun.

The second his fingers let go, Alex lunged. He drove his gun grip into the man's skull. Now it was Jonesy's turn to sprawl. Alex scooped up the soldier's gun and swung around to face Robbie.

"Nice work, ol' boy!" Robbie flashed him a smile and held out his hand. "Give me one."

Alex grinned back. "Sure."

Once again he lunged, this time clouting Robbie in the head. Robbie hit the planks as hard as Jonesy.

Tucking the pistols back into his belt, Alex sidestepped the fallen men and reached for the lantern. The light hung over a barrel of water just in case the thing chanced a fall. Best to assess the situation first, then act, though he wouldn't have much time.

Above deck, a madman reigned with no compunction about shooting on a whim. And down here? Alex strode deeper into the hold, along the center aisle. Big bales wrapped in canvas lined both sides. He frowned. Rockets wouldn't be bundled in naught but fabric and rope.

He set down the lantern and slipped out his boot knife, then cut one of the bindings and sliced into the fabric. His blade dug deep and stuck into a bale of cotton.

Cotton?

What lunacy was this? Had the whole rocket scam been nothing but that—a scam? Had someone double-crossed the double-crosser, or was a triple-cross at play? He yanked out his knife, baffled. This was beyond his reckoning.

His gaze shot to the dark rafters above, and he prayed, for there was naught more to do. "So many lives are at risk, God. The stakes are too high, and I—I—"

His prayer juddered to a stop. So much anguish choked him he could hardly breathe—a feeling eerily like when he'd rotted in the gaol's hole. . .and yet God had been there, as He was now.

He gasped, lungs suddenly filling. What a thick-headed dolt. Had he not learned that already? "Of course, God." He smiled. "You are here, so help me. I cannot do this on my own."

Blowing out a long breath, he cracked his neck, waiting for some kind of wisdom. None came. Nothing but the purl of the water against the hull. The purl of the water... If rows of thick cotton lined this hold, he'd not be able to hear that so clearly.

He pulled down the bale he'd cut open, then hauled out the one below it, creating an opening. Retrieving the lantern, he held it aloft. Golden light landed on the slats of crates. Stacks of them, by the looks of it. Once again he set down the lantern, then worked to probe a crate between the slats. His blade tip first met straw, then snubbed onto metal. Rockets. He'd bet his life on it—and just might.

Backing out of the passage, he snagged his light along the way. Someone had gone to much trouble to hide the crates behind a wall of cotton, probably as a front on the off-chance of an impromptu dockside check. Not that it mattered now. He had to stop these rockets from landing in enemy hands—and the cotton was going to do just that.

Bale upon bale, slice upon slice, he yanked and grabbed and spread a trail of loose cotton from one end of the aisle to the other, the length of the hull. Sweat trickled between his shoulder blades. His hands cramped and his lungs labored. But he worked like a demon, unstoppable—until a grunt ended his crazed dance. Either Jonesy or Robbie would soon be sounding an alarm.

He snatched the lantern and lifted the glass, then touched a piece of cotton to the flame and threw it on the loosened tinder. He repeated the action, working his way back toward the stairs, toward the men. By the time he reached them, flames licked at the bales—and would soon hit the crates.

And the rockets.

Robbie sat up, dazed, moaning, holding his head.

"Time to go," Alex hauled him up.

"Wha. . . ?" It might've been a question. Or another moan. Hard to tell.

Alex shoved him toward the stairs. "Move it, man!"

Robbie started stumbling upward. Alex grabbed a pail and dipped it into the bucket. Hefting the pail, he dumped the water on Jonesy, who immediately sputtered and choked, coming to with great gasps.

Alex threw the lantern toward the inferno then darted up the stairs after Robbie.

Up top, Robbie bent over the bodies on the deck. Louisa's crumpled form heaped atop her father, closer in death than they ever were in life. The sight twisted Alex's gut.

"Fire!" Sailors broke into a dead run toward them—toward the stairway.

Alex grabbed Robbie's arm and dragged him to the gunwale. They both peered over, Alex judging the best place to land. Black water licked up the sides far below them.

Robbie turned to him, the whites of his eyes wide. "I can't swim!"

Alex growled. Did no one consider swimming a skill to be learned?

"Over there!" Overtun's raspy voice hit him in the back.

Alex grabbed Robbie's arm. "There's no time. Hold on to me."

Without giving the man a moment to consider, Alex swung over the rail and tugged Robbie down into the sea.

The coldness sucked his breath.

The darkness was worse.

Alex kicked, struggling to break the surface. Robbie was a dead weight.

God, please!

His head emerged from black into black, but at least there was air. He sucked in until his lungs burned. So did Robbie, every time he bobbed up long enough to snatch a breath.

"Kick your feet, man!"

An eternity later, they worked out a rhythm—though Robbie refused to let go of his stranglehold on Alex's arm. It was impossible to see the shore, despite the eerie light of spreading flames behind them. Hopefully Robbie was right about that rendezvousing ship of his and it would arrive soon. Alex strained all his muscles into plowing through the waves.

Putting as much distance as he could between themselves and the rockets that would soon explode.

Forget the counting. It wasn't working anyway. Neither was fear or worrying about how Mam was suffering on her behalf—for surely

Thomas had told her by now of how she'd gone to look for Mr. Nutbrown. Johanna curled her fingers into fists. There had to be a way to get off this ship of demons. She'd waited long enough for Mr. Quail-Clarkwell to rescue her—if he were even telling the truth.

But what to do? Maybe, if she were able to pry off a lid from one of the crates, or even a single slat, she could whack whoever next entered the door right in the head, then make a run for it. Jumping into the sea was a better option than wallowing in this dark hole.

Feeling about, she set to work. What seemed like hours later, she'd broken three fingernails, and so many splinters needled her flesh, she felt like a human pincushion. But the pain finally paid off, and she worked loose a piece of the wood.

There wasn't much room to practice swinging. More often than not, she smacked her elbow. One time her sleeve caught on a nail and ripped the fabric. Her hair stuck in her eyes and her stays chafed her skin. But she managed to figure out that a chopping motion, slicing downward from high over her head, was the most suitable action. Now, to judge how far to stand from the door.

She crept across the small space, taking care to avoid the earlier rats she'd downed, one hand out to feel for the wood—then stopped.

And listened.

One explosion. Two, three, four. Fives and tens and twenties. Popping, hammering, like the bang of fireworks she'd heard the one time she'd visited London. She clutched her slat, driving splinters deeper into her fingers. These were not fireworks, not on the sea, which could only mean one thing.

The ship was under attack.

Panic tasted like vinegar. No! She had to get out of here. Now.

She sprang ahead, dropping her pathetic weapon. With both hands, she beat against the wooden door. "Let me out—"

The door jiggled in the frame. She paused, hands yet upraised.

A locked door wouldn't jiggle.

She swung the door open wide. Light barreled in from the lantern in the corridor. For a heartbeat, she stood frozen.

Really God? All this time I could've walked free?

Stunning, truly, but no more than the inner voice that answered her back.

Is that not a picture of your life, child?

She gasped. God did have everything in hand—and always had, even when she ran ahead of Him or lagged behind, trying to do things her own way.

"Forgive me," she whispered, tucking the truth away to savor later—then snatched up her jagged piece of crate-wood. After all, if God went through the trouble of opening the door, she probably should go through it.

CHAPTER THIRTY-FOUR

Sharp pain cut into Alex's arm, each tug on the rope agony, but he held. Thank God he held. Robbie clung to him like a woman. They both banged against the hull of the newly arrived ship. Just a few more pulls and they'd clear the gunwale—if his shoulder didn't dislocate before then.

The swim had been brutal, but a far cry better than remaining on the ship behind him. Or what was left of it. The last of the rockets exploded. An eerie orange light violated the darkness. Flashes of red shot out intermittently. How many men had made it off? How many hadn't?

Deliver them, God—and us as well.

A groan ripped out his throat as a last, mighty heave lugged them over the wooden rail. He and Robbie hit the deck like landed mackerels. Wincing, Alex stumbled to his feet. A hank of wet hair fell over his brow, dripping salt water into his eyes. The sting was terrific. Blinking, he shook his head like a dog.

"Well, this is a surprise."

He froze, then stared into a swarthy face, hellish in the fiery glow. Quail. The irony of being saved by a smuggler punched him in the gut, yet a half smile twitched his lips. "I knew you were scum from the moment I met you."

"What a coincidence. I thought as much of you. This is going to be a real pleasure." Quail nodded to his band—smugglers all—lining up beside him. Every one of them pulled a gun from inside their coats, yet none raised their muzzles. A quiet threat, but a threat nonetheless.

"Thanks, ol' boy." On the other side of Alex, Robbie staggered to his feet, then clouted him on the arm—his sore one. "We might be out a load of money, but we're safe."

He smirked. This was safe? Facing six men with guns at their sides?

"What'd ye haul up there, Que? Turn 'em around. Nice and slow."

Throbbing started behind Alex's eyes. The voice, altogether too familiar with its bass bluster, stabbed him in the back. There was *nothing* safe about this.

He and Robbie pivoted. Alex planted his feet.

But Robbie strode over to Blackie and Axe. "Good job, men. I'll take it from here."

Alex sucked in a breath. If luck smiled on him, the remnants of fire on the sinking ship behind him would be bright enough to blind Blackie from seeing his face.

But the villain stood there, leaning on his good leg, riding the canting deck like a sea monster come aboard—and the longer he stared, the wider his eyes opened. So did the red-headed scoundrel a head shorter next to him.

Blackie pulled a pistol. "Well, well, there is a God after all. Look what the deeps spit up." A chuckle rumbled in his throat, garbly and altogether mirthless.

"We been gunnin' fer you a while now." Charlie pulled the axe out of his belt. "But ne'er thought to look in the sea."

Robbie glowered at them both. "Put those weapons down. This man just saved my life."

"And he'll take it as fast." Charlie hefted his axe.

"I'm in charge here. Drop your weapons!" Robbie's voice bellowed, dark and deadly—a surprising tone, coming from the dandy of a man . . . or was he?

Alex scanned the immediate area, scrambling to find an out. Behind him was Quail and his men. That was a no go. In front, sure death. To his sides, cannons lined the decks. If he dove for the cover of one, who would shoot him first—Blackie or Quail?

Blackie belched out a curse at Robbie. "Idiot! You got no idea who you been keepin' company with." His black eyes shifted to Alex. "Tell him."

Despite the cold, wet clothing sticking to his body like a second skin, sweat beaded on his brow. Once his identity was revealed, there'd be no mercy. A lawman's blood was a prize. A trophy. A crown of glory to the criminal that drew it first.

He clamped his jaw shut.

Robbie swung his head toward him. "Do you know these men?"

He breathed in until his lungs burned. What a question. He'd been in sticky situations before, but this one? This just might be his last.

His gaze darted from Robbie to the gun in Blackie's hand, then on to the axe in Charlie's. A sour taste swelled at the back of his throat, one he knew too well. Regret. All his life he'd fought to be the best runner of the squad. To make Ford proud. And now? He swallowed hard. He'd end up the same as his father, gunned down by vermin.

Robbie angled his head in a jerky movement, grotesque actually, as if he were coming unhinged. "Answer me! Do you know these men?"

He sucked in a breath, desperately scrambling for a way to talk himself out of this. Absolutely nothing came to mind. . .except for four small words.

No risk, no gain.

The sentiment he'd spoken forever ago to Johanna barreled back in his mind with startling clarity. Of course the biggest risk was telling the truth. It always was. His whole body pulsed with the rightness of it. He *would* take the biggest risk of all, and while he might still lose, he would not be gunned down without a fight. If this was his day to die, then so be it.

He threw back his shoulders. "Let's just say this is quite the reunion."

Blackie narrowed his eyes. "One I been waitin' on fer too long, Moore."

"Moore?" His name was a blasphemy on Robbie's lips.

"That there's Alexander Moore, Bow Street Runner." Charlie spit on the deck. "Liar. Scammer. And killer."

Despite the black of night, Robbie's face darkened. "Is that true?"

Alex grunted. "Some of it."

"Which part?" The tip of Quail's muzzle jabbed him in the back.

He threw back his shoulders. He might as well go out with bravado. "Axe is right. I am a Bow Street Runner, and you, gentlemen, are all under arrest."

Robbie swore.

Blackie laughed—then sighted along the barrel of his gun.

Charlie hefted his axe, poised to throw.

Behind Alex, the click of six guns was a sound eerily reminiscent of the last ship he'd been on—and that hadn't ended so well.

But then his entire world shifted onto its axis, draining his blood to his feet. Across the deck, a dark figure in a skirt scurried into his line of sight, face pale, hair loose, eyes cavernous.

God, no!

Hiking her skirts, Johanna took the stairs two at a time, her prayers as fervent as her pace. Whatever was happening above deck couldn't be good. The popping explosions grew louder. Men's angry shouts interspersed between the blasts. She clutched her gown tight in one hand, and in her other, the crude club she'd wrested from the crate. If she could make it the short distance across deck to the railing without being accosted, she stood a good chance of jumping overboard—though her odds of swimming to shore were in God's hands. But then, hadn't He just shown her that was the best place to be? She ramped up her prayers and burst through the open door into night.

Or into hell, more like it.

Wicked red light bled onto a macabre scene. Beyond their ship, eruptions of fire shot into the sky from a vessel lying sideways, soon to be swallowed by the sea. Thank God it wasn't cannon fire she'd heard. But with or without artillery, that ship was going down and no doubt taking men with it. Her heart constricted at the thought of the sailors about to lose their lives, whoever they were.

No time to lament now, though. She darted onward, eyes straining to pick out the best route to the rail that would avoid the sight of the men on deck. And the guns. Sweet heavens! So many guns. Was every last man armed and ready to shoot? But why? They were clearly not under attack.

By some miracle, the route to the railing was clear. No one focused on her, for they were all too busy looking at a poor wretch who stood at the center of their attention. All muzzles aimed at the man's guts. But he didn't seem to care a fig. His broad shoulders were thrown back, feet wide, the stance of a warrior about to wage battle. Either he was addle-brained or beyond reason.

Paces from the railing, though, Johanna stopped. Freedom beckoned—but so did the niggling suspicion creeping from her head to heart. Surely, she was wrong.

But she had to be sure.

Slowly, she retreated, craning her neck for a better view of the man. When her gaze landed on him, an invisible tether lifted his face to hers.

Time stopped, as did life and breath. Men in back. Men in front. All hefted weapons. All aimed at Alex.

Her scalp prickled. Her arms. Her soul. Despite the way he'd taken her heart and thrown it back into her face, she couldn't stand here and watch him die, because she'd die too. Such was the love that throbbed in her veins.

"Alex!" It was more a scream than a name, one that competed with the boom of an explosion.

He didn't move, not even as the air vibrated with the last blast from the dying ship. But he saw her just the same. The dark of his eyes slipped ever so slowly to the left, back at her, then to the left again. Commanding. Pleading.

She bit her lip. Even without looking she knew exactly what he asked. The stairs. He wanted her below deck. It was a good idea, and she took a tentative step toward them—then stopped. Was this how it'd been for Mr. Nutbrown? Had he faced death alone, perhaps a needless death because of the inaction of a fearful bystander? How could she hide away and let Alex die without doing something?

Yet what could she—a simple girl with a stick—do against men with guns?

She clenched her piece of wood tighter, the rough grain cutting into the tender parts of her palm. *Assess. Assess.* Repeating the words in her head, she matched her breathing to the rhythm until her heart rate slowed.

Between Alex and the railing stood a line of men. Unruly hair curled out from beneath the hat of the central figure, tall of stature, less burly than Alex, but just as familiar. Mr. Quail-Clarkwell. If the man truly was a revenue officer, he wouldn't harm Alex. Unless he still believed Alex to be a smuggler. But being a lawman, as long as Alex didn't threaten him, the man wouldn't shoot him. . .would he?

She snapped her gaze to the men in front of Alex. There were only three. A dandy of a fellow, who appeared to be unarmed, the axe-wielding Mr. Pickens, and the gun-toting Mr. Cooper—and who knew when that villain would let loose. Behind those three, near the opposite railing, seven others stood with guns raised as well.

Her shoulders sank. The situation was beyond her salvation—but that didn't mean she couldn't try. Perhaps if she got Mr. Cooper's attention, for even the space of a breath, maybe Alex could use it to his advantage.

She crept forward.

Just as five more men emerged out of the hatch from below. She grit her teeth. Wonderful. More guns.

"Stop!" Mr. Quail-Clarkwell's command boomed.

Johanna froze. So did everyone else. Was he speaking to her or to the others?

"As the man said, you're all under arrest." Mr. Quail-Clarkwell and the rest of his men stepped abreast of Alex.

She blinked. Surely she wasn't seeing this, but. . . apparently she'd been wrong. Very wrong. Mr. Quail-Clarkwell and his men hadn't been aiming at Alex, but at the three others in front of him. No wonder Mr. Cooper hadn't pulled his trigger yet.

"If you're lying, Moore, you're a dead man." Mr. Quail-Clarkwell handed Alex one of his guns.

Moore? Johanna angled her head.

So did Alex—a movement she'd learned from living with him the past month that meant he was confused yet still determined to be in charge. He grabbed the pistol, his gaze once again meeting hers, this time with a visible twitch of his head toward the stairs.

Then he extended his arm and aimed the barrel at Mr. Cooper. "You should've shot me while you had the chance."

Grating laughter rumbled out the man's mouth. "Night's not over yet."

"It is for you. Drop your gun."

To her left, near the railing, a man crept toward her, closing in fast. Without thinking, she whaled the board at him.

And missed.

He roared.

A nightmare unleashed. Popping, smoking, curses and hollers exploded. Something hot whizzed past her cheek, grazing a line of fire across the skin.

Was it too late to reach the stairs?

CHAPTER THIRTY-FIVE

One bullet. Just one. Alex crouched behind a cannon, shots pinging off the metal. Smoky haze distorted the scene. Blasts of red dotted the night. Rising slightly, he waited, assessing, judging where best to place his one shot. Thank God Johanna had disappeared below deck. Beside him, Quail reloaded. Why the devil had the man jumped sides?

Burnt gunpowder stung his nose. So did the thick odor of spilled blood. Around the deck, men dropped like swatted blackflies. Except for one man, crouching low, who duck-walked his way toward the quarterdeck. Alex knew his short shape well. He aimed his gun at Robbie's lower half and fired, hoping for a wound, not a kill—just as a bullet whizzed past his own head. He dropped behind the cannon.

The popping died out. Quail and his men reloaded once again. Likely the other side did too. Alex used the lull to rise up and evaluate how many were left. Bodies were strewn about, not the one he'd shot at, but another snagged his attention at center deck. Blackie sprawled in a dark pool, his wooden leg splintered off mid-calf. He didn't move.

Next to Alex, Quail raised his gun.

Alex flung out his arm. "Hold. Look."

Across the deck, smugglers were in various stages of throwing down guns and flinging themselves overboard—and one of them had red hair.

"Grab some rope," Alex ordered, then bolted and grasped the man. Squeezing a mite tighter than necessary, he kept Axe in a chokehold until Quail brought the rope.

Breathing hard, he straightened. Charlie yet struggled at his feet, but he wouldn't be going anywhere—except to gaol.

Around him, Quail's men seized fleeing smugglers. Some slipped their clutches, but most they nabbed and tied up.

"You know your business." Quail clouted Alex on the back. "Looks like you really are a runner."

He snorted, swiping the sweat from his brow with his still-wet sleeve. "And you? Who are you, really?"

Quail's eyes found his, and for the first time, no hint of foolery or scheming glowed in their depths. "The name's Henry Clarkwell, revenue officer, sent to ferret out a guinea gang operating out of Dover." He scanned the deck. "Looks like I stumbled onto something bigger."

"That you did. Sedition, which is why I'm here, though I'm currently missing my traitor." Alex darted his gaze around the ship. No Robbie. Had he missed his mark?

"Come on." Alex sprinted over to where Robbie should've been, then followed a gruesome path. The bloody trail ended at the rear of the ship, portside gunwale, where a few men wrestled with ropes and a ferrying skiff, just about to lower it over the side. Only one man stood inactive, grasping on to the railing to keep from falling over. A dark stain spread from his knee to his foot.

Alex pulled his gun. "Stop right there. Step away from the boat."

A bluff, for he had no ammunition. Would Robbie and his few minions fold, or did they have a last ace to play?

No matter. Clarkwell and his men caught up, fanning out on both sides of him, weapons drawn. He'd never expected a miracle of such magnitude in the guise of bad musicians, and he stifled a laugh. Indeed, God surely did have a sense of humor.

"Deserting again, Robbie?" Alex smirked. Judging by the twitch on Robbie's jaw, the question struck sharper than a well-aimed right hook. "I'd have thought you'd learned your lesson by now."

Robbie unraveled quite a string of profanity as he sank to the deck.

For the first time in weeks, the tension in Alex's shoulders loosened. He lowered his pistol and glanced at Clarkwell. "Can you and your men manage these few without me?"

"I may not play the violin with finesse, Moore, but I do know my way around smugglers." Clarkwell flashed him a grin. "Go. Tend to Miss Langley, for I have no doubt you'll not rest easy until you do."

Shoving the gun in his waistband, Alex turned and sprinted back to the stairs. He took them two at a time, nearly missing the last, but landed on solid footing nonetheless. Lanterns lit a corridor, and halfway down one of them, a lone figure in a gown huddled on the planks.

His step faltered. As much as he wanted to gather her in his arms, she might not wish to be held. Not by him. Especially not when he told her all—for he must. He knew that now. It was time he revealed who he really was, laid bare his soul before her, and risked either her gain or loss, for such was the ultimate power of truth.

Oh, God, go before me. I cannot endure the thought of losing her.

He strode ahead, driven by grim determination, and gripped her by the shoulders, pulling her upward. "Johanna?"

She lifted her face to his, and he staggered back a step. She held a cloth to her cheek.

Soaked with blood.

She'd lived a hundred years this day. Or more. By the looks of it, Alex had too. Silently, Johanna studied him in the dim light. His wet shirt clung to his muscles, alluring, but judging by the bend of his shoulders, he was worn as thin as her. Hair clung to half his face, darkened to burnt honey from seawater and sweat, all snarled and wild. Smoky residue smudged his jaw. Creases at the edges of his eyes disappeared as his gaze narrowed, focusing on her.

"You're hurt." Pain raged in his voice, as if he'd been the one grazed by a bullet.

Slowly, he pulled her hand from her cheek. With a touch infinitely tender, he angled her chin and bent to examine the wound. He smelled of the sea and gunpowder, of salt and man. An awful scent—yet marvelous, for it meant he lived. He breathed. He was here.

For a second, she closed her eyes and whispered, "Thank You, God."

"Indeed," Alex echoed, then he released her and ripped off a strip from the hem of his shirt.

She stood, dazed, too spent to move or even care.

"This is going to sting, but it will help in the long run." His eyes held her gentle, then his voice broke. "I'm sorry."

He pressed the cold, saltwater fabric to her face.

She sucked in air, fighting to shove down a scream. Her cheek burned like a thousand beestings. Tears bled from the sides of her eyes, and she clenched her hands to fists. Merciful stars! That hurt.

Through it all, he held on, applying firm pressure. He said nothing, but a strange, strangled groan rumbled in his throat.

Finally, the pain began to ebb. She unclenched her hands and breathed easier. Maybe—just maybe—this nightmare had come to an end.

"Is it over?" Her voice came out choppy. She cleared her throat and started again. "I mean up there." She lifted her gaze to the rafters, then back to his. "No one's trying to shoot you anymore?"

"No, leastwise not this bunch." His lips curved, a bitter smile, but a smile nonetheless. "What are you doing here? Why are you not safe at home?"

She blinked. How did one explain what'd happened over the space of a hundred years? So much. Too much. "Long story," she murmured. "The short of it is Mr. Cooper wanted to kill me, but Mr. Quail, er, Clarkwell talked him out of it."

Alex shook his head, the damp straggles of his hair brushing against his collar. "I really do owe that man a debt."

Despite the pull on her cheek, she frowned. Why would a gentleman of Alex's wealth and stature owe a revenue man anything? For that matter, what was he doing here instead of courting his betrothed? "I don't understand any of this. What have you to do with the law? Why are you even here?"

His breath huffed out, warm against her brow. "In your own words, it's a long story. The short of it is I'm not who you think I am. I am a Bow Street officer, a lawman, just like Clarkwell, though here for different purposes. I was sent to uncover a plot against the Crown." He tucked his chin, much the same as Thomas when caught in a mischief. "My true name is Alexander Moore."

"Moore?" She tasted the name, rolling it around in her mouth, unsure if she liked the flavor or ought to spit it out. "Not Morton."

"That's right."

The knowledge lodged in her mind like an unwanted guest—one she desperately wanted to evict. He'd lied. Alex had lied. To her. The realization pricked worse than her cheek.

She leaned back against the wall, grateful for the support. How many lies had her mother heard from her father's mouth? Memories surfaced, one after the other, as black as the water keeping them afloat. So many arguments. So many tears.

"Only going out for a bit, lovey. Back in a trice."

"I swear I don't know where the rent money could've gone, sweetling."

"No, of course I'd not gamble away our future, darlin'."

Johanna moaned as a horrid understanding spread from her heart to her head. She'd done exactly what she'd vowed never to do—fall in love with a deceiver. A beautiful, handsome deceiver. What a fool. Just like her mother. Bitterness nearly choked her.

She reached to pull his hand from her face. "Then you are not a wine merchant, either."

"No." His arm was steel. "Please, allow me to hold this a minute more."

She clawed at his sleeve, desperate to get away from his touch. "I suppose you're not a gambler, either, or a rake or a rogue?"

He held firm, but his voice softened. "To my shame, those things are true."

So, a gambler *and* a deceiver. She had almost reconciled herself to his gaming, but now lying too? Her anger flared, and she scowled. "Who are you, really, Mr. Moore?"

A tremor travelled up his arm, trembling his fingers against her cheek. "I'm just a man, Johanna. A sinful man, but one who loves you very much."

He leaned close, closer, a breath away. Surely he didn't mean to—

His mouth claimed hers, and to her horror, she pressed against his wet, solid body. Traitor! She was the deceiver, telling herself she'd never love a man like. . .

Her thoughts, her anger, her everything drifted away on a rising swell of sweet warmth. An ache, not unpleasant and altogether enticing, settled low in her belly. His lips were a whisper, a balm, one with hers—and yet ought not be.

She pulled away, breathless, hating herself for having enjoyed such a forbidden fruit. What was she thinking? Even if he were who he said he was, that didn't change the fact of his engagement. She pushed his hand away, and this time he let her, his brow weighted with an unnamed sorrow.

"Johanna," his voice was a sea of pain. "I lied to you, and for that I am eternally sorry. I thought it necessary because of a sense of misplaced duty, but I know now that my one and only duty is to God first, man second. It is much to ask, but I do. . . I beg your forgiveness for my deception, for so it was. Even though I did so for the sake of an order, that doesn't change the fact that it was wrong. That *I* was wrong."

She froze, unable to move or breathe or think. What was she to do with an apology of such proportion? She'd been right all along, that he was like her father—but then again, not at all. Her father lied too, but he'd never once admitted he was wrong or that what he did was wrong. He always had an excuse, a reason, a crutch. This level of integrity in a man was wholly unnerving—and completely irresistible.

"Johanna?"

Alex's voice pulled her to the present, and she stared at a face she'd never forget, even if she tried. "Though my pardon pales in light of God's, I freely give it, for how can I do any less?"

He pulled her close again. Aah, but she could live here, hearing his heart beat strong against her cheek, wrapped in his arms and—she pulled back. Those arms were not hers to claim. "We should not do this. You are to be married."

"No, I am not."

She frowned, the pull on her cheek a slicing burn. What was she to believe? A fine whine sounded in her head, so high-pitched she winced.

He sighed, and Atlas himself couldn't have sounded more burdened. "Forgive my bluntness, but Louisa is dead."

"What?" She gasped. Would the macabre surprises never stop? "Oh, Alex. I am so sorry for you. How you must feel."

Refolding the square of fabric, he pressed it into her hand. She stared at it, afraid to read the emotion, the grief, that surely must be weighting his brow.

"The truth is, Johanna, that I never had feelings for Miss Coburn, despite my pledge of troth. I tried several times to tell you I'd been ordered to marry her, but. . .well, the point is I overstepped the line. I gambled the one thing I couldn't afford to lose—you. And that is a risk I don't plan to ever take again. My heart has been yours since the day you fell into my arms. Whatever you believe of me, believe this. . ."

He grew silent, and she lifted her gaze to his. Such a burning fervency blazed in the blue of his eyes, a charge ran through her from head to toe.

"I will come for you once this situation is over. I vow it. Wait for me. Only me. Will you?" His fingers reached for her, but a whisper away from making contact, he pulled back, then retreated a step, giving her space. Giving her time, for he stood there, saying nothing more.

But every muscle beneath his wet clothes hardened to sharp edges.

If nothing else, she knew then she held his life in her hands. His heart. His happiness. And hers, depending upon what she said. She swallowed, afraid to speak. Afraid not to. Afraid of the wild beating of her heart and the thrumming in her temples. Had it been the same for Mam?

She bit her lip. First Alex had been a gentleman, too far above her station to notice her—but he wasn't, not really. Then he was engaged—but by compulsion. And now? He pledged his love to her—a door opened by God alone, for she'd not done a thing to earn or encourage it. Should she risk walking through it? Was the gain, Alexander Moore, worth it despite his deceptive past?

She lifted the cloth to her cheek, the hurt as painful as the years her next words might employ, and met his gaze. "I will never stop waiting for you."

And she wouldn't. She would keep her word.

But would Alex?

CHAPTER THIRTY-SIX

Johanna leaned her head against the wall, eyes closed, where she sat in the public room of the Ramsgate Arms. This early in the morning, the inn was just beginning to stir. A pot banged in the kitchen. The stairs creaked with shuffled steps. She really ought to use this opportunity to study the workings of this inn to compare it to the Blue Hedge, see if there was anything she could improve upon, but she was beyond exhausted. After a night of danger and love, her priorities had focused to more important things. . .like simply breathing.

A small nudge to her shoulder popped her eyelids open.

"Excuse me, miss." Mr. Wigman, the Arms proprietor, stared at her with hound dog eyes and a snout as long as a beagle's. "I let you rest as long as possible, but the coach is ready to leave."

"Thank you, Mr. Wigman." She rose, fighting back a yawn. Her cheek ached enough as it was. "Has Mr. Moore arrived?"

Speaking Alex's true surname woke her more effectively than Mr. Wigman's earlier nudge. It felt strange to think of him so.

He shook his head. "Sorry, miss."

"Very well. Thank you for allowing me to wait here."

"Don't thank me, miss. Thank your Mr. Moore when next you see him. He paid more than a fair amount for you to wait here till the coach arrived and paid your fare to boot." Mr. Wigman dipped his head. "Safe travels, Miss Langley."

The innkeeper darted off to the kitchen, where another pot banged.

A small smile quirked her lips, glad she didn't have to deal with the noise. Some poor cook would likely feel the wrath of Mr. Wigman this morning.

But her smile faded as she stepped out into the July sunshine and scouted the Arms' courtyard. At center stood a coach—dust-worn and as travel weary as surely she must look—with a coachman opening the door and lowering the stoop for a couple ready to board. But those were the only figures moving about. A blue-eyed, broad-shouldered Alex was nowhere to be seen.

Disappointment stole what little vigor Johanna had left, and her steps dragged over to the waiting coach. She'd wanted to hear his voice before parting, feel the strength of standing near him one more time, pretend her aching cheek and night of horror had never happened and this was just an outing to be enjoyed.

The coachman stood ready to assist her up the step, when a deep voice boomed behind her.

"Hold up!"

She turned. Alex trotted across the courtyard, bedraggled yet all the more handsome for it. She smiled in full, despite the stinging burn on her cheek.

He nodded at the coachman. "I'll help the lady."

"As you wish, but secure the door behind her. I'm running late enough as is." The coachman turned on his heel.

Yet Johanna couldn't manufacture any interest in the man's movements, for the only man she cared about stood real and warm in front of her. "I was hoping you'd come before I left," she breathed out.

"And I was hoping I'd make it. Arranging transport to London for a traitor and myself was harder than I thought it would be. Granted, the hour didn't make it any easier." He bent, studying her face. "How are you faring?"

"I'm fine. Some of Mam's famous salve and I'll be right as a thruppence in no time. Thank you for all you've done—"

The coachman blew his whistle, cutting off her last word.

Alex shoved back a wild fall of hair from his brow, taken in flight by a morning breeze. "I'll come for you as soon as I'm able. In the meantime, go to the Rose Inn. My belongings are still in room three. There's a wooden chair near the window. Turn it over and you'll find an envelope of money I secured to the bottom of the seat. Take it. It's yours, yours and your mother's, to pay off your debt."

She opened her mouth. "But you've already done so much, I can't—"

His finger pressed against her lips, warm and firm. "No buts, understood? Now off with you. I have a criminal to haul to London."

He grabbed hold of her hand and lent his strength as she mounted the stair.

She turned before he could leave, a sudden desire to leap out of the coach and into his arms rising up from her heart. Despite his promises of last night, what if she never saw him again? Transporting a criminal was no safe thing. "Please be careful."

His gaze held her for a moment—a beautiful, glorious moment. "You as well."

Then he tucked away the stair and shut the door, securing the latch.

Ignoring the other passengers, she sat and pressed her face to the window. The coach lumbered into motion, and she watched the retreating form of the lawman, the gambler, the man that she loved.

Alex counted each *tick* of the massive clock in the office corner, the fixture as dominating as the black-suited man behind the desk. The *tick-tock*s were the only thing left to count, for he'd tired of numbering the magistrate's fingertips drumming on the desk and the varied shouts and hoots outside on Bow Street. Every passing minute in London was one less spent with Johanna. It seemed a lifetime ago that he'd boarded her on that coach in Ramsgate and sent her away to the Blue Hedge, though in truth it'd been less than a week. Aah, but he couldn't wait to hold her in his arms again.

He shifted in his chair, the slight movement drawing the steel-grey eyes of Richard Ford.

Leaning forward, the magistrate planted his elbows on the desk and tented his fingers. "That's quite the tale. I suppose I shouldn't be surprised at the outcome, though I'd have bet my money on the traitor being Louisa Coburn, not Overtun."

"First bets are most often lost, until you learn the playing habits of your opponent." Alex shook his head. "I only wish I'd seen it sooner for the sake of the viscount and his daughter. It's a shame Overtun won't stand trial for their murders."

"He got what he deserved." Ford sniffed. "I'd say it was a very fitting end for him."

A bitter taste filled his mouth as he recalled Clarkwell's report from his revenue reinforcements. Quite a few bodies had washed ashore—leastwise those that had jumped ship, Major General Overtun's among them. The rest lay buried in Davy Jones' Locker, likely burned beyond recognition from the rocket explosions. Alex nodded absently. "At least Robbie shall receive his just reward."

"And likely already has. You know he won't last on a hulk, not with that deserter brand on his back. He'll be lucky to live until trial."

"No doubt." Deserter or not, few survived the horrors of a prison hulk, especially a military vessel. Alex rubbed the tightness at the back of his neck. If the other prisoners didn't get to Robbie, typhoid or some other disease likely would.

"Come now, so morose?" Ford slapped his hands on the mahogany, and Alex jumped. "It was a job well done. I knew you'd pull it off. Congratulations. What you did was no small thing. England is a safer place because of you, and you are a far sight richer."

"Thank you, sir." He sighed. "But it was by God's grace alone I managed it."

"What's this? A new humility in Alexander Moore?" Ford's brows jerked to nearly meet his shorn hairline. "This mission accomplished more than I'd hoped for."

In spite of himself, he chuckled. The magistrate could have no idea all that had changed inside of him.

"Now then, for your next assignment—"

Alex shot up his hand. "With all due respect, sir, there won't be a next."

He stood and reached inside his dress coat. His fingers wrapped around the worn handle of his tipstaff for the last time. For the space of a heartbeat, he memorized the feel of the wood against his skin. So many adventures. So much thrill and danger and justice he'd experienced with this tool. This bit of wood and metal had been an extension of his life and dreams. Was he truly ready to give it up? To cast aside his ambition of becoming the best Bow Street had to offer?

A small smile quirked his mouth. For Johanna, he'd give up the moon and stars were they his to give.

He pulled out the tipstaff and laid it on the magistrate's desk.

"Let me guess." Ford's gaze drifted from the tipstaff to him, a single grey brow arched. "Is this on account of a certain innkeeper's daughter?"

"It is." He smiled, a silly, sloppy grin but one that wouldn't be stopped. "Being the top officer no longer holds appeal. I leave on the morrow."

Ford leaned back in his chair and laced his fingers behind his head. "Hmm. That doesn't give me much time, but I suppose I can be packed by then."

Alex studied the man, but the magistrate's face could bluff even a faro champion—one as well practiced as himself. "What do you mean?"

"I should think it obvious. I'm going with you."

Ford was known for his grapeshot comments, but this one peppered him back a step. "Sir?"

"Oh, have a seat before you fall." His arms dropped to his sides, and he leaned forward in his chair. "I'm sure you have some idea as to my unfinished business in Dover. The question is *what* do you know?"

Alex sank into the chair. As much as he wanted to tie up the last of his London loose ends, this might be his opportunity for a glimpse into Ford's past life. "Mrs. Langley told me some of your story," he admitted. "But not all. I know you married another, a colonial, for the sake of duty."

"That I did. While it wasn't of my doing, nevertheless it was my fault Miss Harrington came to be with child." His right shoulder twitched slightly, the closest the man ever came to a shrug. "What else was there to do?"

The afternoon sun cut a swath of light through the Bow Street window, highlighting a faraway glaze in the magistrate's eyes. His voice lowered to a near whisper. "She died in labor. By the time I returned to England, Eliza had already married William Langley. Not that I blamed her, and I still don't. I'd always planned to rectify that situation, for I've never loved another like her. But the timing never seemed right."

Alex scratched his jaw. Each successive *tick-tock* clicked the assorted facts he'd gathered into place. "So that's why you placed me at the Blue Hedge."

A smile grew slowly, like the first sprig of grass shooting up from a wintery field, until it bloomed into a full grin. "I'd hoped it might get me a foot in the door, though I wouldn't swear to that under oath."

Alex smirked. It couldn't be helped—nor did such an insubordinate tic matter anymore, for he was no longer under the magistrate's rule.

The smirk quickly faded, though. If Ford left Bow Street, neither would the magistrate be beholden to enforcing the law, to mete out justice, to continue in a career he'd held dear above everything else. Alex swept out his hand. "You'll leave all this? Your respected position? Your cherished vocation? That's quite a risky bet for someone you've not seen in years, someone who may not have you. Mrs. Langley is not a woman easily swayed."

"True. She may not succumb to my charms. But what was it you said?" Ford sucked air in through his teeth. "Aah, yes, 'First bets are most often lost, until you learn the playing habits of your opponent.' If so, and I lose, well, then I'll just have to make a study of Eliza until I figure out a way to win her."

Alex laughed. That would be a game he'd love to watch play out. Rising from his seat, he offered his hand across the desk. "I wish you well, sir. Mrs. Langley will be a worthy opponent."

Ford gripped his hand. "Tomorrow, then."

"Yes." He turned and trotted to the door, then paused with his hand on the knob. "I leave at first light. Don't be late."

"I assure you," Ford lifted his chin, "this time nothing will keep me from Eliza."

Alex yanked open the door and stepped out into a firing line of three sets of eyeballs, all gunning for him. He eased the door shut behind him and planted his feet. "This can't be good."

"It could be, depending upon your answer." Nicholas Brentwood, the tallest of the trio, leaned back against the wall and folded his arms. His dark hair was shorter than the last time Alex had seen him, though the man's trademark shaggy ends would not be tamed even by pomade. His clean-shaven face had filled out a bit more, and his dress coat strained against his shoulders. Is this what marriage did to a man, fatten him up and style his hair?

Alex eyed him. "Good for whom?"

"Me!" Killian Flannery, the redheaded firecracker next to Brentwood, thumped a finger against his own chest. "I stand to make the most."

On the other side of Brentwood stood a dark shadow. Alex frowned at Thatcher and shook his head. "Don't tell me you're wagering with these two."

Thatcher's chin jutted out, yet he said nothing.

With a sigh, Alex turned back to Brentwood. "All right, what's the bet?"

"Thatcher here," he tipped his head toward the man, "has been telling me of a certain innkeeper's daughter down Dover way, one who can hold her own against the likes of you."

Alex hid a grin. Showing any kind of amusement would only spark a wildfire of teasing. "What of it?"

Brentwood laughed. "I say you'll be married with a babe on the way inside a year's time."

"Listen, Brentwood." Flannery pivoted to face the man. "Just because a bit o' skirt snagged you don't mean it's the same for ol' Moore. He's a man's man, he is. A sight too smart to get hooked fer life."

Brentwood snorted. "Admit it, Flannery. You're jealous. I see it every time you stop by and dandle my son on your knee or linger over dessert with me and Emily. The family life is what you want, what every man wants if he's brave enough to admit it."

"Bah!" Throwing out his hands, Flannery retreated over to Alex's side. "Tell 'em, guv'ner. Tell 'em you ain't about to fold."

Before Alex could speak, Brentwood's green gaze skewered him. "Am I correct? Did you give Ford your resignation?" Unfolding his arms, he stepped away from the wall and looked down his nose. "Are you not even now sweating about the collar to be off and racing back to Dover?"

Perspiration did dot his brow. Not that he'd admit it to this bunch.

What on earth had Thatcher told them? He frowned at the man. "You know, for a man of few words, you certainly manage to utter the most revealing ones."

A slight smile curved Thatcher's lips, lightening the dark looks of him, yet he said nothing.

Alex turned to Flannery. "You best pay 'em up."

"Blast!" Flannery cursed his luck, his fellow officers, and something about a dog or maybe a potato—hard to tell when the passion lit up and his brogue took over. Even so, he jammed his hand into his pocket to pull out a handful of coins.

Brentwood reached out and squeezed Alex's shoulder. "Congratulations, my friend. You know you've a home whenever you're in town. Emily should be glad of a little female company for once." He frowned over at Flannery.

Alex chuckled. He'd miss this banter. He'd miss these men. "Bring your wife and boy down to Dover, Brentwood. Johanna and I shall run the finest inn in all of Kent. You're all welcome, any time."

"C'mon Flannery." Brentwood cuffed the man on the back, nudging him down the corridor. "I'll help you count out your pennies. Lord knows it'll take some muscle to pry them from your fingers."

Their voices faded down the stairs, until Alex and Thatcher stood in silence. What ought he say to the ghost in the night who'd always been there for him? For once, Alex couldn't put together two words if paid a king's ransom.

Slowly, Thatcher reached out and offered his hand. "Godspeed."

Alex gripped the man's hand, and for a moment, his throat closed. It was hard to let go, to leave behind all he'd known, especially this officer of shadow and dust. But what he was moving toward was even more alluring—something his friend here could have no understanding of. Riding the countryside was a godforsaken lonely job. Would that Thatcher might find a wife as perfect as he'd found.

"To you as well, my friend." He released his hold. "Your day will come, Thatcher. If it can happen to me, it can happen to anyone."

CHAPTER THIRTY-SEVEN

Johanna sat between Mam and Thomas, staring at the taproom door of the Blue Hedge Inn until her eyes burned. Salvation might yet waltz through it. A pack of hungry dockhands or a load of passengers from a late ferry could pile in with empty bellies and full purses. It wasn't wrong to yearn for redemption via a room full of hungry patrons. . .was it?

But all that filled the taproom was Thomas's consistent kicking of his good foot against the chair leg. Tap, tap. Tap, tap.

She sighed. Even so, it was a blessing to be alive. To hear her brother's taps instead of the awful sounds she yet heard in her dreams. Though it'd been little over a week, it seemed like forever ago when she'd been trapped inside the hold of that ship, an eternity since Alex's arms held her protected—and far too long since he'd kissed her. He said he'd come for her. But when? Oh, that it would be today. Staring at the front door, she willed a full-shouldered, tawny-headed man to cross the threshold

Tap, tap.

Pulling her gaze away, she picked at a thread on the hem of her sleeve, trying to push the thing back into the fabric with her nail. A futile endeavor, but it gave her fingers something to do. Drat the Rose Inn! Drat that Mrs. Neville, the innkeeper. The woman had been more stubborn than Tanny Needler about not letting Johanna into Alex's chambers without him being present. A good policy, laudable, even—but one that meant she'd not been able to retrieve the money Alex had hidden. Even after Mam gave Mrs. Neville a good earful, the inflexible innkeeper still wouldn't relent.

She picked more furiously. It was hard to sit here awaiting Mr. Spurge with their shortfall when the full amount was waiting in an unoccupied guest room at the Rose.

Mam reached over and laid her hand atop hers, quelling such industry.

Tap, tap.

The incessant rhythm crawled beneath her skin, and she shifted on her chair, pressing her lips shut. It wouldn't do any good to say anything. The boy was as tense as them all, waiting, wondering, wishing their entire future didn't teeter on a mere five shillings.

Then suddenly, for one blessed moment, the tapping stopped.

Thomas screwed his face up at Mam. "Tell me again why I have to sit here?"

"We will attend this meeting as a family. Your sister has shouldered the financial burden for too long, and for that I am sorry."

Mam's fingers squeezed hers before releasing her hold.

Tap, tap. Tap, ta—

She blinked. Was it her imagination, or had the door jiggled just the tiniest whit? Could just be a gust billowing in off the Channel. . . but no. The door edged open an inch now. A windy blast would've swung the wood wide, not teased it agape at such a steady pace.

"Do you see. . . ?" Her words died as a bloody, yellow-stockinged leg appeared, followed by another, both barely holding up a man who looked as if he'd fallen beneath a miller's grinding stone.

Mam gasped.

Thomas stopped tapping.

Johanna shot up and dashed over to the man. "Mr. Nutbrown?"

He collapsed against her, weighing hardly more than Thomas. Mam joined her and they both bore him up, drag-walking him over to a nearby bench.

"Thomas, bring a drink. Quickly," she called over her shoulder, then lifted the back of her hand to feel for Mr. Nutbrown's breath. Thankfully, warm air collected on her skin. "Mr. Nutbrown, can you hear me?"

His eyelids flickered open, and she drew back.

A world of pain and grief glazed his eyes. His lips moved, but no sound came out.

Her heart squeezed. No matter how eccentric the fellow was, he was still a man, one of God's creations—and a very broken one at that.

Thomas rushed in with a mug while Mam sank onto the bench next to Mr. Nutbrown and helped him guide the cup to his mouth.

While he drank, Mam eyed her. "What do you suppose happened?"

"I don't know. I'm not sure he can speak. . ."

She straightened. Of course. She'd never once heard him talk without Nixie. The smashed puppet was long gone, deposited in the dustbin over a week ago. But upstairs...

"Stay with him. I'll be right back."

She darted upstairs to Mr. Clarkwell's former chambers. Neither he nor his band had returned to claim their belongings. Perhaps he'd ride in with Alex? Hard to say. But it was a boon for now that his pile of puppeteering gear sat heaped in the corner. She snatched up the red-coated Punch and dashed back to the taproom.

Both Mam and Thomas's brows rose as she laid the puppet on Mr. Nutbrown's lap. His head dropped to his chest, gaze fixed on the offering. Slowly, carefully, he lifted one finger and stroked the length of the cape. A giant tear splashed against the felt, and he stroked that away too.

"Oh, Mr. Nutbrown." Johanna's throat closed, and she swallowed. "I am so sorry for whatever befell you."

His shimmery eyes lifted to hers. Mam patted his hand.

But he pulled away, and almost reverently, glided his bruised and scabby hand into the body of the puppet. Punch rose, not nearly as high or perky as his old friend, but enough that the little head bobbed once. "Mr. N–Nutbrown is t–tired."

The puppet flopped to his lap, and Mr. Nutbrown's head leaned back against the wall with a thump.

"Of course you are." Mam tucked her arm around him and hefted him to his feet. "You shall have a good lay down."

The puppet landed on the floor.

Mr. Nutbrown whimpered.

Snatching up Punch, Johanna offered it to him. "I think your new friend is in need of a rest as well."

A weak smile wavered on his lips. He clutched the red felt like a little boy holding on to his Mam's hand.

"I shall be right back." Mam nodded at her, then helped Mr. Nutbrown shuffle off to a room.

Before Thomas could scuttle away, Johanna wrapped her arm around his shoulders. "Come wait with me, Brother. We decided we'd face this as a family, remember?"

"Aww, Jo." Though he flapped a complaint, he allowed her to lead him back to the bench, where in no time Mam joined them once again.

"Did you find out any more?" Johanna asked.

"No. The poor man's eyes closed before his head hit the pillow."

Tap-tap. Tap-tap.

Johanna clenched her jaw to keep from reprimanding Thomas. After having witnessed Mr. Nutbrown's sorry state and with the sure-to-be drama coming from Mr. Spurge, in truth, she felt like kicking her own foot against the table leg.

Without warning, the front door banged open, and her heart sank. All the hoping and wishing for Alex to arrive had done no good. Mr. Spurge entered, reaching to remove a black top hat from his greying head. He paused and eyed them up for a moment from across the room. "The entire Langley clan? This *is* quite an event. Good morning to you all."

"Good morning, Mr. Spurge," Mam and Johanna said in unison.

Thomas tapped all the faster. "Ain't nothin' good about it."

"Thomas!" Johanna hissed.

Thankfully Mr. Spurge let the boy's remark go unanswered. He strode to their table, set his hat down, then as quickly yanked it back up. With his elbow, he bent and wiped off the area—though it was clearly spotless to begin with. Apparently satisfied, he once again set down his hat, then flipped out his coat tails and perched on a chair opposite them. "Shall we be about our business, then?"

Without a word, Mam pushed a pouch of money across the table.

Mr. Spurge's bushy brows hiked skyward. "Well, well. . .I must say I am surprised." He snatched up the bag like a dog might a shank of mutton. Hefting the pouch in one hand, he held it mid-air, jiggling it now and then.

Slowly, his brows lowered, as did the sides of his mouth. "Feels a bit light."

Thomas stopped kicking and leaned forward. "How the scag-nippity would you know that, you old spidery—"

Johanna shot out her arm and pulled Thomas to her side, crushing him against her with her hand over his mouth. "Please excuse my brother, Mr. Spurge. His leg has yet to fully heal and sometimes he's out of his head with pain."

Thomas squirmed. She held tight.

Mam leaned forward. "While the bulk of what we owe is in your hand, Mr. Spurge, you'll find our payment short by five shillings, only five, which we will have to you by end of next week."

Mr. Spurge grunted. "Good."

Good?

Johanna's arm dropped. All the sleepless nights? The angst-filled days? She'd worn her nerves to frayed threads for nothing? Her shoulders wilted, as did Mam's. God had answered! Not as she'd expected, with the blessing of some extra coins, but with the mercy of a white-haired banker. Shame bowed her head.

Oh God, forgive me for not trusting You. Your ways are not my ways.

"Thank you, Mr. Spurge." Mam's voice floated to the heavens, and Johanna had no doubt her mother lifted her own silent prayers as well.

Mr. Spurge pushed back his chair and stood. In one hand he clutched the bag of money. With the other, he reached inside his coat and pulled out a folded document and handed it over to Mam. "You might want to reconsider that sentiment, Mrs. Langley."

Johanna stiffened.

Mam opened the paper, the crispness a brittle crack in the silence. Thomas didn't even tap as she read. Almost imperceptibly, the fine, white document started shaking.

"What is it?" Johanna's question hung like a black cloud.

Mam said nothing. She didn't have to. The creases puckering her face screamed a warning.

Johanna took the paper from her and scanned the contents. It was a legal document, dated and signed, with three names penned in impossibly perfect cursive.

Eliza Langley. Johanna Langley. Thomas Langley—

All due to report to St. Mary's by the end of the day.

Her blood turned to ice, and she shivered despite the warmth of the July morning. She dropped the awful paper and shot up from her chair, scowling into Mr. Spurge's face. "But you hold nearly the entire sum. You would send us to the workhouse over a mere five shillings?"

He clapped his hat back atop his head. "I would and I am."

"Please, Mr. Spurge, have mercy." The world turned watery, and she blinked. "Upon my word you shall have the rest of the payment by week's end. I vow it!"

"Your word, Miss Langley, while encased in very pretty housing, is null and void as far as I'm concerned. Today was the deadline. You have your papers. And I have just acquired a new property. I expect you gone within the hour."

"But we have a guest who is unable to be moved."

His brows pulled into a sharp, grey line. "Then your guest will have to find other accommodation, for this is no longer an inn." With a snap of his heels, he pivoted.

Beside her, Mam rose. "Have you no heart, sir?"

"None whatsoever, madam." His pace didn't so much as hitch.

Johanna reached for Mam, and they clung like two thin yew saplings, desperate for anchor in a storm. Thomas pushed back from his chair and plowed into them.

Mr. Spurge stopped at the open door, a black silhouette against the brilliance of day. "Oh, I forgot to mention...on the off-chance you were thinking of hooking up that decrepit pony cart, think again. Everything here is my property. If so much as a cracked mug is moved off-site, I'll see the three of you in Market Place Gaol instead of St. Mary's. It's a fair walk, should take you all day, so I suggest you start now." He tugged the brim of his hat. "Good day."

At last the road descended, leading to the town nestled between sea and land by great, white cliffs. Alex kicked his horse into a canter, zealous to reach Dover proper—until Ford caught up to him and forced him to slow.

"Ease up, man." The magistrate—*former* magistrate—frowned at him. "I'm as eager as you, but these horses are spent."

"My apologies." Alex squinted as he eyed the buildings hugging the harbor. Afternoon sun glinted bright off the bay. "We are so close."

It took all his strength to hold the reins loose, to not give in to urging his mount faster than a trot. But Ford was right. He had pushed their pace the past three days.

A fresh breeze rolled in off the Channel, carrying a fishy aroma. Likely ol' Slingsby and his crew were even now on the beach, cooking cod over a fire, plotting some new way to lighten a load of tea or rum from some poor vessel.

Alex loosened his collar, reminding himself it wasn't his job anymore to hunt down criminals. Would he miss it? A definitive answer was as elusive as the thin clouds overhead, but he doubted it, not with a dark-haired, brown-eyed woman at his side. His chest squeezed. Aah, but it couldn't be soon enough until he reached Johanna.

He glanced over at Ford as they turned onto the High Street. How different it was to arrive in Dover this time, not moving fast enough to arrive at the Blue Hedge Inn. "So, what's your plan of attack with Mrs. Langley?"

"Nothing."

He arched a brow. "The great Bow Street magistrate has no strategy whatsoever?"

Ford glanced at him sideways. "I didn't say that."

Alex grunted. "You're not going to tell me."

"You never were a patient one." A chuckle shook the man's shoulders. "Oh, all right. If you must know, I intend to allow Eliza all the time she needs to pummel me, hence my doing *nothing*. But by the time I must return to London to finish up Bow Street business, I suspect my charms will have won her over." He faced Alex and winked. "We shall retire on my land up in Shropshire."

"You own land?" His brows shot skyward. "For as long as I've known you, you've lived in London."

"Never had a need for it—until now. As you know, I married an MP's daughter. Her father granted me a small piece of property in hopes we'd eventually settle there one day. Of course that never came to pass, but I still have it. Besides"—a slow grin eased the lines on Ford's face—"you don't really want me underfoot with your new bride, do you?"

"You know me far too well." And he did. Emotion clogged Alex's throat, and he faced forward. "Thank you. You didn't have to take on my provision when my father died, yet you did."

"Alex."

His name travelled on the air like an invitation, one he couldn't refuse. He turned his face back to Ford. Steely grey eyes met his.

"I'm only going to say this once, for we are not men given to sentiment. You were a fine lad and are an even finer man. Johanna Langley is a lucky woman to have you."

His eyes burned. His throat. His heart. He said nothing more, nor could he if a gun were held to the back of his head. They rode in silence the rest of the way until they finally rounded the corner to the Blue Hedge.

"Go on." Ford dipped his head. "I'll give you a moment."

Alex swung out of the saddle and sprinted to the door. "Johanna?"

Bolting inside, he looked for a blue skirt, longing for a flash of her smile. But the taproom was empty.

He dashed into the kitchen, expecting her sweet face might be bowed over a pot of stew. Yet the hearth was cold, and had been for quite some time.

The first hint of alarm prickled at the nape of his neck.

"Johanna!" He strode out of the room, calling her name again and again as he pounded up the stairs. After a search of the guest rooms, he lunged up to second floor, a highly improper action but so be it. He punched open the doors of the women's chambers. All empty. Barren, even. Only the leftover scent of the rose soap he'd given Johanna lingered like a slap to his face.

He charged down the stairs and tore out the back door, rising dread pumping his legs faster with each step. Flinging the stable door aside, he stalked in. The decrepit pony cart languished all alone. The horse was gone.

Alex turned in a slow circle, concocting all sorts of explanations, but the only thing he knew for sure soured in his gut.

Something was wrong. Very, *very* wrong.

He sped back to Ford and vaulted into his own saddle. "They're gone."

Ford eyed him where he stood near the front of his horse, neither mounting nor moving. "What do you mean?"

"The inn is empty, and by the looks of it, they're not intending to return. The hearth is cold. There are no personal effects anywhere. It's not right. Something's happened." His voice shook, but it couldn't be helped. "Come on! We've got to find them."

Ford's hand snaked out and grabbed hold of the headstall on Alex's horse. "Think, man. Don't just act without evaluating. It will accomplish nothing and more than likely waste your time."

He grimaced. What a hypocrite. He'd told Johanna the very same thing that day she'd struggled with the stable door. "You're right." He sucked in a huge breath. Spurge was his first guess, but not the only one. For all he knew Tanny Needler could've had a hand in their disappearance. "Let us go to the local magistrate. Perhaps he might know something."

"Now you're talking sense." Ford released his hold of Alex's horse and grabbed his own mount. Together they trotted back to the High Street—where a familiar figure strolled.

"Mrs. Scott," he called as he dismounted. "A word, please."

Johanna's friend, Maggie, turned toward him, a wriggling babe in her arms. Beneath her bonnet brim, her forehead puckered, then cleared. "Oh, it's you, Mr. Morton."

He let the name slide, unwilling to spend one second more than needed to find Johanna. Forcing a calm tone to his voice, he asked, "Where is Johanna? Where has she gone?"

A small cry garbled in her throat. "You don't know? She and her family are on their way to St. Mary's."

Calm be hanged. The workhouse? But Johanna ought to have had more than enough money to pay her debt—unless Spurge had upped his asking price. Rage lit a fire, painting everything red. "Why? How?" His voice thundered even in his own ears.

Eyes wide, Mrs. Scott retreated a step, clutching her babe tighter.

Behind him, Ford grumbled an admonishment.

"I'm sorry." Alex ran a hand over his face, praying for peace. "Forgive me, but I must know everything. Please, Mrs. Scott."

She blinked, then lifted her chin. "Mr. Spurge called in his loan this morning. To my regret, I hadn't the extra funds to lend them."

"But there was no need. They had more than enough to pay off Mr. Spurge. Unless. . ." his gut sank. Unless the money he'd taken such care to hide had been stolen.

"Surely you are mistaken, sir. My husband is even now driving them to the workhouse. Hopefully it won't take long for them to pay back their debt, though I don't know how they'll manage once they get out and—where are you going?"

"Excuse me, Mrs. Scott," he called over his shoulder as he swung back up into the saddle. "But I have a wagon to catch."

CHAPTER THIRTY-EIGHT

Johanna stared at the dark stain marring the July afternoon. Behind a fence of black iron, St. Mary's grew larger with each turn of the wagon wheels. Situated outside of town in the middle of nothingness, the workhouse hunched like a beast, ready to stretch out a paw and claw in anyone who ventured too close.

A faint smile traced a ghostly pattern on her lips, and she lifted her chin despite the monster ahead. Losing the inn had been hard, but it hadn't been the end—and this wouldn't be either. Now that her worst fear had come to pass, surprisingly she wasn't as crushed as she'd imagined. The sun still shone, the wind still blew, and God yet reigned in the heavens. She lifted her face to the sky, and a peculiar kind of lightness filled her soul.

Could it be that the real demon tormenting her had never been this ugly brick building but her desperate act of holding on to things too tightly, things she had no right to hold on to in the first place?

The wagon lurched over a rock in the road, and she grabbed the side. Mam sat between her and Mr. Scott, wedged in safely. Behind, in the wagon bed, Thomas bumped around. None of them spoke, except for Thomas, whenever he spied another traveller on the road. This far out, though, it wouldn't be likely they'd see anyone.

Johanna patted Mam's leg. "With God's help, we'll weather this, Mam. I feel sure of it."

Mam's hand closed over hers. "I was tired of being an innkeeper anyway."

Johanna gasped. Why had her mother never shared that with her before? "What—?"

"Caw! Look at that cloud o' dust snaking up. Someone's riding hard." Thomas scrambled as best he could to the gate at the back.

For a moment, Johanna was tempted to turn around and focus on the approaching traveller instead of on the open gates ahead. But no, better to face her future—even a challenging one—head on.

"It might be. . .yes!" Thomas shouted. "It's Alex!"

Alex?

Her heart flipped. She yanked her hand from Mam's and jerked forward. "Stop the wagon, Mr. Scott."

The wheels barely slowed before she scrambled down to the dirt. Clutching her skirts, she ran to Alex.

"Hah! Look at her go." Thomas laughed.

Or was that her laughing? Her cheek hurt from smiling, but it couldn't be helped, not when the man she loved hefted his leg over his saddle and his boots hit the ground. She launched into his arms, and the world spun. Her feet left the ground as he swung her around and around, and she buried her face in his shirt. He smelled of hard riding and smoke, all man and muscle and strength. He'd come. He'd really come, just as he'd said. He'd kept his word and for that she wept with joy.

Too soon, he set her down and cupped her face with his hands, brushing away her stray tears with his big thumbs.

"You're here," she said, breathless. She covered his hands with hers, touching his warmth to make sure he was real, that she hadn't been taken by madness. Was she even now dreaming and the next bump of the wagon would jar her awake? "You're well and truly here."

His gaze swept over the remaining scrape on her cheek, and for a moment, his brow furrowed. But then as suddenly, he flashed a smile, brilliant on his sun-kissed face. "I told you I'd come for you, and looks as if I'm just in time."

"I hardly know what to believe anymore," she murmured.

"Then believe this. . .I love you, Johanna. I love you more than life." He bent and for a glorious eternity, his mouth brushed against hers.

"Eew!" Thomas screeched behind them.

She pulled away, smiling, shaking, so wild with emotion she'd fly away were it not for his firm hold on her hand.

With a smirk, Alex led her to the wagon. "Turn this wagon around, Mr. Scott, if you please."

Up on the seat, Mr. Scott lifted his hat and scratched the shorn hair beneath. "Can't. If I don't deliver 'em here," he hitched a thumb at the workhouse, "it'll be the gaol. You an' I both know they'd not last a week in that hole."

Mam frowned, though hard to tell if it were from Mr. Scott's threat or Alex's inappropriate kiss. "He's right, son. We have an obligation, one you cannot change by a simple turn of the wagon."

"There is no more obligation, Mrs. Langley. Your debt is paid in full, leastwise it will be by the time we return to town." Alex looked from Mam to her. "You are free."

Johanna's heart fluttered with abrupt understanding. "You paid it."

"I did, or rather one of my friends is seeing to it now." His gaze slipped from hers and met her mother's—and a queer twinkle in her eye glimmered.

Johanna batted his arm. "I believe, sir, there is much more for you to tell me."

His big grin disarmed her. "Ask me anything, and I'll tell you."

She couldn't help but smile back, and they stood, silent, breathless, beaming at each other as if no one else in the world watched.

"Caw!" Thomas cried. "Yer not going to kiss again, are you?"

"Good idea." His lips warmed her brow like a sweet benediction.

"Eew!"

"Thomas, leave them be." Mam's voice grumbled along with the wooden wheels as Mr. Scott turned the wagon about.

"Tell me, my love." Alex's voice was soft and low, a caress of the most intimate kind. "Instead of being an innkeeper's daughter, how would you like to be an innkeeper's wife?"

Her heart skipped a beat, or maybe more. She wasn't counting—and never would again. As this man's wife, beneath that gaze of love, she wouldn't care if they lived as kings or paupers, innkeepers or—she bit her lip. What exactly was he saying?

"But you're a lawman. Aren't you?"

"Not anymore." He shook his head, the ends of his hair grazing his collar and shaking loose bits of dust from his fast ride. "Thanks to the Coburns, Robbie in particular, I have more than enough funds to buy back the Blue Hedge and make it the finest inn in all of Dover."

"You would do that?" Tears welled in her eyes. "You would sacrifice your career and your money to purchase a run-down hovel of a building?"

The grin on his face broke as large and warm as the afternoon sun. "I would buy the moon and stars if that's what made you happy. Besides, no risk, no gain, right?"

The wagon pulled up alongside them, and he lifted her back to her perch next to Mam—but he didn't let go of her hand.

"You still haven't given me an answer."

Bending, she pressed her lips to the back of his fingers, despite the accompanying "Eew" that was sure to follow from Thomas.

"I can think of nothing better than to be an innkeeper's wife." She met Alex's gaze and held it. "My answer is yes."

HISTORICAL NOTES

Oak Apple Day

Oak Apple Day (sometimes called Royal Oak Day) is an old holiday that is still celebrated in some parts of England every May 29. Its roots go back to the year 1651, when King Charles II escaped the Roundhead army by taking cover in an oak tree. In commemoration, traditional celebrations include parades and the pinning of an oak leaf or an "oak apple" to the lapel in order to avoid a pinch. An oak apple (also called an oak gall) is caused by the larvae of a cynipid wasp. The gall looks a bit like an apple. Nowadays it is also a tradition to drink beer and eat plum pudding.

Bow Street Runners

The Bow Street Runners were the first fledgling police force in London. Founded in 1749 by magistrate Henry Fielding, the original team of men numbered only six. The officers never called themselves "runners," and in fact, considered the term derogatory. At first the men did not patrol the streets but merely delivered writs and arrested offenders as charged by the magistrate. Eventually the force grew to great proportions by expanding into a horse patrol and stretching their jurisdiction to all of England. With the creation of the Metropolitan Police in 1829, the runners eventually became incorporated into their ranks and were completely disbanded by 1839.

Congreve Rockets and the Napoleonic Wars

Believe it or not, rockets were used way back in the early nineteenth century. The Congreve rocket was developed in 1804 by William Congreve and experimentally tried first against a French fleet at Boulogne, France, in 1805. These were the days of Napoleon's threat against England. The rockets were gunpowder-propelled and used incendiary warheads. Think of a giant bottle-rocket and you'll have a rough mental image of one. They were launched from tubes set on special ladder-like frames and could be shot from land or sea. And lest you gloss over this, thinking such information has nothing to do with America, think again. You know the line in the US national anthem: "*And the rocket's red glare, the bomb's bursting in air, gave proof through the night that our flag was still there*"? Yeah, those were Congreve rockets.

ACKNOWLEDGMENTS

I can only do what I do because of the sweet support of some awesome people. Here are a few (though I'm bound to forget somebody). . .

Julie Klassen, you keep me on the Regency straight and narrow, my friend, and for that I'm grateful.

Elizabeth Ludwig, despite your ridiculous writing schedule, I am grateful you take the time to polish my work.

Shannon McNear, I promise I will learn about horses one day so you don't always have to fix my horsey blunders.

Ane Mulligan, your brainstorming is a welcome kick in the pants to get me started every time.

Chawna Schroeder, your keen eye for plausibility and plot holes is second to none.

Annie Tipton, you believe in me and my writing, which is a tough job but somebody's got to do it.

MaryLu Tyndall, you always make me ask why—and that's a *very* good thing.

My cheerleading squad: Linda Ahlmann, Stephanie Gustafson, Cheryl & Grant Higgins, Lucie Payne. . .y'all look so cute in your mini-skirts.

And last but not least, I couldn't do this without Mark, my expert in blowing things up and my best friend.

THE NOBLE GUARDIAN

In memory of my sweet friend,

Bilinda Kelly
April 3, 1964–December 30, 2017

A stalwart warrior of the faith and
one of the most noble women I know...

And as always, to the Author of my faith and
noblest guardian of my soul—Jesus

CHAPTER ONE

Southampton, England, 1815

Was it wicked to say goodbye with a smile? Wrong to feel happy about leaving one's family behind? Surely only a sinner's heart would harbour such uncharitable emotions. . .wouldn't it?

Stepping into the corridor, Abigail Gilbert closed her chamber door, shutting off such reproachful thoughts. This was a day of celebration, not bleak ponderings. Not anymore.

Hand yet on the knob, she hesitated a moment and angled her head. The usual morning sounds—servants bustling, trays rattling, feet padding to and fro—were absent. She'd heard them earlier while she'd sat at her dressing table. Why not now?

But no time to ponder such oddities. She scurried along the corridor to her stepsister's room, tightening her bonnet ribbons as she went. Her other half sister, Jane, would be down to breakfast already, but not Mary. Never Mary. The girl was a perpetual slugabed.

"Mary?" Abby tapped the bedroom door and listened.

No answer.

"Sister?" She rapped again, louder this time. "Are you still abed?"

Pressing her ear to the wood, she strained to hear some kind of complaint, or at least a pillow thwacking against the other side.

And. . .nothing.

Turning the knob, Abby shoved open the door, expecting a darkened room. Instead, brilliant sunbeams landed on a very empty bed. The light needled her eyes, and she blinked. Odd. Mary up so soon? How unlike her, unless—

Abby's breath caught in her throat. Perhaps she'd been wrong, and Mary truly *did* care she was leaving. Even now her youngest sister might be waiting along with Jane in the breakfast room, teary-eyed and saddened to say farewell. La! Abby gave herself a silent scolding. She was a bad sister to assume the worst.

Lighter of step and of heart, she darted back into the corridor and sped down the grand stairway—despite years of reprimands for such hasty movements. Even now her stepmother's voice scolded inside her head.

"Fast feet fly toward folly."

She frowned. Surely that was not what she was doing. Any woman would hurry to be with the man who loved her. Still, she hesitated at the bottom of the staircase and smoothed her skirts before proceeding in a more ladylike manner.

She glided into the morning room, all grace and smiles, a pleasant *adieu* ready to launch from her lips. But her smile froze. She stopped.

No Jane.

No Mary.

Not even any breakfast dishes upon the sideboard. Would there be no one to wish her well on her journey?

Her throat tightened. But perhaps her sisters were already waiting outside by the coach, desiring a last embrace and wave of the hand as she disappeared into the land of matrimony. Everyone knew sisters should part in the best of ways, even Mary and Jane. Abby pivoted, intent on sharing a merry goodbye outdoors with them.

But first she must find Father and give him a final embrace. Besides her stepsisters, he was the last person to bid farewell, for she'd taken leave of her stepmother and stepbrother the night before.

Across from the sitting room, the study door was closed. One more curiosity on this momentous day. Pipe smoke ought to be curling into the hall by now, the scent of cherry tobacco sweetening the morning. Once again, Abby knocked on wood.

"Father?"

Without waiting for a response, she entered.

"What are you doing here?" Her stepmother frowned up at her from where she arranged lilies in a vase on Father's desk. It was a frivolous task, for Father cared not a whit about such trivialities, yet her stepmother insisted the touch added a certain *richesse*—as she put it—to the home. . .though Abby suspected it was more to remind her father what a doting woman he'd married so he wouldn't be tempted to look elsewhere for companionship.

Abby pulled her spine straight, a habit she'd developed as a young girl whenever in her stepmother's presence. "I came to say—"

"You should be gone by now!" Her stepmother crossed to the front of the desk and narrowed her eyes.

"I—I. . ." Her words unwound like a ball of yarn fallen to the floor, rolling off to the corner of the room. Not surprising, really. Her stepmother always effected such a response.

"I asked you a question, girl. Why are you not on your way to Penrith?"

Abby's gaze shot to the mantel clock. In four minutes, the hour hand would strike eight, her planned departure time. Was her stepmother confused—or was she? But no. Father's instructions had been abundantly clear.

Even so, she hesitated before answering. "I am certain that I am not to leave for Brakewell Hall until eight o'clock."

"Do not contradict me." Her stepmother clipped her words and her steps as she drew up nose to nose with Abigail. "Seven, you stupid girl. You were to depart at *seven*."

Abby bit her lip. Was she wrong? Had she misunderstood? Twenty years of doubting herself was a hard habit to break. Yet if she closed her eyes, she could still hear old Parker, her father's manservant, saying, *"Coach leaves at eight bells, miss. Young Mr. Boone will be your driver until you swap out at Tavistock. Charlie's to be your manservant."*

She stared at her stepmother. This close up, it was hard not to. A tic twitched the corner of the woman's left eye, but even so, Abby did not look away. To do otherwise would earn her a slap.

"I am sure of the time, Mother, yet I wonder why you thought otherwise. I am surprised you are not yet taking breakfast in bed. Where is Fath—"

A slap cut through the air. Abby's face jerked, and her cheek stung. She retreated, pressing her fingertips to the violated skin.

"Do not shame me. Curiosity is a vice of the ill-bred. Of all your faults, you cannot claim a mean upbringing, for you have been more than blessed."

The heat radiating on her cheek belied her stepmother's logic. She was blessed to have lived beneath this woman's iron hand for two decades? Abby drew in a shaky breath yet remained silent.

A smile spread like a stain on her stepmother's face, her teeth yellowed by age and far too much tea. "I suppose I might as well tell you, though it's really none of your affair. Your father is taking your sisters and me abroad to see off your brother on his grand tour. They are all out even now, the first to look through a recently arrived shipment of silks and woolens. I expect each of them shall make fortuitous matches as we summer amongst the elite in Italy, surpassing even the arrangement your father made for you."

Abby pressed a hand to her stomach. Gone? All of them? When they knew she was leaving?

Her stepmother clicked her tongue. "What's this? You didn't actually expect anyone to see you off, did you?"

For a moment, her heart constricted. Of course she'd known. She was an outsider. A stranger. She knew that as intimately as the skin on her face or the rift in her heart. A loving family was nothing more than a concept, an idea—one she'd have to learn, for she had no experience of it. Her lower lip quivered.

But she lifted her chin before the trap of self-pity snapped shut. "Of course not." She flashed as brilliant a smile as she could summon. "I merely wanted to thank Father one last time for arranging my marriage to Sir Jonathan, but you can tell him for me. I am grieved you shall all miss the ceremony."

Brittle laughter assaulted the June morning. "Oh Abigail, don't be ridiculous. We have other things to do. Now that we have your association with a baronet, the chances of my daughters marrying better than you are within reach. There is no time to waste."

The words poked holes into her heart. Why had she been so foolish to expect anything different? Abby whirled and ran from the house, praying it was no folly to escape such a hateful woman.

Outside, Mr. Boone stood at the carriage door, ready to assist her, but he was the only one in sight. Her maid, Fanny, was likely already seated inside, and old Charlie, who was to accompany her for the entire trip, was nowhere to be seen.

Mr. Boone held out his hand, but she hesitated to take it. "Are we to wait for Charlie?"

Red crept up the young man's neck, matching the hue of his wine-coloured riding coat. "Pardon, miss, but he will not be attending. It was decided he was more needed here."

Here? When the whole family would be absent for months? Anger churned her empty belly. This smacked of one last insult from her stepmother. If Jane or Mary were traveling cross-country, besides a maid and manservant, the woman would have sent a footman, a coachman, and a hired guard for good measure. Abby frowned. Should she wait for Father to return? He might rectify the situation, provided her stepmother didn't make a fuss. Or should she forge ahead?

She glanced back at the house, only to see her stepmother glowering out the window.

Abby turned to Mr. Boone and forced a small smile. "Well then, let us begin our journey, shall we?"

She grabbed the servant's hand and allowed him to assist her into the coach, then settled on the seat next to her maid. With Fanny and a driver, it wasn't as if she were traveling alone.

"Ready for an adventure, miss?" Fanny nudged her with her elbow. "Soon be queen of your own castle, eh?"

"Yes, Fanny." Cheek still stinging from her stepmother's slap, she turned her face away from the only home she'd ever known. "I should like to be a queen."

Hounslow Heath, just outside London

Gone. For now. Like a demon disappeared into the abyss. Samuel Thatcher shaded his eyes and squinted across the rugged heath kissed brilliant by the risen sun. Shankhart Robbins was out there, all right. Somewhere. And worse—he'd be back. Evil always had a way of returning bigger and blacker than before, singeing any soul it touched. After ten years on the force, with five in the Nineteenth Dragoons before that, Samuel Thatcher's soul was more than singed. It was seared to a crisp.

Behind him, Officer Bexley reined in his horse. "We lost Shankhart's trail nigh an hour ago. What do we do now, Captain?"

Aye. That was the question of the hour. Shoving his boot into the stirrup, he swung up onto his mount and turned Pilgrim about. "Go back."

"You're giving up?"

"Didn't say that." He rocked forward in the saddle. Without a word, his horse set off into a working trot, though she had to be as bone weary as he. Tired from a sleepless night. Tired from humanity. Tired of life.

An hour later, he pulled on the reins, halting in front of a gruesome sight. Draped over the hindquarters of his men's horses were the bodies of two women and two men, covered haphazardly with black riding cloaks. The other two horses, taken down by the highwaymen's shots, lay beneath a gathering swarm of blackflies. Who in their right mind would allow women to travel across this stretch of scrubby land accompanied by only a postilion? And by the looks of the overturned carriage, an inexperienced one at that.

Colbert and Higgins, the officers Samuel had left behind, rose from near the felled chaise, their red waistcoats stark as blood in the morning light.

Colbert turned aside and spit. "No luck, eh?"

Next to Samuel, Bexley dismounted, working out a kink in his lower back the second his feet hit the ground. "It'll take more'n luck to bring down that lot."

The men recounted once again how the attack must have played out, shuttlecocking ideas back and forth. For the most part, their conjectures were plausible. Even so, Samuel gritted his teeth, suddenly on edge. But why? The sky was clear. The weather temperate. And Shankhart was gone for now, so there was no imminent danger to them or any other passing coaches.

All the same, he stiffened in the saddle and cocked his head.

And. . .there. He angled Pilgrim toward a tiny mewl, not unlike the cry of a rabbit kit caught in a snare. Bypassing the ruined chaise and giving wide berth to the downed horses, he followed a small path of disturbed bracken, barely bent. Easy to miss in last night's gloaming, when they'd happened upon the scene. Yet clearly something had traveled this way.

He lowered to the ground, following the delicate trail on foot. The cry grew louder the farther he tracked. So did the alarm squeezing his chest. *Oh God. . .if this is a baby. . .*

Upping his pace, he closed in on a small rise of bracken and rock. Tucked into a crevice, a child, two years old or possibly three, whimpered for his mam—a mother who would never again wipe the tears from the lad's smudged cheeks.

Though relief coursed through him that the victim was not a babe, his lips flattened. One more piece of his charred heart crumbled loose, leaving his faith more jagged than before. It wasn't fair, such suffering for a little one—and he knew that better than most.

Reaching into the cleft, he pulled the child out. Teeth sank into his forearm. Nails surprisingly sharp ripped some of the skin off the back of one of his hands, and kicks jabbed his stomach. Despite it all, Samuel straightened and soothed, "Shh. You're safe now."

The lie burned in his throat. No one was safe, not on this side of heaven. He closed his eyes while the child squirmed.

Lord, grant mercy.

Lately, that prayer was as regular as his breath.

He retraced his route and hefted the child up into the saddle with him. He held the lad tight against him with his left arm, and gripped the reins with his injured right hand, blood dripping freely from it.

By the time he returned to the men, they were mounted as well.

Bexley's brows lifted. The other two officers clamped their jaws and averted their gazes. To say anything would only magnify their failure to discover the lad sooner.

Samuel scowled, as much at his own deficiencies as theirs. If no family could be found, the child would end up in an orphanage. Even so, God knew it could be worse—*he* knew it could be worse.

Bexley edged his horse closer and lowered his voice for him alone. "Don't go too hard on the men, Captain. It were an easy oversight on such a long night."

He'd have to mete out some kind of censure. Good Lord, if he hadn't discovered the child and they'd left the youngling behind—but no. Better not to think it. He shifted the child on his lap, digging out an elbow shoved into his belly, then wiped the blood from his hand on his trousers. He'd come up with a discipline for Colbert and Higgins later, when his bones didn't feel every one of his thirty-one years and his soul wasn't raging at the injustice of the world.

"Move out." He twitched the reins, and Pilgrim lifted her nose toward London.

Bexley fell in beside him. "You've got that look about you."

He slid a sideways glance at the man but said nothing.

"You're not long for the force, are you?"

He did look then, full-on, studying every nuance of the stubbled face staring back at him. "What makes you say that?"

Bexley shrugged. "It's no secret your contract is up in a month."

So everyone knew. But did everyone also know he didn't have enough money yet to purchase the land he wanted? He turned his gaze back to the road.

"Why, Captain?" Bexley gnawed at the subject like a hound with a bone. "You're the best officer we got. You know this road will be more dangerous without you."

He grunted. With or without him, danger would prevail.

"Where will you go?" Bexley asked.

"Far."

"What will you do?"

"Farm."

"You? A farmer?" Bexley's laughter rumbled loud and long. "No. You'll miss this. The action. The adventure. Farming's too dull and lonely a life for you."

"Exactly." He pushed air through his teeth in a sharp whistle, and Pilgrim broke into a canter, leaving Bexley behind.

That was exactly what he wished—to be left alone.

CHAPTER TWO

Abby's eyelids grew heavy as the chaise rumbled along. After only two days of travel, the tedium of the journey wore on both her and Fanny. Even now her maid's head drooped sideways onto Abby's shoulder, the woman's breathing thick and even. Abby shifted slightly, easing into a more comfortable position. It wouldn't hurt to close her own eyes. They still had Hounslow Heath to cross before stopping for the night. There'd be nothing to see but rain-dampened flatlands anyway.

Her chin dropped to her chest, and she gave in to the jiggle and sway of the carriage. For the first time since her father had remarried, she could finally fully relax. No more cutting remarks from her stepmother. No cross looks from her sisters. It was a welcome feeling, this freedom. Decadent and heady.

And horribly shame inducing. She ought to be missing her family, not reveling in their absence. She ought to be praying for them each night as her head hit the pillow, not dreaming of her new life with Sir Jonathan Aberley. As she bobbed along with the rhythm of the rolling wheels, she vowed to be more diligent in prayer for them. Starting tonight.

Guilt assuaged—for the moment—she purposely tuned her thoughts to memorized portions of the Psalms, losing herself in still waters and green pastures. . .one of her favorite ways to drift into sleep.

But a sudden stop jerked her back to reality. Groggy, she fumbled at her bodice for the watch she wore pinned to her spencer, then blinked at the tiny numbers. 'Twas only half past two.

Gently pushing Fanny aside—who mumbled something about scones and jam, or maybe pudding and ham?—Abby unlatched the door and peered out. The postilion had already dismounted from his perch on the lead horse and was brushing mud flecks off his blue jacket as he strode over to lower the steps. He'd stopped the chaise in front of a building that brightened the dreary day by virtue of its whitewashed stones and the lit lanterns in the windows. Above the front door of the inn, gilt letters, chipped and crooked, spelled out THE GOLDEN CROSS.

Abby reluctantly took the driver's offered hand and lowered to the ground. Surely the man couldn't be thirsty nor the horses tired when they'd taken a meal not two hours ago. "Why are we stopping?"

Brown eyes stared directly into hers, for the fellow was her height. Though she'd interacted now with many postilions when they changed horses and drivers at every inn, she'd still not grown accustomed to men no taller than herself. A boon for the horses, not having to haul large frames, but unnerving for her to stand eye to eye with a man.

"Ground's a muddy mess, miss. It'll take too long to cross the heath with the roads such as they are. We'd never make it across by nightfall, and the heath's no place to be caught in the dark. It's better to give it a go early in the morning."

Behind her, feet splatted onto the wet ground. A moment later, Fanny's whisper warmed her ear. "Is there a problem?"

"The roads are too wet. We are stopping for the night."

"Ahh, good. Then you could order us some scones and jam, eh?"

Stifling a retort, Abby gathered her skirt and lifted it slightly. It would do no good to reprimand the woman for such impertinence. It was Fanny's way. The maid's insolence was likely the reason her stepmother had chosen her for Abby in the first place. Still, for all of Fanny's peculiarities, the woman had a pleasant way about her. . . especially when food was involved.

Stepping on flagstones too far apart for comfort, Abby gathered her gown a bit higher and focused on the precarious walkway leading to the door of the inn. A full day of mist coated the world in slippery dampness. The promise of hot tea lured her to up her pace, but a glance at the mucky ground tempered that urge. Sitting with wet shoes would be bad enough. Adding a muddied gown to the mix would prove intolerable.

Inside, she and Fanny stopped at an ancient slab of a bar, darkened by centuries of spilled ale and the elbows of patrons too many to count. Behind it, a round fellow, wiping off the rim of a mug with the corner of his apron, glanced over at them. "What'll it be, ladies?"

"We need a room for the evening and tea for now." Abby dabbed away the moisture on her cheeks with the back of her hand. "For two, please."

"Aye. Room four is yours. I'll have a boy fetch yer belongings." He set the mug down then tipped his head toward an open door across from the bar. "Find a table in the front room, just through there. Tea will be out shortly."

"Thank you." Abby offered the man a smile, then turned and strode through the door. Only one of the five tables was unoccupied, the one nearest the window. The space was likely drafty, but once their hot drink arrived, it wouldn't matter.

Abby sank into the chair, thankful for a seat that wasn't jostling and juddering, then untied her bonnet and lifted it from her hair.

Fanny did the same but stretched her neck to glance around the room. "Quite the full house for this time of day."

"I suppose, with the weather, we are not the only ones holding off our jaunt across the heath." Abby's gaze shifted to the window. Tiny droplets gathered together, forming great tears that wept down the glass. It was sound judgment to stop here for the night, but even so, a growing anticipation needled her for the wasted time.

The closer they drew to Penrith, the more anxious she was to see Sir Jonathan again. She'd met her intended only once, at a dance crowded with people—and even then merely in passing. 'Twas a miracle he'd offered for her. There'd been other beautiful, eligible hands he could have requested. A small smile rippled across her lips. Sir Jonathan must have truly been taken with her to have approached her father before leaving that night.

"Miss?" Fanny's urgent murmur cut into her sweet ponderings. "I don't like the way the fellow at the table behind you is looking at us. Perhaps we should take tea in our room."

"But we are already seated. Do you really think it necessary?" She studied her maid's eyes, trying to detect how much anxiety swam in those brown depths or if the woman was merely angling for a good lie down. Besides food, Fanny's other penchant was napping, and a champion she was. The woman would've made a proficient lapdog.

Fanny leaned across the table, speaking for her alone. "I wager that fellow is eyeing us up for the pickings."

Real fear pinched the sides of Fanny's mouth, and Abby reached out to pat the woman's shoulder. "Do not fret. I am sure brigands have better things to do at this time of day than take tea."

Fanny's gaze burned into hers. "I've heard it said ol' Dick Turpin used to meet with his gang 'round here, maybe even at this very inn, planning his vile attacks. Oh!" Fanny gasped, her voice dropping to a ragged whisper. "He's coming over."

Biting her lip, Abby straightened in her chair just as a tall man pulled up to the side of their table. She lifted her face to a whisker-jawed fellow in a cutaway dress coat, smelling of onions and blue stilton.

"Pardon me, ladies. I am Mr. Harcourt, a local constable in these parts." He hitched his thumbs in his lapels. "Might I have a word with you?"

"You may." Abby snuck a glance at Fanny. The maid leaned as far back in her chair as possible, as if the man might pick her pocket at any moment.

Abby turned back to Mr. Harcourt, preferring to give him the benefit of the doubt. "Is something amiss, sir?"

Mr. Harcourt shook his head. "Not at all. I simply noticed the two of you are traveling alone—unless your gentlemen are joining up with you later?"

For a moment she studied the fellow. He seemed upright enough, with his cream-coloured cravat tied neatly and his silver-streaked hair combed back in a tidy fashion. Still, constable or not, it wouldn't do to admit she and Fanny were alone. She lifted her chin. "Pardon me, but I do not see how that signifies."

"Only that if my summation is correct, and you are planning to cross the heath, then I'd like to offer you my services."

Fanny narrowed her eyes. "What services might those be?"

"Sharpshooting, miss."

Abby pressed her lips flat to keep her jaw from dropping. *Sharpshooting?* Did the fellow think they were off to net big game? "Thank you for your offer, Mr. Harcourt, but we are on a simple journey, not a hunting foray."

"You may not be hunting, but Shankhart Robbins is."

Abby couldn't help but bunch up her nose a bit. Was that a name of a man or an animal? "I beg your pardon, sir?"

"It's like this." Mr. Harcourt cleared his throat and clasped his hands behind his back, as if he were about to launch a tale while employing great oratory.

Abby shifted on her chair, just in case he was.

"A fortnight ago," Mr. Harcourt began, "two women, such as yourselves, set out across Hounslow with naught but a wee lad, a manservant, and a single driver as accompaniment. I warned them against such a rash venture. Why, they sat at this very table when I approached them just like this. I said to them, 'Ladies—'"

"Highwaymen got them," Fanny cut in. "Am I correct?"

Mr. Harcourt's brows sank into a thick line. "I was about to get to that, but yes. Only the lad came back. 'Twas a grisly murder scene, I'm told. Robbins. . .well, he's a blackguard who takes more than gold. He takes everything." He stretched the word so that his meaning couldn't be denied, then he drew back and sniffed. "And that's why you need a hired gun to see you safely across the heath. Three guineas ought to cover it."

Across the table, Fanny's worried gaze met hers. Mentally, Abby tallied her remaining traveling allowance. Paying this fellow would dip deep into those coins, so much so that by the end of the journey, she might have to use the funding given to her by her father for her last-minute wedding needs.

"I, uh. . ." She licked her lips, praying for wisdom.

"Well, what's it to be?"

Mr. Harcourt's bass voice pulled her from her conjecture, and she smiled up at him. "Thank you for the information, Mr. Harcourt. I shall consider your offer."

"As you wish, but don't think on it too long. I generally take the first offer." He slipped a glance at the rest of the occupied tables. "And as you can see, there may be others who will want my services."

"I understand. Good afternoon, sir."

Mr. Harcourt stepped toward the next table but then suddenly turned back. "Oh, and miss? Even if you do have gentlemen meeting up with you, unless they are familiar with a gun and the heath, you ought still to consider hiring me on. Robbins is no respecter of fools. He eats them for dinner and spits out their bones."

Rain drizzled from clouds low enough for a man to reach up and yank down. On a good day, London streets were crowded and smelly. But with the addition of the sooty mist coating one and all, today was a bad one. Not that Samuel minded. The grey June afternoon was a big shadow—and that suited him fine. It felt like home, this murky obscurity.

Rounding the corner, he turned onto Bow Street. Many feet had trod this path to the magistrates' court entrance, usually with trepidation. His steps were no different. Would the chief magistrate grant his contract renegotiation, extending it for only a month instead of the required two more years? Just four weeks more and he'd have money enough to buy the parcel of land that Lord Mabley, needing to raise cash, was selling over in Burnham. Hopefully Magistrate Conant was in a charitable mood, for if he wasn't. . .

Lord, grant mercy.

He flexed his hand and scowled at the remains of the deep scratch from the orphan boy atop it. The gash should've been sewn up, but what was one more scar? The last ten years on this job had been nothing but wound upon wound, in more ways than one.

He reached for the door—just as two hulking shapes stepped out.

The flaxen-haired figure—former Officer Alexander Moore—clapped him on the shoulder. "Speak of the devil—"

"And he doth appear, as I said he would." The darker of the pair, Officer Nicholas Brentwood, shifted his hawklike gaze from Moore to Samuel. "If I don't miss my mark, you're on your way to see Conant. Though judging by the looks of you, you're running a bit late due to an overturned cart loaded with an apothecary's delivery. Am I correct?"

Samuel's scowl deepened to a glower. How in all of God's green earth would Brentwood know that? Narrowing his eyes, he glanced down at his trousers, and. . .yes, there, clinging to the hem and the top of his shoes were small splotches of yellowish goo, too thick and sticky to have been washed away by the drizzle. Hang the man for his overly observant ways.

Part nudge, part shove, Moore turned Samuel about and herded him down the street—away from the courtroom's door. "Come. I've not much time before I must meet up with my wife. I don't often get to London anymore, so this round is on me."

Samuel shook his head. Likely a fruitless rebuff, knowing Moore's penchant for a tall mug and a good jawing. Blast! This would be his only chance for the next week to meet with the chief magistrate, for he was slated to ride the heath again tomorrow. He stopped in his tracks. "I'll catch up. First I must—"

"Don't bother." Brentwood clouted him on the back, bookending him between the two and pushing him into motion. "Conant isn't in, as usual."

Moore cocked a brow. "Not like the old days, eh?"

"Not at all." The words were more of a growl in Brentwood's throat, yet he was right. Things had never been the same since Ford resigned and ran off to Sheffield with his new bride.

"You can tell Ford he is still sorely missed," Brentwood added.

"What, and give the old duff a fat head?" Moore chuckled. "No, thank you. He's barely tolerable when he and Johanna's mam come for a visit. It's all *'I'm the best grandfather this'* and *'never better grandchildren that.'* The man's pride of family is enough to choke a horse."

Samuel stared at his friend, baffled. "Oughtn't you be glad of it? It is your family he's proud of, after all."

"I suppose, though it would be easier to bear were he not as domineering in his child-rearing advice as he was with his former directives. You'd think I'm still a runner under his employ instead of his son-in-law." Moore shoved open the door of the Blue Boar pub and barreled ahead, glancing over his shoulder. "And then there's old Nutbrown, thinking he knows all there is about children just because of his ridiculous puppeteering. . .though I do admit his theatre group keeps the little ones entertained in Dover and beyond."

The reek of ale and sausage wafted out the door, and as Samuel stepped inside, the additional stench of dampened wool and body odour blended with the mix.

Moore hailed the barkeep with a wave of his hand. "Three mugs, over here."

Instinctively, the three of them gravitated to a table in the far corner, each of them vying for the choice seat against the wall with a view of the entire room. But where Brentwood excelled at observation and Moore the use of his cunning tongue, Samuel slid fast and silent into the prized chair. A small victory, but one he'd hold on to with both hands.

Doffing his hat, Moore shook the extra droplets from the ends of his hair, not unlike a great Saint Bernard. And like the big dog, everything about him was powerful yet even-tempered. Samuel would never forget the good days he'd spent in Moore's company.

As if reading his mind, Moore voiced the same sentiment. "As happy as I am in Dover, I have missed you two renegades, though I won't own up to it in a court of law." He chuckled as Brentwood snorted. "But I am glad to find you both hearty and hale."

Accepting a mug from a serving girl, Brentwood took a draw, then swiped his mouth with the back of his hand. "Emily would kill me were I to take a bullet, so don't worry on my account. I'm not much on the streets anymore. With my seniority, the more lucrative security jobs are mine for the picking—which is a boon considering I've got four extra mouths to feed at home. No, Moore, it's this one who ought to concern you." Brentwood's dark gaze slid to Samuel, and he lowered his voice. "Word is Shankhart Robbins is gunning for you. You've been interrupting his business on the heath these past two weeks, and he's none too happy about it."

Samuel grunted. Despite his best efforts, the blackguard was still at large.

"I'm a little in the dark here." Moore slugged back a large swig then set his mug on the table. "Who's Robbins?"

"A dead man, should I find him." Samuel shoved his mug away, thirst for justice stronger than his need for a drink.

Moore's brows shot high. "Must be quite the swine to have you so riled."

"He's vile, I hear." Brentwood leaned forward, an underlying rage deepening his tone. "Sparing no one, not even children. That boy you found a fortnight ago, Thatcher, was a lucky one."

Lucky? Hardly. With no identification, the lad had ended up in an orphanage, just as he'd expected. Perhaps they'd eventually find the boy's father, but each day that passed without a lead, the slimmer the chance.

Tipping back his head, Brentwood downed the rest of his ale, then stood. "Well, as much as I'd like to stay and hear of your plans for capturing Robbins"—he turned his face to Moore—"or your innkeeping exploits in Dover, I must be off on an adventure of my own. Guarding an overnight load of munitions down at Wapping, and it pays to do a preliminary survey."

Moore frowned. "Can't you get Flannery to take care of that for you?"

"Flannery's gone. Back to Ireland to tend his ailing mother. I'm on my own now." He shrugged. "Give my best to Johanna. I suspect next time we meet, you'll have more than two daughters and a son, hmm?"

Moore winked. "I'll get right on that. Godspeed."

"You as well. And Thatcher"—Brentwood paused, his gaze piercing in the dim light of the taproom. "For once, take a care for yourself. Don't let Robbins be the end of you."

Samuel said nothing—for there was nothing to say. Of course he wouldn't go looking for death, but it would come eventually. And he could think of no better way of dying than in the pursuit of justice.

Brentwood's dark form hardly made it out the door before Moore turned to him, all mirth fleeing from his blue eyes. "Look, Brentwood may be a lifer, but you're not. Get out while you can, man."

He rolled the mug between his palms. "I intend to."

"Flit! Life's too short for intentions. Brentwood says you've got only a few weeks left on your contract. Ride it out here. Don't go back on the heath, not with this Robbins fellow at large. You've served too long to be taken out at the last minute."

Setting down his mug, he met Moore's terrible gaze and matched it with one of his own. "You think that frightens me?"

"No. I do not." Moore leaned back in his chair. "And that's what frightens me."

CHAPTER THREE

Sunshine mottled Abby's closed lids, and she fluttered her eyes open. For a moment, dust motes mesmerized her while she swam from the depths of a hard-won slumber. All the talk last evening of brigands and highwaymen, coupled with the jabs of Fanny's elbows and knees—for the woman was a rampaging bed hog—made for a long night. But at least she'd managed a few hours of sleep. Maybe. Reaching for her watch brooch on the small table next to the bed, she glanced at the numbers, and—

Sweet heavens! She flung off the counterpane and shot to her feet, clutching the timepiece. Nine o'clock. They should've been on the heath hours ago.

"Fanny, wake up." She scurried over to a washbasin and splashed water on her face, then darted back to the bed and jostled her maid's shoulder. "Fanny! We are running late. Please, get moving."

"Hmm?" Fanny pushed up on her elbows, blinking. "Oh. . .aye, miss."

By the time her maid finally shimmied into her own gown, Abby had hers buttoned, hair gathered up into a loose chignon, and hat ribbons securely tied beneath her chin. Snatching up her reticule, she strode to the door, then on second thought, turned back to face Fanny. If she didn't spell out the woman's instructions, there was no guarantee her maid might not dillydally over a cup of tea.

"Please see our baggage loaded as soon as you leave the room. I shall secure a driver and arrange for an on-the-road breakfast to make up our lost time. I will meet you at the front door."

"Very well, miss." Fanny glanced at her as she tucked in a last hairpin. "What about Mr. Harcourt? Did you make a final decision?"

"I have." How could she not? She'd been weighing the benefits and deficits of the man's offer ever since he'd proposed it the previous evening. "For our safety, I think it best to employ him, but I had better make haste. Hopefully no one else has hired him. I shall see you outside."

Urged by her own words, Abby hurried out of the room and dashed down the corridor, slowing only to descend the stairs into the taproom.

Behind the counter stood the same burly fellow of the night before, wearing the same stained apron. Upon closer inspection, his shirt was the same too, albeit more creased. She wrinkled her nose. He smelled a bit riper as well. Had he slept in those garments?

"Good morning, miss." The innkeeper dipped his head. "I were just about to fetch a maid to see if you ladies be planning on spending another night."

"No, sir. We are simply getting a late start." She fished a coin out of her small purse and set it on the scarred wood. "Would you wrap up a few rolls and some hard-cooked eggs or cheese that we may take along?"

"Aye. I'll have it packed and sent out to your carriage in a trice." His big fingers scooped up the money, and he turned to open a small strongbox on a shelf behind him.

"Very good. I am also seeking Mr. Harcourt, the tall fellow with side whiskers who took tea yesterday. Have you seen him this morning?"

The man swung back to her. "Mr. Harcourt left with a party earlier, near on two hours ago now. You ladies are the only guests remaining."

She couldn't stop the frown that weighted her brow. If Mr. Harcourt was already hired, were there even any drivers left, or would she and Fanny be forced to tarry another day?

"Oh dear," she breathed out.

"Not to worry, Miss Gilbert. All is not lost. There's still a driver available if you're wanting to cross the heath yet today. One of our most experienced, matter of fact. You'll find Mr. Shambles in the coach house."

Lifting up a small prayer of thanks, she smiled at the man. "Thank you, sir. You have been most hospitable."

The innkeeper tugged his forelock. "Godspeed and safe travels to ye."

Once outside, Abby couldn't help but lift her face to the brilliant June sky. She'd learned long ago to openly savor glorious mornings. And this time there'd be no scolding from her stepmother for such careless behaviour. How grand it would be—it *will* be—when she could greet each morning thus, walking hand in hand with her new husband.

Sighing, she stepped into the cool shadows of the coach house, breathing in horseflesh and leather. Perched on a stool in front of a long workbench was a man-sized grey toad. The fellow's hoary head dipped to his chest, and small snores issued with each inhale.

Abby pivoted in a circle, searching for the experienced driver the innkeeper had spoken of. Yet no one else was in sight. The only movement was the quiet rustle of straw beneath horses' hooves.

She turned back to the old fellow, hating to disturb his rest, but there was nothing to be done for it. "Excuse me, sir. I loathe to bother you, but—"

A great snore ripped out of him, cutting her off and waking him up. With a jerk, he snapped up his head, and she stifled a gasp. Indeed, he was a toad, for a plentiful crop of wartlike growths dappled his face. Bulging black eyes—set wide and somewhat milky—stared back at her.

"Eh? What's that you say?"

Lowering her gaze, Abby focused on the man's faded blue neckerchief instead of his face. "I beg your pardon for disrupting you, but I am wondering if you could direct me to a Mr. Shambles?"

The old fellow chuckled, the movement hunching his back all the more. "Why, that be me, miss."

This was Mr. Shambles? She pressed her lips tight, stopping a moan.

"You be needin' a driver, miss?"

"Y–yes." She stumbled over the word, her admission indicting her for having slept so late. Had she not been such a layabout, she'd have had a better pick of postilions.

"I'm yer man." Mr. Shambles edged off the stool, he and the tall seat tottering a bit. "I'll bring a carriage 'round to the front."

Swallowing her dismay, she forced a smile. "Thank you."

She left the coach house behind, pretending all would be well. And likely it would. It wasn't as if she'd be stuck with Mr. Shambles for the rest of the journey to Penrith. Only across the heath and to the next inn.

Leaving the stable yard, she spied Fanny waiting by the front door—chewing on an apple, her munching and crunching competing with the *chek-chek* of a warbler. A lad loitered nearby, ready to heft her trunk and their traveling bags into the carriage.

Fanny eyed her as she drew near. "Where's Mr. Harcourt?"

"He was not available."

"Hmm." Fanny took another great bite, and after a few lip-smacking seconds, she swallowed the mouthful. "Shouldn't we wait until he is?"

Abby feigned a confident smile. "That could be days from now. We need to move on. I cannot be late for my own wedding."

Tossing aside the apple core, her maid turned to her, worry creasing her brow. "But do you think it's safe?"

Abby pressed her lips flat. Her opinion of the matter didn't make the journey any more safe or dangerous. Still, if she didn't quell Fanny's fears, the silly girl would conjure all sorts of ghastly stories of highwaymen—not the sort of traveling conversation she'd like to hear for the next several hours.

"It is a bright morning." She schooled her voice to a cheerful tone. "We shall cross in plenty of time before dark. And I have been assured that we have hired the most experienced driver the inn has to offer."

Just then, their carriage rolled up. Mr. Shambles sat upon the lead horse. Barely. The hunchbacked man canted a bit sideways, his leather gloves clinging desperately to the reins.

"Pah!" Fanny spit out. "Experienced? Is the old fellow up to the task?"

The question buzzed like a hornet, stinging Abby's good sense. Still, what choice did they have?

"There is one way to find out." She lifted her chin and strode to where the lad had lowered the steps, then gripped his hand as she ascended.

Outside, Fanny hesitated near the door, but eventually she acquiesced—right after the lad hefted up a cloth-covered basket of food.

The coach rolled off, and after stopping at the tollgate to pay the crossing fare, they rumbled into the wilds of the heath.

Fanny heaved a satisfied sigh between bites of cheese and cold meat. "Well, this doesn't seem so bad. Hounslow isn't nearly as frightening as I imagined."

While the maid tucked the basket into a corner on the floor, Abby glanced out at the passing landscape. Scrubby shrubs dotted the expanse. Here and there, rangy trees bold enough to withstand the ever-present wind bowed in deference. Sunshine gilded the grassy plain, and yellow gorse flowers added to the golden effect. Fanny was right. It truly wasn't a frightening scene.

"It is quite beautiful," Abby murmured. "In a primal sort of way."

"It surely is different from Southampton. I wonder what our new home in the north will be like."

She turned back to her maid and studied the woman's brown eyes. "Are you nervous?"

"Not really." Fanny shrugged. "Truth is, with your Sir Jonathan Aberley being a baronet and all, I expect life will be better than ever."

Abby nodded absently. Yes, it would be far better to live with someone who wanted her around. Someone who'd listen to her, *really* listen. Someone who didn't expect her to blend into the background but would cherish her for herself and would love her for who she was, just as her real mother had, God rest her.

With a sigh, Abby turned to thoughts of living in a manor home with a handsome husband. Of candlelit dinners and walking hand in hand. Sharing whispers in the dark. A brazen smile twitched her lips. How long would it be before children came laughing and crying into their world? Would they have her brown eyes or—

Gunshot cracked the air, shattering her daydream. Fanny screamed. So did the horses.

Abby's breath stuck in her throat as she stared out at the nightmare through the window. Mr. Shambles fell sideways, and for one horrifying moment, his boot snagged on the cinch strap. The top half of his body dragged along the ground, bumping and scraping his torso over rocks.

Abby slapped a hand to her mouth, stopping a shriek.

The old fellow's body broke free then, rolling like a thrown sack of potatoes. Abby jerked her face to the side window as they passed him. His eyes were open. So was his mouth. Mud covered half his face. Blood the other.

And then he was gone.

But there was no time to mourn. The horses bolted, and the chaise careened to one side. Abby flailed for a grip as she slid sideways and crashed into Fanny. Without a driver, the carriage bounced wild, the wheels gaining momentum as the horses broke into a run.

Abby clawed her way upright, but only for a moment. Her head hit the glass, her face mashed against the window. Pain smacked her hard.

And the horses picked up speed, smearing the outside world into a blur.

Samuel slid off Pilgrim and looped the horse's lead over a picket, then turned and strode into the Golden Cross on silent feet. Not that he needed to be stealthy this brilliant June morn. No brigand in his right mind would be kicking back with a brew and kidney pie this time of day. Moving as a spectre was simply his way, a habit so engrained, he could no more stop doing it than he could quit breathing.

He slipped into the shadowy confines of the taproom and angled toward the bar. Behind it, innkeeper Willy Gruber worked a rag around the inside of a tankard.

"Mornin', Gruber."

Willy spun, and the mug flew from his hands. The earthenware hit the counter with a crack, then plummeted to the floor, splintering into shards against the greasy oak planks.

"Thatcher!" Willy spat out his name like a curse. "Why the flippity-flam can you not warn me when you come through the door? That's the fifth mug in the past fortnight you've ruined. I oughtta start chargin' ye. Aye, I'll keep a regular tally, I will, chock-full o' numbers. Send it right down to Bow Street and have 'em dock yer pay, that's what."

Samuel held his tongue. Giving in to Willy's drama only frothed it up all the more.

"Bah!" Willy flicked his hand in the air, swatting him away. "Off with ye. Yer men been here and gone already."

He grunted. He hadn't really expected his squad of officers to still be here, though it would've made for an easier ride. "How long ago?"

"Near on an hour and a half now, I figure. Maybe more." Willy tucked his rag into the apron tied around his big belly, then cocked a brow at him. "I were surprised to see you weren't with them."

"Cinch strap broke."

"Well, no doubt the poor sot what fixed it worked at breakneck speed beneath your devilish stare."

His mouth twisted. Willy was right. The *devilish stare* he'd perfected had served him well while facing Mahratta chieftains back in '03.

"Which route did they take?" he asked.

"Din't say, but I'm guessing the Exeter Road. That were the direction most o' last night's guests were headed, leastwise all those what had set out right before yer men arrived. Knowing that horse o' yours, ye'll catch up to 'em in no time."

No doubt, for off the top of his head he could think of at least three different shortcuts to make up for lost time—or more, if he cared to put his mind to it. Which he didn't.

Giving Gruber a sharp nod, he turned to go, but something dragged his steps. Something not quite right. Like the unsettling creak of a floorboard when sitting alone in an empty house.

He reached for the door—then drew back his hand. "*Most* guests?"

Willy flinched at his voice, for he'd already turned to grab another mug. At least this one stayed in the man's meaty paw. Breathing out curses that would redden a smuggler's ears, Willy swung back to the bar where Samuel had backtracked. "Aye, most. Had a few ladies set off not long ago, headed north."

"Who accompanied them? Harcourt?"

"Nay. He were employed by one o' the two coaches what left afore 'em."

Samuel frowned. "Any men with them? Husbands? Escorts?"

Willy shook his head. "Only Shambles."

Scarpin' bodgers! Those women would be easy prey should Shankhart be on the prowl. He tipped his hat and headed for the door.

Willy's voice followed. "And next time, rattle the doorknob or stamp yer feet. I'm done with yer slinking about!"

Samuel waved him off as he strode outside. Willy nagged more than a fishwife. Grabbing hold of Pilgrim's lead, he swung up into the saddle and turned the bay around. Once past the tollhouse, he cut loose onto the northern road. With any luck, he'd find old Shambles and the ladies in one piece.

Gusty breezes tried to steal his hat, but Samuel tucked his head into the onslaught, his worn black felt as much a part of him as his arms and legs. The heath whooshed past. Green. Yellow. Brilliant. Mornings didn't get any better than this.

Or did they? What would it be like to finally trade in his tipstaff for a hay rake? How much more peaceful? No more chasing cullys and killers. No more blood. Or death. As the world rushed by in a smear of green and gold, a small smile tugged his lips. Soon, God willing. Twenty-five pounds more and he'd have enough to—

A gunshot fractured the air, violating the summer morn. Judging by the echo of the report, not too far away. He dug in his heels, urging Pilgrim to top speed.

The wind whipped. Grit blasted his face, and his eyes watered. Samuel dropped closer to the horse's neck, cutting resistance and letting Pilgrim take the brunt of the breeze.

Leaning into a curve, he rounded a stand of gorse bushes, then spied a black lump ahead. Man-sized. Unmoving. Sprawled at the side of the road like a dumped heap of rubbish.

Samuel slowed his mount only long enough to identify the unmistakable face of Mr. Shambles. Part of it, at least. Blood hid the rest, having poured from an entry wound gaping at the side of his temple.

Yanking out a gun, Samuel urged Pilgrim onward, righteous fury burning in his gut. Either this was Shankhart Robbins's day to die. . .or his.

Lord, grant mercy.

Again the road curved, skirting a small rocky rise. When the trail straightened, Samuel growled. Twenty yards ahead, horses screamed to a stop. Barely. Whoever handled them didn't have the sense of a gnat.

Another man stood at the side of the chaise like the grim reaper about to call. One hand on the door handle. The other gripping a pistol.

Samuel yanked on the reins. The instant Pilgrim stopped, he sighted the man with the barrel of his gun and fired.

The scoundrel fell. The horses bolted. And the carriage lurched into motion.

Pushing air through his teeth, Samuel jabbed his heels into Pilgrim's side, but truly neither was needed. After ten years, the horse knew the routine.

The chaise bounced like a child's toy dragged by a tether. Samuel sped past it, gaining on the blackguard who drove the lead horse.

"Stop!" he roared.

Dark eyes swung his way.

So did a gun.

CHAPTER FOUR

She could die here, in this rocking four-wheeled casket—and Abby wasn't ready. Not yet. Not now.

God, please!

The wheels hit hard, and Abby's teeth snapped shut on her tongue, filling her mouth with the taste of copper. She could barely breathe, let alone cry out.

Next to her, Fanny shrieked, her flailing elbow punching Abby in the cheek. The carriage jolted faster, tilting one way, then back the other. Flying up. Crashing down. Abby's fingernail tore as she scrambled for a hold on the seat, the side, anything.

Despite her desperate clutching, her shoulder smacked against the wall, and her bonnet slipped forward, covering her eyes. She batted it away in time to see the galloping hooves of yet another horse streaking past the window. Atop it, a man in a muddied black cloak brandished another gun.

Dear God, is there no end? Save us!

But the chaise rumbled on. The men roared. So did the crack of a shot. The man driving the carriage listed sideways. With a yank on the reins, the man in the black cloak veered his horse into him, knocking the driver to the ground. Before Abby could suck in a breath or Fanny could scream again, the newcomer leapt from his saddle to the carriage horse. The wild ride slowed and, an eternity later, stopped.

That's when the shaking started. Somewhere deep and low. Spreading up Abby's legs to her belly to her arms. As the black-cloaked man dismounted and stalked toward the door, she trembled harder with each of his steps. What was to become of them?

She scrambled like a cat across the seat, crashing into Fanny, both shrinking away from the door. Fanny whispered a ragged rendition of the Lord's Prayer, her breath hot against Abby's ear. Abby bit her lip—heedless now of the blood—wishing she could pray, scream, run.

But all she could do was stare at the latch. It jerked down. The bolt scraped back. The door opened. A shadow-faced highwayman jumped up, blocking light and air and hope. His black gaze violated hers, and she quaked all the more.

He was night, this man. His dark hair hung wild to his chin. His darker hat shaded his eyes, so that all she saw were the sharp angles of his cheekbones, the cut of his nose, the strong mouth flattened to a grim line. Without a word, he stretched out his hand.

For her.

This was it, then. The end of innocence. The end of life—and just when love and belonging were within her reach. It wasn't fair, this ripping away of the gift she'd not yet opened.

And she'd have none of it.

She flattened against Fanny, flung out her hands for balance, and kicked like a wild donkey.

A heel caught Samuel's jaw, jerking his face sideways. Pain shot to his temple. Sweet blessed heavens! Must every person he tried to help lash out at him? The tear on his hand from the orphan boy was not yet completely healed.

Lurching back from the thrashing wildcat, he held up a hand. "Peace!"

The word thundered loud, startling the woman midkick.

"I won't harm you," he murmured, cautious and low, all the while edging slowly toward her. "You need to get out. The horses may bolt again."

God help them all if they did.

Indeed, God. A little help, if You please.

Keeping track of the woman's feet, he once again offered his hand.

Her gaze bounced between his face and his outstretched fingers. Blood trickled down one of her cheeks, marring the porcelain skin. The other woman, ashen-faced and scowling, shoved her forward. And no wonder, for it was a miracle the woman behind the wildcat could even breathe the way she'd been mashed against her.

The chaise rocked, the horses clearly spooked and willing to charge at the slightest provocation. Blast! He didn't have time to coddle frightened women.

Setting his jaw, Samuel reached for the wildcat, prepared for a biting, screaming mass. But she gave way without a fight and, in fact, gripped his hand with nary a complaint. What the deuce?

He helped her to the ground, then turned back to collect the other woman—yet no need. That lady shoved past him and flew from the chaise like a sparrow set free from a cage.

He jumped down after her, his boots sinking deep into the softened muck. Stretching out his arms, he shooed the women away from the road, toward the grassy bank, then gave them each a quick once-over for signs of injuries.

The wildcat stared back at him, quietly indicting him as a rogue, her brown eyes as dark as her scowl. She was a fighter, this one, which was a curious contradiction to her petite form. Or maybe not. Perhaps she'd learned at a young age to defend herself. Other than a swollen lip and the blood riding the curve of her cheek, she appeared to be unharmed.

He shifted his gaze to the bird woman who'd flown from the chaise. No cuts. No abrasions. Except for her rumpled gown, she looked well enough. But all the same, she doubled over, pressing one hand into her belly. "I'm going to be ill."

Samuel wheeled about and followed the crazed carriage tracks carved into the soft ground. Let the wildcat deal with her sick friend. It might work off some of her fury.

Ahead, the man he'd shot in the leg clutched his thigh, his moans an ugly blemish on the brilliant June morning. He tried to scramble away, but with that wound, he wasn't getting very far. The closer Samuel drew, the more frantic his thrashing and the louder his outrage.

"I'll kill ye for this! Ye hear me? Yer a dead man." Groans punctuated the blackguard's threats, rendering them moot.

Samuel reached for his neck cloth, and the man flinched. Samuel smirked. Not that he denounced the fellow for fearing a quick choking, but truly, if he had meant to kill him, the man would already be dead.

"Don't move," he ordered.

He crouched next to the grunting fellow and worked to tie the cloth around his leg, staunching the flow. "Who are you with?"

"I ain't talkin' to the likes o' you, ye filthy runner."

Samuel yanked the knot tighter than necessary.

"Shove off!" the man growled and followed his words with a host of vile epithets.

Rising, Samuel planted his feet wide and stared down at the villain, reminding himself that this was why he was out here. Stopping the wicked. Protecting the vulnerable. A noble endeavor. A needed one. But Lord, he was weary of it.

He turned his back on the scoundrel and continued following the ruts of the carriage wheels. Hopefully the man's partner yet lay in the dirt where Samuel had shot him in the leg. If he'd missed his mark and only grazed the fellow with a flesh wound, no doubt he'd already hied it out of there to attack again another day.

Squinting, he scanned the road as far as he could see. Just beyond a slight bend, a mud-splattered shape hunkered. This one not thrashing about. Who knew? Maybe this fellow would be more cooperative and talk—though it didn't really matter. Whether they admitted it or not, he'd wager his last breath these men belonged to Shankhart Robbins's gang. . .which meant that other members might very well be lurking close by. He upped his pace. It wouldn't be soon enough to his liking to haul in the pair and get the women to safety.

But his steps slowed as he drew near the other man, his gut twisting. Not so much as a twitch riffled the man's coat. No curses sullied the air. He didn't even turn his head to watch Samuel approach. Something wasn't right.

Five yards away, Samuel stopped. Blood bloomed around a hole in the man's calf, where the gunshot had hit. Not a triviality, but also not an injury to keep down such a strapping fellow. Samuel's gaze followed the deep rut of the carriage wheel—right to where it dug into the man's neck. That hadn't been simply a nasty fall from the chaise door.

It had been a deadly one.

He stomped around to the other side of the body and stared into the empty eyes of the dead man. . .then blew out a long breath. By all that was holy, he truly might have a death warrant on his head for this. That glassy gaze belonged to Pounce Robbins.

Shankhart's younger brother.

Closing her eyes, Abby lifted her face to the sun and, for one sanctifying moment, gave in to its warmth while everything in her yet shook. Maybe this was naught but a dream. It might be, especially with all the talk of guns and highwaymen the night before. She could awaken at any moment to the grumbling of the carriage wheels as she had so often done over the past four days. Yes, of course. That was it. This was just a great, awful nightmare. Nothing more.

"He's coming," Fanny hissed. The maid's clammy fingers wrapped around hers, pulling her back to reality. "I told you we should've made a run for it."

Abby frowned at her maid. "And go where? We are no match for a man with a gun. It is better not to anger him. We shall lead him to believe we will cooperate. Then when help is near, we will flee."

The man in the black riding cloak strode toward the carriage, two lengths of rope coiled in his hand. He pulled something big behind him, and judging by the way he strained with each step, something quite heavy. Two objects, rather flat and long and rustling the grass. He stopped far enough away that she couldn't quite make them out, but they appeared to be man-sized.

"Turn around," he bellowed.

That didn't sound good. She didn't know much about men and violence, but it seemed one ought to always keep an enemy within sight. Just because he hadn't harmed them yet didn't mean he wouldn't.

Summoning her courage, she lifted her chin and stared the man down. "What are you going to do with us?"

His dark gaze met her challenge, the set of his jaw stating he'd not be trifled with. "I'll take you to the next inn. Now, do as I say."

She slipped a sideways glance at Fanny, whose brow wrinkled as much as her own. He'd take them to the next inn? As if he were naught but an escort instead of a highwayman? Or was that where he'd meet up with his gang and. . .

She swallowed. Better not to think beyond that.

"I'm waiting," he rumbled.

Fanny turned, and with a huff, so did she.

The man's heavy steps neared, the grass swishing and crackling beneath his boots. Closer and closer. Then his feet stopped. Some grunts. Thick breaths. A thud, accompanied by creaking leather on the back seat outside the chaise. And again. Then more footsteps—slowly fading.

Abby whirled to see the hem of the man's riding cloak swinging in the breeze as he stalked away.

Next to her, Fanny craned her neck toward the back of the carriage. "What did he. . . ?" She stepped closer, angling for a better view.

Abby planted her feet. Though trouble often had a way of finding her, there was no sense in hastening toward it.

"Why, it looks like— Oh! That's Mr. Shambles." Fanny spun, slapping a hand over her mouth. She darted back to the grass and once again doubled over.

Abby turned her back to the chaise, unwilling to witness whatever gruesome sight had sickened Fanny. Even so, the sounds of the maid's heaving and the thought of what she might have seen made her own stomach churn. With stilted steps, she approached Fanny and slowly rubbed circles on the woman's back. "It is going to be all right. We have to stay strong. Surely God is watching over us."

Her chest tightened. He was, wasn't He?

She shoved down a tide of rising doubt and rubbed all the more. "We cannot let that man know he frightens us."

Fanny stiffened beneath her touch. "I am frightened!"

"So am I, but if you show fear, it will only incite him." A bitter frown weighted her brow. How well she knew that truth, branded into her soul by a stepmother who thrived on fear.

Fanny shuddered one last time, then straightened.

Abby reached into her pocket and pulled out a handkerchief. Fanny had already ruined her own. "Here."

"Thank you, miss." The woman accepted her offering with shaky fingers and dabbed the corners of her mouth.

They both turned back to the road when boot steps thudded.

Without a glance their way, the black-cloaked fellow lugged past them a man bleeding from his leg. Vulgarities spewed out of the injured man's mouth, especially when he was hoisted atop a mount. The horse stamped and puffed a harsh breath, no happier than he.

Fanny edged behind her as the other man turned toward them and closed the distance with the stretch of his long legs.

He stopped near the door, the gleam in his dark eyes a wearied sort of dangerous. A crescent scar marred the skin high on his cheek near his left eye. Not surprising, for he'd certainly shown he was capable of violence. How many other marks did that riding cloak of his hide?

He tipped his head toward the carriage. "You ladies need to get in the chaise."

Abby shook her head. He could take them anywhere. Do anything, for he'd shown what he was capable of. But she'd be hanged if she made it easy for him. "We are not going with you."

He rolled his eyes and swung out an arm, indicating the bleeding man who was hog-tied on the horse. "I'm not one of these wretches. If I were, you'd be dead by now."

She gaped. That was supposed to be reassuring? "Surely you do not think I am naive enough to fall for such glib falsehoods."

His lips flattened into a straight line, and he reached inside his coat.

Fanny gasped. So did she. Had she pushed him too far? Would the barrel of a smoking gun be the last thing she saw on this earth?

Slowly, he pulled out a wooden-handled baton, brass at one end and ornamented with a small crown. Abby stared at the tipstaff. Could he truly be a lawman? Or had he stolen that from the body of one?

Her gaze drifted from the truncheon to the man's face. Nothing had changed in his fierce appearance—yet everything had. A gleam of pure veracity shone in his eyes. Not one speck of anything sinister swam in those brown depths. Not a jot of wickedness or cruelty. For the first time, she thought that maybe, perhaps, he could be trusted.

He jerked his head toward the open door of the carriage. "I am a Principal Officer operating out of Bow Street. Now get in the carriage. You're safe as long as I'm with you."

Safe? She trapped a retort behind her teeth. He may be an officer of the crown, but there was nothing safe about him.

CHAPTER FIVE

The Laughing Dog was a ramshackle hovel, barely clinging to the turf at the far end of the heath. It stood like a drunkard, leaning hard to the east, pushed cockeyed by wind and years of neglect. Samuel frowned as he stopped the carriage. This wasn't his first choice of refuge. It was his only one. Turning back to the Golden Cross would've doubled the time, and the next inn wasn't for another fifteen miles.

"Stay put," he growled at the villain on the horse next to his. Likely the command was unnecessary, for the ride had drained the fellow. He merely sat there, stoop-shouldered and ashen-faced, his trouser leg soaked with blood.

Samuel swung down into a thick patch of mud, and a scowl etched deep into his brow. A pox on Skinner for being such a cinch-purse of a proprietor. Two coins out of the innkeeper's profits would dump a load of wood shavings on this mess. And by doing so, perhaps more savory patrons would frequent the place instead of the usual riffraff that congregated beneath the inn's crack-shingled roof.

He rounded the side of the carriage, opened the door, and yanked out the stairs. Without a word, he lifted his arm and offered his hand. Silence proved best in dealing with frightened women, for they often read too many sinister meanings into the most innocent of remarks. And no doubt these women were frightened. They'd seen enough today to make a grown man's bowels turn to water. He coaxed his mouth into a semblance of a smile, especially when the wildcat peered down at him.

Her small fingers pressed against his as she descended. She'd tucked up her loosened dark hair, blown wild by the winds of the heath, but several curls refused capture and dangled free. Her gown was wrinkled, the hem caked with mud. Her crushed bonnet dangled from its ribbons like a dead cat down her back. She'd fit right in with the clientele of the Dog.

But despite her ruffled appearance, she smelled of lavender and something more. Something sweet. He inhaled as she swept past him. Citrus, perhaps? Orange blossom water, if he wasn't mistaken.

He lent his hand to the other woman, and then the wildcat turned to him. "Where are we?"

"North side of the heath, the Laughing Dog Inn."

"What is to become of us now?"

Oh no. He'd not fall for that one. Fluttering eyelashes were sure to follow. Then coy blushes and flattery. He'd seen it before. Women always got far too attached to whoever helped them in a time of need.

"That's up to you, miss."

He stalked toward the inn, his boots sinking into the mud. Lighter footsteps squashed and sucked behind him, the noise kindling a fire in his gut. These ladies should not be here, stamping through the filthy mire. Who in their right mind had sent them out on their own? Allowed them to travel without a manservant? Without any kind of protection whatsoever?

He shoved open the door with more force than necessary, and a belch of smoke from an ill-drafted hearth greeted him. Thin blue haze hovered below the rafters in the small room, stinging his eyes as he entered. Opposite a bar scarred from one too many knife fights, three tables graced the tiny public area. A single window shed light through sooty film. Even on a brilliant afternoon such as this, the Dog lived and breathed in perpetual twilight.

Samuel stalked past a man nursing a mug at the bar—or rather the mug nursed him. The tankard propped up his shaggy head as he snored with an open mouth.

"Skinner?" Samuel called.

A mousey man scurried out of the kitchen door. Skinner's shorn head and clipped beard resembled a pelt of grey fur. His clothes had been washed so many times they were now a perpetual shade of dingy. He twitched when he walked, and his voice squeaked in an off-key pitch. "Aye, Cap'n! Why, I ain't seen ye in awhiles. Got ye some pretties, have ye?"

He didn't have to look behind to know the women stood close at his back. Despite the smoky air, he breathed in a faint whiff of orange blossoms. "These ladies need a place to refresh. Give them your best. I'll need a bed and a surgeon for one man. A gravedigger for the other two."

Skinner cocked his head. "Hit a patch o' trouble, did ye?"

"You could say that."

The little innkeeper darted a look about the taproom, then jerked a step closer. "Were it Robbins?"

"One of them."

The man's eyes widened, black and beady. "Which one?"

"Pounce."

"Pounce!" Skinner jumped back. "Don't tell me I'll be housin' that devil."

"You won't." Thank God. The world would be a better place without that scoundrel. Samuel rolled his shoulders, working out a knot. "Pounce's thieving days are done."

Behind him, the ladies conferred in whispers—hard to make out with Skinner's low whistle filling the small room.

"There'll be a price on yer head, Cap'n. Shankhart will hunt ye down, and that's God's truth." Skinner's nose wrinkled. Were he truly a mouse, no doubt his whiskers would be trembling. "Ye know that, don't ye?"

Of course he knew it—and had since he'd first stared into Pounce's glassy eyes. "Won't be the first time."

"Always were one to live on the edge, eh?" The little man chuckled. "You be riding back today, Cap'n, or staying the night?"

"Depends upon what the surgeon says, how soon that villain out there can ride." He hitched his thumb over his shoulder. "Have someone haul him in, hmm? Oh, and send a lad to see to the ladies' belongings and to my horse."

Skinner's head bobbed. "Aye. I'll have Blotto heave in the ol' carp and the baggage, and I'll send my lad Wicket to tend yer mount. Set yerself down. I'll bring ye a whistle wetter while ye wait."

Samuel took the table in the corner, shoving the chair so his back would be against the wall. Pulling off his hat, he scrubbed a hand over his face, wiping off some of the grime, then winced as his fingers hit the sore spot on his jaw from the woman's kick. Lord, but his bones ached. His muscles. His soul. He was getting too old for this.

Heated whispers floated on the air, somewhere in the cloud just above the heads of the two women. Colour rose on each of their cheeks. Were they sisters? Cousins? Rivals or friends?

The wildcat shook her head then spun toward him. Her steps clipped on the wooden planks, little clods of mud breaking loose from her hem and littering the floor. She stopped at his table, her brown eyes a fierce sort of velvet, far too bold. And worse, far too comely. He shuddered inwardly at what Pounce would've done to such a beauty had he not come upon the scene.

She bobbed a small curtsey. "I wanted to thank you, sir, for your aid. I realize now that you are a noble man of integrity."

He studied her for a moment. What was she angling for with such flattery? Slowly, he shook his head. "No thanks needed, lady. It is my job."

"Even so, you have my gratitude. I am Abigail Gilbert, and this"—she lifted her hand, indicating the woman standing at her shoulder—"is my maid, Fanny Clark. Might I ask your name, sir?"

He stored the information in a mental file. Not that he intended to ever use it, but one never knew when a name might need to be retrieved. Leaning back in the chair, he eyed her, debating if he ought to part with his own name or ignore her. Normally, he didn't engage on such a personal level with those he aided—or anyone else, for that matter.

But then normally women tended to shrink from his scrutiny. Not this one. Miss Gilbert didn't flinch beneath the weight of his gaze, and in fact, tilted her head and stared right back as if she'd spent years facing dragons.

Unbidden, words flowed past his lips. "The name's Thatcher. Captain Thatcher."

"Pleased to meet you, Captain." Her lips curved into a pleasant smile. "I am wondering if, once you are refreshed, you would consider employment as our escort for the rest of our journey."

"The *rest* of your journey?" Sweet heavens! The little wildcat had narrowly missed death only hours ago, and now she was ready to continue on as if the experience had been nothing more than an afternoon ride through Hyde Park?

He set his jaw to keep from gaping. "Lady, you shouldn't be journeying anywhere. Go home, wherever that is. And this time, take a public coach. They are guarded."

The woman at Miss Gilbert's back nudged her, and though she spoke in a whisper, her words sprayed down on the wildcat's head like a curse. "I told you!"

Miss Gilbert brushed at the wrinkles in her gown, ignoring her maid's impertinence. Strange. Why would she do that? Most gentlewomen wouldn't suffer such cheek without censure. Samuel folded his arms, pondering the odd pair.

"Yet if you would consent to hire on as our escort, Captain Thatcher," Miss Gilbert continued, "then we would be guarded every bit as much as a public coach. Would we not?"

He stretched his neck sideways until it cracked, relieving a wicked kink—but it did nothing for the unease that the woman's determination stirred up. Could that same determination be the reason she'd been out on the heath undefended? He pinned her down with a direct stare. "Why are you out here alone, traveling without a manservant or any sort of protection?"

"As you can see, I am not alone." She swept her hand toward her maid. "And not that it signifies, but I am on my way to be married."

"That doesn't answer my question."

Her eyes flashed as if he'd probed too deep. A small satisfaction, that, for truth often welled from the deepest of cisterns.

"If you must know, Captain, at the last minute my family's manservant was needed at home, and there were no more servants to spare."

He shoved down a grunt. Some family. Likely a brood of selfish rich toffs bent on meeting their own needs and forsaking those of others.

But if they were wealthy. . .

He studied her all the more. "Why didn't your family hire a guardian, then?"

"Oh, well. . ." She fluttered her fingers—no doubt trying to distract him from the spreading flush on her face. "They have likely even now left for the continent. There was no time to acquire one before I departed. So you see, Captain, that I am in need of your services."

He smirked. She was an unwavering little firebrand, he'd give her that. Spunky too. Still, he shook his head. "No."

"But you have not yet heard my terms."

"'Ere we are, Cap'n." Skinner leaned around the women and thwunked a mug onto the table in front of Samuel, foam sloshing over the rim. "Be right with ye, ladies. Just scrapin' a bit o' muck out of a back room for ye. Got a pot o' tea on for ye as well, and being as yer friends o' the captain, I'll see if I can scare up a dainty or two to go along with it."

The innkeeper darted off before the ladies could reply.

Samuel collected his mug and slugged back a drink, secretly hoping the women would retire to a table of their own and reconsider taking a coach from here on out.

But Miss Gilbert didn't move. Not a whit. She stood there waiting, as if by merit of her presence alone he might change his mind.

He eyed her over the rim of his mug. "Go home, lady. It is foolish to travel alone."

She tilted her chin. "You will be paid handsomely, Captain. I can give you twenty-five pounds up front, and when you deliver me safely to my intended at Brakewell Hall in Penrith, he shall reimburse you another hundred pounds. Or more. What do you say to that?"

He choked, but not from the smoky air. One hundred twenty-five pounds? He didn't earn that in an entire year of hauling in cutpurses and killers. The sum was enough to not only buy the patch of land he desired but put up some outbuildings and purchase more seed than he'd need for two years. At a good pace, he could get them to Penrith in a little over a fortnight—which would also put a bit of distance between him and the heath. . .where Shankhart would be gunning for him.

The front door slapped open, drawing his gaze. Blotto, Skinner's man, wrapped a beefy arm around the highwayman's shoulders, shoring up the injured criminal as he stumbled across the floor. Reminded of his duty, a great glower pressed deep into Samuel's brow. As much as he needed Miss Gilbert's money, obligation to the crown came first—and that meant seeing the highwayman hauled into goal until a trial could be held.

He tossed back his mug, swallowing the last dregs. The aftertaste was bitter, both from the rotgut and from knowing how he must answer the lady. He reached for his hat, then stood and gazed down at her. "My answer is no, Miss Gilbert. Stay the night here, then take the coach first thing in the morning."

Her chin lifted ever higher. "Very well, Captain. You have been most helpful."

But the sparking gold flecks in her brown eyes and the taut line of her shoulders belied her words. If he didn't miss his mark, the woman had no intention of heeding his counsel. . .and he rarely missed his mark.

Sidestepping the ladies, he stalked off, more rankled than when he'd first entered the Dog.

The woman—Miss Gilbert—was entirely too much like himself.

Abby eased the hem of her gown off the taproom floor, tucking the extra fabric between her legs and the chair. Only God knew the origins of the oily brown residue near her feet. While she and Fanny had frequented a fair number of inns on their journey, the Laughing Dog was by far the foulest. Why had Captain Thatcher brought them here? Her eyes watered and her lungs were beginning to burn, both from the smoke and from not wanting to breathe. The whole place smelled of cabbage gone bad. Very bad.

Seated across from her, Fanny folded her hands in her lap, the beginnings of a fierce frown brewing. For hours now, ever since the failed conversation with Captain Thatcher, her maid had made clear her stance on wanting to take the public coach back home. But each time Fanny brought it up, Abby refused to yield. Not that her opposition had stopped the woman, though. And now, as the maid leaned forward and parted her lips for yet another shot, Abby steeled herself to take the next round.

Thankfully, the proprietor skittered up to them, bearing two steaming bowls. "Here ye be, ladies."

Mr. Skinner set their meals on the crusty tabletop. Abby frowned at the washcloth tucked into the man's waistband. Did he not know how to use it? Or did he not own a chisel? For that's what it would take to chip away the dried remains fossilizing atop the table.

His face squinched into a broad smile, somehow making his pointed nose seem even longer. "Made this meself, I did. Thought you ladies might appreciate something other than a shank bone."

Abby smiled at the man's thoughtfulness. "Thank you, Mr. Skinner."

With a nod, he darted off, disappearing behind the bar where the broad backs of four men hunkered on stools.

Fanny took a bite, screwed up her face, then set down her spoon and shoved away her bowl. "You should have withheld your gratitude."

Abby couldn't help but sigh. The maid had been nothing less than tetchy since they'd arrived. "Oh Fanny, I know this has been a trying day, but are we not in God's debt for even a mean bowl of pottage? And should we not share that thankfulness with the hands that made it? After all, Mr. Skinner did go to the effort of preparing this especially for us."

"Go on, then." Fanny fluttered her fingers toward the bowl. "Take your own bite and see if your sentiment changes."

As Abby lifted her spoon, the rotted cabbage odour intensified, and suddenly she understood the source of the stench. Even so, she determined to give the stew a fair shot. But as the stringy broth landed in her mouth, it took all her willpower to swallow the swill and not spew it out.

Fanny cocked her head, arching an I-told-you-so brow. "Perhaps we should retire. The first coach leaves at dawn, so we'll have an early morning."

Abby set down her spoon. "We are not taking the coach."

"Didn't you listen to what the captain said earlier?"

"We have been over this before." Several times, actually. And with her shoulder yet sore from the crack against the side of the chaise, the repeated dialogue had made for a long afternoon. "Sticking to coaching routes will add over a week to our journey."

"I understand," Fanny clipped out. "But you'll have a whole lifetime with your baronet. Why the hurry?"

"Sir Jonathan is expecting me, and I cannot keep him waiting. Besides, if you were the one on your way to the man of your dreams, would you not also make haste?"

"Not if it cost me my life."

She couldn't stop the roll of her eyes. "Save your drama, Fanny. We have already crossed the most dangerous leg of our journey."

The maid threw up her hands. "And been accosted while doing so!"

"Yes, yet lightning does not strike twice in the same spot."

Three pairs of eyeballs turned their way from the nearest table, and Abby lowered her voice. "Listen, if it makes you feel any better, I will find someone to ride along with us. Surely Captain Thatcher is not the only available guardian for hire."

"That idea is even more dangerous than riding alone. Do you see the men in here?"

Her gaze slid around the ragtag collection of patrons gracing the taproom. Several stared back, interest gleaming in their eyes—the cold and calculating kind. A beast of a man in the corner looked as if, among other things, he wanted to kill her just for the pleasure of it. The rest were so busy wooing their cups, the walls could've collapsed around them and they'd never notice.

She pursed her lips to keep from sighing again—and to keep from admitting aloud that Fanny was right. Not one of these men would be suitable to hire. She and Fanny would be safer on their own.

Turning back to her maid, she curved her lips into a confident smile. "We shall simply travel on to the next inn and employ a manservant there. It will only be another fifteen miles or so on our own. After all, we have made it this far without a hired gun."

Slowly, Fanny shook her head. "While it pains me to do so, miss, if you refuse to take the public coach, I feel I must resign as your maid."

She stiffened. Surely she hadn't heard correctly. "What are you saying?"

"Unless you relent"—the maid pressed her hands onto the table and bent forward—"I will be forced to take the morning run back to Southampton and search for other employment."

Abby drew a sharp breath. "You would leave me to journey on alone?"

"Beg your pardon, miss, but I must. Your determination will not be my downfall." Pushing up, Fanny stood. Without a backward glance, the maid hastened across the small room and vanished up the stairwell.

Of all the arrogance! Abby gaped. Fanny had been the closest thing to a sister she'd ever had. . .and now even she would turn on her? Would this horrid day never end?

Across the room, a dark shape stepped out of the shadows. Captain Thatcher's burning gaze met hers, and her breath hitched, for he looked into her very soul. The man couldn't possibly have heard all that was said between her and Fanny, but all the same, she got the distinct impression that he knew—which both frightened and strengthened her in an odd kind of way. God had provided the captain at just the right time today. Surely He would continue to provide tomorrow.

Abby drove back her chair and rose. If Fanny wanted to return home, then so be it. As for her, she would travel on to the next inn and hire a guardian there. Whatever the cost.

Hopefully it wouldn't be more than she could afford.

CHAPTER SIX

Morning fog muffled everything. The jingle of tack. The nickers of the horses. Even the loading of Fanny's baggage onto the coach was nothing more than a muted scrape followed by a subdued thud. Abby stood silent, watching the action with an equally dull gaze. It seemed like a death, this parting. How fitting that the mists of dawn distorted the world into the unnatural.

Turning to her, Fanny laid a hand on her sleeve. "Are you certain I can't persuade you to join me?"

A sad smile flitted across her lips. As much as she hated to see her maid go, there was no turning back. Not to a stepmother who despised her and half sisters that scorned. The scars of the past were still too raw and fresh, and she had a sinking feeling they would always be so.

Facing Fanny, she forced a measure of courage into her voice that she didn't feel. "I will not return home. Ever."

"Very well then, miss. May God bless you." Fanny's fingers squeezed her arm—and then she let go. "Goodbye."

The woman turned and fled up into the hulking coach before Abby could respond. Her throat tightened against a sob. It was a strange, wonderful, terrifying thing to lose this last connection to her past. So many conflicting emotions squeezed her heart that she could barely breathe. Of course she was doing the right thing. Wasn't she?

Am I, God?

Unwilling to witness the fog swallow her last glimpse of the coach, she whirled—then startled. A pace away from her stood Captain Thatcher, sporting a grim-set jaw and a gaze that penetrated even through the mist.

His eyes flicked from her to the retreating coach, then back. "Why are you still here?"

She chewed the inside of her cheek. How was it that this man could instantly make her feel as naught but an impish schoolgirl?

Stifling the urge to retreat a step, she smoothed her hands along the damp fabric of her skirt. "I will not be here for long."

His head lowered, and his dark eyes studied her from beneath the brim of his hat. "You should be on that coach."

His tone of authority rankled, as irritating as the cold moistness seeping in near her collar. Or was it the way he looked at her, as if his gaze alone could cut through any façade?

Despite the wrinkles she'd create, her fingers bunched handfuls of her gown. "Thank you for your concern, but I have rented a perfectly good traveling chaise, Captain."

He shook his head. "Lady—"

"I have a name, sir. It is Miss Gilbert, not *lady*." The words flew out before she could stop them. La! After all the years she'd spent mastering her tongue in front of her stepmother, why could she not tether her speech with this man?

One of his eyebrows raised. Barely. Had she angered him? Amused him? Given him reason to slap shackles on her wrists and haul her in? Hard to discern by the way his lips tightened into a straight line.

"Don't tell me you intend to journey on by yourself, *Miss Gilbert*."

Ignoring the way he pushed her name through his teeth, she lifted her chin. "I do not see how that is any of your business, for as I recall, you refused my employment."

He blew out a long, low breath. Were the man not already employed by Bow Street, he'd make a daunting head schoolmaster.

"Everyone who travels the roads hereabouts *is* my business. I cannot allow you to—"

"Thatcher! Thank God." The words boomed, nearly drowning out the muted thud of horse hooves and clinking of tack. A grey-cloaked man emerged from the fog astride a strawberry roan with a blaze on its nose. He slid from the saddle and clapped the captain on the back.

Abby used the distraction to whirl and scurry back to the inn. While the captain may be a man of integrity—though she wasn't quite sure of that yet—he certainly had a way of making her feel jittery.

Inside, behind the counter, the mousey barkeep glanced up at her entrance, his dark little eyes widening. "What, you still here miss? I thought ye and yer companion were off this morn."

"I am, or more like I shall be." She loosened the strings of the reticule secured to her wrist. "I should like to hire a postilion and inquire about a possible manservant as well. Someone well acquainted with the roads and able to use a gun."

"Well, miss. . ." The innkeeper paused to scratch a spot behind his ear, loosing a powdering of dandruff onto his shoulder—thank heavens it wasn't lice. "We're a small operation, ye see. Not a regular coaching inn. Still, I suppose I could part with my boy Wicket to ride ye to the Gable Inn, near abouts ten mile off or so, long as he's back afore dark. Can't rightly help ye with a manservant, though."

"I can." A deep voice rumbled at her back.

She clenched her jaw. Why had Captain Thatcher made it his duty to badger her into doing what he thought best? The man was more determined than her stepmother to have his way. She turned, prepared to confront him.

But cold, green eyes—lizard-like and unflinching—stared at her from beneath a shaggy set of brown eyebrows. A wiry man dipped his head toward her, not much taller than herself. He was all sinew and tendons. The type of fellow that could spring up the trunk of a tree before you knew he'd even thought to do so. She remembered him from the evening before as one of the men who'd slipped glances at her from his stool at the bar.

He touched the brim of his hat and gave a slight nod. "Ezra Thick at your service, miss. I heard you be needing a man to hire as guardian. I'm available, if you like."

Though this was what she'd wanted, every muscle in her tensed. He seemed polite enough, his speech respectful, but was it wise to hire a man to guard her when she didn't know if she ought to be guarded against him?

She glanced back at the innkeeper, hoping to find either acceptance or alarm at Mr. Thick's offer. But the mousey man had disappeared through a back door, apparently done with the both of them. She frowned. Surely if Mr. Thick were a rogue, the innkeeper would've warned her. . .wouldn't he?

She turned back to Mr. Thick. "You heard correctly, sir. I do need a manservant, but only until we reach the Gable Inn." Where hopefully she'd find a more respectable fellow. Her shoulders sagged. What if she didn't? Oh, why hadn't she hired Mr. Harcourt when she'd had the chance?

"Then I'm your man, miss. I know these roads like none other." He shuffled his feet, then lowered his voice. "I'll take my pay up front, though. No disrespect intended, but I've been cribbed a time or two."

Her reticule weighed heavy in her hands. If she gave him the full amount, what was to prevent him from simply running off? She fished around for only two coins and held them out. "I shall pay you half now and the rest when you see me safely to the Gable. Take it or leave it."

"Business woman, eh? I like that. I like it a lot." An oily smile slid across his face, and he snatched the gold from her palm. "I'll ready my horse and meet you outside. In the back."

Her heart sank as he bypassed her and vanished out the door. Had she made the right decision?

Samuel gritted his teeth as Officer Bexley's cuff on the back rippled through him from spine to ribs. The man didn't realize his strength—or his insubordination. Samuel let it slide, though. Despite Bexley's poor judgment, the fellow meant as much harm as an overgrown bear cub.

"It were a devil of a ride to track you down, Captain. Had me frettin' like a fishwife when you didn't check in last night." Bexley elbowed him, his blue eyes twinkling brilliant through the mist. "The boys were placing bets that ol' Shankhart had got to you."

"Waste of good money. Hold on." He pivoted to launch a final admonition for Miss Gilbert to reconsider taking the next public coach—only to find the patch of muddy ground empty.

He bit back an oath. Foolish, strong-headed woman! While she hadn't actually admitted she'd be traveling on alone, neither had she denied it. And if she did venture out unaccompanied, a comely young woman such as herself wouldn't stand a chance against any hot-blooded man crossing her path, cutpurse or not.

"What kept you, Captain?"

Despite his unease over Miss Gilbert, Bexley's voice turned him back to his duty. He'd have to see to the woman later.

"Two of Shankhart's gang accosted a carriage." Fog droplets collected into one big splash dripping from his hat down to his cheek. He flicked it away with the back of his hand, annoyed at the damp and the memory of the postilion's body lying dead on the heath. "One of the blackguards didn't make it. The other wasn't ready to travel—till now."

"Humph." Bexley pushed out his lower lip as he digested the information. "Then we'll haul him in together, eh?"

"Maybe." He wheeled about and stalked toward the inn, heels digging deep into the softened ground. He didn't need Bexley to hold his hand while bringing in a prisoner—and in truth, it might endanger his fellow officer's life. Word about Pounce Robbins's death could have already reached Shankhart's ears.

Bexley fell into step beside him, his horse clomping along at their backs. "What aren't you telling me?"

For the love of women and song! After serving so closely for the past eight years, Bexley knew him well. Too well. He upped his pace.

So did Bex. "You know I won't be put off so easily, Captain."

Just before the door of the Laughing Dog, he stepped aside, folded his arms, and faced the man. Better to hash this out here than in the taproom, on the off chance that what'd happened to Pounce hadn't been spread far and wide yet.

"Well?" Bexley's blue eyes searched his.

He looked away, to the eerie mist hovering over the land. It didn't bode well, this chill settling deep in his bones. "It's best if you turn around now. You shouldn't be seen with me on the heath."

But Bexley wouldn't give. Not an inch. The man merely widened his stance. "Why's that?"

It was more a grumble than a question. The tone he'd use himself had he ridden hell-bent across the heath with naught but leftover moonlight shrouded in a rising haze.

He swiped the brim of his hat, warding off any future drips. "It wasn't just any man I took down out there." He met Bexley's gaze. "It was Pounce."

Bexley spit out a curse, loud enough that his horse tossed its head and stamped a hoof. "As if Robbins didn't have enough reasons to kill you, you had to go and give him one more?"

Samuel stared him down, saying nothing.

"What a mess of rotten kippers." Bex blew out a long breath, his cheeks puffing. "Yet there's naught to be done for it now, I suppose. Tell you what, I'll take your brigand in myself. You stay put. Or better yet, move on a bit farther. Go north. Hie yourself up to St. Albans. Stay at the Gable Inn for a while. Give ol' Shankhart plenty of time and space to cool off."

His brows lifted. "Robbins, cool off?"

Another curse cut through the air. "Well, what then? Anything short of you crossing that stretch of land without an armed guard is suicide."

"I won't hide." He shrugged. "Nor will I endanger others."

For a moment, Bexley's jaw worked, then he turned aside and spit. Slowly, he ran his hand across his mouth. "Not surprised. And neither should you be when I say I'm going with you. You know Shankhart's penchant for cat-and-mouse torture. He'll toy with you if you're on your own. Play his wicked games. Drag it out before he strikes. The man ain't right in the head."

Bex folded his arms, leaving no room for argument. A bold move, considering Samuel outranked the man in seniority and position. Bexley was a brave one, he'd give him that. Occasionally foolhardy, yet one of the best on the squad. And he was right on all accounts about Shankhart.

Samuel gave him a sharp nod. "Suit yourself."

A smile slid across Bexley's face, and he looped his horse's lead around a nearby picket. "Come on, then. Let's have us a drink and be on our way."

Samuel squinted into the fog. The first half circle of a sun barely cut through the gloom. Hardly morning, and Bexley wanted to drink? Samuel shoved open the door to the Dog and held it for his friend. Still, he wouldn't think less of the fellow if Bex felt the need for a mug or two before they left. It would take a stout amount of courage for Bex to be seen with him when any manner of killers could be lurking in the mists, all mad-dog possessed to bring Samuel's head in to Shankhart.

CHAPTER SEVEN

Skirting the side of the inn, Abby clutched her small travel bag in one hand and, with the other, held the brim of her hat against a gust off the heath. Between the wind and the hazy outline of a half-circle sun now climbing on the horizon, the fog would be gone in no time. The first smile of the morning lifted her lips. Good. Clear skies would make for safer travel—for her and for Fanny. Wherever she was. *Oh Fanny. . . Godspeed to you.* As cantankerous as her former maid could be, Abby already missed the woman's banter. It would be strange to ride silent in the chaise.

Behind the Laughing Dog, the ground churned up in a sea of mucky gouges and rises. Several chickens strutted about, pecking earthworms too slow to take cover. Near the stable, the yellow carriage she'd rented stood at the ready. At the front of it, a lad bent, checking buckles on the horses.

Abby's smile slipped off as she approached him. The boy could be no more than ten, if that. Surely he wasn't the driver the innkeeper had assigned. Hopefully not, at any rate. "Excuse me, but could you tell me where to find Mr. Wicket?"

The boy straightened, a chip-toothed grin running pell-mell across his face. "Ha! That's a good one. Why, I'm Wicket, m'um. Ain't no mister about me. Not yet, anyways."

"Very well, Wicket." She forced a pleasant tone to her voice—quite the feat when the urge to rail against the universe welled up. Must everything about this journey be ill-fated? "I understand you are to drive me to the Gable Inn. Could you tell me how long of a ride I should expect?"

"Well. . ." His face screwed up, little wrinkles bunching his nose nearly into a bow. "Looks like this fog'll burn off. Roads might be a bit o'a slog yet, though. I reckon. . ." Apparently deep in thought, he angled his head, his lips quirking one way, then the other.

Abby couldn't help but smile at the boy's serious expression.

"I reckon," he continued, "near about two hours. Three tops. Which is good, since my pap expects me back by dinner. We'll be ready to go in a trice. Might wanna heft yerself up to yer seat."

"Thank you." Swiveling her head, she glanced about for the wiry Mr. Thick, but her hired manservant was nowhere to be seen. She turned back to the boy. "Excuse me, Wicket, but have you seen the gentleman, Mr. Thick? He is to accompany us."

"Oh! Aye." The boy smacked the heel of his hand against his brow. "Near forgot. He asked you to meet him in the stable."

She frowned at the odd request. "Whatever for?"

The boy shrugged, the movement dipping his flat cap down over one eye. "Somethin' about needin' to purchase more oats for his horse." He shoved the hat back into place. "Says ye must front him the coin afore we can leave."

Wicket pivoted back to the lead horse.

And a good thing too, for that way he'd be spared the glower that dug deep into Abby's brow. The nerve of the man! Asking for more money before they'd even left the Laughing Dog. Hefting her skirts, she stomped over to the chaise and hoisted in her bag, then whirled. She'd have to nip off Mr. Thick's beggarly ways here and now or suffer his continual petitioning until they parted ways.

Rounding the back of the chaise, she followed the edge of the stable. It was a long building, as windblown and leaning askew as the inn. She stopped just inside, breathing in horseflesh, leather, and the pungent odour of manure. "Mr. Thick?"

A stack of hay lining one wall muffled her query. To her right, the workbench sat unattended, assorted currycombs littering the top of it.

She strode in farther and peered down the shadowy corridor of stalls, irritated that the man wasted her time by thinking to pinch more pennies off her. "Mr. Thick, are you in here?"

Far down in the dark recesses, something shuffled in the straw, followed by a low moan. A man's moan. . .Mr. Thick's. Abby huffed, feeling like moaning herself. Some guard she'd hired. How was he to protect her from ruffians if he couldn't keep himself from getting kicked or stamped on by a horse?

"Oof! My bleedin' foot."

Oh bother. Abby ducked back outside, intent on collaring Wicket to help her aid the man, but the boy was gone. The yard was empty, save for her carriage and the two horses.

Behind her, another moan leached out from the stable.

She blew out a sigh. There was nothing for it, then. She hurried back inside and darted down into the row of stalls. "Mr. Thick, are you—?"

A hand clamped over her mouth from behind. An arm wrapped around her stomach, pulling her backward, into an empty stall. Hot breath hit her ear. "One scream and I cut your throat, aye?"

Tears burned her eyes. Fear. Anger. Stupid! Why had she been so daft as to wander in here alone?

She managed a nod, barely.

"Good."

The hands dropped, and she spun. Mr. Thick's green gaze speared her in place, the whites of his eyes stark against the stable's gloom. He shoved out his palm, and she flinched.

"Now, I'll be taking the rest of that coin you've got jingling in your bag there." He indicated her reticule with the tip of a knife.

Her stomach clenched, the milk she'd taken with her breakfast curdling. What would she do without money? Mr. Thick's brows pulled into a solid line, his scowl deepening, and she trembled. Slowly, she unlooped the small bag from her wrist and handed it over.

A grin slashed across his face as he tucked her coins inside his greatcoat. "There. That weren't too hard, eh?"

She edged sideways, ready to make a run for it. Maybe if Captain Thatcher was still about, she could enlist his help to get her money back.

But Mr. Thick closed in on her, forcing her to retreat. Perspiration beaded on her forehead. He had his money. Why didn't he leave?

Mustering her spare reserve of courage, she lifted her chin. "Let me pass."

His grin grew, a macabre sort of grin, that which belonged carved into a gourd to frighten off evil spirits. "Not so fast, missy. A thank-you is in order, I think. Other men would've lifted far more than your coins." His gaze shot to her skirts. "But I'll only take a kiss."

He advanced, shoving her back against the stable wall.

"Please." Her voice shook, and she swallowed. "Don't do this."

He leaned in, running his nose along her neck up to her ear. "Mmm. You smell nice. All flowery and fresh."

A layer below her fear, a keen rage kindled. She'd put up with torment from her stepmother for so many years, and now that she was finally free of it, she'd be given even worse? No. *No!* Not if she could help it.

She snapped up her hand and dug her nails into his cheek, slicing lines across his flesh. His head jerked aside, and she bolted.

Only to be yanked back by her arm. He whipped her around and crushed her body against his. "So, you like to play rough, do you? Good." He rubbed his bloody cheek against hers. "I like that better."

Samuel followed Bexley into the taproom but only so far as the bar. Bex passed him up and settled at a table.

From his vantage point close to the door, Samuel swept a gaze from wall to wall, hoping to spy the green skirts of Miss Gilbert. He'd not quite finished with his admonition for her to take the next coach, though why he felt such a keen need to do so rankled him. Why should he care what the woman did or didn't do? He'd carried out his responsibility to her by seeing her safely to this inn. His obligation was finished.

Skinner scurried in from the kitchen door, caught sight of him, and darted over to his side of the bar. "Ye be needin' something, Captain?"

"A drink for my friend over there." He nodded toward Bexley. "And I'm wondering about the lady, Miss Gilbert, is she upstairs?"

"Nay." The man shook his head as he retrieved a mug. "She set out not long ago."

"Alone?"

"She hired a fellow to ride along."

Unease crept up the back of his neck. "Who?"

"Ezra Thick."

"And you let her?" The question roared out of him, drawing a raised brow from Bexley way across the room. Did Skinner not have a brain in his head? Ezra Thick was a known lecher!

The barkeep retreated a step, clutching the mug in front of him as a shield. "Weren't none of my nevermind, Captain. Besides, Wicket's driving. He won't let no harm come to the lady."

He squeezed his eyes shut for a moment. It was either that or lunge over the slab of wood and throttle the man.

Turning back toward Bex, he grumbled under his breath, "That boy doesn't even have chin hair yet."

Bexley's gaze cut from the barkeep to him. "What was that all about?"

Ignoring the chair Bexley kicked out, Samuel planted his feet. "Your offer to haul in my prisoner, does that still stand?"

"Aye. Why?"

"Something's come up."

Bexley pinched the bridge of his nose. "Why do I get the feeling this something will be more dangerous than if you invited Shankhart Robbins to tea? And even if you do take my suggestion and hole up at the Gable, he's got men from here clear up there and beyond to torment you."

He fixed the man with a pointed stare. "You worry too much."

Bex threw up his hands. "What do I tell the magistrate? When will you be back?"

"Not long." Hopefully. But the thought stuck in his gullet. His gut told him the lady might be more trouble than she was worth. "I'll send word from the Gable Inn."

Bexley's complaints followed him out the door. Nothing new. The man never agreed with the way he handled things.

But as Bexley's voice faded, a simmering fire kindled in Samuel's gut, burning hotter with each step toward the backyard. He didn't have time for this, truly. Instead of playing mother hen toward Miss

Gilbert, he ought to be helping Bex haul in Shankhart's man. Snipe! The woman was a magnet for trouble, sticking her nose into things she had no business getting involved in. She could have no idea what Thick was capable of once he got her alone.

A yellow carriage stood ready to go in front of the stables, already mud splattered. Wicket, the barkeep's son, stood leaning with his back against it, a clay pipe sticking out of his mouth. As soon as the boy laid eyes on him, the pipe disappeared behind his back. Samuel rolled his eyes. He had bigger concerns than a lad bent on smoking.

The horses stamped at his approach. "Where is Miss Gilbert?"

"In the stable, Captain."

His frown deepened. "Why?"

Wicket shrugged. "She and Mr. Thick are havin' a few words afore we leave."

His earlier unease prickled over his whole scalp. Surely Thick wouldn't be so bold as to accost the lady here. . .though admittedly he'd seen stranger things.

Bypassing the boy and the carriage, Samuel strode to the stable door that gaped open near the end of the slap-hazard building. He entered the work area on silent feet and, finding it empty, paused and listened with his whole body.

Straw rustled down the confines of the horse stalls. Not unusual. But a muted cry was.

A lady's.

He took off at a dead run, pulling out a knife as he sprinted.

Four stalls down, he slowed, then peered around the edge of the next open pen. Two figures scuffled in the scant light. Shadows outlined the wiry frame of Ezra Thick, his body pressed tightly against a skirt. A green one.

Miss Gilbert's whimpers ignited a scorching rage in Samuel's gut. Were there no righteous men left on all of God's vast earth?

Without a sound, he crept into the pen. Then sprang. He grabbed Thick's arm and wrenched it behind the man's back, yanking upward until he felt a pop in the rogue's shoulder.

Thick roared and spun—which gave Miss Gilbert the opportunity to dart away.

With the lady out of the line of danger, Samuel raised his knife—just as Thick lunged with his own blade. But too late. With a wild swing, Samuel cracked the hilt into Thick's skull. Ezra's knife dropped. So did his body.

Chest heaving, Samuel turned to Miss Gilbert. Her hat was askew—again. Several locks of dark hair hung ragged against her cheek. Blood marred the pale skin of her cheek, but judging by the transparency of the smear, it was not her own. A torn collar on her spencer and a missing button appeared to be the sum of Thick's attack. Outwardly, at any rate. Lord knew what kind of anguish was going on behind those brown eyes. The lady stood still as a pillar, save for the slight ripple of her skirts. She stared, wide-eyed and unblinking, like a lost little girl. Did she even see him?

Slowly, he tucked away his knife, then held up his hands. "You're safe now. See?"

A shudder ran the length of her. "Yes," she whispered, then she straightened her shoulders and lifted her chin, drawing from some hidden reserve of bravery. "And I am in your debt, once again. Thank you."

He lowered his hands, surprised at her show of strength. Most women would've plowed into him by now and soaked his shirt through with their tears. Despite her small stature, this one was a fighter—which he admired and pitied all in the same breath.

"Come." He swept his hand toward the open gate. "Let's get you out of here. You have a carriage waiting."

She advanced a few steps, then hesitated at the side of Thick's sprawled body. What the devil? Quick as a flash of ground lightning, she bent and snatched a small bag out of the man's pocket.

Samuel quirked a brow. Not that it was surprising Ezra had purloined the woman's coins. No, it was Miss Gilbert's boldness that stunned. Though it shouldn't have, considering her determination to continue her journey alone after yesterday. What a curious lady, indeed.

He led her out of the stable and into the first true light of morning.

"You were right, Captain." She peeked up at him. "I should have taken the coach. I tremble to think what might have happened had you not stepped in."

So did he. Yet chastising her now would only add to the shame in her voice. He cleared his throat, unsure of how to encourage her. "You did the right thing in hiring a manservant. You just happened to choose the wrong man."

Nearing the open door of her chaise, he turned to her. He might regret what he was about to say, but then he stockpiled regrets as avidly as some men collected fine paintings. "I know someone for hire at the Gable Inn. Someone I'd trust with my life. I will take you there."

CHAPTER EIGHT

Samuel swung off Pilgrim and patted her on the neck. The mare's flesh was warm, but not sweaty. She bobbed her head, then tossed him a saucy look, her front hoof stamping the ground. After this morning's leisurely pace, she was anxious for a real leg stretcher, not a rest stop at the Gable Inn.

"I know." He gave her a final clap. "Not much of a ride, eh girl? And thank God for that."

An ostler approached, nodding a welcome. The young man was so lean, he was hardly more than a collection of twigs wrapped together in a shirt and trousers. Either Hawker was working his men hard or the inn didn't include meals with their wages.

"See to your horse, sir?"

He handed the fellow Pilgrim's lead. "Have her ready in an hour. Oh, and tell me, is James Hawker still the stable master here?"

The man blinked at him. "Aye, sir."

He gave the fellow a nod of his own, then turned at the sound of carriage wheels crunching along the gravel. Miss Gilbert's yellow traveling chaise, dappled with mud and listing to one side on the uneven ground, halted in front of the Gable.

Before the postilion Wicket could dismount, Samuel strode to the door and flipped down the stairs. Lord knew if the boy would even think to perform such a nicety before scampering off for a draw on his pipe.

The lady grasped his outstretched hand, her grip firm as she worked her way down. Her hair no longer hung to her shoulder, which strangely felt like an unaccountable loss. Her spencer was straightened. Her gown smoothed. And when she turned to him, the wild look in her brown eyes and heightened colour of her cheeks had all calmed. Apparently Miss Gilbert had used the placid ride to her advantage.

Late-morning sun, having burned off the earlier fog, shone brilliant against her smile. "Thank you, Captain. I suppose this is where we part ways." She loosened the strings of her reticule and fished out some coins. "I am much indebted to you. Will this cover your service?"

He shook his head. "No payment required."

Gold flecks of determination flashed in her brown eyes. "But I insist."

"As do I." He closed her fingers over her offering. While the few coins would be a boon toward buying his piece of land, it didn't feel right taking her money. He'd long been meaning to get up here to see Hawker. Too long. Miss Gilbert's need had been a means to that end.

He pulled away. "Use your money to purchase some refreshment while I arrange for a guard to see you to Penrith."

"But I. . ." Whatever opposition she'd intended to lob at him blew away on the next gust of wind.

Her gaze met his, direct and unwavering, and the thought struck him like a slap that this might be the last time he ever saw the woman. That rankled. . .yet why the devil should it?

She raised her pert little chin. "I thank you, Captain Thatcher. For everything. God bless you in your service. You are a good man."

He sucked in a breath, her praise stunning and pure—heating him in places he never knew were cold and barren.

Shoving her coins back into her small bag, she whirled and crossed to the front door of the inn, her green skirts swaying. He couldn't help but smile as she marched off alone into the unknown. He watched until she disappeared into the Gable, and curiously, for a few moments after.

Lifting his hat with one hand, he raked his fingers through his hair, then stomped to the back of the inn. Soon, Miss Gilbert would be nothing more than a memory, and the thought stuck sideways in his craw.

Behind the Gable, a long, wood-and-stone structure lined one side of the big yard, large enough to house horses and coaches alike. Several outbuildings dotted the rest of the perimeter. Samuel glanced about for Hawker. By the inn's back door, a few workmen bantered near a barrel. Crossing the yard, two fellows hefted a large pail between them, but neither sported a shock of red hair beneath their caps. A maid hurried past him, an armful of wildflowers cradled close to her chest.

But no Hawker.

No surprise, really. His friend was likely in the stable. Samuel swept through the big open doors, and after a thorough search and several queries, he again turned up nothing. Odd, that. Why was the man not seeing to his duties?

Back outside, Samuel followed the length of the barn to a small lean-to added onto the end, situated on the side nearest the horse pen. He rapped on the door. "Hawker?"

No answer, but the door edged open a bit. The stench of rum and bodily waste wafted out.

Samuel eased through the narrow opening. Dim light angled in along with him, cutting a triangular swath and exposing a broad-shouldered lump hunched over a bottle-strewn table. The man didn't move. Didn't see. Didn't hear. His meat-hook hands cradled his head—a head topped with coppery hair.

Samuel's throat closed. The strong stench of spirits and urine in the small room went down sideways and unearthed ugly memories. Change the man's hair from red to dirt and Samuel was an eight-year-old boy again, sneaking away from his drunken father before another beating ensued. Thank God Hawker didn't have a son of his own on which to take out his demons.

"Hawker!" The name flew out harsher than he intended.

"Wha—?" Like a lazy lion, the big man's head swayed as he looked up. His eyes narrowed to slits, then widened. "Well, I'll be a pig's uncle. Thatcher? Can it be?"

Leastwise that's what he might've said. Hard to tell with all the slurring.

Samuel frowned. "Aye. It's me."

"Come. Come!" Hawker reached for the bottle near his elbow. "Have a drink, for pity's sake."

In three strides, Samuel snatched the bottle away. "What's gotten into you?"

"'Bout a pint o' rum. Mebbe more." A belch rumbled out, and Hawker dragged his sleeve across his mouth. "Not less, though."

Setting the bottle down—well beyond the man's reach—Samuel grabbed a chair and sat opposite his old friend. He'd known the man to imbibe on occasion, but never like this. Not during the day. And especially not when he should be working. "What's happened?"

Hawker swiped for a different bottle, tipped it up and found it empty, then glowered and threw the thing to the floor. Glass crashed. Hawker roared an obscenity. "You wouldn't understand."

Samuel leaned back in his seat. "Try me."

Hawker reached for another bottle—and Samuel blocked his hand.

The resulting scowl could've stopped a battalion of armed dragoons. Hawker's red-rimmed eyes pierced him through. "You ain't no saint."

"Never claimed to be." With a sweep of his arm, Samuel knocked all the bottles to the floor, done with the man's antics. "And I'll have the truth of what's put you into such a sorry state. Now."

Hawker shot to his feet, his big hands curling into fists.

Reaching for his knife, Samuel bolted up as well. He'd hate to hurt his old friend, but the man outweighed him by at least seven or eight stone. And with the liquor skewing Hawker's mind, there was no telling what the crazed bull might do.

Hawker growled, enlarging the red veins in his eyes. His jaw worked for quite some time, his Adam's apple bobbing in his throat. But eventually, the man slumped back into his chair, and a single word oozed out of him like a draining sore. "Tia."

"Tia?" Samuel couldn't help but repeat it. Was that drunken babble or some sort of code word he didn't remember from their service days? Regardless, he tucked away his blade and reclaimed his chair.

"Wish to God I'd never. . ." Hawker's eyes glistened, and two fat tears broke loose. Before long, the man dissolved into a blubbering mess.

Samuel stared, dumbfounded. A charging Hawker he could deal with, but this? What was he to do with this weeping, rum-soaked wreckage? His gaze drifted to the ceiling, and he lifted up a desperate prayer.

God, grant me some wisdom here.

He leaned forward, and employing the same voice he'd used to calm the women the day before, he pulled encouragement from years past. "Remember that time back in Poona? Those were the days, eh Hawk? I thought I was done for when the Peshwa's forces captured me."

Hawker stilled.

Good. This might work. Samuel continued, "But then you came, sporting nothing but a crack-barreled Bess and a six-inch blade. . . that and your own blazing boldness. Ahh, but you were a force to be reckoned with."

With a shudder, Hawker pulled his big hands from off his face and stared into space.

Samuel rolled up his sleeve, the movement drawing his friend's gaze, and pointed at a jagged scar on his forearm. "I made it out of that hell hole with naught but this, and all because of you. You, Hawker. So pull yourself together, man. Whatever's happened to you, you're better than this. You hear me?"

Slowly, Hawker shook his head. "Not this time," he drawled. "You don't understand. Florentia was my world. My everything."

Sudden understanding washed over him. Of course. He should've known this kind of breakdown was because of a woman. He shoved down his sleeve, keeping his voice low and even. "Tell me about her."

"Tia?" Hawker's face lit, and a sad smile rippled across his lips. "She were light and air. A regular flower, she was. Married her, a year ago now."

"You? Wed?" So, it *had* been longer than he'd reckoned since he'd seen Hawk. This big oaf was the last man he'd expect to settle down. He scrubbed a hand over his face. "I never thought to see you take vows."

"Din't think to, not at first, not till a child were on the way." Hawker's face folded, and for a moment Samuel feared the man's tears would flow again.

Hawker cleared his throat. Several times. "Tia died in childbirth."

Samuel sat silent, refusing the platitudes or prayers others might offer. Nothing he could say would bring the woman back. Fix what wasn't fixable. His years on the force had beat that lesson into him time and again.

Lord, grant mercy to this man.

"You know what I wish?" Hawker rasped out. "I wish I'd told her I loved her more. Wish I'd held her in my arms every chance I could, kissed her sweet lips as if it were the last time. Oh God, if I'd known we'd have only those few short years together, I'd have made *every* minute count. Every last one. I'd have spent less time with the horses and more precious hours with her."

Hawker leaned forward, his eyes burning embers. "Promise me, Thatcher! Promise you won't do the same. When you find a woman you love, you'll not waste one second. You'll go after her with all your heart because one day, ahh, one day. . .it will be too late, and you'll be left with nothing but regrets."

Slowly, Samuel nodded, storing away the man's advice, though he'd likely never need it. "Aye."

"Good. Good. . ." Hawker's words trailed off, and he stared into nothingness, memories flinching across his face. Samuel waited him out. He'd come around, eventually.

With a great inhale, his friend finally rolled his shoulders and refocused on Samuel. "Well, don't s'pose you rode all this way to hear me bawl. What are you here for?"

He blew out a long breath. There was no way he could ask his old friend to accompany Miss Gilbert, not with a grief so large and a powerful thirst to drown it out. Blast! Hawker had been the one—the only—man he'd recommend Miss Gilbert hire.

Samuel clenched his jaw, shutting down the host of ugly words begging for release. Suddenly he knew how Jonah felt, prodded into a mission he never wanted to take in the first place. But was this a task from God or a fool's errand?

He leaned back in his chair, considering seriously for the first time the possibility of guarding Miss Gilbert. The money would be more than enough to buy his land. He knew the route. The magistrate would understand his need to avoid the heath until Shankhart cooled down.

So why the foreboding deep in his gut? He curled his hands into fists, fighting the urge to pick up one of Hawker's bottles and guzzle a swig. Somehow he knew, without a doubt, that if he took on the guardianship of Miss Gilbert, it would leave a mark. A deep one.

But if he didn't, that would leave the lady—clearly prone to attracting trouble—to travel on her own.

Rock. Stone wall. And Samuel between.

Pushing back his chair, he stood before he changed his mind. "I'm on my way to Penrith. Thought I'd stop by, but time's wasting. Till next time, Hawk. And lay off the—"

"Penrith?" Hawker bolted out of his chair and advanced so fast, Samuel couldn't reach for his knife.

"Say you'll go through Manchester." The big man grabbed him by his shoulders. "Say it!"

This close, Samuel choked on Hawker's stench. "I could, I suppose," he eked out.

Hawker's hands dropped. So did his eyelids as he lifted his face to the rafters. "Thank You, God."

Samuel clenched his jaw to keep it from dropping. Hawker praying? Something big was up for that man's crusty soul to seek the Almighty. "Why Manchester?"

"My sister lives there." Hawker's gaze met his. "I need you to see my sister."

All this for a family member? Was the woman near death? Samuel narrowed his eyes. "What for?"

"I've got something you need to bring to her. Something I can't. . . Oh God, I can't." Hawker's eyes watered again. "Promise me. Promise!"

Gunshot. Wails and screams. Cannon fire and shouted orders all barreled back from his time in the Indies. Samuel swallowed down the memories. He owed this man his very breath. Whatever it was Hawker wanted him to bring to his sister, how could he refuse after Hawker had saved his life? "All right, you have my word. What is it you want me to deliver?"

Once again, the man's face crumpled, horrific pain etching lines into his brow. Hawker shuffled like an old man over to the only other door in the room and shoved it open. "In here."

Samuel strode to the small chamber, but when his feet hit the threshold, he stopped. Unable to move. Unable to breathe.

In the center of the room sat a cradle, the child inside it bouncing and mouthing on a dried crust of bread. A dirty pink cap dipped low over one of the baby girl's big blue eyes.

Cold sweat broke out on Samuel's forehead. Instantly he was ten years old again. . .the day he'd said goodbye to his little sister.

Forever.

The sweet scent of fresh pastry greeted Abby as she stepped into the Gable Inn. Pausing just inside the doorway, she breathed deeply. Quiet chatter and the tinkle of teacups set to saucers filled the large public room. Sunlight peered through the mullioned windows, bathing the patrons in a cheerful brilliance. Now this was how an inn should be run. The Laughing Dog could learn a thing or two from this establishment.

One of the liveried servants approached her, his blue topcoat and beige waistcoat both ironed crisp and not a stain marred the fabric. "May I help you, miss?"

"Some tea, please."

"Of course. Follow me." He wound a path around the other diners, leading her to a small table in the back corner, perfect for one. He held out her chair, and when she sat, he asked, "Perhaps a slice of gooseberry pie as well, miss?"

She smiled. Who could say no to that? "Yes, thank you."

While she waited, her gaze drifted around the room and landed on a couple near the window. Judging by the way the man leaned forward and whispered tenderly to the lady, they were clearly newly wed. A pretty shade of red bloomed on the woman's cheeks. She gave him a playful swat on the arm, her laughter merry amidst the din of low conversation. His gaze held hers as if she were the only one in the room. His dearest love. His own. Abby's chest squeezed. Soon that would be her. Sir Jonathan murmuring intimate endearments for her ears. Her feigning embarrassment while cherishing his words. His look of complete adoration—for her alone.

"Here you are, miss." The servant appeared with a thick slice of pastry and a steaming pot of bohea.

"Thank you."

She picked up her fork, but after her first bite, she nearly called the fellow back to *really* thank him. The crust melted on her tongue, and the sweet yet tart filling blended into a heavenly mixture. After the terror of yesterday, this was a welcome change. Things were definitely starting to look up.

Soon only crumbs remained on her plate. Not long after, she drained the teapot as well. The couple near the window departed, as did the other patrons, leaving her in an empty room. Glancing at her watch, Abby frowned. Nearly an hour had passed. Ought not Captain Thatcher have arranged for her new manservant by now?

She pushed back her chair, about to go look for him, when the blue-coated waiter approached her once again.

"You're wanted outside, miss."

She gnawed the inside of her lip. Why hadn't Captain Thatcher come to retrieve her himself? Better yet, should he not have brought her new guard in here to discuss traveling details and expectations? Being summoned like a common criminal wasn't very orthodox—or courteous—but truly, having spent the past twenty-four hours in the captain's company, was it any surprise?

"Very well. Thank you." She paid for her refreshments then traded the dining room for the brilliance of the June afternoon. Her chaise stood in the yard, horses hitched, a thin man checking the buckles on a harness. Captain Thatcher's bay stood nearby as well. But that was it. No other horses and no new manservant.

She strode over to the scarecrow of a postilion, for there was no one else around who could have possibly summoned her. "Pardon, but did you wish to have a word with me?"

The fellow turned, the sharp bones of his face looking as if they might break through his skin. "It weren't me, miss. I believe it were him." He tipped his head, indicating the yard behind her.

She pivoted. Marching across the gravel, boots pounding and face shadowed by the brim of his hat, Captain Thatcher advanced like a man set for battle—holding out a small child in front of his body like a shield.

Abby cocked her head at the curious sight. "Captain?"

"Here." He pressed the baby against her, so that she had no choice but to grasp the wriggling child.

"Why are you handing me. . . ?" Her question faded as she held the youngling up, face-to-face. Deep blue eyes sparkled wide above chubby cheeks. A smudged pink bonnet sat askew on her head, a few wisps of downy reddish hair peeking out. The little girl kicked her feet and cooed, her cherry lips parting into a huge smile. Five pearly teeth appeared on mostly barren gums, three on the bottom and two up top. She couldn't be quite a year old yet, but was likely close to it. One plump hand reached out and snagged a piece of Abby's hair. The girl giggled, and Abby's heart melted. "What a sweet darling!"

Captain Thatcher grunted. "Her name is Emma."

Abby lifted a brow at the man. "What is this about, Captain?"

His gaze met hers, his thoughts unreadable behind his dark eyes. "I've decided to accept your offer to see you safely to Penrith, with a brief stop at Manchester along the way."

"That's—oh!" Little fingers yanked her hair, the sharp pain as stunning as the captain's declaration. She pried open the babe's clenched fist and flung back the loose tendril, then speared Captain Thatcher with a pointed stare. Hundreds of questions bombarded her, but only one sailed out. "Why?"

He shrugged as if she were a half-wit. "That's where I'm to deliver the child."

Until this moment he couldn't be bothered with escorting her, and now he wanted to take on both her *and* a child? She frowned. "Why the sudden change of heart?"

From this angle, light accentuated the strong cut of his jaw, stubble darkening the length of it. A muscle jumped on his neck, yet he said nothing. What on earth was he thinking?

Finally, he spoke. "You need me, and I need the money."

No shame rippled at the edges of his words. He didn't even bat an eye. The captain's blunt manner, while refreshingly honest, was astounding.

The girl wriggled, her little hands grasping for more hanks of hair. Abby turned the baby to face the captain. A delighted squeal cut the air, and the child bounced up and down. Suspicion curled through Abby like a waft of smoke. Did he need the money to hire someone to pay for the child's care—*his* child's care?

"Is this child yours, Captain?"

"No!" Despite the denial, red crept up his neck, and he cleared his throat. "Emma belongs to the stable master here at the Gable. I owe him a favor, and it's his wish the girl be delivered to his sister. That's all. So do we have a deal or not, Miss Gilbert?"

The babe swiveled her head side to side, squirming for release—and driving home the scope of what Captain Thatcher was asking of her. Abby gripped the girl tighter before Emma slipped from her hands. When her sisters were little, she'd looked after them on occasion, but this was a far different venture. She'd be a nursemaid, trapped inside a chaise with a wiggly bundle of energy all the way to Manchester, which had to be nearly two hundred miles from here. By the time she finally made it to Sir Jonathan, she'd be a wreck. No, this was out of the question.

She shook her head and held out the child. "I think not. Perhaps you ought to find someone else to accompany you, as will I."

He gathered the girl with one arm, the child looking impossibly small and fragile next to his worn riding coat. Was he disappointed? Angry? Frustrated? Hard to decipher with that even stare of his.

"Good day, then, Miss Gilbert. I bid you Godspeed." Wheeling about, he stalked to his horse. He shifted little Emma to his other arm, clutching her tight to his chest, then reached up to the saddle with his free hand and hoisted them both atop the big chestnut bay.

As the captain settled her in front of him, the girl's mouth opened wide, and a wail crescendoed into a screech—cutting sharply into Abby's heart. It would be a cruel ride for so young a child to travel on naught but horseback. Abby gnawed the inside of her cheek. Should she let the rough-and-tumble captain fend for a little one on his own for so long a distance? Was it really any of her concern? Or had God put her here for such a time as this?

Frustration and guilt nicked her conscience, and she stifled a wince. Truly, she'd be no kinder than her stepmother to ignore such an outright need.

"Wait!" Against her better judgment, she gathered up her skirts and dashed over to Captain Thatcher. She might regret this later, but for now, it seemed the right—the *only*—thing to do.

She lifted her hands. "It appears, sir, that you need me as much as I need you. Hand Emma down and let us be on our way."

CHAPTER NINE

Abby fought a yawn and shifted on the bench in the entryway of the White Horse Inn. It wouldn't be too soon to lay her head on a pillow this night—if Captain Thatcher could secure her a room. Though this particular coaching inn boasted three floors of lodgings, judging by the hubbub of horses and people in the front yard and the loud chatter floating out from the public room, many others sought a night's stay here as well.

She glanced down at the child in the basket next to her on the bench. Long lashes fanned against cherub cheeks. Good. Asleep at last. While little Emma was a pleasant child and had already wormed her way into Abby's heart, her suspicions had been correct. The girl had squirmed about in the carriage all afternoon, eager to explore every last inch of it, with a particular interest in pulling herself up to the window. Absently, Abby rubbed the sore muscles in her left forearm, the one that had repeatedly shot out to catch Emma before the youngling toppled headlong to the floor. The child would be walking in no time—and then trouble would begin in earnest.

Stifling another yawn, Abby pressed her fingers to her lips and lifted her face. Captain Thatcher stood in front of her, and her breath caught. How did he do that? Appear without a sound? The man was more ghost than human.

He held out a key. "Last room."

A frown weighted her brow as she accepted his offering. "And you?"

His dark eyes flashed. "Didn't want to leave my horse anyway. Come. There's an open table."

He strode off before she could comment. She picked up Emma and followed his black riding cloak into a boisterous taproom, the weight of her charge slowing her somewhat. He led her to a table in the back of the room, nearest the door where servants buzzed. Abby took the chair farthest from the opening and tucked Emma between her and the wall, praying that the babe would continue to sleep.

Captain Thatcher dipped his head toward her. "Good night, then."

Her jaw dropped as he turned to go. "Wait! Will you not dine with me? And see me to my room?"

He glanced over his shoulder, the shadow from the brim of his hat hiding most of his face, but there was no mistaking the distinct disapproval in the tone of his voice. "I don't think that would be a good idea, Miss Gilbert."

The babe rubbed a fist against her cheek and squirmed in the basket—though her eyes remained closed. For now, at least. Yet there were no guarantees. Abby's stomach cramped when a waft of stew hustled by, clutched in a servant's hands. Were Emma to wake, dinner would be impossible.

"Please, Captain. At least stay until I have had a few bites to eat, in case Emma awakens."

He stood still a moment longer, a statue in the midst of the humming activity. Before she could blink, he dragged the table away from the wall and scraped a chair behind it, sitting with his back against the stones . . .as far from Emma as possible.

Abby couldn't decide if she should thank him for staying or ask the cause of such skittishness. In the end, she chose neither and remained silent. She could only hope Sir Jonathan wouldn't be as restless around babes—but of course he wouldn't be, or he'd not have asked for her hand in the first place. Marriage was always the precursor for children. No doubt Sir Jonathan wanted as many little ones as she.

A waiter approached, his apron straining around a potbelly. Apparently the food at the White Horse was good. "Evenin' sir, lady."

He nodded toward them both. "We've got a nice kidney pie with mash on the side. Or Cook's made a lovely dish of boiled swedes and roasted up some stubble goose. Can't go wrong with either one. So, what's it to be?"

Abby's mouth watered. "Pie, please."

"The same," Captain Thatcher said.

The waiter dashed off, leaving them alone in a room full of chattering diners. Abby watched the merry travelers, raising glasses and sharing banter. Captain Thatcher watched them as well, but considering the guarded clench of his jaw, he didn't see the same cheer. And for some reason, a great sadness draped over her shoulders. How many burdens did this man carry? What had he seen in all his years to make him so hesitant to smile? A curious desire welled to be the one to put a grin on his face, to lighten the heavy weight—whatever it was—that he carried.

"So, Captain." She curved her lips upward, as if he might follow her example. "How long do you figure until we reach Brakewell Hall?"

His gaze continued roaming the taproom even when he answered. "Little over a week, God willing."

Her brows shot up. *God* willing? This rugged man, lantern light even now glinting off the gun handle peeking from inside his coat, professed such faith? "I did not take you for a religious man."

"In my line of work, you run either from God or toward Him."

Of course. By necessity, being an officer would mean he'd seen things—and likely done things—better left unspoken. Perhaps that was the cause for his restrained personality.

"It must be dreadful," she murmured. "Always seeing the worst in humanity."

His dark eyes shifted to her for a moment before resuming surveillance of the room.

"Have you any family, Captain Thatcher?" The question flew out before she could stop it, and she pressed her lips shut. It wasn't any of her business, not really.

But if he thought her curiosity forward, he didn't let on. He merely said, "No."

She studied him closer, noting for the first time the frayed collar on his dress coat, the missing button on his waistcoat. His shaggy hair was in need of a good trimming, and his skin had the weather-worn look of a man who spent far too much time in the sun. Then it dawned on her. This was a man who had no home to welcome him. No arms to hold him when the brutality of his job got to be too much.

Her heart squeezed. "How lonely for you."

"Loneliness is a state of mind, nothing more."

She leaned back in her chair, astonished by his sentiment. Did he really believe his own words? "Well, thankfully, I will not have time for such a '*state of mind*,' as you put it, but rather one of happiness and fulfillment once we reach Penrith. Sir Jonathan Aberley and I are to be wed straightaway."

His gaze shot to hers, an indecipherable gleam burning deep in his dark eyes. "Is that so? Tell me, how long have you known this man? This *Sir* Jonathan Aberley?"

He spit out the title like a piece of rotted mutton. Did he carry a grudge against the gentry?

She offered a smile to the waiter as he set a mug in front of each of them, and waited until he scurried off before answering. "I met my intended at a ball earlier in the spring."

He snorted then slugged back a drink. "That can't be more than a few months ago. I suspect, lady, that you have no idea what you're getting into."

She clenched her jaw, trapping a retort—a skill she'd honed and employed often with her stepmother. The nerve of the captain. He was the one with no idea of what lay ahead of her. She straightened her shoulders, intent on educating him. "May I remind you, sir, that my name is not '*lady*,' and the truth is that as a baronet, Sir Jonathan is a very busy man. He doesn't have time to waste, so it is no surprise our courtship is a whirlwind."

"Courtship, you say?" The captain folded his arms. "Your man is up north in Penrith. You are coming from the south. How much of a courtship could you have possibly had?"

Her stomach turned—and this time not from hunger. He was right, and that chafed. She straightened on her chair, careful not to bump the basket near her feet. "Admittedly it has not been much of courtship, what with the distance. Yet it is not the length of the relationship that matters, but the depth. Do you not agree?"

His lips twisted into a semblance of a smile. "I suppose you expect to live happily ever after, then."

"I do. Oh, of course I know there shall be hardships, mind you, but with Sir Jonathan at my side, I am certain we shall face each trial as a united front."

"Really." He unfolded his arms as the waiter set down a plate in front of each of them, and when the man had departed, he leaned closer to her. "What do you know of the man, other than he's busy?"

His question was neatly tied with a thick cord of cynicism. Abby closed her eyes and bowed her head, thanking God for the food and asking for strength to keep from snapping back at the infuriating man dining with her. Why had she asked him to stay?

She picked up her fork and jabbed at her pie. "Sir Jonathan runs a lovely estate just outside of Penrith. I am told that Brakewell Hall has two hundred acres. His is one of the oldest families in the area, their baronet title dating back to King James." She popped a bite of kidney pie into her mouth, satisfied with the flavor and with having put the captain in his place.

He merely stared. "And?"

She swallowed. Was that not enough information? But. . .oh. Of course. The captain was an officer of the law. It made sense he'd be more interested in a physical description. "Sir Jonathan is tall, broad of shoulders, with. . ." She stabbed another piece of pie. What colour hair did Sir Jonathan have? Brown? Black? It wasn't flaxen, at any rate. And had his eyes been dark as well. . .or had they been more of a hazel shade? No, they were blue. She was certain of it. Mostly.

She set down her fork and picked up her mug, gazing at the captain over the rim. "He has dark hair and blue eyes."

"And?"

Without so much as a sip, she set the mug back down. "What do you mean '*and*'? I have just told you."

"What you've given me, Miss Gilbert, is a physical description of the fellow and the state of his affairs, neither of which tells me about the man himself."

Frustration roiled the one bite of pie she'd eaten. He was right. She didn't really know much about Sir Jonathan, but living with him had to be better than abiding with her hateful stepmother and stepsiblings in Southampton.

"If you must know, Captain, Sir Jonathan is compassionate, kind, forthright, and generous. His sense of justice is acute, and he is above reproach in all matters. Not to mention he is as handsome as a Beau Brummell fashion plate. There." She lifted her chin. "Does that answer your question?"

"No man is that perfect." A slow smile lightened his usual brooding countenance—and she recanted of ever having wished to be the one to put it there. "You are a starry-eyed dreamer, lady."

"And you are a dour old naysayer," she blurted, then immediately slapped her fingers to her mouth, horrified. What had happened to her years of reserve? Her ability to withstand verbal jabs with nary a retort but a kind word? She wouldn't be surprised if he simply shot up and walked away, never to look back. But his response, when it finally came, was even more astounding.

Captain Thatcher's shoulders shook, a low, pleasant chuckle rumbling in his chest.

A pretty shade of pink blossomed on Miss Gilbert's cheeks. Mortification radiated off her in waves, which amused Samuel all the more. So the little miss wasn't nearly as prim as she let on, eh? And bold. Most women would've run off in tears by now, yet here she sat, not only dining with the likes of him but having invited him to join her in the first place.

Slowly, she lowered her hand and dipped her face to a sheepish tilt. "Forgive me, Captain Thatcher. I had no right to say such a thing."

"No apology required. I stand guilty of the charge, for you see"—he bent closer, speaking for her alone—"I *am* a dour old naysayer."

Her jaw dropped, accompanied by a sharp intake of breath.

Fighting another urge to chuckle at her astonishment, he speared a bite of kidney pie and shoveled it into his mouth. Miss Gilbert was a pleasant young woman, to be sure. Entirely too easy to amuse. He hadn't enjoyed a laugh so freely in years, not since. . .

All his humour faded, blotted out by ugly memories rising from the past. Gunshots. Blood. Death. Who was he to enjoy dinner and laughter with a beautiful woman when his former partner William would never get the chance?

He shoved in another mouthful and went back to surveying the room. One never knew when trouble would walk through the door. Not that he expected it—but more often than not, that's when an enemy struck.

"Tell me, Captain." Miss Gilbert's voice pulled his gaze from the door to her sweet face. "What will you do once you receive your final payment from my intended? A hundred pounds is no small sum."

It wasn't. It was more than he'd prayed for. Once again he silently thanked God before answering. "I intend to purchase a piece of land."

"You would leave the force?"

Hah! He should've left years ago, before he'd been gutted of hope and stained with indelible cynicism. He slugged back a drink of ale, then nodded.

Finished with her pie, the lady pushed aside her plate and dabbed at her mouth with a coarse table napkin. "And what will you do with your land? Horses? Farming? Sheep, perhaps?"

He studied her for a moment, trying to decipher if her enthusiasm was true or merely an attempt to while away her time. Nothing but interest gleamed in her brown eyes, as if she were truly fascinated by what he might say.

"Oats and hay," he answered at length. "After my years spent with horses, I've come to value reliable provender. I aim to produce the best possible feed at an affordable price."

A brilliant smile lit her face. "A noble effort, Captain, but be careful. You are dangerously close to sounding like a starry-eyed dreamer yourself."

Once again the strange desire to chuckle welled in his throat, but he swallowed it. Joy was a habit he couldn't own, not yet. Not when there were still criminals to haul in and brigands to put down—and deep in his gut, he sensed one nearby.

His gaze shot to the door. Steel-grey eyes met his from across the crowded room, hooded eyes, set deep beneath a forehead puckered with a scar stretching from one side to the other, like the man had barely escaped death from a sharp blade.

The same blade now tucked inside Samuel's boot.

Thunderation! Samuel jerked back into the shadow of a passing waiter, but not fast enough. Recognition flashed across the big man's face. Noddy Carper, one of Shankhart's gang. Carper's nostrils flared, hatred purpling his flesh like a bruise.

Then he turned and fled.

Bolting upright, Samuel leapt sideways, causing the table to jiggle—and crashed into another waiter coming through the kitchen door. Bowls plummeted. Soup sprayed on impact, burning through the fabric of his trousers. The waiter barely kept from toppling as he teetered on one foot.

But no time to apologize. Samuel dodged around the man and shot forward. If Carper got away, Shankhart would know where to find Samuel. . .and Miss Gilbert and the babe. None of them would be safe.

"Captain?" Miss Gilbert's voice followed him across the room. So did the other diners' eyes. He could feel the stares, and no wonder. It wasn't every day a man broke into a sprint between bites of kidney pie.

He barreled out of the public room and dashed through the smaller reception hall, banking hard to the right as two gentlemen swapping stories turned toward him. Pulling out his pistol, he reached for the front doorknob—then jumped back as it swung open.

A lady entered, and when her eyes landed on the gun in his hand, she screamed as if he'd shot her.

"What the devil?" shouted the man behind her as Samuel shoved past.

This time he did apologize. "Pardon."

He tore past them both into the night. Torches lit the front yard, casting a ghoulish flicker on the back side of a black horse and big rider galloping out of sight.

Chest heaving, Samuel slowed to a stop. By the time he saddled

Pilgrim and tried to follow, Carper would be long gone and untrackable in the black of night. Of all the rotten turns of luck! He'd just have to gain as much ground as possible tomorrow, putting more space between him and Shankhart—or Shankhart would be breathing down his neck with a gun in hand endangering Miss Gilbert and little Emma.

"Captain?"

He turned. Miss Gilbert stood bathed in torchlight, Emma's basket clutched in one hand, the other fluttering to her chest. "Are you all right? Are you ill?"

He grunted. He was ill all right. Sick at heart that Carper had gotten away. Sick of murderers and thieves.

Sick of it all.

CHAPTER TEN

After two days of traveling—albeit slowed with a woman and child in tow—the uneasy knot in Samuel's gut ought to be loosening. All told, he'd put nearly a hundred miles between himself and Shankhart. That should be a load lifter in and of itself.

But it wasn't.

As he rode through the midlands, sometimes scouting ahead of the carriage, other times—like now—behind, he couldn't help but feel like a coward for running off. He should be back there on the heath, hunting down that killer beast Shankhart, not playing the role of nursemaid and guardian. Should be. Sweet heavens, but he hated *shoulds*.

And worse, the twisting in his gut tightened with each thud of Pilgrim's hooves. Something wasn't right.

Pulling out his pistol, he cocked the hammer and veered off the road, guiding his mount into the tree line. Then he doubled back, scanning the endless maze of ash trunks and ivy carpet. June sunshine filtered through the canopy, painting bright stripes of light. Were they being followed? Easy enough to spot anyone lurking about, yet no dark shapes darted from tree to tree or belly-crawled through the foliage. Nothing but a few random squirrels scampered about.

Blowing out a long breath, he tucked away the gun and chided himself for becoming a skittish old—

"Stop!"

Though faint, Miss Gilbert's voice strained through the trees. Samuel kicked Pilgrim into action, every muscle on alert. By the time he reached the carriage, the postilion had just pulled down the stairs.

Samuel swung off his horse, gun drawn. "Is there trouble?"

The man glanced at him, the whites of his eyes growing large as his gaze landed on the pistol. He threw up his hands. "The lady asked me to stop, sir. That's all I know."

Miss Gilbert's pink-cheeked face peered out the open window of the door. She acknowledged the gun with a sweeping glance yet did not shrink back. "Emma's made quite a mess of herself, more than I can care for in a moving carriage. Would you be so good as to put away your gun, Captain, and hold her while I step out?"

A soiled baby? He'd tensed to kill for nothing more than a fouled clout? If Brentwood or Moore heard of this, he'd be laughed out of service.

But as Miss Gilbert handed Emma down, he suddenly understood the urgency of the lady's request. The babe's gown was sopping, and the stink of it watered his eyes.

He handed the child back to Miss Gilbert as soon as her feet touched ground. Then he turned to the postilion. "Grab the child's bag and spread a blanket over there." He indicated a relatively flat swath of clover next to the edge of the woods.

Before either Miss Gilbert or the driver could move, he strode off to inspect the area. Nothing dangerous met his eye, only robins flittered atop some low-lying branches and rabbits ruffled the undergrowth beneath.

"Are you expecting trouble, Captain?" Worry thickened Miss Gilbert's usual cheery tone.

"Just taking precautions." He turned to find her big brown eyes seeking his. "That's what you're paying me for, isn't it?"

"Yes, I suppose I am." Her lips curved into a brave smile, and she nodded at the postilion as he set down a satchel and shook out a blanket. "Thank you, Mr. Blake."

Miss Gilbert laid down the fussing child, knelt, and set to work. Samuel kept a watchful eye on their surroundings, yet more often than not, his gaze drifted back to the woman. She was an oddity, in a surprisingly pleasant way. Not many gentlemen's daughters would've taken on the charge of a child not quite a year old. And none would deign to clean a squalling, filthy babe, not even if the child were flesh of her flesh. That's what servants were for, yet Miss Gilbert not only snubbed such convention, but pushed up her sleeves and cared for the little one in a way that squeezed Samuel's chest. Judging by the loosened hair trailing down Miss Gilbert's neck, she'd endured quite a ride thus far.

At last, the lady stood and held out a fresh—yet still crying—little one. "Would you please mind Emma while I tidy up? I will only be a moment."

Before he could respond, Miss Gilbert pressed Emma against his chest, and his arms flew up in reflex to grasp the wriggling child. Without a word, Miss Gilbert began collecting the dirty cloths.

Emma's wide blue eyes met his, her lips opening to a big O. For a moment, the crying ceased—then a fresh wave of tears sprouted and the child cried all the harder. Samuel blew out a disgusted breath. There was nothing to be done for it, then.

"Shh," he soothed and started bouncing, startling himself that his muscles still remembered how to calm a wee one. He turned Emma around, cradling her against his shirt, and patted her back. Unwelcome memories rushed him, nearly buckling his knees, especially when the babe burrowed her face into his collar and her soft cheek brushed against his neck. How many tears had he calmed those many years ago? If he listened hard enough, could he yet hear Mary's cries mingled with this little one's?

Somewhere deep inside, an old folk tune rose up unbidden and, before he could stop it, emerged as a low humming in his throat. Emma stilled at the noise, and he swayed from foot to foot to prevent a fresh bout of wailing. One of her little fists broke loose and she clung to his arm, nuzzling her face against his shoulder. He sucked in a breath. This time the memories would not be stopped, though he closed his eyes against them. Mary had been such a frail child. Small. Too small. Definitely not sturdy enough to withstand his drunken father's careless fist when he'd swung for his mother and missed.

"Captain?"

His eyes popped open to Miss Gilbert's raised brow. Clearing his throat, he handed Emma back to her.

But she didn't retreat. She stood there, her brown eyes searching his. "You surprise me, sir. You obviously have some experience with little ones, yet you claim none of your own."

He shrugged. "I don't only rescue fair maidens, Miss Gilbert. Sometimes children are involved."

She pursed her lips, the dimple on her chin scolding him with suspicion. "It is more than that, though, is it not?"

Thunder and earth, but the woman was perceptive. He sidestepped her and stalked toward Pilgrim, who pulled with her teeth at the clover nearby.

Miss Gilbert's voice followed at his back. "This child may not be yours, but I suspect you have lost one very dear to you, have you not?"

He wheeled about, his hands curling into fists as he studied her. How could she possibly know that?

Her brow creased, her brown gaze glinting with compassion. "I do not mean to offend. I merely wish to help, and I am well practiced with a listening ear. Past hurts often lose their sting when shared with others."

He smirked. "There you go again."

"What?"

"Being a starry-eyed dreamer. And you're wrong." His tone lowered to a bitter growl, completely unstoppable. "Some hurts never go away." Well did he know that truth. Some were so deeply engrained, not even a well-meaning woman could uproot them. Once again he turned from her, and in three more strides, he bent and snatched up Pilgrim's lead.

Footsteps patted the dirt behind him. "Who was the child, Captain? The one your heart yet mourns?"

He stiffened. How the deuce could she see into him like that? In all his years on the force, not one of his fellow officers nor his brothers-in-arms back in India had ever guessed as much.

Why her, God? Why now?

"You do not have to tell me, but it might help if you told someone." Miss Gilbert's voice was a sweet addition to the June birdsong. Lord, but she was persistent.

She stepped closer, the scent of orange blossom water wafting over his shoulder from her nearness. "I hate to see you so tortured every time you take Emma into your arms, and we still have a long way to go with her. Should you not make peace with whatever demon it is from the past that yet haunts you?"

He clenched the leather lead in his hand. Should he tell her to mind her own business, or just walk away?

But instead, unbidden words launched from his tongue. "I had a sister."

Stunned, he clamped his lips tight. Not even Moore or Brentwood knew that bit of information. By all the stars in the heavens, what had made him reveal such a personal thing?

"Ahh, I see. . . . Emma reminds you of her. Is that what pains you?"

He gritted his teeth. The woman was more persistent than a sailor bent on a rum run. He stalked over to the carriage, Pilgrim in tow, and called over his shoulder. "It's time we leave, Miss Gilbert."

And it was. Stratford-'on-Avon wasn't far off, and sitting too long in one place was asking for trouble. . .so was answering too many questions.

Abby whispered one more ragged prayer for Emma to go to sleep before pushing herself upright on the bed. But the child continued to cry. It wasn't working. *Nothing* was working. Emma fussed just as much—if not more—than when she'd laid the child down in the little box bed nearly a half hour ago. Abby relit the lamp at her bedside, allowing a sigh to deflate her lungs. Apparently neither of them would rest this long night, and after a hard day of travel, every muscle tight from the jostling carriage, her own sob rose in her throat.

Lord, give me strength.

"All right, my love." She forced her tone to a lilting coo as she padded over to where Emma should be sleeping. Of all the ways she'd imagined how this faery-tale journey to her new husband's waiting arms might be, bouncing a fussy babe into the wee hours of the night had never entered her mind.

"Shall we take a turn about the room and—"

Abby dropped to her knees. "Emma?"

A swath of lamplight stretched out a long finger, pointing at a blue rim spreading in a circle around the little one's lips. Gooseflesh prickled Abby's arms. This was no ordinary illness.

She shot to her feet and grabbed her dressing gown. Pausing only long enough to shove her arms into the sleeves and tie the sash, she whispered one more prayer.

"Lord, grant mercy."

Throwing aside propriety, she dashed down the corridor. She stopped at a chamber just past hers and rapped on the door. "Captain Thatcher?"

A breath later, the door flung open. The captain stood, feet planted wide and muscles straining against the thin white fabric of his shirt. Dark hair peeked out on his chest, just below his collarbone, matching the dark stubble on his clenched jaw. A muscle jumped on the side of his neck. The fierce look in his eyes made her want to run and hide, but she forced herself to remain steady for Emma's sake.

"I fear Emma is ill."

He dipped his head, his voice low. "Take me to her."

Whimpers leached into the corridor and grew louder as Abby re-entered the room. The captain brushed past her and bent over the box bed. Then he knelt and pressed the back of his hand to the little one's forehead.

It was strange to witness the big man so gentle with his touch—and even stranger to see him in naught but his shirtsleeves, half-untucked and spilling over one side of his trousers. His feet were bare. Abby leaned back against the wall, heat rushing to her cheeks. It felt indecent, hosting a half-dressed man in her bedchamber.

But the next whimper pealing out from little Emma banished such embarrassment, as did the flash of concern in the captain's gaze as he stood and faced her. "She needs a surgeon. Keep her cool until I return."

And then he was gone like a ghost into the night, the only evidence of his presence the riffling of her hem from where he'd passed by her in a rush.

The next several hours stretched into an unending routine of dipping a cloth into a basin, wringing it out, then pressing the damp cloth against Emma's skin.

Dip.

Wring.

Press.

Again and again, yet it did nothing to stop the burning, the whimpers, the thrashing. Where was Captain Thatcher? Lost? Hurt? Tired of her and the crying child? Abby smoothed a loose hank of hair flopping in her eyes and stood, arching her back. Her sanity was leaching from her, bit by bit. Perhaps some tepid tea for her and a spot of milk for Emma. It would be good for the girl to drink something. . .wouldn't it?

Her shoulders slumped. What did she know of sick babies? She trudged back to the basin and retrieved the pitcher next to it. If nothing else, some fresh water was in need. Having already traded her nightgown for her traveling dress, she snatched up a shawl and wrapped it about her shoulders, then ventured out into the corridor and down the stairs into the public room.

At this time of night, no patrons remained. A few vigil lanterns burned from hooks on the wall, casting long shadows from the tables and chairs. Abby glanced around the room. Several doors might lead to a kitchen, but which one?

She bit her lip, debating which to try, when the front door opened and two dark shapes entered—one carrying a bag, the other a scowl.

The captain reached her in two long-legged strides, bringing with him the scent of horse and leather and man. The brim of his hat shaded his eyes, but she didn't need to see them to discern the worry clenching his jaw. "Is the child—?"

"She is much the same."

He brushed past her and disappeared up the stairs on silent feet, leaving her and the surgeon blinking.

"Your husband is a determined man, a noble trait in this instance, for I was out on a call and he hunted me down. I am Mr. Harvey, surgeon"—the man tipped his hat without pausing, the spare light glinting off the glass of his spectacles—"and I am guessing your daughter is up those stairs, so if you wouldn't mind leading the way?"

Husband? Daughter?

"I—I. . .er. . ." All the words she wanted to say bunched in her throat.

There'd be no setting the man straight without a lengthy explanation. She turned and fled up the stairway before he could see the flush on her cheeks.

Inside the room, Captain Thatcher had lit all the lamps, flooding the room with light. Abby gravitated toward where he stood, near the bed yet back far enough to give Mr. Harvey clear access to Emma.

While the surgeon knelt at the child's side, Abby looked up at the captain. His dark hair, damp and clinging to the skin near his temples, tossed wild to his shoulders. His riding cloak draped over his shoulders, unbuttoned, half of his collar blown back. Mud dappled the top of his boots. It must've been some ride.

"What were you doing in the taproom?" the captain rumbled low.

"I went downstairs, looking for fresh water," she whispered.

He glanced down at her, his face unreadable as his gaze drifted over her face. "You're weary. Go get some rest in my room. I'll stay with the child until morning."

Her brows shot to the rafters. *He* would tend to the sick girl on his own? "And if Emma should need changing?"

"I imagine I've seen worse on the battlefield."

Her gaze drifted to the crescent scar high on his cheekbone. So, he was more than a man of law, though truly it didn't surprise her that his background included military service. Not with the way he commanded attention simply by merit of standing in a room.

Emma wailed as the surgeon lifted her and laid her on the bigger bed. The little one's mewling cries crawled into Abby's heart and squeezed. While she appreciated the captain's offer to escape to his room, there was no way she could accept it. She cared too much about Emma to leave her.

Clutching her hands in front of her, she lifted one more silent prayer for the surgeon's wisdom before she answered the captain. "Thank you, but I will not sleep until I know how Emma fares."

"Mr. Harvey will soon have her to rights."

Was he speaking to her or to himself? Both, likely, for the pinch on his brow did not go away.

He tipped his head toward her and lowered his voice. "Go. Sleep."

The urgency in his voice, the very thought of stretching out on a counterpane, was tempting. Merely the idea loosened some of the tightness knotting her shoulders. It had been a long day. A never-ending one.

But then Mr. Harvey turned from the bedside and faced them. "It is too soon to tell what is at the root of this distemper. At best, it may only be the beginnings of croup."

Captain Thatcher jutted his chin. "And worst?"

Mr. Harvey's blue eyes darted to Abby, then back to the captain. He beckoned for Captain Thatcher to follow him, then strode to the side of the room.

A flash of anger burned from Abby's belly to her chest as the men left her behind. After caring for the child for hours on end, cleaning and cooling and cooing, did they really think her so weak of heart? She crossed to them with clipped steps. "I am not a frail flower, Mr. Harvey. Whatever you need to say can be spoken in my presence."

Something flashed in the captain's eyes. Censure or admiration? Hard to tell, but he nodded his consent toward the surgeon.

"Very well." Mr. Harvey rolled his shoulders. "Then I shall give it to you straight. The child exhibits the first symptoms of putrid throat."

Abby's heart stopped. So did her breaths. The awful diagnosis stealing both for it was the foulest of thieves—the very one that had taken her mother's life all those years ago.

She swayed, but the captain's strong grip on her arm shored her up.

The surgeon held up a hand. "It may not be, and I pray that it is not, but even so, for the benefit of the public, I shall take her with me at once."

"Take her?" Abby squeaked out, leaning hard on the captain's strength. "What do you mean?"

"Your child, madam, needs to be quarantined until further notice." Mr. Harvey studied them both over the rim of his spectacles. "And at the first sign of any pain in your own throats, you will need to be confined as well."

CHAPTER ELEVEN

Horehound and vinegar. Blood and despair. Abby wrinkled her nose, though that did nothing to lessen the strong odour. While she'd expected the surgeon's office to have a stringent scent, it didn't make the smell more bearable.

She shifted on the small bench in the waiting room, fighting a yawn. After snatching a few hours of sleep, she'd persuaded Captain Thatcher to escort her to Mr. Harvey's office. It hadn't taken much coaxing, though. The lines on the captain's brow had confirmed he was as worried about the baby girl as she.

Fixing her gaze on the door between the anteroom and surgeon's office, Abby willed the thing to open. But it did no good. The oak slab remained shut. She glanced down at her watch brooch, then frowned. The captain had been in there at least fifteen minutes. He'd insisted she wait for him instead of meeting with Mr. Harvey herself, and she hadn't argued. But as the minutes ticked on, she wished she'd put up more of a resistance. She shifted once more, knowing all along that fussing likely wouldn't have done any good anyway. Though she'd known the captain for only five days, she'd learned one thing. When the brown of his eyes deepened to a flinty black, the man would not be moved.

For at least the tenth time in as many minutes, she lifted her fingertips to her throat and swallowed, probing to detect any pain or ache. Just thinking about the possibility of falling ill made little twinges tighten the muscles beneath her touch. But that was all. No tenderness.

Just a scratchy feeling on the inside from forcing herself to swallow so many times.

Just then, Captain Thatcher stepped out.

She shot to her feet before he closed the door behind him. "How is Emma?"

"Much the same."

"Is that good or bad?"

He shrugged and donned his hat. "We should know more tomorrow."

The captain strode past her and held open the door, but Abby hesitated to follow. How could it possibly have taken a quarter of an hour simply to find out Emma fared no differently than when they'd last seen her? Was there something he wasn't telling her?

Narrowing her eyes, she studied the man, looking for clues, but he just stood there. Waiting. The sunlight streaming in from outside painted him in golden light, a chiseled, marbled statue—albeit a bit worn about the edges.

With a last glance at the surgeon's closed door, she exited onto the High Street of Stratford-'on-Avon. The captain fell into step beside her, putting himself between her and the road. Despite the shadow of worry about Emma, Abby lifted her face to the sun and allowed the golden warmth to soak in for one blessed moment. It was a glorious June day. Quite the contrast to the rattling walls of the carriage or the darkened timbers of the inn's public room.

She glanced up at the captain. "Would you like to take a turn about the town? This is, after all, the birthplace of the great playwright William Shakespeare. Perhaps we might take in a bit of history. At the very least, the fresh air would do us both some good."

"It's safer to remain at the inn," he rumbled, his tone as dull as the wheels on a passing dray.

She quirked a brow at him. "Do not worry, sir. I shall protect you."

While she appreciated that he took his role of guardian to heart, could the man not permit himself to enjoy a few brief moments?

His dark gaze snapped to hers. No smile curved his lips, but all the same, amusement sparked in his eyes. Though unspoken, she got the distinct impression her retort had pleased him—which unaccountably heated her face more than the sun.

She looked away, and her step faltered. Then she stopped altogether. After the fear-filled night she'd spent caring for Emma, her mind consumed with worry and flashes of despair, she'd almost forgotten the reason for her journey. There, inches behind the window of a seamstress shop, a beautiful gown made of cream-coloured silk draped over a dress form. Hundreds of embroidered roses in golden thread swirled up from the hem, climbing a vine of small seed pearls. The bodice fit tightly, with no ruffles or braids. Near the shoulders, the sleeves puffed a bit, then followed the arm in a sleek line. This time Abby's throat did ache—with longing. This gown was a dream. *Her* dream. Completely unlike the flouncy gauze and taffeta creation her stepmother had insisted upon and persuaded her father to purchase for Abby's wedding day.

"Oh my," she breathed out. "The woman who wears a gown such as that will be a picture of elegance."

"Waste of money," the captain grumbled beside her.

"How can you say that?" She flung out her arm as if to uphold the gown and her opinion in the palm of her hand. "Anyone wearing a gown like that would surely be the most beautiful bride in all of England. Would you not wish your future wife to be so adorned on your wedding day?"

"What makes you think I'm not married?"

"But you said you had no family!" Her brows knit into a knot as she tried to decipher the captain's question. Had he lied to her before? To what end? Yet all she'd experienced from this man for the past five days had been nothing but honor. Why would he—

She gasped as a sickening truth sank to her belly. "Oh! How careless of me. You *were* married, were you not?"

His eyes actually twinkled. "No." Half his mouth curved into a faint smile. "Never have been. You are entirely too easy to tease, Miss Gilbert."

The rogue! Her fingers curled into fists to keep from swatting the amusement off his face. Captain Thatcher was as incorrigible as her younger stepbrother. In fact, the softened lines near his eyes and jaw made him look almost boyish—and entirely too handsome.

She pinched her lips into a mock scowl. "Why do you torment me so?"

He leaned closer, angling his head. "Why do you fall for it?"

Her scowl slipped, giving way to a small chuckle. "Fatigue, I suppose. And it is unfair of you to take such advantage."

She turned back to the gown for a last look, powerless to stop a sigh from barreling out. "Simply lovely," she whispered.

"You don't need a gown to make you beautiful."

She jerked her gaze back to him, only to see his long legs already striding down the pavement. Had that been a compliment? From the dour captain?

Lifting her hem, she dashed to catch up. "Thank you, Captain, but I hope you do not think I was fishing for praise. There are simply certain expectations of how the bride of a baronet should present herself. Sir Jonathan Aberley will wish me to play the part, and I intend to meet his expectations."

"Sounds like a production on Drury Lane." He glanced at her sideways. "What kind of man cares more about the wedding than the marriage?"

"I am sure it is not like that at all. Of course the baronet cares about the marriage, about me, not just the ceremony."

A breeze kicked up a puff of dirt from the road, and the captain angled to block her from it, his head shaking as if he didn't believe a word she said.

She frowned, determined to change his obvious sour opinion of the man she was to marry. "Sir Jonathan Aberley is the highest-ranking landowner in the area. A man of his station must maintain the decorum people expect."

His eyes narrowed. "Are you marrying for a title, then, Miss Gilbert?"

"No!" How dare he even voice such a question? Was he teasing her again? She cleared her throat and forced a pleasant tone, unwilling to take his bait. "It is a love match."

"Love?" He scoffed. "You've only met the man once. You hardly know him, nor he, you. Not a very solid beginning to a marriage. Such a union can only be ill-fated."

She stopped and popped her fists onto her hips. Many the time had she sparred with her stepmother, but never did anger burn so fervid within her chest. This was beyond teasing. "Must you always expect the worst, Captain?"

His dark gaze challenged her in ways she couldn't begin to comprehend. "Must you always expect the best?"

She stared right back, refusing to be the first to look away. His assumption was wrong—*completely* wrong—for at this moment, she was having a hard time expecting the best of him!

Samuel's mouth twitched, a smile threatening to once again break loose. This was new. Entirely new. He couldn't remember the last time a lady inspired so much amusement—if ever. Then again, Abigail Gilbert was no ordinary miss, the way she held her ground, neither shrinking nor wavering. How tenderly she cared for little Emma, concerning herself for the child's well-being. The easy manner with which she'd laughed off his teasing. Was this how it had been for Moore or Brentwood when they'd first met their respective brides-to-be?

Gah! What was he thinking?

Miss Gilbert was right. If she could blame fatigue for her skewed thoughts, surely he could as well. He turned on his heel, calling over his shoulder as he resumed stalking down the High Street. "Come along, Miss Gilbert. I daresay neither of us will change the mind of the other."

Rows of dark-timbered storefronts rose up on each side of the road, standing shoulder to shoulder, like comrades bellying up to a bar. Halfway down the block, a crowd began to gather, forming a ring around a scuffle. He glanced into the road to cross, but coming up from behind them, a lacquered carriage pulled by four high-steppers clattered down the lane. He'd have to wait until it passed before leading Miss Gilbert to the other side.

But apparently the woman hadn't noticed his hesitation, for she continued on.

"Miss Gilbert, wait."

He darted after her, nearly crashing into her back when she stopped at the edge of the onlookers.

At the center of the ring of spectators, two men circled each other, knees bent, fists up. The smaller of the two struck first, uppercutting with a strong right hook to the jaw. The bigger man staggered—a bit too theatrically—then whumped to the pavement, eyes closed.

Samuel shook his head, disgusted. If the Stratford constable didn't put a stop to this kind of crowd gathering, the whole village would soon fall to cutpurses and pickpockets galore.

Miss Gilbert's big brown eyes lifted to his. "You are a man of the law. Can you not do something?"

Her fresh-faced innocence was beguiling. Sweet mercy! How he hated to be the one to introduce her to the ways of this conniving world. But so be it. He lifted a finger and gently pushed her chin for her to witness what would happen next.

The victor raised his fists into the air, strutting rooster-like around the inside of the circle. Behind him, the fallen man sprang to his feet. The crowd gasped, likely expecting the smaller bully to take a good cuff to the back of the head.

Miss Gilbert clutched his arm. "Captain Thatcher! You must stop this before one of them gets seriously hurt."

Her confidence in his ability to break up such a brawl did strange things to his gut, but he set his jaw. "Keep watching," he ordered.

With one meaty hand, the big man swiped blood from his split lip. With the other, he pulled out a cloth banner from his waistband. Snapping it open, he held it up for all to read a painted advertisement for Jack Henry's Boxing Club. "Don't take a beating like I did, mates. Learn to fight back. A new bout of lessons starts today, on Quigley and Main. Affordable and necessary, aye Billy?"

The short man grinned back at him. "Aye!"

Miss Gilbert, pretty little lips parted, stared up at Samuel. Ahh, but he could get used to that look of reverent amazement.

"How did you know?" she whispered.

"Part of the job," he murmured, then swept out his arm. "After you."

She paused a moment more, other questions surfacing in the lines on her brow, much like a curious tot marveling over the discovery of a world beyond her chamber door. Then she turned and began weaving her way through the dispersing bystanders.

He followed, until a small child scampered between them. Samuel stopped to avoid kicking the lad with his boot.

The child stopped as well, blinking up at him like a fawn to a hunter. Slowly, the boy's face squinched into a wicked grin, then he bolted, laughing as he tore between pedestrians. What the deuce? Why would a boy—?

Gut sinking, Samuel jerked his gaze to Miss Gilbert. Sure enough, a tattered old woman held on to her sleeve, swaying on her feet. The woman's words screeched a layer above the din of the remaining people.

"My pardon, a thousand times o'er! Why, I ne'er meant to bump into so fine a lady as you, miss. Don't be cross, miss. Don't be cruel."

"Of course I shall not. It was only an accident. Go in peace." Miss Gilbert's innocent voice stabbed him in the heart. She had no idea.

Samuel shouldered his way past the few dress coats between them.

"God bless ye, mum." The old woman turned.

But Samuel flung out his hand and grabbed her arm, yanking her back. "Not so fast."

Miss Gilbert frowned up at him. *Him!* Not at the old woman who deserved her scorn. After years of such looks, he'd built up a rawhide skin to misunderstanding scowls, but this time, from this woman, it stung like a slap to the face.

"Captain Thatcher! How can you be so harsh? Release that woman at once."

Ignoring Miss Gilbert, he shoved his hand out toward the old thief. "Give it back."

The woman, surprisingly agile, wrenched one way then another, wriggling to break free. Satan himself couldn't have spewed such vile obscenities.

Samuel dug his fingers deeper into the fleshy part of her arm. "Mind your tongue, woman. There's a lady present."

"Pah! Lady or no, I'll say what e're I flip-flappity want to say, ye gleeking gudgeon. I ain't done nothing. I'll call the law on you, that's what. Now let me go, ye hedge-born clotpole!"

Her grey eyes widened as he shoved his greatcoat open with his elbow, exposing the brass end of his tipstaff.

"Now," he growled. "Hand it over."

One more curse flew out, but so did the old woman's hand. Miss Gilbert's golden watch brooch sat atop the thief's gnarly palm.

Miss Gilbert sucked in an audible breath as she snatched it away. This time when she gazed up at him, sheepish repentance shimmered in her eyes, and something more. He sucked in his own breath when he realized what it was.

Admiration.

"How did you know?" Miss Gilbert clutched the pin to her chest. "And do not tell me it is part of the job."

"Sometimes, Miss Gilbert, it *does* serve to expect the worst."

Still gripping the old woman, he fished around in his pocket and retrieved a farthing, then held it out to her. "See that you hold on to this coin instead of busying your fingers with other people's property, or next time I won't be so lenient."

He let go. The old woman narrowed her eyes for a moment, then seized the coin and darted off.

Frowning, he turned to Miss Gilbert. "Tuck your brooch away. Such a valuable keepsake ought to be kept out of sight."

Her eyes widened, glistening with unspent tears. "How do you know it is a keepsake?"

"One doesn't weep for the loss of a simple brooch. Where did you get it?"

"It was my mother's. And you are right. There is nothing simple about it. This is my last connection to her." She clutched the pin in a death grip. Clearly there was more attached to that bauble than grief.

Sighing, he softened his tone. "You know, Miss Gilbert, someone once told me that past hurts often lose their sting when shared with others. You rarely speak of your family. Why is that, I wonder?"

"There is not much to say. My mother died when I was five. Father gave me her watch shortly before he remarried. And a good thing too, for my stepmother would have cast it out of the home as she did with all of my mother's belongings." Miss Gilbert ducked her head, the dimple on her chin curving into a frown. "But enough about me. I. . .I owe you an apology, sir. I had no right to question your abrupt handling of the old woman, for you are far wiser than I."

A twinge of compassion squeezed his chest. Miss Gilbert couldn't possibly look more like a forlorn little girl if she tried.

"You owe me nothing, Miss Gilbert, save for my payment when we reach your baronet's manor. I pray your future husband is more educated in the ways of the world than you are, for your own safety."

Scarlet brushed her cheeks, almost feverish in intensity. While he'd meant no disrespect, had she taken his words the wrong way? Then again, such heightened colour could be the remnants of excitement from the near-robbery. A distinct possibility. Or. . .

His throat tightened. It could be Miss Gilbert was starting to exhibit the first signs of illness.

He blew out a long breath and offered his arm. Despite saying otherwise to the lady, he was tired of expecting the worst.

CHAPTER TWELVE

Pins. Needles. Abby sat up in bed, her heart sinking as she swallowed again, and this time shards of glass scraped the inside of her throat. Heart sinking, she eased back against the pillow, her pulse beating loud in her ears. She'd been trying to ignore the increasing ache all night. But now, with morning light seeping between the cracks in the drapery, there was no more denying the truth.

Whatever illness little Emma suffered, she now had it.

Dragging her body from the bed, she went through the motions of dressing, all the while vainly trying to hold worry at bay. It could be nothing, as the surgeon had said of the babe yesterday. A trifling malaise of some sort, or naught more than a seasonal discomfort.

Or it could be putrid throat, the killer. The murderer.

Abby's fingers faltered as she cinched the front of her bodice. Even were she stronger than her mother and survived such a dreaded disease, the illness and resulting recuperation would add weeks, if not months, to her journey. Must everything impede her from reaching the man who would love her forever? She'd already tallied several extra days to her journey. Was Sir Jonathan even now so concerned that he'd send out a search party?

She sat on the small stool in front of the dressing table and pinned up her hair, peering at her face in the mirror as she worked. Scarlet didn't flame across her cheeks, nor did her skin pale to a deathly hue. Heat didn't burn through her, and she didn't shiver with chills. Those had to be good signs. Didn't they? But what if they weren't? What if those symptoms crashed down upon her all at once, any minute now?

This was ridiculous. She pushed the last hairpin into place then bowed her head. She'd learned long ago while enduring the hurts of her stepmother that only through prayer would she find peace.

Lord, I confess I am anxious and fretting and altogether not trusting in Your great providence. It is not You who are in my debt, but I in Yours. . . for everything You give. If this be putrid throat, then I will trust You for the best outcome, whatever that may be, for I can do no more. But even so, Lord, I pray You would grant healing for little Emma and for me.

She lifted her face, then on second thought, once more dropped her chin to her chest.

And keep Captain Thatcher hale and hearty as well. Amen.

Trying not to swallow, she rose and collected her watch brooch from off the bedside table. This time—and forevermore—she'd pin it on her gown and wear her spencer over it. Reading the time would be a bit more inconvenient, but the placement would also serve to confound thieves.

She fastened the golden keepsake to the fabric, then absently rubbed her finger over the tiny glass face. The captain had brushed off her gratitude and praise yesterday, saying he was only doing his job as her guardian, but he could have no idea how truly thankful she'd been to keep this treasure. If it hadn't been for his fast action, all her tangible ties to her mother would be gone.

She pulled her spencer from off a peg on the wall and shoved in her arms, then tied on her bonnet, taking care to keep the ribbon from digging into her neck. Though she hated to admit to the captain that her throat ached, there'd be no hiding it if Mr. Harvey's worst suspicions proved true.

Leaving her chamber, she padded down the corridor to the captain's door, prepared to suffer his censure for not telling him sooner. But after three raps, he still didn't answer.

"Captain Thatcher?" She knocked again.

No response. Strange. He always answered her call barely before the words left her mouth.

Leaning her ear to the wood, she listened for any sign of movement.

But there were no footsteps thudding. No rustle of clothing. No anything. Just the low chatter of morning patrons climbing up the stairs from the taproom below. Where could the captain be at this early hour? Unless he'd gone down to breakfast?

Of course. She should've thought of that sooner. She descended the stairs and paused on the last one, gaining a wide view of the public room. Her gaze drifted from table to table, but no strong-jawed, dark-haired man looked up at her—as Captain Thatcher always seemed to do whenever she entered a room. Well, then. She clutched her reticule with both hands and stepped off the last stair.

She'd simply go see Mr. Harvey alone.

Sun and wind. Air and light. Samuel bent and gave Pilgrim free rein. The horse surged into a gallop. Here in the English countryside, the world blurring into a green line, God spoke in the roar rushing past his ears.

"Peace. Be at peace, My son."

The words goaded him, and he dug in his heels, ramping Pilgrim into a frenzy. For a few breathless moments, Samuel gave in to the solid muscles beneath him, carrying him far and fast. Trying to forget. Straining for that peace.

And failing miserably.

As he neared the Stratford outskirts, he slowed the horse, but the same burdens weighted his shoulders. The latent anger simmering in his gut—so much a part of him he didn't know how to live without it—flared hotter. How was he to grab hold of peace when so much responsibility bound him tightly?

Swinging off Pilgrim, he seized the horse's lead and walked the rest of the way to the inn's stable, cooling down his mount and himself. He rebuffed the stable boy with a scowl, preferring to see to Pilgrim's care on his own. After watering, untacking, and a good brushing, his old friend nudged him in the shoulder with a playful nose jab.

Samuel patted the bay on the neck. "Yes, my friend. It was a much-needed ride, though I don't think it did any good for me."

He strolled from the stable to the inn, purposely restraining his stride to a slow gait—despite the urgency to discover if Miss Gilbert was up and about yet. The desire to see the woman's smile etched a frown on his face. Why care a whit about a woman betrothed to another man? He wouldn't. He didn't. But all the same, he stomped up the stairs to his room, completely distracted by glancing down the corridor to her chamber. She'd not been in the public room. Was she even now lingering over a cup of tea in her bedchamber, her dark hair undone, in naught but her dressing gown?

Bah! He'd spent far too much time in Moore's and Brentwood's company, their soft tendencies toward their wives influencing him overmuch. He stopped in front of his own door, shoved the key into the lock and turned it. The movement rotated without friction. The tumbler didn't click. Clearly the thing was already unlocked—and he *always* secured his room.

Tensing, he reached for his gun.

But not quick enough.

The door flew open, and Noddy Carper's hulking shape barreled out. His beefy forearm slammed into Samuel's windpipe, cutting off air and driving him back. Before Samuel could react, the back of his head smacked against the corridor wall. Pain seared into his wrist, splaying his fingers. His gun fell with a sickening thud.

The world blackened at the edges. Samuel jammed his knee up, hoping to connect with soft tissue. But once again he was too late. Carper wrenched aside, sticking out his leg and ramming Samuel in the shoulder, toppling him off-balance to the floor.

Samuel gulped in air, coughing—until a sharp crack hit his skull.

This time the world did turn black.

Seconds later, his best guess, the fuzzy outline of his bedchamber furniture sharpened into view. A rough grip yanked the back of his collar, hauling him to his knees. Pain bounced around in his head like a steel ball gone wild. Sucking in a breath, he pushed upward.

Then stopped breathing altogether.

An arm's length in front of him, a ruddy-skinned monster sat on his bed. A slow smile opened his big maw, revealing yellowed teeth clinging to mottled gums. Dark hair stubbled over the beast's shorn head, misshapen from years of hard living and too many blows. And in the brute's lap, a knife lay gripped in one hand, the blade cradled in the other. Sunlight glinted off the freshly honed metal, impossibly sharp.

Despite the cold gun barrel shunted against the back of his head, Samuel squared his shoulders and faced his nemesis.

Shankhart Robbins.

This time when Abby entered Mr. Harvey's outer foyer, she was prepared for the vinegary scent. But as she stepped into the surgeon's office, nothing could have readied her for the sights. As a gentleman's daughter, she'd never had cause to visit a working surgeon's theatre. Now she understood why the captain had commanded she wait for him on the bench the previous morning. She could only imagine the suffering the yellowed walls in here had witnessed.

At the center of the room sat a raised wooden slab, long enough for a body, darkened and splotched from years of blood. Small divots were worn into the edges, right about where hands had likely clutched and squeezed and clawed in pain. Various saws and pincers of assorted sizes hung from hooks on one wall. Bottles filled with different liquids stood on a nearby table. A large velvet-lined box yawned open on that table, and though she didn't want to, Abby couldn't help but stare at the large syringes lined up inside, ready to pierce flesh.

"Ahh, Mrs. Thatcher." Mr. Harvey glanced over his shoulder as he hung a stained apron on a peg. "I was just finishing up and about to make a call on you and your husband. You've saved me a trip."

Heat rose up her neck, and she thanked God the surgeon yet had his back toward her.

"Oh, he is not my—"

She bit her lip. Which was worse? Allowing the man to think she and the captain were married, or refuting him when Mr. Harvey had clearly seen them together in her bedchamber?

"Hmm?" Mr. Harvey turned.

She smoothed her skirts, giving her hands something to do other than flutter about from mortification. "I. . .uh. . ." Despite the biting pain in her throat, she swallowed. "I am glad I saved you the trouble, sir. I came to inquire after little Emma and also to ask, if you have a spare moment, if you might look at my throat?"

His brow folded, dipping his bushy grey eyebrows into his spectacles. "I was afraid of that. Let's see what the trouble is."

He advanced, sidestepping the table, and with a gentle touch to her chin, guided her face upward into a ray of sunlight beaming in from one of the many windows. "Now then, Mrs. Thatcher, open your mouth and say ahh, if you please."

She obeyed.

He mm-hmmed immediately.

"Yes. Yes, I see," he murmured while tipping her face to one side and peering closer. Then he released her and stepped back. "Thank you."

He said no more, but something flashed in his eyes. Concern? Worry? Frustration over how to tell her she'd succumb to a mortal disease within hours?

Clutching her skirts, she braced herself for the worst. "Your verdict, Mr. Harvey?"

"Unfortunately, I'd say you're well on your way to feeling as poorly as your little girl."

Her hand flew to her throat. "Is it. . . ?" But she couldn't bring herself to even think the words let alone say them aloud. She swayed on her feet.

"Now, now, Mrs. Thatcher. Don't go swooning in a surgeon's office, though I suppose if you must, this would be the best place for it, eh?" He guided her out to the waiting room with a gentle nudge to her back and led her to the bench.

She sank, grateful for the support and to be away from the operating room.

"Allow me to put your fears to rest, madam. Your daughter suffers from a bad case of the croup, not the putrid throat. And neither do you."

She snapped her face up to his, relief pumping through her veins with each beat of her heart.

He reaffirmed his words with a nod. "I suspect you've contracted some form of the girl's ailment, though it will likely pass from you much faster than it will for little Emma. Some white horehound syrup for the both of you, and you'll be on the mend in no time. The girl will likely fuss a bit longer, but she should be back to rights within the week. Wait here, please, while I retrieve her for you."

Mr. Harvey disappeared through a different door, and Abby sank back against the wall, sighing. Thank God! No deathly illness for her or little Emma. She'd collect the child and they could be on their way this very morning, incurring no more delay.

Wouldn't Captain Thatcher be surprised when she showed up back at the inn with the babe in her arms?

CHAPTER THIRTEEN

Staring at death was nothing new. It was a way of life. A companion Samuel frequently clasped hands with. In a freakish sort of way, he was comfortable knowing each breath might be his last, for he'd been facing his own demise since the day he'd screamed into this world. No, the sickening clench of his gut had nothing whatsoever to do with the possibility of dying. It was that he'd slipped up. Been caught unawares. Fallen headlong into his enemy's snare. And that rankled more than the ugly grin slicing across Shankhart Robbins's face or Carper's gun drilling into the back of his skull.

In front of him, Shankhart's big hulk sagged the mattress in the middle, where he sat on the bed, defiling the counterpane beneath him. A breeze wafting in from the window directly behind him carried his sweaty taint.

"Well, well. If it ain't my old friend, Sam'l Thatcher. Thing is, though, I have to keep asking myself. . ." Shankhart's misshapen head hinged eerily sideways, as if it might topple off. "I say, 'Self? For the love of money and women, why would Thatcher go and kill my own brother?'"

Ignoring the gun Carper jabbed into his head, Samuel locked gazes with Shankhart. " 'Cause *you* weren't within reach at the time."

"I am now." The man blinked, his eyelids never quite shutting. It was an unsettling defect, the moist crescent of his eyeballs showing at all times. God only knew how many victims had stared at those lizard-like slits as he sliced their throats.

Shankhart tapped his blade against his palm in a deadly rhythm. “Looks like I’ll be the one doing the killing today.”

“Have at it, then.” Samuel lifted his chin, the muzzle sliding to a higher point on his skull. “If you’re able.”

Coarse laughter rolled out of the highwayman, jiggling Shankhart’s meaty shoulders. “Big talk for someone down on his knees.”

He had a point. Samuel clamped his jaw shut while mentally ticking off any possible assets to use for his escape. White muslin curtains riffled in the breeze behind Shankhart. The window he usually kept shut was now open—likely reserved for Shankhart and Carper’s exit. But it could prove useful to him. To his left, a pitcher sat on the washbasin, a formidable weapon if shattered against one of these brute’s faces. And he still had his boot-blade tucked away. All in all, if the timing were right, he stood a chance, albeit a very slim one.

“I won’t be here for long.” He forced confidence into his tone—more than he had a right to own at this moment.

Shankhart sucked in his lips, then released them, making a smacking noise. “Not to be difficult, Captain, but I beg to differ. This could take all day. You see, I’m going to carve you up, bit by bit, piece by piece. Real slow,” he drawled.

Samuel steeled every muscle as Shankhart lifted the knife. But the big man merely raised the blade to his own chin and scraped the sharp edge lightly against his dark stubble. Again and again. The rasping noise more unnerving than when the blade slipped and opened a small line of red on the man’s jaw.

Shankhart’s lips curved as he studied the blood on his knife, tilting it one way then the other in a ray of sunshine beaming through the window. Then he lowered the weapon to his lap and skewered Samuel with a pointed stare. “Oh, I know. I see it in your face. Anxious for the revelry to start, are you? Not yet, though. Time’s not right. You wanna tell him why, Carper?”

The gun dug into the back of his skull. Carper’s snicker was as foul as his breath, wafting thick upon Samuel’s head. “We bein’ gentlemen, and all, why we gots to wait on that lady of yours.”

The words slammed into him like a hammer blow. They knew of Miss Gilbert?

God, have mercy.

Shankhart chuckled. "That's right. We know about the woman you're running off with. It pains me you never told your ol' friend about the bit o' skirt you've taken up with. Never introduced us proper like." Shankhart leaned forward, close enough that Samuel could feel the heat of him. "And a child too. My, my, but you've been a busy boy, chasing me down by day and tumbling yer doxy by night."

Samuel's hands curled into fists, the slur to Miss Gilbert lighting a wildfire in his chest. "Leave her and the child out of this. Your quarrel is with me."

"You should've thought of that sooner," Shankhart growled. "Things changed when you killed my brother. It's only justice that your loved ones should be taken just as you've taken mine."

"Justice?" Samuel snorted. "You don't know the meaning of the word."

"What I know is that you've been a thorn in my flesh for far too long. This ends now."

Lifting a last, frantic prayer, Samuel ground out, "So be it."

He lurched sideways. Carper's gun fired.

The shot lifted the hair on the side of Samuel's head as the ball passed. A hot trail grazed across his temple—but sank into Shankhart's chest.

Shankhart roared, the bullet punching him back.

Victory—maybe. No time to gloat.

Samuel jumped to his feet and lunged for the pitcher in one motion. He swung the heavy porcelain at Carper's skull. But the man twisted at the last moment, the vessel shattering against the brute's shoulder instead of his head. Before Samuel could regain his balance, Carper drove his elbow into his face. Cartilage gave. Blood flowed. Pain stabbed.

So, this was going to turn ugly, then.

Samuel swiped for his blade—but Carper's boot cracked into his forearm. He stumbled from the force, then pivoted back with an uppercut to Carper's jaw.

Carper grunted.

Followed by a sharp rap on the door.

"Captain?" A feminine voice leached through. "Are you all right?"

Samuel's heart skipped a beat. *God, no!* Not Miss Gilbert. Not now.

A wicked grin split Carper's face, and he lunged for the doorknob.

Samuel sprang. If he didn't take Carper down before the man grabbed Miss Gilbert, there was no telling what violence she might suffer.

He snagged Carper's arm and yanked him back, wrenching the man's elbow upward so sharply, his wrist nearly connected to his armpit.

Carper howled.

Before he could swing around, Samuel shoved his foot in front of the man's boot, knocking him off-balance, then thrust him to the floor, riding the villain down.

Jamming his knee against one of Carper's arms, Samuel ground his forearm against the man's neck and cut off his air supply. Carper writhed. Samuel held. Just as the body beneath him slackened into unconsciousness, Samuel shot back to his feet and whirled, snatching out his knife. If Shankhart were still alive, the fight was only beginning.

The curtains fluttered like unmoored ghosts. Blood smeared across the counterpane in a deadly line toward the window.

The bed was empty.

Samuel ran over to the window. No wounded body lay on the ground. No corpse. No Shankhart.

Just a bloody trail that ended where horse hooves had dug into the ground.

An anguished cry rumbled behind the closed door, the low growl terrible and altogether too familiar. Abby's pulse thumped loudly in her ears. Something was wrong. Horribly wrong. She clutched little Emma tighter with one arm and pounded her fist against the wood. "Captain! Please answer."

Boot steps thudded, and the door yanked open. Captain Thatcher stood, chest heaving, dark hair wild and hanging over one eye. Blood oozed down his temple and snaked out of his nose, running over his lips before it dripped from his chin. He swiped the offense with his sleeve, as if the flow were no more than a mild inconvenience.

She gaped.

He frowned—then winced. "Why do you have Emma?"

"You are hurt!" she cried. "What happened?"

Behind him, a body on the floor moaned.

The captain glanced over his shoulder, then his dark gaze shot back to hers. "Go to your—"

Feet pounded behind her, the heavy wheezing of the innkeeper rattling off the walls. "What the briny carbuncle is going on up here? Ye don't pay me enough to be shootin' the place to bloody ribbons."

Captain Thatcher tipped his head toward her chamber. "Go to your room, Miss Gilbert. I'll meet you there straightaway."

"But—"

"Now." His voice was flint. Arguing was out of the question. And as the bloodied man behind the captain groaned louder, she wasn't so sure she wanted to put up a fight anyway. Clearly enough battle had already taken place.

Emma shifted against her shoulder, and with one last look at the wearied captain, Abby turned away. For the child's sake—and hers—it was likely best to obey his command.

Once inside her chamber, she laid the babe in the middle of her bed, grateful Emma had slept through the commotion. Abby untied her bonnet, fingers trembling, then sank down next to her, more shaken than she cared to admit. First her carriage had been attacked, then that awful man at the Laughing Dog had cornered her in the stable. Now this. Maybe she should've gone home with Fanny.

Forcefully shoving her doubts away, she straightened. No sense wallowing in maybes or what mights or should haves, a lesson she'd learned long ago when her stepmother took over the house. Oh, the long nights she'd spent in vain weeping as a child, wishing for her real mother, craving for arms that would hold her. But Father had been too preoccupied with his new wife, and her stepmother truly had only space for one love in her heart—herself.

Abby glanced up at the ceiling, as stained and cracked as she felt on the inside, and closed her eyes.

Lord, give me strength.

Rising, she retrieved a leftover cup of cold tea from the bedside table and gulped the remains, somewhat calming the fire in her throat. She set the cup down and picked up her small book of Psalms, then settled on the only chair in the room. Peace came slowly, but it did come. And the longer Abby read, the more it seeped into her soul. At last, fully relaxed and replenished, her head bobbed. She laid the book in her lap and closed her eyes.

Knuckles rapping against her door jerked her awake, driving the Psalms to the floor. Retrieving it, she set the book aside then crossed to answer.

Captain Thatcher's big frame filled the doorway. No more blood flowed from his wounds, though splotches of deep red marred his skin where it had dried.

His brown eyes blazed into hers. "The child, how does she fare?"

Here he stood, beaten and worn, and his only thought was for little Emma? What kind of man was Captain Thatcher?

She narrowed her eyes. "What happened to you, Captain?"

His jaw clenched, his only response. He was quiet for so long, she was sure he wouldn't answer.

"Nothing to concern you," he said at length.

Nothing? Did he really expect her to believe that?

"The man I hired stands at my door a bloodied mess, and you think it does not concern me?" With a sigh, she stepped aside and swept out her hand. "Come in and use my basin, sir. I will consider it a fair trade to tell you of Emma's condition if you tell me who that man was in your room."

He didn't move. Not directly. But eventually, for a reason she couldn't guess, he strode inside as if he owned the room and stalked over to the washbasin. His footsteps roused little Emma. For propriety's sake, Abby left the door open wide and collected the child. No more fever burned Emma's brow, nor did she cry, but a cough rumbled in her little lungs. Abby propped the child upright against her shoulder and patted her back as Emma barked in spasms.

The captain filled the basin then shot her a raised brow. "The babe is still ill. Why did you bring her back here?"

"I went to see Mr. Harvey this morning because my own throat started to ache and he—"

Captain Thatcher slammed down the pitcher and faced her. "Are you ill too, then?"

His tone was harsh, and his brows pulled together into a fierce line. An angry façade, but just a veneer, she suspected.

Abby shifted Emma to her other shoulder, glad when the child's coughing eased. "I am fine, Captain. A few days' discomfort and I shall be right as rain. Apparently little Emma suffers from nothing more than a bad case of the croup, hence the cough she has developed. She is not to be exposed to night air, and I purchased an ample supply of horehound syrup to keep her comfortable during the day."

The lines of his face softened—mostly—yet the grim set of his jaw remained. "So, neither of you are in danger?"

"No, we are not." She lifted her chin. "But clearly you have been."

He turned his back to her and bent, cupping his hands and splashing water. A small smile twitched her lips. Did the man really think she'd be put off that easily?

She padded over to the washstand, keeping a firm grip on Emma. "Why did that man attack you?"

After a few more splashes, the captain reached for the drying cloth. He dabbed at his temple and nose before answering. "A few unwelcome visitors came to call. Nothing more."

She frowned. Did he harbour some dark secret, or was he trying to protect her?

Emma squirmed in her arms, and once again she shifted the child. The babe would be hungry soon, which would cut a swift end to any conversation she hoped to have with the captain, for she'd have to go in search of milk and porridge.

"There's more to it than that," she persisted. "You and I both know it, and I take you for an honest man. So tell me, Captain, what transpired in your room?"

He balled up the cloth and dropped it onto the washstand. Then, blowing out a long breath, he faced her. His nose was still swollen, but no more blood leaked out. "It isn't a burden meant for you."

A bitter laugh welled, but she swallowed it—despite the pain in her throat. Would that her stepmother had owned the same sentiment.

"I respect your caution in sparing my sensibilities, sir, but I believe God provides us with fellow sojourners to help lighten our heavy loads through prayer and encouragement. And for the time being, we are fellow sojourners, are we not?"

He recoiled—or was that a wince? Hard to say, but the cloth of his suit coat tightened across his broad shoulders. Either she'd surprised him or he completely disagreed with her theology. She stood silent, awaiting his verdict.

Finally, he spoke. "You are a singular woman, Miss Gilbert."

"Is that good or bad?"

A small smile ghosted one side of his mouth. "I haven't decided yet."

Slowly, he folded his arms and widened his stance. "All right, since you insist, but remember, you pushed for this information. The man who attacked your carriage—the one who didn't make it—was the brother of a very powerful highwayman, who is now out for revenge. I am the target."

The knowledge wasn't surprising, but it was heavy, and her shoulders sagged, jostling the babe. How many times in the captain's life had he fought off violence of such magnitude? Her gaze drifted over his face. His features had no doubt been handsome once, a strange mix of boyishness and masculinity. But now, after years of weathering the darkest whims of man, he wore the scars of past battles, from the swollen, purple bump on his nose to the angry red abrasion cutting a line at his temple. Her own awful upbringing began to pale in comparison. Verbal jabs were one thing, but the scrapes and bruises marring the captain's flesh were quite another.

"I see," she murmured.

"No, lady, you don't." His gaze sharpened into a dagger, slicing into her in ways she couldn't understand. "The man gunning for me is a killer of the worst sort. He'll stop at nothing to hurt me—*nothing*—including going after you or the child. It would be better, Miss Gilbert, if we parted ways."

The harshness in his voice shivered through her—as did his words. He was right. After witnessing the effects of the beating he'd suffered, it would be better for her if she found a different guard and made haste to Brakewell Hall.

But why did the thought of saying goodbye to this rough-and-tumble man feel like lightning struck her soul, leaving behind a hollowed trunk that might not stand without him?

CHAPTER FOURTEEN

Each jolt of the carriage over the rocky road magnified the pounding in Abby's head. Pressing her fingertips to her temples, she tried to shove back the pain, but to no avail. The veins beneath her touch pulsed with a crazed beat. Apparently this grand and glorious headache had unpacked its bags and moved in, settling for a lengthy stay no matter what she did to evict it.

The carriage tilted to the right, and Abby grabbed the side of the large basket at her feet to keep it from banging into the wall. Emma had finally fallen asleep, and thankfully, her eyes remained closed as she lay nestled in her blanket. Small rattles wheezed with each of her exhales. Just thinking about tending to Emma once she did reawaken made the ache in Abby's head throb all the more.

Leaning sideways, she glanced out the window at the passing greenery, hoping for a glimpse of the upcoming inn. Surely they would be arriving soon. . .wouldn't they? She'd trade her life for a hot cup of tea right now, and the hotter, the better, judging by the next shiver that shook her bones. Despite the sunshiny day, she was cold. So cold. Tea would be just the thing to warm her, and maybe a scalding drink would burn away the pain raging every time she swallowed.

But staring out the window didn't make an inn appear. Only rows of trees passed by, their trunks lined up like soldiers at attention. Abby frowned. Perhaps it had been a mistake to continue traveling after the trauma of the morning. Yet remaining in the same building where the captain had been attacked was out of the question—especially knowing the villain had gotten away and might still be lurking about, injured or not.

The coach lurched over a bump. Flinging out her hand lest she crack her head against the wall, Abby turned away from the glass and glanced down at Emma. The sweet girl rubbed one chubby fist against her cheek yet did not open her eyes.

Sighing, Abby sank back against the seat. Only God knew if she'd made the right decision to remain with Emma and the captain—leastwise until they reached Manchester. She'd been too weary to choose otherwise, even when the captain had insisted on finding her a new guard. The mere idea of hiring another man had drained the last of her strength. Even now her eyelids grew heavy and her chin dipped with the thought of it. Perhaps if she just gave in to exhaustion, the headache would go away, and she'd be able to think more clearly.

Seconds later, the carriage stopped, and her head jerked backward. Groggy, Abby fumbled for her watch brooch, then blinked at the glass face. She'd been wrong. It hadn't been seconds but nearly a half hour since she'd last checked the time.

The lowering of the stairs rattle-clunked outside the door, and she straightened on the seat. Every muscle screamed to be left as is—then screamed louder as she bent to pick up Emma. Just before scooping up the babe, another shiver rattled through her, and she pulled back. She hated to admit it, but she simply didn't have the strength to lift the girl. It would do neither of them any good if she tumbled out of the carriage with Emma in her arms.

As soon as the door opened, Abby peeked out. Shadows from the captain's hat shaded his eyes and covered the wound on his temple, but nothing could hide the jagged abrasion ripping across his nose. Though she was loath to trouble him more than necessary, the weakness in her arms reminded her this *was* necessary.

"Would you mind retrieving Emma after you help me down, Captain? She is asleep in her basket, but she will wake soon enough."

His dark gaze drifted over her face. Many a time her stepmother had studied her as intently, but beneath the captain's searching, compassion surfaced in his eyes, so genuine that it stole her breath. Heat flashed through her—a welcome warmth.

With a nod, he held out his hand.

His fingers wrapped around hers and she stepped out, his strength a bulwark to lean on as the world swirled and her head pounded. When her feet hit the ground, she planted them firmly to keep from swaying, then pulled away. Or tried to.

The captain held on with an unrelenting grip.

She arched a brow at him. Why would he not release her?

His brown eyes merely bored into hers, offering no explanation. Then, as suddenly as a spring tempest, he let go.

"We'll stay here for the night," he rumbled.

She glanced at the sky. No storm clouds sullied the horizon, nor did the sun lay low. Puzzled, she met his gaze. "But we can easily reach the next inn."

"Not with your fever."

Fever? Her fingers flew to her forehead. A bit moist, but the skin surely didn't feel any hotter than her hand. She'd confess to a headache and sore throat if need be, but not to a fever.

She dropped her hand and smoothed her damp palm along her skirt. "You are mistaken."

His trademark smirk lifted one side of his mouth. "Your hot skin says otherwise."

There'd be no arguing the point with him, not the way his jaw hardened into a strong line. La! What was she thinking? She didn't feel up to arguing, anyway.

She forced a small smile, for she'd learned long ago how to hide her true state. "I am certain that after a cup of tea I shall be fine. Besides, we have lost enough time already."

"Then it won't matter if we delay further."

Stubborn man. She'd stamp her foot if she knew the jolt wouldn't climb up her leg and join the throbbing inside her skull.

"While I appreciate your concern, Captain, I assure you I can manage a few more miles today. After all, a bride cannot be late for her own wedding."

He grunted. "I'm sure your Lord Fanciness won't mind."

"It's Sir Jonathan *Aberley*." She scowled—then repented of it as the movement heightened the pain behind her eyes. "And of course he will mind."

"Not if he knew you were feeling poorly." The captain folded his arms, his black riding cloak stretching taut at the shoulders. "If the man is worth his salt, he'd insist you rest for a while."

Would he? What a lovely thought, to be so cherished that time and schedules could be tied up and placed on a shelf, awaiting her renewed strength. But—illness or not—one simply didn't keep a baronet waiting.

She shook her head. Bad idea. The world spun, and she flung out her hand to shore herself up against the carriage. "I can rest as easily in the carriage as I can at an inn."

"Hogwash."

One of the horses whickered, apparently as astonished as she. Why was the man so unyielding? She blew out a sigh. "Fine. Then think of yourself. That man, that highwayman, he is still out there. We have not traveled very far from Stratford. You need to put space between him and. . .and. . ."

Her words trailed off as the world tipped. Strange, that. She angled her head, straightening things out for the moment, leastwise visually. Her thoughts, however, would not be as easily ordered. What had she been saying?

The captain narrowed his eyes, then unfolded his arms and offered her a hand. "Let's get you inside. I'll come back for Emma once you're seated."

She stared down at his outstretched palm, mesmerized at the way the darkness closed in around it. Like the drawing shut of a great set of draperies, daylight slowly vanished. She blinked, unable to think why or how or—

"Miss Gilbert?"

Her name was an annoying blackfly, buzzing around her head, adding to the pounding inside. She reached to swipe it away—then tilted sideways.

Oh dear.

Something wasn't right.

Strong arms broke her fall, lifting her up against a chest that smelled of leather and horses and man. Her face pressed against a warm neck, and for the first time in her life, she felt safe. Protected. As if the arms of God Himself held her aloft. Ahh, but she could live here.

Slowly, the wooziness ebbed away, and as it did, the pounding in her head crept back. So did light and the sound of Captain Thatcher's low voice.

". . .a room. Now!"

She winced. Why was he so loud? Who was he upbraiding? Summoning all her strength, she lifted her head. The blurry outline of a public room sharpened into focus, as did a pungent waft of ale. Her stomach flipped, and she laid her head back down.

The ends of the captain's hair brushed against her cheek as he strode across the room and mounted some stairs. Somewhere toward the back of her mind—far, *far* back—she knew she ought to protest this cradling of her body against a man who wasn't her intended. But he was so warm. So solid. The captain's sturdy embrace held her together and mended holes in her heart she hadn't known were torn.

Still, that didn't make it right.

Once again she forced her head up, immediately regretting the loss of the comforting nook between his neck and shoulder. "I can walk on my own, sir."

"You can fall on your own too." His voice grumbled against her ear.

His boot kicked open a door, and several breaths later, he laid her down on a cloud. Her eyelids drooped. It would be so easy to give in to this pampering. To lie about like a queen with this handsome knight to do her bidding.

Heat jolted through her, and her eyes popped wide. Handsome? Captain Thatcher? Her gaze sharpened on the worried brown eyes staring down at her, the swollen nose, the scars and lines. His was no conventional beauty, but that didn't make him any less striking. Indeed, she'd never seen a more attractive man.

The thought burned through her from head to toe. What kind of bride was she, thinking so fondly of another? She pushed up to her elbows, and the ceiling spun in a wide circle.

"Be at ease, Miss Gilbert." The captain's big hand guided her back to the counterpane. "I'll get you to your baronet soon enough. I vow it."

"But I. . ."

She what? The draperies began to pull shut again, making it hard to see and even to think. Yet she had to tell him. Something urgent. Something important. . .but what was it she wanted to say?

"Shh," he murmured. "Rest now."

"You are so kind," she whispered. That was it! He *was* kind, despite his gruff exterior. And now that she'd told him, she could let go.

So she did.

Women had called Samuel many things over the years. Cold. Taciturn. Cagey and evasive. But kind? He frowned. Miss Abigail Gilbert could see the best in a baited bear about to rip off a man's head.

Fine dots of perspiration glistened on her fair brow, and he clenched his fingers to keep from brushing back the damp tendrils sticking to her temples. Even ill, the woman was a beauty. Almost angelic the way her long lashes curved shut against her pink cheeks. His gaze drifted, pausing for a moment on the full lips so easy to coax a smile from, on to the fine line of her neck, then swept the rest of her body. Alarm rose in increments the longer he studied her. She was still. Too still. Sweet heavens! Was she yet breathing?

He dropped to his knees and leaned over her, practically cheek to cheek, praying to God he'd feel a flutter of breath against his skin. If she died, here, now, he'd have no one to blame but himself for exposing her to such illness. How had things spiraled so out of control?

Faint as a faery's whisper, a warm wisp of air kissed his face. He sank back on his haunches, blowing out a long breath. She'd be all right. Of course she would. He'd settle for nothing less. Besides, when the babe had first taken ill, hadn't little Emma appeared as close to death's door as—

Emma!

He shot to his feet and stalked out of the room. The child was likely even now squalling up a storm for having been left alone in the carriage.

Hawker would have his neck for being so careless with the babe.

A few patrons dotted the public room. Their eyes burned through his riding cloak as he blazed past them and stormed out the front door. As soon as the wood slapped shut behind him, he stopped. Ten yards ahead, where the carriage should have been, nothing but empty gravel met his gaze. Had a dull-witted stable boy retired the coach without first checking inside?

He veered left, his boots pounding the ground with each stride. Hopefully Emma still slept in her basket and she'd be no worse for the wear of having been left behind.

Breezing through the wide stable doors, he swept the area with a wild gaze, all the while listening with his whole body for a whimper or a cry. A few hooves stamped the ground. Straw rustled. Pilgrim's ears flicked and her nose raised at his entrance. He'd have to tend to her later.

Over in one corner, two ostlers rehashed their exploits of the night before as they worked on brushing down some horses. But other than their chatter and the normal sounds of a working stable, not a single baby wail rent the air.

Samuel swung right and closed in on the yellow carriage. Had Emma slept through the ordeal, then? He yanked open the door and peered in. No basket. No baby.

Blast!

Wheeling about, he stomped over to the men. "Have you seen a babe in a basket? She was in that carriage over there." He hitched his thumb over his shoulder.

Only one paused from his work, his head shaking. "No, sir. Weren't no little 'un in there, leastwise not when the coach were brought in."

Samuel's chest tightened. He tipped his hat to the man and beat a trail back outside. Had the postilion taken her inside the inn? But if so, why hadn't he seen the man or Emma in the taproom?

Fear for the child's safety punched him in the gut, and he increased his pace, eating up the ground with long-legged steps. This time he shot toward the back entrance of the inn, rather than the front. A stone stairwell led to the lower level, and he flew down the flagstones. He'd start at the bottom and work his way to the top. If he had to tear the inn apart floor by floor, so be it. He *would* find the child. He had to.

But what if he didn't?

Please, God.

Pushing down doubt, he shoved the door open—and a blessed, barking cough pealed out from a room down the corridor. He dashed along the smoky passageway and flew into a large kitchen. Near a wall lined with shelves of crockery, a plump woman on a stool patted Emma on the back, little puffs of flour wafting off her sleeves with the movement.

Samuel's shoulders sagged, tension draining.

At the center of the room, the cook looked up from where she stood chopping a chicken, and aimed the butcher knife at him. "Guests aren't allowed down here. Best be off with you, then."

"That's my child." He nodded toward the babe and advanced.

At the sound of his voice, Emma turned, her rosy cheeks splitting wide in a grin. She flailed a chubby fist toward him, greeting him with a rattling coo.

He reached for the babe and nodded at the woman. "Thank you."

The woman handed Emma over with a cancerous gaze. "For shame, sir! Leaving a little one unattended, and an ill one at that."

The cook chimed in from her post at thc table. "Aye. What's this world coming to when a father leaves behind his baby like a forgotten loaf of bread?"

It was reasonable to believe the cook assumed he was Emma's father. Unreasonable, however, was the queer catch of his breath and lonely ache in his soul—especially when Emma reached for his hat and tugged it sideways. What would it feel like to hold a child of his own?

One by one, he removed Emma's fingers from the brim of his hat and retreated, as much from the strange notion as from the cook, who yet brandished her big knife. "I assure you, ladies, that it was necessary. Good day."

He ducked out the door, the last of the cook's words stabbing him in the back.

"That child needs a mother."

He winced. She couldn't be more right. Emma did need a mother, and well did he know it. Going to live with an aunt didn't guarantee a happy ending, a lesson he'd learned the hard way long ago.

Gaining the servant's stairway, he ascended, keeping a strong hold on the girl wriggling against his shoulder. No doubt she'd be hungry soon. Thunderation! Should he turn back and once again face the two women of wrath to beg a bowl of porridge?

He paused at the top of the stairs, but as luck would have it, the wire-haired innkeeper swung around a corner and headed his way.

The man's eyes narrowed as he drew close. "This part of the inn is not for guests. Have you lost your way, sir?"

"No, just retrieving something I lost. Could you send up a bowl of porridge, some tea, and a mug of warm milk?"

The innkeeper eyed him for a moment. "I could, but I have yet to see a coin from you."

Really? The man wanted to quibble over coins while he stood here with a squirming babe? He dug in his pocket with his free hand while Emma once again yanked his hat sideways, cutting off half his vision. Even so, he held out a shilling—one of his last. "Will this suffice for now?"

The innkeeper snatched it, the offering easing the creases on his brow. "Aye."

"Good." Samuel brushed past him and worked his way upward to Miss Gilbert's room. Once inside, he set Emma down and pulled off his hat, giving the worn felt to her. The girl immediately bit into the brim, her big blue eyes smiling up at him.

Samuel couldn't stop his own smile from wavering across his lips. Emma was a charmer—and Hawker was a fool for having sent her away.

Turning from Emma, he eyed Miss Gilbert. She lay exactly where he'd left her, cheeks unnaturally flushed, eyes closed. His smile faded—then disappeared altogether when she suddenly thrashed her head side to side.

"No. No! Do not shut me away. Not again!" Her eyes flew open, glassy and abnormally bright. "Please, I beg you. . ." She looked right at him but not really. Whatever she saw wasn't him. "Why, Papa? Why did you send me off alone?"

Her *father* sent her on this journey alone? Samuel fisted his hands, a fire hotter than Abby's fever burning through him. He'd ask what sort of man would do that to his daughter—except he knew all too well.

Her voice softened to a whimper. "You just left. Did not even say goodbye. Do you not love me?"

Her words knocked him sideways, his gut hardening to a sickening knot. It wasn't right, this pain of hers, this anguish, and now he finally understood her determined flight to Penrith.

Dropping to his knees at her side, he blew out his tension through his nose and brushed back the damp hair sticking to her face. "Shh, Miss Gilbert. All is well. You're not alone. I'll not leave you."

At his assurance, her eyes rolled back and she went limp. Alarmed, Samuel bent closer, praying to God for breath and life. So fair a frame should not have to bear the fire of such a fever—especially for one who'd apparently come from a hellish existence.

God, please! Would that I might take this illness in her stead. Grant her peace, God. Grant her Your peace.

Minutes passed, and thankfully, Miss Gilbert's breathing evened. Perspiration yet dotted her brow, but she lay serenely enough that he pulled back.

With Miss Gilbert quieted, food on the way, and the child entertained, Samuel left the lady's bedside and sank onto a chair. Scrubbing a hand over his face, he took care not to touch the tender part of his nose. He'd been on some hair-raising journeys in his time. But this one? His hand dropped to his lap. This one was beginning to trouble him the most. It scared him, this growing need to protect the woman and the child as if they were his own.

And he wasn't afraid of anything.

CHAPTER FIFTEEN

Abby's eyes opened to blurry outlines in a fuzzy world. Was this another dream? She blinked and—slowly—all the blobby shapes began to separate into individual objects. The table by her bed. The basin atop it. The man sleeping on a chair with a babe sprawled across his chest.

What? She blinked again. This might be a dream, for never would she have imagined the sweet way Captain Thatcher nestled Emma in his arms. His stubbly cheek rested against the top of the baby's head, a contrast of fair and rugged, dark and light. Asleep, the hard lines of the captain's face softened, erasing cares and years and burdens so that he was a young man again—albeit a bit battered. His nose yet sported a gash, and a purple bruise spread from his temple to his eye.

Abby shifted, and a cloth fell from her forehead. She reached for it and pulled the nearly dried bit of rag away, trying in vain to remember if she'd been the one to put it there. Had she forgotten, or had the captain been bathing her brow? Either way, the treatment had apparently worked, for she no longer shivered or sweated with a fever.

Emboldened, she risked a swallow. No sharp pain. No more fire burned, no tenderness or swelling. Only a slight ache remained.

"How do you fare?" The captain's low voice crept across the room, his eyes open now and studying her with a worried gaze.

"Better—" Her voice garbled, and she cleared her throat. "The room no longer spins."

And it didn't, leastwise not while she was lying prone. Tentatively, Abby pushed up to sit—and still no dizziness swooped in. Light did, though. A sunray cut through the length of the room, beaming in a straight line from between the nearly closed draperies to her eyes. Judging by the slope of it, she estimated the day was well spent. Had she slept several hours, then?

Turning from the brilliance, she faced the captain. "You must think me a pampered princess. I am sorry to have wasted the day away."

"It's been two."

Stunned, her lips parted, but no words came out. *Two* days? Surely she'd heard wrong. "Pardon me, but what did you say?"

Emma stirred, rubbing her face against the captain's shirt. Then she planted her chubby little hands against his broad chest and pushed up, craning her neck to peer at Abby. A coo burbled out of her.

The captain rose. In three strides, he swiped up a chunk of bread from off a table near the window, then settled the girl on the floor with it. Emma gnawed the crust—until he started to walk away. Big tears shimmered in her eyes, and her mouth opened in a wail.

Without a word, Captain Thatcher turned back and pulled his hat off the table, then handed it to the girl. Immediately, Emma crushed it to her chest, forgetting all about her upset.

Abby couldn't help but smile at the scene. Whether he'd admit it or not, a big heart beat beneath the captain's wrinkled waistcoat.

He dragged the chair to the side of the bed and faced her. "We arrived yesterday afternoon. You slept the night through and most of today."

La! Then she had heard right. Abby sank into the pillow, the reality of the captain's words seeping in. Surely by now Sir Jonathan was worried sick by her late arrival and was out searching the highways and byways for her. "I stalled our journey," she murmured, then looked up at the weary captain. "And left you alone to tend to Emma."

"And you."

Her nose wrinkled in confusion. If she'd been sleeping the whole time, what kind of tending could she have possibly needed?

"What do you mean?"

He scratched the side of his chin, the raspy noise a reminder of his manhood. "You were delirious into the early hours of the night. Thrashing about. Mumbling about your Sir Fanciness."

"It is Sir Jonathan and—" She gasped. The *early* hours of the night? "Do not tell me, Captain, that you spent the entire night alone with me in my room."

"You were ill." His hand dropped, and he shrugged. "I couldn't very well leave you by yourself."

Did the man have no sense of propriety whatsoever? She pressed her lips to keep from gaping. "You could not have hired a serving girl to sit with me?"

A storm brewed in his eyes, a dark warning that she'd pushed him too far. "Believe it or not, lady, the day I set out for work on the heath, I wasn't expecting a journey to the north, especially not one that would take more than a fortnight. I don't carry as much coin on me as your Sir Fancy—"

"Jonathan!"

She winced at her shrill tone, shrewish as her stepmother's. By all that was righteous, was she turning into the ill-tempered woman?

The captain flattened his palm against her brow. True concern pulled at the sides of his mouth. "Is the fever returning?"

"No." She pushed his hand away, overly aware of the warmth of his skin against hers. "I should not have spoken so forcefully. Forgive me for such ingratitude. I thank you for your care, truly, but I have a reputation to uphold. If anyone should find us thus and report back to the baronet, he would not have me."

The truth tasted bitter. Whether Sir Jonathan loved her or not, his social station demanded he avoid any hint of scandal. He was taking a big enough risk marrying her, a nobody with naught to offer but her dowry.

Captain Thatcher's jaw hardened. "That, Miss Gilbert, would be his loss."

No. He was wrong. It would be entirely her loss, for she had nothing to go back home to.

"You do not understand." Her throat tightened, and for a moment she feared that the illness really was returning. There was no way the captain could grasp how horrid her life had been, dressed in the trappings of a beloved daughter yet living each day reviled and berated. Just thinking of going back to her stepmother's sharp tongue and her sisters' digging remarks sent a shiver across her shoulders.

"After last night, I understand far more than you credit." The captain's gaze burned into hers. "You are running from an unhappy existence toward a man you hope will value you for the gem that you are."

She sucked in a sharp breath, unsure what shocked the most—that he could so easily sum her up in so few words. . .or that he'd earnestly called her a gem. But no. It was neither. What really stunned was the casual way he meted out truth with no pretense or guile whatsoever.

But that didn't mean she'd admit to it. Not to him. Not to anyone.

She lifted her chin. "Suffice it to say, Captain, that a lady never—ever—shares a room with a man who is not her husband, illness or not."

He said nothing for a long while, then ever so slowly, he nodded. "All right. Don't fret. It's highly unlikely anyone here holds the ear of your baronet, so rest assured not a soul will go telling him of your sordid night alone with me. Besides, no one knows us, and frankly, I doubt that anyone cares."

A sharp rap on the door belied his words.

Though still fully dressed in her gown of yesterday, Abby yanked the counterpane up to her chin. Heaven help her. Ill or not, were she to be found in a bedchamber with a man, it would be her ruination.

Samuel sprang to his feet. Scoundrels didn't usually knock so politely, but that didn't stop him from unsheathing his knife. He'd not be caught off guard again—especially not with a woman and child within range of harm.

He cracked open the door and peeked out, every sense heightened. Nothing met his gaze—leastwise not at eye level. Standing only as tall as his waist, a smudge-faced boy gawked up at him. The lad retreated a step when their gazes locked.

"Y–you be Cap'n Thatcher?"

He frowned. Such trepidation didn't usually bother him, but this time it nicked him in the heart. Since when had he grown tired of being feared? It was a protection. A shield. His frown deepened. So much time spent with Miss Gilbert and Emma was changing him in ways he couldn't fathom.

He scanned the length of the corridor behind the boy, on the off chance the lad was a setup. No one lurked about nor were any doors cracked open. Nothing moved, save for a tree branch casting a shadow on the wall from a window at the end of the passageway.

Satisfied for now, he finally answered. "I'm Thatcher."

"Then this be for you, sir." The boy held up a folded slip of paper.

The instant his fingers pinched the note, the lad whipped around and tore down the passageway. His untucked shirttail flew behind him and was the last thing to disappear down the stairway.

Samuel stared a moment longer, making sure no ill surprises popped up, then tucked his knife back into his boot and closed the door.

By now, Miss Gilbert sat on the edge of the bed, gripping the coverlet with both hands. Little Emma rumbled a cough and started crawling his way.

"Who was it?"

The lady's voice was a shiver. It wasn't right, this fear he'd brought upon her. She never should have been caught up in this mess. A pox upon Shankhart!

Samuel allowed a small smile, hoping to calm her worry. "It was just a boy. Don't fret."

The coverlet dipped an inch. "What did he want?"

He left the question dangling in the air. Sometimes the better part of valor was silence. Turning the paper over, he scanned for a name, a seal, anything to hint as to who'd sent the note, but it was blank on both sides.

A tug on his trousers drew his attention away as Emma pulled herself up on his leg. He stood poised to snatch her should she totter backward and crack her head. She wobbled—yet held tight to his leg, baby chatter burbling past her lips. She'd be fine.

He focused back on the note. Unfolding the paper, he read three hastily scratched words, barely legible:

I see you.

One by one, the hairs at the nape of his neck stood out like wires. Without moving a muscle, his eyes darted around the room. He knew in his head no one could possibly see him inside these four walls, but that didn't stop his heart from racing. The weight of a thousand pairs of unseen eyes pressed down on him, making it hard to breathe. For the sake of Emma and Miss Gilbert, he fought the urge to rave about like a madman, knife bared, looking for a killer who wasn't there.

"Despite your earlier reassurance, Captain, apparently someone knows you are here. Or is the message for me?"

Would to God that it wasn't! He crumpled the paper and shoved it into his pocket, then forced a soothing tone to his voice. "No, it's nothing."

Liar!

The dip of Miss Gilbert's brow concurred.

Bending, he peeled Emma's fingers from his trousers and eased her bottom to the floor. As soon as she sat steady, he strode to the window and slid back an edge of the drape with one finger.

Their first-floor chamber overlooked the front of the inn. There were no outbuildings from this view, so no one could possibly be secreted inside a shadowy corner, peering out a window at him, or worse, aiming a muzzle. Only a stand of trees stood opposite the drive, maybe ten yards off. He narrowed his eyes, staring so hard his eyes watered. Branches. Greenery. Nothing large enough to suggest a villain hunkered down for a shot at him.

Behind him, footsteps padded on the floor. "Clearly there is more to that note than you are telling me. What did it say?"

He pulled back his hand and the drapes fell shut, sealing them off from the world outside. A blessing and a curse, that.

Turning, he faced Miss Gilbert, hating that he couldn't tell her the truth—and hating the truth even more. Her skin glowed white, a contrast from yesterday's flaming patches of colour on her cheeks. She was definitely on the mend, but had all of her strength returned?

"Do you feel equal to watching Emma?" he asked.

A small crease lined her brow. "You are frightening me, Captain."

"There is nothing to fear. I only need to step out for a while."

Her big brown eyes searched his face. "Why?"

He clenched his jaw. He'd rather take on a rock-fisted brawler bent on smashing his brains out than answer that question.

So he parried with one of his own. "Do you trust me?".

Her nose scrunched, as if the query smelled of something rotten. Which it did. Truly, it wasn't fair of him to twist the conversation back onto her like this, but it was necessary.

Her lips parted, closed, then parted again. "Yes, Captain. I do trust you. Implicitly."

The conviction in her tone was stunning enough, but the veracity in her gaze stole his breath.

He reached out, tentatively. She held still. Assured she wouldn't flinch or recoil, he stroked his knuckle along her cheek. Skin soft as the babe's warmed beneath his touch, more delicate and velvety than he imagined.

"Believe me when I say, Miss Gilbert, that I will allow nothing bad to happen to you or Emma." The words came out husky, and he swallowed against the thickness in his throat.

"Very well." She nodded and pulled back. "I shall tend Emma."

Hard to tell what shook him more, the foreboding note or the loss of their connection. Giving himself a mental shake—what *was* he thinking to have caressed her so?—he sidestepped the woman and gathered his hat from off the floor. He jammed it on his head, then shrugged into his coat and grabbed his gun. Hopefully he wouldn't need it.

Behind him, a hand rested on his sleeve.

"Be careful, Captain."

This time he pulled away, unsure if he should feel angry that she plagued him to be cautious or touched that she cared enough to warn him. He settled on neither, choosing to ignore the host of foreign emotions the woman kindled in his gut.

He stopped at the door and tipped his head at her. "Stay in the room."

Then he slipped out of the chamber and stole down the corridor, using all his powers of stealth. Keeping to the edge of the stairs—less chance for squeaking a loose board—he descended into the public room. Two men shared a pipe in one corner, but he quickly discounted any danger they might pose. Both were grey-headed and incapable of wrestling with a cat let alone him. The rest of the tables sat empty.

Near the kitchen door, a boy strolled out, chewing on a pastry. . . the lad who'd delivered the note.

Samuel collared the boy before he could see him coming. He guided the lad to a shadowy corner, away from prying eyes. But to be extra cautious, he kept his tone quiet as he crouched to eye level. "Who gave you that message?"

Fear rampaged over the boy's face. "D-dunno," he stuttered.

Samuel narrowed his eyes. "How can that be? Was it a ghost?"

"No, sir." The boy shrank until his back hit the wall. "Never seen him afore, that's all."

"So, it was a man, hmm?"

The boy nodded. "He gave me a shilling to bring that note to you."

Suspicion prickled across his shoulders. Most would only pay a ha'penny or maybe a thruppence to have a note delivered. But a whole shilling? The sender was either very careless with his money—or had a good supply of coin. Had Shankhart mended and tracked him here so soon? Or had he sent one of his henchmen to torment him?

"This man, tell me of him."

The boy's lower lip trembled, but to his credit, his voice didn't crack. "Can't, sir."

"Why not?"

"I din't see him. He stayed in the shadows, out in the stable."

Samuel shoved his hand into his pocket and pulled out one of his last shillings—for he'd not be bested by a scoundrel even in the paying of a lad.

"For your trouble." He held out the coin.

Eyes widening, the boy snatched the money quick as a pauper—which he wasn't. Not anymore. It was he who was well on his way to the workhouse if he kept parting with the sparse amount he had left.

He rose, and the boy scurried past him with a hasty, "Thank ye!"

Leaving the inn behind, Samuel strode across the backyard, pulling out his gun yet keeping it concealed. It wouldn't do to go scaring any ostlers lurking about the stable, but neither would he run headlong into an ambush.

He slid around the door on silent feet, immediately easing into a shadow. No one moved, for no one was about. Not here in the large work area, anyway. The scene was eerily reminiscent of a week ago when he'd gone in search of Miss Gilbert back at the Laughing Dog.

Satisfied no one hid beneath the workbench or behind a line of tack hanging on a wall, he padded over to the long corridor lined with stalls and began methodically searching each one. The first two were empty, standing ready to house the next horses arriving at the inn. A beauty of a black Belgian eyed him warily in the third. And at the fourth, where Pilgrim lodged, a roar ripped out of his throat.

"No!"

White-hot rage flamed in his gut as he flung open the half door and dashed inside, trading his gun for his knife. Pilgrim lay on her side, hooves tied, rope biting tight into the horsey flesh of her forelegs. A single crude word was painted in whitewash on her belly:

SOON

Samuel sliced through the ropes, barely able to thank God that his horse yet breathed, so keen was the fury burning through him.

If war was what Shankhart wanted, he just got his wish.

CHAPTER SIXTEEN

A knife to the kidneys. A shot to the head. Maybe even a fast drop from a short rope. Samuel scowled. No, none of those were good enough.

He slackened the reins as Pilgrim tramped along the rocky trail. If God called him home today, he feared the gates of heaven might not open to him—not with such molten anger simmering inside his veins. It was wrong, of course, to clutch on to these cruel thoughts of vengeance against Shankhart, but sweet mercy! He was a mortal, was he not? Flesh and blood. More sinner than saint, for though he tried, he could not let go of his rage. Not when his best horse yet favored her front foreleg where the rope had sliced into it, nor when he witnessed the fear in Miss Gilbert's eyes. And especially not when he thought of the threat hanging over all their heads. Shankhart or his lackeys could strike at any moment—or not at all. . .and that was almost worse.

Keeping the carriage well within sight, Samuel eased Pilgrim down the rise. For two days he'd had to temper their pace, slowing their progress, hoping and praying all the while that the gouge on his horse's leg would heal quickly. Besides, Miss Gilbert and little Emma were still on the mend themselves, so the sluggish pace suited. Leastwise, that's what he told himself. But were he honest, the real reason he plodded along and kept to the shadows was to remain vigilant while nursing the hatred he bore toward Shankhart. Next time they met, he'd have no qualms about shooting the blackguard right through the heart.

He hung his head, conviction bubbling sour at the back of his throat.

God, have mercy, on Shankhart and on me.

A rumble of thunder lifted his head, and he studied the horizon. While the entire day had been sullen, now the pewter sky deepened to an unholy blackness. A dark bank of clouds advanced like a shield wall and would soon bear down upon their heads. He sniffed, then frowned as a pungent tang hit his nostrils. Earthy. Acrid. Pilgrim's ears twitched, indicating the horse sensed the same.

This was more than a summer rain. A tempest was about to break, as potent and ugly as his rage.

Carefully, Samuel urged Pilgrim to up the pace. By his best judgment, they were halfway between inns, so even if they did turn around, they'd not outrun the storm by the time they reached shelter. Yet pressing on only brought them closer to the menacing—

Lightning struck. Deafeningly close. The zing of it raised the hair on his arms. The accompanying boom reverberated in his chest. Pilgrim reared, and Samuel held tight, flattening forward against the horse's neck while working to get his mount under control.

Ahead, the carriage horses bolted.

Blast it!

Samuel dug in his heels, coaxing Pilgrim into a controlled run. He trailed the bouncing coach by twenty yards, wishing to heaven he could give Pilgrim free rein, but any faster and he'd lame his friend for certain.

Another crack boomed. The carriage lurched sideways, careening over rocks. Crashing into ruts.

God, protect Miss Gilbert and little Emma.

The space between him and the coach lessened in increments, until miraculously, the carriage stopped. Samuel heaved back on the reins, halting Pilgrim barely a pace or two behind it. Thankfully, the thing was still in one piece—but a very lopsided piece at that. The carriage listed hard to the right, the entire back end jutting down toward the rear left wheel.

Samuel swung off Pilgrim and neared the broken coach just as the postilion rounded the side and joined him. They both crouched as the wind picked up and the first stabs of rain fired down from the sky.

The postilion's curse rang out with the next peal of thunder. "I knew this carriage weren't sound! But did old man Herrick listen to me? No, not a bit of it. Carpin' crow! I should've insisted on a different coach."

Samuel was inclined to agree. Only God knew how many years and miles this carriage had seen. Judging by the looks of it, far too many. He narrowed his eyes and trailed his finger along the curve of the spring—leastwise as far as he was able. The bolt holding the spring arm had completely sheared off so that the casing had ripped loose.

Rising, he met the postilion's gaze. "Is there shelter nearby?"

The man made a grab for his hat as the next gust of wind lifted it. Holding tightly to the black felt, he bobbed his head. "Farmer Bigby, up past Bramble Creek."

Samuel tugged down the brim of his own hat as the sky turned to an unnatural shade of greenish grey. Hopefully Bramble Creek wasn't far off. "We best make haste, then. Unhook the horses. I'll see to the lady and—"

"No need, Captain. Emma and I are accounted for."

The sweet voice in his ear was as startling as the next peal of thunder. He jerked aside. Barely an arm's length away stood Miss Gilbert, Emma blinking wide-eyed in her arms. "How did you. . . ?"

He shook his head. No sense asking how she'd managed to crawl out of a crook-sloped hulk of a carriage with a baby in tow, for such was the wonder of Miss Abigail Gilbert. Glancing about, he spied a boulder just about the right size to employ as a mounting block.

"Come along. This storm is about to break in earnest."

She followed, but not without questions. "What about the carriage? Will you be able to fix it? Where are we going?"

He stopped and reached for Emma, letting Miss Gilbert's queries blow away in the wind. Clutching the child to his chest with one arm, he offered Miss Gilbert his hand to aid her atop the rock. "Climb up."

She frowned at his upturned palm. "Surely you are not suggesting I ride your horse."

Big plops of rain began to hammer harder, popping like grapeshot as they hit his riding cloak. He grabbed her hand. "It's not a suggestion."

"But I cannot manage your horse!" She pulled back.

He held tight. "I'm not expecting you to. Now mount."

Fear flashed in her eyes. Odd. Surely being a gentlewoman, she had riding experience. Didn't she? He squeezed her fingers. "Don't worry, Miss Gilbert. I'll be with you the whole time. I'll keep you and Emma safe, I vow it."

"Do not tell me you intend to ride along with me." Her nostrils flared, indignation as thick in her tone as the humidity in the air.

"Propriety be hanged, lady! Do you see this lightning? If we don't get on my horse soon, you'll have more than proper etiquette to worry about. Now grab the saddle and hike yourself up."

Thunder boomed an accompaniment to his order, and a breath later, the sky ripped open, unleashing a downpour. Without another word, Miss Gilbert heaved herself atop Pilgrim. He handed her Emma, then swung up behind them. For a moment, he fumbled with the wet tie on his riding coat, then whipped it off and flung it around the lady and child, covering most of her and all of Emma. They'd still get wet, but not nearly as much.

Miss Gilbert turned her head, her warm breath puffing against his cheek. "Thank you, but now you will be wet and cold."

Wet, yes, but cold? Not a chance, not with the feel of her body tucked against his.

"This way." The postilion shouted above the roar of wind.

Samuel urged Pilgrim into line behind the man, who'd tethered the other carriage horse to his mount. As they worked their way along a cow trail, the storm pitched wicked gusts of wind and rain, sharp and frigid.

But Samuel paid the harsh weather no heed. How could he? The only thing he could feel was the woman pressed against his chest. The softness of her. The heat of her body. The way she fit so perfectly against him.

Though he ought not, Samuel leaned closer and inhaled her orange-water scent, the sweet fragrance mixing with the wildness of the storm. If he bent any nearer, his lips would be against the bare flesh of her neck, and the craving to taste that skin charged through him, settling low in his belly.

He tensed. What was this strange urge? He'd doubled-up with women before, hauling them to safety more times than he could count. Such was his job.

He clutched the reins tighter as a new realization slapped him hard. This wasn't a job anymore. Not with this woman.

Involuntarily, his arms tightened against her, encircling her, drawing her close, sheltering her from the storm—or so he told himself. Were he honest, the physical reaction stemmed from so much more. And that scared him more than facing Shankhart. For the first time in his life, he was unsure what to do with or how to manage the mounting desire to make a woman—*this* woman—his own.

He frowned—yet he didn't pull away. He couldn't. Such was the magnetism of Miss Gilbert. If her baronet could read his thoughts, the man would more than reconsider his proposal.

He'd challenge Samuel to a duel of honor.

Abby clutched the squirming Emma tightly against her chest. How terrifying it must be to endure such a tempest cloaked in the darkness of the captain's riding coat. She ought to be squirming with fright herself, seated atop the man's fearsome horse, riding headlong into rain that cut sideways.

But oddly, fear wasn't a consideration, not with the captain's strong arms holding her firmly in place. She shifted as the horse climbed a rise, and the captain's strength pulsed through her. He guided them through the blackest of storms as if nothing but a few pesky drops of water fell from the sky.

With each step of the horse, she tried not to feel the ride of his body behind her. A worthless effort. She could think of nothing else but the hard muscles pressed against her back or the touch of his thighs bumping into her. It was licentious, this position. She ought to lean forward, put what distance she could between him and her. But God help her, she didn't want to. Didn't *ever* want to, such was the draw of the man.

Heedless of propriety, she turned her face and pressed her cheek against his chest, seeking a measure of shelter from the pelting rain.

Without his cloak, the soaked fabric of his shirt and waistcoat moulded against his flesh, and she breathed in his scent of horse and leather and possibility. What would it be like to be loved by the untamed Captain Thatcher? Tingles shivered through her, and in response, he tucked his chin, protecting the top of her head.

Using the wriggling Emma as an excuse, she leaned into him, telling herself she needed such closeness to balance as the horse fought for footing against the storm. It was wrong, though, and she knew it. If her stepmother witnessed her brazen behaviour, she'd be struck with more than a tongue-lashing. The surety of a stinging slap needled the cheek not shielded by the captain's warmth, and Abby forced herself to turn away and face the rain instead.

She blinked as water blinded her view. What a cow-eyed schoolgirl she'd become. What was wrong with her? Inwardly, she scolded herself as soundly as her stepmother might. Yet surely, once she arrived at Brakewell Hall and reached the arms of Sir Jonathan, all these unbidden feelings for Captain Thatcher would vanish. Yes, that was it. Of course they would. She entertained naught but a silly infatuation for the man because she'd paid him to look out for her. Any woman in her place would feel the same. In fact, had Fanny remained, the woman would've been positively moonstruck in his presence.

That settled, she eased little Emma around and rubbed the child's back with one hand, a motion that soothed her as well. Shortly thereafter, the postilion ahead of them halted, and they dismounted in front of a whitewashed croft. Hardly bigger than the nearby stable, the squat building braved the onslaught like a stalwart sailor, used to lashing winds and driving rain. Loosened by a wild gust, a few pieces of the thatched roof near the corner waved a greeting.

Not so the man who flung open the door. He welcomed them with the barrel of a musket.

Immediately, the captain sidestepped in front of her and Emma, blocking them with his wide shoulders.

"Be ye daft?" A woman's shrill voice from inside the cottage blended with the howl of the storm. " 'T'ain't fit for beasts out there, let alone travelers. Let them in, man!"

Captain Thatcher raised both hands, his wet frock coat riding the strong lines of his back. "We mean no harm. We only ask for shelter."

Abby huddled closer to him, seeking haven from the captain's big frame just in case the crofter wouldn't allow them in. A few grumbles later, the man pushed the door wider and stepped aside. And thank goodness, because Emma started to cry.

The captain ushered her and the child in first, keeping close behind them as they entered. Abby warmed immediately from his watchful care and from escaping the cold rain. The postilion followed suit.

And the woman howled again. "Why, stuff my goose! That be you, Darby Cleaver?"

Doffing his hat, the postilion shook his head like a dog, water droplets flying everywhere. "Aye, m'um. We broke down on the road just afore the storm picked up."

"See?" The woman turned to her husband, planting her fists on her hips. "And you about to send them to glory."

"Wheest!" The man blew air through his teeth, his hook nose bunching from the effort. He lowered his gun—though he didn't let go of it—and pinched the woman's cheek. "Just protectin' my fair beauty."

"Ach! Off with ye." She flicked her fingers at him, yet despite the action, the warmth in her voice radiated volumes of love.

As she bounced Emma, quieting the child somewhat, Abby studied the woman. A ruffled cap, which at some point might've been white, clung to the top of the woman's head. Lines carved into her face at the sides of her mouth and near the creases of her eyes. Those eyes might have shone a brilliant blue once but were now bleached to the colour of a sun-washed August sky. The woman wasn't old, but neither was she young. Rather, she was timeless, her apron holding in an eternity of love and life and laughter. She was the kind of woman with whom you could share a pot of tea and your deepest secrets. Abby's heart swelled. Would this be what her mother might've looked like had she lived?

As if the woman sensed her perusal, she swooped over to Abby and corralled her with an arm about the shoulders, pulling her away from the captain's side. "Come along, child. We'll get ye and yer little one into some dry clothes, then some hot broth is in order, I think."

Abby tried to keep up, but with wet skirts sticking to her legs and the woman's brisk gait, she was glad for the fleshy arm guiding her across the small main room. Dry clothes would be heaven, but anything more seemed like an imposition. She glanced sideways at the woman. "Please do not trouble yourself about the broth."

Just then a sharp cough barked out of Emma, and Abby recanted. Though the child had made amazing progress in regaining her health, it wouldn't do to extend a calling card for her illness to repay a visit.

"On second thought, some broth would be nice." She smiled. "And thank you."

The men's low talk about horse stabling and carriage repair faded as the woman ushered her into a back room. A bed with a rumpled mantle filled nearly the whole space, save for a small table with a candle, a crooked chair in the corner, and a battered chest against one wall with a shelf above it.

The woman flung open the chest's lid and yanked out a shift and a gown, both the colour of sand. Straightening, she faced Abby and shoved out her offering with one hand while collecting Emma with the other. "No doubt the garments will be too big and not nearly as fine as yer used to, but all the same, they will serve ye well until we get yer gown dried. I'll see to yer wee one while you change."

The woman bustled past her and laid Emma on the bed. For a moment, Abby froze, wondering where exactly she was supposed to shed her clothes and don the dry ones. But as a shiver shimmied across her shoulders, all modesty fled, and she began the arduous task of peeling off the drenched fabric.

"Thank you for your hospitality, Mrs. . . . ?" She fished for the woman's name while she worked.

"La, child! No such formalities under this humble roof. The name's Wenna. And you be?"

Wenna? Ahh. . .so that explained the leftover Cornish lilt in the woman's voice. But what in the world was the woman doing this far north?

Shoving the wet pile aside with her foot, Abby reached for the fresh shift. "I am Abigail Gilbert, but please, call me Abby."

"Well then, Abby, pleased I am to—"

A desperate wail squealed out of Emma, cutting the woman off. Despite Wenna's murmurs and shushings, the child would have none of it as she wrangled Emma into what was likely one of her husband's shirts. Strange, that. Usually Emma was such a placid little girl.

Wenna swung the child up into her arms and faced her, bouncing Emma as she spoke. "As soon as you're dressed, let's get you, your fine man, and your youngling fed and put up for the night. We'll tuck ol' Darby Cleaver out in the byre and the rest o' ye can sleep upstairs in my boy's loft." She jerked her head toward the rafters. " 'T'ain't much, but 'tis snug and kept at the ready for my Georgie to return."

Heat crawled up Abby's neck, though she was hard-pressed to decide if it was from the woman's misunderstanding that Captain Thatcher was "her fine man" or from the niggling wish that she might want him to be. She ducked inside the billowing fabric and pulled the ample cloth over her body, mulling over what to say.

"I appreciate your offer, truly." As soon as her head popped out of the gown, she smiled. "But there is no need to put yourself out. We are more than grateful for the shelter you are providing while the storm rages, but as soon as it breaks, we shall be on our way."

"Ach! None of it." The woman wagged her head and juggled the fretting Emma to her other shoulder. "That storm's like to bluster and blow till the wee hours. Ye'll be staying the night, no doubt, and I'll not hear another word on it."

Abby bit her lip as the woman bustled past her, humming a folk tune to quiet Emma. It had been bad enough back in Stratford when the surgeon had assumed her union with the captain, but they hadn't had to share a roof with him. How was she to tell the headstrong Wenna they weren't married?

She followed the woman's swishing skirts, scrambling for the right way to broach the subject, and settled on simply being direct. "We are not married."

Wenna stopped and turned so quickly, Emma's head bobbed from the ride. "What's that you say?"

"The captain and I. . .well. . ." Abby withered beneath the woman's narrowed eyes. Perhaps the direct approach hadn't been the best idea, but she couldn't rescind it now. So, she lifted her chin. "We are not married, but I can explain—"

The woman's hand shot up, cutting her off. "Faith and honor! Then ye can't be staying here after all!"

CHAPTER SEVENTEEN

Samuel stopped on the threshold of the croft's front door. Outside, sheets of rain swallowed Farmer Bigby and the postilion, Darby Cleaver, as they dashed toward the stable, horses in tow, Pilgrim last in line. His horse needed his attention, especially that wound on her foreleg, yet Samuel turned back and shut the door behind him. Pilgrim would have to wait, for a bigger squall was about to break in here. The remnants of the older woman's harsh tone yet resounded from wall to wall. What the devil had Miss Gilbert done to offend her so?

The lady in question clutched her hands in front of her, dressed in a gown two sizes too large. Miss Gilbert's dark hair curled past her shoulders, wet and loose as a wayward girl's. Patches of colour pinked her cheeks, and her big eyes blinked wide. A smile twitched Samuel's lips. Even garbed in homespun, the woman was a beauty.

"Please, Wenna, hear me out." She dared a step closer to the farmer's wife—Wenna, apparently—and Emma nearly launched out of the woman's arms to get to her. But Miss Gilbert kept her gaze fixed on Wenna and measured out her words, slow and even. "I assure you that we bring no shame to this house. Captain Thatcher is my hired guardian, nothing more. Believe me when I say that there is not a nobler man on the face of this earth."

Samuel planted his feet to keep from staggering. He'd taken blows to the chest before, even fell out a first-story window once, landing flat on his back in a pile of crates, but none of those incidents stole his breath quite like Miss Gilbert's passionate defense.

The older woman humphed. "That may be, but this child is yours." She handed over the weeping Emma, who immediately buried her face into Miss Gilbert's neck and quit crying.

Before Miss Gilbert could respond, Wenna folded her arms, clearly not done with the battle. "I'll not be condoning no unwed mothers, no matter how fancy yer clothes be. You can stay the night, but off with the likes of ye come morning, and may God have mercy on yer soul."

Miss Gilbert's face flamed. So did the anger in Samuel's gut. While he couldn't fault the farmer's wife for jumping to such a torrid conclusion, neither could he allow it to stand unchallenged.

He stalked over to the women, his boots hitting the planks harder than necessary, and pulled up next to Miss Gilbert. Drawing from years of experience, he faced down Wenna with a stern set to his jaw. "The lady is innocent of your charge, madam. The child belongs to a friend of mine, who wishes us to deliver her to his sister. Your censure is not only unmerited but ill-mannered, for Miss Gilbert's character is above reproach. An apology is required."

Rain beat against the windows, and the glass rattled in the frames. On the hearth, an occasional ember popped out from the fire. Other than that, silence reigned, for Wenna stood mute. Her shoulders deflated in increments as his words sank in, until finally, her hands flew to her cheeks and her washed-out eyes sought Miss Gilbert's. "Mercy and grace! And me, going on so, grizzling like a badger. I beg your pardon, miss. It weren't kind o' me to think such a thing, let alone say it aloud."

Her gaze drifted to him, the droop of her floppy cap as repentant as the woman. "Nor ought I have thought poorly of you, Captain. I'll catch a scolding from my husband when he hears of it, for sure and for certain."

The sheepish tuck of Wenna's chin radiated her shame and subsequent angst over her husband's expected upbraiding. Amusement flickered through Samuel that for such a headstrong woman, the farmer's wife cared deeply about her man's opinion of her.

A small smile lifted his lips. "Then we shan't tell him."

"Well said!" Miss Gilbert laughed. "And I agree. All is forgiven,

Wenna. It was naught but a silly misunderstanding. How about I settle Emma on the floor then help you with the broth, hmm?"

"Aye, and I'll be glad for the help." A relieved grin curved the woman's mouth. "When those men come in, no doubt they'll be hungry as the horses they've settled, eh?"

Wenna winked up at him, then scurried over to the hearth, apron strings riding the current of air behind her.

Miss Gilbert turned to him, and once again his breath hitched as their gazes locked. Admiration ran deep in those brown eyes. Deep and pure. Ahh, but he could get used to that look, to the resultant twinge that charged through him from heart to gut, arousing a hunger for more. It was heady, this new craving, this reckless yearning to pull her into his arms and hold her close.

And altogether far too dangerous.

He scowled and stalked away, leaving the queer feelings shut tight inside the cottage as he strode into the storm. The drenching rain slapped him hard in the face, and he relished the sting of it. Better to lose himself in a torrent than hand over his heart to a woman.

Inside the small byre, Cleaver and Bigby yet worked to remove the coach horses' tack. Pilgrim stood to the side, casting him a poisonous eye as he pulled off his hat and shook the water from it. He patted his old friend on the neck, and Pilgrim tossed her head, making a point. "Now, now. . .you didn't think I'd leave you for long, did you?"

Crouching, he ran his fingers gingerly along the animal's foreleg, inspecting the muscles and examining the wound. Despite the harried ride through the storm, the rain had washed the gash clean, and as he peered closer, he thanked God silently that pink skin formed at the edges. A day or two more of salve and slow going, and Pilgrim would be set to rights.

Rising, he unbuckled the girth strap and called over his shoulder to the other men. "How safe is that road where we left the carriage?"

Bigby turned his head, the shorn hairs on his scalp giving the stout fellow the appearance of a great, bristly scrub brush. His large ears added to the picture, looking like handles. If you tipped the man over, he could be used to scour the floor with the top of his head. "Why do ye think I answered the door with the tip o' me musket? Been a great load o' thievin' hereabouts lately. But ne'er fear. Ye and yer lady are safe as can be now."

Thieves? He sighed. If only it were that simple. Hefting the saddle off Pilgrim, he faced the farmer. "Maybe so, but the lady's chest, all her belongings, are ripe for the picking."

Cleaver spewed out a curse as he eased off the coach horse's bridle. "It'd be a half-witted fool to plunder on a night like this."

True, but all the same, a glower weighted Samuel's brow. He'd seen one too many half-witted fools in his time, and the worst were those bent on wrongdoing. He set the saddle on the stone floor near the door, then doubled back. "All the same, soon as this storm lets up, I'd appreciate the use of your wagon outside to collect Miss Gilbert's chest."

"I'll not be refusin' ye, but neither will I venture out on this wicked night." Bigby cocked his head at him as if he were the half-wit. "Have at it on yer own, if ye like."

He nodded and returned to Pilgrim. Hauling the lady's chest on his own would be an arduous task, but a necessary one. Not only would it save the lady from a possible theft, but it would also erase any ties to them and their location.

Ties that Shankhart or his toadies might come across.

Abby pulled off the borrowed gown and folded it while Emma watched from the bed, flat on her back and chewing on her toes. It'd been a long day for the girl, and as a yawn stretched Abby's own jaw, she had to admit it'd been long for her as well.

Farmer Bigby had entertained them well into the evening with stories around the hearth, a pleasing way to pass the time while the tempest continued to rage outside. The captain, however, had seemed distant after his defense of her virtue. He'd been polite and answered when spoken to, yet Abby got the distinct impression he'd listened more to the storm than to what was going on inside the cottage walls, and the lack of his attention was a great, gaping loss.

What sort of a frivolous female was she turning into?

Casting the strange thoughts and feelings aside, she laid Wenna's gown over the back of a chair, taking care not to bump into the small table next to it and disturb the contents. The blue porcelain washbowl already sported a chip in the rim, and Wenna had made it clear that her son's belongings were not to be moved. Abby glanced at the shaving kit next to the bowl, candlelight cutting a steel-grey line along the edge of the razor. All of the man's accoutrements stood at the ready, but how long had it been since he'd used them? On a peg nearby, a white shirt hung against the wall like a ghost in the night shadows, just waiting to drape over its owner's shoulders. Though the room was sparsely furnished, the spirit of the Bigbys' son permeated everything, so pristinely did Wenna preserve it in anticipation of his return.

Cupping her hand, Abby blew out the candle, a splash of wax burning her skin from the force. All the love and hope embodied in that hung shirt and dish of soap standing at the ready sliced into her heart. No doubt her stepmother had charged the servants at home with scrubbing down her former bedroom, washing away any possible traces that Abby had ever inhabited the space. Would the woman go so far as to order the housekeeper to remove her small portrait from atop her father's desk? Would her father even miss it if she did? She frowned as she stared at the spectre of a shirt in the darkness. What would it feel like to be as loved and missed as the Bigbys' son?

She padded over to the bed, huffing out a long breath and expelling the ache in her soul lest any bitterness take root. Grousing over past ill treatment was a waste of time. Was she not on her way to a man who would cherish her? One who was even now likely fretting like a wild man over her delayed arrival?

Emma reached for her with both arms, and Abby pulled the child close, kissing the crown of her head. Snuggling them both beneath the counterpane, she traced a finger along the downy skin of Emma's cheek. However many days she had left with this sweet girl, Emma would know love and know it well.

"Sleep sweet, precious one," she whispered.

Emma's long lashes fanned against her cheeks, and Abby couldn't help but close her own eyes and dream of a dark-eyed man who, more often than not, hid beneath the brim of his hat.

What seemed like only minutes later, raised voices growled downstairs, rudely pulling her from the depths of slumber. Abby blinked her eyes open, surprised to see morning light streaming in from the loft's single window.

Rising, she shrugged into Wenna's gown once again, straining her ears to decipher the heated words bandied about below her. The captain's low tones only occasionally added to the mix. What could he possibly be quarreling about so early in the day?

Emma rolled over on the bed and made a crawling dash toward the edge. Abby snatched her up, noticing her bottom end sagged heavier than normal. "My, my, little one! You are as wet as the green grass outside."

Emma gurgled a reply and smacked her lips—signaling she cared more about a warm drink of milk than her soiled clout.

Carefully, Abby picked their way down the ladder leading to ground level. As soon as her feet hit the wooden planks, Wenna turned from the hearth.

"Ach! I knew they'd wake ye." She aimed her finger at the bickering men near the door. "Take yer squabbling outside. Ye've gone and waked the ladies!"

Wenna's husband flicked his hand in the air, batting away his wife's words as if they were no more than a swarm of gnats. But even so, he yanked open the door. "Come along, Captain. We'll check on that horse o' yers afore church. Cleaver, ye can do as ye like, and may God have mercy on yer soul."

"Bah!" The postilion jammed on his hat and stalked past all of them, muttering under his breath.

The captain shot her a look before he followed Farmer Bigby out the door, his brown eyes a mix of humour and irritation.

Abby lifted a brow at Wenna. "What was that all about?"

Wenna chuckled as she hefted a pot of porridge to the scarred wooden table. "The Cleavers ne'er were the kind to grace a pew with their backsides. 'T'aint setting right with ol' Darby that my man and yer captain see fit to worship as is fitting fer a Sunday morn. He were all fired up to get to work on that broken carriage of yours. But don't ye fret none about it." She wiped her hands on her ever-present apron and reached for Emma. "Let's get you and the little one fed, then off we'll be to church."

Emma let out a wail, and Wenna shifted the babe to her shoulder. "I'll get this one into some dry wraps, and you can don yer fine gown again. It's waiting for ye on that stool near the fire. Unless you prefer a fresh one?" She tipped her chin, indicating something behind Abby.

Abby turned, and her jaw dropped. Her mud-spattered hulk of a chest sat safely against the wall. "How did that get here?"

"Yer captain slogged through the mud late last night soon as the rain let up, and like as not had a devil of a time o' cleaning his boots when 'twas all said and done."

Warmth shot through her, and she was glad Wenna turned away with the crying Emma so she'd not witness the red flushing her cheeks. How thoughtful of the stoic captain!

By the time they were both changed and fed, Emma's tears ceased, and Abby carried her outside to a world washed fresh and smelling of meadowsweet. Wenna hooked her arm through her husband's, coaxing him away from the captain with a warning that if they didn't quit jawing, they'd all be late and have to suffer the vicar's evil eye. Abby followed behind the pair, not wishing to earn such a reprimand from Wenna, and the captain fell into step at her side.

"Hand over Emma. She's too much for you to bear on a hike through the woods." He reached for Emma, and the girl fairly leapt into his arms.

Abby smiled at the twitch of the captain's jaw, a valiant attempt to hide his own grin, no doubt. Whether he admitted it aloud or not, clearly the man was smitten with the child. Beneath that gruff exterior, a heart of compassion beat pure and strong.

Keeping to the gravelly part of the path, she lifted her hem as they skirted a puddle. Good thing she had the option to change into a fresh gown when they returned. The trek to and from church might very well leave the bottom of this one soaked and muddy. She peered up at the captain. "Thank you for retrieving my chest. It must have been a frightful task in the dark and wet."

He shrugged. "I've seen worse."

Her gaze fixed on the crescent scar near his temple. Indeed. What kind of troubles had this man seen?

Emma made a grab for his hat, and he gently pulled her grasping fingers away from the brim, then turned her around and cradled her in the crook of one arm. She bounced, clearly enjoying the ride, and Abby smiled at the scene. The captain managed little Emma with such tenderness, it was hard to reconcile with his frequent dour moods and steely looks. Surely he must owe Emma's father some kind of enormous debt.

Abby's gaze drifted from the bouncing Emma back to the man. "I am curious, Captain. . .had not Emma's father been one of your particular friends, would you have taken the girl into your care anyway?"

He cocked his head as they walked, a single brow lifting beneath his worn hat. "Tell me, Miss Gilbert, if you had the opportunity to do good for someone, would you not do so without a second thought?"

She hid a smile. She would—and had—time and again. Fixing her sister's embroidery when it turned knotty. Playing shuttlecock with her brother when no one else could be bothered. Bearing her stepmother's tirades with naught but a kind word in return.

"Yes," she answered. "I suppose I would."

"There is no supposing." His dark eyes sought hers. "I see it daily in your care of Emma."

She grinned. "Emma makes it easy, for she is a sweet little lamb."

As if Emma understood the praise, her cherub cheeks turned her way, a happy squeal bubbling out of her. Emma *was* sweet and far too easy to love.

But as they walked along the trail to morning worship, Abby's grin faded. Despite it being hardly a fortnight since the captain had hefted Emma into her arms, already the girl had made an indelible mark on her heart.

One that would bleed when they handed Emma over to her aunt.

CHAPTER EIGHTEEN

Samuel put all his muscle into pounding the final nail into the newly fashioned springboard. It wouldn't last long, formed out of rowan wood instead of steel, but it ought to at least get them by until they reached the next inn and could change carriages. He set down the hammer, then offered the layered strip of board over to Cleaver. "Want to ride out and see if this fits?"

The postilion nodded, his earlier ill feelings about the morning's delay pacified by a thick slice of Wenna's partridge pie when they'd returned from church. "Aye, and if so, I'll be back for your muscle to help put it on."

Cleaver's exit ushered a small breeze into the stable, but not enough to stop a drip of sweat from trickling down Samuel's brow. He swiped it away, shoving back the damp hair sticking to his skin. How long had it been since he'd made the effort to visit a barber?

He paused a moment to roll up his sleeves, chiding himself for not thinking of doing so sooner, then glanced over to where Bigby shaved down a thick strap of leather to attach the springboard—if it fit.

"You need my help?" he asked.

"Nay. I'm near to finished."

Good. If God's grace held, they'd have the carriage fixed by dark and be on their way come morning. A blessing that, yet one he held lightly. Putting too much stock in an expected outcome was never a good idea.

Grabbing a currycomb off the workbench, he sought out Pilgrim, who stood tethered just outside the door. The horse bobbed her head at his approach, then went back to munching on the green shoots nearest the stable wall.

"Someday, my friend," he breathed out in a soothing tone, matching the words to the pace of his strokes. "Someday soon, God willing, you'll not be driven so hard. No more heaths to roam. No highwaymen to hunt. Only sky and fields and wind. Just you and I and a stretch of land as far as the eye can see."

The chant was familiar, a common litany he used when grooming his horse, but this time it struck him as empty. Lonely, somehow. As friendless as a solitary tree left to weather on its own in a vast sweep of moorland.

Shoving the odd thought aside, he crouched and studied the wound on Pilgrim's foreleg. Pink skin, not inflamed or swollen, knit the injury together. Soon new hair would cover the damage, leaving the gash naught but a memory.

Even so, Samuel scowled. The damage never should have happened in the first place. He stalked back into the stable and flung the currycomb onto the bench, drawing in a deep breath to calm the ever-present rage that flared whenever he thought of the wicked man.

"The day off did yer horse good, no doubt. Aye?"

Bigby's bass tone crept up on him from behind, and he turned to face the man. "Aye."

"Then what's got yer blood still aboil?"

Samuel clenched his jaw, wielding silence like a great, grey blade. More often than not, the tactic worked, causing the inquirer to back down from the sheer discomfort of the moment.

Yet Bigby stepped closer, peering at him right in the eye. "There's no hiding it, lad. Ye've got a fire in yer belly"—he aimed a stubby finger at his gut—"and secrets enough to keep that blaze stoked hot."

He forced his brows to keep from raising. The farmer was bold, yet with an outspoken wife like Wenna, he likely had to be.

"Maybe." Samuel folded his arms and widened his stance. "Or maybe not."

Bigby chuckled, his ale belly jiggling beneath his work apron.

" 'T'aint no maybe about it, though I respect yer silence. Never have known me a lawman what didn't hold his cards close."

Samuel sucked in air through his teeth. How the blazes had the canny farmer figured that out? Not that he'd admit to it, though. He narrowed his eyes, prepared to scan the slightest twitch on the man's face. "What makes you think I'm a lawman?"

"The gleam o' yer tipstaff." Bigby nodded toward Samuel's hip.

Samuel's gaze followed the movement, only to see the hem of his waistcoat hitched up on the brass end of the wooden baton he kept tucked in his waistband at all times. In one swift movement, he yanked the fabric over the instrument.

Bigby's ready smile faded, mirth replaced by pity in his watery blue eyes. "Ahh, son, don't let the worst of man ruin the best o' you."

Hah! The sentiment, while likely well intentioned, stuck in his craw like a glob of gristle. The old fellow had no idea of what he spoke—or to whom he was speaking. Living here in the heart of England, secluded by hedgerows and fields of wheat and rye, Bigby couldn't possibly understand all the vile crimes he'd seen or the depth of depravity no one should have to witness. . .all embodied in the slit-eyed, square face of Shankhart Robbins. The mere thought of the man coiled his hands into fists.

Samuel turned away, finished with the ludicrous conversation.

But a strong grip on his shoulder stopped him. "Ye keep holding on to such anger, Captain, and it'll do you in."

He wrenched from the man's grip. "This has nothing to do with me. There's danger out there on the road, one Miss Gilbert and young Emma shouldn't have to face."

The farmer jutted his jaw. "Ye're a God-fearin' man. Leave that danger to Him."

Pah! If only it were that simple. "All that woman and child have is me and my gun standing between them and a man more ruthless than I've ever known."

"Yer not God." Bigby's voice lowered to an ominous tone. "So quit tryin' to be."

He stared at the man, seeing yet not seeing as the words barreled into him, booming as loudly in his heart as if God Himself thundered the message down from heaven.

"Yer not God, so quit tryin' to be."

Sweet everlasting! Was that what he'd been doing?

Shame left a nasty taste at the back of his throat. When it came down to it, he was no better than Shankhart. Not really. Just two sides of the same pence. While pride drove the highwayman to boast of his conquests of the innocent, was it really any different than the smugness Samuel harboured in his own heart every time he hauled in a villain? For ill or for good, did not pride always precede destruction? And by harbouring unforgiveness, was he not destroying himself, just as the farmer suggested?

Oh God. . . He swallowed hard.

Bigby cuffed him on the arm. "Don't take it too hard, Captain. It's to yer credit that ye care for the woman and child, but ye can safely leave them in God's hands. Not that He can't use yer gun, though, mind ye. There's no sin in wanting to protect them. The fault lies when ye think ye're their *sole* protector. Aye?"

The sharp edge of the farmer's words cut deep. He'd taken beatings before, but none so brutal as this. His shoulders sagged. His head. His soul.

Forgive me, Lord. The old man couldn't be more right, and for that I beg Your forgiveness.

Bigby shuffled his feet, his big boots rustling wisps of straw littering the ground. "But it's well beyond caring now, ain't it, Captain? Leastwise where the lady's concerned. Have ye told her?"

Samuel jerked up his head, stunned by the man's continued perception. Were the farmer in need of an occupation, Bow Street could well use his abilities. Donning a mask of indifference, he stared the man down. "There's nothing to tell."

Bigby chuckled. "Why, it's plain as a bleatin' goat stuck in a briar patch that ye love the woman. What's keepin' ye from claiming her? She's a right fine female."

Love? He clenched his jaw tight lest he gape. Surely that wasn't what these foreign urgings were. Were they?

No, he wouldn't—he *couldn't*—allow it.

He pivoted and snatched up a hoof pick from the bench, Pilgrim's mute company much preferred.

But Bigby was a hound with a bone, his footsteps dogging his every move. "The woman deserves to know, lad."

"I'm not the man for her," he rumbled.

"Ye ought to let her be the judge o' that."

He clenched the pick so hard, the metal shook in his hand. Even if this burning in his heart were love, there was no way he could admit such an offense to Miss Gilbert. For an offense it surely would be. He couldn't compare to a baronet, not in wealth or stature, and surely not in temperament. He was no fine dandy, serene and mollycoddling.

And even *if* he did have feelings for her, would Miss Gilbert return them? An impossibility, of course, but on the slightest chance that she did, he could offer her nothing save a rugged life with a very broken man. And oh, blessed heavens, she merited more than that.

He shook his head, refusing to turn around and face the farmer's all-seeing eyes. "There's too much at risk."

"Flit! Did not our own Lord risk His very life for the likes o' us? It's more noble to love, even if it's not returned, than to live without it. Why, 'tis one o' the greatest of all the commandments, man!"

"You don't understand. She's promised to another."

"Ahh, but she's not yet married to the man now, is she?"

Samuel scowled. The farmer mucked up so many sentiments, he couldn't begin to name them were he asked to at gunpoint. It was safer by far to embrace the anger he'd kept company with these past years.

"No." He spit out the word, then turned once again to face the farmer. "I will deliver her to her baronet, and that's the end of it."

"For her, maybe, but not for you." Bigby arched a brow at him. "Ye'll be heart-sore a good long time, I reckon. It's a cold ache. An empty one. And well I know it, leastwise till my Georgie comes home." Bigby's gaze strayed out the stable doors, focusing on some undefined point in the distance. "Aye, ought to be any day now, ol' Georgie will be riding up the road to home." The farmer's face softened, erasing years of toil and worry. How long had the man been missing his son? And why had the boy not returned?

"Where is he?" Samuel asked.

"Wanted to see the world afore he settled into farming alongside me. Georgie picked up and joined the queen's finest."

Samuel cocked his head. "Navy?"

"Aye. Sailed fer America the spring of '13, proud as a full-feathered peacock to patrol and keep safe the waters of Lake Erie. Ought to be home any day now."

A sick twinge tightened Samuel's gut. The year '13 had been notorious for British losses in the fledgling country of America, especially in the north. "Do you know the name of his ship?"

"The *Queen Charlotte*." Bigby shifted his gaze back to him. "Georgie's last letter home were from late August o' that year, saying he were proud to be on deck of one o' the best in the fleet." The man's bushy brows drew together. "Been nigh on two years though, since. He's like to be too busy to put pen to parchment, I reckon, but he ought to be home any day now."

Despite the summer heat, a chill leached into Samuel's bones. He nodded, then escaped out to Pilgrim. A report of the damages from that particular year had crossed the magistrate's desk. Devastating damage—especially on Lake Erie. If George Bigby had indeed been aboard the *Queen Charlotte*, he was either captured or missing. Or worse . . .killed. Samuel gathered up Pilgrim's front hoof and glowered. Ought he tell the Bigbys what he knew?

Or let them go on staring down that road, watching with love in their eyes for a man who may never come back?

Abby jabbed the needle into the fabric of the breeches she was mending, promising herself she'd not look out the window. Not again. She'd already been caught in the act of staring at Captain Thatcher as he brushed his horse. Not that Wenna had said anything—which might've been worse. The knowing gleam in the woman's eyes had unleashed Abby's imagination to entertain all sorts of accusations and innuendoes. Which was silly, of course. There was nothing between her and the captain, so the woman could have nothing to say on the matter. Truly.

Ignoring the squeeze of her heart, Abby wove the thread in and out, forming a tight seam.

"Ye're a fine hand with a needle. Ye'd ne'er be in want of employment should ye need to get by on yer own, and that's a fact." Wenna winked at her from her chair near the hearth. No fire crackled today, for the late June afternoon was warm enough.

But even so, heat flared in Abby's belly from the woman's praise. Of all the years she'd spent sewing in her stepmother's and sisters' company, not once could she remember such a kind word—and to this day she prayed to forget all the harsher cuts.

"That seam is as puckery as those little lines by your mouth, Abby."

"Keep your back straight when you sew. La! You hunch like a decrepit fishwife."

"Do you see Mary and Jane creasing their brows while they embroider? No man will want you with such wrinkles, girl!"

She straightened in her chair, correcting her posture out of habit, and glanced down at Emma, who yet slept sweetly in her basket. Would that Emma might never bear the same hurtful scars she suffered.

Outside the window, a movement from the corner of her eye snagged her attention. A shadowy figure. Dark and tall. Commanding enough to warrant a second and third look.

Don't do it. Don't give in.

But the pull of the man was too strong. Abby turned her face to the glass, making sure to keep her needle moving, and stared out at the fine lines of the captain.

He bent near his horse, shirtsleeves rolled up. The thick muscles on his forearm flexed as he worked to clean something out of his horse's hoof. His waistcoat stretched across his back, the flesh beneath rippling with his effort. He could conquer the world, this man, were he of a mind to. Did he know it? Or did the latent humility that was so much a part of him keep him unaware of his inherent power?

For a moment, she allowed herself to relive the feel of his arms pulling her close, the heat of his body as he'd shared his horse with her and Emma during the storm. He'd sheltered. He'd protected. He'd been soaked to the skin from wrapping her and Emma in his riding cloak.

"He's a good man, that one."

Her thought exactly—but Wenna's voice.

Abby jerked her gaze back to her sewing, dipping her head slightly so the woman wouldn't see the flaming of her cheeks. A big knot snarled her thread, and she was glad for the distraction to pick at.

She stabbed the knot with the tip of her needle, working to free the twisted mess. "Captain Thatcher is a good man. Were it not for him, I shudder to think of what might have happened to me."

Indeed. He'd rescued her and Fanny from highwaymen. Come to her aid in the stable from that brute of a false guardian. When she'd fallen ill, he'd been the one to nurse her back to health. And countless times he had put her and Emma's comforts ahead of his own. She wrangled the knot, which only seemed to tighten it further, and sighed. The captain had saved her from trouble so many times, she would have to beg Sir Jonathan to give him more compensation than what had been promised.

"If ye'll humour an old woman?" Wenna nipped her own thread with her teeth and added the repaired shirt she'd been working on to a growing pile of garments. Despite the woman's earlier praise, her worn yet nimble fingers put Abby's skills to shame. It was Wenna herself who could get by on her own with all the sewing she did for the manor house and tenant farmers hereabouts.

But Wenna didn't reach for the next torn shirt. Instead, she fixed her gaze on Abby. "Why are ye running off to marry another when there's one who cares for ye right in front of yer face? With all the pretty girls in church service this morning, the captain had eyes for none but ye."

She chuckled at the woman's misguided notion. "No, Wenna, 'tis not like that at all. I pay Captain Thatcher for his care, and being the noble guardian that he is, I am sure he was merely keeping an eye out for me. He would do the same for anyone."

"Pish! Ye really believe that?"

"Without a doubt." What a silly notion!

Finally, the threads on her knot parted. Abby licked her thumb and forefinger, then ran them along the kinked strands to straighten them out. "Besides," she continued, lest Wenna think any more on the topic of her and the captain, "I am promised to another and am on my way to happiness, you see."

She smiled at the woman.

"Are ye?" Wenna frowned. "Tell me of that man, then."

"Sir Jonathan Aberley is a baronet, lord of Brakewell Hall, a manor home on two-hundred-plus acres near Penrith. I have it on good authority that he is well respected." She tugged at the thread, fighting against another knot, the kinks from the former tangle straining to overtake the smoothness she'd worked to achieve.

Wenna's eyebrows arched. "That be nice, miss, but that doesn't tell me much about the man."

The words were an unnerving echo of the same Samuel had voiced to her not long ago, and suddenly she was glad for the threat of a snarl in her thread, for it meant she didn't have to look over at Wenna. It was hard to remember what the baronet was like, and even harder to keep believing he was truly in love with her—but she must.

She pulled back her shoulders and stabbed the needle into the knot. "Sir Jonathan has dark hair. Brown, I think. He is taller than I, and he dances quite well."

There. She pulled the thread through, victorious with the stitch and her description.

"Fine qualities, all." Wenna leaned forward in her chair, her gaze seeking Abby's. "But what captures yer fancy about the man?"

Abby dipped her head, focusing on the worn bit of breeches as if her life depended on it. How was she to answer that? How could she possibly fancy a man she hardly knew? One sweep around a ballroom while changing partners at intervals was barely grounds to know what it was about Sir Jonathan that she might admire.

But Wenna's eyes bore into her. She could feel it. Searching. Probing. She'd have to answer.

"He asked my father for my hand," she said simply.

"I'm wondering if it's you he wants or yer dowry," Wenna mumbled.

Leastwise that's what it sounded like. Abby lifted her chin, her brows pulling tight. "Pardon?"

The emotions on Wenna's face pieced together like a homespun quilt. Patches of pity coloured the woman's cheekbones. Concern basted tucks at the sides of her mouth. Yet compassion blanketed her tone as she softened her voice. "Allow me to be plain with ye, Miss Abby. Yer baronet may very well want ye. Who am I to say? But that's not solid ground for ye to be committing the rest o' yer life to him. A hungry lion might pursue ye with the same eagerness, but to devour, not to love."

The needle slipped, pricking her fingertip as sharply as Wenna's words stabbed her heart. Immediately, she pinched her thumb against the pierced flesh, stopping a drop of blood, and frowned at Wenna. "Why are you telling me this?"

"Flit, child! I'd hate to see ye throw away yer life on a man who didn't care enough to come and get you himself. Allowing ye to traipse the countryside on yer own. Not even providing a guard to keep ye safe."

The truth she'd been trying to ignore for so long stung the back of her eyes, and the world turned watery. Blinking, she stared at the fabric on her lap.

Footsteps padded, and an arm wrapped around her shoulder, giving her a little squeeze.

"Here be the way of it, miss. Ye say ye're on yer way to happiness, when all along it's been right under yer very nose. The truth is, ye *are* wanted, by the Creator of the stars, no less. Ye don't have to run across the country to find love when every minute of every day it's being offered to ye in God's wide, open arms. Do ye know that, girl?"

Setting down her sewing, she pulled from Wenna's touch and stood. Did the woman really think she was that much of a heathen? "Of course I know God loves me. I have been to church every Sunday of my life."

"Ahh, but do ye *know* the truth of God's love in yer heart, daughter? Have ye been in His presence, dropped to yer knees by the power o' His love?"

Slowly, she turned and faced the woman, afraid to ask what she must—but more afraid not to. "What do you mean?"

"Ahh, child." The ruffle of Wenna's mobcap dipped along with her brows. "It seems ye're setting yer expectations on earthly things, such as yer happiness with yer baronet. But ye'll not find it there. Not in man. Not in any man. Until ye're fully satisfied with the love God gives ye, freely and without question, ye'll not be satisfied at all."

Abby sucked in a breath, stunned. Was that what she'd been doing? Striving so hard to find love—first in her family and now in the man she was to marry—that she'd ignored what God had to offer? She pressed a hand to her stomach, the sick feeling beneath her touch a testament to the truth. But how to change? How to really *know* God's love, as Wenna said?

"I—" She cleared her throat and dared a peek at Wenna, bracing herself for the sympathy that was sure to glisten in the woman's eyes.

"I do not know how," she admitted.

A huge smile brightened Wenna's face. "Well, God be praised! Then yer one step closer."

Abby frowned. "What do you mean?"

"It's not by yer own strivin' that ye'll find God's love. All ye have to do is ask. Our faithful God will do the rest." Picking up Abby's sewing, Wenna shooed her with her other hand toward the door. "Go and talk to yer Creator. I'll finish up these breeches and mind the wee one for ye."

She shook her head, astounded by the woman's suggestion. "It cannot be that simple."

Wenna's grin widened. "If little Emma were to lift her arms to you, would ye not gather her to yer breast and hold her?"

Unbidden, Abby's gaze drifted to the sleeping babe as the woman's words sank in. Could it truly be that simple?

Slowly, she turned toward the door. There was only one way to find out.

CHAPTER NINETEEN

"You shouldn't be out here alone."

A charge ran through Abby at the deep timbre of the captain's voice behind her back, and her eyes shot open. Even more jarring were the last rays of daylight painting Farmer Bigby's field a golden green. How could that be? It seemed like only minutes had passed as she'd poured out her fears, her longings, and all the hurts she'd thought were buried deep enough to never remember. But from the moment she'd whispered, "God, are You there?" time had stopped. Tears had flowed. And a peace she'd never before experienced watered, soothed, and healed the cracked soil of her soul.

Clutching the rough wooden gate, she stared out at the turnip field a moment more, the land a verdant sea of thick leaves. Nothing had changed in the time she'd been out here. Yet everything had. How could she possibly tell the captain she wasn't alone—and never would be again?

Her lips curved into a smile, and she turned to face him, surprised to see he stood but a few paces away, with Emma riding atop his shoulders. "Do not concern yourself, Captain. I am perfectly safe."

"No one is ever safe this side of heaven, Miss Gilbert." His jaw hardened, tightening as if all his bones strained beneath the weight of the sentiment.

Compassion swelled in Abby's heart. She reached toward him, as if by touch alone she might transfer some of her newly found peace and confidence in God.

But at the sudden cock of his head and narrowing of his eyes, she realized this was not a man who welcomed pity, but rather might slap her hand away. Reaching higher, she tucked in a stray strand of hair, hoping he'd think that'd been her intent all along.

Emma laughed, her sudden outburst causing several sparrows to take flight from a nearby hedge. The girl shoved Captain Thatcher's hat brim over his eyes, and with one big swoop, he freed her from her perch on his shoulders and swung her to the ground. She clung on to his big hands, refusing to let go, and bounced on her toes.

Abby's grin grew. "She looks as though she is ready to take her first step." Crouching, she held out her arms. "Come, sweet one!"

The captain squatted as well, then breaking free of Emma's grip, shot out his arms in case the child teetered one way or the other.

Emma's eyes widened, and for a breathless eternity, she wobbled. Slowly, one leg lifted then landed, the momentum tilting her body forward. Abby leaned forward too, lest Emma fall face-first in the dirt. But the girl's other leg jerked ahead, and in one more stilted step, Emma squealed and lunged into Abby's arms.

"Well done, little one!" Abby laughed, nuzzling her cheek against the crown of Emma's head, then she turned the girl around. "Try it again, dear heart. Walk to the captain."

When Emma balanced upright, Abby let her go, stretching out her arms so that her fingertips were barely a hand span away from Captain Thatcher's. If Emma did fall, she'd not have far to go. Once again, the child took off, her legs a bit jerky, her little hands flailing in the air. Gleeful gurgles burbled out of her mouth. The big, strong captain stood at the ready to catch her should she miss her footing.

And suddenly Abby's eyes stung with tears. Was this not the very picture of how God had just held out His arms to her during her fledgling steps toward Him?

Emma laughed again, but with too much gusto. She veered sideways like a tightrope walker, off-balanced on one leg. Abby gasped and, in reflex, lunged ahead. But no need. The captain swept little Emma up and stood, swinging her around and chuckling.

Chuckling?

Both Abby's brows rose. Surprisingly, laughter suited this man, erasing the sharp lines and angles that usually hardened his face. He looked years younger and entirely too attractive.

Planting his feet, the captain swung Emma back up to his shoulders and gazed down at Abby. "Soon there'll be no containing her." He gripped the girl's legs tighter as she bounced against him. "You'll have your work cut out for you until we reach Manchester."

She smoothed her damp palms along her skirt, focusing on his words instead of his handsome face. "A labour I gladly accept."

His eyes glimmered with approval, or dare she hope. . .admiration? A sudden yearning welled in her to have this man look upon her with his full heart in his gaze, cherishing her above all other women.

She turned away, cheeks heating at such a wayward thought. Surely it had only been the angle of the sun painting him in a charitable warm glow. Nothing more.

The captain strode past her, leading the way to the main road, then paused and waited for her to catch up. As she fell into step beside him, Emma bent from her perch and shoved a chubby fist her way. Abby kissed the girl's fingers, and Emma cooed.

The captain slid her a sideways glance. "You'll miss Emma when she's gone, I think."

He couldn't be more right. In truth, it would be harder to part with the sweet girl than it had been to say goodbye to her own family.

"I will miss her," she admitted. "Dreadfully. Though I am not her mother, she has stolen my heart. I cannot imagine the pain the Bigbys must have felt when parting with their son, nor how happy their reunion shall be when he returns."

All humour fled from the captain's face, more sudden and drastic than yesterday's storm. What on earth had she said to exact such a change? Did he harbour some secret about Emma? Emma's mother? The Bigbys?

She dared a light touch on his sleeve. Hard muscles rippled beneath his shirt, and he glowered down at her hand. She almost pulled back, but by will alone she kept her hold, determined to be as courageous as him. "There is something you are not telling me, Captain. What is it?"

His boot sent a rock skittering, yet he said nothing.

She squeezed his arm. "Well? You should know by now, your silence will not work with me."

A muscle jumped on his neck, and he muttered something too low for her to hear.

"A little louder, if you please."

His face turned to her, his eyes once again lost in the ever-present shadow of his hat. "You know, with your persistence, you'd make a fine officer yourself."

"I shall take that as a compliment, sir." She grinned. "But I will not be put off."

He blew out a long breath and faced forward again. For several paces, she wondered if the conversation was over before it began. Far too aware of the silence—and how warm and solid his flesh felt beneath her fingertips—she pulled back her hand.

Finally, he murmured, "All right. Since you insist, it's about the Bigbys' son, George. I suspect he won't be coming home."

She pursed her lips. How could he possibly know that? "Surely the man is not an acquaintance of yours. Is he?"

"No, but I am familiar with the ship he served on."

An ominous undertone moved swiftly through his words, and despite the heat of the afternoon, a shiver skittered across Abby's shoulders. She turned to him and stopped, the movement halting his steps.

"What do you know, Captain?"

Emma rested her cheek against his hat, her sweet cherub face a stark contrast to the captain's flinty stare. "His ship—the *Queen Charlotte*—was taken by the Americans two years back. The captain was killed, as were many of the crew. Some may have escaped. The rest were chained as prisoners. If George hasn't made it home by now, he isn't coming."

The truth knocked her as off-kilter as Emma's earlier misstep. How awful! How horribly cruel. Even now if she closed her eyes, she could envision the man's shaving kit, his shirt and trousers, his tin mirror shined and ready for his return. Wenna would be crushed by the weight of such a sorrow. And what of Mr. Bigby? The man not only desired but *needed* his son to help him on the farm. The pain of knowing George wouldn't be back could send the old man to his deathbed.

She peered up at the captain. "But you do not know this for certain. Do you? Can you say beyond a shadow of doubt that George was killed or captured? Why could he not have been one of those who escaped?"

"I'm no stranger to war, Miss Gilbert. If he made it out of there, he'd be home by now. The chances of that man returning are little to none." His lips pressed into a grim line. "And the Bigbys deserve to know."

Her jaw dropped. "You would cause them great pain for something that may not be true?"

"Is it not more cruel to let them live out their days staring down the road for a son who might never come back?"

"No, it is not, for I know what that feels like. You can have no idea how empty it is to be told what you hope for is not within reach. My stepmother certainly taught me that truth well, for despite my hope of a loving relationship with her, she squelched my efforts at every turn. Worse, she belittled my attempts." Righteous anger flared in her chest, and she lifted her chin. "So you will pardon me, Captain, when I insist that it is never cruel to live with hope, even the smallest portion. It is a weak comparison, but if someone came along and stole your hope of buying some land, farming your own fields, how would that make you feel? Hmm? Tell me."

A shadow darkened his face, and he wheeled about so quickly, Emma swung sideways. He pulled her down to his chest, saying nothing.

Abby bit her lip. Had she pushed him too far? Then so be it. She'd rather irritate the man than have hope snatched away from the Bigbys.

She upped her pace to gain his side. "Will you at least consider what I have said?"

For a long while, he didn't answer. Maybe he wouldn't at all, but could she fault him? The passion she'd just let slip likely made her sound like a raving lunatic.

They rounded the last curve in the road, and as the cottage came into sight, the captain slanted her a sideways glance. "Very well. I will consider it."

She hid a smile. Why that felt like such a victory was a mystery, but did not God work in mysterious ways? Was God even now working in the captain's heart? Glancing up at the leafy canopy, she silently prayed.

Lord, give this man wisdom to know what, if anything, to say to the Bigbys—

Her appeal ended abruptly as the captain shoved Emma into her arms, then stepped in front of her, blocking them both.

Abby froze, clutching Emma, wanting yet fearing to raise to her toes and stare over the captain's shoulder. What danger had he spied?

"Captain, what—?"

He spun around, jamming his finger against her lips. Without a word, he commanded her to stay put, and then he pivoted back and stalked ahead.

Every sense on high alert, Samuel's gaze snapped from the fallen branch in the middle of the road to the tree line at the side of the road. A maze of dark trunks, thick enough to conceal an enemy, spread as far as he could see—which was a precious short distance. Even so, he scoured the ivy blanketing the ground, looking for a trail, flattened greenery, anything to hint at an entrance or escape route someone might've taken when putting that chunk of wood on the road. But the woodland appeared as unspoiled as the day God had called it into being. Clearly no one had trampled through this swath of undergrowth recently.

Even so, he pulled out his gun. Tree branches didn't fall for no reason, not in the middle of the road where nothing but sky opened overhead. It surely hadn't gotten there by itself.

Choosing his steps carefully, he advanced, his gaze bouncing between the forest on one side and the hedgerow on the other. Sparrows chattered and flitted inside the shrubbery, quivering the leaves. The topmost canopy of trees swayed in a gentle breeze. Other than that and a few squirrels scurrying about, nothing moved. He frowned. Whoever had been here was long gone now—*if* anyone had been. Was he looking for demons when none threatened? Could the branch simply have fallen and rolled?

Lowering to his haunches, he studied the piece of wood, as long as his arm and just as thick. One end was jagged, crumbled by rot. The other stretched out fingers of dead wood. Thunder and turf! He could've sworn the thing hadn't been here when he'd passed by on his way to find Miss Gilbert, but maybe—just maybe—it had?

He felt sick in his gut. Perhaps he had been distracted by Emma or overly preoccupied with how to tell the Bigbys about George. Neither were a good excuse, though, and suddenly his pistol weighed heavy in his hand. What kind of captain of the horse patrol would pass by such an obvious hunk of wood without even noticing it?

Footsteps padded behind him. The rustle of a gown. The cooing of the child. Soon a question about his erratic behaviour would shoot him in the back. How was he to explain pulling a gun on nothing but an insignificant hunk of tree limb?

Angry at himself, he shoved his gun back into his belt and swiped up the branch. He was about to toss the thing aside when he froze. Something didn't feel right. But what?

Slowly, keeping his back to the advancing woman, he turned the wood over. Three crude letters scarred the wood, formed by cutting away the ash-coloured bark to the lighter flesh beneath:

YOU

You? He narrowed his eyes. For all the effort and stealth it took to put this message in his path, that's all it said? Or had the sender been scared off before finishing the message? His gaze drifted back to the tree line. Still, he detected nothing out of place. Whoever had delivered this curious dispatch was good at what he did, a professional, likely well paid from deep pockets.

And there were none deeper than Shankhart's.

"What is it?"

The whispered question shivered behind him. He hefted the branch and flung it into the woods, then turned. "Nothing." He forced a pleasant tone and a sheepish tilt to his head. "My mistake."

Miss Gilbert pursed her lips, a small crescent dimpling her chin. Either she didn't believe him or she inwardly condemned him to madness.

"While I appreciate how seriously you take your responsibility toward me and Emma, Captain, did you really feel it necessary to pull out your gun for naught but a fallen branch?"

He shrugged. "As I said, my mistake."

"Hmm. Obviously you are expecting trouble."

Sweet heavens! How could this woman read him so thoroughly?

"Yes," he admitted, then turned about and called over his shoulder. "We'll suffer Mrs. Bigby's wrath if I don't get you back for dinner."

Thankfully, they hadn't far to go, for Miss Gilbert shot out questions in rapid fire—and he thanked God for years of experience in dodging bullets. As soon as they stepped through the cottage door, Wenna pulled Miss Gilbert aside, enlisting her help in serving up bowls of pottage.

The rest of the evening passed by uneventfully, though he kept a sharp ear for any telltale noises outside, purposely manning the chair nearest the window for such a purpose. While the Bigbys, Cleaver, and Miss Gilbert chatted amongst themselves, his mind wore ruts with alternately trying to decide if he ought to say anything about George and his unlikely return, and the message on the log and what it could mean.

". . .morning, Captain?"

He snapped his gaze across the small room, where Miss Gilbert's brown eyes pinned him in place. Clearly she'd been speaking to him, but he'd not heard a word. "Pardon?"

"I asked if we are to leave early in the morning."

"Yes. Daybreak." Standing, he swiped his hat off a peg on the wall, jammed it on his head, then dipped a farewell. "Good night."

He strode to the door—and the floorboards creaked behind him. His hand paused on the latch when the faint scent of orange blossom curled over his shoulder.

"You did the right thing," Miss Gilbert murmured low.

His brow folded, and he turned, surprised to see she stood hardly a breath away. "What's that?"

She stepped closer, pressing her hand against his sleeve. "You let the Bigbys keep their hope. You are a good man, Captain, and I thank you."

The admiration glimmering in her gaze crawled in deep. And her touch. . . Lord have mercy. Against his better judgment, he leaned into it, and his heart skipped a beat. Ahh, but he was starting to crave this woman's nearness. Her warmth. Her smile. All the delicate fierceness that made up the petite form of Abby Gilbert.

Abby? Heat settled low in his belly. Since when did her Christian name come so easily to mind?

Without a word, he turned and fled into the night, glad for the slap of cool air against his face. The sooner he delivered Abby—Miss Gilbert—to her baronet, the better.

CHAPTER TWENTY

Outside the stable, crickets chirruped. Inside, Cleaver snored. Samuel lay wide-eyed, annoyed by both.

Some nights just weren't meant for sleeping. He'd learned that lesson as a young lad, when long after his father's shouts had ended and his mother's weeping had subsided, he'd lain awake. Staring in the darkness. Wishing he were somewhere else. This night was no different save for the reason—a brown-eyed vision chasing off his sleep. Even now he could hear the thick emotion in Abby Gilbert's voice as if she lay right next to him.

"You are a good man, Captain."

Rising slightly, he punched the straw into a thicker wad and whumped back down. Good man. Him? Oh, not that he didn't yearn to be—try to be—but that same little boy who lived deep inside him still huddled in a corner of his heart, crushed by his father's words of long ago.

"Get your worthless backside out o' my house! I'm done with you."

And so, at only eleven, he'd left to live on the streets, vowing to never turn into the same drunken bully as his father.

Though no one could see it, a small smile curved his lips. Apparently, leastwise in Abby Gilbert's eyes, he'd succeeded. And that one, singular truth prodded him to flip over yet again. He should run from the tenderness he'd heard in her voice, flee the fondness he'd read in her eyes. He knew it in his head, the same as he knew he should've left his father's house sooner than he did. But in his heart, ahh, that misguided organ. . . His heart demanded he not only stay but also win Abby over to him alone.

He flung his arm across his eyes. It wasn't good, this growing attraction he harboured for the woman, not when she belonged to another. Though Farmer Bigby had told him—hardly two paces away from where he now lay—to love with abandon, whether returned or not, somehow it felt wrong. Abby Gilbert deserved more than a worn-out lawman with enemies skulking around every corner. She should have a quiet home filled with love and peace, especially after escaping such a dismal existence with a family that neither cared for nor valued her. Indeed, a man of means such as her baronet was exactly what she merited, not a broken horse patrol captain. . .and the sooner he got her to her baronet, the better, before he did something stupid like fall in love and ruin her chances with the man.

He punched the straw again and tossed to his other side, then stilled, listening past Cleaver's heavy breathing. A solitary bird chirped. Then another. Soon the farmer's rooster would cock-a-doodle-do the official start of morning.

Weary to the marrow of his bones, Samuel stood and arched his back, working out a kink with a satisfying pop. He moved on to his neck, stretching one way and the other until it cracked. One stall over, Pilgrim stuck out her head, eyeing Samuel's movement. A horsey smirk twitched the animal's nose, mocking his creaking body. Condemning him as an old man. Samuel smirked back. He couldn't agree more.

Grabbing his riding cloak off the workbench, he threw it over his arm and snatched up his hat. Then he stalked over to where Cleaver yet lay snoring and nudged the postilion with his boot. "Time to move."

Cleaver bolted upright, bits of straw sticking to his coat like a poorly stuffed scarecrow. After a curse and a "What the. . . ," his gaze followed the length of Samuel's leg up to his body, then finally to his face. "Oh," he yawned. "Aye."

Outside, early-morning vapors rose like prayers, blurring the countryside into a mystical softness. Samuel glanced at the sky, pregnant with the promise of morning. Still a deep grey, but no clouds. A good day to travel. A better day to put space between them and whoever left that carved message in the branch yesterday.

The next hour passed in a flurry of hitching horses, reloading Miss Gilbert's chest, and downing as much porridge as Wenna could possibly ladle into their bowls. Emma surprised them all by finally allowing the farmer's wife to hold her without crying, though it lasted for only a moment before she wrenched around and shot out her arms toward Abby.

Thunderation! She should be Miss Gilbert to him, not Abby!

After helping her and Emma into the carriage, he strode over to Pilgrim. Farmer Bigby followed him while Wenna darted to the coach's side to say her goodbyes at the window.

The farmer clapped him on the back. "Keep in mind what I said, Captain. Don't let that one"—he hitched his thumb over his shoulder, aiming at the carriage—"slip from your hands."

Samuel turned his back on the man and his advice and swung up onto his horse. Grabbing Pilgrim's reins in a loose hold, he looked down at Bigby, purposely changing the subject. "Thank you for your hospitality. You and your wife have been more than generous."

"Just sharin' what the good Lord provides." Bigby squinted up at him. "Godspeed, Captain."

Samuel gave the man a sharp nod, then trotted ahead, getting a lead on the carriage horses. No branches in the road would miss his observation today. In fact, just to be safe, he sped ahead, intending to scout the length of the Bigbys' curvy route all the way to the main thoroughfare.

Leftover mist clung low to the ground, but only in spare hollows where the land dipped at the sides of the road. As the sun rose higher, nothing but shimmery dewdrops remained. Samuel gazed past the beauty, scowling as he urged Pilgrim onward. It didn't seem right to ignore God's handiwork in favor of looking for evil, yet that was his job, *always* his job. And by all that was righteous, how it wore on him. It wouldn't be soon enough to receive the baronet's payment and retire on his own piece of land.

Pilgrim's ears twitched. Samuel stiffened and listened beyond the thudding of his own horse's hooves. Rounding the last bend to the main thoroughfare, he peered into the distance—and saw what had snagged his and Pilgrim's attention.

To the east, a cloud of dust rose above the brush along the main thoroughfare. A horse and rider. And by the looks of it, coming fast. The sight wasn't that unusual. Maybe someone rode hard for a surgeon. Or perhaps the rider tore hell-bent for a midwife, his first child on the way. Any number of innocent reasons could drive a person to move at such a frenzy this early in the day.

But when the rider turned off the main road and onto the Bigbys' lane, all his speculations darkened to a dangerous shade. No one should be eating up ground that quickly to get to an old farmer and his wife.

Unless the rider wasn't coming for them.

In one swift movement, Samuel snatched out his gun and dug in his heels. Pilgrim shot ahead. Thirty yards away from the approaching rider, he angled Pilgrim sideways and stopped the horse perpendicular in the middle of the road. A blockade of sorts—made all the more deadly when he jerked up his arm and steadied the pistol muzzle on the crook of his elbow.

"Stop!" he yelled.

The rider didn't.

No choice, then. Samuel pulled off a warning shot—the *only* warning he'd give.

With one hand, the rider yanked on his reins. Too hard. The horse reared, and the man fell.

Samuel leapt off Pilgrim, pulling his knife with one hand and flipping his gun around with the other to use the grip as a bludgeon. All the while, he sprinted to where the rider rolled to a stop. He planted his feet wide, ready for anything. "Who are you?"

The man pelted him with curses. "You'd better have a good reason for threatening me on my home land!"

Samuel cocked his head, wary yet curious. *Home* land?

The man shoved up one-handed to his knees, still calling down brimstone and all manner of other oaths upon Samuel's head. His other sleeve was empty, pinned to his chest. And when Samuel caught full sight of the man's face, he gasped.

A jagged scar crawled like an earthworm from his chin to his cheek, stopping briefly at an eye patch, then emerged out the other end to disappear into his scalp. But it wasn't the wound that punched Samuel in the gut. It was the man's ears, sticking out like handles on his head, and a hook nose that might serve as a sparrow's perch. . .the very image of a young Farmer Bigby.

George? No wonder the man hadn't returned home in two years. With those wounds, it was a wonder he'd returned home at all.

Samuel lowered his gun and knife, yet kept a grip on them in case he was wrong. "Do you live in the farm cottage down the lane?"

The man glowered up at him. "Not that it's any of your business, but aye."

Samuel stored his weapons and offered his hand, relieved he'd been wrong about George not coming back—and even more relieved that he'd said nothing about his suspicions to the Bigbys.

George slapped his offer away and rose to his feet, a bit wobbly but on his own power.

Allowing the man a moment to collect himself, Samuel turned and snagged the lead of George's horse, then returned the animal to his master.

George snatched the lead from his hand. "Who the devil are you, and why gun me down?"

If looks could kill, Samuel would be bleeding out on the dirt. He lifted his hands and backed away, edging toward Pilgrim. "I beg your pardon, Mr. Bigby. I made a mistake. Please, continue on your way."

George narrowed his eye. "Do I know you?"

"No." Just then, the carriage rounded the bend, and Samuel tipped his head in that direction. "We were simply passing by, and your family took us in. I daresay you will be a welcome surprise. Once again, my apologies."

He swung up on Pilgrim and cantered down the road, chagrined by his blunder. Of course his drastic precaution had been a necessary evil. What were the odds of George Bigby returning home on the very day he rode out looking for trouble? His offense had been the right thing to do. The *only* thing to do.

So why did his gut twist and his heart burn?

Putting pressure on the reins, he guided his horse onto the main road. Thank God he hadn't shot the man. From now on, he'd be more careful. Use a bit more discernment before pulling out his gun and—

"Easy," he rumbled and put pressure on the reins, halting Pilgrim at the side of the road, hardly believing his eyes.

There, on a rise of thicket grass that led up into a stand of trees, strategically placed rocks spelled out letters, three feet high. Two feet wide. Vindicating his gun-pulling. The single, ominous word kidney-punched him:

DIE

A morbid enough message, but when added to the previous two he'd already received, his pulse took off at a breakneck speed.

Soon. You. Die.

Abby fanned herself with her hand, debating yet again if she ought to ask the driver to stop so she could retrieve an actual fan from her chest at the back of the coach. Oh, why hadn't she thought to remove it when the big chest had sat in the Bigbys' cottage? Even with both carriage windows down, the air stifled, making her want to crawl out of such a heated cage. Or maybe it was Emma who she really wanted to escape. Ever since discovering her mobility yesterday, the girl was a scrambling squirrel.

Instant remorse pinched Abby's conscience, and for at least the twentieth time in the past hour, she shot out her arm to block Emma from diving off the seat.

"Gee!" Emma squealed and bounced, then, thankfully, lunged for the opposite window and pulled herself up to peer out.

Abby leaned back against the seat, closing her eyes as the wheels rumbled along. Was this what it felt like to be a mother? To be driven to such extremes, loving wholeheartedly *and* desperately wishing for a minute alone? Or was she being selfish? Either way, God bless each and every self-sacrificing mother on the planet.

Exhaling her frustration, she tucked up a hank of hair loosened by

Emma's grasping fingers. The child truly had at least four arms, each of them out of control. With a last look to make sure Emma's feet were safely anchored away from the edge of the seat, Abby leaned sideways and poked her head outside the opposite window, not caring that she probably looked like a beagle riding with its ears flapping in the breeze. Propriety be hanged! The wind on her face was so worth it.

Ahead, the captain rode tall on Pilgrim and glanced over his shoulder as if he detected her breach of decorum. But he didn't see her. Not really. She'd learned that hours ago when she'd waved at him and received no response. Ever since they'd left the Bigbys' cottage early this morning, he'd been looking back, and sideways, and straining to see up front—where he'd been riding all day.

Abby narrowed her eyes and studied his broad shoulders. In the heat of the afternoon, he'd forsaken his riding cloak, shoving it into the leather bag he kept strapped behind his saddle. He rode loose, his body rolling with the horse's movement, his muscles slack. Still, it didn't fool her. Pulling a gun on nothing but a branch. Pitching rocks away from the side of the road. Scanning his surroundings like a spinster bent on finding a husband. Something festered inside that man. Something he wouldn't tell her, no matter how many times she peppered him with questions.

A squeal ripped out of Emma. "Ah-be-da! Ah-be-da!"

Abby pulled her head back inside the carriage, curious yet dreading what might've caught Emma's attention. *Ah-be-da* could be any number of things. Scooting sideways on the seat, Abby neared the child and peered past her.

The road gave way to a large field, and on the opposite end of the big clearing, all manner of coloured tents, flags, people, and animals spread out. As the road curved and they drew closer, the sounds of music and laughter, hawkers clamoring about their wares, and showmen begging for an audience all filled the air. Abby smiled. Ah-be-da, indeed! She'd always wanted to visit a country fair.

Once again, she shoved her head out the window. "Stop the carriage!"

The postilion slowed the coach to a stop and barely had the step out for her to exit when the captain rode up, his usual glower in place as he swung from his mount.

"We're nearly to the inn. Why stop here?"

She peeled Emma's fingers from her face, then turned the child around and angled her head toward the merriment. "The fair, of course."

His dark gaze drifted to the revelry, then cut back to hers, sharp as a knife. "No. Absolutely not."

Truly, he needn't have said anything. The steely set of his jaw and stiff way he held his neck screamed he'd rather be drawn and quartered than escort her and Emma to a fair.

Abby pursed her lips. Good thing opposition was a commodity she'd learned long ago to trade in deftly. She blinked up at him, determined to win the battle. "While you have enjoyed the fresh air all day, Emma and I have been slowly cooking inside the carriage. She needs this outing, Captain. As do I."

A tic twitched at the side of his eye. "It's not safe."

"Maybe not, but that is why I hired you, hmm?"

He glanced around, his eyes slowly grazing the entire length of the fairgrounds. His mouth flattened into a straight line, and he shook his head. "It's a bad idea."

Abby shifted Emma to her hip, stalling for time. How was she to convince him? Her sisters would've fluttered their eyelashes or maybe let loose a single, fat tear, but that wouldn't work with this man.

So she met his gaze, hard and even, and softened her tone. "Please, Captain? Despite any dangers you may perceive, I know that Emma and I shall be perfectly safe in your company."

As if on cue, Emma stretched out her arms toward him. "Ah-be-da?"

Finally, he broke.

A growl rumbled in his chest, and he pulled Emma from her arms. "Very well. But we're not staying long." He turned toward the postilion. "See to my horse and the lady's belongings, then secure us two rooms. Also, arrange a carriage and fresh horses for the morning. We'll settle with you later."

"Aye, Captain." The driver dipped his head.

Abby hid a smile, lest Captain Thatcher saw how much her victory pleased her.

The captain set off toward the rows of merchants displaying their wares, likely assuming that would fancy her most. Given that she had lived in the great harbour of Southampton, where such merchandise shipped in daily, he couldn't have been more wrong.

She tapped his sleeve. "Might we go see the performers?"

One of his brows lifted. "Truly? A woman who scorns shopping?"

This time she allowed her smile to run free. "I have no need of anything at the moment."

His other brow shot up as well. "As you wish."

They roamed past food vendors, and though her stomach pinched at the savory scents of spiced nuts and meat pies, she'd not give in to the temptation. Eating was an everyday occurrence, and she didn't want to waste one minute on such a mundane activity when she could be watching musicians and jugglers, slack rope walkers and tumblers.

The captain paid scant attention to any of it, his gaze never landing long enough to enjoy the performances. But that was his loss. Abby clapped and exclaimed along with the rest of the crowd. And Emma squealed with delight, especially when a monkey in a jester's suit did backflips all the way up to the captain's legs.

Abby grinned at the child. "Did you like that, sweet one—oh!"

Her gaze shot downward at a tug on her skirt. Big brown eyes gazed up at her, set wide into a furry little face. How dear!

But then she gasped when the monkey scampered up her gown, all the way to her shoulders. He reached behind her ear and pulled out a shiny, gold coin, holding it out for the crowd to see. Those around her gasped. Some laughed. The captain narrowed his eyes.

The monkey's handler, dressed in matching harlequin silk, stepped up to her and extended his arm with a flourish. The furry scamp leapt from her shoulder to dangle off the man's sleeve with one paw. With the other, the monkey offered her the coin.

His handler laughed. "Why, he likes ye, miss. Take it!"

She peered up at the captain. Not that she needed his permission, but did he suspect anything untoward about the transaction?

At his single nod, she bent and took the coin. "Thank you."

The crowd cheered, and both the monkey and his master doffed their hats and held them out.

Pennies clinked into the red velvet as patrons passed by. Abby reached into her reticule and fished out a thruppence, then tossed it in along with the monkey's gold coin. No doubt the traveling entertainers could use the money far more than she needed.

"Thank you, miss." The handler winked at her.

"No, no. Thank you."

She turned back to the captain, and for the first time that day, something other than suspicion glimmered in his eyes. "You are a generous soul, Miss Gilbert."

"As are you, more than you will admit to. I know you do not wish to be here, but I thank you for escorting me and Emma. I have never had such a wonderful time." She grinned up at him.

And he smiled right back at her.

For her.

Suddenly shy, Abby bit her lip, trying to ignore the tripping of her heart—until a barrel-bellied man stepped up to them, waving a red rose:

"The rose is fair but fairer still,
true love that binds and twines the will,
of lovers' hearts, and melds to one.
Try your luck and beat Big John!"

He pointed toward a raised platform not far from where they stood, where a shirtless man sat at a table at center. His greased brown flesh glistened in the sun, enhancing the muscles rippling on his chest and in his arms.

The man in front of them angled his head at the captain. "Best Big John in a fair-and-square arm wrestle and win your lady a flower, *if* your arm is as strong as your love."

Heat flared on Abby's face. "Oh, but you are mistaken. I am not his—"

"All right." The captain shoved Emma into her arms and stalked off.

Abby stared at his broad back, clutching Emma, unsure if she should follow or faint. Was the dour Captain Thatcher seriously going to take part in a frivolous fair game?

Just for her?

CHAPTER TWENTY-ONE

A shadow kept pace with them. Off to the left. Stopping when they did. Moving at their speed. Yet every time Samuel snapped his gaze that way, he was met only by innocent stares.

He thrust Emma into Miss Gilbert's arms and shot into the crowd. Not that he was eager to arm wrestle, but that platform would give him a broader view. He took the stairs two at a time, and at the top, he spun back to scan the edge of the people gathering closer.

Two young boys chased a pig past people's legs, sending a ripple through the swarm. Miss Gilbert, clutching Emma, shouldered her way through men and women alike, plowing a furrow right up to the front of the platform, God bless her. A long-limbed man with a brilliant green cap darted through the throng, taking bets for the upcoming wrestling match. Samuel frowned. Though he couldn't ask for a better vantage point, no one seemed suspicious, leastwise in this direction.

He pivoted, and—there. Possibly. Behind an apple vendor's stack of empty crates, he could barely make out a dark shape. Was someone hiding? After this morning's blunder, he'd need clear cause to go chasing a man down. He tugged the brim of his hat lower against the late-afternoon sun, shading his eyes, and—

"Don't back out now, man! Yer lady is a-watchin'."

An arm around his shoulders corralled him away from the edge of the platform and propelled him into a chair. Opposite him, a monster of a man assessed him as he might a carcass on the side of the road, his eyes like two black pebbles pushed deep into the sockets. He reeked of sweat and ale and far too much arrogance. Samuel jutted his chin. If he had the time, he'd be more than happy to school that pride right off the man's face.

The other man—the one who'd propositioned him in the first place—stepped to the front of the platform and faced the crowd with upstretched arms, beckoning with fluttering fingertips. "Step close, ladies and gents! See if Big John Banyan will retain his title, or if this fellow here"—he swept his arm toward Samuel—"will win his love a red, red rose. Is love strong enough to vanquish such solid brawn and muscle?"

Hoots and hollers—and even a few whistles—blew through the crowd like a gust of wind. Ignoring all the hubbub and Big John, Samuel jerked his gaze over his shoulder to catch another glimpse of those crates while the announcer kept on trumpeting about the match.

"That's it! Gather 'round! Don't be shy. Here's your chance to win and win big. But before ye place your wagers, ye ought to know, Big John ain't ne'er lost a match, not a one. Gentlemen, begin on my mark."

Samuel offered his arm without a glance, too busy studying the apple vendor's stand to even flinch when Big John's anvil-sized hand clamped on to his.

"Go!"

The black shape behind the crates moved. So did his arm. Just a second more and he'd see the face of whoever—

His shoulder wrenched, and he snapped his attention back to Big John. A wicked smile slashed across the brute's face, like a badly carved gourd on All Hallows' Eve. And no wonder. Samuel's arm was a breath away from being smashed into the tabletop right there in front of God and man. He'd look like a half-weaned stripling if he lost this quickly.

Ahh, but he didn't intend to lose at all, not if he could help it. True, Big John had at least ten stone on him, all bulging and steely, but for all the man's muscle, he was a compact fellow—and most importantly, his forearm was shorter than Samuel's.

Samuel gritted his teeth and twisted his wrist, turning his palm toward his face and slightly edging his opponent's hand into a direction he couldn't defend. Then, manipulating that angle, Samuel rotated his body, lining up his shoulder with the spot on the table he wanted to grind Big John's arm into. His muscles burned. This wouldn't be easy. With a quick prayer, a sharp thrust, and using all his body weight for leverage, Samuel whumped the man's arm over and pinned it to the oak.

The crowd roared. Big John's coal-black eyes burned like embers, his whole beefy face reddening to a deep shade of astonishment and rage.

Samuel sprang from his chair, craning his neck to peer at the apple crates. Sunlight leached through the slats. Each of them. Whoever had been there was gone now. Could've been nothing. In fact, he *hoped* it was nothing—and that was a new feeling. Lighter, somehow. He flexed his aching hand, ignoring the quivering muscles in his arm, while behind him, angry voices simmered into a hot, bubbling mix.

"He's a bleatin' cheater! Big John shoulda won!"

"Undefeated? My ever-loving backside! I want my money back!"

"This match were fixed, I tell ye!"

Alarm crept up his backbone. He'd seen riots before, humanity frothed up into foaming-mouthed dogs. Snarling. Snapping. Devouring. Abby and Emma wouldn't stand a chance in a mob like that, not once fists started flying.

He darted toward the stairs, plucking the rose from the announcer's hand. The man probably didn't even notice. He stood with his arms akimbo, his mouth opening and closing like a landed trout.

As soon as Samuel's feet hit the dirt, he shouldered his way over to Abby and grabbed her hand. "Come along," he shouted above the raised voices.

She followed without complaint, keeping close to his back. Once free of the crowd, he kept going and didn't release her hand until they neared a roped-off area, where a man led a spirited white Barbary horse on a spangled strip of leather.

Abby shifted Emma to her hip and smiled up into his face. "Well done, Captain! Such showmanship. For a moment, I feared you might lose."

"Have I not told you to never fear when I am around? Tip your head a bit. Here is your prize."

He snapped off the long stem of the flower—crushed beyond

salvation, anyway—and tucked the rose behind her ear, securing it between her bonnet and hair. But as he began to pull away, his fingers grazed the skin of her neck, and he sucked in a breath. He'd never felt anything so soft. So warm. So vibrant and pulsing with life.

Without thinking, he ran his thumb along the line of her jaw and brushed over her mouth. Heat flashed through him. What would it be like to touch those lips with his own? To pull her close and taste the sweetness and fullness of her?

Blessed heavens! What was he thinking?

He yanked back his hand and retreated a step, his heart beating loud in his ears.

Colour deepened on her cheeks, matching the red rose nestled against her dark hair. "Thank you, Captain. I am honored."

Her eyes gleamed with all the brilliance of a starry night, emotion shimmering in those brown depths. . .emotion stirred by him.

He swallowed—hard—and set his jaw. "We should leave."

And they should. Danger lurked somewhere on these fairgrounds—and in his own heart, for there was no denying it anymore.

He was in love with Abby Gilbert.

He turned away, then jumped back a step as a pig squealed past his feet. The two boys he'd seen earlier kicked up clods of dirt as they tore after it, arms outstretched, hollering all the way. The animal raced its stubby legs into the makeshift horse pen, and the boys followed right along, ducking under the rope.

Samuel's stomach rolled, churning a warning all the way to the back of his throat. That Barbary had been high-strung enough simply being led around the paddock. If the pig got too close—

It darted between handler and horse. The Barbary reared, breaking free of the man's hold. Thankfully, the boys scattered before the deadly hooves crushed their skulls to bits. The handler reached for the horse's lead, but the animal jerked from his reach and raced ahead.

Straight toward Abby and Emma.

Emma squirmed and screeched, her flailing arms knocking Abby's bonnet down over her eyes. At times, the child sounded just like a squealing piglet, especially when fatigued. The captain was right. This would be a good time to leave the madness of the fair.

Shuffling Emma to her other hip, Abby pushed up the brim of her bonnet, then gasped as the captain barreled into her, violently knocking her sideways. She stumbled away, frantically trying to regain her balance so she and Emma wouldn't topple to the ground. Why would he—?

A horse screamed. Close. Too close. She spun toward the sound. Then froze, horrified. The captain stood in the exact spot where she'd been.

And horse hooves plummeted toward his head.

He twisted, but a hoof caught him in the shoulder. The captain hurtled to the dirt with a whump. So did the horse's front legs, narrowly missing his face.

She gasped for air—then quit breathing altogether as the horse reared again.

Abby shrieked. Emma bawled. A few men rushed over, the horse's handler among them, but they stopped a safe distance from the wild animal, their arms flailing helplessly. Hot fury burned in Abby's heart. Why didn't they help the captain? Surely something could be done!

The dangerous hooves plummeted once more.

With all that was in her, Abby desperately wanted to close her eyes. Shut out the shocking gore that was sure to happen. But God help her, she stared, frozen, unable to blink let alone breathe.

God, no! Please!

With the deadly hooves inches away from the captain's head, he rolled and sprang up. Before the horse's legs landed, the captain grabbed the bridle with one hand. His other snagged the lead. He spoke into the animal's ear as he pulled the horse aside, leading it in a tight circle. Again and again. Finally, the frenzied horse calmed, and so did Abby's heartbeat.

Applause rippled around her, and she glanced sideways. A crowd had gathered. Surely they didn't think this was a show. . .did they?

The captain led the horse to his handler and offered over the lead without a word. The man took it, wide-eyed, slack-jawed. Was he amazed at the captain's skill or woefully shocked by his own lack?

"Well, now." The handler cleared his throat and tossed back his shoulders. "That was quite a show of horsemanship. I've a job for you, if you will have it. We could use a man like you."

"No thanks, I've already got one." He turned his back on the man and strode toward her.

Once again, her heart took off at a gallop. Dust coated the captain's shoulders and his suit coat. A hank of dark hair hung over one of his eyes, and sweat cut a trail down the dirt on his face. But even worn and beaten, his step was sure. His head held high. His dark gaze belonging to her alone. It didn't take any more to convince her that no matter the odds, this man could move a mountain by the strength of his will alone.

He stooped to pick up his hat, then stopped in front of her, shoved his wayward hair back, and jammed the worn felt onto his head.

Emma reached out a plump hand toward him, still sniffling from her crying bout. Abby shifted her away from him. The last thing he needed right now was to hold a wriggling child.

"Yet again you saved my life, Captain. You saved *our* lives."

"That's what you hired me for." He swiped his mouth with the back of his hand, rubbing off leftover dirt, as if he'd simply taken a tumble on the ground instead of nearly getting killed.

Which only endeared him to her more. If Sir Jonathan turned out to be half the man as Captain Thatcher, she couldn't help but live happily ever after.

"You are far too modest, sir. I thank you for risking your life for ours." Just like Emma, she reached toward him, wanting—*needing*—to feel the solid muscle beneath his sleeve. She'd nearly lost this man, and the thought sent a ripple through her soul.

Her hand landed lightly on his upper arm—and he winced.

She pulled back. "You are hurt!"

He looked away, scanning the ground around them. "Just a bruise, likely. It's getting late. Have you seen enough of the fair?"

A shiver shimmied across her shoulders. "More than enough."

His gaze shot back to hers, and he held out his arms. "Then hand over Emma, and let's be on our way."

She shook her head. "After what you have just been through, I cannot allow you to—"

"I insist." He pulled Emma from her arms, and Abby couldn't help but note that he held her far away from his injured shoulder. She frowned. The big oaf. That was more than just a bruise.

Before she could protest any further, he pivoted and set off through the merrymakers. By the time they got to the inn, the hunger pangs in her stomach surely ached as much as the captain's shoulder.

After a dinner of pease pudding and bacon, throughout which the captain said hardly more than five or six words, both she and Emma yawned. Strange that the captain didn't seem weary, especially after his ordeal. While stoic, he didn't sag in his chair, nor did his eyes droop. He sat as alert as ever.

Narrowing her gaze, Abby studied him. Not fatigued, but definitely preoccupied. By what?

He stood and pushed back his chair, then gathered Emma against his chest. "I'll see you ladies to your room."

Abby followed his broad back toward the stairway. The chatter of the taproom lessened as they ascended to the first floor, and faded even more as he led her down to the farthest door at the end of the passageway. It was a tight little corridor, not much wider than the captain's shoulders. When he turned and handed over Emma, his arm brushed against hers.

Though propriety dictated she shy away, she didn't. Nor did she move so he could open the door. There was something precious about this moment. Something she didn't want to give up so soon. She peered up at him, memorizing the strong line of his nose, his firm mouth, the defined cut of his jaw. Even the small scrape to his chin that he must've earned while capturing the wild horse charmed her.

Finally, fully, he met her gaze. Curiosity darkened his eyes to the shade of polished mahogany, and he angled his head. "You look at me as if I might disappear. What are you thinking?"

"I would ask the same of you, Captain. You hardly put two words together during dinner. Clearly there is something on your mind. What is it?"

His jaw worked, yet no sound came out. Emma laid her head against Abby's shoulder, signaling she was ready for sleep.

But Abby held her ground. She'd learned long ago how to outwait a stubborn mule.

The captain sighed, his breath warm and feathering against her cheek. "Has anyone ever told you how persistent you are?"

"You have. Many times." She tipped her chin. "And though your bluster makes it sound as if that is a bad thing, I get the distinct impression that you somehow admire me for it."

His Adam's apple bobbed. "Would it matter?"

She frowned. "Would what matter?"

"If I admired you." He bent close, his brown eyes searching parts of her she'd never shared with anyone. . .until now.

Sudden warmth flooded her from head to toe, and she held her breath. The truth was that this man's good opinion of her *did* matter, more than she could possibly understand. She leaned toward him, and despite the barrier of a small child in her arms, she craved the captain's touch, desiring far more than his admiration.

She froze. What was she thinking? She had no right to share any part of her heart with the captain. But how could she take back what she'd already given?

"I—" All the words she should say, the denial of him she must give, stuck in her throat, and she swallowed.

He rested his worn, calloused finger on her lips. "There is no need to answer. I shouldn't have asked the question to begin with. Good night, Miss Gilbert." He edged past her and stalked down the corridor.

She stared at his retreating form, clutching Emma. Each of his steps away from her was a great, gaping loss, like someone carving a hole in her chest in the exact area that her heart ought to be.

"Good night," she whispered, the words tasting as dry as ashes in her mouth.

As hard as it was going to be to say goodbye to Emma in two days, she suspected that when the time came, it was going to be impossible to voice a farewell to the captain.

CHAPTER TWENTY-TWO

The next days flew by, far too fast for Abby's liking. Her mouth twisted with the irony of it as she stared out at the Manchester streets. How eager she'd been a lifetime ago when Fanny had accompanied her, zealous to cover as many miles as possible in a day. Now if she could grab the hands of time and stop them, she would.

The carriage bumped over cobblestones then dipped into a pothole. She held Emma closer on her lap, her arm wrapped snug around the girl's tummy. Surprisingly, Emma sat still and had for some time. It was almost as if the girl knew her life was about to change and was as reluctant to let go of Abby as Abby was to release her to a family unknown.

She pressed a kiss atop Emma's head, then looked out the window, trying to guess which house might be the girl's new home. Rusty brick row houses paraded by, straight as a school matron's posture. They were neat and tidy, but the doors opened right onto the street. There'd be no green grass for Emma to run around on, no space for her to explore, and oh, how she loved to move. Hopefully they wouldn't stop here.

The coach turned, leaving the brick houses behind, and relief loosened the muscles in Abby's shoulders. Emma deserved a cottage house, one with a great field and possibly a pony, where she could grow up running free and breathing fresh air. That was an impossibility here in the city, of course, but at least they might pull up in front of a town house with a small patch of yard.

But the carriage turned again, this time onto a narrower lane stinking of eggs and fish brine. Abby scrunched her nose. Surely this was only a shortcut on the way to a better part of town.

It wasn't. The farther they traveled, the closer the sides of the road drew, choking out light and air and hope. Houses leaned one against the other, like drunken sailors holding each other upright. If one fell, the rest would lie down and never get up again. Abby grimaced, silently praying for mercy on Emma's behalf. She'd hate to leave the girl in one of these hovels.

Thankfully, the carriage made a sharp right, and she flung out her hand to balance against the wall. Emma laughed, and after one more kiss to the little one's downy head, Abby once again looked out the window as the coach jolted to a stop—and her heart dropped to her shoes.

The captain flipped down the stairs and opened the door. When he offered his hand, Abby debated if she ought to shrink back and hide Emma behind her skirts.

His dark gaze met her hesitation, commanding her to come out with nothing more than the tilt of his head. She stepped down into an alley courtyard, surrounded on three sides by buildings made up of weathered boards that were held together more by misguided will than nails. Ropes crisscrossed overhead, from one window to another. Those that had glass were cracked. Patched garments hung like graveclothes over the lines, colourless sleeves dangling, grey trousers languishing. . . or were those rags? None of the clothes rippled with movement, for not a breath of a breeze crawled into this hole.

She peeked up at the captain. "Are you certain you wrote down the correct address?"

His jaw hardened, and he nodded. Without a word, he handed Emma to her and retrieved the girl's basket and small traveling bag. Three steps later, she stood by the captain's side as he pounded his fist on a pitted door. Abby felt dirty just looking at the place. Maybe no one would answer, and they wouldn't have to—

The door opened a crack. A smudge-faced boy with a black eye peered out, saying nothing.

Captain Thatcher stared down at him. "I'm looking for Margaret Gruber. Is she your mother? Is she at home?"

The lad's nose twitched, then he shut the door—or tried to. The captain shoved the toe of his boot in the gap.

Inside, a reed-thin voice leached out the opening. "Who is it, Tim?"

The boy stiffened. He darted a look over his shoulder, then licked his lips. "Ain't s'posed to allow no one in. Father's orders."

Captain Thatcher took a step closer and bellowed into the house. "Margaret Gruber? I'm here on behalf of your brother, James Hawker. I'm a lawman, madam. You have nothing to fear."

Tim glowered up at him, the purple around his eye deepening to a shade of fury no young lad should own.

"Let him in, Timmy." The voice inside was little more than a whisper.

"But we ain't s'posed to—"

"You heard your mother." The captain used his stern tone, and Abby straightened her own spine in response.

With a scowl better suited to an overworked longshoreman, Tim flung the door open and retreated into darkness. The captain followed, and for a moment, Abby hesitated at the threshold, holding Emma tight, afraid to enter. Afraid for the girl's future. Afraid of the thick dread knotting her stomach.

Pudgy little fingers cupped her chin, pulling her face down. Emma's big blue eyes stared up at her. "Ah-be-da?"

Abby's throat tightened at the only word Emma knew—whatever it meant. Swallowing back tears, she willed herself to be strong. If she started to cry, no doubt Emma would wail, and the captain would surely have no patience for such a display.

She brushed back the girl's reddish-blond hair and whispered, "Ah-be-da, little one."

Summoning all her courage, Abby stepped into a room not much bigger than a crypt. Daylight barely seeped through a soot-filmed window, casting shadows over a few sticks of furniture. A table stood at center, which was really just some planks propped atop two crates. An off-kilter bench, large enough to seat only two, sat next to a small hearth. On the floor in one corner lay a poorly stuffed sack with a threadbare lump of fabric balled atop it. Their bed, perhaps? Tim stood next to it, arms crossed. A strange stance of protection for naught but a wad of bedding. . .unless he had some treasure hidden there? But where was the owner of the thin voice? There were no other rooms and no ladder leading up to a loft.

The captain strode to the foot of the mattress. "Are you Margaret Gruber?"

Abby dared a few more steps into the room, narrowing her eyes upon the crude bed. What she'd mistaken for fabric slowly moved, lengthening, rising. A waif of a woman sat up, one arm pressed tight against her stomach. Stringy hair hung down over parchment skin, her eyes deep set and yellow. Her lip was split as if someone had punched her in the teeth.

"I am Margaret," she rasped. "What of my brother? Is James well?"

Abby huddled closer to the captain's back, seeking solace that she knew he couldn't provide. Everything inside her screamed to make him turn around, to plead with him to take her and Emma out of here, to ride hard and far away from this place of despair. Not that he'd listen, though. It was his duty to carry out his friend's wishes, and above all, the captain was a man of honor.

But none of that mattered to Abby. Not now. Not ever. How could she possibly leave Emma in the care of a woman who was little more than a collection of bones and blue veins?

"Your brother is. . .he lives." There was only a slight hitch in the captain's words, but enough that Abby caught the slip. He knew something about the man, something he wouldn't share with the woman. "James charged me with delivering his only child into your care."

The captain glanced at Abby over his shoulder, and with a nod of his head, he indicated it was time to hand over Emma.

Abby's gut clenched, feeling as sick as the woman on the pallet looked. She'd known all along this moment was coming. Tried to separate her heart from the babe she'd learned to love as her own flesh and blood. But now that it was here?

She turned and fled out the door, clutching tightly to Emma.

Of all the foolhardy moves!

Samuel dropped Emma's basket and bag and took off, chasing

Abby's blue-striped skirt outside. What on God's green earth was the woman thinking? That wasn't a kitten she held. Emma was not a pet she could cosset and make her own.

He grabbed Abby by the shoulder and spun her around. "What do you think you're doing?"

Her brows folded into a fierce frown. "We cannot leave Emma in that place. We cannot!"

The words were choked. Desperate. As ragged and ruined as the pathetic scrabble of a courtyard they stood in.

Samuel yanked off his hat and raked a hand through his hair, tugging hard and relishing the sting. It was a stalling tactic, one he employed on those rare times he felt helpless, and sweet blessed heavens, his hands were tied in this wretched situation. He let loose a breath, praying for the right words to convince Abby—and himself—that leaving Emma here was the right thing to do. That there was no other option.

For there wasn't.

He tugged his hat back onto his head, just as Emma reached out to him.

"Ah-be-da?"

His gut clenched, sickened by the guileless blue eyes staring up at him. Trust lifted the girl's brow. Innocence as pure as that of a newborn foal radiated from her. His hands curled into fists. How could he possibly go through with this?

Steeling his jaw, he gently pushed Emma's hand away and looked only at Abby. "I know this is hard. This isn't what I want for Emma either, but the child is not ours. We cannot keep her from her kin. Say goodbye."

"But—"

"Say goodbye!" He snapped out the command, hating himself for his harshness, hating even more the instant tears shimmering in Abby's eyes.

The small shards of his heart that were left broke into a million jagged-edged pieces as Abby lifted the child, face-to-face, and wept openly. Little gasps for air punctuated her words.

"Goodbye, little one. You be a good girl for your new"—her face contorted and she gulped—"for your new family."

Emma planted her palms on each of Abby's cheeks, pulling their faces together.

And Samuel clenched every muscle in his body to keep from crying himself.

God, how am I to bear this? Give me strength, Lord. Give me Your strength.

From an act of sheer will, he pulled Emma from Abby's arms, refusing to look at the girl, staring only at Abby's teary gaze. "Stay out here if you like." His voice lowered an octave, and in truth, it was a wonder he could force out the words at all. "I'll be back shortly."

He wheeled about. Footsteps padded behind him, each tamp of leather against gravel accusing him. She blamed him for doing this—yet she needn't have. The nightmares that were sure to follow this day would sear his soul for years to come.

His step faltered as he neared the door. He'd had to do hard things before. It came with the job. Dragging mangled bodies out of crashed coaches. Hunting down killers who'd think nothing of slicing open his throat. But stepping back into the rat hole the Grubers called a home topped them all.

Sucking in a breath for courage, he strode into the dim interior. For the first time ever, the gloomy shadows that wrapped around him didn't comfort, and he suspected they never would again.

He stalked over to the pallet in the corner and held Emma out. "This is Emmaline Hawker, your niece."

Hawker's sister looked up at him, her face softening, and for the briefest moment, the ravages of whatever disease she suffered from lessened. "Ahh, such a lamb. Give her to me."

"No, Mother!" The boy dropped to all fours, pleading with the woman practically nose to nose. "You can't. Send them away before Father returns."

Samuel tensed—and suddenly he was ten years old again. Begging his mother to snatch up his sister and run away with him. Tugging at her apron to get her out of the house before his father came home, drunk, loud, and swinging his fists. Cold sweat beaded on his forehead. The similarities here were far too many. What kind of wicked jest was this?

Margaret patted a bony hand atop the boy's head. "It is my brother's wish. I owe him this, at least."

Samuel eyed the woman as Emma kicked her legs, angling to be free. What had Hawker done for his sister that she felt so beholden to him?

Tim sank back to his haunches as his mother held up her arms to receive Emma. The neck hole of the woman's thin shift drooped with the movement. Paste-coloured skin peeked out, dotted with red spots.

Samuel bit back a curse, knowing full well but not wanting to admit what the woman suffered from. . .wasting fever. He'd wager ten to one on it. Margaret Gruber would be dead within a week. Two, if she were lucky—which she wasn't. Luck didn't live in this wretched backstreet fleapit.

Clenching his teeth so hard that his jaw cracked, he stooped and handed Emma down to the woman, not releasing her until Margaret Gruber's skeletal arms wrapped around her.

Emma craned her neck, gawking up at him. One of her hands snaked up in the air, reaching for him. "Be-dah?"

He shook his head, refusing the request, and betrayal wailed out of the girl's mouth, punching the air from his lungs.

Folding his arms, he turned to the boy, vainly trying to shut out Emma's cries. "Where is your father?"

Tim didn't bother standing. He stayed crouched, only his eyes moving. "Out selling apples."

Apples? Samuel frowned. Only cripples sold—

"What's this?" A foghorn of a voice entered just before a thump-step, thump-step drew up behind him.

Samuel swung about, and Abby darted to his side. Two steel-grey eyes bored into his. The man was his height, slightly smaller of frame, and propped up by a rag-topped crutch shoved beneath one armpit. Only one leg and the stick of hickory held him up. A sour stench wafted off him. From a morning of drinking or from whatever it was he held in a canvas sack.

The man's cold gaze slid from him to Abby, drifted down to where Hawker's sister tried to shush a snotty-nosed Emma, and finally landed hard on Tim. Purple crept up the man's neck. "I told you, boy, ne'er to let anyone in."

Samuel sidestepped, blocking Tim from his father's deadly stare. "The boy had no choice in the matter. I am Captain Thatcher, principal officer of the Bow Street magistrate."

Gruber bared his teeth like a wolf. If hatred were a living thing, the size and breadth of the monster living inside the man would devour them all.

"What's a filthy runner doing up in these parts? Not enough men to harass in London? Bloody thief catcher. Bootlicker to the crown, that's what you are."

Samuel rolled with the jabs. He'd heard worse. These weren't even particularly creative. He met the man's stare head-on. "I was charged to deliver your niece into your wife's care."

Curses thickened the air, punctuated by the thwack of the man's bag landing on the table. "I can't feed a squalling brat! I can barely feed these two worthless sacks of horse—"

"Mind your tongue," Samuel growled. "There are ladies present."

Scarlet spread up the man's neck and bled across his pockmarked face. "I'll not be told what to do in my own home, *runner*."

"You will as long as I'm here." Pulling free of Abby, Samuel stepped up to the bully and squared his shoulders.

Footsteps trembled behind him. Abby gained his side and fumbled with the strings of her reticule, drawing all their attention. She dumped the contents into her palm, the coins jingling into a small pile, then held out the offering to Gruber. "Here. Use this for Emma's care, for all of your family's care, that she may not be a hardship to you."

The man snatched the money away so quickly, he wobbled on his crutch. "All right. But soon as this is gone"—he looked past him and Abby, narrowing his eyes on his family huddled in the corner—"the child will be eating from your portions, not mine."

Fury quaked through Samuel, shaking him to the marrow of his bones. Should not a husband, a father, *any* man born in the image of God die to self for the sake of a loved one? Ahh, but there was the truth of it. Gruber loved no one but himself—just like the man who'd sired him thirty-odd years back.

Gruber shoved the coins into his pocket then turned on him. "Well, runner? Have you further business with me?"

Aye, he'd like to give the mongrel a sound thrashing. Teach him what it was like to be knocked about for no reason other than the whim of the moment. Samuel's fists tightened into iron knots. He could use a real bloody knuckle toss-around right about now, and in his younger days, nothing would've held him back. But Emma's mewls did. So did the trembling of Abby's skirts.

"No," he ground out.

Gruber's mouth twisted into a snarl. "Then shove off."

Without another word, Samuel wrapped his arm around Abby's shoulders and guided her toward the door, forcing each step. There was nothing else to do. He never should have given Hawker his word.

And Emma's wailing cries drove home that ugly truth, each one stabbing him in the back.

CHAPTER TWENTY-THREE

Merry chatter bubbled in the taproom, boxing Abby's ears. Laughter clanged in her head, overly loud. This inn was a rash. The *world* was a rash. Irritating. Rubbing her raw. How could everyone be so cheerful when all was not right?

She stabbed a piece of roasted pork and popped it into her mouth, knowing the thing would stick in her throat, as had the few bites she'd barely managed before. All she wanted to hear was Emma's coos or babbles. She'd even listen to the girl's cries and count herself blessed. But never again would she hear that little one's sweet voice.

The pork landed like a rock in her stomach, and Abby set down her fork. Who was she kidding? She ought to rummage through her chest and pull out her mourning crepe until her heart healed. But would it ever? And if it did, would that not be dishonoring to the child whom she'd come to love so much? It seemed a hideous blasphemy to simply forget Emma like a castoff mantle.

A pang of guilt churned the meat in her belly. She hadn't grieved the loss of her own family as profoundly as this.

Across from her, the captain shoveled in his last bite then pushed away his plate. Amazing that he could eat so heartily. Did he not miss Emma as keenly as she?

Abby searched the captain's face for an answer. His dark gaze met hers, but nothing moved behind his eyes. He was a house shuttered tight against any unwelcome visitors.

"A farthing for your thoughts, Captain."

"Trust me," he grumbled. "They're not worth that much."

"They must be of some kind of value. You've hoarded them since we delivered Emma."

Leaning back in his chair, he folded his arms across his chest, a stance she knew too well. He had no intention of answering.

So it astonished her when he opened his mouth. "You are—"

"I know." She cut him off with a flutter of her fingers. "I am persistent. And *you* should know by now that I will not rest until I hear what it is that worries you so."

His lips clamped shut, pressing into a firm line.

Abby shoved down a sigh, for she knew that expression intimately as well. The captain was done with the conversation before it even began. His stubborn streak was as long and broad as her persistence. She might as well bid him good night now, for they were at a stalemate. Pulling the napkin from her lap, she set it on the table and edged back her chair.

But before she could rise, the captain's voice rumbled low, catching her off guard once again. She scooted closer to the table, straining to hear over the clatter of forks scraping against plates and dinner conversations much more pleasant than this would surely be.

"I have no idea why I'm telling you this." He looked past her for a moment, as if he searched for words at a far table in the room. Then his gaze shot back to hers, swift and sharp as any arrow. "It's Emma. She'll die there, in that house. I might as well have killed her with my own hands."

Abby bit her lip, unsure of what to say, how to comfort the pain riding ragged in his voice. Yet she must say something. Put him at ease somehow.

She clenched her hands in her lap, hoping to squeeze out some form of consolation. "Surely God will watch over her."

There. She'd done it, said something. . .but what exactly had she said? Even to herself her words sounded small in the big room—or maybe it was the sentiment that felt so absurdly tiny in the face of such a loss.

The captain apparently agreed. His jaw hardened, and his eyes narrowed upon her, making her feel even more minute and ridiculous.

Tipping his chin, he looked down the length of his nose at her. "The only thing sure is that man Gruber will run them all into the ground."

She stiffened. No. She couldn't believe that. She wouldn't.

She met his rock-hard stare with one of her own. "You do not know that, Captain. Can you not hope for the best?"

He snorted. "Can you?"

He shoved back his chair and stalked toward the front door, leaving her alone to fight the monster of a question he'd loosed upon her. Coward!

She jumped up and followed him outside. Sconces burned brilliantly against the night, set at intervals on the brick wall of the inn, welcoming any late travelers. The captain, however, strode beyond the yellow glow, his boots pounding hard on the courtyard's gravel. He stopped when he reached a stone wall, standing as high as his waist, then bent and propped his elbows on it. But he didn't turn as she drew up behind him, though he had to know she stood close. He just stood there, staring into the darkness, no acknowledgment whatsoever.

Abby clenched her hands, her nails digging little crescents into her palms, angry with the obstinate man. Angry with herself too. What had gotten into her? Now that she was here, what was she to say to the captain's broad back? That he was wrong? That Emma was even now likely tucked safely into a soft bed with a full tummy?

Despite the chill of the evening, fury burned all the hotter in her chest. Deep down, the truth roiled her few bites of pork roast to rancid bits. The captain was right. Though she'd been trying all afternoon to hope for the best, going so far as to search the scriptures before dinner, she couldn't do it. She was anxious, despairing, and annoyed with searching for hope. No, worse. She was chained and fettered by a lack of it, unable to move or breathe.

She clenched her fists tighter until her arms shook. How was she to be hopeful when the outcome for Emma would be a life of poverty? Or death? No. There was no possible way she could churn up any morsel of hope for the girl she loved.

"But I can, child."

She tensed, every muscle in her locking tight. Had she heard right?

But how could the captain know what she'd been thinking? Why call her a child? And how on earth did he propose to help restore her hope when he rarely partook of the sentiment?

She dared a step nearer to him. "What did you say?"

He glanced back at her. "There is nothing to say except go to bed, Miss Gilbert."

She cocked her head. She could've sworn she'd heard—

"Hope in Me, child. Emma is Mine, as are you."

Wonderful. Now she was hearing things. Tiny prickles ran down her arms, raising gooseflesh. Had she not begged all afternoon for guidance and wisdom, to hear some measure of comfort from God's mouth alone?

She lifted her face to the black sky.

Is that You, Lord? Is that Your voice I hear?

She stood there for a long time, the captain's broad back to her, stars blinking down on them both. No more whispers came, but that didn't stop an urgent prayer from welling up in her soul.

Oh God, will You take my ugly hope of You protecting little Emma and change it into a peaceful hope? A strong one? Maybe even a joyful hope? Because I do believe, with all my heart, that Christ is the Victor, that You are Emma's Protector no matter what, and in that truth will I abide.

The same peace she'd felt days ago draped over her shoulders, and against all reason, she knew—she *knew*—that somehow Emma's future would shine as brightly as the stars twinkling overhead.

In the dark, the captain's shoulders bent, his silhouette black upon black. "I shouldn't have left her there." The words were quiet, more of a groan, really. His bleak confession dared her to drift back into despair.

She laid a hand on those bent shoulders, wishing with all that was within her to relieve some of the weight this man carried. "You did what you promised, Captain, and that is always a good thing."

"Maybe." He turned to face her. "But maybe I never should have promised such a thing in the first place."

Sidestepping her, he stalked toward the inn and disappeared through the door.

For once, she didn't follow him. She planted her feet and looked up to the heavens. It was going to be a long night for the captain—and for her. She had a lot of praying to do on his behalf.

Regrets always attacked worst in the darkness. Springing out from the midnight shadows. Drawing blood as the witching hours slowly ticked off. By the time Samuel swung his leg over Pilgrim the next morning and led the carriage through the streets of Manchester, he was battle sore and bone weary from an evening of wrestling with guilt.

He shouldn't have left Emma at the Grubers'.

He shouldn't have taken her on in the first place.

And he definitely shouldn't have said anything to Abby about it.

Scrubbing his hand over his face, he fought a yawn. He couldn't afford this fatigue, for it might cost his and Abby's life if Shankhart or his men were about. And they would be, sooner or later. If only he had enough funds to buy another gun, arm the driver, or even hire on another man to ride with them.

Shops thinned out as he neared the Manchester city limits. Beyond, fields stretched into a green patchwork. He urged Pilgrim with a nudge to her side to up the pace. Soon they'd pass by a gibbet with some blackguard's body in a state of decomposition, swinging in the breeze, which was no proper sight for Abby to witness should she chance a glance out the carriage window.

Clouds smothered the countryside, punching down from the sky like mighty grey fists. A bleak day, as dreary and miserable as his mood. Abby had been right when she'd called him a dour old naysayer.

Off to his left, in the field, a boy cried out. Samuel narrowed his eyes. A big man held the lad in the air by the collar with one hand. The other clutched a switch, striking the boy on the backside. Again and again. Far too many times for whatever crime the lad had committed, if any. Men like that often didn't need an excuse to torture those younger and smaller, those like Emma. *Oh Emma. . .*

His throat closed, and he lifted his face to the sullen sky. "God, what have I done? Emma won't last long in that place. Some guardian I turned out to be."

"Peace, My son. I am her Protector."

The truth of the unspoken words hit like a hammer to the head, stunning, smarting, and rankling in a most unholy fashion. He clenched the reins to keep from raising a fist to the heavens. "But how? How will You protect a child I left defenseless with a monster?"

"You."

He cocked his head, suddenly unsure of his sanity. But more words whispered on the wind.

"You are my means."

Sweet heavens! He was going mad. Surely a righteous God would not condone him breaking a vow. "But I swore to bring her there. I promised—"

The boy's cries stopped. So did his heart. The truth of his own prayer zapped through him from head to toe, leaving a line of prickles in its wake. He had promised to deliver Emma to Hawker's sister, and so he'd fulfilled his pledge.

But he'd never once said he'd leave her there forever.

He tugged Pilgrim's reins, stopping the big bay, feeling lighter. Freer. And more determined than ever to rescue Emma. But first he swung his gaze back to the field and narrowed his eyes toward the boy, intent on helping him.

Half a smile lifted his lips. The lad had wriggled free and was even now hightailing it out of the barley, the big man with the switch losing ground as the boy sprinted. The cruel master wouldn't catch him again, not today, and maybe not ever if the boy kept running.

Clicking his tongue, Samuel guided Pilgrim in a tight circle, then bolted back to the carriage and pulled up next to the postilion with a raised hand.

"Turn around," he ordered.

Alarm widened the man's eyes. "Something wrong, Captain?"

"Not anymore." He kicked Pilgrim into a canter, purposely avoiding the bewildered look on Abby's face as he rode past the carriage window.

It took every last bit of his self-control to keep from galloping. Tearing into a town as if the devil were at his heels was asking for attention, and that was never a good thing.

The Grubers lived near the cotton mills, where the rich broke the backs of the poorest of the poor, working them to death and making profit during the sparse years they laboured. Soot blackened the nearby buildings, windows, hearts, and souls. But this day as Samuel rode into the alley on Mudlark Lane, the oppression of the bleak courtyard didn't smother him. In fact, he sprang off Pilgrim as if he'd lost ten years.

The postilion eased the coach to a stop, and Samuel strode over to the man. "Turn the carriage around and wait."

"Aye, Captain." He gave him a sharp nod.

And Abby gave him a sharp look as she stuck her head out the open window. "What are we doing back here? Are you going to—"

He shot up his hand, staving her off. "Stay in the carriage, Miss Gilbert."

"But—"

Thankfully, the postilion ordered the horses to walk on, carrying away Abby's questions and protests.

Samuel drew near the door, rage lighting a fire in him as Emma's pitiful cries leached through the thin wood. If Gruber had harmed that girl, may God have mercy on the man—for he surely wouldn't.

He pounded his fist against the door, rattling the wood like bones in a coffin. "Open up! Captain Thatcher here."

Emma screamed. "Ah-be-da!"

That did it. He rammed his shoulder against the door, forcing it open. The wood smacked into the wall, startling Emma, and she stared up at him from where she sat on the floor, mouth open, face smudged, and her bonnet gone. The clean gown Abby had dressed her in the day before was now soiled with ash, grease, and the contents from an overflowing clout.

But he didn't care. Samuel swept her up and cradled her against his chest, rubbing his cheek against the top of her head. Her fingers clawed into his waistcoat in a grip that would be impossible to pry off.

"Ah-be-da, little one," he whispered against her hair.

With a last, shuddering breath, she quit crying.

Samuel lifted his face, surveying the small room. His gaze landed near the hearth, where Margaret Gruber lay on the floor still as a stone, despite the commotion of a man breaking into her home and snatching up the babe in her care.

He pulled off his hat and peeled Emma from his chest, setting the child down with the old piece of worn felt—her favorite plaything. Two paces later, he dropped to his knees and bent over what might very well be Margaret Gruber's corpse. Strands of greasy hair hung over her sharp cheekbones, her skin the colour of wax. Her eyes stayed shut, and though he looked, he couldn't really detect any rise or fall of her chest.

"Mrs. Gruber?" He pressed his fingers against the side of her neck. A weak pulse fluttered beneath his touch, for now, anyway.

He scooped her up, her body weighing hardly more than Emma's, and as he laid her on the flattened sack of straw in the corner, her eyes flickered open.

"Captain?" Her voice was a wisp against her cracked lips. The air rattled in her lungs. But she'd recognized him, a small victory, that, but a victory nonetheless.

"Yes, madam, it's me. Let me get you a drink."

He collected a dipper of greenish water from a pail with scum climbing up the insides. Not good, but better than nothing. . .hopefully.

Emma scooted over, grabbing onto his leg and pulling herself upright, so that he had to hobble back to Mrs. Gruber with the child attached. Once again he pried Emma's hands from him, then aided the sick woman to sit, lending her his strength as she drank.

"Mmm," she murmured as she took little sips and finally downed it all. Her yellowed eyes blinked up to his. "Thank you. I am much revived."

He eased her back down and set the dipper aside while Emma pounded on his back, cooing. Then he faced Mrs. Gruber. "Is there anything more I can do for you?"

"No, I. . ." She swallowed, her throat bobbing with the effort, but when she spoke again, her voice came out much clearer. "You came at a fortunate time. I was trying to stop Emma from getting too near the hearth, but I. . .I couldn't do it." Her brow folded, and she swallowed again. "Why are you here?"

"I'm taking the girl." With one arm, he swept Emma from behind his back and drew her forward. "I'm taking Emma back to your brother."

The woman's eyes glistened. From sadness or a return of her fever? "But James wished me to care for her."

He hugged Emma tighter in the curl of his arm. "We both know you can't, madam."

"You don't understand. I owe him this." Thin tears broke loose, just a few, for she likely couldn't produce more. "My brother is the one who got us out of debtors' prison."

Samuel stifled a scowl. Would that Hawker could've saved his sister from her brute of a husband as well.

"Mrs. Gruber," he softened his tone, "I am certain that if your brother knew you were ailing, he'd not have sent Emma in the first place. I shouldn't have left her here yesterday. The burden is too much for you to bear."

"You are"—her voice hitched, and she gulped in a breath—"very kind, sir."

Reaching with his free arm, he pushed back the matted hair from her brow, wishing he could do more for her. But it was too late. It would be a miracle if she lasted till nightfall.

"Rest now," he whispered. "I'll gather Emma's things and let myself out."

Her hand shot out, grabbing his arm with more strength than he'd credited. "Thank you."

Torment twisted her face, stabbing him in the heart. It wasn't fair, this ruined life of death and destruction. "May God bless you, Margaret Gruber."

Her lips parted, and for one spectacular moment, a brilliant smile lit her face, erasing the ravages of disease and hard living. "He already has, Captain, for I am assured I will go to a better place because of Christ."

Her eyes closed, and she drifted into a peaceful sleep.

Blowing out a long breath, Samuel gripped Emma tighter and stood, hauling her up along with him. Her basket lay overturned on the floor near the door, and her bag of belongings spilled out clouts and tiny gowns onto the table. Samuel scooped both up in his empty hand and strode to the door—just as it opened.

Tim stood on the threshold, blood dripping a trail from his nose to his upper lip, then smeared across his cheek where he'd obviously been swiping at it with his sleeve.

"Best be on yer way, sir." He ran his arm across his nose once again. "My father's not far behind."

Fury throbbed a vein in Samuel's temple. No doubt the boy had his cullion of a father to thank for that bloody nose. He set down the basket and crouched, keeping a good hold on Emma. Then he fished in his pocket, pulling out the last of his coins and the end of his hope to purchase any land in the near future.

"Hold out your hand, Tim."

The boy sniffled and cocked his head, but slowly he obeyed. Good boy. Too good for the likes of Gruber.

Samuel pressed the money into the boy's hand and held on.

The boy's blue eyes searched his, questions creasing his forehead as blood continued to ooze from his nostrils.

Samuel squeezed his hand. "Take this money and hide it. It's a tough truth, but you need to know. Your mother isn't long for this world. She'll be lucky to make it another day. When she's gone, leave here. Immediately. Use these coins to take a coach to Warrington. When you get off, seek out Farmer Bigby, about six miles from town. Tell him you have my recommendation. You'll be safe there. Do you understand?"

Slowly, the boy nodded. "Aye, sir."

"Good." Samuel released him and snatched up Emma's things. Indeed, no place this side of heaven was truly safe, but that never stopped God from being a protector. And maybe—just maybe—God had allowed him, a tired, worn-out lawman, to make the world a little safer for one young boy.

CHAPTER TWENTY-FOUR

Eyes watched them—and had been since they'd left Manchester two days ago. Close but unseen. Ever present. Samuel couldn't prove it, despite his best efforts, but the queer twist in his gut was all the evidence he needed.

So he alternated between scouting ahead of the carriage, then doubling back and trailing behind, as he now rode. To his right, fields stretched just beyond an abrupt dip that led to a small river. To his left, death. In what had been a vibrant pine forest, charred trees stood like skeletons. The larger ones, at any rate. The rest scattered the blackened ground like dead men's bones, eerily rising up from the grave in spots where boulders lifted the ends of them into burnt pikes.

Pilgrim's ears twitched, and Samuel bent forward, patting the horse's neck. "Easy, girl. That fire's long gone."

He straightened and continued plodding along. Prudence demanded he up his pace, but even so, he held Pilgrim to a slow and steady stride. Within the hour, the manor home of Sir Jonathan Aberley would loom large on the horizon and steal Abby away from him. Forever. The thought of it cut deep in his soul. While it would be a relief to deliver her safely, he could not make himself hasten to that hideous end. He wasn't ready to part with her—and never would be. He'd grown accustomed to the woman, and he'd miss her as sorely as he would his arm or his leg. Somehow over these past weeks, she'd scaled his best defenses and become a part of him.

But in his heart he knew it was time to let her go. Release her into God's care and that of the baronet He'd provided for her. True, the man hardly knew her and likely didn't love her—yet—but he soon would once he learned of Abby's family background and saw how precious the woman truly was.

Shadows stretched longer as the sun sank lower in the sky. Would that he could stop time from passing, that he wouldn't be traveling this same road tomorrow in the opposite direction with Emma shored up in front of him. After a quick stop at the Bigbys' to check on Tim—for surely the lad would be smart enough to go there—he'd make the trek back to Hawker's. And when he dropped off Emma, he'd be alone.

More alone than he'd ever been in his life.

Ahead, the carriage stopped, and he pressed his heels into Pilgrim's side, shooting forward. The way the road bent, this was not a good place to loiter. Any manner of danger could come at them with little warning. Half-wit driver! He'd had reservations about the postilion's aptitude the first time he met the fellow. It was a foul twist of fate that the fellow had been the only available postilion.

Drawing near, Samuel rolled his shoulders, vainly trying to ease some of the tension eating at him. A felled tree blocked part of the road in front of the coach, a valid enough reason to slow the horses—but not stop them. The man could easily have driven around the impediment. And why the deuce had he dismounted and was even now walking away from the carriage, toward him?

Samuel halted Pilgrim in front of the fellow. He was a jittery man, like too many nerves were bundled inside his skin and were wild to break free. Or maybe it was because the man's lanky arms and legs didn't quite fit his stub of a body, and the spidery feel of it drove him to constant movement. Either way, Samuel didn't like it.

Samuel stared down at him. "What's the trouble?"

The man flicked a glance over his shoulder, indicating the felled tree. "Road's blocked, Captain."

Pilgrim shied sideways, and Samuel heeled her in with a jerk on the reins, irritated more at the man than the horse. The driver could try the patience of a frock-coated saint. "I see that. I can also see there's enough clearance to go around it."

"Yes, but. . ." His arms jerked up in an overzealous shrug.

Samuel shoved down a growl. "But what, man? Drive around it! This is not a good place to stop."

The driver stepped closer, putting distance between himself and the back of the carriage. "I've, um. . ." He cleared his throat, then lowered his voice for Samuel alone to hear. "I've some *personal* business to attend to down by the riverbank, if you know what I mean."

Sudden understanding flared. No wonder the man seemed particularly animated—which only peeved him all the more. He gave the fellow a sharp nod and edged Pilgrim aside. "Be quick about it."

The man darted off and skittered down the embankment.

"Why are we stopping?" Abby's head poked through the carriage window, her brown eyes seeking his.

Samuel eased his horse ahead several paces, keeping the riverbank in his line of sight. "The driver needed a respite."

The words, spoken aloud, circled back and slapped him in the face. Any postilion worth his salt wouldn't need to stop, especially this close to arriving at their destination—even one as half-witted as their particular driver.

He reached for his gun.

"Captain?" Alarm pinched the edges of Abby's voice. "Why are you—?"

Two shots cracked the air. Blistering pain ripped into his upper arm, and his gun flew from his grip.

"Get down!" he shouted. He turned Pilgrim toward the wood line, reaching for his knife with the only arm that worked.

Too late.

A blade sliced into his thigh and a demon from hell reached for his arm, yanking him down.

The world exploded, spattering Abby's cheek with hot droplets. Blood. The *captain's* blood. Her heart stopped. So did her breath. She froze, helpless, staring at a living nightmare outside the window.

A grey-cloaked monster of a man pulled the captain from his horse, and he whumped to the ground. Another man stood a few paces back, trading his gun for a knife. Fear stabbed her in the chest. The captain could die here, now, right in front of her eyes.

God, no. . .please!

A screech rang in her ear, and it took her a moment to realize the echoes weren't from her own throat. She ripped her gaze away from the fight outside to a tearful Emma. The girl had pulled herself up on Abby's arm, standing on the seat, eye level with her—and a clear target if another shot should fire out.

Grabbing the child, Abby plummeted to the floor, huddling them both into the small space. Curses blasphemed the air. A growl. Several grunts of fresh pain. Abby clung to Emma as tightly as the girl dug her fingers into Abby's neck.

"Shh," she breathed out, hoping to calm Emma. What a farce. How could she expect the girl to settle down when chaos clashed and gnashed just beyond the thin carriage wall?

The captain roared—and Abby's heart sank. For all she knew, that could be his death cry. . .and she'd done nothing to help him. What kind of coward trembled in a heap on a floor when the man she loved—*loved!*—was in the fight of his life?

She pried Emma's fingers off her neck and tucked the girl into the corner. "Stay!" she ordered.

Turning away from the child, she swept a desperate gaze around the carriage, ignoring the crazed beat of her pulse and the madness of what she intended to do. What could she use to help the captain? What might serve as a weapon?

Her eyes landed on the curtain rod just above the window on the door. If she snuck up behind one of the captain's attackers, one good wallop with that iron bar could dent the brute's skull. It might work. No, it *had* to work.

She shot toward the door—then gasped. A horse and rider tore up from the riverbank, riding straight toward her. Behind her, Emma's cries crescendoed. Abby bit the inside of her cheek, stopping her own scream.

The captain would have to hold his own for now.

She dropped back down, shoving Emma aside and sorry for the harshness. Propping her spine against the wall, Abby curled up her legs, prepared to kick wildly and slam open the door at the slightest hint of movement on the handle. Timing was key. Too soon and she'd open the thing wide, giving the man access without an effort. Too late and he'd grab ahold of her, pulling her out for whatever wicked deed he had in mind. Either way would not be good.

She fixed her gaze on the brass door handle, watching for movement. Narrowing her universe down to a small hunk of metal that, at the slightest quiver, would mean life or death.

And prayed as never before in all her life.

CHAPTER TWENTY-FIVE

Samuel's face mashed into the ground, gravel cutting his cheek. Fire burned in his arm, and life seeped out of his thigh. But he couldn't give in to pain now. Lying there meant death, for him *and* for Abby and Emma.

Harnessing momentum, he rolled, then slashed his blade in a wide arc as he rose to his feet. The knife caught. Slicing through flesh and muscle. Coming away slick and sticky.

His attacker stumbled back and fell, spewing out curses and clutching his belly—or what was left of it, anyway.

Ten paces behind the felled man, a guttural cry tore across the afternoon, from a cavernous mouth on a misshapen head.

Shankhart.

Samuel sucked in air. So this was it, then. Kill or be killed. . .unless he could get the better of the man and haul him in.

Oh Lord, make it so.

The brute barreled forward, his gaze narrowed on Samuel. "You're a dead man, runner!"

"God numbers my days, Robbins. Not you." He charged to meet him, knife at the ready, and at the last minute before contact, swerved sideways, forcing Shankhart to spin toward him—leading the villain away from the carriage and toward the charred wood line.

Putting most of his weight on his good leg, Samuel pivoted and crouched, grasping the hilt of his knife tighter. Already he felt his strength draining down his leg and spilling onto the ground. He'd not last long. That gash on his thigh had to be deep, but he dare not pull his gaze from Robbins.

A little help here, God, if You please.

Curses belched like hot tar out of Shankhart, and he edged sideways. Samuel did too. It was a macabre dance, this circling of mortals and murder, working their way off the road and into the ruined woods. Each of them took measure of the other. Looking for an opening. Ticking off weaknesses. If he could strike Shankhart on the upper part of his body, find the place where that bullet of a few weeks ago had torn flesh, he might gain the advantage. And judging by the way the man favored his left arm, up near that shoulder would be the best place to thrust his blade.

Robbins lunged. Samuel threw himself back, and his boot hit a rock, knocking him off-balance. With a wild swoop of his arms, he caught himself before a sharp spire of pine sticking up from the ground could skewer him through the back.

He barely recovered when Robbins slashed again, carving into him, the metal snagging the flesh of his arm—the same one the bullet lodged in.

Samuel roared.

Shankhart struck again. The beast was unstoppable, his blade cutting through the air like lightning. Samuel feinted one way, then as Robbins lurched forward, he darted back the other, slicing the man on the meaty part of his shoulder.

They both spun, exchanging places, and before Shankhart could strike again, Samuel stabbed upward.

Shankhart jumped back, just as Samuel had moments before, and the man's foot hit the same rock. But the force of Robbins's recoil was too much. The ungainly bulk of him too off-center. Flailing his arms for balance came too late. The notorious highwayman arced backward.

And the blackened point of a charred pine branch speared through his back and jutted out his chest, just below the rib cage.

Sickened, Samuel spun away, shutting out the grisly sight—but not able to keep from hearing the last gurgle of Shankhart's final breath. That awful death rattle would haunt him for years to come.

God, have mercy on that man's soul. . .but even as he prayed it, Samuel knew it was too late for the black-hearted sinner—and that was a fate worse than death.

He staggered from the thought as he wiped off his knife. It was always like this, the heave of his stomach, the squeeze in his chest, every time a criminal died unrepentant, no matter how abominable their offenses.

Sucking air through his teeth, he hobbled from the gruesome scene, spent and worn. Darkness closed in at the edges of his vision, and he blinked, desperate to remain conscious. But he had to. If he fell here, he'd never stand again. All he had to do was get to the carriage. Stumble or crawl the distance if he must. Once Abby tied up the gaping flesh on his leg and staunched the flow on his arm, he could think more clearly. Assess what action to take next. Or maybe close his eyes for one blessed moment and rest. Had he ever been so tired in all his life?

Fighting to remain upright, he pressed on. Every step ignited fresh agony as he worked his way from the wood's edge. He bypassed the other blackguard lying still on the dirt, permanently curled into clutching a gut that spilled onto the road.

A movement caught Samuel's eye, but not from that man. On the river side of the byway, a foreign horse stood on the rise leading down to the water. Four paces away, its rider stalked toward the carriage, the man's hand rising to yank open the door. His other hand clutched a pistol.

Sweet blazing stars! Were all the forces of hell against him today?

Biting back a growl, Samuel used every skill he owned to silently scoop up his gun where it lay in the dirt. Sweat broke loose, dripping down his brow and stinging his eyes. White-hot pain blistered from his knee to his waist. He gritted his teeth to keep from crying out as he fumbled to reload his gun. The fabric of his sleeve stuck to his skin, heavy with blood, and his fingers shook. No, his whole body did, coaxing him to lie down and give up the ghost.

Focus. Focus!

He cocked open the hammer and, with a quivering arm, lifted the gun.

But not soon enough. The man's hand already gripped the door handle and—

The door exploded open, slamming into the man's face and jerking him backward. His arms shot out. His gun plummeted to the ground.

Samuel took aim and pulled the trigger.

The man crumpled like a wadded-up rag, clutching his knee and howling on the dirt.

For the first time in the past eternity, Samuel heaved a sigh of relief as he strode over to the man and clouted him in the head with the butt of his gun, just to be on the safe side. No sense giving the fellow an opportunity to put a hole in him when he wasn't looking. Then he stepped back and scanned the area for movement of any more attackers.

Abby climbed down from the carriage, her skirts giving the man on the ground a wide berth as she raced over to Samuel's side.

"Oh Captain." Her voice was as wobbly as he felt. Tears shimmered in her eyes, wide open with pity and fear. "You are hurt!"

Despite the effort, he smirked. "A little. Are you unharmed? Is Emma safe?"

"Yes, but you—" A small cry cut off her words, followed by a gasping breath.

"I'll mend." He wavered on his feet, his own body calling him a liar. "If you could just..."

Just what? His thoughts scattered like chaff. He swiped the back of his hand across his brow, hoping the movement might straighten out his tangled thinking. "You should..."

He gave himself a mental shake. *Hold it together, man!*

"Captain?" Abby eyed him, fear glinting in her eyes.

Beyond her shoulder, a dark shape rose from the river embankment. Or was he seeing things? At this point, anything was possible. With another swipe, he shoved the hair from his brow, praying to God it would push away the confusion as well.

He narrowed his eyes and stared past Abby.

Blood-smeared and pale, the captain swayed as if he might topple to the ground. He looked over her shoulder as if she weren't there. Did he know she was? Could he still think straight? Or was his spirit even now packing bags, about to depart?

Abby clenched her jaw. Not if she could help it. She reached for him, hoping to guide him gently to the ground and get that leg and arm of his to stop bleeding.

He sprang to life, sweeping her behind him and pulling out his knife, the movement so sudden, she teetered on her own feet.

"Stop right there!" His voice was a bear's growl, and she retreated a step from the fierceness of it.

"Put your hands up where I can see them," he commanded.

A debate raged fierce inside her. Huddle down behind the captain's broad back and hide from whatever danger approached? Or peek around his shoulder to see what threat loomed?

"Be-dah!" Emma's shriek tore out of the open carriage door. If the girl toppled out headfirst, she could break her little neck.

That did it. Abby rose to her toes. If she had to, she'd snatch up a rock and fight alongside the captain.

She blinked, confused. Ahead, the postilion stood wide-eyed, fear draining the colour from his face. Slowly, he lifted his long arms high into the air, like he might grab the sky and pull it down over their heads. "I don't want no trouble, Captain."

"Seems you've avoided that so far, like you knew it was coming." The captain's words stabbed the air, and with each one, the postilion winced. "You did, didn't you? You knew Robbins was going to attack."

"I—I—I—" The man stuttered to a stop.

"Didn't you!" the captain boomed.

"I did." A guilty tot couldn't have looked more penitent for having been caught with his hand inside a biscuit tin. Even from this distance, Abby could see his Adam's apple bob.

The captain advanced. "How much were you paid to endanger the life of a woman and child?"

"It's not like that." The driver retreated a step, terror etching lines on his face. "I didn't—"

"I ought to cut you down where you stand."

Abby frowned. Didn't he see the man's fear? Couldn't he understand that the postilion posed no threat? After a glance at the carriage to make sure Emma was yet inside, Abby gathered up her skirt hem and bolted forward. "Captain, please. Put down your knife."

He waved her away, blood glossy on his hand and dripping off his fingers.

"I didn't make a farthing. I swear it!" The postilion looked from the captain to her. "They said they'd kill my wife, miss, and my little ones, if I didn't stop your carriage here. I don't wish any ill on you, on *any* of you. That's why I run off. I couldn't bear to witness any violence against ye."

Desperation shook the man's words and his lanky legs, rippling the fabric of his trousers from his boots all the way up to his riding jacket.

Even so, a low rumble vibrated in the captain's throat. His knife raised higher, sunlight cutting a line off its sharp edge.

Abby darted between the men. "You heard the driver, Captain. His family was in danger. You would have done the same for me and Emma. You *have* done the same for me and Emma, time and again."

She dared a few steps closer, blocking the postilion from view. "Put your weapon away. We are safe now, Emma and I. You have kept us safe."

His brow creased into a hundred questions. "You are safe?" he mumbled.

Her heart broke at the bewilderment in his tone. She'd never heard such uncertainty from this man of muscle and confidence. She forced a smile, hoping it looked more than just a baring of her teeth. "I am safe."

"Thank God," he breathed out.

His knife dropped. His arm lowered. And the mighty captain sank to his knees in the dirt.

Abby reached him as he pitched forward, dropping down to her own knees and catching him in her arms. The sudden weight of him knocked her back a bit, and she cast a wild glance over her shoulder. "Help me!"

The postilion snapped into action, relieving her of the bloody burden and easing the captain to sit on his own.

Turning her back on them both, Abby lifted the bottom of her gown and frantically tore at the petticoat beneath, ripping off a strip. Then another. And another. And if that wasn't enough, then to the devil with propriety and she'd start ripping her gown. Anything to stop the captain's bleeding.

She sucked in a breath for courage then knelt by the captain's injured leg. Blood oozed out like a cancer that would not be stopped. If she didn't get the bleeding stopped soon, he'd die. Pushing away the thought, she hefted up his leg so that his knee bent. He didn't cry out, but his fingers grabbed great handfuls of dirt, white-knuckled.

She started wrapping slowly at first, tugging the fabric tight despite the captain's grunts. Then as the gaping flesh pressed together, she worked faster, winding the makeshift bandage around his thigh. While she worked, he spoke to the postilion, charging him with tying up the brigand felled by his gun and tossing him into the outside seat of the carriage. The baronet could send some of his men to bury the other two.

The postilion didn't have to be told twice. He dashed off, and Abby scooted from the captain's leg to his arm.

He twisted away. "Leave it. It's not. . ." He sucked in air. "The shot needs to come out."

"But it still bleeds!"

"I know." He closed his eyes, a wave of pain creasing lines near his temples. "Just. . .leave it."

An argument rose to her lips, but she pressed her mouth flat. He needed a physician, not a quarrel. She shoved her shoulder beneath his armpit on his uninjured arm. "We will stand on three. Ready?"

At his nod, she counted off, and somehow, staggering and grunting, she got them both to their feet and over to the carriage, just as the postilion jumped down from where he'd tied up the other fellow on the back seat.

"Help me get him in."

"Aye, miss."

Between the two of them and with the last of the captain's strength, they hefted him inside. Before Abby climbed up, she raced around the back of the carriage and retrieved the captain's hat from the dirt where it lay, as beaten and ruined as he was.

The driver lent her a hand up, and before she ducked inside, she turned to him. "Thank you. Please see to the captain's horse, then make haste to Brakewell Hall. There is no time to spare."

He nodded. "You can count on me, miss."

She edged past the captain's sprawled legs and reached for Emma. The girl had clutched his arm and pulled herself up to stand—thank God it was the uninjured one she'd grabbed.

"Here, love." She handed the girl the captain's hat—still her favorite plaything—and settled her on the floor in the corner. Then she turned back to the captain and sank beside him on the seat.

His eyes watched her. Barely. His head lolled back against the wall as if he hadn't the strength to lift it—and likely he didn't. His skin was ashen. His breath wispy and smelling of copper.

"Oh Captain!" Whatever strength she'd mustered before failed her now, and a sob rose in her throat. "Please, stay with me. Stay right here with me and Emma."

One side of his mouth curved, and slowly, so gradually that she didn't notice it at first, his hand rose, and his worn knuckle brushed along her cheek. "Abby," he whispered. "Sweet Abby."

Her name on his lips was a kiss, and she gasped from the intimacy of it. Did he truly think of her so? She leaned closer, memorizing the feel of his hand now cupping her jaw, her gaze searching his.

Without warning, his hand dropped, and his eyes closed.

No! She pressed her ear against his chest, praying, hoping, weeping that she'd hear his heart beat. That he'd live to someday call her Abby again.

The carriage jolted into motion, the wheels overloud against the gravel. Stopping up her other ear, she pressed closer, straining with her whole body to listen for a sound—*any* sound—beneath his shirt.

And. . .nothing.

Tears broke. *She* broke, grief and rage swirling a great, dark tempest in her soul. She clutched the captain's shirt with both hands and buried her whole face in his waistcoat. "Do not die, Captain!" she sobbed. "Do not leave me. Please, I cannot bear it."

A hint of a sound rattled in his lungs. Small, but it was something. . . wasn't it? She lifted her head and was startled to see his brown gaze burning into hers.

"Not Captain," he rasped. "My name is Samuel."

Then his eyes rolled back into his head.

CHAPTER TWENTY-SIX

This wasn't how Abby imagined she'd arrive at her future husband's manor, with a baby on her shoulder, a criminal tied up at the back of the carriage, and the man she loved bleeding to death on the seat next to her.

Oh Samuel.

His Christian name lingered bittersweet in her mind, and she pinched the bridge of her nose, warding off another bout of tears. Likely she already looked a hideous, puffy mess, bloodstained and bedraggled—not the sort of bride the baronet would expect. Or maybe not even welcome. And he must. For the captain's sake, Sir Jonathan *must* take them in immediately.

The coach lurched to a stop in front of Brakewell Hall. While she waited for the postilion to lower the step, she hefted the sleeping Emma and gazed one more time at the captain's still form. Not once since he'd spoken his name had his eyes opened. His chest continued to rise and fall, thank God, but though she longed for it, no more whispers passed his lips. Her heart twisted. Would she ever hear his commanding voice again?

No, better not to think such a morbid question. Better to simply focus on what needed to be done, here and now. It was her turn to be the strong one, and she would be. She owed him that much, at least.

She handed Emma down to the postilion's waiting arms, then carefully worked her way out into the darkness. Night had fallen, and she stepped gingerly onto a drive composed of gravel and weeds, her leather soles landing with a muffled crunch.

Golden light poured out the manor's ground-level windows, most open to usher in the evening air. Gossamer curtain panels hovered like passing ghosts near the glass. A few of the shutters hung crooked, or maybe it was only the play of night shadows. Hard to tell, especially with Emma rousing. If Abby didn't collect her immediately, the baronet would be greeted with a howling child.

She reached for the girl, yet she needn't have—the driver all but thrust Emma into her arms. "Shh, sweet one. Go back to sleep."

Emma rubbed her face into the crook of her neck, and thankfully, her little body once again went limp. Abby clutched her tightly and strode ahead. The sooner a physician attended the captain, the better his chances of survival.

Three stairs led up to a stone landing, where she stopped in front of a big wooden door streaked dark from weather and years. She rapped the knocker hard against the brass plate. Again and again. And wouldn't stop pounding until—

The door flew open, ripping the knocker from her grasp so forcefully, she stumbled forward. In front of her towered a man wearing midnight blue livery and a disgusted scowl. Judging by the wide cuffs on his sleeves and overly long cut of his coat, he was either a rebellious butler refusing to change with the times or he simply didn't mind that his dress was outmoded and unbefitting of a baronet. Neither was a good portent—of him or Sir Jonathan.

But neither did she care. Abby lifted her chin. "Please, I must speak with Sir Jonathan at once."

His lips tightened, and the longer he studied her, the flatter his mouth drew into a disapproving line. "The foundling hospital is in Penrith proper. Continue down the road."

The door started to close—but not if she could help it. Shielding the sleeping Emma, Abby wedged her body into the narrowing gap. The wood smacked into her shoulder blade, but the effort was worth the pain. The door stayed open.

Splotches of red mottled the butler's face. "Step aside this instant!"

She frowned up at the man. "You are making a grave mistake. I am not this child's mother. I am Abigail Gilbert, soon to be Sir Jonathan's wife. He is expecting me, and I implore you to summon him at once."

His gaze grazed over her, from head to toes, then back up again. Wrinkle upon wrinkle gathered on his nose as he sniffed in disdain. "The baronet's intended is a lady, not a disheveled imposter with a child on her hip. If you do not step aside, madam, I will be forced to bodily remove you."

She narrowed her eyes, hoping desperately to mimic the same kind of imperious stare that the captain oft employed. "Do you really wish to risk that I am not who I say I am? For I will be the lady of this manor soon, and when that happens, you will be out of a job—unless you let me in. Do you understand?"

Something moved behind his eyes, a hesitation of sorts. Ahh, but he was a dogged, bullheaded man. By faith! She didn't have time for this—*Samuel* didn't have time for this! But she held her ground, waiting, hoping, praying.

"Very well," he grunted. "We will let the master settle this." He opened the door wide, yet grumbled under his breath.

Ignoring the butler's rude manners—for now—she entered a small foyer, expecting to follow the man to a sitting room, but he stopped and turned to her at the entryway's arch, blocking her advance. "Wait here."

He stalked down the corridor, the breach of etiquette stunning, but not surprising. If the butler truly did believe her to be naught but an unwed mother in search of charity, he likely also supposed she'd pilfer the silver or secret the knickknacks into the folds of her gown.

While she waited, she shifted the dead weight of Emma to a better position and prayed for God's mercy on the captain. All the times she'd told him to hope for the best, expect the best, haunted her now... yet trust she would. Nothing that happened took God by surprise or was beyond His reach to heal. She'd cling to that. She must.

Turning, she peered out the narrow glass pane at the side of the door. A useless endeavor. The night was so black. But somehow, just staring at the dark shape of the carriage where Samuel lay was a connection to him—one that comforted.

"Miss Gilbert?"

She whirled.

Striding toward her was a Greek god clad in green velvet. Abby swallowed, suddenly shy. Though she'd remembered Sir Jonathan to be a handsome man, it'd been so long ago since she'd seen him, and then for such a brief time. Here in the flesh, he stood taller than she recollected. His eyes blazed bluer. His shoulders stretched wider. His smile flashed more brilliant than humanly possible.

He stretched out his arms as he approached, the butler tagging at his heels. "So you have finally arrived." A few paces from her, he slowed, then stopped, his gaze fixed on Emma. "What is this? A child?"

Behind him, the butler edged closer, eyes glinting with interest in the sconce light. The talk belowstairs tonight would be rabid, no doubt.

Abby closed the distance between her and Sir Jonathan, lowering her voice for his ears alone. "I will explain everything in private, but first, please send for your physician."

"Are you ill?" His head reared back as if the air between them were diseased. "Or is it the child?"

"Neither. We are both well. But there is an officer dreadfully wounded out in my carriage who will die without immediate attention."

Spoken aloud, the gruesome words taunted mercilessly. Though she'd wrestled with the possibility in her mind the entire drive here, voicing the awful words to the baronet somehow breathed life into them. Samuel could die—could be drawing his last breath even now—and the thought of living in a world without him burned a fresh wave of tears in her eyes.

Sir Jonathan cocked his head, no doubt studying her very physical reaction, then called over his shoulder. "See to the injured officer in the carriage, Banks. Have Mencott tend him."

"Yes, sir." The butler—Banks—pivoted and strode down the long hallway, not fast enough for Abby's liking, but at least he moved toward getting Samuel some help.

"Come." Sir Jonathan swept out his hand. "You are overwrought."

La! He couldn't be more right. Clutching Emma—who by now sagged in her arms like a leaden weight—Abby followed the baronet past the foyer and through the first door. Two large settees flanked a wide hearth. A single table with an oil lamp rested between them. Off in the corner, several cushioned chairs huddled near one another, and in the other, a sedentary dumbwaiter stood like a three-tiered sentinel, with various coloured bottles and crystal glasses on the shelves. No artwork adorned the walls. No trinkets sat on the mantel. Apparently Sir Jonathan cared nothing about displaying his wealth. . .unless, perhaps, his funds were tight? Abby shook her head, confused. Neither her father nor stepmother had made mention of any lack.

"Be seated while I ring for a maid," he instructed.

She sank onto the nearest settee, glad for the support. Emma stirred, lifting her head. Truly, it was a wonder she'd slept this long. Tendrils of damp hair stuck to her brow, and Abby pushed them back. The child craned her neck for a moment, but seeing nothing of interest, she nuzzled her cheek against Abby's shoulder and popped her thumb in her mouth.

Across the room, Sir Jonathan busied himself with a decanter, pouring amber liquid into a tumbler. His long legs were clad in well-tailored buff trousers, and above that, his green dress coat narrowed at the waist and broadened at the shoulders. His sandy hair was brushed back neatly, the curled ends riding just above a hint of his cream-coloured cravat. There was no denying he cut a dashing figure, a desirable one, this man who would be hers.

Hers?

A strange thought, that, though it shouldn't be. For so long she'd looked forward to this moment. To finally be near the man who loved her. But now that it was here, it didn't quite feel right, like a gown that fit properly yet somehow looked ill-suited when glancing at a reflection of it in a mirror.

But that was a trifle compared to the injured captain. Careful not to jostle Emma, she edged forward on the cushion. "Are you certain your butler will carry out your instructions posthaste? Time is of the essence in the matter of the captain. I should like to attend him until the physician arrives."

"Banks is a bit rough around the edges, but he will do as I say, my dear. And as for you, a drink to calm your nerves is first in order, I think." His words were honeyed, his step even more fluid as he turned and crossed the room, holding out a drink for her.

Abby shook her head. While her brother liked his brandy and her sisters hid sherry bottles in their rooms, she'd never acquired a taste for strong drink—and wasn't about to start now.

The baronet crouched, face-to-face. "I insist."

She tensed. Of all the times the captain had commanded her to do something, never once had she felt so coerced as she did now.

"You are wound too tightly, sweet Abigail. This will do you good, hmm? You have been through much and are rightly disturbed." He angled his head, the glass in his hand never wavering. "I wish your first night beneath my roof to be pleasant."

Slowly, she reached for the tumbler. Of course he was right. After the events of this day, she was out of sorts. It was kind of him to notice and wish to ease her distress.

The horrid liquid burned a hot trail down her throat, and she spluttered, shoving the glass away from her. Ack! How could anyone drink that?

Frowning, Sir Jonathan took the tumbler and retreated to the dumbwaiter. Turning his back to her, he poured another glass.

Glad for the moment of privacy, Abby ran her hand across her lips, wiping away any last burning remnants, then resettled Emma on her other shoulder.

Sir Jonathan tossed back his head, slugging down his entire drink, then refilled his glass and joined her on the sofa—on the side farthest from Emma.

His leg brushed against hers, and a hint of a smile curved his lips. "I expected you a fortnight ago, my dear. It appears you have had an eventful journey." He tipped his glass toward Emma, then took a long pull on his drink.

Abby bit her lip and leaned away from him. The man was a tippler. Had her father known of his habits before agreeing to give the baronet her hand? Then again, most men drank, often to excess. . .didn't they?

Yet she'd never once smelled hard liquor on the captain's breath.

Behind a second set of doors, leading to what she could only assume would be a dining room, a burst of laughter leached through the gap near the floor. Abby's gaze bounced from Sir Jonathan to the sound, then back to him. "Am I interrupting something?"

He shrugged. "Some friends are here for a house party. I would invite you to join us but. . ." He eyed the bloodstained traveling gown. "Well, you were going to tell me about the child, were you not?"

A party? His bride-to-be was more than a fortnight late in arrival and he dined with friends instead of frantically searching for her? Abby closed her eyes for a moment, desperately trying to calm the riotous thoughts stabbing one right after the other—for surely these thoughts were all wrong. There had to be an explanation for the baronet's apparent callousness.

"Abigail? Are you certain you are well?" Sir Jonathan's hand rested warm on her thigh, his fingers giving her a little squeeze.

Her eyes flew open at his touch. Betrothed or not, the captain would have never taken such a brazen liberty. But when her gaze met Sir Jonathan's, concern etched crinkles at the side of his eyes—not desire. He loved her. He did. She *was* overwrought.

"I am well," she assured him, inching from his grasp. "How Emma came to be in my care is too long of a tale for me to tell tonight. The short of it is that the man I hired to be my guardian—a captain in the service of the Bow Street magistrate—agreed to deliver this little one to her home, just as he agreed to deliver me to mine."

"Hmm." Sir Jonathan tossed back the rest of his drink and set the glass on the floor. "And that man—that guardian of yours. . .he is the one who is critically wounded?"

"He is." Her heart squeezed. Hopefully even now the captain was resting in a cushioned bed, kept warm by a coverlet, kept company by a. . . By whom? No one knew him here. No one cared.

She stood so quickly, Emma startled. "I hate for the captain to be left alone until your physician arrives, and I assure you that I am much refreshed now. If you would direct me to his room, I should like to wait there. I owe him that. He has saved my life, several times. He has saved *our* lives." She hugged Emma tighter.

"Has he?" Sir Jonathan eyed her as he rose to his feet, his chiseled face a mask hiding what he might think of her singular request. "Then I suppose I also owe him my gratitude for bringing my bride here in one piece."

He reached for her, brushing a lock of wayward hair from her cheek. "Yet you need not concern yourself on the captain's behalf any further. My man Mencott is attending him. All that matters is that you are here now, safe and sound. We have a wedding to prepare for, do we not?"

"But I—"

"You rang, sir?" A maid entered, cutting her off.

Sir Jonathan pulled away and faced the woman. "Have a fire laid in the green room. I will see the lady up there directly. Oh, and take this child to Mrs. Horner. Tell her to make provision for the girl until she leaves, which may be a day or two."

"Yes, sir." The young woman bobbed her head, then marched over to retrieve Emma.

Abby threw a wild glance at her future husband, clutching Emma so tightly, the girl squirmed. Didn't he see how attached she was to the child? "I prefer Emma to remain with me. I am afraid she shall give anyone else a difficult time."

"I assure you, my love, Mrs. Horner is quite capable."

"But she does not know Emma like I do." A sob caught in her throat. *She* was the only mother Emma had for now, not some stranger of a housekeeper. She patted Emma's back and lifted her chin. "The child is new here, as am I, and we would both do better if—"

"I think not, darling." Though he softened the blow with an endearment, it still nearly knocked her from her feet. "We would not want people getting the wrong impression of my soon-to-be wife, would we? Tongues will wag if you insist on favoring the babe as your own. You have my word that the child will be well cared for, and if you wish, we will house her in the very room our own children will one day occupy. You may visit her as often as you like."

A headache started, throbbing a painful beat in her temple. As much as she didn't want to part with Emma, how could she prevent it? She *wasn't* Emma's mother, and though her heart yearned otherwise, she could never be. The baronet was right. It wouldn't be proper for her to be seen caring for a child that wasn't his.

Heart breaking afresh, she planted a kiss on Emma's downy head, then handed her gently into the maid's waiting arms. As the young woman strode from the room, Emma peered over her shoulder. Her little face screwed up into a big wail, the cry colliding discordantly with another burst of laughter from the dining room.

Abby grabbed great handfuls of her skirt, unsure of what to do. She felt like throwing up. Throwing things wildly. Throwing her body down onto the floor and pounding the carpet with her fists.

"Come." Sir Jonathan's arm wrapped around her shoulders. "I shall see you to your room. Clearly you are in need of a good night's rest."

That much was true. She was tired. More than tired. Her bones wanted to lie down and never get up again.

She allowed Sir Jonathan to guide her across the carpet. This was surely not the romantic reunion she'd hoped for—nor likely what Sir Jonathan had expected either. She peered up at his clean-shaven face, the fine cut of his jaw every woman's dream, and tried to ignore that he wasn't her dream. Not really. She'd grown to prefer the captain's shadowy stubble.

Shaking off the inappropriate image, she forced a pleasant tone to her voice. "I apologize, Sir Jonathan, for arriving in such a distressing fashion. I shall make it up to you, somehow. I promise."

He turned to her, tipping her chin with the crook of his finger, and his blue gaze searched hers, intimately deep. "Drop the *sir*, my sweet, for I am your Jonathan. And yes," he drawled, "you will make it up, no doubt."

She froze. All the times she'd stood this close to Samuel had felt like a warm embrace. Somehow, this didn't.

"Pardon me, sir." A male voice entered the room this time, and they both turned.

The servant standing at the door dipped his head. "Banks says to tell you that Mencott has things under control. The captain is attended and the other man has been secured until the constable arrives."

"Other man?" He shot her an arched brow.

"Yes, sir," the servant continued. "Apparently the captain apprehended a criminal during their scuffle. The driver says the man also dropped two other brigands on the road back near Thacka Beck and we ought to send a few men to bury the poor souls."

"I see. Tell Graves and Hawthorne to go. You are dismissed." The baronet waved him away.

The servant hesitated. "There is one more thing, sir. Lady Pelham asks for you."

"Does she?" Sir Jonathan glanced at Abby for a moment, then unexpectedly, pulled her into his arms and brushed his lips lightly across her forehead, right there in front of God and the servant. "If you will excuse me, my dear, duty calls," he whispered against her skin. "I am sure you understand."

He strode from the room, leaving her wobbling. Before he disappeared down the corridor, he called over his shoulder. "See Miss Gilbert to the green room."

Abby stood barely breathing. Sir Jonathan was wrong. Horribly wrong. She didn't understand anything. Not the gnawing angst in her heart for Samuel. Not the ache in her arms, longing to hold Emma.

And she surely didn't understand why the man who claimed to love her attended to another woman when he should be at her side.

CHAPTER TWENTY-SEVEN

Sleep came hard, but when it did, it crashed into Abby like a load of falling bricks. She woke the next morning to grey light, a head that still pounded, and an insane urge to run through the manor, collect Emma, and lay them both down by the captain's side. Only by breathing in his scent of leather and horses and, yes, even gunpowder, would she feel at home here in this foreign manor. The baronet had forbidden her from attending him last night, but today was a new day—and she *would* see Samuel, one way or another.

Without waiting for the aid of a lady's maid, she hurried into her traveling gown of the day before and tried to rub off the worst of the bloodstains and grime. A quick splash of water on her face and some pins in her hair was the extent of her toilette. It was the best she could do, anyway, for her chest had not yet been delivered to her, nor even her traveling bag. She frowned as she brushed out the wrinkles in her gown with the palms of her hands. The captain had slogged through a storm to make sure she had use of both her bag and her chest, and the memory squeezed her heart.

She dashed to the door and set off down the corridor. When the passageway ended, leaving no choice but to go right or left, she paused and stared down the length of one then the other. The bare wooden walls and planked flooring of each mirrored the other. Oh, why had she not paid better attention last night?

She hesitated a moment, then veered right. Halfway down that corridor, she turned right again and entered a wider hallway. Remnants of what might've been flocked wallpaper spread like diseased arms. Smoke stains streaked up to the rafters, where darkness collected into black clouds. Not far ahead, a staircase with a warped balustrade led downward, and above it, a large, round window blistered out from the ceiling toward the sky. Light seeped in, barely. Ivy and moss covered most of the glass.

Abby narrowed her eyes as she neared the first step. A tattered carpet runner clung to the wooden risers in spots—the only spots that hadn't been mouse chewed. Flecks of plaster and mould collected in the corners. She'd have to be careful where she put her feet. *This* was a baronet's home? Why hadn't his servants cleaned here? The home she'd left wasn't as large, but for all her stepmother's faults, she made sure to keep a tidy house.

Gripping the bannister with one hand and hefting the hem of her gown with the other, she picked her way downward. Of only two things was she certain. She definitely hadn't come this way the night before. And the need to see the captain's and Emma's familiar faces was now as vital as air.

Her feet touched the ground floor, and she stopped and turned in a circle. Cracks ran through the tiles like black veins. Three doors, all closed, punctuated the walls. She strode toward the double set, for surely that would lead into the main part of the house.

The handle of one was broken off, and the other wouldn't turn. Bother! Working her way back up the stairs and trying a different route would waste more time. She frowned. There was nothing for it, then.

Turning a bit, she sucked in air for strength and rammed her shoulder against the wood as she'd once seen the captain do. The door gave way with a groan, but only a little. So, she did it again. And again. Pain shot through her bones, and eventually, with effort and grunts, the wood inched open just enough for her to peer through.

Oh my...

Absently, Abby rubbed her shoulder as she stared at weeds run amok, choking the remains of charred stone walls. Window holes gaped like empty eye sockets on one side. The other crumbled to nothing but a hump where a wall should've been. Grey clouds were the only ceiling.

Grabbing the handle with a tight grip, she yanked the door shut, closing out the sickening sight. Hopefully nothing other than the manor had been hurt during that blaze. Sympathy welled in her empty belly. In light of the destruction she'd just witnessed, the rest of the home didn't seem nearly as austere as she'd first judged it last night. Poor Sir Jonathan, to have suffered what surely must have been a devastating loss.

She hurried as fast as she dared across the ruined tiles and chose a different door. This one swung open easily. The pounding in her temples eased a bit as she stepped into a narrow yet well-kept corridor. A smaller staircase led down to her left, plain and hardly the width of her hem. A servants' stair. She pressed on, and when the corridor turned into a wider, well-lit passage, hope rose—especially when the murmur of a woman's and man's voices wafted out through an open door only paces ahead.

A servant exited as she neared—the same fellow who'd seen her to her room the previous evening. He dipped his head in greeting and scurried past her, clutching a silver urn in a white cloth.

Abby upped her pace, eager to see Sir Jonathan—though a twinge of guilt pinched her for her motivation. She ought to be keen on breakfasting with him as her future lover, but all she could think of was asking him how the captain fared and where she might find him. What kind of bride did that?

God, forgive me.

Forcing a pleasant smile, she swept into the room and scanned it from corner to corner, then froze when the only gaze that met hers was green and overly curious.

A black-haired lady sat at the head of a dining table, looking at Abby over the rim of a rose-petal teacup. She was a trim little pixie, sitting there in a white organza day dress, making Abby feel like an overgrown slattern in a wrinkled sack of a gown. The woman's green eyes held secrets, hiding them deep while probing Abby for hers. It was an unsettling scrutiny, as if the lady searched for a weak spot, a broken wing perhaps, so that she might reach out and break the other.

Shoving aside such uncharitable thoughts, Abby bobbed a small curtsey, trying desperately not to let her smile slip. "Good morning. I am Abigail Gilbert."

The lady set down her cup yet didn't rise, nor did she dip her head as custom required. She merely arched a brow and continued her inspection. "Good morning, Miss Gilbert. I am Lady Pelham. You appear to be looking for someone—a tall, handsome someone, perhaps?"

Her smile faded as the woman's bold implication sank in. "I am, actually. Have you seen Sir Jonathan this morning?"

"Heavens no!" Lady Pelham laughed, and while Abby wished she could dislike the sound as much as she disliked this woman, she couldn't. The lady's merry chuckle was entirely intoxicating.

"Unless there is a hunt, Jon—*Sir* Jonathan does not rise until well in the afternoon." The lady reached out a slim hand and patted the chair adjacent to her. "Come. Take a seat. I shall pour you some coffee. . . unless you prefer tea?"

Abby glanced over her shoulder, debating what to do. Stay and possibly find out from this lady where the captain was? Or search the grounds for him on her own? Yet it had been luck and not her skill that had brought her to this room.

She crossed to the offered chair and sat at the edge of the cushion. She'd query the lady and go from there. "I will have whatever you are having."

"La!" The lady grinned. "You are an easy kitten to please. I see why the baronet chose you. We shall be the best of friends, shall we not?"

Best friends? With this woman? Abby pressed her lips tight as the woman poured steaming brown liquid into a teacup and passed it over. The scent of bergamot hit her nose as Abby lifted the cup to her lips. Better to occupy her mouth than to answer that question.

Lady Pelham sat back and studied her afresh. "There are many questions in your eyes, Kitty. I know! Let us play a game. I will answer yours without you having to speak a word. Would you like that?"

Abby set down her cup. No, she wouldn't like that at all. "I do not think—"

"Excellent! Then the game begins." Lady Pelham clapped her hands and stood, circling the table while she talked. "Though I have told you my name, you no doubt wonder who I am, do you not? That is an easy one to answer. I am Sir Jonathan's cousin, so you shall have to get used to seeing much of me." She paused opposite Abby and tossed her a glance. "We are very close, you know."

Her hands fluttered out and she continued following the curve of the table. "Of course you cannot help but wonder at the state of the manor. I would, and in fact did, the first time I came to visit. The home is a bit sparse and the west wing is in dire need of repair, but soon after your marriage that will all change, and the manor will be restored to its former glory. It has been in the family for seven generations now." She stopped directly behind Abby and bent, breathing into her ear. "Did you know that?"

Abby tensed. Why had her father not told her of this? Had he even known?

Lady Pelham laughed again and circled the table a second time, running her index finger along the chair backs as she went. "Of course you must have many questions about your soon-to-be husband, hmm? Fortunately for you, he is not too complicated. Sir Jonathan prefers green, so I suggest you have gowns made in varying shades of it. He does not take snuff, likes his brandy warmed, and on the rare occasion when his temper runs short, he has an endearing little tic near his left eye."

Abby clenched her hands in her lap. While the information was helpful, it rubbed her against the grain. She should be finding out this information on her own, not from another woman. And it was getting her nowhere closer to finding out about the captain or Emma.

She pushed back her chair and stood, done with the game. "Lady Pelham, I—"

The lady held up her hand, eyes twinkling. "No need to thank me yet, Kitty. There is more you are likely dying to know. The butler, Banks, is a goat. Cook is a magician. And the housekeeper, Mrs. Horner, is never—*ever*—to be trifled with. The rest of the staff members are spineless bootlickers."

Abby gripped the back of the chair. "While I appreciate your—"

"Tut, tut! Save that gratitude, for you will want to know who else you will cross paths with today. There are several guests in residence, whom

I am sure you will meet, if not this morning, then at dinner tonight. They are Colonel Wilkins and Amelia, his wife; Parker Granby; and Parson Durge, though he is not really a parson." Lady Pelham finished her circle and sank into her seat, a pleased grin lighting her face. "Well, how did I do? Does that answer all of your questions?"

Abby skewered Lady Pelham with a direct stare. "It answers all save one."

"Good! Then the game continues." The lady leaned forward, folding her hands on the table as if she held court. "Pray, what is it you want to know?"

"When I arrived last night, I was not alone. I—"

"Ahh, yes! I nearly forgot to mention the mysterious injured captain, the wounded brigand, and the young girl. You would like to know where they are, hmm?" The lady laughed again, but this time the merriment of it chafed, and Abby stiffened.

"Oh, do not look so surprised, Kitty. I daresay I know more about what goes on beneath this roof than Sir Jonathan does."

Abby clenched her jaw, trapping a salty remark. If she offended the woman now, she'd cut off her main source of information—as catty as it was. Though it sickened her to have to rely on Lady Pelham's intelligence, she had no choice. "Yes, I should like to check on both the captain and the girl."

The lady smiled indulgently and pointed toward the floor. "The child is in Mrs. Horner's care, belowstairs, just past the kitchen. The captain, I am afraid, has been put out in the stable."

Anger flared hot in her belly. The stable? They put the beaten and bleeding captain out with the animals? Why would he not be housed in the manor? Why offer such rude accommodation, unless. . . Her heart stopped as an ugly realization hit her hard.

Only a corpse would be kept in an outbuilding.

Tears burned her eyes and she spun, unwilling to let Lady Pelham witness her reaction. "Thank you," she forced out before her throat closed. Then she sped to the door.

"Leaving so soon, Kitty? You have not yet taken a bite to eat."

Abby stumbled into the corridor. Eat? She could barely breathe—and might never again if Samuel was stretched out in a burial shroud in the stable.

Even half-dead, Samuel could tell a lot about a man by the way he handled three things: old age, trousers that wouldn't stay up, and strangers. Judging by his slit-eyed observation of the grey-haired man across the room, the fellow was a saint. The man's tread had been purposely light since he'd entered the small chamber. He'd set down a mug on a trestle table without a sound, clearly trying to keep noise to a minimum. Rheumatism gnarled his knuckles into craggy walnuts, growing all the larger as he patiently adjusted the leather braces holding up his breeches. But he didn't wince or moan or make any sound at all—until his gaze landed on Samuel.

"Well, well! Ye're not dead, then, eh Captain?" The man retrieved the mug and the only chair in the room.

Samuel pushed up to sit, and a groan ripped out of his throat. Fire burned in his arm and agony flared even hotter in his leg. He sucked in air like a landed fish. Sweet blessed heavens! Death would've been far less painful than this.

"Where am I?" he gruffed out.

The old man dragged the chair across the floor, then straddled it at Samuel's bedside. "This here be the stable house of Brakewell Hall, home to Sir Jonathan Aberley. Ye're in my quarters. I'm Winslow Mencott, stable master, at yer service." He dipped his head in introduction.

Ahh. . .slowly things started to make sense. The lingering dreams of whickering horses and stomping hooves. The familiar scent of horseflesh and oiled harnesses that were as much a part of the room as the gap-spaced boards and cobwebs on the high windows. Apparently the baronet kept strict rules about broken bodies and blood sullying his fine manor home.

Samuel scrubbed a hand over his face, and stubble rasped against his palm. When was the last time he'd shaved?

"How long have I been out?" he asked.

"Tish! Not long enough. I reckon ye could use a good sleep. Ye lost a lot o' blood, man." Mencott leaned close and offered the mug. "Here, drink this. 'Tis my old mother's recipe."

Thirst unleashed at the man's suggestion, and Samuel gripped the cup. He swigged back a big swallow, and a queer stench met his nose—which would've stopped him were his body not a desert and this the only watering hole to be found. Several mouthfuls drained down his throat before the flavor of the swill registered. Dead badgers soaked in lye would've tasted better than this swampy liquid.

He turned aside and spit the nasty concoction onto the floor, the accompanying stab of pain from the quick movement worth the effort. He shoved the mug back toward Mencott. "Are you trying to kill me?"

Chuckling, Mencott retrieved the cup and set it on the floor. "Looks like somebody else already gave that a go and failed. Far be it from me to finish the job."

Samuel rubbed his mouth with the back of his hand, thankful for the truth in Mencott's words. He *had* survived. The ordeal with Shankhart was finished. He'd come away broken but not dead, and Abby and Emma were. . .well, surely since he was here at Brakewell Hall, they must've arrived safely along with him. Hadn't they?

He eyed Mencott. "The woman and child that I traveled with, are they safe?"

"Aye. They're up at the house." He tipped his head toward the door, as if the manor home lay just on the other side of the wood.

Reaching with his uninjured arm, Samuel rubbed a knot out of his shoulder. The assurance of Abby's and Emma's welfare eased some of the tension in his muscles, but not all.

"And my horse?" he inquired.

"Ahh, now she's a real beauty." Mencott nodded, his gaze drifting, and no wonder. Pilgrim was the sort of animal that few horse lovers could forget once they laid eyes on her. Even mud-spattered and burr-speckled, Pilgrim was the finest animal Samuel had ever owned.

"Brushed her down me'self, I did. Gave her the best provender we have." Mencott glanced over his shoulder, then leaned closer. "But don't let the baronet get wind of it. He buys only so much of the choice feed for his racehorse. The rest get last year's hay."

Samuel nodded, irritated that the baronet didn't see fit to provide quality feed for all of his stock, yet pleased for Mencott's favor upon Pilgrim. He shifted on the bed and stifled a wince from a stabbing reminder that his leg was torn up. At this point, Pilgrim no doubt fared better than him and was itching to get back on the road. Which they should. He'd never intended to house beneath the baronet's roof to begin with. His heart faltered at the thought of leaving Abby behind, but truly, his mission was finished. He'd delivered her safe and sound. It would be wise to collect his payment and Emma, then head back south—and no doubt the baronet would agree.

"Thank you, Mencott, for all you've done. I won't trouble you any further." He swung his legs over the edge of the bed and gritted his teeth. Pain sliced deep as the bone in his thigh, and a universe of stars flashed across his vision. He blinked them away, clutching the side of the mattress so tightly, the small scar on his hand from the orphan boy he'd rescued an eternity ago whitened to a thin line. If he kept this up, he'd be nothing but scar upon scar.

Mencott reared back his head. "Now, Captain, I wouldn't do that if I were you."

He grunted. How many times had he heard that in his life?

Filling his lungs with air, he rose. So did the fires of hell, up his leg and straight to his gut, pushing nausea to his throat. The room spun. Darkness closed in.

And he crumpled like dead wood fallen from a tree.

Mencott's sinewy arm caught him and eased him back to the mattress. "It's too soon, man. Rest yer bones another few days. If that leg o' yours takes to flamin', ye'll lose it."

Samuel groaned. The truth of the man's words hit him like a bludgeon, and his stomach lurched. He might as well lose his life as a leg. He would *not* join the ranks of the empty-eyed cripples begging for pennies in some waste-filled gutter of London's streets.

Mencott adjusted the thin pillow behind Samuel's back, then leaned over him. "I'll bring ye up some breakfast directly, if ye think ye can keep from spewing it out on the floor."

Weary beyond his years, Samuel nodded. "Aye, as long as you keep that drink away from me, I'll be fine."

Chuckling, the man retreated and shut the door behind him. Samuel let his head sink back against the cushion and closed his eyes, desperate to end another wave of dizziness.

Moments later, a knock rapped on the door. His eyes shot wide as the wood cracked open a few inches. Out of habit, he reached for his knife—a moot endeavor. His fingers met nothing but the cloth of his shirt.

"Captain, may I enter?" Abby's voice crept out from behind the door, and his breath hitched at the sweet sound. Traitorous body.

He dragged the thin coverlet up to his waist, covering his bare legs. Hopefully some servant somewhere was patching his ruined trousers.

"You can now."

The words barely passed his lips when the door flew open, then banged shut as Abby raced to his bedside. Her gown flounced into a big poof as she dropped to her knees. Emotions he couldn't begin to name rippled across her face, one after the other, too fast to identify. She grabbed his hand in both of hers and pressed it against her cheek. "Oh Captain, I was so afraid. I thought you were. . .dead—"

Her voice caught, and for a flicker of a moment, the shimmering of a hundred suns welled in her eyes. Tears broke loose then, in a torrent, one after the other, baptizing their entwined fingers.

He swallowed a huge lump in his throat, and though pain slashed an intense trail from shoulder to fingers, he reached with his injured arm and wiped away her tears with his thumb.

"Shh," he soothed. "Don't fret on my account. I'm not that easy to get rid of."

She nuzzled her face into his palm. "I thank God for that, and for you."

Warmth spread across his chest—but this time not from pain. He could die satisfied now, having known the admiration of such a fine woman. Did the baronet have any idea what kind of a jewel he was about to marry?

The thought slapped him hard. Despite the very real attraction between him and Abby, the ugly truth remained that she still belonged to another.

Slowly, he pulled his fingers away from hers, diverting her from his retreat with a question. "How is Emma faring?"

Abby drew in a shaky breath. "I have not seen her yet this morn."

Strange, that. Unless. . . He cocked his head. "Emma did not stay the night with you?"

"No. The baronet did not. . .well, he did not think it prudent for me to remain as Emma's caretaker." Sorrow tightened little lines at the sides of her mouth, but then just as quickly, a small smile erased them. "He did say, however, that I may visit her as much as I like, which I intend to do as soon as I leave here."

"Perhaps you can bring her by, then. Looks like I'll be laid up for a day or two." He flicked his fingers toward his wounded leg.

"I would be happy to." Abby smiled. "Emma would like that."

He grunted. "It's the hat, not the man, that the child prefers."

"You are wrong, you know. It is entirely the man that enchants." Her voice thickened, and her smile faded. The blush of a June rose flushed her cheeks.

A charge shot through him. Abby Gilbert mesmerized like none other. He'd remember her like this. Forever. Brown eyes shining into his. A wayward spiral of hair dangling down to her stately neck. The curve of her collarbone kissing the bodice of her blood-flecked gown.

Hold on. *Blood-flecked?*

He leaned forward, cupping her chin and studying her face. "How are you faring? And speak the truth. For I know this is the same gown you wore yesterday. Do not tell me your baronet put you up in the stable as well."

"Of course not." She frowned. "I have a lovely accommodation, and I cannot complain."

He tilted her face higher, looking deep into her eyes, to where the soul could not deceive. "So, you are happy?"

"I—I am. . ."

Little liar! Such a ragged tone did not denote happiness—*and* she never finished the sentence.

The door flung open, nearly as forcefully as when Abby had entered. Pulling away from his touch, Abby shot to her feet.

A man strolled in, clad in a worsted woolen dress coat and ivory trousers. A white cravat spilled out of his collar, as unsullied as the smooth skin on his hands. Clearly the man didn't work for a living. His blue gaze was direct and disturbing, like too much power given over to a tot, dissecting both Samuel and Abby with one glance.

The man closed the distance between him and Abby, then he draped his arm around her waist. "I thought I might find you here, my dear." He pecked a kiss on the top of her head, then stared down at Samuel. "It is a pleasure to finally meet you, sir. The illustrious Captain Thatcher, I take it?"

The muscles on Samuel's neck hardened to steel, and it was all he could do to answer in a calm fashion without flying from the bed—injuries and all—and pry the man's hand off Abby's body. "I am he."

A thin smile flicked across the man's lips. "My bride here speaks highly of you." He pulled Abby closer. "I am Sir Jonathan Aberley, baronet."

Of course he was. The pompous dandy.

Instantly he regretted the harsh thought. How many times had Abby admonished him to hope for the best? Expect the best? And oh, how dearly he did wish for the best for her sake. Besides, did it not bode well for her that the man paid her such loving attention? Surely the baronet would make an attentive husband—which is exactly what Abby deserved.

Samuel dipped his head in polite respect toward the man. "I have heard much of you as well, sir, and I thank you for your charity while I mend. I assure you I will not be here long."

"I should think not. A man of your profession," he drawled out the word as if it were a dirty sheet to be boiled, "is likely used to such inconveniences. You are, no doubt, adept at maneuvering about while wounded, are you not?"

He met the man's pointed stare and upped the intensity of it. "I am."

"Well then, we shall let you get back to your. . .er, *mending*, as you put it." His hand slipped from Abby's waist to capture her hand. "Come, my dear. Let us leave the captain in peace."

"But—"

Before she could finish whatever it was she wanted to say, the baronet swept her to the door, where she cast Samuel a backward glance as the man ushered her outside.

As soon as the door shut, Samuel grabbed the pillow and threw it to the floor, then whumped flat on his back, glad for the blinding pain cutting him to shreds. This wasn't right. None of it. Not his torn-up leg or the hole in his arm. Not the insane urge pumping strong through his veins to steal Abby away from a life that would provide her with ease and security.

And especially not the animosity curling his hands into fists with the desire to thrash Sir Jonathan Aberley, baronet.

CHAPTER TWENTY-EIGHT

Abby gripped her skirt hem up in one hand, taking care not to trip headlong down the stone stairs. At the rate Sir Jonathan whisked her along, such a fate was a real possibility. What was his hurry?

He stopped once they reached the gravel of the stable yard, and turned to her, running his hands up and down her arms. The intimate gesture ought to make her heart flutter, her cheeks warm, but the only twinge she felt was a slight irritation that she'd not gotten to say goodbye to the captain.

"Such a strange little mouse you are, rising early, scurrying off to the stables." Sir Jonathan lifted his chin and stared down the length of his nose. "When we are wed, you shall lounge about all day, drinking chocolate and eating dainties, as befits a woman of your station."

Her brow puckered. Not even her coddled stepmother loafed around in her nightgown all hours of the day. "But there will be a household to run—*your* household. I cannot do that from my bedchamber."

"Oh, I think it can be managed." He winked and dropped his hands, then held out his arm. "Come, let us take a turn about the garden."

"I would like that," she murmured halfheartedly, then glanced past his shoulder toward the manor. Surely by now, Emma was beyond consolable. It must be frightening for her in new surroundings with new people.

Abby lifted her face to Sir Jonathan's. "But first I would like to see Emma."

Reaching for her fingers, he placed them on his sleeve. "In due time, my sweet. I would have you to myself a moment more." He patted her hand, then guided her across the gravel, away from the house.

It was a pleasant morning, truly. July sun kissed the earth. Bluebirds sang. Crickets chirped. Yet it took all Abby's strength to keep from screaming. Why did she feel so patronized by this man? Was it not a natural desire for him to wish to spend time alone with his bride? Should she not be grateful for his attention?

Shame settled thick on her shoulders. Her stepmother had been right. She was a thankless wretch.

Oh God, forgive me.

She snuck a peek at Sir Jonathan. He stood a head taller than her—almost as tall as the captain. She curved her lips into a pleasant smile. "I am surprised to find you up so early. Lady Pelham says you rarely rise before noon."

His teeth flashed white as he chuckled. "Lady Pelham paints her version of the truth with wide strokes. Get too near her, and you shall be splattered."

Her smile faltered. What was that supposed to mean? She tucked away the strange remark to mull on later. "Well, this much is true. The lady seems very fond of you."

"Does she?" Stooping, Sir Jonathan swiped up a wild daisy midstride and handed it to her.

Abby's smile disappeared altogether. He had to know his cousin admired him. She'd discovered as much in a five-minute conversation with the woman. Did Sir Jonathan perhaps harbour feelings for Lady Pelham as well? Yet if he did, how could Abby possibly cast a stone when, in her own heart, she longed to be kneeling at the bedside of a rough and rugged lawman?

She pulled her hand from Sir Jonathan's sleeve and twirled the daisy in her fingers. "I was also surprised to find Captain Thatcher lodged above the stable. I realize parts of the manor are in need of repair, but is there not a more comfortable room to which he might be moved?"

Sir Jonathan turned onto a pea-gravel path, too narrow for them to walk side by side. She followed at his back, noting for the first time the colour of his dress coat. Green. At least that much of Lady Pelham's information had been correct. But must he wear the same shade every day?

"It is easier, my dear, for Mencott to attend your captain by housing him in the stable master's quarters. He is in the best possible place for now."

She bit her lip. Why was her thinking so contrary? Clearly Sir Jonathan really did care about the captain. She lifted the daisy to the sunlight, admiring the white petals and thoughtfulness behind the gift.

"It is kind of you to show such hospitality. I should have known you would move him to the manor once he is mobile."

"Nothing of the sort. Once the man is able to stand without keeling over, we shall say our goodbyes."

The baronet's words blended with the sharp trill of a woodcock, both grating to her ears. Of course the captain would be leaving—but that didn't mean she had to think about it right now.

She dropped the daisy into the dirt. It was naught but a weed anyway and blended in with the rest. Most of the garden was overgrown with ivy and lamb's ears running rampant. She'd seen better tended plots on Fisherman's Row in Southampton.

The narrow path ended, opening onto a stretch of ankle-high grass that swept back to the manor. Once again, Sir Jonathan offered his arm and smiled down at her, sunlight glinting off the blue in his eyes. A woman could get lost in that gaze, that handsome face, the strong lines of his jaw and dimpled chin.

But not her. She rested her fingers as lightly as possible on his sleeve.

He covered his hand over hers, his touch cool. "Now that you have finally arrived, I expect you are anxious for the wedding. With the banns already read in my parish and in yours, there is no need to wait. Does the day after next suit?"

"So soon?" She gasped, then pinched her lips shut. Such a churlish response might put him off, and then where would she be? Packing to go back to her awful family?

She blinked up at him, feigning innocence as the cause for her hesitation. "But you see, Sir Jonathan—"

"*Jonathan.*" He squeezed her fingers.

"Jonathan." She pushed out the name. "I cannot possibly be ready in only two days. I have not yet finished my trousseau. I was hoping for a day or two in Penrith to purchase the last of my needs."

He arched a brow at her. "Have you extra money for such trifles?"

"Yes, my father gave me a goodly sum."

"I see." He stopped and, facing her, captured both her hands in his. "Well, you must transfer that money to my safekeeping. No wife of mine need trouble herself over worldly matters such as finance. That is what a husband is for, darling. I will accompany you to town, of course." He leaned close and whispered against the top of her head. "I should like to see what fancies you in the shops."

A shiver crept down her back, and she told herself the sensation must be a good response to his affection. Yes, naturally her body would react in such a fashion. Any woman would tremble to have a handsome man speak such intimate words to her alone.

Even so, she pulled back a bit. "Might we go visit Emma now?"

His blue eyes narrowed. "You seem inordinately attached to the child."

"I am the only mother she has ever known. Granted, it has only been for a few weeks, but we have been through a lot together." A smile curved her lips as memory after memory surfaced. Emma's first steps. Her *ah-be-da* baby gibberish. The smell of her salty-sweet skin after sleeping hard against Abby's shoulder.

She squeezed his fingers, as if by touch alone she might make him believe. "You will adore Emma as well. Once she gets to know you—"

"You forget, my sweet." He dropped her hands and pinched her cheek. "I have houseguests to attend to. The men and I are taking in a spot of fishing today. See to the child, if you must, but I expect you to be dressed and down for dinner by seven. Will you do that for me?"

The conversation moved from Emma to fishing to dinner so fast, she stuttered. "I—I. . .of course. I look forward to it."

And she should. Dinner with the man who would be her husband in the manor that would be her home was a dream come true.

But deep down in her heart, she wished she were back on the road with the captain, looking forward to a homely meal in a smoky pub with a sleeping baby on her shoulder.

Dinner with Sir Jonathan and his guests did not change that sentiment. The four-course meal lodged like a brick in Abby's stomach as she sat on the sofa in the drawing room. Next to her, the colonel's wife, Mrs. Wilkins, chattered away like a magpie. Abby picked at a thread on the hem of her sleeve to prevent her hands from stopping her ears. The woman hadn't come up for air since she'd latched arms with Abby immediately following the baked apple pudding.

As the woman droned on, Abby's gaze drifted to the corner of the room, where Colonel Wilkins and Parker Granby engaged themselves in a quiet hand of picquet. The colonel was a man of few words, as was Mr. Granby, and both were likely quite pleased Mrs. Wilkins had found a new victim to regale.

Opposite them, Parson Durge—aptly nicknamed for his strange penchant to wear a black cassock over his trousers—bent over another table close to Abby's side of the sofa. He held a large magnifying glass in one hand as he studied a book on entomology, exclaiming aloud now and then on some wonderful quirk of insect lore.

But none of these guests interested Abby nearly as much as Sir Jonathan and Lady Pelham. They congregated near the pianoforte, riffling through sheet music. An innocent enough occupation, especially since they stood a good arm's length apart. All the same, Abby frowned. Other than a gut feeling and several offhand remarks by Lady Pelham, she had no evidence of anything illicit between the two. Still, suspicion gnawed away in the corner of her mind that far more than kinship drew them together.

". . .wouldn't you say, Miss Gilbert?"

Abby snapped her attention back to the colonel's wife, painfully aware she'd neglected the last several minutes of the woman's conversation. "I. . .er. . ." How was she to answer a question she hadn't heard without offending the older lady?

Think. Think!

Forcing a fake yawn, she lifted her fingers to her lips. May God—and Mrs. Wilkins—forgive her. "I beg your pardon, Mrs. Wilkins, but with the excitement of finally arriving here yesterday after such a long journey, I confess I am still a bit fatigued."

"Of course you are." Mrs. Wilkins leaned over and patted Abby's knee, the movement wafting a somewhat musty smell of overripe melons. Everything about the woman was beyond seasonal, from the outmoded cut of her floral gown to the tight pull of her grey hair, styled in a fashion that died twenty years ago.

"It was a champion thing of you to travel so frugally, my dear. Rented chaises are so unreliable. Perhaps once the manor is restored, Sir Jonathan will once again be able to own a carriage of his own."

Ignoring the woman's queer odour, Abby dipped her head closer and lowered her voice. "Are you saying the baronet has no carriage?"

Mrs. Wilkins shook her head so quickly, her silver earbobs jiggled. "Not a one."

Abby pursed her lips, thinking back on her earlier visit to the captain above the stable. While she'd not entered the bottom half, she'd swear in a court of law that she'd heard horsey whickers and shuffling hooves.

"Yet he owns horses," she thought aloud.

"Only for racing." Mrs. Wilkins glanced aside to the pianoforte, then scooted nearer to Abby. "I think you should know, dear, that the baronet's luck is dismal. However, I am sure that will all change now you have arrived. I had always hoped a valiant woman would come along to save the baronet from his money woes."

Abby pressed her lips flat to keep from gaping. Did Sir Jonathan really love her, or did he love the dowry she came with? Had he chosen her that night at the MacNamaras' ball because she'd captivated him or because he'd learned she was the daughter of a wealthy merchant?

Resonant laughter pulled her gaze back to the pianoforte. Whatever jest had been shared between Sir Jonathan and Lady Pelham heightened the colour on the lady's cheeks, painting her face a becoming shade of scarlet. Her green eyes twinkled in the sconce light, her black hair framing her pixie face in perfect spiral curls. She was a picture, this woman. A masterpiece. The sort to beguile and mesmerize any warm-blooded man.

Parson Durge's book slammed shut, and Abby startled from the sharp *thwap* of it. In four great strides, the man left the table and took up residence next to Abby on the sofa. Still clutching his magnifying glass, he gestured in the air with it, emphasizing his words. "Did you know, ladies, that the female praying mantis eats her mate? Head first. In fact, some begin eating the male's head before the mating process is finished."

"Oh dear!" Mrs. Wilkins gasped. "Such scandalous talk!"

Abby blinked. She'd suffered through many a gathering of her stepmother's eccentric guests, but Parson Durge outshone them all.

He drew the glass close to his eye—enlarging the brown orb well out of proportion—and stared at her as if she were a beetle to be dissected. "I would say, Miss Gilbert, that you have saved Sir Jonathan from a very painful fate. The mantis Lady Pelham would have shown him no such mercy."

So she wasn't the only one to harbour such suspicions about Sir Jonathan and the lady's relationship. But true or not, it wouldn't do them any good for rumours to travel outside the walls of Brakewell Hall. Gossip, once birthed, often grew into a deadly cancer.

She forced a pleasant smile to her lips. "Pardon me for disagreeing, Mr. Durge, but you are misinformed. The lady is Sir Jonathan's cousin. They could not marry even if either were so inclined."

The parson's bug-eyed stare swung toward Mrs. Wilkins, and the two exchanged a glance. Without another word, he rose and strode back to his book, the hem of his cassock swaying with each step.

Mrs. Wilkins reached for her teacup on the small sofa table, averting her gaze. Was she afraid Abby would take her to task as well?

"I am sure, Miss Gilbert, all the parson meant to say is that it is a good thing you are doing, that *you* are a good woman."

Heat warmed Abby's cheeks. Had she jumped to a conclusion? Was she overly sensitive?

"What is this? Are we speaking of my bride's goodness?" Sir Jonathan approached and held out his hand to her—and Abby's face flushed all the hotter. How much of the conversation had he overheard?

Accepting his offer, she placed her hand in his, and he pulled her to her feet, then bowed over her fingers and kissed a benediction atop them. As he straightened, his voice curled out in a low caress. "You are goodness and light, you know. Kind to a fault."

All eyes turned their way, the parson's magnified behind glass, Lady Pelham's brow arched with avid interest. Even the card-playing duo swiveled their gazes away from their game.

Abby pulled back her hand and ran her fingers down her skirt, abhorring all the attention. "Thank you, Sir Jonathan, but there is nothing special about me. I am certain that if you had the opportunity to do good for someone, you would, without a second thought."

"Ahh, such precious naivete." He chuckled and waved a hand in the air. "One must always count the cost and determine how much such an act would cut into profits, be that monetarily or emotionally. You will never be a success if you give away more than you have, my sweet."

Her brow crumpled. "I do not mean to be disagreeable, but did not our Lord do that very thing? He gave His life, defeating hell and death. I can think of no greater success than that."

"Yes, well," he snorted, "if you believe such tales to be true."

"You do not?" A sudden coldness sank in her belly.

Sir Jonathan threw back his head, his laughter shaming. "Such gravity for a dinner party? Come." He held out his arm. "Lady Pelham has agreed to play for us. Let us sing and save such dreary topics for a rainy day, hmm?"

A slap across the face couldn't have stunned her more. What kind of irreverent man was she engaged to? The urge to run into the night and seek the quiet, solid sanctuary of the captain's company coursed through her veins, growing stronger with each beat of her heart.

Bypassing his arm, she pressed her fingers to her lips, once again feigning a yawn. "Forgive me, Sir Jonathan, but I am really rather weary. Perhaps another time."

She flashed a smile at the rest of the guests. "I bid you all good evening."

Murmurs of good night followed her to the door, and when she finally stepped into the corridor, some of the tension of the long evening fled from her shoulders—

Until a deep voice warmed her ear.

"I will see you to your room." Sir Jonathan looped his arm around her waist and guided her toward the stairway.

She clenched her hands against an irrational desire to bat away his touch and peered up at him with a tight smile. "No need. I do not wish to rob your guests of their host."

"It is no inconvenience whatsoever, my sweet." His fingers pressed against her side. A possessive type of embrace. The kind she'd hoped for ever since Father had spoken of Sir Jonathan's offer of marriage.

Even so, she pulled away and grabbed the bannister.

Undaunted, he kept pace at her side. "I have arranged for a ride into Penrith five days hence. Will that suit?"

"Yes. I should like that."

"Good. Then we shall wed the day after your purchases arrive."

Her slipper hit the riser on the last step, and she stumbled onto the first-floor landing.

The baronet's arm shot out, steadying her. "Take care, darling. I would not want you tumbling down the stairs."

Though he spoke of concern, a shadow of foreboding draped over her.

He pulled her close again, this time tightening his grip. His thigh brushed against her gown as he led her toward her room. His hand rubbed up and down her waist. Being alone with this man in the garden was one thing, but here? In the shadows of a sconce-lit passageway? A chill shivered down her spine, the involuntary reaction nothing at all like what she'd experienced when standing close to the captain. Though she had no familiarity with intimacy or passion, she was certain the odd sensation had nothing to do with physical desire.

They stopped in front of her door, and before a "good night" could pass her lips, the baronet swept her into his arms.

She gasped. "I really do not think—"

His mouth came down hard on hers. Wet. Hot. His long arms wrapped around her like steel bands, entrapping her. She wanted—*needed*—air.

Space. Freedom. But his hands cupped the back of her neck, forcing her head up so that he could deepen the kiss.

She'd heard tales of her sisters' stolen kisses, but none of them had mentioned the clenching of one's gut or sudden rise of nausea.

"I have been waiting a long time for this," Sir Jonathan whispered against her skin as his lips trailed down the curve of her neck. His hands drifted, moving down her back, to her waist, to her—

She planted her hands on his chest and shoved him away with all the strength she possessed. "Sir Jonathan, please! We are not yet married, sir."

His blue eyes smouldered to a smoky shade. "You will be mine within the week. Why trifle over a few days?"

He reached for her again.

She arched away, searching for the doorknob behind her. "Yet I insist. Good night, sir."

As soon as her fingers met brass, she yanked open the door and darted inside, slamming it shut before he could follow. Shaking, she leaned against the wood and braced herself, on the off chance he might try to gain entry.

Silence hung thick and heavy, the tick of the mantel clock and beat of her heart overloud in her ears. Had he gone?

"Soon, my innocent dove." The baronet's muffled voice leached through the door.

She stiffened.

"*Very* soon." His husky words seeped into her like an unholy prophecy.

A breath later, his footsteps padded down the corridor, then disappeared altogether.

Abby pressed her fingers against her lips, hating that the baronet had taken such a bold liberty. Hating even more that as his soon-to-be bride, she would have no choice but to welcome such advances.

But most of all, she hated the unstoppable desire to find out what it would feel like to be kissed so passionately by the captain. . .for that could never be.

CHAPTER TWENTY-NINE

Time and the full-hearted embraces of a child were the best elixirs in the world, diminishing Abby's revulsion of the baronet's advance four days ago. Thankfully, since then, Sir Jonathan had been nothing but the utmost gentleman—seating her first at dinner and making it a point to include her in the conversations of his guests. Most importantly, he kept his caresses to a simple brush of his fingertips against her cheek or a light peck atop her hand when seeing her to her room at night. Perhaps she had been a bit harsh with him. After all, he'd merely been showing his eagerness to have her as his bride. What woman wouldn't want that kind of attention?

And so she fell into a pattern of sorts. Her days were filled with enjoying Emma's silly grins and sloppy kisses as they spent afternoons with the captain. Her evenings were occupied by the baronet and his houseguests. All in all, it was a perfectly pleasant existence—save for the nettling feeling that would not go away whenever Lady Pelham entered the room.

Abby shoved aside all thoughts of the woman and swung Emma to her other hip, then pushed open the back door to the stable yard. Sunlight washed the world in a golden glow, and she squinted. It took a moment for her vision to adjust to the brightness—and when it did, she did a double take.

Across the yard, the captain hobbled down the stable's stone stairway—without use of the makeshift crutch old Mencott had fashioned for him.

She clutched Emma tighter and dashed across the gravel. "Oh, you are doing better!"

Emma squealed, from the wild ride *and* the sight of the captain. And Abby didn't blame her. It was all she could do to suppress her own squeal.

Abby caught up to him as his boots hit the cobbles. He said nothing, but he didn't have to. The flash of a wince tightening his face said enough.

She stifled a sigh. Every day he pushed himself too much, asked more from his body than it could give. And each time pain flickered in his eyes, another piece of her heart broke off.

She frowned. "Shall I help you back upstairs?"

"I am not a fragile flower, *lady*." He winked—knowing full well the name ruffled her—and reached for Emma.

Abby twisted aside, keeping the girl beyond his grasp. "Do you really think it is a good idea to hold this squirming worm?"

"You worry too much," he grunted. "Life is more than good ideas. It's the risks that return greater results."

He stepped to the other side of her and pulled Emma from her arms, swinging the child up high into the air. "How's my girl?"

"Ah-pa!" Emma shrieked, and when he lowered her, she wrapped her arms around him and giggled into his neck.

Joyful tears filled Abby's eyes, blurring the scene. She'd never tire of watching this man love this girl and vice versa—especially since they'd nearly lost him. Swallowing, she dabbed away the dampness at the corners of her eyes with her knuckle.

The movement pulled the captain's gaze toward her. "Are you all right?"

"I am." She grinned and swept her hand toward the old workbench just outside the stable doors. "Shall we sit and let Emma play?"

He shook his head. Emma giggled and planted her hands on his cheeks. "I came down here to stretch my leg, not sun myself like a lazy alley cat."

"Do you mind if Emma and I join you?"

"Not at all." He peeled Emma's hands away, but each time he succeeded in releasing one and reached for the other, she slapped her freed palm right back again.

Abby's grin grew. "Good. I would have joined you even had you denied me. Come, little one."

Before the captain could protest, she retrieved Emma and swung her down to the ground, keeping tight hold of the girl's hands. Emma bounced a moment, then kicked out one chubby leg after the other, eager to walk. Abby followed behind, now and then letting go so Emma could practice walking on her own.

The captain's hobbling step joined her side. "She grows more every day."

"That she does. Mrs. Horner tells me she is quite the handful, especially when I am not around." She gazed up at him. "Will you be able to manage her on your own when you take her back to her father? I will not be traveling along to care for her, you know."

His lips twitched into a smirk, his silence and the accompanying scolding from an overhead martin speaking volumes.

Heat crept up her neck. "I suppose that was a ridiculous question. You round up highwaymen and bring them in. One small girl should be no challenge for you."

"I think, Miss Gilbert, that you're finally getting to know me." A slow smile brightened his face, and sight of the rare appearance tingled in her belly.

As they rounded the back of the stable and moved onto the grassy path leading to the garden, laughter floated on the air. Abby's jaw tightened reflexively at the merry chuckle, for the origin was unmistakable.

On the far side of a vast stretch of creeping ivy, a green-coated man and a blue-skirted woman batted a shuttlecock between them. Lady Pelham and the baronet, unattended by anyone else, appeared to all the world as if they were a happily married couple.

A hot mix of shame and anger boiled in the back of Abby's throat. Why couldn't Sir Jonathan employ better discretion? She swooped up Emma and turned to the captain, intent on suggesting they take a different route before he witnessed the sight.

But too late. He narrowed his eyes at the pair.

Abby forced a light tone to her voice. "Emma would like to see your horse, I think. Shall we go back to the stable?"

His gaze swung to her, a dark glint deepening the brown of his eyes. "Tell me, Miss Gilbert, how are your wedding plans coming along?"

"Oh…um…" Shifting the kicking Emma to her hip, she sidestepped him and headed back toward the stable, calling over her shoulder, "I am not quite ready yet."

Despite his injured leg, he caught up to her. "I should think you'd be more than ready. Your baronet was all you could talk about on our journey here. Or is it, perhaps, your groom is the one who is *not quite ready*?"

La! Neither of them were. But after the hardship of the cross-country journey, she couldn't very well admit aloud that the captain's astute guardianship all the way across England may have been in vain. Besides, once she married the baronet, of course he would send Lady Pelham away.

Wouldn't he?

She flipped Emma around, allowing the girl to face forward, and wrapped her arms tight against Emma's middle. "Do not be silly, Captain. There are a few more necessaries I must purchase in Penrith, that is all. Then everything will be set for the wedding."

He eyed her as he might a potential criminal, searching for truth between the thin spaces of her words. She looked away, the scrutiny too much to bear.

"Who is the lady with your baronet?"

The directness of his question startled her, and her step faltered. His strong hand gripped her arm, righting her.

She pulled back, scorning her own awkwardness. "Lady Pelham. She is his cousin."

"Hmm." The gravelly sound grumbling in his throat indicted and condemned without a word.

Frowning, she stopped and turned to him. "What does that mean?"

"Maybe nothing. Or maybe everything." A murderous shadow darkened his gaze. "The baronet…is he treating you well?"

Instantly her mind slid to the stolen kiss. The force of Sir Jonathan's embrace had been brutal. His lips had devoured her like an animal, not a loving and tender suitor.

Abby nuzzled her cheek against the top of Emma's head, banishing the ugly memory to the past where it should be buried. After all, the baronet had not been untoward since then. So why did it still chafe to be in his presence, while being with Samuel felt so comfortable?

She lifted her face to the captain. "Sir Jonathan is all politeness and decorum, and I have nothing more to say on the matter."

A muscle on his jaw pulsed as he studied her, indicating some kind of mental battle raged inside his head. She didn't dare look away, though. Any semblance of retreat on her part might label her a liar. And who knew what he'd do if he believed the baronet was mistreating her, for she'd witnessed the captain's raw strength when unleashed.

Finally, he blew out a long breath. "I should head back."

Her brows pinched together. Was his face paler? His breath laboured? Had he overtaxed himself? "How are you faring?"

"I'm fine. I promised Mencott I'd help him mend some of the tack, that's all." He reached out and rubbed his hand over Emma's head, mussing her hair. A slight smile lifted the corners of his mouth, but when he pulled back, it faded—then completely sobered as he stared into Abby's eyes. "You know we'll be leaving soon, Emma and I."

"I. . .I know." Her throat closed, the admission tasting as bitter as horseradish. She didn't want either of them to leave. Ever.

A wild impulse rose to her lips, and without thinking any further on it, she blurted, "Say you will come to dinner tonight, at the house. We have so little time left, you and I, and I do not want to waste a minute of it."

Reaching, he kneaded a muscle at the back of his neck. "That's probably not a good idea."

"Did you not just tell me life is more than good ideas? That it is the risks that return greater results?" She nodded toward the manor. "This will soon be my home as much as the baronet's, and I should think I may invite whomever I like to dine with us. After all, his friends are here. I deserve to have mine as well."

"Well, I am glad to see your spunk is still intact." A grin broke over his face like a ray of August sunshine—the effect stunning and ruggedly handsome.

Three smiles in the space of a quarter hour? That *was* a victory.

"So you will come?" She rose to her toes. "Please?"

He sighed. "Just this once."

He stalked off without another word, his step determined but a bit stilted each time he put weight on his injured leg.

Abby squeezed Emma tighter and whispered against her downy hair. "What will we do without him, little one, when he leaves us behind?"

Slowly, Abby lifted her head. That was a battle for another day.

For now she must convince the baronet to allow the captain to dine with him and his guests.

A firing line would've been easier to face.

Samuel tugged at his collar and slipped a covert glance across the table at Abby. Which fork would she pick up? Ever since sitting down in the baronet's dining room, the long line of silver flatware in front of him blasted grapeshot into his confidence. He had no idea so many different-sized forks or spoons existed, let alone which one to employ for which course. This type of dainty banqueting was better suited to Brentwood or Moore. Oh, sweet mercy. If they could see him now, sitting here sweating over the selection of a butter knife, they'd laugh him halfway across the continent.

Just as he fingered the farthest utensil on the left, the man across from him speared him with a direct gaze.

"I don't suppose a man like you is used to this sort of gathering."

Samuel set his jaw to keep from grinding his teeth. It took a lot of gall for the long-gowned fellow to pretend to know what a man should or should not be like. When Abby had introduced him as Mr. Durge instead of parson, Samuel had thought she might've made a slip of the tongue. But after listening to the fellow's colourful language and heretical ideas, no doubt remained. Mr. Durge was no saint and, in fact, blasphemed the clergy by wearing a cassock.

He met the fellow's gaze. "What kind of man would that be, sir?"

"I am sure you do not need me to spell it out."

"By all means, enlighten me."

The man narrowed his eyes, a wicked flash sparking like that of a cat about to bat around a mouse. "The kind of man, Captain, to eat with a fork and knife at a fine linen table, set with imported porcelain. Surely this is an oddity for you."

Samuel upped the intensity of his stare, a skill he'd honed over the years of interrogating criminals. At this point, offense was his best defense—and he intended to be as offensive as possible. "You're right. Usually I gnaw raw meat off a bone, bare handed. I'm surprised the baronet allowed me in here."

Next to him, a strangling choke burbled in Mrs. Wilkins's throat, and she shot out a jeweled hand for her water glass.

Nervous laughter tittered out of Abby. "Oh Captain, such a jest! I assure you all"—she swept her gaze around the table—"that I have never once seen the captain gnawing on bones of any sort."

Next to her, at the head of the table, Sir Jonathan Aberley leaned aside and caressed Abby's shoulder with a possessive touch. "You cannot expect a man who deals in ruffians and rogues to maintain sweet manners, my dear."

The fish in Samuel's gut sank like a lead weight. He'd like to show the baronet some of his manners, right at the end of his fist—especially if the man's fingers slid any closer to the bare skin just above Abby's bodice.

Seated at the so-called parson's elbow, a living, breathing weasel perked up. Parker Granby, his eyes two black beads set close to a nose better used as a parakeet perch, angled his head toward him. "Well, I, for one, would not want to ride roughshod along the highways and byways of the wilds. It must be a hard life, I imagine."

"Must it?" Samuel stabbed a bite of meat and lifted it to his mouth. "Fresh air quite agrees with me."

"Yes, well, I suppose simple pleasures are to be enjoyed now and then." A sneer rippled across Granby's lips. "I find that the simple are often the most content, unruffled by avarice or ambition."

Samuel bit down hard on the chunk of meat. A bullet taken sideways often did the most damage. Clearly this fellow was an adept marksman with his mockery, and this was exactly why he preferred the dust of the road to the carping of upper society.

Abby gasped and leaned back in her chair, shooting her own daggered look at Mr. Granby. "Surely you are not suggesting the captain is a simple man, sir."

"I should think not, Miss Gilbert." Mr. Granby speared a bite of his food. "I hardly know him."

Patches of colour deepened on Abby's cheeks, and it took all of Samuel's restraint to keep from leaping over the table and popping the man smack in the middle of his weaselly nose. Baiting him was one thing. Toying with Abby, quite another. One more word from the fellow and—

A light touch on his sleeve jerked his gaze to the right.

Lady Pelham angled toward him, a single black curl caressing her shoulder like the snake she was. God forgive him for such a harsh judgment, but it'd only taken a few minutes to see beyond her polished façade into the reptilian scales of her soul.

"Tell me of your home, Captain." Her lips parted into a sultry smile. "I find London to be an exceedingly exciting city."

Of course she did. Most strumpets thrived there. He reached for his glass and eyed her over the rim. "I don't live in London."

"But you are a runner." She launched the derogatory term more accurately than a French mortar shell. "Do you not operate out of Bow Street?"

"I do." He slugged back a drink of wine, then set the glass on the tablecloth, relishing the burn down his throat. "Yet I house in Hammersmith."

"Oh. . .I see," she drawled.

He gritted his teeth. By the curl of the lady's lip, what she saw was a poor man unable to pay the high rent in the city—which goaded even more, because she was right.

Two servants moved in, removing plates and setting down bowls of greenish soup. The pleasant twang of lemon and parsley erased some of the bitterness of the lady's words, but not all.

The baronet picked up a wide spoon and indicated Abby with the tip of it. "My bride here informs me that you are quite proficient with a gun."

Samuel's gaze shot to Abby, who took a sudden interest in her soup.

Why on earth would she have said such a thing to the baronet?

Opposite the baronet, at the far end of the table, Colonel Wilkins planted his elbows on each side of his bowl and laced his fingers over it, his interest clearly piqued. "What do you shoot, Captain?"

He gazed at the grey-haired fellow. If the parson was not really a clergyman, was this fellow truly a colonel? Only one way to find out. "I carry a nine-inch land pattern, sixty-two calibre."

One of the Colonel's thick, white eyebrows lifted. "Ahh, light dragoons, perhaps?"

So the man did have military experience. Samuel nodded. "The Nineteenth."

"Well!" The colonel blustered and dropped his hands to his lap. "I am surprised you survived. If I recall correctly, that regiment was not known for their quick thinking."

The slur lit a blaze in his belly, driving heat up his neck and over his ears. "Wellesley would've lost Assaye were it not for our detachment."

"Yet you must admit, Captain, that the assault was not of your own contrivance, but under orders from my colleague, Colonel Maxwell."

"That has little to do with it," he gritted out. *He* was the one on the front line. *He* was the one dodging a rain of deadly fire, losing brothers, facing hell—and bearing a crescent mark on his cheek to remind him daily of the carnage.

"I should think it has everything to do with it." The colonel dabbed at the corner of his mouth with a napkin. "Last time I checked, a colonel outranks a mere captain."

Beneath the table, Samuel's hands curled into fists. This was not to be borne.

The baronet tapped his spoon against his goblet. "Back to the subject at hand, gentlemen. I myself have little use for pistols. Real damage is done with a Girandoni, though they are not for the faint of heart. Have you ever tried one, Captain?"

Samuel swung his gaze back to Sir Jonathan, unsure which man aggravated him more—the pretentious baronet or the know-it-all colonel. Though he might as well add the pretend parson and

Granby to the mix.

"No, sir, I have not," he answered, and for good reason. That particular rifle was expensive, accurate, deadly—and frowned upon by most militia, for the usage of such most often targeted officers, a grievous breach of the rules of war.

"I thought as much." Sir Jonathan bent to sip a mouthful of his soup, then set down his spoon and leaned back in his chair. "Besides being costly, such a weapon requires special training to operate. No slur intended, Captain, but the Girandoni is not a firearm for the common man. If you like, I will show one to you after dinner, for I do not suppose you have ever had the opportunity."

That did it. One more insult and he'd take them all on—and revel in the pleasure of bloodying their arrogant noses.

"Thank you, but no need to trouble yourself." He pushed back his chair and tossed his napkin onto the table. "If you'll excuse me, it's been a long day."

Made even longer by this lot.

He stalked out, leaving behind murmurs and hissed breaths, hating that his injured leg slowed him down. The sooner he made it out of Brakewell Hall, the better. If that was the company Abby wished to keep, then God help her. He'd rather share a crust of stale bread in the stable with Mencott than suffer one more minute with those finely dressed vultures.

Taking care to favor his stitched-up thigh, he hobbled out into the middle of the stable yard and faced the sky. A three-quarter moon cast a white glow in the blackness, blotting out the nearby stars with its brilliance. Samuel closed his eyes and filled his lungs with the damp night air, then slowly blew it all out, easing some of the tension in his shoulders—until footsteps once again cinched his muscles.

He turned. Abby's ivory gown soaked up moonlight as she floated toward him, a being of light in the darkness. She stopped in front of him, saying nothing, bringing her sweet scent of orange blossom water and lazy summer afternoons. He watched her warily as her eyes welled and pity swam laps in their depths.

Pity? For him?

Disgust rolled through him all over again. Folding his arms, he steeled himself against her tears. "Go back to your dinner party, Miss Gilbert."

She shook her head. "They had no right to say such things."

"Why not?" He snorted. "Everything they said was true."

A ruffled hen couldn't have looked more perturbed as she planted her fists on her hips and lifted to her toes. "You do *not* gnaw on bones with your bare hands!"

"All right, I'll give you that." He threw back his shoulders. "*Almost* all they said was true."

"What they said were lies! They painted you a barbarian. An animal."

He advanced, going toe to toe, eye to eye, and stared her down. "Maybe I am," he growled.

Most women would've tucked tail and run, or called him out for the beast he really was. At the very least, they'd have burst into tears. But not this stubborn little sprite. Slowly, she reached up a slim hand and caressed his cheek, her touch hot against his skin.

He stiffened.

"No, Samuel," she whispered, a thousand possibilities thickening her words. She lifted her face higher, her mouth a breath away from his. "You are not anything like they insinuated, and I thank God for that. You, Samuel Thatcher, are the most compassionate man I have ever met."

The veracity in her gaze, the huskiness of her voice, the way her fingers slid over his face, pulling him closer. . .it was too much. More than a mortal man could bear.

"Abby," he breathed out.

Then he pulled her into his arms and fit his mouth onto hers.

The heat of an August sun burned through him. She tasted sweet, spicy, hinting of promises and distant horizons. He'd kissed women before, and kissed them well, but this? He staggered, fully intoxicated, moulding his body against hers. This was dizzying. Heady. Dangerous. Especially when she moaned his name and grabbed great handfuls of his suit coat, burrowing into him.

Alarms tolled in his head, but the thrumming in his veins and throbbing in his body overrode reason. His mouth traveled from her lips, to the curve of her neck, then lower, tracing a line to her collarbone, to the very flesh that would not—*could* not—ever belong to him. Unless . . .did he dare?

"Samuel." She arched against him, a passionate invitation—one neither of them had any right to issue or accept.

Sobering, he pulled away, breathing hard. Her chest heaved as well, and slowly, she lifted one trembling hand to her lips. Was she remembering? Wanting more?

Or regretting?

The need to know cut into him like a knife. What were her feelings toward him, her *real* feelings, not just some physical response to a well-placed kiss? He drew in a deep breath, desperately trying to regain equilibrium, and pinned her in place with his gaze.

The fire blazing in her eyes lit with a passion to match his own.

"Promise me, Thatcher! When you find a woman you love, you'll not waste one second. You'll go after her with all your heart because one day, ahh, one day. . .it will be too late, and you'll be left with nothing but regrets."

Hawker's words barreled back with stark clarity. It'd been easy enough to agree with his friend then, but now? There was no more denying that he loved this woman, but how could he possibly pursue her when he hadn't even a shilling in his pocket? No, asking her to be his wife was out of the question, for now, anyway—but that didn't mean he had to leave her here in this nest of vipers, not if she wanted out. And if she did wish to leave, maybe someday—with a bit of hard work and the smile of God—he would have the chance to make her his.

"I'm only going to ask you this once, Abby, so take care with your answer."

Her hand dropped, her eyes shimmering wide and frightened. "Very well."

"Do you want me to take you away from here?" He measured the words out like a lifeline. "Emma and I will be leaving soon. Do you want to leave as well?"

Her mouth opened, then closed. Moonlight brushed over her face, draining the colour from her skin.

"I. . ." Her throat bobbed. "I—"

A sob broke off her words, and gathering up her skirts, she spun and sprinted back toward the manor.

"Abby!"

He sucked in a breath. Was that ragged voice bouncing off the cobbles truly his, or some wounded animal heaving a death groan?

The door slammed. Abby vanished. He stood speechless, breathless, hopeless.

Crushed.

Movement at an upstairs window snagged his attention, and his gaze climbed the stone wall of Brakewell Hall. In a candlelit window, the back of a green dress coat stepped away from the glass.

Samuel stiffened, what was left of his heart nothing but ashes now. Had all Abby's talk of a loving family and home life been but a means to urge him to deliver her safely here?

He gritted his teeth. If the baronet, that pompous coxcomb, was the man that Miss Gilbert truly wanted, she could have him.

CHAPTER THIRTY

The morning breeze wafted through the open stable doors, unreasonable in its carefree tussling of Samuel's hair. Scowling, he tossed back his head, shaking the annoying swath away from his face. He should've thought to grab his hat.

With a nod to Mencott, who perched on a stool near the workbench, Samuel grabbed a currycomb with one hand and snatched up Pilgrim's lead in the other. As he guided the horse out into the sun, pain stretched a tight line across his thigh, but not the sort that broke a bead of sweat on his brow. Not anymore. Thank God he was on the mend, and none too soon. After last night, even the thought of seeing Abby again was an exquisite agony.

Just outside the door, he looped Pilgrim's lead to an iron ring, then patted her on the neck. "You are a constant, my friend. A true and faithful companion."

Pilgrim shoved her horsey nose against his shoulder, then perked up her head, ears twitching.

Samuel wheeled about.

Sir Jonathan Aberley clipped across the cobbles, the buckles on his black leather shoes catching the light and bouncing it back. "Good morning, Captain."

Out of respect for the man's station—and nothing more—Samuel dipped his head. "Sir Jonathan."

The man stopped several paces from him, a pair of kidskin gloves held loosely in one hand. With the other, he shielded his eyes and glanced up at the sky. "Yes, indeed, it is quite a fine morning today, is it not?"

Samuel cocked his head. Never once had the baronet sought him out like this. Something was up—and more than likely it had to do with what the man had seen out the window last evening. . .a topic he'd rather not discuss. Ever. He turned back to Pilgrim with a grunt and started brushing.

Behind him, footsteps thudded, and the baronet circled into Samuel's line of sight. "This is a beauty of a bay you have here."

Shoving back a sigh, Samuel dropped his hand idle at his side. "I think we both know you're not here to appreciate my horse or supply me with a commentary on the weather."

The baronet's gaze hardened, his mask of pretense falling to the dirt. "You are correct. I have come on Abigail's behalf."

Samuel gripped the currycomb tighter. Why would she send Sir Jonathan to do her bidding? She wasn't one to avoid confrontation. Unless, for some reason, she wasn't able to venture out here.

A ripple of unease spread like unsettled waters in his chest, making it hard to breathe. Merciful heavens, had she taken ill? Had she somehow been injured?

"Is she all right?" he asked.

The baronet's brow pinched. "She is no longer your concern. You appear sufficiently able to ride, so I suggest you collect the child and leave at once. In short, Captain, Abigail wishes you gone, as do I."

She wishes you gone. She wishes you gone. She wishes. . .

The words buzzed like angry hornets, stinging mercilessly. A bayonet to the belly would've been a kinder act than this abrupt dismissal. After all they'd been through, the danger, the passion, she hadn't the decency to part from him herself? The currycomb in his hand shook beneath his death grip.

"Very well," he ground out, surprised the words could even form the way his jaw locked. "But first I'll thank you to pay me what is owed."

Pursing his lips, the baronet slowly pulled his gloves onto his hands, working each finger hole snug against his flesh. "I should think your room and board are sufficient payment."

The muscles on Samuel's neck hardened to steel. He needed that money, now more than ever after having given the boy in Manchester the last of his coins. "Miss Gilbert and I agreed that I would be paid—"

"And so you have been, Captain." The man's gaze jerked to his. "You have been compensated in the medical services rendered by my stable master, in the roof over your head these past six days, and in the food filling your belly. Not to mention the care and feeding of your squalling brat. I will not give you a penny more, nor will I allow you to continue to suckle at my breast. I want you off my property within the hour. Is that quite clear?"

Astounding. Absolutely astounding. The man was more tight-fistedly bold than most cutthroats roaming the roads.

"Quite." Samuel shot the word like a bullet, wickedly wishing it were a deadly ball of lead.

"Good." The baronet flexed his hands in his skin-tight gloves, a sneer slashing across his face.

Without another word, he skirted both Samuel and the horse and strode into the stable.

Closing his eyes, Samuel clenched his jaw, sickened that it had come to this. He'd done hard things before, performed distasteful duties and inglorious tasks. But traveling halfway across the country, his body held together by catgut and willpower, with nothing but a baby he must keep fed and dry, well...that would surely be a challenge, even for him.

But not nearly as demanding as trying to forget the betrayal dealt him by a brown-eyed snip of a woman and the arrogant rogue she'd chosen over him.

Hope for the best? Expect the best? No. He never would again.

Abby ran her finger aimlessly over a bolt of muslin. Early-afternoon light slanted through the linen draper's large window, highlighting the fine green-and-gold stripes on the fabric. Any woman would be proud to own a length of such fine material, but she didn't reach to loosen the strings on her reticule. It was a fruitless pursuit, this shopping. She'd not made one purchase for her upcoming marriage the entire morning she'd been in Penrith. How deep would the baronet's scowl be if she returned empty handed to Brakewell Hall? He'd been so insistent she take Lady Pelham's carriage to finish purchasing her needs for the wedding, practically shoving her out the door right after breakfast . . .alone. . .though earlier he'd said he'd accompany her. Not that she minded, but why the sudden change of heart?

A sigh deflated her. This should be a happy outing, an exciting one. Not all brides were as fortunate as her to be marrying a baronet, shopping with his blessing.

So why the dead weight hanging heavy on her chest, smothering the life from her?

Pulling back her hand, she fought the urge to once again lift her fingers to her lips and remember all over again—though she needn't, really. The taste of the captain's kiss lingered like a lover in her mind. She'd never forget the feel of his arms moulding her against him, the heat of his body, or his exotic spicy flavor. A delicious twinge rippled through her belly. She'd found a home in his embrace, a sense of belonging, and something more. Something eternal. Samuel's kiss had been an unspoken promise that he would cherish her more than his own life, even beyond the grave.

Which was nothing at all like what she'd felt in Sir Jonathan's arms.

The shop clerk closed the ledger she'd been tallying in and wove past a table of lace. An inquiring smile lifted the older lady's mouth. "Have you made a decision, miss?"

The question hit her broadside, and she gasped. Indeed, she *had* made a decision—a forbidden and altogether irresistible decision—one she should've told Samuel and the baronet long ago.

Her own grin spread wide and free on her face. "I have, thank you."

Then she turned and bolted out to the carriage.

"Brakewell Hall, with all haste," she told the driver as she gripped his hand. "Deliver me to the stable yard, please."

"Aye, miss." The man nodded as he helped her up, a curious tilt to his head. Likely Lady Pelham had never instructed him so, or returned from a shopping excursion without excessive packages or parcels.

But no matter. Abby was going home. Home! To a dark-eyed,

sometimes grim-jawed captain who, more often than not, was a sort of gruffly man—but the only man she wanted. Though the road leading out of Penrith was worn smooth and the wheels turned easily, she couldn't help but bounce on the seat, imagining the flash of a smile on Samuel's handsome face as she flung her arms about his neck. She could practically hear his laugh rumbling deep in his chest when she told him she loved him and to please take her away with him and Emma.

Turning her face, she gazed out the window at the passing greenery, anticipation fluttering her heart, not unlike the eagerness she'd felt when leaving behind her home in Southampton. Of course her stepmother and father would be horrified at her wayward behaviour, running off with a captain of the horse patrol, but so be it. They'd made their choices, lived their lives as they'd seen fit. It was time, for once, that she did so as well, for had not God Himself extended His love to her by offering the deepest desire of her heart—a loving home with Samuel?

When the carriage barely slowed, she leapt from her seat, practically crawling out of her skin for the door to open and release her to her future. The second her feet touched ground, she hiked her skirts and ran up the stone steps to the stable master's quarters.

"Samuel?" She gave the door a cursory rap then, without waiting for an answer, shoved it open.

A wedge of sunlight cut in through the opening, highlighting a swath of dust motes in the air. She rushed over the threshold, then stopped. Blankets fit snug on the cot where the captain had lain. The crutch he'd used leaned forgotten against the wall. No leather pack of belongings troubled the floor by his bed. She frowned. Why did it look so empty? So forlorn? So. . .final. A shiver spidered down her spine.

Abby straightened her shoulders, casting off the ridiculous foreboding. Silly girl! He was likely in the garden, stretching his legs, or perhaps testing his strength by taking Pilgrim for a ride. In the meantime, she'd see to Emma and prepare the child to leave.

Shutting the door firmly behind her, she retraced her steps down to the stable yard, then stopped short as Mr. Mencott swung around the corner and blocked her path.

"Miss Gilbert." He nodded. "Is there anything I can help you with?"

"I was looking for the captain. Have you seen him?"

Yanking out a handkerchief, the old man ran the soiled cloth across his brow, then tucked the thing away. "You haven't heard, then, eh? The captain is gone."

"Gone?" The word stuck sideways in her throat. "What do you mean?"

"Sir Jonathan and him had words this morn. The captain and the child left shortly thereafter and—miss? Miss!"

The older man's voice faded as she tore across the cobbles to the manor's back door. She flung it open and dashed down the corridor, loosening her hat and her hairpins in the mad race. By the time she neared the sitting room door, where the baronet's deep voice and Lady Pelham's laughter rang out, her hair broke loose and fell to her shoulders, her bonnet hung down her back by the ribbon at her neck. Regardless of her crazed appearance, she bolted into the room.

Green eyes batted up at her. Lady Pelham sat like a princess on the settee, carefully balancing a teacup. Sir Jonathan stood behind with one hand draped across her shoulder, bending so that his lips nearly touched her neck.

He straightened, a quirk to his brow. "Well, it looks as though your shopping trip nearly did you in, my sweet."

Swallowing a red-hot rage, Abby stormed to the middle of the room and skewered the lady with a glower. "Excuse me, Lady Pelham, but I would have a word with Sir Jonathan. Alone."

"Hmm. . .perhaps the kitten does have claws." The lady set down her teacup and rose, then cast Sir Jonathan a look over her shoulder. "Until later."

"Mmm," he murmured, his gaze following Lady Pelham as she sashayed past Abby. Once she exited, he sidestepped the sofa and crossed the rug to stand in front of Abby. The lady's lavender scent clung to him like a second skin.

His gaze bore into hers, iciness flashing in those blue depths. "I have been very patient with you, darling, but it is bad form for you to dismiss one of my guests so casually."

"Yet you dismissed my dearest friend!" Her voice shook, and she breathed in deeply to steady herself. "What did you say to the captain to make him leave so abruptly?"

"That is what this is about? Your precious captain?"

He pulled her to him so quickly, his mouth coming down hard on hers, that her protest stuck in her throat. Squirming, she planted her hands on his chest and shoved with all her fury.

"Stop it!"

She jerked back her arm to slap him, but he caught her wrist and held fast.

"Listen, you little fool." He shoved his face into hers. "I saw you and the captain last night, in the stable yard. You should be thankful I sent him away instead of you."

She staggered. Of all the hypocritical, double standards! "And what of you and Lady Pelham? You are not cousins! Were you going to tell me that before or after the wedding, *darling*?" She drew out the word like the slice of a knife.

"Ahh..." A dangerous smile slashed across his face. "It comes down to managing our indiscretions so soon, then? Very well. It will be easier not to pretend."

Though she'd known it all along, the admission hit her hard, stealing her breath. "Why?" The question shook out of her, sounding as forlorn as a lost little girl even to her own ears. She tipped her chin and forced steel into her tone. "Why did you ask to marry me if you had no intention of loving me?"

"Love?" His laughter bounced off the walls, mocking her from every direction. "What has love to do with status and a fine home? It was a fair enough trade, my dear. Your dowry for my name. Your family certainly did not raise any objections and, in fact, were quite eager for the arrangement—as were you, if I recall."

She stiffened, horrified. What a naive little lamb she'd been. "I had no idea," she ground out. "I thought you cared for me, that you cherished *me*!"

"Oh kitten." Pity was tied by a thread to the end of his endearment, and the lines on his face softened. He brushed away the hair that'd fallen across one of her eyes, and his fingers lingered near her ear. "You are upset. Let us put this behind us. I very well might come to love you. Stranger things have happened."

Her jaw dropped. She stared into his hollow blue eyes, hopelessly and completely speechless. What was one to say when a dream finally heaved its last, shuddering breath?

But no. The impeccably dressed man in front of her was not her dream at all—and honestly, never had been.

She shook her head, disentangling her hair from his grasp. "I cannot go through with this. I *will* not. I am done with waiting for love to find me, when all along it was within my grasp."

He grabbed her arm before she could sidestep him. "Do not do this, Abigail." For the first time since she'd known him, panic whined in his voice. "Do not throw away what you have for what you think you want. It is never a good idea to base one's life on the whim of passion."

A whim? Was that the only value he put on love? Compassion rose up, tightening her throat. How awful it must be to live with such a shallow understanding of the very thing that caused a heart to beat.

"Someone once told me that life is more than good ideas. It is the risks that return greater results. I hope, sir, that one day you too will learn to risk all for love, for that is what our Lord did for us." She pulled from his grasp.

"You are more an innocent than I credited." His brow folded into a sneer, then as suddenly, faded. "But you are young, and you will learn. Come. You are weary. I shall walk you to your chamber and you may rest. Things will look different after a good sleep."

"No. All the sleep in the world will not change my mind." She lifted her chin. "I bid you goodbye, Sir Jonathan."

His eyes narrowed. "This is no small thing you are doing, Abigail. If you walk out that door, your father will hear of this. Do not think for one second it will go well for you. We have an understanding, he and I, and you will be sent back here immediately. You *will* be my wife, so save yourself the trouble of an unnecessary journey."

Without another word, she turned and strode from his threat, hopefully hiding the hitch in her step as his words hit home. He was right. Leaving behind Brakewell Hall and facing her father when he returned from the continent was no small thing.

And neither would be finding Samuel and Emma on her own.

CHAPTER THIRTY-ONE

Rain showered down, unrelenting in its ability to drip off Samuel's hat and find a crevice to crawl under, usually between his collar and shirt. Emma sat on the wet ground next to a pine tree, crying, while he scrambled to collect boughs to make some meagre refuge. Their first night on the road, and it had to rain?

He scowled. He should've expected as much. All of Abby's "hope for the best" folderol was a load of manure. Life was hard, hope was for dreamers, and the dirt of the highway was the best he could expect for the next ten years.

One by one, he propped up bough after bough, crafting a lean-to—until Emma crawled over and threw herself against his leg, catching him off-balance. Flailing his arms, he managed to stay upright, but the shelter didn't. His arm caught against one of the branches, and the whole thing imploded into a soggy heap of pine needles and sticks.

Emma pulled herself up his trousers and wailed into the storm. He didn't blame her. He felt like howling himself.

Blowing out a disgusted sigh, he scooped up the child and held her close to his chest, wincing at the pain in his leg, his arm, his soul. She burrowed into his waistcoat, sobbing. And he couldn't fault her, not one bit. Bedding down with an empty stomach in the wilds of the woods was not for the weak of heart—and certainly not for a child.

"Very well, little one." He kissed the top of her wet head. "Let's get you dry and fed."

He trudged to the tree where he'd tethered Pilgrim and unloosened the length of rope. Hefting himself and Emma into the saddle cost him a stitch in his thigh and a grunt, but he made it, then maneuvered the horse in a tight roundabout and set off for the road.

The rain made for hard going, Emma nearly slipping from his grasp several times, all a sickening but apt picture of his life. He'd tried to hold on to hope—for funding, for a farm of his own. . .for Abby—but look where all those fine thoughts had gotten him. Riding a mud-slicked horse with a crying baby, penniless and injured.

Where's that peace You promised, God? I could use a smidgeon of it now.

He tucked his head against a sideways blast of wind, no better off on his journey back to London than when he'd started out that fateful day on the heath. No, that wasn't true. He was worse off, his heart more jaded, his faith more ragged.

God, have mercy.

Strengthening his grip on Emma, he urged Pilgrim onward, willing his broken spirit to do the same. Two sodden miles later, he neared a coaching inn and turned into the front drive—where it appeared half the population of the county congregated, or at least their carriages and horses did. The Blue Bell was apparently the place to be on this wet and wicked eve.

He slid from Pilgrim, and keeping a tight hold on Emma, he tied his faithful mount to an iron ring on a post. He'd have to see to his horse later. For now, he pushed open the studded oak door of the Blue Bell and strode into chaos.

The taproom boiled with people. Men lifted mugs, calling for refills. Women chattered, some tittered. One of them held a yipping pup with a red bow on its head. Emma twisted in his arms, craning her neck to stare at the ruckus. Her whimpering subsided as she forgot her soiled clout and empty belly—but that wouldn't last long.

With Emma clinging tight around his neck, Samuel plowed through the merrymakers toward a man in an apron, who now and then barked orders to a red-cheeked serving girl.

"Pardon." He tapped the man on the shoulder and loosened Emma's grip, drawing in a much-needed breath. "Have you a mug of milk and a corner of the stable to spare?"

"Aye." The man pivoted, long flaps of skin on each side of his chin wagging with the movement. He held out a meaty palm. "Five shillings."

Five? For a small patch of straw? Robbery! Samuel scowled at the man's open hand. Even if he had the coins in his pocket, he wouldn't share them willingly with such a greedy goblin. The fellow was nothing more than a highwayman garbed in the trappings of an innkeeper.

He slipped his gaze up to the man's shrewd face. "A trade would be more to your benefit, I think. I am skilled with horses, and judging by the amount of patrons packed in here, I suspect you could use a hand out back."

"You're right. I do need some help." Reaching behind his back, the man fumbled with the ties of his apron. "This is an unexpected mob, and I'm short a serving wench." He yanked off the soiled fabric and held it out. "Bring the child to the kitchen and get to work."

Samuel shook his head and recoiled a step. "I don't think—"

The innkeeper shoved the apron closer, cocking his head like a raven before it pecked. "Take the offer or leave. I've not the time to cater to you."

A growl lodged in his throat. He didn't know the first thing about serving mugs of ale or plates of beef, nor did he want to—but once again Emma's whimpering surged, making his decision for him.

He grabbed the apron and stalked into the kitchen, savoring the ache in his leg. Pain was better to focus on than anger, and he had a whole lot of rage simmering in his gut. A pox on Sir Jonathan Aberley, the miserly cur.

Inside the large room, a wide-hipped woman bent over a steaming pot at the hearth, stirring with a wooden paddle. Cooks were notoriously ill-tempered, and no wonder. Considering the dark stains spreading out from her armpits, she'd likely been bucking cinders and heat all day. Samuel shied away from her and instead pursued the red-cheeked miss, who breezed in through the door.

"Pardon me, but—"

"No time." She snatched up six bowls of stew—*six!*—and balanced them in her arms as she whirled back toward the taproom.

He followed. "Could you just direct—?"

"I couldn't just *anything* right now."

She darted out the door and disappeared into the crowd beyond.

Well, so much for a polite approach. Shifting Emma to his other arm, Samuel stalked over to the cook. "I'm to serve," he declared as if he were addressing a new recruit. "This child needs milk and a safe corner in which to stay."

The woman stiffened, her shoulders flinging back like a crossbow ready to shoot. She whirled from the pot and pierced him and Emma with a narrow-eyed stare—one that could curdle cold milk.

"Are you daft, man? I'm a cook, not a nursemaid."

He swung out his free arm, indicating the bowls of pottage lined up on the table, cooling as they waited to be served. "Yet you need the help."

The red on her face deepened to burgundy. If she blew, it wouldn't be pretty. He held his ground, steeling himself for what might be a blood-drawing battle.

"More sausages, Mary!" the innkeeper hollered in through the kitchen door. "And keep that stew flowing or it'll be the devil to pay."

"Pah!" The woman reached for another apron on a peg, then shoved it toward Samuel. "Use this to tie the child to the cabinet leg in the corner and give her a bowl of the cooled pottage. Milk will have to wait."

She turned so quickly, the hem of her skirt puffed up a cloud of spilled flour.

Samuel snapped into action, anxious for this night of humiliation to be over. He secured Emma to the cabinet, giving her a bit of lead for movement, but not much. She stared up at him with shimmering blue eyes, accusing him in ways that cut deep.

Squatting, he lifted her face with the crook of his finger. "My pardon, Emma. You are of more value than being tethered like a horse, but chin up and bear it, hmm? Can you do that for me?"

Her lower lip quivered—a sure sign she was about to go on a full-fledged crying jag.

He shot up and snatched a dish of stew from the table behind him, then handed it to her with a wooden spoon.

Emma wobbled for a moment, then threw down the spoon and planted her face in the bowl, coming up with a smile and stew dripping down her chin. A messy triumph, but a triumph nonetheless.

Heaving a sigh, he tied the apron the innkeeper had given him around his waist and sucked in a breath. Chin up and bear it, indeed.

He stalked into the public room, armed with grim determination and two bowls of pottage. At the very least, no one should know him in this part of the country. A blessing, that. Should his fellow officer Bexley catch wind of him prancing about in an apron, there'd be no end to the jesting.

Three hours later, he wore more broth than he'd served, the pains shooting up his legs howled like angry beasts, and he'd heard a rash of inventive curses more creative than the time he'd run a night watch at the Wapping docks. But slowly, finally, the taproom emptied of patrons. Sloop-shouldered and weary beyond measure, he trudged into the kitchen, where the other serving girl hung her apron on a peg then slipped out the back door with a nod to Cook.

"Well, well. . ." The cook eyed him. "Still standing, are ye?"

"Barely," he breathed out as he glanced at Emma. The girl had curled into a ball and slept with the overturned bowl as a pillow. Stew matted her hair into clumps.

He reached to unloosen the knotted apron ties at his back, when the innkeeper's voice bellowed through the kitchen door. "One more to be served."

Samuel clenched his jaw. Would this woeful day never end?

The cook's gaze shot to his. "There's but a scraping of deviled kidneys and spoonful of pork jelly for you to offer. That's all that's left."

He nodded. Hopefully this far into the evening, the late rider would be more anxious to visit a soft mattress than to fill his gut.

Samuel strode into the public room, his brows raising as he approached the table nearest the door. It wasn't a man who demanded service after all, but a straight-backed bit of skirt perched on a chair. His own empty belly cinched. A woman wouldn't be traveling alone at this time of night, so no doubt her companion would soon join her. What kind of wrath would he have to parry when they found out the only food to be had was nothing but scraps? Thunder and turf! He'd rather face a bare-fisted bandit keening for a knockdown than a hungry, quarrelsome woman.

He neared the table and, with the last of his willpower, forced a soothing tone to his voice. "Pardon, miss, but the kitchen is—"

She turned, and the air punched from his lungs. Two brown eyes bore into his, blinking with shock.

Abby gripped the table with one hand, stunned. She hadn't expected to catch up with Samuel so soon—and certainly not with an apron tied around his waist.

She swallowed her surprise and raised her eyebrows. "What are you doing wearing an apron?"

A shadow darkened his face, heralding a coming storm. "What are you doing here with your baronet?"

The question seethed through his bared teeth, indicting and condemning her in the same breath—and it rankled her to the core.

She'd done nothing wrong! She was the one who'd risked everything by leaving Brakewell Hall, pushing herself to travel far past sunset, stopping at every inn along the way. He had no right to stand so rigidly imperious, making her feel more of a wayward imp than ever her stepmother had. This was not the reception she'd expected. Why did he not welcome her with open arms?

"I travel alone." She emphasized each word then jutted her chin.

Lamplight slid along the captain's hardened jaw. "You should know better, and so should your man."

"He is not—"

"Enough!" The captain's face tightened into a mask of steel. "What trickery is this? Why would Sir Jonathan Aberley, *baronet*, allow his bride to roam the roads at night?"

The headache she'd been ignoring all evening broke loose and banged around in her skull. So be it. If a quarrel was what the captain wanted, then she was in a mood to serve. She poked him in the chest with her finger. "The baronet has nothing to do with this. You are the reason I am out here—you and Emma, and—Emma! Where is she?"

He grew dangerously still. "Even now you doubt my ability to care for the girl?"

"You know that is not what I mean!" she huffed. Why was he being so obstinate? Where was the man of the previous evening, all tenderness and passion?

"Emma is asleep in the kitchen, if you must know, but why come all this way on your own? Unless. . ." He ducked his head like a bull about to charge. "Feeling guilty about not delivering on your promise, are you?"

She scrunched her nose, a most unladylike action, but it was not to be helped. Promise? She'd not even given him an answer last night let alone vowed anything. "What are you talking about?"

"Playing the innocent ill becomes you, Miss Gilbert. Just pay me what is owed and be on your way."

"Owe?" That's what this was about? Money? She frowned. "After what the baronet already paid you—"

"Oh yes. Six days of food and lodging. Quite generous, that baronet of yours." His brown eyes turned to stone—so did his voice. "Which is why I'm standing here in an apron. So Emma can have supper and a dry place to sleep."

She sucked in a sharp breath. He'd not been paid. Not one ha'penny. And after all his hard work, suffering, bleeding. . .oh my. What a horrid mess this had all become.

She rubbed her temples, the pounding in her head worsening, then gestured toward the chair next to her. "Please, sit. There are things we must discuss."

A pot clanged in the kitchen, and he glanced toward the door. For a moment she wondered if he would stay at all or might dash off. And he had every right to, after the unjust treatment he'd been given.

Eyeing her warily, he scraped back the chair and angled it to face her. His posture remained taut as a sail in the wind, but beneath it all, she could tell he hoarded fatigue. Surely his arm must ache, and his leg, especially after standing for who knew how many hours, rushing between the now empty taproom and the kitchen. . .all because Sir Jonathan had sent him away penniless.

She swallowed down the lump in her throat. "Look, I do not know why the baronet did not pay you nor what he said to make you leave

Brakewell Hall with such haste, but believe me, I had no part in it."

His eyes narrowed, yet he said nothing. What in the world was he thinking? Why did he not respond?

"Please, Captain. Why did you leave without saying goodbye?"

He winced. A sign he was softening, perhaps?

So, she prodded him. "What did the baronet tell you?"

"You should know. You're the one who sent him to me to say you wished me gone."

She flinched, his icy reception of her suddenly making sense. Of all the wicked, scheming plots the baronet had manufactured—offering marriage to her because of her dowry or claiming Lady Pelham as his cousin—this one was by far the worst.

"I would never wish you gone. Never! I was dreading the day that you and Emma would have to leave."

He stared at her, a terrible stare that could cleave truth and lies from the most protected of hearts, and finally his chest deflated as he blew out a long breath. Unfolding his arms, he leaned forward and planted his elbows on his knees. "All right. Tell me what happened with you and your baronet."

She bristled. "Please, stop calling him that. Sir Jonathan is not mine, nor ever shall be."

"But he is the man you chose, that night we. . ." His gaze drifted to her lips.

Heat climbed up her neck and spread over her cheeks. "I never said such a thing."

His eyes snapped back to hers. "Neither did you say you wanted me to take you away, nor that you wanted to leave."

"I did not say anything!" She threw up her hands. "I was so torn, so conflicted, that I ran off without giving you an answer. You told me to think carefully before I answered, remember? I needed time for that."

"You needed time to talk yourself out of loving the baronet?"

"No, Samuel." Her voice broke, and she leaned toward him, laying her hand over his. "I needed time to listen to my heart. Do you not know? Can you not see? It is you that I love, *only* you. Despite the baronet's title, you are the true nobleman, not him."

His breath hitched, yet he pulled away. Something unsettling charged the air between them, rife with words that should've been spoken long ago. Her throat closed. Was it too late? Had any feelings he might've had toward her cooled and vanished like a mist?

Sorrow pulled at the corners of his mouth. "Oh Abby. . ."

Whatever words he'd intended to say languished into silence. Was he struggling to turn her away? To tell her goodbye? Hot tears burned behind her eyes at the possibility.

"Forgive me," she murmured, then licked her lips, her mouth impossibly dry. "I see my declaration is unwelcome. I should not have spoken so boldly."

"No." He stood and averted his gaze, his face twisting into a grief no man should have to bear. "It is I who is the real criminal here. I stole your heart from a man who could provide for you. I had no right to ask you to give that up for me."

"You cannot have stolen what was freely given."

"Go back, Miss Gilbert, while you still can. Go back to a man who can give you what you deserve."

"Don't you see? I am *never* going back." She shot to her feet and cupped his face in her hands, forcing him to look at her. "You are the man who can give me what I deserve."

His jaw flexed beneath her touch, the rasp of his whiskers prickly against her palms, and for a moment, he said nothing, merely studied her with that same unnerving, brown gaze of his.

Finally, he spoke. "Then you do not know what you truly deserve." He pulled away. "If you will not return to Brakewell Hall, then I will see you safely to London."

Turning, he stalked into the kitchen, each of his steps driving another nail into her heart. She stood alone in the big room, with nothing but unanswered questions and a hole in her chest, bleeding out the last of her hopes and dreams. Apparently love was never meant to be hers. Her stepmother had been right all along.

She was a stupid girl.

CHAPTER THIRTY-TWO

Samuel pounded each step hard into the gravel of the Blue Bell's courtyard, relishing the pain in his leg. He deserved it, this torment, and the closer he drew to the carriage where Abby waited with Emma, the deeper he dug in his boots—especially when Abby turned at his approach.

Grey morning light draped her figure, the cloudy day as sullen as the stiffness in her spine and hurt in her eyes. He'd caused that injury. His words. His resolve. Yet by all that was holy, he'd had no choice in the matter! He couldn't provide for her. At the moment, he couldn't even provide for himself. But as he closed the distance between them, with the waft of her citrusy scent and the way her gown rode soft along the curves of her body, he wanted her so badly, his teeth ached.

Stopping in front of her, he schooled his face into a blank slate. It would do neither of them any good to unleash his true feelings. "Are you ready?"

Emma popped her thumb into her mouth and turned her face away from him. Was he to be shunned by the child as well?

Abby threw back her shoulders. "I am, but what about Emma?"

He ground his jaw, hating the iciness in her voice, hating even more the estrangement hanging thick between them. But it wasn't to be helped, not until he could figure out a way to care for her. His best hope at the moment was to take her to Brentwood's and see if his wife might keep Abby on to help tend their brood. Abby was certainly good with children, and he could properly court her there while he earned some money out on the heath. Or maybe, if God and Brentwood smiled upon him, he could take on a few of those lucrative security jobs of Brentwood's. And if not. . .well, he would turn London upside down if need be to find Abby a safe place. Anything to keep from returning her to a family who didn't love her until he could claim her as his own.

Emma reached up with her free hand and rubbed Abby's cheek, as if by instinct the child sought to console her.

"We'll stop at the Gable Inn and return Emma to her father." He turned on his heel to retrieve Pilgrim. Let the driver help her into the carriage, for no doubt she'd slap away his hand should he offer.

And she probably would have. For the next five days, Abby held herself aloof, shutting him out at every possible turn. The one time he did hold up his gloved hand to aid her into the coach, she'd gazed at his fingers as if he held out a black adder, then she'd sniffed and hefted herself up unaided. Each night at dinner, she ate in her room with Emma, her door securely locked. When they stopped to change out the horses and the driver, she handed Emma over to him and took care of her personal needs without a word. The tension was taut enough to stretch across a river gorge and walk upon it from one bank to another.

And with each mile they traveled, the worse he felt. Should he tell her of his plans before he even asked Brentwood if it was a possibility? Would it not be cruel to dangle such a hope before her?

Clicking his tongue, he guided Pilgrim onto the last stretch of road leading to the Gable Inn, helpless to stop the raging in his soul. He was less than a man. He was a beast, for any man worth his salt could provide for a wife. But not him. He'd had to rely each day on the graces of Abby's purse strings for the food in his belly and the roof over his head—*and* over hers and Emma's.

Self-loathing and the grime of travel crawled into every crevice of his skin as he swung off Pilgrim. He brushed away the worst of the dirt on his trousers while waiting for the carriage to catch up.

In front of him, the Gable Inn stood as proud as ever. He tethered his mount to the front post, busying his hands until he heard the carriage door open and Abby's footsteps draw near. He turned, and the shimmer of tears in her eyes nearly dropped him to his knees.

She clutched Emma to her breast, nuzzling the child's head with her cheek. "Shall I say my goodbye here?"

His chest squeezed. He knew this moment was going to be hard, but now that it was here, he realized just how wrong he'd been. It would be impossible for Abby to let the child go without tearing out yet another piece of her heart.

"No, come with me." He strode to the stable yard, biting down so hard, his jaw crackled.

God, please, have mercy. Abby can't do this. I can't do this!

But sweet blazing fireballs, what else was he to do?

Filling his lungs with air, he prayed for courage and strode into the coolness of the Gable's big stable. Ahead, a familiar set of broad shoulders hunched on a stool near a workbench.

"Hawker, we're back."

The large man turned at Samuel's approach, the sour stink of an unwashed body and cheap rum clinging to him like a Shoreditch harlot. He narrowed his red-rimmed eyes. "Thatcher? What are you doing here?"

Abby stepped beside him. Hawker's terrible gaze landed on Emma and hardened. Emma stared back, then turned and burrowed against Abby's shoulder, rubbing her face into Abby's neck.

"What's *she* doing here?" Hawker bellowed.

Samuel clenched his hands. Lord, but this would not go well. He took a step away from Abby, in case his old friend should snap and go on a rampage.

"It's about your sister, my friend. She. . ." He swallowed. How to say this gently? "Well, she died peacefully."

Hawker sat deadly still, his face tightening to granite. Samuel held his ground, unsure if the man would spring or just sit there and never move again.

Slowly, Hawker rose, his stilted steps crushing straw beneath his boots. He held out one hand toward Emma, but a pace away, he stopped and dropped his arm. A ragged sigh ripped from him, blowing out a demon or two.

Then his bloodshot gaze swung to Samuel. "No, I can't keep her. I won't. When I look at the girl, all I see is her mother, the woman I'm drinking myself into the ground trying to forget. You take her. You and your lady. She's your child now."

Samuel shook his head. "But you can't—"

"Don't tell me what I can't do!"

Hawker dodged past him and stalked into the light, leaving him and Abby in the shadows of the stable, a cloud of questions in the air too numerous to even think about answering.

Abby turned and blinked at him. Her mouth parted, yet no words came out. How could they? He hardly knew what to say himself.

So he pivoted and strode outside as well, as big a coward as his friend. "Hawker, wait—"

"Well, stars and thunder, Captain! And here I was thinking I'd have to haul my hide halfway across England to find you." Officer Bexley's familiar voice pulled up alongside him, and his patrolman clouted him on the back. "Good to see you alive."

Turning, Samuel frowned, unsure which he needed to attend first—the retreating Hawker or the interest in Bexley's eyes as Abby joined Samuel's side.

Bex cocked a brow his way. "It seems, Captain, that you hunted down more than just Shankhart, eh?"

"Now's not a good time, Bex," he breathed out. "What do you want?"

Bexley lifted his meaty hand and scratched behind his ear, one corner of his mouth turning up. "The magistrate says you're to return at once. He's got something for you. Says it's urgent."

Samuel grimaced. Sure he did. A contract to shackle him for the next ten years. . .but if that meant enough income to marry Abby, then so be it. She was worth having no matter what job came his way.

Abby's gaze pinged between them both and finally landed on him. "Emma and I will wait in the carriage, Captain."

She whirled, the hem of her gown swishing with her steps.

Bex watched her go, his brows pulling into a line. "Why is the lady still with you? Unless. . . Ahh." A slow smile spread across his face, stretching from one edge of his side whiskers to the other. "Ho ho! You've gone and fallen for a skirt?" A chuckle shook his big shoulders, drawing the attention of a passing ostler.

Samuel ground his teeth, needing to explain but wanting to ignore—especially when Bexley slugged him in the arm.

"Never thought to see this happen. And a child to boot? You old hound!"

Samuel's fists shook with the effort of holding back from punching Bexley straight to kingdom come.

His laughter spent, Bexley folded his arms. "Makes sense though, I suppose, now that you're a man of means."

Samuel angled his head, studying the man. "What say you?"

"Huh? Oh, I suppose you've not heard, eh? Wrapping up the Shankhart affair and all. Remember that lad you rescued off the heath? The one we nearly left behind but you found?"

How could he forget? The lad's scratches had scarred the back of his hand. "The orphan, yes?"

Bex nodded. "Turns out the boy isn't an orphan after all. He's the son of a wealthy fellow, an earl or some sort, who was out of the country on business. The lad was en route to the man's estate for safe-keeping in his absence. Apparently their hired guardian took a fall and broke his arm. Not wishing to be delayed, the foolish women decided to go it on their own across the heath with naught but their driver and manservant, thinking to hire a new guardian at the next inn."

Samuel shook his head. Funny how one seemingly small decision could affect the lives—or deaths—of so many.

"When the boy never arrived," Bex continued, "the boy's father offered quite a reward for his return. The magistrate got wind of it and checked into the missing lad of Devonshire. You were the one what found him, so you get the reward. But the earl isn't long for London, and peers don't like to be kept waiting. That's why I was sent to fetch you. The man wishes to reward you in person."

The words circled slowly, coming to roost as gingerly as the sparrows atop the peak of the Gable's roof.

But he didn't believe a word of it.

He narrowed his eyes at Bex. "This is a poor jest."

Another laugh rumbled in Bexley's throat. "'Tis no jest. You're a moneyed man now, or soon will be. Why, I figure ye ought to have more than enough to buy that land you been scarpin' about."

Moneyed? Him? He clenched his jaw to keep it from dropping and lifted his gaze to the sky, shame burning a hole in his gut.

Forgive me, God, for casting aside hope and wallowing in a lack of faith. You have answered my prayers for mercy time and again. Truly, Lord, Your goodness knows no bounds.

Then he took off at a dead run.

Tears came easily these days, as prolific and never ending as a spring rain. Sucking in a shaky breath, Abby fought back another round, tired of weeping. Tired of life. Tired of everything.

She cuddled Emma closer to her breast, next to the place where her heart used to be, and strode past the carriage to a green patch of lawn in front of the Gable. Who knew how long it would take for the captain to sort things out with Emma's father—if things could be sorted at all. The man had seemed adamant in his rejection of his daughter, and oh, how Abby ached for the girl. She knew firsthand what it felt like to be spurned so cruelly by a parent who should have loved her. What was to become of Emma? The uncertainty of the girl's future was as nebulous as her own.

"Oh little one." Tucking her chin, Abby murmured against the top of Emma's head. "We are an unwanted pair, are we not?"

Emma squirmed. "Ah-ma?"

"Yes, my sweet." A sob welled in Abby's throat, choking her voice. "I will ever and always be your *ah-ma*, no matter what happens."

The child was too wriggly to hold on to any longer, so she let her down and pulled out a small felt rabbit from her reticule—the one and only purchase she'd made while wedding shopping in Penrith. Emma clapped her hands and reached for the toy, having no idea that her fate was likely even now being decided by the captain and her father—or would be, after the captain finished his business with the bearlike man who had joined him.

Oh Samuel. Would that we might have been able to come to an understanding of our own—a lifetime of an understanding.

But that hadn't happened, nor ever would. She sighed. The captain had spoken little the past five days. Not that she'd given him much of a chance. What was the point? Clearly he'd decided she was not the woman for him, and once his mind was made up, there was no turning him.

While Emma played at her feet, alternately gnawing on the little bunny then lifting it up to the sunlight, Abby leaned back against a tree and stared out at the road. How different things had been a month ago when she'd first traveled that dusty path. She'd been a naive girl then, full of hopes and dreams, so certain of a happily ever after.

She flattened her lips. And now look at her, backtracking to a home she'd vowed never again to see. Already she could envision the pinch of her stepmother's face and hear the screech in her voice once she found out Abby had refused the baronet. Her father would likely wash his hands of her, pensioning her off in some small cottage as a spinster to grow old all alone. Despite the warmth of the summer afternoon, she chilled to the core.

No, that would never happen, not if she could help it. She was good with children. Perhaps in London, she might find occupation as a governess—though without references, that might be a stretch. Better yet, Wenna had commented on her skill with a needle. Employment in a dress shop might be a more attainable situation. But how to keep herself until such a job might be found?

Absently, she reached up and fumbled for the watch brooch beneath her bodice. Her throat tightened as she rubbed her thumb over the glass face. Could she truly part with this last piece of her mother to begin a new life?

Boot steps crushing gravel broke into her misery, pulling her gaze as the sound grew louder. Captain Thatcher dashed past the carriage and closed in on her and Emma. Something had been decided, though she wasn't sure she wanted to know what exactly.

Bracing herself, Abby stepped away from the tree trunk and straightened her shoulders. For Emma's sake, she'd stay strong, no matter the outcome.

The captain stopped in front of her and yanked off his hat, then wiped his brow with the back of his hand. His brown gaze held hers, yet he said nothing. He stood silent, the afternoon breeze lifting wisps of his dark hair, his fingers turning his worn felt hat in a slow circle. A muscle clenched on his jaw. Whatever he had to say clearly cost him in ways she couldn't begin to understand. Did he fear to tell her, perhaps, that Emma was to be given over to a foundling home?

Abby glanced down at the sweet girl, then back up to him. "Has something been decided?"

He shook his head. "Not yet."

"Thank God," she breathed out, but a wave of uneasiness still washed over her. He hadn't hurried over here for no reason, for the captain was ever a man of intention. She angled her face. "Then why are you here? Should you not be speaking with Emma's father?"

"No, you're the one I need to talk to."

His fingers continued to pinch his hat, moving it inch by inch, 'round and 'round. Emma threw her rabbit and crawled over to it, then threw it again. And again.

Another carriage rolled in, passing them by and stopping at the inn's front door, and still the captain said no more.

"Well?" Abby prodded.

He blew out a sigh. His head dipped, and he pinned his gaze on the ground, as if he might find whatever it was he wanted to say lying there in the dirt.

Abby tensed, uneasiness prickling the skin at the nape of her neck. What was this? The captain wasn't one to mince words. He was a man of action, of command. One who said what he must and hanged the consequences.

"You frighten me, sir."

He jerked his face up, pain etching lines at the corners of his mouth. "Forgive me. I know my silence has caused you much hurt, Miss Gilbert, and for that I am grieved. But I hope to put an end to it here and now."

"And how do you propose to do that?"

"By asking you to marry me."

Her jaw dropped. Her breath stopped, clogging somewhere in her throat. Surely she had not heard him correctly.

"Pardon?" her voice squeaked.

He turned away and crouched by Emma, handing her his hat, then rose and swung back to Abby, catching both her hands in his big, calloused fingers.

"That night you came to me at the Blue Bell and told me you loved me, I could hardly fathom it. Lord knows I am not an easy man to love. But you, sweet Abby. . ." His lips thinned, and he shook his head. "You have held my heart in your hands from the day you stood brave and tall on the heath, threatened by highwaymen yet holding your ground. There can never be another woman for me but you. The truth of it is I love you, Abigail Gilbert, and I will never love another."

The healing balm of his words slipped into the cracks, the hurts, the years of dry ground that had longed to hear such endearments—until one single question stopped the flow.

She narrowed her eyes. "Why did you not tell me this five nights ago?"

"I. . ." He squeezed her fingers, gentle, firm, warm, as if to drive home some unspoken point. "I didn't want to get your hopes up, not until we reached London. I wanted to find you a home with one of my colleagues first. Give you a safe place to stay while I earned money for lodgings of our own."

Lodgings of our own?

Samuel's words nestled into her heart. All this time, when she had thought he had rejected her, he was only planning how to care for her. *Her.* The immense weight of responsibility he must have carried the past few days swept over her. Because he loved her.

"But things are different now. *I* am different, and there is no more need to wait. So. . ." He cleared his throat and looked at her almost sheepishly—a first, that. A very handsome first. "Will you have me? Will you be my wife?"

Tears filled her eyes, turning the world to yet another watery mess. "Oh Samuel," she barely managed to choke out.

A slow smile flashed across his austere face, instantly changing him into a young man full of life and vigor and love. "So your answer, my lady, is yes?"

Pulling free of his grasp, she lifted to her toes and planted a resounding kiss on his lips. Satisfied, she stepped back and grinned. "Yes!"

Low laughter rumbled at their side, and they both turned.

The bear of a man who'd rode in to find Samuel chuckled at them both. "If Brentwood or Moore could see this."

"Indeed, my friend." Samuel laughed too. "Would that they could." Then he glanced at her, a sultry gleam in his brown eyes, and once again caught up her hand in his. "I will never be the same, you know. You have made me very happy."

She beamed at him. "Do you realize, Captain, that you have just taken on my guardianship for the rest of your life?"

"I would have it no other way."

Emma clapped her hands, and Abby's heart soared.

"Neither would I, my love." She lifted Samuel's fingers to her lips and pressed her mouth against his knuckles. "Neither would I."

EPILOGUE

One year later,
five miles west of Burnham, England

Abby set down her sewing and shifted in her chair, preparing to rise. Nowadays simply standing took all her effort. But before she pushed upward, Emma dashed across the room, ginger curls flying, and plowed into Abby's legs.

"Baby sleep?" Emma pressed her cheek against Abby's swollen middle.

A resounding kick from inside pushed back against the girl's sudden attack.

"No, Emma." Abby smiled. "The baby is most definitely *not* sleeping. Be a good girl, now, and gather your Bibby. It is time we begin making dinner for your father."

"Papa!" Emma squealed, then spun on her heels and ran to the corner of the bedchamber where she'd left a heap of blankets and a cloth baby doll. Ever since Samuel had brought home the little toy last week—which Emma promptly named Bibby—the girl had hardly let the doll out of her sight. Lord only knew what Emma would do when she had a real babe to hold.

Abby pressed her hand against her big belly as she stood, struggling for balance. Sweeping aside the sheer window curtain, she peered out at the hay field, and her heart instantly melted. Ahh, but she'd never tire of watching the long lines of Samuel's body stride across the land.

He'd thrived since they'd moved here, wrangling with dirt and sun and rain instead of cutthroats. He smiled frequently, laughed often, and his brooding good looks took on an even more handsome shine.

Lowering her hand, she let the curtain drop. He'd reach the house soon, likely bringing with him an appetite. Heat flushed over her cheeks, and a slow grin curved her lips. No doubt he'd want more than dinner.

Her grin suddenly faded as a knock on the front door carried in past the sitting room. They didn't receive many guests out here in the country, especially not in the minutes before dark.

She hurried as fast as her large girth allowed, Emma running on her tiptoes right alongside her, and opened the front door—

Then wished she hadn't. Her stomach lurched, and she leaned one hand against the doorframe.

A man in a dark blue riding coat stood on the stoop, the grime of the road dusting his shoulders. His blue eyes were all too familiar, for she looked into the same shade each day.

"Mr. Hawker?" The name barely made it past her lips. What in the world was Emma's father doing here? Now?

"Mrs. Thatcher." He dipped his head toward her, then pinned his gaze on Emma. "May I see her?"

A chill cut straight to Abby's heart. She'd feared this day. Awakened at nights in a sweat, fighting with the counterpane from a nightmare such as this. Though Samuel often reassured her otherwise, she'd always suspected Emma was only theirs on loan, a gift that would be snatched away some future day.

And now the future was here, standing at her door in a black felt hat and riding boots.

She drew in a breath for courage and fumbled for Emma's little hand. "Of course you may. Will you come in?"

Without pulling his gaze from the girl, he shook his head and crouched, eye to eye with Emma. He fumbled in his coat pocket and retrieved a small, hand-carved horse, then held it out. "For you."

Emma's eyes widened. "Horsie?" she breathed, then glanced up at Abby.

"Yes, Emma. A horse for you." She bit her lip before her voice broke.

"Horsie!" Emma shrieked and snatched the toy from her father's hand.

Mr. Hawker reached out and patted the girl on her head, then rose. "Is your husband here?"

For one wicked moment, a lie bristled on her tongue. If she told the man Samuel was away, he'd leave and Emma could stay. . .but that would only delay the inevitable.

She pulled back her shoulders, hoping good posture would provide some measure of courage. "You should find my husband out back. He was nearing the house only moments ago."

Mr. Hawker tucked his chin. "Thank you, madam."

He strode away, and Abby pressed the door shut behind him, a bit wobbly on her feet but this time not from pregnancy. Emma galloped around the sofa in a circle with her new toy, squealing, "Go, horsie! Go!"

Abby skirted her and sank to the sofa cushion. Would this be the last she'd hear of Emma's sweet laughter? Had last night been the final time she'd ever tuck her into bed? Had the plate of cheese and bread she'd shared with the girl at noon been her last meal with her?

God, no! How am I to part with her?

The loss was too great, and she hunched over, bowed by the weight of such a dreadful prospect. Her chest squeezed, feeling as hollow as if a giant hand had reached in and yanked out the roots of her deep, rich love for Emma, a love that'd been growing ever since the day Samuel had handed the girl over to her.

The door jolted open, and Samuel poked his head inside. "Bring Emma outside, please."

Tears burned in her eyes. Was this shearing pain in her heart what it felt like to lose a child? She rubbed both hands on her belly and stood. Though another was on the way, there would be no consolation for losing Emma.

With a bravery she didn't feel, she held out her hand and forced a light tone to her voice. "Come, Emma."

Emma trotted over to her, horse in hand, and wrapped her small fingers around Abby's. "Go? Ride?"

"No, my sweet. At least, I hope not—" A sob cut off her words. Her head pounded as she delivered Emma outside, fighting to keep a great, wailing cry from breaking loose.

Samuel and Emma's father turned at their approach, and once again, Mr. Hawker crouched. "Come, child. Come to me."

Emma looked from the new horse in her hand to the man and apparently decided it was worth the risk to allow him to gather her in his arms since he'd brought her a toy. He walked off with her, but not far.

Abby turned to Samuel, unable to contain the misery welling inside her for one second longer. "Oh Samuel!"

His brow folded as he studied her, then suddenly softened. He pulled her to him and pressed a kiss against her forehead, smoothing back her hair with his big hands. "All is well, my love. He merely wants to say goodbye."

Her breath hitched, especially when the babe inside gave another good kick—as was the child's custom whenever Samuel held her close.

She pulled back and tipped her face up at her husband. "But where is Mr. Hawker going? Why such a formal parting?"

"He sails for America, and thank God for that. I feared he'd drink himself to death, but he's finally decided to leave his past and pain behind and start a new life."

"And Emma?" Abby held her breath, dreading but needing to know what would become of her girl.

A grin flashed across Samuel's tanned face, vanquishing any fear she might ever bring to him. "She stays with us." He reached out and placed his hand on the bulge of her belly. "Emma will be the finest older sister our son could ever know."

Closing her eyes, she breathed in blessed relief and thanked God.

Then she snapped her eyes open and arched a brow at Samuel. "Do not be so sure it is a boy, husband. You might very well have a daughter."

"If it is"—he smirked—"then I will be sorely outnumbered."

Boot steps neared them, and they both turned. Mr. Hawker set Emma down, and the girl ran right into Samuel, wrapping her arms around his legs. He stood solid, a broad beam holding up both of their worlds.

Mr. Hawker's blue eyes—so hauntingly the same as Emma's—stared directly at Abby. "You're doing a fine job of raising her, ma'am." Then he dipped his head at Samuel. "Thatcher, take good care of your family, all of them. Goodbye."

Samuel nodded. "Goodbye, Hawker. Godspeed."

Emma's father wheeled about and retrieved his horse, swinging up into the saddle the same time as Samuel swung Emma up into his arms.

He winked at Abby. "He needn't have told me that, you know. I will care for my girls until my last breath."

Abby grinned. "And *if* you have a son?"

"And *when* I have a son"—he bent and kissed her on the nose—"I shall teach him to care for my girls as well." Settling Emma up on his shoulders, he reached for Abby's hand. "But until that day, I guess I'll have to do as your sole guardian."

"I would have none other." She grinned. "For you, husband, are the most noble of guardians a woman could have."

HISTORICAL NOTES

One of my favorite parts of writing historical fiction is the research. I love learning tidbits and weaving them into the story. Here are a few pertinent facts I came across in the writing of *The Noble Guardian*.

Highwayman

A highwayman is simply a thief who steals—usually at gunpoint—from travelers on the road. Not all, but some of those attacks turned deadly, the robbers not wishing to leave anyone behind who could identify them. Others wore masks for the same purpose. Hounslow Heath was a notorious haunt for highwaymen because criminals would choose remote stretches of highways that supplied regular traffic going to and from major destinations. Dick Turpin is one of the most notorious English highwaymen, a villain who roamed the wilds in the 1730s.

The Magistrates of Bow Street (especially Richard Ford)

Bow Street Runners began with only a handful of men under the direction of Magistrate Henry Fielding in the 1750s. The force grew to eventually branch out into a horse patrol in 1805. This consisted of around sixty men who were charged with guarding the principal roads within sixty miles of London. Their most successful achievement was to rid Hounslow Heath of highwaymen.

In *Brentwood's Ward*, *The Innkeeper's Daughter*, and even in this story, an update is given on Magistrate Richard Ford. There really was a Bow

Street magistrate with this name, but alas, he died on May 3, 1806, at age forty-seven. For the sake of this story, however, I chose to keep him alive a bit longer *and* give him a wife. The magistrate mentioned in this story, Sir Nathaniel Conant, served from 1813 to 1820.

Physicians vs. Surgeons vs. Apothecaries

During the Regency era there was a clear distinction between physicians, surgeons, and apothecaries. Only physicians were labeled with the title of doctor, and they usually attended only wealthy families. They were the gentlemen of caregivers and were deemed socially acceptable.

Surgeons, on the other hand, were the general practitioners of the day, so they didn't get such a high and lofty title but merely went by *mister* instead of *doctor*. Because surgeons performed "physical labor" by treating patients, they occupied a lower rung on the social ladder. Apothecaries were the pharmacists who concocted and dispensed drugs.

Croup and Putrid Throat

What we think of today as croup—barking cough and wheezing breaths—isn't necessarily what people of yesteryear believed it to be. In fact, croup was a catch-all phrase that could be applied to many illnesses at the time, such as the deadly diphtheria. The most common treatment during the Regency era was white horehound syrup, which was used to alleviate any cough or lung issues. It is known to have a pleasant taste.

Putrid throat is another historical all-inclusive phrase that meant a severely inflamed throat that put off an odor and included tissue destruction. Generally a high fever, delirium, and hallucinations also accompanied such an illness. Most likely this was either strep throat or, once again, diphtheria. Back in the day, diphtheria was a very common cause of death.

Coaching Inns

Before the advent of the railroad, the best way to travel across country was by carriage. Though not everyone owned a carriage because the upkeep of horses was expensive, travelers could still rent a carriage and horses at coaching inns. In fact, that was the main function of a coaching inn (besides providing lodging). Inns hired out fresh horses, post-chaises (sometimes called traveling chariots), and drivers, who were called postilions. Inns were anywhere from seven to ten miles apart and could be any size, ranging from small, family-run affairs to large, several-storied buildings manned by plenty of staff.

BIBLIOGRAPHY

Beattie, J. M. *The First English Detectives: The Bow Street Runners and the Policing of London, 1750–1840*, reprint ed. Oxford, England: Oxford University Press, 2014.

Bleiler, E. F., ed. *Richmond: Scenes in the Life of a Bow Street Runner, Drawn Up from His Private Memoranda*. Mineola, NY: Dover Publications, 1976.

Cox, David J. *A Certain Share of Low Cunning: A History of the Bow Street Runners, 1792–1839*, 1st ed. London: Willan, 2010.

Harper, Charles G. *The Old Inns of Old England: A Picturesque Account of the Ancient and Storied Hostelries of Our Own Country*, vol. 1. London: Forgotten Books, 2017.

Protz, Roger. *Historic Coaching Inns of the Great North Road: A Guide to Travelling the Legendary Highway*. St. Albans, England: CAMRA Books, 2017.

Tristam, W. Outram. *Coaching Days and Coaching Ways*. Amazon Digital Services LLC, May 1, 2011. First published 1893.

ACKNOWLEDGMENTS

While writing is a solitary profession, a book is never written alone. I have so many to credit with holding my sweaty hand on this writerly journey. Here are a few of those that make up my tribe. . .

Critique Partners: Yvonne Anderson, Julie Klassen, Kelly Klepfer, Lisa Ludwig, Ane Mulligan, Shannon McNear, Chawna Schroeder, MaryLu Tyndall

First Reader: Dani Snyder

The Team at Barbour: Mary Burns, Liesl Davenport, Nola Haney, Annie Tipton, Shalyn Sattler, Bill Westfall, Laura Young, and editor Becky Durost Fish

Awesome Readers & Bloggers (just a smattering of the many): Perianne Askew, Crystal Caudill, Elisabeth Espinoza, Robin Mason, Deborha Mitchell, Trisha Robertson, Susan Gibson Snodgrass, the Tantalizing Tea Ladies

Cheerleading Friends: Linda Ahlmann, Stephanie Gustafson, Cheryl & Grant Higgins, Sal Morth, Darrie & Maria Nelson

And last but not least, my family: Mark, Joshua, Aaron, Callie & Ryan, Mariah

But the biggest of all shout-outs is to you, dear readers, who faithfully read story after story.

More than likely I've inadvertently left off someone important to mention, so if that's you, consider yourself heartily thanked because to one and all, I ám grateful.

ABOUT THE AUTHOR

Michelle Griep's been writing since she first discovered blank wall space and Crayolas. She is the Christy Award–winning author of historical romances—*A Tale of Two Hearts, The Captured Bride, The Innkeeper's Daughter, 12 Days at Bleakly Manor, The Captive Heart, Brentwood's Ward, A Heart Deceived,* and *Gallimore*—but also leaped the historical fence into the realm of contemporary with the zany romantic mystery *Out of the Frying Pan*. If you'd like to keep up with her escapades, find her at www.michellegriep.com or stalk her on Facebook, Twitter, and Pinterest.

And hey! Guess what? She loves to hear from readers! Feel free to drop her a note at michellegriep@gmail.com.

Other Books by Michelle

The Captive Heart
The Captured Bride
12 Days at Bleakly Manor
A Tale of Two Hearts
Once Upon a Dickens Christmas (a collection)
Ladies of Intrigue (a collection)
The House at the End of the Moor
The Thief of Blackfriars Lane
The Bride of Blackfriars Lane
Lost in Darkness – Of Monsters and Men series
Man of Shadow and Mist – Of Monsters and Men series